last first

kiss

W Winters

broken

Heartless. Ruthless. Stone Cold Killer.

That's me. I destroy anything in my path to get what I want.

Then she showed up. Olivia Bell. She's sweet and innocent,
and in the wrong place, at the wrong time.

Now she's mine. *My property.* I *own* her. Given to me
as a bargaining chip.

She's not a part of my plans, but plans change. Her pouty lips and
gorgeous curves beg me to break her.

Taking her lush curvy body, and ravaging it for all its
worth would be easy, but I want to earn her submission.
It's addictive. I want it. I want *her.*

They wanted me to break her. I am. And I'm enjoying it.
Now they want to take her from me.

Over my dead body.

Let them come for us. I'll kill them all.

By the time I'm done, everyone will know. *She belongs to me.*

**This is a DARK romance. A full-length standalone novel
with HEA and no cheating**

Prologue

Olivia

THE COURTROOM IS QUIET. I CAN HEAR SOMEONE IN THE BACK of the room clear their throat. I swallow thickly and try to avoid their gazes. But I'm on the witness stand, I can't avoid them or any of this.

They're all watching me. Waiting for an answer. I feel like I'm suffocating. This is too much.

It reminds me of being in the room with him. With Kade. My eyes dart to him, and my mouth parts slightly as I remember the time I spent with him.

The other men would watch. He said I had to be perfect, and if I was he'd give me my freedom. And he did. He's a man of his word. But this freedom feels empty and hollow. I wish I could take it back. Not our time together, just my wish to be set free.

"Miss Bell?" asks the prosecution, snapping me out of my reverie.

"Yes?" I ask warily. My fingers twist in my hand. My heartbeat picks up. I don't want to be here. I'd give anything to go back.

They're waiting for me to talk, to testify against him and give evidence that Kade's a bad man. That he deserves to be imprisoned not only for what he did to me, but for everything else.

But I can't. He did it to protect me. He *had* to do it. My voice is caught in my throat. My blood heats and chills at the same time. The thought of turning against him makes me sick.

My eyes focus on him, and all I want to do is to run to his side. I wish he could just take me away. Instead he's on trial, and I'm left alone to deal with the aftermath of how my life has changed forever.

Tears prick my eyes as Kade nods his head and gives me a small, sad smile. He wants me to answer them. He wants me to be a good girl and tell them everything they want to know so I can go free. *It's time to let go, angel.* I hear his words and I hate them. I don't want to let go of him. I was his, and now I feel like I'm no one.

"Do you need me to repeat the question?" the old man says as he stares at me through his spectacles.

I shake my head. I know what he asked. I know what they want from me.

My body relaxes as I remember how he broke me down bit by bit. Now it seems calculated, as though he knew what he was doing. Like he used me. That's what they keep telling me, they say that's why I feel this way about him. But back then, it felt different. It felt as though he was helping me. I thought he needed me. *He did need me.*

His fingers gently slid down the curve of my hip. *"My angel,"* he whispered. His lips barely touched the shell of my ear, his hot breath sending chills down my shoulder. As his hand slid farther down, he groaned with satisfaction. I was always ready for him. I learned to love what he did. I learned to be perfect for him.

"Miss Bell, answer the question." The judge's voice rings out and makes my body jolt in the seat.

I clear my throat thinking about where I should start and what all I should tell them. My heart clenches in my chest. I don't want to share it with them. Right now these memories are mine. They'll ruin them. They'll make me think my recollections are something they aren't.

They want me to believe he never loved me, and that the feelings I have for him are false.

I don't know what to do. I don't know what to believe.

The only thing I know that's true is I fell in love with Kade and that now, because of him, I'm utterly and completely broken.

Chapter 1

Olivia

Three months earlier…

I FEEL SICK TO MY STOMACH. I WISH I COULD JUST THROW UP AND be done with this feeling, but it's not from drinking too much, or food poisoning, or anything like that. I'm just sick of my life and the shitty position I put myself in. Getting turned down for your ninth job interview sucks. And it was for a hair salon. Like, really? All I'd be doing is bookwork. It can't be that fucking hard. I'm starting to think there's no hope. That's what makes me so damn sick. Like there's nothing I can do, and I'm just screwed.

It's been three weeks since I got expelled from the university. It was all over alcohol. They have a zero tolerance policy. So of course getting kicked out also meant losing my scholarships. And losing my scholarships meant losing my income, plus my part-time job in the registrar's office. Which means when the rent is due, I'm fucked if I can't hurry up and land a job already.

As if this wasn't already the worst month of my life, my mother won't even answer my calls. It's her idea of tough love. Yeah, I know I fucked up. I don't need to hear it again. It's not like this is what I usually do. Like I went to college and suddenly became a horrible person. I was in all the honors classes in high school. I was a teacher's pet.

I've gotten straight A's my entire life, except for that one C in Advanced Literature. Fuck English, I only took the class because I had to in order to fulfill my graduation requirements.

I've always been a brown-noser, as Cheryl calls me.

Fuck, Cheryl. It's her fault!

I bite my lip and cross my arms over my chest to warm myself up. I shake my head, trying not to be bitter about it all. It's not really Cheryl's fault. She may have put the bottle in my hand, but she didn't make me drink. She was only trying to help. After all, it's not every day that your first real boyfriend, the man you gave your virginity to, dumps you for someone prettier.

Tears prick my eyes, but I'm sure as shit not going to cry over him. I'll cry over my self-esteem though, because that shit hurt. When I asked him how he could just break up with me like our relationship meant nothing to him, he just shrugged and said her tits were bigger. Fucking asshole. How did I ever fall for him?

Daniel Croast is hot and athletic, and really knows how to lay on the charm.

But he's a fucking dick. I knew this, yet I still fell for him. I still spread my legs for him and let him take every last piece of me that he wanted.

Curse my fucking hormones. Tall, with broad shoulders. He played on the rugby team and there's just something about men crashing into each other and taking those brutal hits; it makes my pussy pulse with desire. I'm not a biology major, but it was definitely my fucked-up hormones.

I fell in lust, not love.

I finally had a boyfriend and friends. Real friends who liked me for me. Cheryl may be a bad influence and not have a clue about how the real world works, but deep down I know she cares about me. Drinking on campus in the dorms was stupid though.

Real fucking stupid. I just went there to cry to Audrey about everything, and instead we ended up drinking. I even thought, *No, we should go to our apartment if we're going to be drinking.* Shit, that's the entire reason we got the apartment off-campus.

But I felt horrible, and my friends were all around me, and I just wanted to feel better.

I fucking hate that RA prick that busted us. I swear he's got a stick shoved up his ass. He can go to hell for all I care.

I turn twenty-one in two months, and Cheryl in three. That RA's so fucking pretentious and likes to pretend he did this for the "right reasons" but seriously, he can go fuck himself. He's never liked Audrey since she turned his scrawny ass down during freshman orientation. That's really what it was about, his dumb fucking vendetta.

Luckily for Audrey, she left to go get more booze. And while she was walking to the liquor store, campus security showed up. She got a strike, and we got booted.

So now I'm at the lowest point in my life.

What kills me the most is that my parents aren't talking to me, which I don't understand. I know they're disappointed and all, but the silent treatment is just not helpful. All it's doing is hurting me. I stop at the edge of the sidewalk and wait, standing in the chill of the fall night, hugging my arms tighter around myself. My legs are freezing since I wore a black A-line skirt to my interview, but at least I grabbed my cream chenille sweater.

I stare up at the red hand on the crosswalk sign and just wait.

There aren't any cars this late at night. But the hand is red. And that means you can't go, so I don't. I'm not a fan of breaking the rules.

I huff a laugh at this train of thought. The one time in my entire life I break the rules, and of course I get caught. And now everything I've worked so damn hard for is crumbling all around me. Tears prick at my eyes again, and this time one escapes.

I breathe out slow and steady, calming myself. I wipe the stray tear with the cuff of my sweater and start walking as soon as I get the green signal to go. Mascara covers the end of my sleeve now, but I don't care.

I feel like I'm balanced on the edge of a razor. One one side, I care entirely too much about everything, and my heart aches with all the disappointment I've caused, not to mention the disappointment I feel in myself. But on the other side, I don't give a fuck about any of this. I've hardened my heart with hate for everyone around me that doesn't care enough to try to help.

I swallow thickly. They don't have to help me. No one owes me anything, and that's just fine by me. I have a plan.

This isn't going to ruin me.

Yes, I got kicked out of one of the most prestigious universities in the country, but I can get into another. If I can just get a job, I can survive until February for sure. That's when I'll find out if I got in anywhere else. I'm sure another school will take me. They can't hold having a drink over my head forever, especially since I'm sure this kind of thing happens all the time. I'm just happy they decided not to press charges, and it's not on my legal record. As for my academic record, it was embarrassing as hell to have to explain that I got kicked out for drinking on campus. But I'll do whatever I have to do.

I've already filled out twenty applications for other colleges. I filled out nearly forty for jobs.

I'll keep applying myself until someone gives me a break. I'm sure my professors are disappointed, but at least they were kind enough to offer their recommendations.

My heart twists in my chest. I hate disappointing people. Especially those I look up to. In my mind, I see Dr. Griffins shake her head slightly, mouth parted in shock as I told her I had to leave.

Disappointed.

Well, you and me both, I guess.

I keep walking down the sidewalk and I start to get a real uneasy feeling creeping over me. It's so fucking quiet. There's no one around. It's just dead. I'm pretty used to walking everywhere, even late at night, but not on this side of town. I don't even know what time it is.

I should be home this late at night. I shouldn't be here. It's obvious this isn't the safest part of town. But I just couldn't go back to the apartment and have nothing to tell Cheryl.

I'm the one who looks out for her. But right now I've got nothing for either of us.

I couldn't tell Cheryl that I didn't get the job, and that I have no plan for us.

She's freaking out about money. She's kind of a wild child, and she's never had a worry in her life. I love her free spirit and all, but that needs to take a back seat when your parents cut you off. She isn't like me though. She's never worked a day in her life. Between all my savings and the scholarships, I was able to pay for college on my own. Not Cheryl Fletcher. I don't think her perfectly manicured hands have ever performed any sort of manual labor. Which is fine if you don't have to, and it's not like she's a spoiled brat who throws it in your face.

But her parents were pissed about the expulsion and completely cut her off. And it's not like she isn't trying—she's filled out more job applications than I have. Partly because she doesn't plan on going back to school. She was undeclared anyway since she doesn't know what she wants to do with her life.

But the best plan we have to make rent this month is to start selling our shit. And by our shit, I mean hers. A purse or two from her collection would be enough to do it. I'm not going to ask though. My everyday purse is a clutch I bought on clearance from Target a few semesters ago. Hardly glamorous, and hardly expensive. Nope, not like Cheryl's newest purse, a Michael Kors hobo with buttery soft leather. Still, I'm not going to ask and put her in that position.

It's the only option I can think of though.

I see a few guys walking two blocks up from me. They're on the opposite side of the street and heading in my direction. I don't like it. They're talking and laughing, and having a good time. They don't seem threatening. But still, a young girl walking alone and three men… I just don't like it.

There's an alleyway on my left that lets out a few blocks down from the main road where our apartment is. As I stand in the opening, I can see it opens up on both walls of the alley halfway through and that there are some cars farther down on the other side. It's empty.

I don't even hesitate to take the left turn and walk toward more people. Toward safety. I'm pretty sure it's an even faster route home—I think, anyway.

It's dark, and things look different when it's dark.

I pick up my pace with my eyes straight ahead on the light at the opening to the other street.

I'm about halfway through, right near the openings on both sides of the alley when I hear shouting.

My heart jumps in my chest, and my breathing stalls. I instinctively take a step back and nearly fall on my ass with fear.

It's *angry* shouting. More than two men arguing in what I think is Russian. Or maybe German. I don't know. All I know is that I don't understand anything they're saying, and I shouldn't be here. I look behind me for a moment, but I don't know where those three men are. Fuck. Fuck.

I don't know what to do. The yelling gets louder and closer. My heart hammers faster in my chest. I feel lost and trapped as my throat closes with fear.

I could just run as fast as I can through the opening. It's large enough that a car could get through. But they sound so close. If they saw me, they'd definitely be able to catch me before I made it out the other side.

I take a deep breath and chance a look, just a small glance to see what's happening.

My breathing slows, and the only thing I can hear is my blood rushing in my ears. My heart *thumps, thumps, thumps* way too loud. They're going to hear me; they're going to see me.

I feel a small sense of relief as I see a row of trashcans blocking the path. I can see past them though. Maybe twenty feet from me, there's a group of men gathered in the parking lot of a warehouse.

I don't know what's going on, but it's not good. So far, no one's spotted me since I'm peeking around the corner with just part of my head showing. I could still get down on the ground, try crawling in the dirt and gravel, and hope I get through unnoticed.

Instead I watch, paralyzed with disbelief at what I'm seeing.

A man's standing apart from the others. It's not the fact that he's in a custom-tailored suit when they rest of them are all in wrinkled khakis or worn-out jeans. He's one of the tallest men, with broad shoulders that stretches the rich fabric tight across his gorgeous frame. But that's not it either. His very presence is a dominating force. It's the air around him.

He's a dangerous man. The other men may be mean, or even pure evil. But this man is ruthless, calculated, and something tells me he can get away with it. He's a man who isn't denied, and for good reasons. The shadows on his face only make his high and sharp cheekbones even more severe. A light dusting of rough stubble lines his hard jaw.

He's handsome in the most sinful ways, but he'd break you without thinking twice. Maybe even intentionally.

He straightens his crisp white shirt from under his dark navy suit with a gun still firmly in his hand, his finger on the trigger. His barely contained anger is evident even at this distance. He's listening to the man screaming, the one being dragged over on his knees to the center where the other men are circling.

Another man, Ricky, is yelling back. At least I think that's his name, since that's what it sounds like they're calling him. Ricky is obviously in charge of the group of men who are mostly dressed in dark denim jeans, and Henleys or hoodies.

All but *him*.

All of them are under Ricky's control, except the man with the absolute power.

Their guns are pointed at the one man who's unarmed and on his knees. Two men are pushing down on his shoulders, forcing him to maintain that position.

"Fuck you! Fuck all of you!" the man on his knees yells out and spits on the ground.

"So it's true!" yells one of the men holding him down.

"Fucking pig! Fucking liar!" the men are yelling, practically chanting. I realize with a start that the man being forced to kneel must be an undercover cop. I fumble in my clutch for my phone. I need to get help.

"What did you tell them?" asks Ricky. *Bang!* I almost scream and have to cover my mouth with my hands as the sound of a bullet cries out and echoes through the alley. My phone drops to the ground, and the screen cracks from the impact.

My heart stills as Ricky yells out and grabs the cop's shoulder.

Somehow I don't think they heard me, or saw me. Their focus is on the cop who's still on his knees clutching his leg and wincing in pain.

"The next one will be in your skull." Ricky walks closer to the man and puts the gun up to his temple, twisting the barrel of the gun to taunt him. "What did you tell them?"

The kneeling man attempts to laugh although he's in obvious pain. "Just do it. You'll never get anything from me." He sneers as blood soaks through his jeans. It's so dark, it almost looks black.

No! No! I need to do something. As I bend down to get my cracked phone, the man in the dark suit moves forward. A hush falls over the men. The only exception is Ricky, who's cussing and making threats that don't seem to affect the undercover cop.

"Is it true?" a deep, rich voice asks so calmly that it doesn't seem real. The loud click of his gun cocking makes me take a step forward. My head shakes. No. No.

It's silent. Everyone's waiting for his answer, even Ricky.

"Fuck you, you fucking criminal."

"What did you call me?" The man's voice raises with a deadly tone. He points his gun at his target's head.

"You really going to make me say it again?" the man on his knees asks, but his voice cracks. The fear of imminent death is finally coming through.

And with that, his death sentence is complete. One shot, *bang*, and he falls to the ground. The man in the suit moves his arm again and aims at the ground this time. I can't see, but I hear the shots ring out, again and again. *Bang, bang, bang!*

I shake my head with disbelief, tears leaking from the corners of my eyes. They killed him, and I saw the whole thing. My blood runs cold, and the sickness I'm feeling threatens to come up my throat.

And then I do scream. I shriek louder than I ever have before.

A pair of hard, unforgiving arms wrap around my waist and chest before a hand covers my mouth. I struggle against what feels like an unmoving brick frame holding me tight, my back to his hard chest. Caught. I've been caught. I fight for my life; my nails dig into his skin, piercing and scratching. But it does nothing. He's so much taller than I am, so he easily picks my body up off the ground and wraps his hand around my throat, suffocating me. I struggle as much as I can. But it's hopeless, I'm already losing consciousness. The last thing I see, before my world goes black, is the man in the suit looking down the alley. His intense gaze is focused solely on me.

Chapter 2

Olivia

I WAKE WITH PAIN RADIATING IN MY SHOULDER. MY THROAT FEELS bruised, and my head throbs with an unrelenting ache in my temples. Zip ties dig into the flesh of my ankles and wrists. They're so tight it feels like every move against them, no matter how small, cuts my skin.

My heart skips a beat, and I struggle not to open my eyes as I realize what's happened. I've been taken. I register I'm not alone when I hear voices. I need to be still. I need to be quiet. I need to get the fuck out of here. I can't risk drawing unnecessary attention to myself until I can figure a way out of this.

"Who let him in, Ricky?" I recognize his voice immediately, the voice of the man with power. The dangerous man from earlier, the man in the suit, and right now he sounds pissed. The sound of his anger alone is enough to paralyze my body.

"It's a mistake anyone could have made, Kade." Ricky's words are hard. The man in the suit might be in charge, but it's clear Ricky is as well.

"It's a mistake that could have ruined me."

"You never made more than a handful of contacts. He would've had nothing on you," Ricky says dismissively.

"It's unacceptable." Kade's words are sharp, and nearly make me jump. But I'm too scared to move. I have to remind myself to breathe as I begin to feel lightheaded.

"Well, we found out before anything got leaked," Ricky grumbles.

"Are you sure?" Kade asks.

"We're positive." I gather my courage, and slowly open my eyes to find myself in a cramped and dirty office. It's really small with drop ceiling tiles covered in dust and a flat wood laminate door.

Kade's sharp blue eyes are narrowed and hard. He obviously doesn't belong in this cramped, dirty office. There are cardboard boxes stacked in the corners, and a dirty old chair behind what looks to be an even older desk. Nothing in here is expensive. It's cheap and filthy. The other men belong here. But the man in the suit doesn't. He's as out of place as I am.

Two other men are seated in the far corner, while Kade and Ricky are standing in front of the desk to my left. Ricky leans against the cheap desk piled high with papers and folders, feigning a casual position. But the air is tense around the two men.

Ricky yells sharply at the men in the corner. It's something in Russian, definitely Russian. The only word I understand though is a name, Vic. The two men shake their heads, but only one replies. Of the two, he's taller and more built. His voice is deep, and he has a thick accent. After watching their exchange, I'm assuming he's Vic.

It's obvious they're obedient lap dogs. Now that I look at them more closely, I can see that both of the men in the corner are young. The short and pale one could be eighteen or younger. The other, Vic, is maybe in his early twenties. Vic looks deadly though. If you saw him walking down the street toward you, you'd run in the opposite direction. He looks like he'd love to take his anger out on someone. He probably does. He has a toothpick in the corner of his mouth, and he keeps looking at my body like he wants to be alone with me. Inwardly I shudder.

I need to get the fuck out of here.

Ricky responds to Vic with rapid-fire Russian, and somehow he seems even angrier than before. I don't want to make myself a target for that anger, but I can't help staring at Ricky during his tirade. His face is sunken in, and he has dark bags under his eyes. They don't look like the kind you get from lack of sleep though, more like the kind that come with age and alcohol.

Vic's eyes bore into me. He ignores his boss and looks intently past both men at me. I can feel his hatred. Whatever happens, I cannot be left alone with him.

Kade and Ricky continue to argue and Kade takes a step forward, blocking Vic from my sight. I heave in a breath I didn't know I was holding and try tugging uselessly on the zip ties binding my wrists. I wince as they bite into my skin.

It's useless.

As the weight of my situation starts to suffocate me, I feel Kade's piercing stare. My body trembles, and I slowly move my eyes to meet his. Somehow I already knew they were on me.

I'm struck by his masculine beauty. To say he looks like a sex god and CEO wrapped into one would be an understatement. But there's more. There's an edge of danger that's undeniable. His frame is domineering—tall, with broad shoulders and narrow hips. But it's his expression that's the most intimidating. My eyes sweep over him from his dark hair and piercing blue eyes, to his plush lips, slightly downturned with disapproval.

My eyes lift to meet his again, and I'm entrapped. As much as I want to look away, I'm forced to stare back.

My shoulders hunch inward with fear, and I feel like I can't breathe. It's as though he's choking me.

"And what of her?" Kade asks with his eyes still firmly on me. "His partner?" My eyes widen and I try to shake my head to deny it, but I can't. I'm paralyzed.

"No, just a dumb bitch," Ricky says scornfully. Kade whips his head around to face him. Kade takes a step forward and the two men cower slightly, shifting in their seats. Vic attempts to right himself, but it's obvious he feels threatened. Ricky stands his ground, but I swear I see a flash of fear cross his eyes.

"Tell me you did a background check on her?" He speaks slowly, and with menace dripping from his voice. "'Just a dumb bitch' isn't good enough."

Ricky keeps his gaze on Kade and gestures behind him toward the two men in the corner. The younger one looks to Vic with worry evident on his pallid face. Vic starts to respond in his heavily-accented English, "It's in—"

"Fucking get it!" Ricky snaps, causing the younger lackey to jump up and scurry from the room. Vic doesn't move, but he averts his eyes from Ricky and stares fixedly at the door where the other man went through.

Ricky's sallow skin turns red with anger as his veins swell in his neck. As explosive as his anger is, Kade's the one that scares me more. I don't think Ricky would appreciate the comparison though.

"Doesn't matter who she is." Ricky looks at me with a crooked smile exposing his yellowed teeth. "We're sending her with you." He looks back at Kade with a wicked glint in his eyes.

If he's trying to get a rise out of Kade with that comment, it's not happening. I look to Kade to gauge his reaction, and he's completely expressionless. It's clear he's utterly disinterested.

My body shakes harder, and I open my mouth to speak. "I—""I—" I try to speak, but my throat is so dry. It croaks, and I stutter. I shake my head. My blood seems to boil, and my breath falls short. Heat overwhelms me.

"You—you—you—what?!" Ricky yells, and I instinctively jolt back. I scoot backward on my ass, my hands awkwardly and painfully dragging on the dirty linoleum floor until I feel my back against the wall. A sharp pain shoots through my shoulders and ankles. I can barely move with the zip ties holding me hostage. My heart beats chaotically, and it's only then that I realize I'm crying.

"She's not even trained," Kade sneers. I don't know what he means by that, but for some reason his disapproval of me hurts. My chest aches, and my face falls with sadness. Please, please don't leave me here with them.

His anger may scare me, but I feel as though I'd be safer with Kade.

"That's for you to do. You're supposed to be an expert in this field, yet we've never seen your work," Ricky says as he leans against the desk once again and crosses his arms. Kade shoots him one arrogant, icy look before he speaks.

"For a good fucking reason. If I'd worked with Barrow like you pushed me to, I would've been fucked."

"Well you weren't," Ricky says as he dares to take a step forward, closer to Kade. Kade doesn't budge. "And now I'm not feeling very trusting of anyone."

Kade tilts his head and cocks a small but threatening grin. "You expect me to accept her, train her and show her off to you? When for all I know, she's a fucking cop!" Kade's shoulders lean forward with the last words.

Ricky's eyes turn cold and it's clear he's not shy about his hatred for Kade. "She's not a cop. We have her license and paperwork done. I'm sure of it." I want to speak; I want to plead with them to let me go. But I'm frozen with fear, my eyes darting between the two of them. "She goes with you, or she gets shipped off."

I break into a cold sweat, and I have to force myself to keep breathing when I hear what Ricky says. That option can't happen. I don't want to get *shipped off*, because whatever the fuck that means, it's not good. It can't be good. "If you don't take her, you can take another. I don't give a fuck, but it's time we see what you can do."

Kade turns away from Ricky and looks at me for a moment before walking forward. I've still got my back up against the wall. My arms and wrists ache from being held behind me with zip ties. I can feel a trickle of blood from the plastic cutting into my skin.

My skirt has ridden up and my pale thighs are exposed. With my ankles bound, I'm trapped.

He crouches in front of me and seems to inspect every inch of me. He licks his lips as his eyes travel down my body. His masculine smell fills my lungs.

"Please," I beg in a whisper. "I won't tell anyone."

Ricky smiles wickedly at my words. He moves to the door as the man from earlier finally comes back. He hands a yellow folder to Ricky. "That's what they all say." He mimics my voice and mockingly says, "I won't tell a soul." Ricky, Vic, and the pale toady laugh, and all hope leaves me as hot tears fall down my cheeks.

Kade doesn't laugh, instead he continues to watch me. I lick my dry lips and try to wipe away my tears by brushing my face against my shoulder. I want to plead with him to take me away from them, but when I look up at him, there's no sympathy there. Only hard and cold blue eyes seemingly made of ice. My head falls to my chest, and I wish I could disappear.

"So, what will it be?" Ricky asks, drawing Kade's attention from me. He rises and walks away from me and I find myself trying to crawl toward him. I can't stay here. Not with Vic looking at me like a predator and the threat of being *shipped off*.

Kade grabs the folder from Ricky and opens it. I don't know what's in there, but whatever he's looking for, I hope he finds it. I watch as his eyes travel down the page and then the next. Suddenly, he looks back at me with an expression of dissatisfaction.

"You're on birth control?" he asks.

My cheeks flame. I swallow the spiked lump in my throat and try to verbalize an answer, but I can't, so I nod my head.

They must have my school records. I just went to the gyno on campus a few months ago, after I decided to give myself to Daniel. I went with the shot because it seemed easier than having to remember to take a pill every damn day. I almost didn't get the last injection since we broke up, but I went and got it since I'd scheduled the appointment.

He shuts the folder and shoves it against Vic's chest.

He looks at Ricky and then back at me. I can't read his expression. I don't know what he's going to do or say, so I do the only thing I can do at this point. I wait with bated breath.

"After today, I could use a distraction." Kade turns back to Ricky and nods once as he says, "I'll take her. And then you give me what I want."

Ricky's lips pull into a wide smile and he says, "Deal."

Chapter 3

Olivia

MY THROAT'S HOARSE FROM SCREAMING THROUGH THE GAG, and I'm getting tired. I'm starting to really feel the exhaustion weighing down on me, but fear is keeping me wide awake.

I've tried to kick the trunk open to no avail. I've been kicking this entire time, hoping that maybe someone would see the thumping. It's not really kicking though since my ankles are bound. So I'm pushing all my weight to my chest and thrusting my legs upward. It hurts. The zip ties rip into my skin with each blow. But I have to try.

It's been a long time since he put me in here. I don't know exactly how long, but I'd guess hours. The first time he slowed to a stop, I thought he would get out and try to stop me and shut me up. But he didn't.

He either doesn't care, or he's confident that my struggling and muffled screams are useless. The soft sounds of the car rumbling and moving effortlessly against the smooth asphalt make my eyes shut. My fate's no longer mine, but I still have fight in me. I can't give up hope. I heard my phone go off in the front of the car a while ago. It rang a few times, but there's been nothing since.

I don't know who it was, or if anyone else has called wondering where I am. Maybe he's just shut it off. For all I know, he threw it out the window.

My eyes feel puffy and swollen with tears. I hate this. I hate how helpless I am. I'm bounced around painfully as the car passes over an uneven patch of gravel and then slows. My heart hammers against my chest, and the heavy weight of sleep vanishes, replaced with intense anxiety. We've stopped.

I keep perfectly still as he opens and closes his door. I wait to hear where he's going. Part of me hopes he'll forget I'm back here, like that's even a possibility. Still, if that were the case, I could try to get the fuck out of here.

That stupid dream crumbles into dust as he opens the trunk. I bite down on the gag in my mouth and shake my head, trying to move away from him.

He looks at me with an intense stare that makes me want to cave to him. Something in his look sparks an electric current between us, but in a flash it's gone.

I don't fear him, not like the others. Some part of me feels safe with him. It's a false sense of security, but it's there, keeping me somewhat calm although anger is coursing through me.

He grabs my waist, hoisting me over his shoulder. I try to struggle, but his large hand smacks hard against my ass. *Slap!* His hand meets my bare skin underneath my skirt, and the shocking pain shoots through my body. My back bows, and a scream rips through my throat, muffled by the gag.

"Stop it." His harsh admonishment makes my body go limp. I struggle to take a breath as I look around. There's nothing but woods. I can't see anything but woods.

He's going to kill me. My heart hammers frantically and I nearly vomit, but then I see pavers.

Gorgeous stained concrete pavers make a perfect path surrounding a garden of lavender and rose bushes. Lush green grass trimmed to the perfect height separates the tiles. As we walk up some steps, I see columns with ivy growing up the side and over the roof of a pavilion.

I don't have a chance to see anything else, but we're at a house at least. I know that much. A home with a perfectly manicured, and well taken care of lawn. Which means other people will be here. Hope ignites within me.

I may be in the middle of the woods. But if someone comes, I can yell for help. If I find a way out, I can hide in the trees. The fight in me strengthens as he carries me through the doorway and shuts it behind us with a loud bang.

I look up and see the massive French doors that we walked through. They have a colonial touch to them, all classic lines and stark white coloring. The hardwood floors are dark, with wide planks. If this were any other day,

I'd admire the architecture. But this isn't any other day. And this isn't a place to admire, it's a place that induces fear. It's beautiful, but it's still a prison.

Before I have a chance to look around and take in more of my surroundings looking for exits or anything I can use as a weapon, Kade carries me up the stairs and through a dark hallway. A room. He's taking me to a room. My heartbeat picks up.

I can't freak out. I need to pay attention and keep track of where the exit is. We walk much longer than I thought possible. If my count is correct, we pass six doors and an open hallway with a balcony that overlooks the entrance. It's hard to tell how many doors we pass exactly since the hallway is so dark, but when we get to the balcony I'm able to use the lighting to my advantage as I look around.

This house is huge. No, not a house. A mansion, maybe?

All too soon the balcony ends, and once again darkness takes over. I can barely make out a door to my left, and then he stops.

He lowers me to the ground more gently than I thought he would. The zip ties dig deeper into my ankles because of the angle, and I hiss in a breath. I hear keys jingling, and I look up to see an old set of keys in his hands. The keys look like they're made from cast iron, and I'm guessing he pulled them down from a nearby hook on the wall. I hadn't noticed earlier due to the distracting and excruciating pain in my ankles, but I can't make that mistake again. I need to stay alert if I'm going to get out of here alive. Kade carefully selects one key from the bunch although they all look alike to me. With a clink, the door unlocks and he pushes it open.

He looks down at me for a moment, but I'm too scared to look up.

I feel his eyes on me, but I keep my own trained on the ground.

I let out a yelp of surprise as he quickly picks up my small body and takes me into the room, cradling me in his arms. I resist the urge to rest my head against his hard, muscular chest.

My stomach hurts, and the exhaustion hits me harder than before.

He leaves the door open and carries me across the room onto a soft bed before setting me down gently.

He leaves me there, bound, gagged, and lying on my side. I close my eyes, listening to him moving through the room. It's dark, but I can clearly make out a dresser in front of me. It's an antique with glass knobs. I imagine the pulls have screws on the ends. I've seen them before at the hardware store. If I get a chance, I could unscrew them. I could use one to stab him in his jugular and get the fuck out of here. I just need him to untie me first.

I hear him gather items throughout the room and take them out to the hallway.

It seems like forever, listening to him rearranging the room. And then nothing.

It sounds like he's gone. But he's left me bound. I try to look around, but I can't see anything besides the dresser. I wish I could move, but with my hands bound behind my back, I can't. I try again uselessly to get out of the binds, but it only makes the pain worse.

I still as I hear his footsteps in the hallway. They grow closer and louder until he's standing in front of me, his hips by my head. I can see the buckle of his belt, and his crisp white shirt that now has a smear of blood, no doubt from when he carried me.

He grips my forearm and with a quick slice, cuts the ties. Relief flows through me, along with new aches and the need to move. But I'm stiff, waiting for him to cut the ties on my ankles. As soon as he does, I fucking bolt.

I jump up and push against him with all my weight, and by some miracle, it forces him far enough away that I'm able to jump from the bed. I sprint as hard as I can, but I don't make it more than a few feet before his hand grips the hem of my sweater. I let out a shriek, landing hard on my side, palms slamming against the floor as he drags me toward him. All the while I fight. I kick my legs blindly and scream for help.

My foot lands hard against his chest, but he doesn't even flinch. Instead he grips my hair at the base of my skull, and I yelp in agony as he yanks my head back. Tears leak from my eyes at the sharp pain, and my hands instinctively move to try and pry his fingers from my head. He releases my head, but the momentary relief I feel is quickly eclipsed by intense pain once more as he grabs both of my wrists. The stinging pain from the cuts intensifies.

With my wrists secured in one hand, he wraps his other arm around my waist and carries me back to the bed.

He pushes me face down on the bed, his large frame pinning me beneath him, forcing me still. He seizes the nape of my neck and squeezes until I go limp beneath him, surrendering the fight I so badly lost. Tears roll down my cheeks, every part of my body aching, and my soul crushed with hopelessness.

"This is your one warning." His hot breath leaves chills down my spine, his lips barely touching the shell of my ear. A shiver runs through my body and the deep cadence of his voice makes my pussy clench with sinful thoughts. "There is no escape from this."

Chapter 4

Olivia

I CAN'T SLEEP FOR MORE THAN A FEW MINUTES AT A TIME. I JUST can't. I'm afraid to move, afraid to even breathe too loudly. But I have to. I have to look and see if there's a way out.

He has my phone. I hope he still has it. I know I heard the ringtone earlier, so I can only hope Cheryl or someone tracks it and finds me here.

But how long would that take? Too fucking long.

I can't wait for a knight in shining armor to come and save me. Every second I'm here is another second Kade could decide to just kill me, or worse. I shudder as I think back to Ricky and Vic. Some things are definitely worse than death. The first thing I need to do is move. I haven't budged an inch since he left me.

I'm terrified that the moment I move off the bed, he'll burst through the door and beat me. I remember his weight on top of me, and the way he gripped my hair. I can't fight him. It's an uneven match.

He's not going to save me. It was stupid for me to even hope he would. No one's coming to my rescue.

I have to try to save myself.

Without realizing it, I've gathered handfuls of the down comforter. It's fluffy and soft, but the intricate stitching chafes against the cuts on my wrists. With a small sigh I let the comforter fall and gently run a fingertip along my wounds.

I can't stay here and wait for more.

I slowly pull the blanket away from me. I'm still fully clothed in my sweater and skirt. There's no way I'm taking anything off of me. I need as much between me and that asshole as possible.

I gently climb off the bed and head over to the one thing I've been thinking about all night. The windows.

There are two large windows on either side of the large bed. They're both covered by curtains that run from the floor to the ceiling. The fabric is thick and rich, although with such little light in the room, I can't tell for certain what color the curtains are. I place one foot on the cold hardwood floors and pause before placing my full weight down slowly.

The floors creak, and I wince. My eyes dart to the door and I hold my breath, waiting for a sign that he's heard. It's been hours since he left me alone here, I think. He must be sleeping by now.

We're high up on the second story. I'm sure he's certain I can't escape. I fucking hope he's that confident.

I take another step, trying my best to keep the creaking to a minimum and walk with slow, deliberate steps to the nearest window.

My heart beats loudly in my ears. It climbs up my throat, threatening to suffocate me. What if he finds me trying to escape? What will he do to me?

I shake my head slightly and walk quicker to the window. I can't think like that. I can't let fear keep me from saving myself. I pull back the heavy curtain and nearly cry at what I find. My shoulders sink inward. There are bars on the windows. Thick steel bars. They're on the outside, so I could open a window, but then I'd have to try to squeeze myself through. I don't even think my head would fit, let alone my wider parts.

I swallow, and my dry throat aches from the wretched screaming that did nothing for me. I can't give up. I imagine he locked the door, but I haven't checked. I take two steps toward it, but then I stop as I spot the dresser, remembering the thought I had earlier. The knobs. I need a weapon; I need more than one.

I brace one hand and hover over the knob. I see his tall frame; I feel his lips on my neck. I shouldn't think twice about hurting him. He *deserves* it. He can't do this to me! But I do. I question if I should. I question if I really want to.

The thoughts are gone just as quickly as they came, and I hold on to the anger of being taken and the fear of being trapped.

I quickly try to unscrew a knob, but the first one I try is on so fucking tight. I grip it harder and twist it to the point that it hurts my hand, but it doesn't give at all. I breathe frantically and try the other one on the top drawer. But it doesn't budge either.

I crouch lower to try the next, and hope lights within me as it loosens. I unscrew it, but instead of the glass pull being attached to the screw, the screw itself is still in the drawer. I try opening the drawer as silently as I can, but the thing is old. There aren't any tracks, and it's loud as hell trying to pull it out.

I get it open just enough for my hand to fit inside. The drawer itself is empty, which I find odd, but I don't give it much thought.

I try to get the screw loose, pushing my thumb against it and twisting, and when that doesn't work, I try using my nails. But it won't fucking move.

Useless.

I lick my lips and drop the knob into the drawer, not bothering to close it as I take a look around the room.

I need to find something else.

The room is massive. Compared to the dorms and my cramped apartment, it's ridiculous in size.

I search the room for closets, but there are none. There are two wardrobes that look identical to the left of the room, however.

As I walk toward them to see what's inside, I nearly trip. A rug I hadn't noticed before is under my feet. I must have fallen onto it earlier, but I hadn't noticed. I steady myself and stare at the door, hoping he didn't hear. Minutes pass with no sign of him.

I walk as quietly as I can to the wardrobes, and pray there's something in there I can use against him.

It doesn't take long for me to get there and find the first one empty. Hope dwindles inside of me, but I have to try the other. With shaky hands, I open the second wardrobe and I find the same. Empty. The feeling of defeat washes over me. That leaves only one other thing to try, and I shouldn't even be getting my hopes up.

I look to the door to the room, and pray it's unlocked. What are the odds he would be so foolish?

And if it isn't locked, maybe he's waiting for me. Maybe it's a test.

Either way, I have to try. I won't stay here and make this easy on him. I can't. I need to get the fuck out of here. That's the only truth I need to hold on to.

Chapter 5

Kade

THE ICE CLINKS IN MY GLASS AS I LIFT IT OFF THE COFFEE TABLE. The fire across the room roars and crackles. Those are the only noises in the room, but the noises I'm hearing are different. I can't stop hearing James' last words. The bang of my gun. Over and over, the sounds won't stop.

Criminal. It was our code word. I keep hearing him say it. We chose that word together, but I'd hoped neither of us would ever have to say it.

"You really going to make me say it again?" My heart twists in my chest as I hear James' words over and over in my mind. I knew this was a possibility when we signed up for this. We both did. It was only supposed to be months, but it turned into years. But if either of us ever had to say that word, I was hoping it'd be me. Not James.

My official record lists thirty-eight confirmed kills overseas. And he had twenty-six. We were something else, so fucking good the government came to us with an opportunity we couldn't pass up. One last job, and we'd earn enough cash we could live off it forever.

We were ready to go in, excited even. It sucked having to go in separate, but it made sense.

Fucking Ricky Stone was harder to crack than they said he'd be. He's a hotheaded fuck, but he still hasn't shown his cards.

Two years ago, one of the biggest sex trafficking trades went down, but neither of us found out about it until it had passed even though we were supposed to be in on it. We—I can't seem to get close enough.

I front the money for the cartel, I'm their largest investor. My fake background has me passing myself off as an ex-con. As far as they know, I served time for money laundering, and the connections I made in prison led to my current interest in dealing in women. That's how the cartel found me, actually. Buying women. Of course the women all went free and are now safe and recovering. But they think I killed them when I was done.

That's what the cartel does. It's what's expected.

Ricky and Vic are sick fucks; they're behind the biggest and most profitable sex slave and drug trafficking rings across the globe. From the United States, to Thailand, and plenty of places in between.

I was so close to getting more information about Ricky's informants and business partners overseas. Or at least the locations where they store the women.

I wonder what James found out. I wonder what he did that tipped them off. Tears prick my eyes and I slam the glass down. Fuck!

And *she* saw. Olivia. She saw me kill him. It's against protocol to do anything illegal when you're undercover. Every action has to be approved first, which is bullshit, and everyone knows it. Even though James told me to kill him, they can't find out. If she went to the police and told them, they'd pull me out in a heartbeat. If she got out and told, this entire operation would be a wash. Years of hard work would be gone, just like that. I could live with that. But my best friend's death would be for nothing. I can't let that happen to James.

I would have killed him for nothing.

For a split second, I considered turning the gun on Ricky, at that cold-blooded, hotheaded prick. I considered just killing him and dying alongside James. It would have been an honorable death.

But the rest of them would have lived, including Vic. And the girls would still have been shipped off. Ricky dying, and maybe one of his henchmen—it wouldn't have been enough to take them down.

And James said it. He said the one word that meant I needed to pull the trigger.

Criminal.

I swallow the whiskey straight from the bottle this time. My head hurts and my throat burns, but my heart hurts more. I'm in too deep to turn back now.

I need to end this, and the date for the sale is quickly approaching. I know it is.

For him, I'll make sure they all die. I'll make sure they pay.

I hear the floor creak above the study. She got out of bed. I grind my teeth, hating the position I'm in.

When I saw her, I thought for a moment I'd done it. I thought I'd pointed the gun at the real enemy, that I'd died. She looked like an angel with her white sweater and sun-kissed skin. Her eyes pleaded with me to save her. They were taking her from me. My angel.

I look down into my empty glass.

There's no angel out there for me.

If I'd left her there with them, I know what they would have done. I know they would have beaten her and used her body. They would have passed her around before selling her off.

They would have broken her, just like they've done with so many others. I couldn't let it happen, but now I've fucked myself.

I've been trained on what to expect. I know what I need to do so they'll believe me and let me in closer.

I have to break her myself.

Chapter 6

Olivia

I HEAR HIM COMING DOWN THE HALL, AND MY HEAD WHIPS TO THE door. Fuck! I bolt to the bed. I don't have a damn thing to arm myself with.

I get under the covers and lie there. But then I remember the knob. Motherfucking fucker! I want to scream. I ball my hands into fists under the covers and squeeze my eyes shut as the door creaks open.

Why am I so fucking stupid?

I stay as still as possible as he moves closer to the bed. I hear his footsteps as he approaches and my stomach sinks. At the same time though my pussy clenches at the threat of him taking his anger out on me. My cheeks flame. I don't know what's wrong with me that I could want something so demeaning.

The bed dips with his heavy weight and my body rolls slightly, even though I'm stiff.

I bite down hard on my lip.

My mind runs away with the most sexual images. I don't want this. But some sick part of me does.

A sob rips up my throat, and I wish it hadn't. His hand lands softly on my hip, and I just barely resist the urge to take a swing at him and push him away from me. I could try to run again. I *should* try to run again. But at the same time, the thought of him pinning me down makes me equally turned on and fearful.

"I should punish you." His calm, deep voice stops my thoughts where they were.

I shudder and curl slightly away from him.

"Do you think what you've done wasn't defying me?" he asks in an even voice.

His weight shifts and he lifts off the bed. I don't turn to see what he's doing, but my eyes pop open wide and my breathing pauses as I realize what he's noticed. I hear him snort and push the dresser drawer in.

Fuck. Fuck. He walks over to the window and moves the curtains.

I left a fucking trail for him. I feel him behind me and I want to cower, but I remain still.

"I asked you a question." His voice is soft, as though there's no threat. But I know there is.

I take a ragged breath. "Yes."

"Yes, you thought you weren't defying me?" he asks with a lowered tone, daring me to confirm what he's said. I hesitate to answer. I don't know what to say.

In a flash he rips the sheets from me and I cower from him. My body trembles as he grips my hips and brings me closer to him. My pussy heats, and I can't stand it. I hate how my body is betraying me. I shouldn't be so turned on by him, but I can't help the effect he's having on me.

"Please!" I cry out as I resist the urge to fight him.

He whispers in my ear, "What did you think would happen, Olivia?"

I shake my head. I don't know what to say, so I say nothing, and it angers him.

"Answer me!" he yells as his hand comes down hard on my ass. He pushes me down on the mattress, his large hand splayed against my shoulder blades, pinning me down. I struggle against him, trying to get away.

"You're only making it worse on yourself." His words register and I try to stay still.

"Please don't." I swallow my pride as I beg him. I may be turned on. I may find him handsome, and a sick part of me thinks this could fulfill a fantasy I've never shared with anyone before. But I don't want this.

"What did you think would happen when you defied me?" he asks.

"I didn't." I respond with the truth as a small sob escapes my lips. "I didn't think."

"You should've, angel." He lowers his head to mine and gently kisses my hair. His pet name for me seems off, but comforting somehow. "With everything you do, there will be consequences. Good and bad."

He moves back as his hand leaves my ass. His fingers gently walk up my thigh, pulling my skirt up and exposing me.

"Please don't," I beg him again. I can't help that the shivers that run up my spine harden my nipples and make my clit throb with need. The threat of him using me leaves me breathless with both desire and fear. I don't know which outweighs the other. But I won't give in. This is wrong.

"There are consequences," he says confidently. "I told you that."

Smack! His hand comes down hard again as he spanks my ass and the pain rips through me. I scream and take the blow. And then another. The weight of his body holds me down.

"What were you going to do with whatever you were looking for?" he asks. It's a trick question. I know it is.

I shake my head and part my lips to answer, but instead a shriek comes out as his hand whips my ass again.

"Do not lie to me." His words are hard.

"Defend myself!" I manage to bite out. That's the truth and if he doesn't like it, then I guess he can just beat me. Fighting against him is the same thing as defending myself. So long as I'm here, I'll fight.

"Oh sweetheart," he whispers as his lips graze my neck. My body betrays me yet again, and I hate the wave of arousal rolling through me as he plants a sweet kiss on my neck.

"There's no fighting this." He pulls my body toward the edge of the bed, holding me under him. "There's no way out."

"Please," I say, but I'm not sure what I'm pleading for as his hands lift my skirt up.

"Do you know who I am, angel?" he asks as his thumb rips through my cotton panties. Kade tears the thin pair as though they're nothing, exposing me to him.

I shake my head into the pillow, denying everything. This isn't real. This isn't happening. He takes the opportunity to answer his own question.

"I'm a bad man. And now you *belong* to me." His words shatter any hope I had. My throat closes as fear threatens to overwhelm me.

"This," he says as his hand cups my pussy, "this belongs to me."

As he says the words, I smell whiskey on his breath, but it only adds to my arousal for him. Goddamn traitor body.

He pulls back quickly with shock, and then pushes his fingers against my heated core.

"You're fucking soaked. You *want* this." Shame washes through me again. It's one thing to be turned on, but it's another thing entirely for him to know. It's my treacherous body. My own depraved fantasies. But this is reality.

I shake my head. "I don't." I barely push the words out.

He pulls his hand away and yanks my sweater over my head. I try to fight against him, but it's useless. I cross my arms over my chest feeling so demeaned and helpless. My tank top and bra are the only things keeping me from being completely bared to him.

"You will remove them." His voice hardens as he adds, "Or I will." He stares at me, waiting for me to comply. I don't want him to. But I don't want to do it either.

Slowly I pull the tank top away and unhook my bra, letting it fall. I can't look at him.

He balls all of my clothes in his hands and moves off the bed. Leaving me there naked, embarrassed and completely fucking soaked for him.

I wait for him to do something—anything. But he just watches me.

"Do you know about BDSM or anything at all about Master slave relationships?" he asks.

My blood boils. I know all about them. I've read about them in books, but this shit is real life. "Yes." I push the word out through my teeth.

"Do you know what you are to me now?" he asks.

I barely shake my head as his eyes pierce into me.

"All you are is mine. All you will do is what I say. I am your *Master* now. There is no safe word, there is only you obeying what I tell you to do."

I bite my tongue and resist the urge to snap at him.

"I will always keep you safe. I will never do anything to hurt you. I won't push you beyond what's needed. I promise you that." I don't believe a word he says.

"You'll behave now, or things will only get worse for you," he says in a voice laced with sympathy. He's not sorry though. He did this to me. He chose to do this. He *wants* to do this.

I swallow thickly, hating that every part of me is begging to make him happy. I can't avoid the inevitable, but maybe I can prolong it, if I behave.

"You need to be good for me," he says with a low voice. "You're going to learn how to be the perfect slave, pet, fucktoy. Whatever it is that's required from you." My breath halts in my lungs, and fear freezes my body.

"You're a reflection of me, and you *will* be perfect. Is that understood?"

"Yes," I answer him, feeling completely defeated. The word is choked as it leaves my lips.

"Good girl." His hand gentles on my back. "Tomorrow you'll have another chance. Don't disappoint me."

The seconds pass slowly and finally he leaves the room. As soon as he's gone I cover myself, hiding underneath the duvet.

Anger replaces my shame and fear. I don't care what he does to me, I'll never break for him. Never.

Chapter 7

Olivia

I WAKE UP TO THE SOUNDS OF KADE MOVING IN THE ROOM. I STAY perfectly still under the covers; hopeful he hasn't noticed I'm awake. I can't see him, so I don't know what he's doing. I just want him to leave.

I've barely slept at all. I have no way to get out of here, and no hope of leaving. *Yet,* I tell myself. I just need to get out of this room first. One step at a time.

"I know you're awake." His words ring out clear in the quiet room. I hear him push a drawer shut and walk closer to the bed.

"I brought in breakfast. Come." He gives the order and it pisses me off.

"No," I say from under the covers, like a petulant child. But I don't care. I'm not going to go to him.

Silence greets me.

"You're disobeying me?" he asks in that low threatening voice that somehow fools my body into thinking I should get wet and hot for him. I bite my bottom lip, ignoring him and my arousal.

"Get up and get on your knees."

I ignore the part of me that's dying to obey him and hold on to the sane part of me. I grit my teeth. I'm not doing that. I fucking refuse to let him use me. I poke my head up beyond the covers and look him in the eyes.

They're the softest shade of blue; they could be cold and callous, or forgiving and sympathetic. He could use them to charm women and convince them to be his. They're eyes filled with deceit. I don't trust him. I'll never trust him.

"Fuck you." I hold his eyes as they narrow and heat with lust. It shocks me to the core. Desire. His eyes flame with desire, and I can't help that his look makes my own needs flare.

"Is that what you want?" he asks in a deep, menacing voice that only manages to turn me on as he unbuckles his belt. The hardness in his features softens, and a small grin forms on his face as he slides the belt from the loops.

"I wasn't going to fuck you just yet. But maybe that's why you're having such a hard time realizing what you are now."

My mouth tries to part with lust, but I slam it shut. The tension between us is thick. But it's wrong, and I hate it. This isn't supposed to be like this.

He loops the belt in his hand. "I said get on your knees." With a flick of his wrist he whips the belt in his hand with a loud *smack!* It makes me flinch and my pussy clench.

I grind my teeth and shake my head. "No."

Smack! The belt falls hard onto my thighs. I scream out and he pulls the covers back.

"Knees!" he yells at me, and I bury my head into the mattress, huddling into a ball.

He grips my hips and pulls me toward him. I scramble to get away, but he holds me there and presses his chest to my back. I try elbowing him and the first time it works, I hit something, but it fucking hurts me more than it seems to hurt him.

He pushes his weight against me and shushes me in my ear. Like I'm a wild animal, and he's trying to calm me.

"Let me tell you a secret, angel." He speaks clearly as I still beneath him. "I don't want to hurt you." Liar. He's a fucking liar.

He continues talking as if he read my mind. "I have no choice but to train you. You may not understand why, and honestly, you don't need to know. But I don't have to hurt you. This doesn't have to be a fight."

His words are soothing, and I almost start to relax a little, but the next thing he says comes out hard. "But you will listen to me. And I've found it's best when punishment is severe."

"Fuck you!" I scream again.

"Don't make me punish you." "Do whatever the fuck you want, asshole." I sneer.

"What I want is to feed you," he says simply. "But you disobeyed me. So you need to be punished first."

"Please stop this." The words come out without my conscious awareness. "You don't have to do this." I sound weak and pathetic as I beg him.

I expect him to laugh. I expect him to tell me he won't stop. Instead he hesitates. For a moment, I feel something. I feel hope.

He moves away from the bed and I look back at him, praying he'll set me free. But there's no mercy in his expression.

"I do," he finally says. He nods his head slowly, keeping my gaze with his intense stare. "I have to do this. And you have to obey me, either by choice or force. That's entirely up to you. But it's going to happen."

My eyes fall. "Just kill me then." Again I speak without thought.

"I can't do that." He speaks so quietly I barely hear him say, "I need you." The way his voice comes out with so much sincerity makes me believe him.

"Now come over here and eat."

I eye him warily. "You said I had to be punished first."

"I did. And I changed my mind." He leans closer to me. "You should move quickly, before I change my mind again."

I look up at him, not knowing what to do. In an instant, my anger dissipates. My throat seems to swell with a lump that won't go down. "I have a mother." I try to speak confidently, but my voice comes out raspy. I look down and try to calm myself.

I back away as he sits next to me and pulls me closer to him. I try to resist, but it's no use. He gently pets my back.

"You have family. You have friends," he says calmly, and it kills the last bit of hope I have, like an ice shard through my heart. "I know you do. I know their names. I know where they live." My eyes pop open and my body chills with fear.

"Don't worry, I don't have any plans to hurt them. I meant it when I said I didn't want to hurt you, either." He tilts my head up to force me to look into his blue eyes. "I mean it. But you *need* to listen."

He stares at me for a long time, waiting until he has my full attention. "You've gotten yourself into the middle of something very serious. There's no way you can get out."

I shake my head, wanting to deny it, wanting to plead with him.

"Hush, angel." He rubs his thumb along my jaw and I subconsciously lean into his touch. "There's no changing that now. The only thing you have control over is how you respond to me."

I stare into his eyes, trying to understand. "They want me to train you. You know that, don't you?"

I barely nod my head as I accept that reality. "I've trained sex slaves before. Some willing, and some not so much." He pushes the hair out of my face. "It's easier when they're willing."

I can't look at him.

"If that's the way you want it, we can do it that way, too." He moves away from me and I scoot closer to the headboard, keeping my eyes on him as prey watches a predator.

"You need to eat," he says simply.

"I'm not hungry," I whisper.

"Do you need to use the bathroom?" he asks.

I shake my head and hug my knees to my chest. My entire body feels hollow. I don't need anything other than a chance to get away from him. As I shake my head, I become acutely aware of the pressure in my bladder. But I'm not having that fucker watch me go to the bathroom. I'll hold it as long as I have to. I'd rather pee in the corner.

He sighs angrily and presses his lips into a straight line. "If you need something, you'll need to knock loudly. Do you understand?" His voice is hard.

I nod my head as I say, "Yes."

He leaves the plate from the tray and walks out of the room without another word. I wait a moment, thinking he's left it unlocked and quietly move to the door. I'm halfway there when I hear the click and see the knob rattle as he tests to make sure it's locked.

My heart falls in my chest.

He's going to train me for them. That's all I am now. And there's no escape.

I suppose one would experience many different emotions when faced with something like this, the first being denial. And maybe that's what I spent the last few hours and yesterday doing. But the second emotion is anger.

I look around the room and let the rage consume me. And then I do something very, very stupid.

Chapter 8

Olivia

HE CAN'T JUST TAKE ME AND EXPECT ME TO BEND TO HIS WHIMS. He thinks he's my *Master*. He can go fuck himself. I'm not some sort of sweet little thing, so desperate to live I'll let him whittle me down into nothing. I refuse to give in to him. I take out the bottom drawer of the dresser. Or rather, I rip it out. I pick it up by the handle.

It's fucking heavy and made of real wood, but I'm able to swing it with all my weight against the side of the armoire. It barely breaks, and that makes me even angrier. I scream out and swing it again. This time it cracks and splinters, and falls into large pieces. One board almost lands on my foot, but I move it in time.

I pick up a small splinter that split off and shove it under the duvet in the bed. I'll start storing weapons.

I breathe heavily, staring at the armoire. I want that fucking door. I can see myself smashing it over his head. Or maybe using it as a shield to break down the bedroom door. It looks heavy, but I only need one chance. I toss the board onto the floor and grab the door to the armoire, tugging it, trying to bring it down.

I hold onto the door as the armoire tilts and gravity takes over as it falls to the floor with a loud crash. My hand on the door slips, and it smacks my arm as it falls. Fuck! That hurt like a bitch. It's definitely going to leave a bruise. I almost kick the damn thing in my rage, but that'd be worthless.

Instead I grip it and pull, trying to break it off. I'm tearing this fucking door off, and then I'm smashing through the door to the bedroom keeping me prisoner. I'll fucking break my way out of here.

"What the fuck!" The door slams open and Kade stares back at me with a look of contempt.

"What the fuck are you doing?" he sneers at me. My chest heaves. I don't know. I have no fucking clue what I'm doing, but it doesn't matter. It was my choice. And I'll do whatever I want.

He stalks toward me and I grab a piece of the drawer that broke off. I point the jagged edge at him. He wants to tame me, break me, fuck me… well then he's going to have to fight me first.

"What are you going to do with that, angel?" His dark voice sends a warning that makes my breathing come in frantic pants. I ignore the pulsing desire deep in my core.

I can see him overpowering me, ripping my weapon from my hand and making me pay for disobeying him. But he just punished me last time. Tears prick my eyes and my throat closes as a lump grows. I don't want this. I don't want any of this. This is some fucked up twisted mix of a nightmare and fantasy.

Kade pauses on his way to me, sensing my anger starting to wane. He holds his hand up like he's approaching a wounded animal. And maybe that's what I am. But he made me this way. It's his fault. I fucking hate him.

"Olivia, put it down." No fucking way. I shake my head and hold up the board with my trembling hand. I try to steady it, but I can't.

The reality of the situation hits me like a ton of bricks. I'm fucking dead. I can't fight him. Even with this board, I don't stand a chance. But at least I'm trying.

I shake my head again and the second I blink away the tears, he's on me. I scream as his body slams against mine and he pushes me down onto the rug. He grabs the board before I can do anything and pulls it from me.

I thrash under him, but his weight is too heavy. He cages me in, leaning his chest against mine.

"Shh, it's alright. Calm down." He whispers comforting words into my ear. His hand rubs along my hip and up my side then back down in soothing strokes. His lips barely touch my neck with his head safely nestled in the crook of my neck. The position also forces me still, unable to move much at all.

Minutes pass. My racing heart starts to slow, and the adrenaline rushing in my blood begins to melt away. I lie still under him, not knowing what he's going to do next.

"You shouldn't have done that, angel," he says after a long while. His hand steadies on my hip.

"I'm sorry." The words slip past my lips instinctively. Am I sorry? No, I'm not sorry. Not right now. I don't know what the consequences will be, but right now, I'm not sorry.

"Did you really think having a tantrum was going to help you at all?" He tsks in my ear.

He slowly rises, pinning my wrists down at my side. It's only then do I feel his raging erection against my hip. My eyes widen, and I force myself to look anywhere but at him.

I can't breathe.

"Get on your knees, angel." I shake my head, but I'm not given any choice. He flips me over and splays his hand on my shoulders, leaving me prostrate and completely vulnerable to him.

My breathing comes in ragged pants. "This would hurt to spank you with, angel," he says as he places a piece of the broken armoire against my bare ass. I hold my breath waiting for the blow. But nothing comes.

"You've already hurt yourself with your display of disobedience, haven't you?" His fingers gently touch my arm and I wince. I can't see, but I'd be damned if there isn't already a bruise there.

His fingers run along my spine and down to my ass. He leans down and plants a tender kiss on my neck. "I understand, angel. I do. But you can't behave this way." My pussy heats, and my back bows. I instantly regret it, but he doesn't seem to notice. Shame replaces my arousal. He places another sweet kiss on the nape of my neck this time, pushing my hair out of his way.

"I can't allow it," he says with a deep voice laced with regret.

Smack! His hand comes down hard on my ass. *Smack!* The pain shoots through my body. It's a sharp, stinging pain. My skin reddens with his repeated blows until I'm crying hysterically into the rug.

My ass and thighs sting. My eyes are swollen with tears. "Shh," he tries to comfort me, leaning down to kiss me again, but I pull away. I hate him. I hate him with everything in me.

"Now now, angel, you knew this would happen. Didn't you?"

I hate how he makes it seem like it was my fault. How could anyone blame me for trying to get out of here? I don't want this.

"I told you, you need to be good for me." I bite my tongue to keep myself from telling him to fuck off. I don't want any more punishment. He leans down to comfort me again with his hand still on my stinging ass, and again I move away from him.

"Let me comfort you, angel." No, fuck that. He hurt me, I won't seek shelter from him. No matter how much I want it. He pulls me into his arms and although I don't fight back, I don't lean into him either.

My ass burns as he moves me closer to him. I try not to whimper and hold it in. I won't let him see how much it hurts.

"I don't want to hurt you, angel." I hate that he keeps saying that. If he didn't want to hurt me, then he wouldn't. It's as simple as that.

"I wanted to keep you to myself, but now you've given me no choice." My heart rate picks up. "I don't have much time, and it's obvious you're going to fight me."

I risk a glance back at him as he says, "I'm sorry, angel." I don't believe him for one second. I know the sympathy and compassion in his eyes are complete bullshit. "I didn't want this for you." He's a liar.

Tears roll down my cheeks and I don't even bother to brush them away. He lays a hand on my cheek and I hate that it brings me warmth. "Please," I beg him again, "just let me go."

"If only you knew." I turn away from him, hating how he's acting like this is out of his control.

He huffs a humorless laugh. "I'm taking you to a place where you won't get away with this. You'll be running to me to keep you safe."

My body chills at his words.

"I won't let them hurt you." I look deep into his eyes and some naïve part of me believes him.

"But you won't get away with this shit over there."

Chapter 9

I LOCK THE DOORS ON THE CAR AND THINK ABOUT CHECKING THE trunk. It's been quiet, but I don't trust her being quiet. It's been five hours. I drove straight through the entire time. I'm sure she needs to relieve herself and stretch. But maybe she's quiet because she's asleep. I fucking hope that's it. She's going to need to be well-rested so she can take this in.

I remember the way she struggled in my arms trying to get her back in the trunk. I'm a sick fuck, but feeling her naked body writhing against me made me want to overpower her even more.

I thought about just letting her go. Leaving the door open and letting her leave.

But they'd just give me someone else at this point.

The meet is coming up fast. He needs to trust me, and this is how that'll happen.

I need this to work. There's no turning back.

And they gave me *her*.

I have to will away the image of me punishing her. Fuck, I groan and lean my head back. I still can't believe what I wanted to do to her.

I'm on the edge of unleashing a side of me that I don't want others to see. A depraved part of me I'm scared to unleash.

When she opens that smart mouth of hers I want so badly to put it to good use.

Last night was a turning point for me, with her acting out and the constant disobedience. On one hand, I understand it; I respect it even. On the other, I want to spank her ass raw and then give her what she really needs. What we *both* need.

I didn't used to be a bad man. I'm not sure at what point that changed for me. But seeing her look up at me with heated desire in her eyes and continuing to push me, knowing she was going to be punished begs me to release a beast inside of me that's clawing to get to her.

I stare up at Gabriel's mansion and admire its beauty. The intricately carved columns and flagstone pathways grace his home. It's luxurious outside, and even more lavish inside. But it's a house of pure sin and decadence of every sort. My dick starts hardening as I walk up the steps.

My handler, Gates, keeps saying I'm in too deep. He's threatened to pull me twice. I've never once thought he was right until I started thinking about my relationship with Gabriel Durand, a French entrepreneur who brought his expertise here stateside.

He owns this place, and runs it and the illicit parties that occur inside. He doesn't deal in women, but he keeps them. Not for him, but for others. It's not just a brothel, it's something much more. Dirtier and dark. This mansion is a place of pure sin.

I remember the first time I came here, to see how the women were trained. Men and women bring their own *pets*, or they come and pay for their choice.

Olivia needs to see what's expected of her. This is only going to help her to learn faster. I want to see how she reacts. I want to know what she really thinks of this.

If she's terrified and still fighting, I'm fucked. I won't do it. I can't do this to her. I'll have to find some excuse and get her the fuck out of here. I can at least save her.

But there's a chance she'll react like other women have here. I've seen the way Gabriel handles them. She could do that for me. I hope she enjoys it. I hope it turns her on. If the desire in her eyes is any indication, this will make the transition easy for her. The idea of her willing to be my pet should make me relieved. It would mean this will be easier and I can move forward with my mission.

Instead it makes me hard as fuck. I'm practically leaking in my pants at the thought of her on her knees and at my mercy.

I close my eyes and will the images away.

This is a mission. I need to stay focused. This isn't about any twisted fantasy I have. This isn't about either one of us.

I'll be quick and make the necessary arrangements so I can begin her training as soon as possible.

I walk quickly up the steps and bang on the hard, maple doors with the cast iron knocker. There's a doorbell, but I never use it. I prefer the feel of the knocker. The raw metal and hard bang remind me of that first night that I spent here when I was doing my research.

The door opens and a short woman with smooth, milky skin answers. Her long, straight blonde hair is pulled into a tight ponytail. Her clear blue eyes shine out with happiness once she registers me.

Her soft voice is just barely audible as she bows her head slightly and moves to the side for me to enter as she respectfully greets, "Good to see you, Master K." I gently set my hand down on her shoulder and step inside.

"You look lovely, Talia." She's in a floor-length silk charmeuse navy dress. It's loose on her. And no doubt will be taken off once evening approaches and the nighttime festivities start.

Talia is different from the others; she belongs to Gabriel. *She* is his most prized possession.

"Is your Master home, Talia?" I ask as she closes the door.

"Yes, Master K," she answers obediently. She raises her head and gestures gracefully with her hand to the right. "May I?" she asks.

The foyer is large with textured walls the color of soft cream, and sconces that give an Old World feel. The curved stairway has a cast iron railing that contrasts with the pale gray and white marbled floors. In the very center is an ancient table, and above it hangs a large crystal chandelier.

Decadence at its finest.

"Lead the way."

Talia's been with Gabriel for nearly a decade now. She didn't come here willingly like the other women. I often watch her and Gabriel. She is his *esclave*, French for slave. At first I was pissed to hear him call her a slave constantly. It took me a long time to realize it, but to the two of them it means something else, something more. Our steps echo off the floors. It seems empty, but I know there are others here. This place is never empty, and at night it truly comes alive.

"Are you well?" I ask her as she leads me to a room I've been in before many times. Gabriel's office is just as spacious as every other room in his home. It smells of wood oil and cigars. The room appears dark due to the rich mahogany furniture and deep red handwoven rug that covers most of the floor. But the thick curtains in front of the windows are also drawn, heightening the effect.

A faint blushes rises to her cheeks. "I am. And you?" she asks.

"You've brought me an unexpected guest, *esclave*." Gabriel stands from behind his desk and smiles wide at me.

Talia waits patiently by the door with her head bowed, and her hands clasped as he walks over to me.

Gabriel's a tall man. He's not muscular, but toned—it means he's not an obvious threat, but he's still lethal. He's ruthless in business. And he makes everything his business. I came here first when I went undercover. I had to become part of the scene, and that meant being talked about.

Talking is what Gabriel does best.

His dark hair is slicked back, and his brilliant smile is just as white as his crisp button-down shirt.

He gives me a quick hug along with a hard pat on the back. "I've been waiting for you to show your face in here again."

I never know how he's able to suck me in. No one knows me anymore; I don't even know who I am. But Gabriel does. He has a way of putting me at ease. It's a false sense of security, but it feels… thrilling.

A darkness I've tried to suppress creeps up on me. I need to contain the person I am when I'm here. For Olivia.

He lets a short, throaty laugh out from his chest and looks back at his desk.

"Have a seat, my friend." At first when I met him, I assumed he called all of his guests his friends. I found out very quickly he doesn't.

"Talia, come." He takes a seat and waits as Talia lowers herself beside his desk and sits her knees down on a pillow. He puts a hand on her shoulder and rubs soothing circles over her bare skin.

Her eyes close and she relaxes under his touch.

"I have a problem, Gabriel." I look at Talia as I use Gabriel's first name. It's a rule in his mansion that first names aren't used around pets or slaves. He once told me that for training purposes it's important they only ever know you as Master. But his favorite pet knows him by all his names. And he seems to give her more and more exceptions every time I see them.

"And does that problem have a woman's name?" he asks with a humorous glint in his eye.

"She does. Olivia Bell." Saying her name makes my heart still in my chest. A part of me wants to keep her a secret. To make sure she's safe. But she's not. I can't keep her safe. "I wasn't prepared for her. And she's quite…"

"Difficult?" he asks with a smirk. "The best ones always are." He looks down at Talia and she must feel his eyes on him, because she looks up. She gives him a small smile and rests her cheek on his thigh.

"I need a room, if you have one available."

"For you? Of course," he replies. Gabriel's always willing to lend a hand. But I'm sure he keeps a record of everyone who's ever owed him anything. I try to lean back in my seat, but I'm too anxious.

"Thank you. I appreciate it." I imagine this is going to cost at least 200 grand. Maybe more, depending on how long she takes.

"You're just in time, too," Gabriel says. I raise my brows in question. "I'm having a celebration tonight."

He reaches down and cups Talia's chin, giving her a small, chaste kiss before looking back at me.

"You've never brought your own before. This should be fun."

Chapter 10

Olivia

I slowly wake, feeling groggier than I did when I passed out in the trunk. And hot. So fucking hot. I try to sit up, but then I realize I'm on the floor. My eyes pop open and adrenaline shoots through me. Memories of yesterday come flooding back. Fuck, no. No. I close my eyes and wish it was a dream. But it's not. This is real. Was it yesterday? Or two days ago? How long has it been?

I see movement to my left, and I instinctively jump back.

"Now, angel, that's no way to greet me." His eyes hold a threat I haven't seen before.

"Get on your knees."

His words haunt me. Scenes from yesterday flash before my eyes. I lower myself to my knees slowly and wait. Outside the bedroom I can hear noises. Other people, although I can't make out what they're doing. At first I get the inclination to scream for help. But then I realize he brought me here for a reason. Whoever's outside that door is on his side, not mine.

"You can listen to me," he says with feigned amusement. Fucking prick.

He holds out a glass of water in front of me. But I'm not a fucking idiot. I'm not drinking that, or eating anything he gives me. I don't know what he might have put in it. "Drink," he commands with a deep voice that makes me question my resolve.

I take the glass in my hand and hold it, but I can't bring it to my lips.

He takes the glass from my hands and waits for me to look at him. When I do, he keeps my gaze and takes a sip before handing it back to me.

My cheeks burn. I hate that he can read me. Not that anyone in my position wouldn't be easy to read. I'm an emotional wreck.

"Olivia, I'm trying very hard to make this easy for you. You need to obey me."

My blood boils with his bullshit. *Make this easy on me.* My bottom lip trembles, but not from sadness, from anger.

I bring the glass to my lips, but I still don't drink. I can't look at him. I can't look at the glass. I let it fall, and it drops to the ground. The glass doesn't break, but it spills the water on the floor, splashing my leg.

He grabs the nape of my neck with a bruising force, lifting me to my feet so that my head is closer to him. So close, his lips barely touch my cheek. I can feel the heat of his hard body pressing down on top of me. He leans forward, growling in my ear. "Why do you always defy me?"

His hard, chiseled body presses against me. I close my eyes as I feel his erection dig into my stomach. A warmth flows through me as my nipples harden. "You will listen to me."

"Yes, Kade." The words stumble from my mouth.

"Master," he whispers in my ear with a deep, rough voice. "Master K." His grip loosens.

"Yes, Master K." I swallow thickly, waiting for him to release me.

"You're going to learn quickly to obey me. I want you to be perfect. And tonight, you'll see what that means."

Kade reaches into his pocket, and before I can see what he has, he snaps it around my neck. It's not tight and hangs just above my collarbone, but it feels as though it's strangling me.

My heart clenches with betrayal. I don't know why I keep waiting for him to let me go, but I do. I keep hoping he'll see how wrong this is.

"You will obey me," he says sternly, but I don't look at him. I don't respond at all.

"Angel, don't make me angry." He crouches down so he's level with me, and I'm forced to look into his cold blue eyes. But I'm surprised to see they're not cold at all. They're heated, and he stares at me as though he's holding back something dangerous.

It steals my breath from me.

"I'm trying very hard to go easy on you. I want to make this transition as easy as possible. But if I need to remind you of your punishment earlier, I will."

He holds my eyes for a moment, but then backs away. He leaves me on the floor, grabbing a thin piece of fabric from the dresser behind me.

"I want you to wear this tonight." His voice is soft and sincere.

He picks the garment up so I can see. It's a somewhat sheer shift dress with thin silver straps that cross in the back. The straps also look like they would wrap around my throat like a necklace. The dress is a pale blush color—so pale, it's almost white.

He raises his brows and waits. Clothing. Yes, I want that. I'm quick to lift my arms, although that means my breasts are just hanging there for him to see. His eyes travel along my body with appreciation. My pussy clenches despite myself, and I bite down on my lip. I look away as he slips the dress over my shoulders. I just need to cover myself with something.

The soft fabric feels lavish against my skin, although my ass is still raw from yesterday.

He circles me and pulls my hair out from under the dress. His hands linger on my skin and make my eyes close from the comforting touch.

He sighs and sounds disappointed. "Next time I'll be more prepared." I'm not sure if he's talking to me or to himself.

"You still look beautiful, but next time I'll make sure you're ready for them." His eyes linger on my breasts and I realize my nipples are hard.

"Are you cold?" he asks with a smirk. *Asshole.*

I don't respond, and have to seriously resist showing my anger.

He leans his head down and whispers against my neck. "You look utterly fuckable, Olivia. Especially when you tempt me like that." His hand fists the hair at the nape of my neck. He pulls slightly, just to the point of pain and exposes my neck to him.

He plants gentle kisses behind my ear and down my neck. "You make me want to do bad things when you disrespect me like that."

He pulls back and stares at my lips. They're parted, and I swear he's going to kiss me. But he doesn't. He pulls away from me and walks to the dresser. I watch him as he adds cufflinks to complete his ensemble.

"Would you like that, angel?" he asks.

"Would I like what?" I ask him warily.

"If I did bad things to you?"

My eyes linger on his broad shoulders and then down his muscular frame. The faint smell of his scent lingers, a mix of woodsy pine and cigars. I would. Some fucked up part of me wants him to do very bad things to me. But those aren't the words that come out.

"No," I answer with bated breath, and he pauses his movements, looking at me expectantly. "Master K." He gives me a small, approving smile.

"Good girl." He looks in the mirror and then back at me with a devilish glint in his eyes. "I wish you wouldn't lie to me though."

My cheeks heat and I look away to avoid his gaze. It's the first time I really take in the room.

It's luxurious, and by far the most beautiful room I've ever stepped foot in. All the furniture is modern and dark with clean lines. But the linens are a soft white with silver threading. The overall feel is bright and airy, with a fresh atmosphere. It's a con though. I may as well be in a fucking dungeon.

I hear noises outside the room, and for a moment I think it's someone coming in here. I shuffle closer to Kade and grip onto his leg, staring at the door, but the noises pass and no one comes in.

He looks down where my hands are and then to my face. I'm quick to take a step back and flash him a hateful look.

He doesn't like that, and I wish I could take it back. My cheeks heat and I look down, hating that his approval is something I need for survival.

"This is your home for the time being. I'll make sure you have everything you need." I nod my head once, although I don't really consider what he's saying. Anxiety is still racing through my blood.

"We're going downstairs. You will not say a word. Do you understand?" I don't know what it is, his anger, maybe his dominance, but something about the threat in his voice makes me want him even more. It shouldn't, but it does.

"Yes, Kade," I answer. His eyes narrow, and my heartbeat picks up with fear. I don't know why he's upset.

"Master K," he corrects me.

"Master K," I repeat as quickly as I can, and he relaxes his shoulders.

"When we're here you can call me Kade, so long as we're alone. But down there, you will call me Master K."

I nod my head, keeping my eyes on him. He said not to speak, so I won't. Even though I feel like I should. It's confusing.

Something shifts inside of me. I don't mind his anger so much when I know what I've done to cause it. I expect it. I can't help that I want to fight him. And he should fucking expect it. But the fact he got angry and I didn't know why... I don't like that. Not at all. I don't want it to happen again. At least when I'm pushing him I feel like I have some control. I need that. I need to know what to expect from him, and that's dependent on what I do.

I look up at him and realize I've taken a step closer. My hands are outstretched, ready to touch him.

"It's alright, angel." Kade pets my hair as I try to back away from him. I hate myself for doing that. I don't know why I keep thinking he's the one who's going to save me. He's the reason I'm here.

"Hands out," he says gently, and I slowly will my arms to obey. In an instant both of my wrists are bound in thin silver shackles that are more like bracelets from Pandora than handcuffs, but they're attached by a loop and he's quick to set a lock to bring them together. The snap of the lock makes my pussy clench. This is so wrong.

I stare down at my wrists not wanting to accept it, but somehow I have.

Kade attaches a leash around the loop on the bracelets and leads me from the room.

"I want you to walk beside me." Kade speaks to me as though I have a choice. My body seems to move of its own accord.

"I'm going to show you something tonight, angel. I'm going to show you lots of things, in fact." He brushes the hair out of my face and cups my chin.

"I want you to try to enjoy this. If you don't, this is going to be much harder for you than it has to be."

Chapter 11

KADE OPENS THE DOOR, AND A FLOOD OF SOUNDS POURS INTO the room. At first all I hear are the sounds of laughter and chatter. The faint sounds of music and people moving about, like this is all normal. If I didn't know any better, I'd think I was hearing just a normal party. I search his face for any sort of indication that this is dangerous.

If he was nervous I'd think I could maybe escape. There'd be some hope left. That I could somehow get away. He's nothing but confident. He turns to face me and looks me in the eyes. "Behave, angel."

A flood of arousal pulls between my legs, and my chest reddens with a flush of excitement. I try to ignore it, but I'm painfully aware of the effect he has on me.

It's the tenor in his voice, the way he commands me and my body. It's wrong. But it tempts me to give in to him.

I look out across the hall and it almost seems like we're in a hotel. There's a row of numbered doors across the way.

One door is open, and inside a woman is on a swing. It'd odd and made up of steel bars, almost like a chair. Her legs are spread wide and strapped to each end of the legs of the chair. As I realize her wrists are bound to the ropes of the swing, a man steps into view stroking his dick and circling her.

Chills run down my body.

I take a step back and want to fucking run.

I'm not going out there. I pull away, and the chains on the leash clink together. Kade looks back at me with a scowl.

"I need one thing," he growls as he slams the door shut behind him. I try to take a step back, my heart racing in my chest. I've never seen him like this. He's angry as he approaches me.

He takes a step toward me and I take a step back, with my hands bound in front of me and the leash attached.

Kade stops in his tracks and takes a moment to breathe. The hard lines of his face soften, and he inhales deeply before letting out a long exhale. "Olivia." Hearing my name on his lips loosens the fear in me.

He starts to say something, but I interrupt him.

"I'm scared." I shake my head and swallow thickly. "Please," I say. The fear is more real now than it's ever been. When I'm alone with Kade, this situation doesn't seem real. Maybe it's my attraction to him. Or something about him taking me from those other men. I don't know what it is, but it's different.

But seeing the other man and knowing there are more here? I don't want that. I'm terrified.

Kade takes a step forward with his hand out to cup my chin, his fingers are gentle on my neck. "It's going to be a bit of a shock, angel." I stiffen under his touch. No! I don't want to go down there. His other hand grips the back of my neck and he leans forward, his lips nearly touching mine. His low voice responds to my unspoken words. "You don't have a choice. Neither of us do."

I close my eyes, both hating him and what he's doing to me. He leans back and tips my chin up with his fingers. My eyes slowly open and I'm surprised to find pity in his gaze.

"I promise you, angel. You're only mine." He searches my face looking for understanding or acceptance, but I'm sure he won't find either. I don't trust him, and I don't know what to believe. My breathing is still coming in short, shallow spurts, and my heart feels like it's in my throat. "They all know that. No one will touch you."

I try to come to terms with the fact that I'm going down there. Like this. With them.

"Just stay beside me, and keep quiet." He runs his thumb over my jaw until I meet his gaze. "You'll be safe with me, and if you listen, I won't have to punish you." Even with the fear of going down there, the idea of him punishing me sends a wave of want to my core.

I let out a heavy breath, and watch as Kade's eyes widen with lust and his lips kick up with a small smirk. He leans down and hesitates before taking my lips with his.

I cave at his comforting touch, leaning into him and needing some kind of reassurance. My lips soften against his as his fingers spear through my hair. My pussy heats, and I lean my body toward his.

Maybe we can just stay here. I can hide here and just be his.

As the thought enters my mind, Kade pulls away from me and I instantly miss his touch, and the soothing balm he gave me with it. As he moves away, my hands move up to grab him and keep him here, but I hesitate.

The sense of calm is completely gone, and I find myself moving closer to him.

"Don't leave me," I whisper as his hand rests on the doorknob. He turns around to look at me and I almost expect him to scold me for giving him a command, even though we both know it was a plea.

Instead he wraps a hand around my waist and plants a small kiss on my forehead.

"Never, angel. Just stay by my side."

Kade opens the door and steps out. I follow him quickly, but I don't look up, keeping my eyes trained on the floor and that's where they're going to stay. Still, I can see the couple from before in my periphery. I can hear the sounds of her muffled moans and the man grunting and groaning as he pounds into her echoing in the hall. My heart races, and I nearly trip on Kade's feet.

"Angel," he says and gives me a low warning. I look up with wide eyes. He lays a hand on my head, letting it slowly smooth my hair. "Just relax."

I nod once because I can't speak. I just want to disappear. A few men in suits walk behind us at the top of the stairwell. I can feel their eyes on me, but I don't look up. I'll just look at the floor and try to stay next to Kade until he's done parading me around.

Fear and anxiety race through me, but I can't let them show. I'll be good.

I just need to stay by his side. I feel as though I'm in imminent danger of being devoured, like I'm bleeding out in the middle of shark-infested waters and on death's door. And I know the only thing keeping me alive and safe right now is Kade. Yet he's the most dangerous predator there is.

As I follow him down the stairs, watching my feet and only my feet, I see several shiny, black shoes of men but also the small, bare feet of women walking the opposite direction, up the stairs. Women like me. My eyes slowly rise, and I'm nearly petrified to see a woman completely naked with rope wrapped around her throat and midsection.

I look at her eyes, but she doesn't look back. Her shoulders are squared, and her back straight. She walks with dignity, and it's then that I notice she's smiling and her hands aren't bound.

My lips part to ask a question and my head turns of its own accord and I nearly trip and fall down the stairs as Kade's grip on the leash pulls me forward. I nearly bump into his back as I catch my steps.

My heart beats faster with fear as several men around us turn to stare. Kade turns around and cocks a brow at me, as if daring me to say something.

The world around me stills as I look up at him. I'm lost and confused and scared. I just need him on my side.

"Do you need help, Master K?" I hear a man's voice offer to my right. My lungs stop, and I stare at Kade's shoes. My shoulders turn in and I want to run as the man steps closer. I can feel him next to me. He chuckles and says, "She's new. And it looks like you've got your hands full."

"You'd like that, wouldn't you, Master A?" Kade says.

The man laughs and his fingers brush my shoulder, moving the hair to my back. My eyes widen with fear and I stare straight into Kade's eyes, but he's not looking at me. He's looking at the other man with a smile, as though everything is just fine.

My heart races faster when he turns to me and the smile falls. My body's paralyzed.

"She'll warm up soon enough," Kade says to the man, although he's still looking at me. The warmth on Kade's features still hasn't returned.

"I'm sure you'll do an excellent job with her," the man replies as a woman wearing a short, simple black dress passes behind him. She's balancing a silver tray in her hand carrying several champagne flutes filled with the sparkling liquid.

The man moves in my periphery, and I instinctively look at him.

He reaches out to the woman's tray and sets an empty glass on it. He's in a suit like Kade's but it's dark grey with a perfectly folded, bright white handkerchief in his pocket. He flashes the woman a dazzling, bright smile and shakes his head as she turns and lowers the tray for him to take a new glass.

"No thank you, love," he says with a boyish charm. The woman smiles and turns, leaving the man to look back at me. He has rich brown eyes and a classically handsome face that's freshly shaven.

"Say goodbye to Master A, Olivia," Kade says with a hint of admonishment in his voice, bringing me back to reality.

I open my mouth, but my throat is so dry, I have to swallow and clear it before I can say anything. I look up at the gorgeous man, and I can barely breathe. "Goodbye, Master A," I say in a rush as the words tumble from my mouth.

The man groans and pinches his forehead, looking at Kade as though I've just teased him. "You did that on purpose, you fucker." He says the words with humor in his voice.

Kade chuckles low and says, "You're an easy target."

Kade leans into me and asks loud enough for the man to hear, "Do you want him to be your Master?"

I quickly shake my head as fear grips my body.

Kade places a hand on my shoulder and rubs soothing circles on my body with his thumb. "Call him sir," he says simply.

"Sir." I'm quick to correct myself. I am not giving him permission to take me away from Kade. I have to actively resist the urge to cling to Kade.

"Say goodbye, *correctly.*"

I look at the man who has a sad smile on his face. "Goodbye, sir."

"Goodbye, Olivia." He smirks and raises his brows with his hands in his pockets as he says, "You may change your mind later." He gives me a wink and looks back at Kade.

"Enjoy your night, Master K."

Kade nods and replies, "And you as well."

I expect Kade to start walking again, but he doesn't. Instead his eyes are focused on me, and I'm forced to look up at him.

His eyes flash with power and lust. He takes a step forward, and I'd take a step back, but I feel caught in his gaze and the steps are behind me.

"He'd love to have you, Olivia. They all would." His eyes travel my body with obvious appreciation. He licks his lips and then meets my gaze again. "You will call them sir, unless I tell you otherwise." He wraps the leash around his hand once, and then grips my chin in the same hand. His thumb rests gently on my lips.

"You did well, angel." With his words of approval he drops his hand, and tugs gently on the leash. I'm quick to follow, feeling as though I've passed some sort of test of his.

I don't want tests though. My feet continue to move as he leads me through a hall. My bare feet patter against the floor, but I can barely hear it. Dozens of people are talking and moving about. It's surreal. I try to breathe, but my body isn't cooperating. Kade leads me through a large set of dark wooden doors with intricate carvings, and the atmosphere seems to shift from lighthearted to something more dangerous and thrilling.

A sick feeling overwhelms me, but when I look up, awe replaces the negative emotions threatening to take over.

The room is like a ballroom. It reminds me of Beauty and the Beast in some respects, with large chandeliers and an expansive empty space with marble floors that shine in the dim light. But it's dark. So dark. There's faint music, but it's not the sweet classics they dance to in fairytales. The beats are low and dangerous. They're meant to entrance you.

The walls of the room are painted a dark grey, and the large floor-to-ceiling windows are draped with thick, dark red curtains. There's a large mahogany bar in between the two windows, and servers dressed in simple black pants with tight, white t-shirts. It takes a moment for my eyes to focus, but there are cages lining the back wall. They're large with a few square feet inside, and each one is nearly eight feet tall. With the low lighting it's almost hard to see the women dancing in the cages. The shimmer of their silver dresses catches my eye as they move in rhythm to the beat of the music.

In the cage closest to me, a woman's small hands are wrapped around the bars, making her look even more delicate. Her eyes are closed, and she's lost in the music. Her hands move to her body, traveling up to her neck seductively, then to her hair. Her movements are sensual and mesmerizing.

It's only when Kade takes a step forward and the chain pulls on my wrists do I realize I've been staring.

This room itself is a drug. It's intoxicating, frightening, and electrifying all at once. Had I stepped into this room by my own volition, I would sway my hips to the music. I would close my eyes and get lost in the divine pleasure this room crafts. It seems like most of the people are on the outskirts of the room, staying close to the walls and talking and drinking. They're hardly paying any attention to the stimulating sensations overwhelming me.

There are a good number of people, a few dozen at least, dancing in the center of the room. Some women are dressed in clubwear and heels, while others, like me, are in bare feet and barely any clothes at all. The sea of swaying hips and hands caressing bodies is accompanied with couples grinding against one another.

I fixate on a couple at the very edge. The man is in low-hung pants and he isn't wearing a shirt. He's holding his partner up with his hands on her ass, and her legs wrapped around his waist. Her head tilts back, and he kisses her neck as he pumps his arms up and down to the beat while she moves against him. My breathing comes in heavy pants as her lips part. They look so intimate that they must be fucking. But in a flash, they're lost in the crowd.

My feet don't stop moving as Kade tugs the chain around my wrists. He's wrapped the chain around his hand so much I'm forced to stay close to him. It's not until I hear the sounds of moaning and strangled cries that my feet stumble, and Kade's there to catch me, as though he anticipated my fall.

The music dies as we move away from the dance floor and closer to a thick curtain that divides the room in half. Guarding the area where the curtain splits are two tall muscular men, wearing the same black pants and tight white t-shirts as the bartenders. The curtain is made from the same deep red fabric as the ones covering the windows.

As we approach, I can hear several women's strangled cries, but I'm not certain if they're from pleasure, or pain. I grip onto Kade's side, my nails digging into his muscular back. He wraps an arm around me, but even as my feet refuse to work, he continues to push me to move.

My body is a confusing mix of fear and curiosity, jumbled up with arousal and anxiety.

I only move because I have to, and as I walk in Kade's embrace and see what lies in front of us, my blood runs cold.

Behind the curtain is a room of debauchery.

Anxiety races through my blood. I feel lost, just like Alice when she fell down the rabbit hole. There are multiple small areas separated by a thick, red rope, but each division is taken by a couple while spectators stand around watching. Some men are completely clothed, but a few have their pants undone and they're openly stroking their erect cocks.

I try not to stare as I see a man standing in front of a scene with a woman on her knees in front of him. Her head bobs up and down his length. On a small stage before them the woman is being taken by two men. The woman at the spectator's feet doesn't bother to look at the scene. Her one hand balancing herself on his thigh and her other stroking him. She eagerly takes him into her mouth as his hand spears through her hair and he looks between her and the woman in front of him.

"They want that, angel." I look up at Kade, scared and wanting to cling to him to save me. I want to plead with him not to leave me here. "They *asked* to be in this room." He tilts my head back so I'm forced to take in the room and this time I watch the scene playing out to my left.

The woman closest to me is completely naked and shackled to a bench. Her beautiful blonde hair is disheveled, but still partially pulled back in a ponytail.

I watch as her eyes close and she obeys her Master. He's standing in front of her, with his hands resting on her arms as another man grips her hips from behind and thrusts himself deep inside her. Sounds of pleasure spill from her mouth as she takes the relentless thrusts. Her mouth parts, and her body trembles. The man behind her groans and pulls away from her, cumming violently on her lower back.

I watch her Master.

His eyes never leave her face. Another man comes up behind her and forcefully pounds her, making her entire body jolt forward as he fucks her with a ruthless pace.

She gives a strangled cry and reaches out for her Master. He holds on to her, supporting her head in his hands. I watch as he kisses her passion-ately, capturing her cries with his lips.

His other hand runs along the curve of her waist, trailing down between the bench and her body. He keeps his eyes focused on hers as he rubs her clit.

"Cum, *esclave*. Show them how good you feel, *esclave*," he whispers into the space between them. She moans into his mouth and takes the punish-ing fuck from the stranger behind her. I'm entrapped in their passion; I've never seen anything like this before.

Kade pulls me away, and I refuse to look at the other scenes. I'm over-whelmed with my own varied emotions and concerns.

Does that woman even know who the man behind her is?

Does her Master? Has he given them permission ahead of time, or would he let anyone fuck her?

The questions race through my mind. But the truth is, I'm not dis-gusted; I'm enthralled. My skin heats and tingles, and my pussy grows hot with need.

This is wrong. This is terrifying. But for a moment, it's intoxicating. The erotic thrill confuses me, and makes me genuinely afraid.

"Come, angel," Kade says as he pulls the chain tight on my wrists. "Your training starts tonight."

Chapter 12

KADE LEADS ME THROUGH A NARROW HALLWAY AND PAST A SET of rooms. They're small, and each have a large square window that lets the people in the hallway see the entire room. There are small benches in the center of the hallway, but no one's sitting. A few windows have curtains pulled shut, but most are open so anyone can watch. I try not to look. I try not to listen to the sounds. But every one of my senses is flooded with sex. *Sex* is everywhere.

"You'll watch tonight," Kade says, stopping in front of a window.

His hands rest on my shoulders as I peer into the window and take in the scene. A redheaded woman with beautiful curls that drape down her back is turned away from us. A man stands to the left, circling her; he's appraising her.

His hand settles on her hip and he pulls her backward so her back hits his chest. His head lowers and he whispers something into her ear.

I want to ask Kade if everyone here is like… us. If she's forced to be there with him. She doesn't look it. Neither has anyone else. This isn't what I expected.

The woman in the room molds her body to his and nods, making her red locks bounce. I have so many questions. Kade told me to be quiet though. My heart sinks slightly. I resist the urge to turn in his arms and plead with him. I feel so lost and confused. I don't know anything.

The man leaves the woman standing with her back to us and approaches the window. He flicks a switch, and I hear a loud click.

"Tonight, my Sara will show her submission to me, and devotion to our lifestyle." He walks to the far edge of the room and picks up something off the floor. It's a paddle. My heart races faster in my chest. He's going to beat her!

My legs move naturally in an attempt to protest and save her. My body heats. I can't stand by and watch this. *I won't.*

Kade's hands dig into my shoulders, forcing me to stay where I am. "He's not going to hurt her." He says the words simply, but I don't trust him. I don't believe him. A man to my left turns his head and stares at me. I almost look up at him and sneer, but Kade grips my chin and lowers his lips to my ear.

"You're being such a good girl, angel." His words make my body melt into his. I can't deny his approval makes me weak. "Just watch." He loosens his grip and takes my hips in his hands, keeping me in place.

"Kneel spread." The man gives a forceful command, but he also raises his hand and then lowers it with his fingers fanned out.

The woman drops to her knees and spreads her legs wide. I try to look away, but Kade holds the nape of my neck. I can see *everything.* Her ass rests on the heels of her feet, and her back is straight. I try not to look, but my eyes are drawn to her glistening sex. A violent heat floods my face as I blush. I search her face for anything, but she's completely neutral with her eyes on the floor.

"This position is excellent for display, but also for both punishment and reward due to the difficulty in maintaining the position, and the ease of access to her body, respectively" The man talks as he walks behind her. He sets the paddle down onto the bench and kneels next to her. He pinches her nipple and pulls outward. Her lips part slightly as her eyes close then slowly open, as she looks directly at his face.

"Good girl," he says as his hands roam her body while she remains perfectly still, giving him full control to do whatever he wishes.

As she stays still, he spreads her lips for us to see. Her nipples harden, and her breathing picks up as his fingers pump in and out of her. Once, twice, but after the third time he stops. Her body shudders as he moves his fingers to her clit. He stands and offers her his fingers, covered with her arousal.

"Suck," he commands, and before the word is even fully spoken, she takes them greedily into her mouth. She looks him in the eyes as she sucks and licks his fingers clean.

He smiles down at her and pets her hair before circling her body again and repeating the same routine again and again. Each time her legs seem to tremble more and more. Her breathing becomes ragged as she takes his fingers into her mouth. But she never finds her release. Instead he tells her to get into a different position, like the sitting position, which is exactly what I'd naturally assumed it would be.

I watch as she quickly moves from position to position as he orders her to do. Most seem to make sense, like the first. But others I wouldn't expect. She knows each one perfectly though, and confidently maneuvers her body so she's on display for him however he's commanded.

What strikes me most is how at ease she is. She knows she won't be punished; the presence of the paddle, even as he smacks it in his hand, doesn't faze her in the least.

She stays in each position until told to resume a different position. I keep waiting for her eyes to catch mine. For some reason I need her to see that I'm watching. I feel as if I could tell she was okay, if only she would look at me. But she never does. Her eyes stay on the floor, or on her Master. Not once do they move to anyone else.

"Present down." As he says the words, his submissive lowers her body forward with her arms at her side. The man circles her once, but I can already tell something's wrong. His forehead is pinched, and his breathing quickens.

"You know this one, little bird. Are you doing this deliberately?" he asks her. It's the first time his voice has taken an edge of authority.

The woman lifts her head. A blush rises to her cheeks. "It's the last one," she says hesitantly.

He cocks a brow at her and crouches in front of her, but to one side so we can see her face. "Did you think you needed to fail one?" he asks.

She did it on purpose? My heart beats so loudly, it nearly drowns out all other sounds. I hear a rough chuckle from the man to my left. But I only faintly register it.

"I thought they should see the whip position," she whispers. He leans forward and takes her chin in his hand. He plants a quick kiss on her lips.

"Then get into position, my pet." She gives him a small smile and raises her ass in the air.

"My Sara deliberately disobeyed me. She also decided to top from the bottom." Sarah's body tenses on the ground. I don't know what his words mean, but I can at least tell she wasn't expecting them. "She will be properly punished."

He turns and picks up the wooden paddle off the bench.. He turns it over in his hands, examining it. He leans down and gently places it flat against her ass. He lifts it high and I close my eyes, waiting to hear a loud *smack!* But there's nothing. My body is tense. I slowly open my eyes and let out a shaky exhale.

Kade kneads my shoulders and says, "Relax, angel." His voice is soft and smooth.

I watch as the man pushes the handle of the paddle in and out of her pussy. I can't see everything, but I know that's what he's doing. His other hand is on her back, keeping her shoulders down and he's watching her face intently.

He withdrawals the paddle suddenly, and the submissive whimpers. "You'd be cumming by now if you'd done what you were supposed to do, Sara." He puts the handle of the paddle to his mouth and tastes her juices. Her eyes stay forward, unaware of what he's doing behind her. I watch as he unzips his pants and steps out of them, his large, erect cock on full display. He bends down behind her and runs the paddle along her spine, and over her ass.

My breathing picks up as I watch the man lift the paddle and then swing it down, hitting the woman's ass and leaving a bright red mark. Her head flies up and she screams out with obvious pain.

In a quick movement, the paddle slaps against her ass again. *Smack!* My body jumps as Sara lets out a wail. Again and again he swings the paddle. Her face is scrunched up and she tries to muffle her noises as he spanks her over and over.

My eyes refuse to close, and I struggle to breathe. My fists clench. *She knew this would happen,* I repeat to myself over and over. *It's okay. She knew.*

And then something changes. Her back arches, and she seems to greet the paddle invitingly, rather thanstruggling to stay in position. Her face relaxes, and she screams out a sound of pure pleasure.

Smack!

"Yes!" she screams, and I stand in shock.

Kade's arm wraps around my waist and he pulls me close to him so my back is pressed against his chest. I feel his hard erection digging into me at my back. My eyes close, and I swallow thickly as my nipples harden and arousal pools between my legs.

Intellectually, I'm confused with a range of emotions. But my body isn't. And it's betraying me.

Kade whispers in my ear, "That wasn't so bad, was it?"

The man gentles his hand on her ass, right on the bright red mark, and she winces. He shushes her and sets the paddle down on the bench again. He strokes his cock as he examines her ass. A moment passes in silence. "Present down, correctly this time!" her Master says.

Kade's hand slowly travels to my hip, pausing for a brief moment and then continues moving lower.

"Answer me, angel," Kade says in a smooth voice.

Other spectators gather around as the woman moves to her knees. She spreads them wider than the last time and lowers her upper body flat against the floor, her arms straight out and her palms up.

"No, Master K." The words fall from my lips as the man in the room settles on his knees behind the woman and lines his dick up at her opening. She rocks her pussy against him and moans before he's even touched her. He shoves himself inside of her and her head lifts with her mouth shaped in a perfect O. He thrusts behind her with an arm bracing her body. His other hand wraps around her throat, and he lowers his chest to her back.

"Good girl," he says as his pace picks up. His other hand rubs her throbbing clit. He kisses her neck and nips her ear. "So fucking good," he breathes into her ear as he fucks her with a relentless pace.

Kade's own fingers travel to my heat. "Oh, angel," Kade groans as his fingers spread the moisture up to my clit. He kisses the tender spot behind my ear as the man grips the woman's hips and lifts her body off the floor to push deeper into her with each hard thrust.

I close my eyes as Kade's fingers dip into my soaking wet pussy.

Kade nips my ear and hisses an admonishment. "Open your eyes."

As the man fucks the woman bowed before him, Kade finger fucks me. Each thrust is perfectly in time with the scene before us.

"Yes!" the woman screams out, then bites her lip to quiet her moans of pleasure as her body rocks with each powerful movement from the man behind her. His hand grips her hip and smacks her ass as he mercilessly fucks her.

My own body leans forward as my body heats and my legs tremble. My pussy clenches around Kade's fingers, and I struggle to contain my silent scream. Arousal leaks down my leg as my pussy spasms around his fingers with my own orgasm.

I look up, barely able to catch my breath and find the woman panting on the floor.

The man stands with their combined cum on his cock. He grabs a blanket from a nearby shelf and covers her before lifting her into his arms and kissing her on the lips. Kade turns me in his arms and starts leading me away.

My legs hardly function and I try to lean against him as my eyes threaten to close.

"Not yet, angel," Kade says and kisses my hair. "You need to walk back to the room on your own. I can't carry you yet."

Chapter 13

I STARE AT THE CHAINS ON THE FLOOR NEXT TO A LARGE FLOOR pillow. It's time to sleep. And apparently, I'll be sleeping on the floor.

"Do I need to use the restraints?" Kade asks. I feel numb looking at the chains bolted to the floor. They're such a contrast. The room is spacious and luxurious, yet it's designed to be a prison. "If you killed me, you'd have to go out there with them."

My eyes slowly find Kade's as I say, "I don't want to kill you." *Kill him?* I'm so confused by everything. I don't know what to think anymore. My heart sinks in my chest.

"Until you submit to me, I think it's best you sleep here." Kade gestures to the large pillow on the floor. It's long enough that my body will fit however I want to lay, but it's not a bed. I part my lips to ask him what it means to submit to him so I can sleep on a real bed, but then I slam them shut. I know what it means, and that's not happening. My anger is short-lived as I stare at the bed.

My heart slowly falls and I nod my head and slowly lower my body to the floor.

"Tomorrow, I'll get you ready before training." My shoulders hunch forward. Every step back to the room was a step back to reality and away from the fantasy I'd conjured in my head. I breathe out deeply, trying to maintain my composure.

"Yes, Master K." I keep my eyes on the floor pillow, my fucking bed until I'm able to get the fuck out of here.

"You can call me Kade here, Olivia." His voice is soft, and I hear him just fine, but I can't give him a verbal response. So instead I just nod my head.

"Go to sleep, angel." With a loud click, Kade locks the doors and turns off the lights. A faint stream filters through the room from under the door. It gives me just enough light that I can see him lift his shirt over his head and drop his pants to the floor.

The bed groans as he climbs in and gets under the sheets.

It's better this way. I can sleep here, and I can do as I'm told until I can figure out some sort of escape.

I take in a deep breath and try to calm myself. This is temporary. I can fine a way out of this. I tell myself over and over, but I know it's false. My chest aches, and my throat closes. I know it's not true. I just don't want to admit it to myself.

I hear the faint music and soft laughter. Occasionally there are footsteps. Some are close to the door. I lie on the pillow facing the door, but I can't breathe.

I try to sleep for maybe hours, I don't know. But every time I hear the steps come close to our door I jump, and the fear keeps me wide awake.

"Angel." My body tenses as Kade's voice pierces through the night.

"Y-Yes, Master—" I try to speak. I can't begin to know why I'm so emotional. Why now of all times, I'm struggling.

He climbs off the bed and comes for me. My initial thought is to push him away, or to run from him. To hit him.

But I do nothing. Instead I let him lift me into his arms and carry me into the large bed.

He covers both of us with the blankets and pulls my naked body toward him. "Hush, angel."

I close my eyes, waiting for him to use me however he wants. I can't fight anymore. Not here. I feel helpless. Like the illusion of freedom has been ripped away from me.

"It's alright." He kisses my shoulder and settles in behind me, splaying his hand on my belly. "Go to sleep now. You're safe."

My body relaxes slightly, but I don't believe him. I wait with my eyes open. But the only movement he makes is to gently stroke my hair with his other hand.

My eyes feel heavy, and the part of me that's stopped fighting takes over. I lean against Kade and fall into a deep sleep.

Dreaming of cages and whips, chains and collars. The images flash before my eyes. I feel his hands on me and I enjoy every second. I hear the sounds of the whips and I arch my back, welcoming the exotic feel.

I wake with my heart pounding and my pussy clenching in the middle of the night. It's dark, with only faint bits of light from the moon filtering in through the curtain. I search the room, but there's nothing. Only Kade behind me, holding me close to him.

For a second I think I should run. I should leave him.

But then I hear footsteps in the hall. Heavy ones.

I settle back into Kade's embrace.

Bringing me here was deceitful. He's forced me to look at him as a savior rather than my captor. I can't forget who he really is. No matter how much I'm starting to crave his touch and this darkness he's introduced me to.

Chapter 14

Olivia

I WAKE UP TO THE BRIGHT LIGHT AND INSTANTLY BOLT UPRIGHT. I pull the covers around my naked body and slowly take in the room. I'm flooded with the memory of the night before, and my heart races frantically. A shiver runs through my body as I realize it's all true. It wasn't a nightmare or a depraved fantasy.

This is real.

The door cracks open and I turn sharply, watching Kade enter with a plate balanced on his hand. He closes the door behind him and keeps his eyes on me as he walks to the bed. I slowly scoot away until my back is pressed to the headboard, and I pull the blanket tighter around myself.

"Whenever I come in, you will greet me appropriately," he says with his icy blue eyes staring straight into mine. The comforting touch of last night is gone, and in its place is absolute authority.

A lump grows in my throat and I try to respond, but my voice croaks. I bow my head slightly and ball the blanket in my hands. I cower, like a pathetic little bitch.

"It's alright, angel. I haven't taught you yet." He's calm in his response and he climbs on the bed. He sits next to me and gently pulls the blanket away as though that's just fine. It is to him.

He owns me.

"You need to bow and keep your eyes lowered to the floor until I address you." He splays his hand across my back and pushes me forward. I let him move my body into a bow. I know the position from last night's lesson.

"And don't ever hide your body from me." I close my eyes and stay still as the bed dips and he moves away.

"That's better."

I slowly open my eyes as his hand cups my chin. He tilts my head up and runs his thumb along my lower lip. "You're doing so well, Olivia. You have no idea."

Again his approval makes my tense body ease with slight comfort.

"I've seen a lot of training, and you would make an excellent example for all of them."

My heart sinks and I pull away from his hand, hating that he's touching me at all. *How many women is a lot?* Anxiety, fear, and disgust all overwhelm me in a minute.

"Angel," he says with a threatening tone. My body stills and my heart slows. "You cannot move away from me. Do you understand?"

I nod my head once and let out a small, "Yes." I can feel his eyes on me, but I don't look up at him. I can't.

"What's bothering you?" he asks after a moment. My blood heats, and I bite my tongue. Is he fucking serious?

"When I ask you a question, you will answer it." Kade's voice is hard and I want to snap at him in return. But I clench my teeth and finally look up and respond by asking, "What happened to the others you trained?"

"Once they're trained, they're given to their owners." There's no remorse in his voice. He must sense my disgust though because he adds, "I know the ones I've trained have enjoyed their positions, angel. It's not all the horrors you've conjured in your head."

"Will you sell me?" I ask before I lose my nerve. I have to know.

"No," he's quick to respond, and I stare back at him with apprehension. *He's lying to me.*

"You're mine, and only mine." Something about the conviction in his voice eases a pain deep inside of me. I feel my defenses fall, and my armor seems to chip.

But I don't want to be owned. Not by him; not by anyone.

Kade pulls me closer to him. His hands grip my hips as he settles me in his lap. I'm tense and completely naked, yet he's fully clothed.

"I'll make you a deal, angel." Kade reaches to the plate sitting on the end of the bed and grabs a small slice of strawberry before he commands, "Open your mouth." I stare at his fingers for a moment, but then I obey.

I'll save my fight for when I truly need it. Right now I'll bide my time and play along with this shit.

I part my lips and let his thick fingers slip the small bit of fruit into my mouth. I close my eyes and practically moan at the sweet taste. It's only then that I realize how hungry I am. I haven't eaten in over a day.

"You do as I say," Kade instructs and reaches for another piece while I eagerly wait for him to bring it to my lips. "You show them that I can create the perfect slave, and I'll give you your freedom." He pushes the fruit into my mouth, but I can't chew. My body feels frozen.

He'll give me my freedom. Lies! He must be lying to me.

"Until then, I'll give you everything you need. I'll keep you safe, and you'll obey me." I have to work hard to keep my hands from fisting. I'm not going to willingly roll over and let him fuck me. But he hasn't tried yet. He could have, but he hasn't.

"How does that sound, angel?" he asks as I finally chew and swallow the small piece.

"It sounds like a lie." The words tumble out of my mouth without my permission. My eyes fly to his and widen with fear.

Much to my surprise, the corners of his lips pull up into an asymmetric grin. "I won't lie to you." He purses his lips for a moment and then adds, "Things aren't quite what they seem to be."

I don't get his cryptic meaning, but I'm also not interested. I don't believe he'll let me go. Not for one second.

"I can't tell you much, but I can tell you that very shortly, I'll be traveling soon. I won't be in the U.S., and if I sent you on your way back home, you'd be safe and I'd be safe from prosecution." He brings a slice of orange to my mouth and I have to open my lips wider. I take in the succulent slice and hold his eyes.

"I don't have a need for you where I'm going, and I won't mind sending you back home." I search his eyes and his face, but he seems sincere.

"I need you right now though." He looks away and his hand hovers over the plate before deciding on another slice of orange. For the first time, I see a sliver of vulnerability from him.

"I need you to be perfect for me, and then I can leave and you can go home."

I want to ask him what he means. I need a concrete answer and plan, but I already know he won't tell me.

"You can't tell anyone I offered you this deal, my sweet angel." I nod my head and swallow before promising, "I won't."

He gives me a small smile, but it's sad. He cups my chin in his hand and leans forward and whispers, "They'll kill me and most likely you."

My heart lurches in my chest. "I shouldn't have said anything, but I'm truly sorry you're in this situation." I look up into his eyes and I believe him. I may be naïve or stupid, but I do.

"So just be quiet and be good for me, and everything will be alright."

I nod my head and say, "I will." I speak the truth.

"Olivia," he says firmly, "don't ever speak of this again. Not to me; not to anyone."

I nod my head and let the fear of what would happen wash over me.

Chapter 15

"Kneel." Kade's voice is calm, and I'm quick to sit down on my heels. My legs are firmly pressed together. My back is straight, and I keep my eyes forward. I've had days of practice. I know these positions by heart now. It's easy to listen and obey these commands. They're all I've done, and thankfully, all that Kade has asked from me. I've obeyed everything without question, only thinking about being set free.

He leans down and gently brushes my nipples with the backs of his fingers.

My pussy clenches, and my nipples harden at his touch. This is a part of training, but I'm not giving in to him or his touch. I can't let myself be fooled. I'll play the part and do what I have to do to survive. But that's all this is. It's just me surviving until I can get out of here.

"Spread," he says in a low voice.

My knees move to the side, exposing myself to him. My heart races faster, but I do my best not to show it.

"Good girl," he barely speaks above a murmur. My lips part with his approval. I almost said thank you. Before I can think too much on my thoughts and the effect his approval has on me, I hear a zipper. The sound fills the room. I don't look up, but I don't have to. Kade's pants drop to the floor in a crumpled heap. The belt smacks the floor with a clank and I watch as he steps out of them.

"Look at me, angel." My eyes raise to his. They beg me to look straight ahead. His cock is right there, proud and large. Precum is already glistening at the head.

My breathing comes in frantic pants. "This is something they'll want to see."

I nod my head once. I knew this was going to happen eventually. I slowly open my mouth for him. But he doesn't move. I'd rather just get this over with. A moment passes and I hesitantly look up at him.

"Stay," he says. And with that simple command he leaves the room.

I close my mouth and finally breathe. My body sags forward and I want to collapse on the ground, but I don't. I need to be in this position when he returns.

I don't know how long we've been in this room, but it feels like forever. It's nearly empty and nothing like the bedroom.

This room was made for training. The walls and floor are cement. Neither are painted, and it gives a grim atmosphere. That, combined with the tools on the back wall and machines in the room makes it feel like a room designed for torture, although Kade informed me otherwise.

They can be used for pleasure, angel. "Can" being the operative word.

I could try to kill him. The thought sneaks into the crevice of my mind. There are paddles and whips and other tools of the trade at my disposal. I could grab one and try to overpower him. If I hit him just right when he walked back in, maybe I would be able to kill him or at least knock him unconscious.

But then what? I'd have to sneak up the stairs and try to find my way out without anyone noticing. And then run? I don't even know where I am, or what's outside. And I'm completely naked.

There are so many fucking people here. Men I've never met all know my name.

And if they found me running…

Kade said he'd give me my freedom. He said he'd protect me from them, and he'd be the only one to touch me.

And I believe him. I tear my eyes away from the back wall and concentrate on the concrete floor.

As horrid as this room is, I can't deny I'm turned on. It's Kade—his hands, his voice, his authority. Everything about him turns me on.

Every time I got into a position, he'd move me slightly. His firm grip would spread my legs wider, and then they'd linger on my body. Every touch was like a jolt of electricity. But I've done my best to keep my mind on the training.

I just need to do this right, and then I can leave.

As the thought hits me, the door opens and I quickly move back to the right position. I stay perfectly still and stare at the ground.

I hear Kade's footsteps, but then the faint pitter-patter of bare feet.

I have to seriously resist the urge to look up and see who else is with him. But I don't have to wonder for too long.

"Talia, kneel in front of my angel." Kade sounds confident and sure of himself.

I lift my eyes but not my head as the beautiful woman displays herself in front of me. At least she's wearing a dress. Our knees touch for a moment and then she sits back on her heels.

He brought in someone else.

I remember her from the first night. Anxiety races through my blood. I have to blink back my tears.

"Talia," Kade says, "Olivia has been a very good girl. I'd like you to comfort her."

I watch Talia cautiously as she reaches out to me and gently places her hand over mine. My body tenses at her soft touch.

My heart races, and I look up at Kade. I don't understand, but I don't like this. I don't know why he brought her in here, and I sure as shit don't need her comforting me.

Talia takes my hands in hers and gently rubs circles on the backs. "It's alright, Olivia. You're doing so well." It's the first time I've heard Talia's voice. It's low and soft, but also soothing. "He's so very proud of you." My eyes reach hers and my brow furrows. I don't like that she knows anything about us. Her eyes flash with fear as she takes in my expression, and her smooth motions falter.

Her lips part and then close, and she clears her throat before looking up to Kade. "I don't know how, Master K."

Master K. I remember how Kade said to call the other men sir. That calling them Master meant you wanted to be theirs. The memories of that night flash before my eyes. Those men who fucked her that night. Did she call them all Master? Anger slowly courses through my blood, at her and then at this situation. At Kade.

But mostly because I'm fucking jealous. She's staring up at Kade, a man I'm trying to keep at bay, and she wants him. I know she does.

I'm fucked up in the head for being jealous, but I am.

I rip my hands away from hers and scoot back so that my back hits the wall behind me and I pull my legs into my chest.

He brought her in here to hurt me. That fucking bastard.

"Angel?" Kade says my pet name, but I ignore him. I can't respond right now. I've worked so hard to be *good*. I was even going to suck him off! Tears prick my eyes. I was going to be his good slave, and he brought in another because why? I didn't move fast enough for him?

"What's wrong, Olivia?" Kade asks, but his voice is stern.

"Did I hurt you?" Talia asks with sincerity.

"Yes," I croak out and harshly wipe at the unshed tears before they have a chance to show themselves. *Try to be good. Earn your freedom.* Somewhere these thoughts are in the back of my mind, but *fuck them both* is the voice that takes over.

"Why don't you just take her if you want her?" I sneer at Kade. My eyes snap to his, and I instantly regret the decision.

His eyes narrow and heat with anger. Talia's eyes go wide and she folds in on herself, bowing and lowering her head to the floor. She's completely submitted.

My heart races as Kade's hand whips down and grips my mouth. My heart beats frantically in my chest.

Stupid! Stupid! What the fuck is wrong with me? Fuck! My breathing falters.

"You will apologize to me and to Talia, or you will be punished." Kade's voice is low and threatening. He rips his hand away with such force that I nearly topple over.

"I'm sorry." I'm quick to spit out the words as my palms smack against the concrete and I brace my body and move into a bow like Talia. "I'm sorry, Master K. I'm sorry, Talia." I mimic her position as perfectly as I can.

Blood rushes in my ears as I watch Kade pace the room. His hand runs through his hair with frustration.

"I didn't bring her in here for me. I brought her in here for you!"

I can hardly believe what he's saying. What the fuck was he thinking? A long moment passes, and finally I hear Kade drag a chair across the room. The feet scratch against the concrete until he moves it directly between Talia and me.

"Talia, do you enjoy getting off?" Kade asks. My heart races faster. I'll never forgive him if he touches her. Never.

"I do." Talia's answer is simple.

"Do you want to help me train angel?" he asks and quickly adds, "It would please me if you would."

"I do, Master K." Talia uses his name again, but the anger hardly registers this time. My mind races with possibilities.

"Talia, kiss my angel." Kade gives the command, and I tense.

Talia rises, her blonde hair swinging in front of her shoulders. She crawls over to me and gentles her hand on my back, peting my hair before leaning down and kissing my forehead. Her lips are soft, and the motion is over quickly. It's almost like a mother kissing her child good night.

But I don't see the point.

Kade stands and walks to the shelf in the back of the room. He comes back with what looks to be a microphone at first, but it's not. It's a huge ass vibrator.

"Thank you Talia, but that's not going to work." Kade sets the vibrator on a low speed, and I can hear it humming as it comes to life.

"Lean back and pleasure yourself," Kade says as he holds out the vibrator but doesn't give it to her as she tries to take it. "But don't you dare cum until you're permitted to," he says before letting her accept it.

Talia nods her head once and obediently says, "I understand."

She pulls her dress up slightly and lies on the floor with her legs spread. She isn't facing either of us, so I can't see her pussy and I'm grateful for that.

She lets out a low moan and starts moving the vibrator against her clit in slow circles.

"This can be pleasurable." Kade moves to the ground next to me. "There's no shame in enjoying this."

I try to stay still as his arm wraps around my waist. "Watch her, angel." I swallow thickly and look straight ahead. Talia's pebbled nipples show through the thin material of her dress. Her eyes are almost closed, and her lips are parted as she takes shallow breaths.

She bites down on her bottom lip and her legs snap back as she pulls the vibrator away from her clit. Her eyes open and she looks to Kade. "May I cum, Master K?" she asks with desperation.

The sight of her on edge makes my body heat.

"Ask my Olivia." Kade's words make my heart race. What the fuck?

"Mistress, please, may I cum?" Talia's blue eyes hold my gaze.

"Yes," I answer quickly and then look up at Kade, but he scolds me.

"Keep your eyes on her." His words are hard.

I grip my fingers in my lap and watch as Talia rocks her hips in motion with the vibrator. It doesn't take long before her back bows and she lets out a soft cry as her orgasm shoots through her body.

She starts to set the vibrator down, but Kade stops her with a firm, "No."

She doesn't hesitate to move the vibrator back to her heat. Her brow furrows, and her head thrashes. She's already primed for another.

"Please, Mistress," she begs me.

"Yes," I say and turn toward Kade. "Can she please stop?" I ask him.

I feel hot all over. And I can't help that the sight of her own orgasm turns me on. I have no interest in her whatsoever, but the sight of her finding her pleasure is tantalizing.

"If you'd like," Kade replies simply.

I nod my head and watch as Talia cums again. Her eyelids flutter, and her legs shake as she finds her second release. She gently lays the vibrator on the floor and rises to the waiting position. Her skin is flushed, and her hands tremble slightly.

"Good girl, Olivia." I look up at Kade with confusion. "Would you like Talia or me to give you your reward?" he asks, and I look between the two of them, not knowing what to say.

My mouth opens and closes. I hesitate. We've been over this, and hesitation isn't okay. I need to respond. With anxiety shooting through me, I answer, "You."

Kade gives me a stunning smiles and nods his head.

"Lie back then, angel."

Nearly numb, I gently lower myself to the floor. Talia's eyes are trained on the ground, somewhat giving us privacy. My cheeks heat with a violent blush.

"Grab your knees so I can see you better." I do as I'm told and pull my knees back, exposing my glistening sex. I'm so turned on and desperate for a release, but it still feels wrong.

"You enjoyed watching her before." Kade talks as he pushes my legs open even farther. The cool air touches my heat and makes me even more aware of how ready I am.

"I thought maybe it was Talia." He pushes two fingers into my hot, wet pussy. My mouth parts and my back bows as he strokes my G-spot and presses his thumb against my clit.

"I would have given you as many women as you wanted," he says as he pumps his fingers in and out of me. A strangled cry leaves my lips. As I turn my head to the side, I see Talia watching. Her fingers dig into her thighs and she's practically panting as she watches Kade finger fuck me.

Her eyes widen as Kade's head lowers and he takes a languid lick of my pussy.

"But it wasn't her, was it?" Kade asks before blowing on my clit. The chill makes my legs shake with the need to cum. I'm so close.

"No," I answer without thinking.

"No, it was how the men fucked her one after the other." My pussy clenches around his fingers, and I cum. I hold my breath and close my eyes as my body trembles. Waves of pleasure move from my core and shoot outward.

"Oh," a deep voice says from behind me. I whip my head up to look at the door. It's open, and Gabriel is standing there. I'm still on my back, naked and because of that he's upside down. I'm quick to look back down at Kade.

Fuck! I swallow hard and wish I could disappear.

"Well, if you ever need help…" A shudder runs through my body at his words. I want to close my eyes, but Kade's gaze is holding me. I'm trapped in the heated look he's giving me.

"I didn't plan on sharing," he says with his eyes still on me. I hear Gabriel's shoes smacking against the concrete as he walks over to Talia. Kade finally looks up to Gabriel, and he clenches his jaw and adds, "But then again, I didn't think she'd want that."

Gabriel chuckles as he pets Talia's hair.

"Come *esclave*, I need you." He holds his hand down and she slips her small hand in his. She's graceful to stand, but her legs are still shaky. He gives her a warm smile and puts his arm behind her back, wrapping it around her waist.

I turn to look away as he moves his gaze to me. I want to cover my body since I'm naked and I don't want him staring at me, but I don't. I can't. That's not allowed.

I only breathe once the door clicks closed.

"How do you feel, angel?" Kade asks as he scoops my body into his arms. He holds me against his chest and sits back in the chair.

How do I feel? Confused, scared, *aroused*. I'm tired because I've barely been able to sleep on that damn pillow. The first night I finally slept with him holding me in bed. But he hasn't brought me back to bed with him since. He's asked me every night, but I refuse.

"I don't know," I answer honestly. It feels like there's a hard lump in my chest. It's pressing against my heart and making everything uncomfortable.

A small voice inside my head is whispering to just let go. That if I stop fighting and just put my faith in Kade, everything would be easier. *It would be. Everything would be easier.* But then I'd lose myself. I can already feel that I'm on the brink of a steep cliff. If I fall, I'd shatter at the bottom, completely beyond repair.

I move my hand to my throat and tilt my head into Kade's chest.

He's so warm, so strong. What's worse is I feel safe with him. I don't feel on edge. It's not how I thought it would be. He's in complete control, and there's no doubt in my mind I have to listen to him for my very survival. But the commands are few, and mostly common sense.

Kade takes a deep inhale and I look up into his eyes. I can see he wants to say something, but instead he leans down and he kisses me.

His lips press against mine. His tongue glides against the seam of my lips and I part them. His hand splays across my back and he pushes me closer to him. My breasts press against his chest. He moans into my mouth. I can feel his hard dick pressing into my ass.

And I want it. I want *him*. As sick as it may be, desire stirs low in my core.

His power may arouse me, but it's this side of him that makes my defenses crash hard around me. His soft touch makes me weak. It threatens to destroy my very being.

He pulls away from me and I slowly open my eyes. My breathing is ragged, and my skin hot. "Not yet, angel. Not yet."

Chapter 16

Olivia

I HEAR THE DOORKNOB CLICK AND IT'S ENOUGH TO WAKE ME. My eyelids open as I hear the door creak open. I move quickly to get on my knees and kneel for Kade. I can't help the yawn, but luckily my face is down so I doubt he can even tell.

I don't think he'd mind much if he did see. Kade doesn't seem to mind much at all, really. He's held up his end of the deal. I behave, and he teaches me how to be a good slave. A shudder runs through my body as I think the word. *Slave.* I'm not much of a slave though. Not in the way I thought. He rewards me when I'm good, which is every day. I don't have a chance to run, and I'm not going to push him until I have that chance.

Instead it seems like I'm watching everything from afar. Like I'm not really here. It's not really me that he commands, *Spread yourself for me.* My body obeys, but in my mind I'm simply surviving. It's not my body that he lights aflame with desire. When he pushes his fingers inside of me and tells me to beg him to let me cum, I'm only doing what I need to do. Even if I enjoy it. Even if I crave it. I can't deny that I look forward to him touching me. I love seeing the desire and lust flicker in his eyes. His hands on my body are like a drug. Every day that passes I have to remind myself this is all just an act. *Isn't it?*

But it feels so good. I can't deny how I look forward to it now. With every position that exposes me to him, he makes me cum over and over.

He hasn't made me do anything to him though. I know it's coming. It has to be. That's the point of what I am. Still, he hasn't even hinted at it. It's almost like that first day he pulled out his cock never happened. At times I felt him on me and my body pushes me to give him pleasure, but I can't. I have to wait for his command. I'm eager for it as I wait on edge for my own release.

But then training ends and I seem to remember everything. It's like a switch. Only now I don't much fear the darkness.

Kade's hand gentles on my head and I know that means I can get up, but I don't want to. I'm tired. I've been sleeping on this damn pillow every night to stay away from him as best I can. My body is pleading with me to sleep in bed with him. To beg him. But I don't want to risk it. If I lie next to him, I'll want more. And so will he.

I pull my body up and look into his soft blue eyes. My core heats, and I'm already growing wet for him. He did that. He trained me to be this way. "I need you to be a good girl while I get ready for dinner. I'm taking you downstairs."

My heart races, and I'm instantly awake. I haven't been anywhere other than the training room and the bedroom for however long it's been. Maybe a week now? No, longer. I'm not sure.

I nod my head, keeping my eyes on his although apprehension races through me.

"I got you something to wear tonight," he says and smirks at me, "but I want you in it now." My heart speeds up. I have no idea what he means. When we're alone, I'm naked. Maybe it's a collar or cuffs. Nothing else. Outside of this bedroom, I wear what he tells me to. Which is usually a short thin dress.

"Get on the bed, Olivia." The way he says those words makes my pussy clench.

I sit on my knees with him behind me.

He shows me the wide, black leather collar with several silver loops on it. It's new. He fastens it to my neck, the smooth leather gently sliding across my tender skin until it's in place. I stay still as he attaches a thick silver chain to the back of it. My hair tickles my shoulders as he lifts it out of the way. It's a leash.

He bucks his hips into my ass and I slide forward on the bed with a small gasp. His hard dick is still pressed against my pussy. Only the thick fabric of his pants is between us. Shamefully, I feel myself heat for him. I want him. I want to know what it's like. He tempts and teases me every day and night, never taking from me.

My hands slip across the soft sheets, and the cold chain lifts from my back but before I can bow completely, he pulls the chain and I'm pulled back slightly by the collar around my neck. It tightens, but not to the point of pain or limiting my breath. I stay exactly how he has me positioned, my back arched and my fingers digging into the mattress to support this pose.

I hear him groan in satisfaction as his fingers gently glide down my waist, hip and then thigh, leaving goosebumps along the way. He shifts behind me and a chill runs up and down my spine. I hear the chain fall before I feel the cold metal on my back. He lays it down against my spine with care and then over my ass, letting the remainder pool between my legs and onto the mattress.

He splays a hand on my lower back while his other cups my pussy. I close my eyes in shame, knowing just how hot and wet I am for him.

"You're such a good girl, angel." He bends down and plants a kiss on my lower back. He moves the long chain between my pussy lips and up my stomach. I hear the clinking as he threads it through one of the silver loops in the collar and then tightens it.

My lips part with a gasp as the cold metal presses against my throbbing clit.

"Stay," he commands me and I obey. The bed dips, and I resist the urge to turn and look as he opens and then quickly closes a dresser drawer.

He moves back behind me and settles a hand on my lower back.

My forehead pinches as he slips an egg-shaped device into my slick pussy. It has a curve on the end that just barely touches my clit and bumps up against the chains. If I'm still, there's hardly any sensation, but the slightest movement feels so intense. Every nerve ending is on edge and ready to explode. I'm already primed from the training session today.

"Be a good girl and keep this in while I get ready." He starts to leave, but then he asks, "Do I need to chain you? I don't want you to move at all."

"No, Kade," I answer quickly. I almost said Master. I almost forgot we're in the bedroom.

"I mean it, angel. Be a good girl and just enjoy this." I turn slightly to meet his eyes as he clicks a button on a remote.

My mouth opens with a gasp and my body almost collapses as the device starts to vibrate in my pussy and against the thick chains. The humming movement of the chain makes my body heat, and pleasure stir within my lower belly. I drop my head to the mattress and moan into the sheets.

I'm on edge and dying for a release within seconds.

I lift my head to plead with him to make it stop or to give me more, I'm not sure which one. But he's not here. As my toes curl and the pleasure rises, the urge to grind against the chains is strong.

I moan Kade's name with desperation.

But he's already gone.

Chapter 17

I DON'T THINK I'VE EVER SHOWERED SO QUICKLY IN MY LIFE. I SPENT more time jerking off than anything else. I've had to ease my baser needs myself. I can't be hard around Olivia. I want to fuck her every second of every day, but she's not ready for that. I can't take advantage of my sweet angel. She's trying so hard, and doing so well. I only need them to see how good she is. She can do this. She's still holding back, but she trusts me. She's even turned on by being my pet.

I'm a sick bastard for enjoying this as much as I am.

Fucking her would only condemn me further. It's going to happen. It *has* to happen. But I want her to truly desire it.

I could hear her moaning and panting the second I walked away.

I smile slowly as I dry my hair with the towel. I heard her cum more than once while I stroked myself off in the shower. Even over the pounding of the water splashing against the tile.

I've memorized the way she bites down on the tip of her tongue when it gets too much for her body to handle. When she explodes with pleasure and her head falls back, each time it's because of me. I give her that pleasure. I want to give her more. I need to feel her pussy spasming around my cock and not my hand.

It's wrong, but I want it. I desperately need to fuck her.

Fuck! I'm rock hard again. Just the thought of Olivia makes me ache for her. Every day she submits to me more and more easily drives me to take her.

She'd let me. I know she would. All I'd have to do is ask. But I don't know if it's because she's just trying to survive, or if she truly wants me. In the heat of the moment, she'd give me anything I asked of her. The beast inside me wants to reward her as a Master should.

Instead I'm being a pussy about it all. This *needs* to happen. I won't be able to save her otherwise. My hands fly to my hair and grip tightly in frustration. I need to take this to the next step, but it'll solidify something I don't want.

I wish it didn't have to be like this.

I know they'll be here soon. Gabriel's told me they've called more than once to see how she's doing. I clench my jaw hating how they even know about her.

But that's the reason she's here. I can't forget that. Yet it constantly slips my mind. I'm ashamed that I keep forgetting. The thoughts of everything I've been through, of everything that's been sacrificed, thoughts of James fill my head and I'm quick to shut it all down. I don't want to think about it.

I hear her soft moans and I'm drawn to them. She's a beautiful distraction and so much more.

I drop the towel and open the bathroom door.

I walk out slowly, and look at my angel; my dick stands at full attention when I see her.

Olivia's on all fours with her ass raised high in the air, just how I left her. I circle the bed and see her hand is holding the vibrator in place. Her arousal's leaking down her thighs and her entire body is trembling. Without her holding it in, it would have easily fallen out.

"Please," she begs me.

"Please what, angel?" I ask her calmly, at complete odds with her desperation. I know what she needs. I should replace that vibrator with my dick. That's what we both need.

"Please," she moans louder with her forehead scrunched. She doesn't want to beg me to fuck her. She simply doesn't want it badly enough. She doesn't want *me*. My heart squeezes painfully in my chest, but I don't give myself time to think about it.

I climb on the bed and ignore my desire to push my dick into her hot cunt. Fuck, I want her. I want her more than anything else. As my hand settles on her lower back, she moves her hand away and steadies herself on the bed, raising her hips so I can take care of her needs.

I gently pull the vibrator out of her heat. She's so wet and hot. I watch as her pussy clenches around nothing, and I have to close my eyes.

She's *mine*. She was given to me. And she agreed to be my slave as long as I set her free when I can.

Mine. Mine to do with as I please. I grip my cock in my hand and slowly open my eyes. She's fucking gorgeous. Her cheek is pressed to the mattress, and she looks back at me with half-lidded eyes. Her skin is smooth and flushed.

"Tell me what you want angel." I barely speak the words. My heart hammers in my chest. She turns her head away from me and takes in an unsteady breath. I can hear the words begging to be spilled from her lips. But she doesn't say them. She lets out a long exhale with her eyes closed tight. "Please," she whimpers.

I push two fingers into her hot cunt and stroke against her G-spot with my thumb pressing down on her clit. I'm fighting against my desire and it's a hard battle to win. It doesn't take more than a few pumps until she's cumming. I feel her pussy pulse around my fingers and groan. My dick leaks with the need to be inside her. My heart pounds in my chest.

Her head tilts up, and she lets out the sexiest moan with her eyes barely closed.

I pull away from her quickly, before I do anything stupid.

I'll hold her in a minute. I'll give her the aftercare she needs.

But first I need a release.

When I get to the bathroom, I close the door and lean my back against it.

My breathing is frantic as I wipe my brow with the back of my hand.

I fucking want her. This is a dangerous game I'm playing. I'm in too deep. But all I want is her.

Chapter 18

Olivia

I T'S BEEN DAYS SINCE I'VE REALLY SEEN ANYONE ELSE. I FEEL protected with Kade. When he takes me to the training room I know other people are here. I can see them in my periphery as Kade leads me through the house. But I keep my eyes down. Sometimes I hear them talking. Occasionally Kade stops to talk to them.

I've seen Master A more than a few times. He seems to be very close to Kade. Almost as close as Gabriel. I've talked to them a few times. As in, I've said hello and thank you.

Whenever I see anyone other than Kade, it's only in passing, and nothing like this.

The dining room is large, with an oval mahogany table in the center of the room. There are over a dozen seats at the table. Next to each seat is a plush pillow with a dark red damask pattern on it. The dark red and gold accents give the room a warm and rich feeling.

Although the room is large with many chairs, there are only three people in the room. Gabriel, with Talia by his side, and another man I don't know at the chairs.

"You've finally decided to join us?" Gabriel asks Kade as we walk through the stained-glass double doors. Gabriel's at the head of the table and farthest away from us. Talia's seated on the pillow beside him. I can only see a bit of her hair until we walk farther into the room and Kade takes a seat next to Gabriel. I kneel onto the pillow beside him. My heart hammers in my chest.

"I think she's ready for a bit of socializing."

Kade's hand settles on my shoulder, his thumb rubbing soothing circles. I finally look over at Talia, and she seems perfectly content. Her hand rests on Gabriel's thigh, and his hand is on top of hers.

Her eyes meet mine and she gives me a soft smile. She closes her eyes and when she opens them, she's no longer looking at me. "It's about time," I hear Gabriel say. "More guests are coming tomorrow. It should be fun."

"Stone?" Kade asks.

Gabriel shakes his head. "He called again though." Irritation laces Gabriel's voice. "He's an impatient asshole, isn't he?"

I watch a woman walk into the room and hear her set something down on the table. Because I'm seated on the floor, I can only see her lower half. "Who's an asshole now?" says a voice I recognize, and turn to my left. Master A walks across the room and sits to the left of Kade, directly next to me.

"No company tonight, Master A?" Gabriel asks.

"There's plenty of company in here," Master A says. I quickly turn to face the ground as he looks at me with a smile.

"Isn't that right, Olivia?" Master A asks me.

I look up as my heart races. I swallow thickly and try to respond. My body heats with anxiety.

"It's alright, angel." Kade's calming voice puts me a bit at ease.

"She's scared, Master," Talia says, looking up at Gabriel.

I look between the men as I try to breathe normally. They're all looking at me, and I don't know what to do. I weakly respond with a "Yes, sir."

"Come up here, *esclave*." Gabriel puts a hand down for Talia and she easily slides into his lap, molding her body to his and letting her legs dangle over his.

Kade reaches his hand down. "You, too."

I do the same as Talia, mimicking her pose and look to her for clues on what I'm supposed to be doing. Her eyes are fixed on the large bowls and platters in the center of the table. The smell of butter and salmon fills my lungs. My mouth waters as I see the crusted fish on a silver tray with bowls of asparagus and potatoes next to it. Salmon is one of my favorite meals and the fillets look perfect, as though they came straight from a picture in a recipe book. The man across the table uses the tongs to dish some greens onto his plate.

Gabriel puts a fillet on his own plate and passes the utensil to Kade.

I lick my lips at the sight of the fillet. I want to reach out and dig in, but I don't. I resist. I watch as Talia picks up a fork and starts eating. Gabriel pets her hair and continues a conversation with the man across the table. I keep my hands in my lap, knowing I shouldn't do anything until Kade allows me.

Every meal I've had here so far he's fed me. I peek at Talia as she picks up a piece of asparagus with her fingers and nibbles delicately on the tip. She leans back against Gabriel and watches him and the other man as they talk.

"I didn't mean to make you uncomfortable." I hear Master A's voice and I turn to him and try to respond. I don't know what to say though. I'm at a complete loss. I know how to do what I'm told, but I don't know how to talk to anyone or what I can do if I'm not given direction.

Other than to call them sir, since I sure as fuck remember that. I need to know the rules for socializing, but I don't. I feel lost.

"Well I know she's keeping you busy, Master K, but do you even talk to the poor woman?" Gabriel asks with humor. Kade lets out a humorless laugh. My breath stills in my lungs, and tears prick my eyes. I'm supposed to be perfect for him. I'm failing.

Talia reaches across the table and takes my hand in hers. She wipes her other hand on the napkin. Her eyes are full of remorse. "It can be hard at first, but you're doing so well, I mean it." She gives me a smile, and part of me wants to hate her for condoning the way I'm being treated; the other half wants to hug her for her kindness.

I swallow thickly and give her a tight smile. "Thank you."

"She'll learn," Kade responds simply. He leans forward and my body is pushed against the table as he grabs a bottle of wine. "This will help." As he leans back, he wraps his arm around my waist and pulls me closer to him. He pours a large glass of wine and moves it closer to me. He kisses my hair, and when I look up at him he seems happy.

He's not upset with me, which is a relief.

He jostles my body as he leans back, and I have to put my hands out and brace myself against his chest to steady myself.

"Honestly, I'm sure she's ready," Master A says. *Ready for what?*

"I'm not." Kade answers quickly before Gabriel can respond. "I want her to be perfect."

My body chills at his words. I don't know what they're referring to, but I've done everything he's asked.

"I'm trying," I barely manage to say. Kade looks down at me, and his face softens. "You're doing perfectly, angel." His praise makes my tense body relax. "You just need a little time."

"I have to say I'm impressed, Master K," the man I don't know says from across the table. "My pet took much longer to come around."

"Where is she now, Master W?" Gabriel asks him with his eyebrows raised.

"In bed," Master W replies with a smirk. "She had a long day."

The men all chuckle, and Talia lets a smile play at her lips, as if she's in on some joke.

"We do enjoy the training lessons, but they exhaust her."

Master A takes a napkin off the table and smooths it over his lap before reaching for the bottle of wine. "Master W and his wife started coming here a few years ago." He lowers his voice and leans in closer to me as he says, "Their situation is a little different from yours."

My body tenses, and I look back at Master W with adrenaline racing through me. Kade stiffens and holds me a bit tighter.

Master W and his *wife*. My heart pounds with the need to escape. Wife, not slave. My eyes dart from the table to the man, and my hands grips onto my thighs as though they'll fly away if I let go.

Maybe he doesn't know. Maybe he could help me.

I want to scream and tell Master W I need his help. I want to plead with him to call the cops. I remember the party and how I wondered if the women were there willingly or not. Am I the only one here by force? How stupid have I been not to try to run?

My chest tightens with pain as I think about the days I've spent wanting to be free, but too scared to run. Maybe I could've escaped already. My body turns to ice as I open my mouth.

My throat dries as I look back at Master W. His eyes are fixed on his plate as he picks up his fork. Kade lowers his lips to my ear and grips on to me tighter as he says, "Think very hard about what you're going to say, angel." My body freezes with fear.

I feel a pang of guilt and I'm nearly overwhelmed with anxiety. I feel like I'm betraying Kade, I know that..

I swallow thickly and prepare to scream for help. I have to try. I have to. My heart clenches in my chest. I have to at least try. I'm acutely aware in this moment that I feel something for Kade, but I'm not his property. I need to get the fuck out of here.

"Help me!" I barely get the words out as they rip from my throat. Kade's hand closes over my mouth tightly, and he forces my head back so I'm staring at the ceiling.

The legs of Kade's chair squeak against the wooden floor as he pushes us away from the table. His legs wrap around mine as I kick out and hit the hard table. It hurts, but I barely register the pain. Kade's arm wraps around mine and effectively holds me completely still. My heart races, and my body is a mix of hot and cold, a sickness threatening to lose itself.

"Whoa!" Master A yells out, and stands up from the table. I see his wine spill across the dark wood and onto the floor. "No worries," he says, putting his napkin on the table.

My heart stills, no one's reacted at all to my cry for help. My chest feels hollow as I see the man across the table looking at me with pity as he picks up his glass of water.

Useless. It was for nothing.

Tears leak down my cheeks. *Help me.* My heart lurches in my chest.

"You were right," I hear Gabriel say. "She's not quite ready, but still, she's doing wonderfully considering how new she is." He's speaking casually, as though I didn't just scream for help. As though Kade's not holding me still because I was flailing my body and screaming.

My body goes limp in Kade's arms. There's no use fighting.

"Are you done?" Kade asks with a low, threatening voice. My eyes squeeze shut. No, no. I wish I could take it back.

I try to nod my head, but his hand over my mouth is so forceful that I can't move my head. He slowly drops it to my throat and I'm quick to answer, "Yes, Master."

I feel defeated, betrayed, alone, and ashamed. My breath is unsteady as I try to calm myself. The three other men continue to eat as though nothing's happened, and everything is alright.

Talia looks at me with sympathy in her blue eyes. She sets her fork down and leans against Gabriel, refusing to meet my gaze. Her plump lips are turned down and it makes me feel so alone.

No one here is going to help me. Even worse, I feel guilty.

"Well that was bound to happen," Gabriel says in a casual voice as though he's trying to lighten the mood.

Kade's tight hold on me loosens, and I see the man across the table nodding while chewing whatever he just put in his mouth.

My body's stiff as Kade sets me back down in his lap. Everyone else has resumed to normal, although Talia's not eating. I watch as Gabriel picks up a piece of asparagus and puts it to her lips, but she shakes her head and leans against him, burying her head under his chin.

I stare at her and will her to look at me, but she does nothing. I feel sick to my stomach.

"What are you thinking, Master K?" Gabriel asks. He takes a bite of the asparagus and chews it as he waits for Kade to answer. I lower my eyes to the floor. Fuck. I try to breathe in and out slowly, but even doing that is hard.

"It's her first offense since we've been here." Kade's voice sends a chill up my back.

"But it was a grave offense." I watch as Talia shifts in Gabriel's lap, uneasy with the topic of conversation.

I can feel Kade nodding behind me. "I'll finish my dinner first."

"And then what?" Master A asks.

Kade picks up the tongs and dishes out a few spears of asparagus onto the plate. His movements jostle my body, but I try to stay upright. They're talking about me as if I'm not in the room. Talking about my punishment. I close my eyes and wish I'd never done it.

I had to though.

My body freezes at Kade's response. "When I'm done eating, we'll go to the basement."

Chapter 19

Olivia

I WALK BEHIND KADE OBEDIENTLY, EVEN THOUGH HE'S LEADING ME to my punishment. I can hardly breathe, my chest hurts so much.

Kade stops at a door to the right of the stairs. His hand rests on the knob as he turns to me. "I understand why you did that, Olivia. I do. But you know it was bad, don't you?"

My stomach churns as I nod my head and answer, "Yes, Master K."

No, no it wasn't. I *had* to. He grips my chin in his hand and forces me to look into his narrowed eyes. He looks pissed. My heart stops in my chest.

"Don't lie to me, angel." His words are hard and unforgiving. "I'm thankful it happened in that company. Had it been different…" he trails off as he opens the door and takes in a slow inhale. He doesn't finish what he was saying, leaving me to imagine the worst, but instead walks down the steps.

I take a peek into the basement. It's different down here. It's not luxurious at all. The walls are cinderblocks that have been painted grey. The steps are wooden and also painted, although they're black and have texture to them. My heart races as Kade descends the stairs. I look to my right and I know the front doors are close. They're just down the hall. I could try to run. A very large part of me wants to.

I take an uneasy step toward the basement door and grip the handle. I could close the door and try to run.

My heart races and thuds in my chest.

"Don't make me wait for you, angel." Although Kade's voice is low and laced with a threat, it eases something inside of me. I let go of the door and walk slowly down the wooden stairs. When I look to my left I can see the room for what it is. It's mostly empty. The floor is painted black, and the walls are the same grey-painted cinders. There's a drain in the center of the room, and nothing else. It's empty.

My heart slows as I think of what this room could be used for. I nearly trip on the last stair as my heart tries to leap out of my throat.

Murder, death. The drain is for blood. That must be it. My hand grips the railing, but my feet are bolted to the ground.

"Olivia, calm down. It's okay." Kade puts his hands up and his eyes soften. "It's alright, angel." His voice is meant to calm me, but it's not working. He walks to me with even steps, and it takes everything in me not to move away from him. "I'm not going to hurt you." He sounds so sincere. I lift my eyes to meet his, and he slowly drops his lips to mine. His hand cups the back of my head.

His comforting touch feels so welcoming. I lean into him and deepen the kiss. I'll be good. I can be good. My heart swells in my chest. I want to make this right.

He pulls away from me and wraps his hand lightly around my throat. "Olivia," he begins and pauses to take in a deep breath. "You weren't supposed to do that." Sadness clouds his eyes.

"I'm sorry." I really feel like I betrayed him. I remember what he said, and his promise to free me. I'm so fucking stupid. I take in a ragged breath.

"Please, Kade," I say and place my hand on his hard chest as I beg him. "I won't do it again. I promise."

"Angel, I wish it were that easy." He takes my hand in both of his and leads me across the room. Under the stairs is a bench covered in a wipeable material and on either side of it are two storage containers.

"I want you to lie down on the bench." Kade doesn't even look at me as he gives me his order. I walk slowly to the bench and lie down on my back. The bench is wide enough to easily fit me, and long enough so that there's plenty of seating left over.

My heart races as Kade opens a box and then the other. I want to look at what he's getting, but I don't. I'm terrified. I close my eyes tight and clench my fists.

Just obey, and soon I'll be free. I can do this.

My eyes pop open as I hear chains above my head. I look up, and sure enough, two chains with shackles are now dangling from the stairs. Kade adjusts them so he can easily lock the shackles around my ankles, then he raises and spreads them wide. Each side of the staircase has a chain affixed. The thin dress I'm wearing slides up, and the cool air breathes against my bared pussy. I swallow thickly, knowing I'm completely vulnerable like this.

"Kade," I breathe out.

"Yes, Olivia?"

"What are you going to do to me?" I ask. I need to know.

"I'm going to deny you, angel."

"Deny me what?" I ask as he places a thick strip of cloth over my torso before wrapping and locking a chain around it. Now I'm chained to the bench with my legs in the air, completely spread wide open for him.

He gives me a soft smile and pushes the hair out of my face, but he doesn't answer me.

"You don't have to chain me," I say as he reaches into one of the boxes. He looks at me with a cocked brow. "The chain around my stomach," I say and clear my dry throat. "I promise I won't move." I won't. I'm going to be good for him.

He smirks at me and shakes his head. "You won't intend to move, but you will. That chain is for your safety. I don't want you to fall." He closes the box and looks to the stairs as he takes something out of his pocket. My eyes widen. It's the egg from earlier.

I breathe out as he slips the egg into place. He has to pump it in and out before it's fully in place. I'm not at all aroused.

"I'm not used to you not being wet for me," Kade remarks as he reaches back into his pocket and grabs the controller. "You must really dislike being punished."

No shit. Nothing like thinking you're going to die to turn you off.

I hold onto my snarky remark and try to forget everything. *Just obey.* I can do this.

Kade flips the switch and a gentle hum fills the room.

It doesn't feel the same as earlier. It's on a low speed, and I'm not anywhere near on edge.

My fingers twitch at my sides, and Kade sees. He's quick to cuff my wrists to the chain around my stomach.

"Are you comfortable?" Kade asks. The shackles on my ankle bite a bit into my skin, but other than that I am, yeah. I nod my head and search Kade's eyes for answers.

The humming seems to get louder and the vibrations more intense. It's just enough that my pussy heats, and desire spikes, but then it's gone. I try to readjust, feeling off-balance, but I can't. I can't move anything. "I have to blindfold you now," Kade says, and I shake my head out of instinct. I don't want that. Not being able to see terrifies me.

"You don't have a say in this, angel," Kade says as he slips a black blindfold over my eyes. I hold in a moan as the vibrations increase again and my forehead scrunches. I try to twist my hips, but I'm limited, and it only makes my ankles hurt from putting pressure on them.

In an instant, the sensation is gone again and I feel on edge. I can tell there's light, but other than that, I'm blind.

"Kade," I whisper. There's no response. "Kade?" I call for him with desperation.

"I'm here, angel." I wish he'd hold me.

I scream out as the vibrations pick up again and I try to buck my hips to get away, but I can't. My body heats as I get closer to my heightened orgasm, but then it dies.

My heart races, and my pussy clenches.

I breathe out slowly.

I swallow and attempt to ignore it. I try to ignore the arousal pooling in my core, the heated tingles along my stomach and legs. My nipples have hardened, and every small movement against the dress seems to elicit a shock of electricity straight to my clit.

The vibrations intensify again, and this time I try to rock my hips. I just need a bit more. It's so close, yet so far away. I whimper a small moan as they die down, leaving me feeling needy and helpless.

When it doesn't come, I lie limp and try to remember to breathe.

And then again, and again.

I clench my teeth as each time my orgasm approaches, I almost fear the moment I fall off the edge. My toes and extremities tingle with need. My body feels as though it's going to explode, each time greater than the last… yet nothing happens.

My arousal drips down my ass and onto the seat. I want to move. I pull against the chains, but I can't do anything. I'm forced to scream out as the next one comes and goes. Leaving my body to fight against both the up-coming release, and the inevitable denial of it.

"Kade!" I cry out for him. But I hear nothing. "I'm sorry!" I scream as it comes again.

I buck my hips and try desperately to find my release.

My body heats and cools as a thin sheen of sweat covers every inch.

And then nothing.

My head thrashes, and my heart beats up my throat as I try to both fight and conquer the heated sensation.

The faint hum of the vibrator is the only noise in the room.

And it's the only sound other than my own moans and screams for god knows how long.

It feels like hours.

Tears leak down my face as it comes again, with the relentless sensation, but this time there's more. A strangled cry leaves my mouth as I get closer than I ever have before.

Relief blooms in my chest. The intensity picks up and just as I begin to fall, the vibrations stop completely.

I scream out in both anger and frustration. I feel delirious.

The room is quiet other than my frantic breathing. Even the hum I've listened to the entire time has left me.

I try to calm down, thinking maybe it's over. My punishment is finally done with. But then the faint hum comes back with the soft vibrations, and I lose all sense of composure.

I scream out for Kade until my throat hurts. Sweat covers my heated body and I pull against the chains and thrash on the bench as my punishment seems to last and last.

I don't know how long it's been. But each time it hurts more and more to be teased and denied.

I focus on trying to accept it won't come. This is my punishment.

I'm only distracted by the small sounds of footprints coming down the stairs.

"Kade?" I call out for him in a choked voice. "Please!"

"Shh!" a soft feminine voice says as the egg is pulled away from me.

Relief. Oh, fuck! Thank fuck.

I turn my head to the side as my body goes limp although my legs are still trembling.

The blindfold is pulled away, and I wince from the light.

"Talia?" I blink several times until she comes into focus. "Please let me out," I whisper harshly.

"I can't. Please. I just came for a moment." A sob is ripped up my throat.

"I can't stay here," I whimper.

"It's okay," she says sweetly, wiping the tears from my face. "He just left, so I thought I'd sneak in."

I don't understand what she's saying. "Who?"

"I'm sure he'll be right back, and hopefully he'll end it soon."

"Kade?" I ask her, my body tense.

She nods her head and wipes my face with a cool cloth. It feels so good. So good. I feel so hot. "The first time is the worst." I don't know if she's talking to me or to herself.

"Please!" I scream out, and she covers my mouth with her hand.

"Shh! I'll get in so much trouble for coming down here if I'm caught." The nervousness in her voice makes me try to calm my breathing and listen for any new sounds, but there's nothing.

She slowly lifts her hand away from my mouth and I beg her, "Please, please let me out."

"I can't. I'm so sorry, Olivia."

"You don't know what it's like," I say and take in a ragged breath. "I don't want this like you do."

She scoffs at me and it catches me off-guard. "I know exactly what it's like." There's a moment of silence as she looks up the stairs. My body is begging to move. I'm still so close. I try to ignore it, but part of me shamelessly wants me to beg her to get me off. I bite down on my lip and ignore the intense need claiming my every thought.

"It was much worse for me, trust me. It wasn't always this way." Her voice sounds lost. "It's really not so bad, is it?" she asks.

I can't answer. I turn my head to look away. Partly because of her question, and partly because of my debilitating needs.

After a moment, she starts talking again. "Master A feels really bad. He didn't think you'd do that."

"Did he tell you that?" I ask weakly. My body calms slightly as the absence of stimulation lengthens. I turn back to look at her; I'm grateful for the distraction.

She shakes her head and looks back up at the stairs. "He was talking to Master G."

"They were talking about me?" I ask weakly, still partially out of breath. Fuck, that can't be good.

She lets out a small giggle at my worried look and explains, "They were hoping your master would let them help."

"They want to punish me?" My heart lurches in my chest. My body is still on edge and I'm trying to ignore it. The fear of her confession helps.

"No, no, afterward. They thought he would spank and then fuck you at the table."

My pussy clenches at her words, and the small movement makes my clit throb. I throw my head back and moan. I can see him doing it. Fuck, it's so wrong, but the thought turns me on. I wish he'd just done that. My back arches as I think about what she said. *How they wanted to help.* And then I realize it's her Master and he said that to her.

"He'd do that to you?" I feel so bad for her.

She arches a brow. "Spank and fuck me? Of course," she says and practically rolls her eyes.

"No, fuck... fuck someone else in front of you." It feels weird talking to her about this. But they seem like a couple. I can't imagine how much it must hurt her.

She gives me a soft smile. "He would." She leans in and adds, "I like to help, too."

I can feel shock the moment the meaning of her words hits me. My mouth pops open slightly, and I don't know how to respond. I try to speak, but I don't know what to say.

"It's okay, I'm not sad that you don't want to fuck me. I prefer the dicks, too." She winks at me, but I'm stiff and unsure of how to respond at all.

"I have to go; he'll be back soon," she says hastily, as if this conversation wasn't uncomfortable.

If I could I'd grip her arm to keep her from leaving, I would, but I can't.

I see her reach down the bench as the humming comes back to life.

"No!" Fuck, no! I can't. I can't take this any longer.

"Please don't ask me to do something I can't." Her forehead is creased, and her clear blue eyes are so sad. "It's going to be okay, Olivia. He'll make sure you're taken care of. I promise you."

She quickly places the blindfold back over my eyes and I pathetically begin to cry.

"It's okay, it's going to be okay," she reassures me.

"But it's not," I manage to choke out. She slowly puts the egg that's still vibrating back into place, and I start crying again. I can't take it. I can't help it.

"I'm so sorry." I can hear the sorrow in her voice. "Please, don't worry. It'll be okay."

I listen as she leaves, and try to rein in my pathetic sobs. She quickly climbs up the stairs and gently closes the door.

As I strain against the cuffs feeling a wave of arousal come I know will only heighten and torture me over time, I swear I hear the faint sound of the door opening.

I listen as hard as I can, but I don't hear his steps. I hold my breath. Finally, I hear a creak on the stairs and then the next, and then nothing.

"Kade," I call out. "Please—" My words are cut short as I struggle against the intense vibrations yet again. My body heats, and my back bows. So close. So close. Please.

And then nothing.

"Shh, angel."

"Kade," I say and turn toward him as best I can, which isn't much. "Please," I beg.

He doesn't answer me, but in an instant the egg is removed and in its place are his fingers. He pumps them in and out of my slick heat and pushes his thumb against my clit. It doesn't take long until I'm close to the overwhelming edge of my impending release. My body heats with a vengeance, and every nerve ending quickly goes numb before exploding with pleasure. My mouth falls open, and my body shudders as wave after wave courses through my body. A white light flashes before my eyes as he pulls my orgasm from me. In an instant it's over and I quickly crash, feeling drained and numb.

My body falls limp, feeling nearly paralyzed. He unchains one leg and then the other, and they fall heavily into his arms. He lowers them to the bench, and I feel the wetness on the back of my legs.

It takes a long time before I register what's happening. My eyes are heavy, and so is my body.

I groan as he massages life back into my legs.

"Kade," I whisper in a soft voice.

He removes the cuffs and then the chain around my stomach. And again he massages my arms and shoulders.

I cry silently with relief as he lifts me into his arms and wraps a blanket around me. Finally, he slowly removes the blindfold and I bury my head into his chest.

"Shh, it's alright, angel. It's over."

He whispers into my hair and kisses my forehead as he carries me to the bedroom.

The last thing I remember before I pass out is him laying me gently on the bed and pulling my back against his chest.

He plants a small kiss on my neck. "It's alright, angel. I've got you."

Chapter 20

Kade

Last night was too much. I don't know why, but I couldn't get James out of my head. I fucking killed him. I shot him in cold blood, for fuck's sake. I should be more focused on the case. I should be more invested. But something about this house, something about *her*, is keeping me from wanting this to end.

It's wrong. It's fucked up. But somehow my focus has switched. I close my eyes and try to calm myself. This had to happen. I *have* to play the part. And I am. I'm playing it damn well.

After I left her asleep last night, I went back downstairs. I thought I handled it well, and I was right. They're impressed more than anything else. Even Olivia is playing the part perfectly. She doesn't even know it.

She's doing so well, I think as the hot water from the shower flows down my body. She's so fucking perfect. They saw her fear and anxiety and how she obeyed me regardless. And now she's the perfect example of obedience. Well, other than her little outburst. I hope she got that shit out of her system.

I knew it would happen. I don't blame her in the least. That's why I chose last night to test her when I knew it would only be a few people. Close friends. Except for William. I could have done without him being there.

I know she's on edge. She's feeling trapped and uneasy. She's practically walking on eggshells every time I bring her outside the bedroom. She doesn't trust anyone else, but she sure as fuck trusts me. She just needs to let go and realize she doesn't have to think about it so hard.

I'll take care of her. All she needs to do is trust me. And she's so close.

My heart pumps faster in my chest and my dick twitches as the water runs down my body. Punishing her was harder than I thought. I wanted to do so much more than deprive her. Every moan and twist of her body made me want to pound her tight pussy. But I haven't taken it that far yet. I need to. They need to see it. It's much harder to resist her when she's fully submitting to me. And she did that last night. Fuck, just the memory of it has my dick at full attention.

I open my eyes as I hear the door creak open and a breeze disturb the comforting heat around me. It closes quickly, and her bare feet patter against the floor.

"Angel?" My brows raise as I see her slowly walk toward the shower. I move the glass door open and watch as she lowers herself into the tiled floor. She's completely naked. I took off her clothes last night and her collar. Everything needed to be cleaned after her punishment.

She looks so fragile and delicate.

My heart slows in my chest. This is new. It must have taken a lot for her to approach me. She's learning that she doesn't need to wait in order to things that would please me. That's a good sign. I wait for her to speak.

"Kade, I—" She clears her throat before looking up at me with wide eyes. "I'm sorry."

"You're sorry you were punished." I keep my voice even and hard. I could see it in her eyes before I took her downstairs. She wasn't sorry she tried to get away. She was sorry it didn't work. I'm not sure she'd do it again though. I'm not positive either way, and that's a problem.

She shakes her head. "I'm sorry," she barely speaks; her voice is choked. Her small whimper breaks my heart. The need to ease her worries is strong. She needs me, almost as much as I need her.

"It's over now, angel."

"Can I—" her voice cuts off as her eyes dart to the ground then back up to mine. "Can I come in with you?" she asks with a small voice. She looks nervous and vulnerable.

This is the first time she's initiated any interaction with me. I need to make sure I reward this behavior. She needs the comfort, too. She needs to know I'm not angry with her, and that she's completely forgiven. And she is. There's nothing that truly needs to be forgiven. I don't want her to worry. That would be detrimental for both of us.

I answer her question with a simple nod. "Come."

She rises slowly and I open the door wider so she can walk in. She stands in the steam a moment. The hot water splashes against her feet as she hesitantly holds her hand out, testing the temperature. Without her body full immersed, her nipples begin to harden. She takes a small step forward, and her milky white skin turns pink with a beautiful flushfrom the heat.

My dick immediately starts hardening.

Her small hands rest at my hips, and she leans into me resting her head on my chest. I turn her slightly so the water runs along her back and into her hair.

I reach for the soap, and she turns to watch. "Can I wash you?" she asks.

She's in such need, my poor, sweet angel. "You can."

She eagerly pours a bit of soap into her hands and rubs them together to make a frothy bit of suds. I watch her face intently. She seems so serious, like she needs to do this perfectly. She's scared still. I want to ease that fear. I place my hand on her lower back and pull her body close to mine.

My hard cock presses against her lower belly. She looks up through her thick lashes, with her plump lips parted and I give in.

I can't resist giving us what we both need.

I lower my lips to hers and push her back against the tiled wall.

Her back bows, and she pushes her breasts against my chest. Her mouth parts for me and she moans into my mouth. Her hands grip onto my shoulders, pulling me closer to her.

I grip her thighs in my hands and lift her up. She wraps her legs around my waist and digs her heels into my ass. With one hand on her ass and the other in her hair, I pull away from her and look down at her. She's panting with half-lidded eyes.

There's nothing but lust in her gorgeous eyes.

She wants me.

I leave open-mouthed kisses on her neck and rock my hard dick against her clit.

"Uh!" She lets out a strangled cry as I nip her neck. Her blunt fingernails dig into my shoulders. "Kade," she whimpers. I kiss and suck and bit along her neck and up her jaw. I angle my hips so she's steady against the wall, and move my hand to her breast.

I kiss her soft and gently as her breathing calms.

She fits perfectly in my hand. I roll her hardened peaks between my fingers and pinch.

"Ah!" she exclaims as she throws her head back, and I feel her pussy clench down on the side of my dick, nestled between her lips.

"Tell me you want me, angel," I whisper into her ear. The sounds of the water splashing is loud, but she hears me.

Her hand settles on my jaw and she looks deep into my eyes. "I want you," she breathes out quickly.

In one swift move, I push all of myself deep inside of her. Her body slams hard against the tile and her head falls forward, her forehead pressed to mine. Her mouth opens into a perfect O as she holds in a scream of pleasure.

I stay deep inside of her tight cunt as her pussy spasms around my dick.

A low rough groan is forced from my throat. She feels so fucking good. So hot and tight.

I give her a moment to adjust to my size and push my lips against hers. Her forehead is still pinched and her lips are hard at first, but she softens them. Her breathing picks up as I thrust my hips, pulling almost all the way out and then pushing all the way back in. I slide as deep as I can each time.

I force soft moans out of those plump lips with every pump. I fucking love the sounds she's making.

I dip my tongue into her mouth and she eagerly kisses me back. I deepen the kiss as I pick up my pace, fucking her ruthlessly against the cold, hard wall. Yes! I struggle to stay in control. I've wanted her for so long.

Her moans and the sounds of the water streaming in the shower are the only things I can hear as I buck my hips against hers over and over. My spine tingles and my balls draw up, but I need her to cum with me.

I angle my hips so I'm pushing against her clit and thrust shallow pumps into her heat. She bites down on her lip and throws her head to the side. I fucking love the sight of her so vulnerable. So close to pleasure, yet it's a dangerous edge, letting go and allowing it to overpower her. She knows she'll be shattered, and she's fighting it. She has the urge to race to the end and be overwhelmed with the sensation of cumming with me, but also the desire to prevent it from happening altogether.

"Please," she pushes the word out, and I cave into her desires.

I push harder and faster, and make sure each thrust hits her throbbing clit. I slam my dick into her all the way to the hilt and still deep inside of her as jets of hot cum leave me in waves. My spine tingles, and waves of pleasure flow through my body. I feel her body stiffen and her walls tighten, then the most beautiful sounds I've ever heard spill from her lips. Her head pushes against the wall as she cums violently. Her eyes are closed and I stare at her face, loving how fucking beautiful she is like this.

If I could keep this moment forever, I would. But this moment doesn't belong to us. I gently kiss her full lips as the high of our lust dims.

I wish things were different. I wish she really was mine to keep. But she's not.

I wish I could keep her forever, but I can't.

My eyes slowly open and I stare at her gorgeous face. Her eyes are closed in complete rapture. I can try to keep her though. I have to try. I don't want to let her go.

Chapter 21

Olivia

"YOU NEED TO GET READY FOR TONIGHT," KADE SAYS AS I brush my hair. I set it down on the vanity. It's filled with new makeup and expensive perfumes and lotions I'd never dreamed of having. There are clothes in the closet too, although I've barely worn any of them.

Kade prefers me in the same handful of dresses when we're outside of the bedroom. But he said we'll be leaving soon. And I'll need them once we leave here.

I haven't forgotten what this place is. It's a gilded cage. Although it is a comfortable one.

The thought of getting away from here brings back my desire to run full force. I keep the thoughts at bay as best I can so I don't slip up. I need to be perfect and leave this place unscathed. I'm so close, just days away now until he takes me back. I know his guard is down, and I may be given the chance to take my own freedom, rather than waiting for him to gift it to me.

"You look beautiful, angel." His soft praise interrupts my thoughts, and I look up into his blue eyes as he grips the top of the chair behind me. My heart swells. I don't know how fucked up I am, but there's something wrong with me. I crave his approval. And I love it when he gives it to me.

I kneel on the floor next to Kade. There are several chairs in the large room, although most people are standing closer to the stage. We're on the side wall with an unhindered view. To my right is Kade, his hand on my shoulder, rubbing soothing circles as I sit perfectly still in the kneeling position. Gabriel is on my left, and next to him is Talia.

I keep wanting to look at her, but I don't. I haven't had a moment to talk to her since… my punishment. I want to thank her; I haven't had a chance to though.

In the center of the stage is a slave and her Master. I'm not certain if she's like me and Talia, or like Master W's wife. I know not to ask.

She's shackled to a post in the center of the stage. Her Master's fingering her and she's pulling against the chains. His corded muscles ripple as he shoves his fingers into her soaked pussy. He pumps them in and out and kisses her neck, biting and moving up her jaw. Her back tries to bow, and she screams out sounds of pleasure.

The dim lights are centered on them, and the rest of the room is practically pitch black. But I can see the audience just fine. My eyes have adjusted to the darkness. Some couples watch as the Master covers her eyes with a sash and pulls a toy from his pocket. Other couples engage in their own activities. The man on stage commands her to open her mouth, and she does so eagerly. She sucks on the plug, warming it and getting it wet before he inserts it into her ass. She squirms slightly as he works it in and out.

That's one thing Kade hasn't done with me. Of all the things he's done, he's never done anything other than spank my ass. He said he wants my pussy. And I'm his alone, so there's no need for me to be trained otherwise.

The woman screams out as he smacks her clit with a riding crop, spreading her pussy lips and doing it over and over. His movements are harsh, although the crop is barely touching her with light flicks. But I imagine the sensation of not knowing when they're coming is nearly too much to bear. I know when he's done with her she'll be limp and sated. But that could take hours, and there's no telling what all will happen between now and then.

"When will Olivia be ready for us?" I don't react to Gabriel's question. I anticipated this.

It's like a fucking graduation ceremony. Although I'm nervous and feeling a little uneasy about the idea of everyone watching, I trust Kade. He's not going to let anything happen to me. He'll keep me safe and take me away once all this is done. And a darker part of me is looking forward to it. When he trains me now, it's just like this. My core heats as I think about yesterday.

He didn't have to tie me up. I'm much better now at resisting the urge to move away. He made me wait to cum. He brought me to the edge, and I was able to hold it there. I waited until he said I could. It's much easier to do when he's simply hitting my clit like the Master's doing on stage. I can go for a long time without cumming then. But the vibrator or Kade fucking me is much more difficult. Both are just so intense. Too intense to control.

It took days of practice to get to this point. He said it was his fault though that it took so long for me to learn. Every time I came without his consent he fucked me mercilessly. But that's not a punishment. Not that he's ever punished me beyond the one time. As long as I'm trying, and as long as I submit to him, then I don't deserve any negative consequences.

"I think she's ready for us right now," Master A says as he walks closer to us. I hadn't seen him in the room. My eyes widen slightly when I see the look in his eyes.

My pussy clenches as I realize the double meaning of their words.

A soft rumble comes from Kade's chest as I close my eyes and look at the ground.

"Are you ready for me, Olivia?" Master A asks.

My breath stills in my lungs as I peek up at him.

"I'm ready when Master K tells me I am, sir." I keep my voice low and my face neutral, but the thought of being commanded by Kade on the stage only makes me even more turned on. I try not to show it, but judging from Gabriel's chuckle, I've failed.

For some reason, knowing this is all going to end soon, and feeling so safe with Kade, I almost want to answer differently. I almost call him Master, but I don't.

Master A pouts comically and leans against the wall to Kade's right.

"Well, you can't blame a man for trying."

I lean against Kade's leg and he runs his hand through my hair, petting me.

As the night continues, I consider just how completely broken I am. The sight on the stage doesn't affect me in any way other than to arouse me. *I want to be her.* At what point did I come to trust a man who's dangerous and took me as a sex slave? When did I start desiring being used? But most importantly, why am I not in a hurry to leave?

Chapter 22

Olivia

I TAKE KADE'S HAND AS I STEP OUT OF THE SHOWER. THE HOT STEAM with the scent of lavender fills my lungs as I step onto the cold tile floor. It's so relaxing.

Every night he's done this for I don't even know how many days now. It's always the same routine. He feeds me, trains me, bathes me, and then takes me downstairs. He says dinner and the show are for training. But I don't do anything. I don't understand. It's simple, I obey him. Always. He's never pushed me to do anything other than stay beside him.

When we get back to the bedroom, the atmosphere changes. I get lost in his touch. The heat in his eyes is so intense that I feel alive and vibrant. He commands me, but not in any way that seems unnatural to our relationship. Nothing that makes me want to say no. I want everything he gives me. And he gives me everything I want. I fall asleep feeling safe and warm beside him.

But it's the same thing every day. Nothing has changed.

He never leaves my side, which I both love and hate. I need the security; this house itself still scares me. Sometimes I feel like Kade's my bodyguard, and other times he's my warden.

"Why do you always come in with me? I'm not going to do anything stupid." I don't know if that's completely true though. Even knowing my freedom is close, I've thought about doing something stupid a time or two. But I'd never do it.

The idea that he's going to let me walk away does strange things to me.

I push down the emotions threatening to creep up on me and ignore it. It's still days away. Possibly more before we leave here, and then who knows if I'll be able to escape. If not, I'll have to wait.

The idea of waiting doesn't make me tense or anxious. It's a different emotion, one I'm not comfortable exploring. I should want to leave, and I do. But the thought still makes me upset. I want to leave, but I want to bring Kade with me. It doesn't make sense.

Kade chuckles low and deep. Being in the small confines of the bathroom makes it sound even sexier somehow.

"Because I like touching you." My nipples pebble as I lift my arms for him to wrap a towel around me.

"Tonight," Kade starts but stops as his forehead pinches. "Tonight you're going to be on the stage, angel." He doesn't look at me as he takes a deep breath.

"What do you think about that?" he asks. I'm surprised he's asking me my opinion.

"If you think I'm ready, then I'll be perfect for you. I'll do the best I can." I search his face and will him to look at me, and he does.

But there's a hint of fear there I've never seen before.

"You're different from the others, angel." Kade sits on the windowsill and pulls me between his legs. "I never should have offered you freedom."

My heart stills in my chest, and I almost take a step backward.

"No, no, it's yours. I would have given it to you regardless." He lowers his nose to mine with his eyes closed. "I made you that promise, and I meant it."

"I don't understand." Why is he saying that?

He stares into my eyes. "You didn't fight me. Only that once."

"Isn't that a good thing?"

He takes a deep breath. "They're going to want me to push you, they're going to want to see that I'm taking you to your limits."

"Do you trust me?" Kade asks.

I nod my head. I do trust him. I don't know why, and I know I probably shouldn't, but I do.

"If I ever put you in a situation you don't want to be in, I want you to give me a sign, angel."

My heart's beating faster and I start questioning if I can do this. "What are you going to do?"

"I can't tell you, angel. It's not for me to decide." What? I don't like that.

"Gabriel gets to pick what's done on the stage."

My breathing stills, and my pussy clenches.

Kade arches a brow at me. He grips my hips in both his hands and pulls me close to him. He whispers in the crook of my neck, "That doesn't upset you, does it?"

I know what he's really asking, and I'm quick to answer, "I'm yours, and only yours."

"There's no doubt in my mind that's true."

I don't know what to say. It feels so wrong to have these desires. It feels like betrayal to even consider admitting it. I open my mouth, but he puts a finger against my lips.

He searches my eyes for a moment before saying, "If you don't want it, I need you to bite me."

My eyes widen with surprise. "Hard?"

He shakes his head with a grin. "It doesn't have to be hard, but it needs to be obvious. They have to see it, angel. But then I can stop it and punish you instead."

I whisper, "I don't want to bite you." I don't. I don't want to be punished, and I don't want to bite him.

"I don't think it will come to that, but if it does, you have a choice." Bite me, hit me, scream at me. Do something worthy of being taken away. He gently sets his forehead against mine and kisses the tip of my nose before taking a deep breath.

"Tonight will be hard, but tomorrow may be a little harder."

"Why?" I ask. I don't understand. We should be leaving soon. Tonight is the last step, or so I thought. This is just for them to see how well he's trained me.

"I have a meeting tomorrow, and you'll have to come." I nod my head. That doesn't sound so bad.

"Just know you'll be safe. Always." His eyes are sad, and it's making me worry.

"Kade?" I don't know what the question is that's on the tip of my tongue, but whatever it is, it's hurting my chest.

"It's alright angel, I didn't mean to worry you."

"Is everything going to be okay, Kade?" I get the very strong sense that something's off.

"You're going to be fine, I promise you."

"What about you?" I ask him. Tears prick my eyes when his eyes go sad and he doesn't respond.

"Even if something happens to me, you're going to be safe. I made sure of it." Goosebumps flow down my back and I move away from Kade as he tries to pet my hair.

"You promised me that—" I don't know how to word this, but if he's not alright then he's broken his promise somehow, I know he has.

"Olivia." Kade's voice turns hard, and my eyes widen. My heart beats faster and I instantly lower myself to the floor. I stay upright on my knees and wait for him to tell me what I did wrong, just like I've done in training. Although I already know this time. The towel pools around my body, exposing my breasts to him.

Before he has a chance to admonish me, I speak the truth. "I'm scared, Kade."

His hard expression softens, and he sighs. "Come here."

I walk back into his arms, leaving the towel behind.

"I didn't mean to scare you." He kisses my hair. "I tell you too much."

I shake my head in his chest and reply, "You don't tell me enough."

He chuckles, and it eases something inside of me. I pull away from him and look into his eyes as I ask, "We're going to be okay? After tomorrow, I mean?"

I search his eyes and watch as he answers, "Of course we are. And after that we're going to leave."

Through the course of all this, I've done nothing but watch Kade as he talks with the other men at dinner. I've noticed every small detail in his expressions.

I know when he lies.

And for the first time I can recall, he just lied to me.

I wish I knew which part he was lying about.

If we're going to be okay, or if we're going to be leaving.

Chapter 23

I CAN FEEL THEIR EYES ON ME AS I WALK INTO THE ROOM. USUALLY we come in later and the room is already full. I was expecting it to be empty when Kade said it was time to come down here. But it's not. It's already packed, and we have to walk through the crowd. My cheeks heat and my breathing comes in short pants.

They're going to watch.

I need to do this, and then we can leave. I'll be free soon. I swallow thickly and keep walking.

Kade pulls the thin chain and it tugs against the clamps on my nipples. It's a new toy, just for tonight. The slight pain sends an immediate bolt of pleasure to my clit. I'm primed to go off again already. I'm on edge and needy. He holds his hand out for me and I climb the single step onto the stage and prepare to obey my master for all of them to see.

The chains barely make any noise compared to the chatter in the room as I walk to the center of the stage. My dress is nothing but a piece of soft silk that's so thin it's nearly see-through. The delicate fabric is loose and Kade easily slips it off my shoulders, baring me to everyone.

He kisses my neck and says, "You're so beautiful." His hands caress my shoulders and his fingers linger on my body as they move down my back. I close my eyes and moan as they travel farther down and slip between my pussy lips.

"So wet, my angel," he whispers in my ear. "Do you enjoy this?" I breathe out slowly and open my eyes.

The entire crowd is watching us. The confidence I had when it was just the two of us slips.

"I don't know," I answer honestly. It's exhilarating to be up here and know they're watching. But I'm not sure I like it.

"Fair enough." He circles around me and blocks them from my view. "Are you alright?" he asks in a low voice.

I nod my head easily. I am. I can do this. A part of me is even excited to do this.

"I am, Master K." He smiles with my response and crouches down so his head is at my breast.

"Good girl," he says and looks behind him to nod at Gabriel. I swallow thickly and wait for my orders. I can do this. Just a little bit longer and I'll be free.

"You look beautiful tonight, Olivia," Gabriel says from across the room. "I have every bit of confidence in you." A flush of pride flows through me at his praise. Talia nods her head slightly, and leans onto Gabriel's leg.

"What do you say, angel?" Kade asks.

"Thank you, sir," I answer and see a flash of worry in Gabriel's eyes.

Kade's eyes find mine and hold my gaze. "Stay still, angel."

"Yes, Master K." I keep my shoulders squared and chin held high.

He crouches down with his hands on my hips and takes the clamp and my nipple in his mouth. They're sensitive and walking a razor's edge between pain and pleasure. He lowers one hand to my pussy and groans around my hardened nipple when he slips his fingers between my wet folds.

At the same time, he pushes his fingers into me and and uses his teeth to release the clamp.

"Ah!" I scream out and resist the urge to grab my breast. The pain of the clamp being removed and the pleasure from his touch combine into something so intense I nearly collapse, but I don't. I stay as still as possible and force my eyes open. In front of me are Gabriel and Master A. Talia is in Gabriel's lap, and his hands are between her legs. He's whispering in her ear and kissing her neck as she watches Kade prepare to do the same thing to my other breast.

I hold my breath and wait for the pain to come. I stare straight ahead, focusing on the wall behind my audience and ignore their sounds. It's dark and difficult to see them anyway. I imagine we're alone.

It's just the two of us. As my orgasm builds with every stroke of Kade's fingers against my G-spot, I prepare for the pain. The only move I make is curling my toes.

Out of nowhere, Kade releases the remaining clamp and sucks my nipple as my release tears through my body. It's completely unexpected, and I scream out a strangled cry of pleasure. Kade pushes his palm against my clit and gently sucks each tender nipple until both the pleasure and pain subside.

After a long moment, I feel like I can breathe again and Kade stands in front of me. He gives me a small kiss on the shoulder and tells me to turn around. I obey him on shaky legs.

Behind me is a simple and small bench. Kade pushes gently against my lower back and I obey the unspoken command. It hits my hips and I lean over. It's bolted to the floor, and so are leather straps.

"Lean over, Olivia," he whispers in my ear. I do as I'm told. It's only a few inches wide and offers little support. He kicks the inside of my heel gently with his shoe, and I spread my legs for him. I swallow thickly as the men move around in my periphery to get a better view. I have to close my eyes as my heart races faster and he attaches a leather strap to my ankle.

"Now your wrists," Kade says before kissing my thigh. I look back at him, not understanding. We've never done this before.

"Bend further, angel." My blood heats as I lower my shoulders and lean down so my hands nearly touch the floor. The thin bench keeps my ass in the air. It's only then that I realize the padding on it is for my hips.

My breath comes in shallow pants as he buckles the straps tightly around my wrists. They're a few inches long so I have a little give, but not much. And with that, I'm bound and bent over, completely bared for all of them to see. I'm completely vulnerable and relying fully on my trust in Kade. My anxiety peaks.

I feel Kade's hand on my lower back and that's the only warning I get before he slams into me from behind.

"Uh!" I bite down on my bottom lip as Kade pounds into me. His fingers dig into my hips. Over and over again he thrusts all the way into me. He's so deep. Each time is so deep. I almost can't stand it.

"Let them hear you," Kade says loudly as his hand grips the nape of my neck. "Let them hear how loud you are when I fuck you like this."

"Fuck!" I close my eyes as he tears through me without mercy. I have to be careful. I can't scream out his name, Kade. Master K. Master K. I have to remember. But fuck! My toes curl and my legs tremble as he pushes in and out of me repeatedly with a relentless pace.

"Yes!" He pushes against my clit and I spasm around him as my mouth falls open and I cum violently. My body heats as the pleasure pulses through me. My vision goes black as Kade pumps into me a few more times before pulling out completely. I keep my back straight and hold that position as he circles me.

I see his dick in front of me covered in my arousal and I anticipate him pushing his large cock down my throat, but he doesn't.

He cups my chin in his hand and he brings my lips to his. It's a struggle to maintain this position with my wrists bound, but I do it. My breathing comes in shallow pants as he crushes his lips against mine. His tongue dips into my mouth and massages mine. It's a passionate, yet dark dance that makes my heart beat faster. He breaks the kiss and nips my bottom lip before releasing me.

I fall some, but I pull myself back up. My wrists pull against the shackles as I keep my upper body nearly parallel with the floor.

Kade moves behind me and again the only warning I get is his lower hand on my back, right before he slams into me. My arousal drips down my leg as he continues the punishing fuck. Over and over. Each time, he gives me my release.

By the time he's done with me, my legs won't stop shaking and I'm out of breath completely, barely able to hold myself upright. I do though. I push through the trembling need to pass out and stand tall once the shackles are removed. Kade rubs my wrists and ankles, kissing them each before moving on to the next.

He takes enough time doing so that I finally feel centered and as though I can continue.

Kade leads me to the exit of the stage and I look at his back with hesitation. The performance generally lasts for hours. It hasn't been that long. Has it? I follow him without question although I'm feeling uncertain. My cheeks are burning furiously with a blush as we walk past the onlookers.

Before we leave the room, Kade pauses at the exit and waits for Gabriel and Master A.

Talia's nearly passed out in Gabriel's arms. Judging from the blush on her chest and cheeks, she's sated as well.

"I need to put my Talia to bed." Gabriel walks easily with her in his arms. "I'll meet you three in just a minute."

My eyes widen as I take in the meaning of his words.

It's not over yet.

Chapter 24

I SIT ON MY KNEES IN THE QUIET AND DIMLY LIT OFFICE. MY HANDS rest on my thighs and my eyes are on the floor. I can hear the ice cubes clinking in Gabriel's glass as he lifts it to his lips. I'm trying to breathe, but it's hard.

"Relax, Olivia." I still don't know his real name. Master A. I've seen him so many times now, but I have no idea what his name is.

I stare into his eyes, willing myself to come up with a response, but I can't. I can hardly breathe. I swallow thickly and part my lips, but still nothing.

Kade's hand settles on my shoulder and I instantly close my eyes. My tense body relaxes.

"Come sit in my lap," Master A says as he pats his legs with both of his hands. I look up at Kade over my shoulders. I don't know what to do. I thought I was only supposed to listen to Kade.

His eyes are on Master A. He cocks a brow and then looks back down at me.

"Go ahead, angel. I'm right here."

I slowly rise and walk to Master A. He leans forward and grips my hips, pulling me down onto his lap before I have a chance to sit.

I let out a small gasp, and the men in the room chuckle.

"Be honest with me, Olivia," Master A says in my ear. His hot breath greets my neck and I lean my head so he has more access to the tender skin.

He groans and rocks his dick against my ass. "I'm trying to be good here."

Kade lets out a small laugh and leans forward, resting his elbows on his knees. "She makes it hard to resist."

Master A runs a hand down his face before pulling my small body closer to his chest. "Are you scared, or just nervous?" he asks loud enough for everyone in the room to hear.

Nervous. I'm so fucking nervous.

I lick my lips and answer him honestly. "Nervous."

He groans in my neck and presses his lips against my skin. "Thank fuck," he says as his hands slip up the sheer fabric of my dress. His fingers slowly rise on my inner thighs until they're almost pressed against my core.

My eyes dart to Kade's. My lips part and my back bows slightly, moving away from Master A.

"It's alright, angel." Kade's watching us intently.

I don't know if I should believe him. This feels wrong.

"What's my name, Olivia?" Gabriel asks from across the room as he sets his glass down.

"For tonight," Kade says with a hard edge. I look between the two men with slight anxiety.

Master A chuckles in my ear as his thumbs slip closer up to my clit.

Kade looks me in the eyes and asks, "What are you going to call them tonight, Olivia?"

The meaning of Gabriel's question hits me with clarity. "Master," I whisper.

"Say it louder," Kade demands. "I want them to hear you calling them Master." He turns back to Gabriel and repeats, "For tonight."

Gabriel grins and says, "I understand." His eyes find mine. "You're *ours* tonight." My pussy clenches, and Master A nips my ear.

"You like that, don't you?" Master A asks me. Yes. A part of me does. The idea is so forbidden and exotic, and I want it. But I want Kade more. I don't want to ruin whatever this is between us. I *need* him.

I nervously look back to Kade again. I move my hand to reach out to him and then put it back on the sofa.

"Stop." Kade's hard voice echoes off the walls.

Master A looks up at him, letting a chill blow in the crook of my neck and slowly rests his back against the chair, leaving me sitting nervously on top of his lap.

"Come here," he demands. His words are hard. His chest rises and falls with his steady breathing. The idea I've upset him makes my blood race with adrenaline and anxiety. I slowly slip off Master A's lap. He holds my hand until I'm steady on my feet.

I keep my eyes on the ground as I walk over to Kade. Even if he's angry with me, that's okay so long as I'm still his. I start to lower myself to the ground in front of him, but he stops me.

"Over here, angel." My eyes fly to his at his soft words. He pats the armrest of the sofa. I walk to the side of it and he holds his hand out. I slip mine into his and he gently tugs. My hips butt against the arm of the chair and my upper body falls into his lap.

He brushes the hair away from my face and rests his arm over my lower back. He rubs gently as Gabriel and Master A rise from their seats one after the other. Kade lifts my dress and exposes my pussy to them.

"Look at me, angel." I lift my head and wait with bated breath.

"Now would be the time to say no if you don't want this." His eyes hold mine, and I can tell neither of us are breathing.

I hear a zipper and the sound of the men walking closer. My lips part as I search Kade's eyes.

He grips the hair at the base of my skull and lifts my head up. My pussy clenches with the slight pain. He lowers his lips to mine and takes them with his own. I moan into his lips as hands grip my hips and tilt them slightly. My eyes pop wide open.

My heart stills as my pussy clenches around nothing.

This is really going to happen. Holy fuck!

Kade gives me a smirk. "I'll be right here." He leans back and gives a nod to whoever's behind me.

"She's so fucking wet, I think you've been depriving her, Master K." I recognize Master A's voice. He tightens his grip on one hip and uses the other to stroke his dick. I jump forward slightly as the head of his dick pushes through my pussy lips, running up and down before slipping deeper into my hot entrance.

I turn my head to look back at Kade.

His mouth is parted, and his heated gaze stares back at me. I bite down on my bottom lip to hold in the noises threatening to leave my lips, and Master A pushes deeper inside me.

Gabriel's voice rings out as a hand smacks against my ass. "Spread." The stinging pain is directly connected to my clit and the mix of pain and pleasure makes me moan. I quickly spread my legs apart wider and look to Kade for approval. He pets my back and plants a kiss on my shoulders.

"Oh fuck, you're so tight." Master A's hands slip under my hips and he pulls me back some. He slowly pulls out and then pushes back in, stretching my walls.

A heavy breath leaves my lips as he moves in and out of me slowly.

"Open your mouth, Olivia." I turn my head at the sound of Gabriel's voice to my right, and my eyes widen. My body jolts as Master A picks up his pace. Gabriel rests his right knee on the sofa, bringing his body closer to me. Gabriel grips his thick cock and strokes it once before smacking it against my cheek. "Open."

I part my lips and open as wide as I can to fit him. He pushes his massive girth past my lips and I try to cover my teeth with my lips. "So fucking good," he says.

Gabriel groans, pulling my hair into a ponytail with his fist. His other hand grips my throat to keep me still. All the while Kade rubs soothing circles on my lower back. Gabriel pushes in deeper, so deep I have to breathe through my nose. My body heats with the pleasure of being used and filled. Master A slaps my ass as he pounds into me. His balls slap against my clit with each thrust.

Gabriel pushes in deeper, and I feel like I'm going to choke. I try to hold it back though and continue to breathe through my nose. A long moment passes as Master A thrusts behind me, pushing me deeper and deeper onto Gabriel's dick before he pulls out of my mouth. I take in a breath and dig my fingers into Kade's thigh, trying desperately to hold on. I'm at a steep edge of heightened pleasure.

Gabriel reaches behind me, and I'm not sure why. His hand slips between the armrest and my pussy. He ruthlessly rubs my clit and Kade holds me down as my body thrashes with my impending release. My body feels so hot. Too hot. My legs shake, and Master A only fucks me harder and faster.

"Cum for him now," Kade commands me, and I obey.

My pussy squeezes around his dick as the intense pleasure rolls through my body, but before it's done, before the waves let up, Master

A pulls out of me completely and Gabriel takes his place, thrusting all of himself deep inside me.

"Fuck!" I scream out.

"Good girl," Kade says as I hear Master A groaning. Kade's hands leave me for the first time as Gabriel fucks me with a force so hard, it's nearly too much. Gabriel adjusts me so he can get in deeper and I let out a strangled cry. He's pushing me to the point of pain. My arousal leaks down my thighs and my clit rubs against the armrest with every forceful thrust.

My body feels so hot. My hands fly to Kade's arms for support, I need him.

"It's alright, angel." His voice is unsteady and full of lust. Gabriel pulls me away from Kade enough that Kade can reach his pants. I grip onto the armrest, realizing he's not leaving me. I try to pick my body up enough for him to unleash his cock, but Gabriel's thrusts are so hard, I'm jolted forward.

Gabriel reaches his arm around to my front, bracing my body on his forearm. He slows his pace slightly and leans down, kissing my shoulder as Kade strokes his dick.

"You feel so good, Olivia," Gabriel says before moving away and slowly letting his arm slide down my body until he's only gripping my hip.

Kade moves his dick to my lips and I eagerly take him in my mouth. His hand fists in my hair, but he doesn't control my movements. I anticipate him pushing my head down or bucking his hips, but he doesn't. I massage his dick with my tongue as I push my head down and move up and down his length.

I pull back, letting Kade's dick pop out of my mouth as Gabriel thrusts deep inside me and stills. I scream out from the intense sensation. My pussy pulses around him, and my body trembles with pleasure. My legs are so weak they give out, but Gabriel's hold on my hips keeps me upright.

Kade gently moves me back to him. I suck on his dick and hollow my cheeks as I do everything I can to get him off.

Gabriel's fucking me so deep and hard, I know I'm going to lose it any second. I resist and hold on, wanting to cum with Kade.

He hisses with pleasure as I shove him down my throat as deep as I can and try to swallow. My eyes sting and I can't breathe, but I'm as desperate for his release as I am my own.

It only takes a few minutes until Kade groans and bucks his hips, once, twice, and then a third time. Hot jets of his cum shoot in the back of my throat, and I swallow as quickly as I can.

Gabriel pulls out and all I can hear is his heavy breathing as he furiously strokes himself until he's reached his own climax. His hot cum splashes on my lower back as I swallow Kade's and wipe my mouth and find my release with them. The numbing pleasure wrecks my body, but both men keep me still with their firm grip on me. I'm breathless and exhausted. I lower my chest against Kade's thigh and hold on to him as I close my eyes.

Gabriel leans down and plants kisses along my spine that leave a chill. I shiver slightly and smile when I hear him chuckle.

I'm barely aware of what's going on around me. I jump slightly as Gabriel wipes my lower back clean and Kade instantly pulls me into his arms. My body is still trembling.

Kade holds me close to his chest as I come down from the intense orgasm. I shift in his lap and the movement makes my clit pulse with a sated need. I bury my head into Kade's chest and moan. But I'm spent. I can't take anymore. Exhaustion weighs heavy on me.

I feel a hand push my hair away from my face. I hesitantly look up as Master A leans down. He plants a small kiss on my forehead. A violent blush hits my cheeks as he looks down on me.

His lips kick up into a smirk and he says, "If you ever want a new Master, you just let me know."

Kade huffs a laugh. "You must have a death wish."

"Sleep well, Olivia," Gabriel says from across the room as he opens the door. He nods at Kade, and Master A walks toward the door.

The door closes behind them and Kade kisses my hair.

My heart beats a bit faster realizing it's over. I slowly raise my eyes to meet his and when they do, I feel nothing but comfort.

He has a soft smile on his lips. "Are you alright, angel?" he asks.

I nod my head and move my hands to his chest. The tips of my fingers play with a small bit of chest hair peeking through his shirt.

He lowers his head to the crook of my neck and whispers in my ear, "I enjoyed that more than I should have."

I bury my head under his chin to hide the grin growing on my lips. A strange sense of pride washes over me.

But then something changes, the fantasy and illusion that seems to slip into place when I'm with Kade and in need shatters, and I feel lost and vulnerable. I shouldn't be enjoying this. I shouldn't feel *loved*. He doesn't love me. I can't love him.

But I do. Not only do I feel loved by him, I'm painfully aware in this moment that I love Kade.

Chapter 25

Olivia

KADE TAKES A SEAT IN THE SMALL SITTING ROOM AND I obediently kneel next to him. I'm not sure what this meeting is about, but I want it to be over with. I haven't forgotten our conversation, and I'm ready to get over this hurdle so we can leave.

Master A walks into the room, and my breathing is caught short. My cheeks burn as he walks past me. He takes a seat in the chair next to Kade so that I'm kneeling on the floor between the two of them.

"Good morning, angel," Master A says with a wink. Talia giggles from her position on the other side of the room.

"Good morning, Mast-sir. Good morning, sir!" Master A claps his hands once and bellows out a laugh.

"I will kill you. Don't think I won't," Kade says from my right. I look up at him and he has a sexy smile on his face. He places his hand on the outside of my shoulder and scoots me closer to him. I settle between his legs and lean my head against his knee. I look at Master A from the corner of my eye, and he winks at me.

A small smile graces my lips. That warmth in my chest comes back, but I wish it didn't.

I wish I didn't feel so comfortable here.

Gabriel comes back into the room and a young woman follows him. Her simple strapless black dress flows as she walks quickly behind him. Her short hair is nearly as black as her dress.

"Alright then, let's try this out."

In the center of the sitting room is a device I've never seen before. It's a simple rope pulley although the ropes themselves are woven with gold chains with cuffs on the end. The pulley is already set up and dangling from the ceiling. Gabriel lowers the cuffs with the rope, and the young woman stands and instantly raises her arms.

"There's no support?" Kade asks with uncertainty. I look at Master A, and he has his forehead pinched and his jaw is clenched.

"Lydia will let us know how it feels," Gabriel answers smoothly.

Master A sits back in his seat. "I'm sure it'll only be for the red rooms."

Gabriel nods his head. "And that's why Lydia's testing it out, and not my Talia."

Gabriel walks to the rope after fastening the cuffs and slowly pulls. Lydia's arms are pulled upward until she's on her tiptoes. Her body sways, but being held up so high, she can't balance herself with just her big toes. Gabriel lowers it slightly and waits for her to steady herself, then raises it higher again.

"How do you like it?" he asks her.

Master A cocks a brow as the small woman answers, "It would hurt after a while, but for a quick fuck, it'll do the job." Gabriel lets out a rough chuckle.

"We'll have to get a few then." He looks at his watch as a loud chime rings out. Talia stands and exits gracefully. She doesn't wait for orders. The rules between her and Gabriel are much different than they are for everyone else.

"Fifteen minutes then?" Gabriel looks up at Lydia, who nods her head and answers simply, "Yes, sir."

I don't want to get in that thing. That's all I can think about as Gabriel pushes against Lydia's hip and she swings slightly. Her big toes slide across the rug as she lets out a squeak and then a laugh.

"It could be fun," Gabriel says with a smile. The room feels light with laughter. It does look… interesting, but I have zero arm strength and that looks like it would tire me out quickly.

The laughter dies the second Talia returns to the room. Her head is down and her hands are clasped in front of her as she returns to her seat on the floor in front of Gabriel's empty chair.

Vic follows her into the room and stands in the doorway.

Ice pricks down my skin as he looks at the woman dangling.

Lydia's smile slips, and she goes silent as Gabriel steadies her.

"Victor. I wasn't expecting you so soon," Gabriel says. I keep my eyes trained on the ground as Victor walks across the floor. His black boots thumping across the ground are the only sounds until he slumps in Gabriel's seat. He spreads his legs wide and his boot hits Talia's leg. She doesn't move and simply allows it.

My eyes dart to Gabriel's. He's staring fixedly at his foot.

My breathing picks up and anxiety ignites within me. I can't see all the men's faces, but the tension in the air is thick.

"What's this?" Victor asks. His voice is low and rough. He gestures with his hand although he seems bored.

"A new toy we're considering installing." I watch as Victor stands and pushes the small woman. Lydia's silent as she swings and struggles to steady herself. Her hands wrap around the rope to support her weight since her toes are no longer touching the ground.

Vic huffs a laugh and then he walks closer to me.

"Kade."

"Victor." Kade replies with the same temperament, cold and disinterested.

"Ricky wanted to know how you were handling the gift." I can see past Victor's legs and Gabriel seems to be having a silent discussion with Talia. Gabriel looks back toward my direction, his eyes on Victor as he walks to a side table and opens a drawer. I watch as he lays a gun on the side table. My heart speeds up faster, but he leaves it there and continues to watch.

"Ricky could've called and asked himself."

"I wanted to come and see for myself. She should be trained by now, shouldn't she?"

"She is." Kade rests his hand on my head and gently pets my hair, but it does nothing to calm me. "As you can see."

"Fantastic. I've been ready to fuck this little bitch since we caught her."

"You'll have to get in line then, Victor," Gabriel says from across the room. "I'll call first dibs." Gabriel's trying to keep the mood light, but it doesn't work.

"What the fuck does that mean?" Victor asks.

"She's mine. That's what the fuck it means. And I'm not willing to share her just yet."

Victor clenches his fist like a petulant brat, but then seems to calm himself.

"How about you come with me to the meet in a few days?" Victor offers. "You can get rid of this one and get yourself some fresh stock?" It's difficult to stay still as he talks about me as though I'm disposable. My heart clenches in my chest and I have to remind myself this is fake. I'll be free soon. Very soon. I breathe in deep. I just need to stay calm.

"You can pass her to me then. Once you've had your fill." Kade makes no move to respond as Victor stands and takes a few steps toward me with confidence. I keep my eyes on the ground, but my body trembles with the need to run.

"For now, I'll just see how well she obeys." His voice takes on a hard edge, but then he says easily, "Just to let Ricky know how well you've done. *If* you've trained her right."

I don't want to. I consider turning around and biting the shit out of Kade's knee or doing anything I can to get out of this. I don't want to obey Victor. I don't trust him. I don't want anything to do with him. It's more than that though. I'm terrified.

"Within this room, I give you permission to give her simple commands," Kade says.

"Simple commands?" Victor sneers. "And you expect me not to leave the room?" He snorts and looks to Master A for support, but judging by how his face falls, he obviously didn't get any support from Master A.

"She's *mine*." My body tenses at Kade's hard words although his claim on me affects me differently. "She is not to leave my sight."

I can feel Victor's eyes on me in the silence. I remain still and wait with bated breath.

"Come on then. Crawl to me," Victor commands me. I don't want to. I hesitate even though I know I shouldn't.

"Go on, angel," Kade finally says, and I feel betrayed. I don't want to. "You can do this." Kade's voice is soft. I swallow thickly and nod my head.

"Bow and kiss my boots, slave," Victor says with a smug confidence in his voice as I crawl toward him. I'm afraid to. The thought that he's going to kick me in my face is a very real fear of mine. But I do it. I crawl to him and bow on the floor and put a kiss on each boot before laying my head down next to his feet and waiting.

"She's a wonderful pet," Kade says from behind me "Very easy to train." I don't like the way he's talking. This is a different side to him; one I've never seen. I want to believe it's fake. But I don't know for sure. My heart tries to climb up my throat, but I swallow it down and continue to wait to be commanded by this man I detest.

I hear Victor unzip his pants and my eyes pop wide open. I can't do this. I won't. I won't let this fucker touch me.

"You will not use for her anything other than simple commands. I'm not in the habit of sharing." Kade sounds pissed.

I can practically see Victor's sick smile. "I have no plans to touch her." He sounds casual and cocky.

"If you cum on my property," Kade's voice is even but deadly, "I'll slit your throat."

I chance a look up. Victor's dark eyes stare back at Kade who's still seated behind me, and I can see he's weighing his options.

"What good is she then?" he asks with disdain.

Victor snorts and steps over me, moving to the woman dangling in the center of the room.

"Come here now," Kade commands me to crawl to him and I try to obey and crawl back to him, but the loud smack of Victor's hand against Lydia's body stops me.

Lydia whimpers as I look up and see her body swinging from the ropes.

"Victor!" Gabriel calls out a low warning. "This is in testing, and she's not prepared for you."

Victor completely ignores Gabriel. I keep my eyes on the ground, but I can see Gabriel stand and walk toward the center of the room. My heart thumps loudly in my ears.

"Don't fucking disrespect me, *Master G.*" Victor taunts Gabriel by using the name we call him. Victor's pissed and apparently done with listening to anyone. "This bitch is a whore, and I'll fuck her like a whore."

Everything happens too quickly. Gabriel moves to the ropes and Master A to Talia, standing in front of her.

Gabriel yells something in French I don't understand and Lydia cries out.

Victor's hurting her, grabbing her roughly toward him and yanking her arms against the rope. My heart lurches in my chest and I instinctively reach out to stop him. Fear and disgust cripple me, but I fight them and reach out to grab Victor's leg. I can't let him do that. Kade grabs my hips and pulls me away, my fingers barely touching Victor's pants and doing nothing to stop him. I hear him yelling. The other men yelling. Lydia's crying. The horrific chaos hits me at once.

One moment is clear though. Victor looks down at me with a sick, twisted smile and pulls Lydia even closer to him with a violent yank. My heart refuses to beat, and time moves in slow motion.

Lydia screams as Victor pulls her. She screams a sound of horrid pain as I hear a loud *pop* and her arm pulls from the socket in her shoulder even though the rope is being lowered. Gabriel was too late. Her upper body drops, but her arm is limp at her side.

Kade picks me up swiftly and moves me behind him and onto the chair. I'm disgusted and want to do something. I have to try to help her.

I watch as Kade reaches into his waistband, but before he can pull out his gun, my body jolts with each loud sound of a gun going off. *Bang! Bang!*

My head whips to the side and I see Talia holding the gun, pointed right where Victor was standing. Her body is still as Victor falls lifeless to the floor. His cold dark eyes stare at the ceiling. His face is contorted, and blood bubbles from a neat hole in his throat. His dark black shirt sticks to his body as blood spills from the wound in his chest.

My eyes stay on him, until I hear the pounding of footsteps and a squeak from Talia.

Gabriel grabs Talia by her throat, stopping her from kneeling. The gun falls from her hand and hits the ground with a loud thump.

"You will not hide behind your submission, Talia." Gabriel sounds pissed. Talia lets out a small sob and keeps her eyes on the ground.

"Get her down." Gabriel's low voice sends the command throughout the room. He's not talking to Talia, but I'm not sure who the order was directed toward.

My eyes are still locked on Talia's face. She's scared. It's the first time I've seen her look unsure and upset. It's also the first time he's scolded her. And for what? Killing a man who deserves to die? Blood pools around his neck and seeps into the carpet.

Kade moves to go to Lydia, but I grip onto his leg. I don't want him to leave me. Kade looks down at me registering my needs, and then to Master

A. Master A stands and quickly moves to Lydia, unfastening the cuffs and cradles her in his arms. He shushes her and carries her out of the room.

Kade pulls me off the ground and holds me to his chest. He tries calming me, he tries keeping me from looking at Talia and Gabriel, but I turn away from him.

The only sound in the rom is Talia's soft cry. She doesn't deserve to be crying.

"*Esclave*, did you think I would let him get away with that? Do you think that little of me now?" His voice is low.

"No Master," Talia replies quickly.

My heart hurts for her. I move to push away from Kade. I'm not going to watch her be punished for doing the right thing, but he digs his fingers into my hips, stopping me.

Gabriel loosens his grip on Talia's throat and cups her chin. "You will never put yourself in danger again. Do you hear me?" Gabriel's voice is soft, but absolute.

She finally looks into his eyes and sniffles.

"Answer me, *esclave*." Gabriel's eyes dart across her face, searching for something.

"If you want something done, you will tell me. You will not make yourself a target, ever." His voice raises with each command. "Is that clear? You will stand behind me always. Don't you ever do that again."

My breathing slows as I understand why he's upset. My anger wanes, and the fight in me dies.

"It's alright, angel," Kade whispers, pulling me closer to him and petting my back.

Talia nods her head and hunches her shoulders. "Yes, Master."

Gabriel pulls her into his arms. "Don't you dare do that again, Talia," he whispers in her hair and then kisses her. He rubs his hand along her back as she sniffles.

I watch as he soothes her pain and both of them relax slightly. He doesn't stop looking at her and wills her to look at him, but she buries her face into his chest.

It's quiet for a long time. I want to leave. I want to get out of here.

Kade finally breaks the silence. "She has very good aim," he says to Gabriel.

Gabriel turns toward us and huffs a laugh. "Just because she can shoot doesn't mean she should. I was taking care of it."

Talia looks at the ground with a frown and wipes her eyes. "I'm sorry," she says. She sounds so weak.

Gabriel pulls away from her and grips her shoulders. "Don't be, *esclave*." He comforts her. "Try to stay behind me next time," he says in a soft, comforting tone.

She nods her head and asks in a small voice, "Are you mad at me still?"

He shakes his head and plants a soft kiss on her lips. Gabriel whispers, "Never. I love you, *esclave*."

She buries her head into his chest and whispers, "I love you, Gabriel."

Gabriel rubs her back and looks over his shoulder at us.

I pull my eyes away from them and lower my cheek to Kade's chest.

"I'll take her upstairs and come down to clean this up," Kade says. Gabriel looks back at us and then down to the dead body on the floor. "Victor was never here. We need to make sure Ricky doesn't find out."

Kade's deep voice rumbles in his chest. "Of course not. He was never here."

Chapter 26

Olivia

"**I** want to leave, Kade." That's all I've been thinking since this morning. I can't sleep. I'm wide awake, lying on the bed. I've been in this room all day while Kade's been gone 'cleaning up that mess,' as he referred to it.

I keep seeing Victor's lifeless eyes.

I'm not okay.

"Soon, angel." I shake my head as Kade dries off his hair and drops the towel on the floor.

I was quiet when he came back in. I laid still in bed while he got undressed and went to shower. But I'm not okay. I can't just be quiet and wait for him anymore.

I need to get out of here.

"I can't stay here any longer."

He walks to the bed and stands in front of me. Just being close to him again calms a part of me, but I'm still ready to bolt. I'm done waiting

Kade climbs on the bed and cups my chin in his hand, lifting my eyes so I have to stare into his. It's a motion he does often and usually I lean into his touch, but not now.

He starts to speak, but I interrupt him.

"I've never seen a dead man up close before. I can't. I can't stop seeing it. And the way he looked at me." I shake my head nearly violently as the fear comes back, squeezing my lungs of their breath.

"You'll be alright, angel. I'm here now." His voice has that calming tone he uses with me, but I don't want to be calmed down.

He walks to the bed and takes a seat next to me. Just being close to him again calms a part of me, but I'm still not okay.

"I'm sorry I had to leave you today. I would have stayed, but I had to take care of that."

His eyes search mine, but I can't give him the acceptance I know he wants. I can't cave into him. I need to leave.

"The only other person I've ever seen die is the man you killed that night, and—" Before I can finish, Kade leaves me. He quickly sits up from the bed and turns his back to me, reaching for the towel on the floor and going back to the bathroom.

My body stiffens. "Kade?" I call out for him and move the sheets off of me as I scoot closer to the edge.

He's never done that before, just leave me like that. I start to question my resolve. I think back on what I said and I regret saying it all, although I don't know why. I don't want him to leave me.

As the time passes and he doesn't respond, my heart beats faster with worry. I can't lose him. I need him.

I let out a breath as he comes back into the room. He doesn't seem mad or upset. I part my lips to ask him what I said, but I'm afraid to. I wait for him.

"I'm sorry I've done such a horrible thing to you, angel," he says with sincerity as he comes back into the room. "I promise I'll take care of you. I'll make this right." His voice is firm. But something's wrong. He's holding something back from me.

"What's wrong?" I ask hesitantly. I've never seen him like this before. Fear overwhelms me. "Did Ricky find out?"

Kade shakes his head. "I wish I could tell you. I want to tell you everything." He bends down and kisses me. "Ask me for something I can give you. Anything."

"I want to leave."

He lowers his head, his forehead pressed to mine and sighs. My heart sinks in my hollow chest.

"I will never let any of them hurt you." He speaks barely above a murmur.

"He did hurt me though. Victor hurt me." Kade's eyes close tighter as I continue my plea. "I don't want this anymore. I can't do that again." I don't know how to explain it to him.

I can't do that again. I don't want to. I don't want any of this anymore.

"I'm sorry. That was a mistake. I thought it would prevent things from getting out of hand." He takes a deep breath. "I thought wrong."

I don't know what to say to him.

"I'm sorry, angel." His soft blue eyes look deep into mine. "Please forgive me, tell me you'll forgive me."

My heart swells with the need to soothe his pain. I don't like seeing him like this. "I forgive you."

Kade's lips press gently against mine the second the words leave my lips. I moan softly, accepting his gentle touch. His hands move to my lower back and mine spear into his hair. A calmness settles over me. This is what I need. I need Kade.

Kade breaks our kiss and looks at me with a spark of lust in his eyes.

"Lie back," Kade commands me, and although a part of me doesn't want to, I obey.

My breath is shaky as Kade grips my hips and pulls me to the edge of the bed.

"Relax, angel. I've got you." I put a hand over my face, trying to calm myself as he spreads my knees farther. I'm a mix of emotions and I feel as though I'm being pulled in too many different directions. He lowers his lips to my pussy and my body shudders as he takes a languid lick.

I'm not prepared for him, not like I usually am. My head falls to the side as he sucks my clit into his mouth.

I heat for him instantly and close my eyes with a small moan. My fingertips dig into the mattress, and I have to work hard to keep my body still. I want to wrap my legs around his head and rock my pussy into his face. But I don't.

I stay still and let him do with me as he wants. His large hands grip my ass and angle me for him. He spears his tongue and fucks me with it over and over. My mouth falls open as my belly stirs with desire and need.

He takes me to the edge and I'm almost there, but this isn't what I need. I need *him*.

"More, please." I do something I've never done. I reach down and pull him on his shoulders. I need to feel him. I need to be as close to him as possible.

My eyes widen as I realize what I did, but the heat in Kade's eyes as he climbs over my body erases the momentary fear of acting out. He pulls me across the bed under him and devours my lips with his.

I can faintly taste myself on his tongue, but I don't care. My hands travel up his muscular body and I wrap my legs around his hips. He moans into my mouth and moves his hard dick to my opening, pushing in slowly.

His girth stretches my walls and I throw my head back and moan into the cool air. His lips suck at my neck as he pushes himself deeper inside of me. He stills deep inside of me, buried to the hilt, and captures my lips. It's almost too much. I feel so full and desperate for him to move. He doesn't though.

He kisses me as though he needs the air in my lungs to breathe.

I feel his passion, and it consumes me. His hands grip my hips tighter and he pulls out for a moment and then slams into me. Fuck! My mouth pops open with a silent scream. It's so good, but too overwhelming. His eyes stare into mine as he does it again and again.

Each hard pump heightens the edge of my release. My body tenses and heats.

"Kade," I whimper, and that's his undoing. A low growl erupts from his chest and he buries his head in the crook of my neck as he fucks me relentlessly into the mattress. He pounds into me over and over again. Each hard thrust smacks against my clit and makes my body that much hotter.

My head thrashes, and my fingernails dig into his shoulders. I struggle not to cry out.

"Mine," he growls into my neck.

My eyes close and my head falls back as he fucks me harder, owning my body with each hard thrust.

"Mine." He nips my neck and then my shoulder.

I can't contain the strangled scream of pleasure as he pushes my legs out wider and thrusts deeper inside of me, pushing me to a point of slight pain that's overwhelmed with pleasure.

"Kade!" I scream his name as he loses control and ruts between my legs with a savage need. My lungs refuse to work as my temperature rises, and waves of pleasure rock through my body with a paralyzing force. My mouth opens with a silent scream and Kade's quick to bite my bottom lip and then my throat as he rides through my orgasm, racing for his own release.

He stills deep inside of me and groans from deep within his chest. He thrusts short, shallow pumps that only seem to prolong my orgasm. My body shudders with a chill as he pulls out of me and leaves me for a moment. I feel overwhelmed with a hot, tingling sensation rippling through my body in waves.

The aftershocks dim as Kade wipes between my legs with a warm cloth and I settle into the mattress.

Kade holds me close to him. His warmth settles into every part of me, calming me and letting me relax into the bed.

A calmness washes over me and I begin to think that everything will be alright, but then Kade's phone beeps from the nightstand. He pulls away from me, rolling onto his back and picking it up. I miss him instantly. I need him to come back to me, but he doesn't. I watch his face as he looks at the message.

The softness in his features vanishes and the cold façade returns.

He gets up from the bed without saying a word and walks to his dresser.

I slowly sit up and watch as he dresses himself.

"Kade?" I ask him. He can't leave me. I need him.

He looks at me as he pulls his pants up and zips and buttons them, but he doesn't say anything..

"Are you alright?"

"I'm fine, angel. Go to bed." I can tell from his voice he's not fine. A weight settles against my chest, threatening to suffocate me.

"Kade, please don't leave me." I pull the covers tight around me and up to my chest. I don't want to be left alone.

He walks to the bed and gives me a look of sympathy mixed with something else… longing. It's a look of longing. He plants a soft kiss on my lips and I move my hand to the back of his head to deepen it, but he pulls away before I'm able to.

"I'm sorry, angel." His thumb brushes along my cheek and then he leaves me.

I stare at the door, waiting for him to come back. Unable to sleep, and unable to stop seeing the longing in his eyes.

Chapter 27

Kade

I SIT ACROSS THE DESK FROM GABRIEL. HE'S AT EASE, AND I'M TENSE. I need to get her out of here. The text confirmed what my handler said two days ago. I'm fucked, and I can deal with those consequences. But not my angel. I need to get her safely away as soon as possible.

He picks up his glass and takes another sip. He cocks a brow at me as he sets the glass down and asks, "Are you sure you don't want one? You look as though you need it." His voice holds the same humor I see sparkling in his eyes.

I shake my head and clear my throat, finally spitting out the reason I'm here. "I need you to take Olivia." I have to leave. I have to go to this meeting tomorrow. But she can't come. She needs to be safe by noon tomorrow. And I need Gabriel's help. I fucking hate that I do, but I have no one else to ask. I've played my cards all wrong. And now I'm a dead man.

"You can't be serious, Kade. You don't want her?" he asks incredulously.

I'm quick to shake my head. Gabriel continues speaking as I try to find the right words without giving him too much information. He's going to find out sooner or later.

"I care for Olivia, but it would hurt my Talia. I know it would. I don't understand why you don't want her."

I do want her. I want Olivia more than anything. I wish I could take her and run away with her. But I can't. I can't put her in danger. And I'm right in the middle of it. I need to get her away from me. I need to know she's safe.

"I have to leave tomorrow, and I don't think it's safe to take her with me." I tell him the truth. I wish I'd planned what to say to him. But I have no plan. Just the urgency to make sure she'll be alright. I shake my head, trying to figure out how to tell him without giving him too much information. He's going to find out sooner or later. If I leave now, they could follow me. Intel is sure it's just Ricky that knows. But I don't trust him or anyone who works for him. He could have men here or others on the way. I can't risk her getting caught in a shootout. I need protection while I get her to a safe place. Or for someone else to do it.

"You're going to have to be more specific then, Kade." Gabriel's patience is waning.

"I need her to go home." I hold his firm gaze. "I need her to be safe." That's all he needs to know.

Gabriel purses his lips for a moment and knocks his knuckles against the desk.

"You need to tell me what's going on before I agree to anything." Gabriel lowers his voice, and I see distrust in his eyes. Fuck, I don't want to tell him. I need him to do this regardless. I trust him. I *know* him. I know he'll do the right thing for her. He'll help her. Even if he slits my throat, I know he'll help her. He's done it before. I know he will. And I have no other choice.

"I'll tell you. I'll tell you everything. Just promise me that you'll find a way for her to get home."

"You're going to leave her in that condition, Kade?" he sneers. "You broke her, and now you're sending her back?" He sounds disgusted.

"She's not broken," I respond evenly.

"You're delusional if you think that."

"They're going to kill me, Gabriel, I have no choice." My body trembles with anger, but also fear for her. I can't tell him the truth until he promises me. "You've done it before. You've given them their freedom before."

"So you want me to take her home because someone's going to kill you?" Gabriel asks with disbelief.

I nod my head once. "But only if I can't. I don't know how much time I have."

"And can I ask why you're so sure you're going to die?" he asks.

I stare into his eyes. "Because Stone is going to kill me."

"I never quite liked Stone." He taps his fingers on the desk again and looks past me as if he's debating something. Are you going to tell me why?" he asks.

"She has nothing to do with this." My blood rushes in my ears. "You'll help me take her home regardless of what happens between us?" Although it's a question, it comes out as a statement.

His eyes finally meet mine. "I will." He nods his head with certainty.

"Whatever you want to do to me when you find out, it'll be on hold until she's safe." He nods his head once again, keeping my gaze.

"I'm a man of my word, Kade. Now out with it."

My chest tightens with anxiety. My hands dig into the armrests even though my gun is burning in my waistband, begging me to take it out. I won't though. I need Gabriel's help. If for nothing more than to make sure I can leave here without a tail and get Olivia safely back home. "Stone received information," I start and then readjust in my seat, exhaling deeply. "Information that implicates me as a cop."

Gabriel clucks his tongue. "Do you know when and how he received that information?"

I'm caught off-guard by the question, but I take a moment and then answer him honestly. "A little over two months ago, one of his men was discovered to be an undercover cop and at some point, information that linked the two of us together also pointed to me being a cop."

"I could see how that would be a serious problem." He presses his lips into a thin straight line. "He knew you were here, and yet he said nothing to me." I nod my head once. It was only discovered two days ago, but it was confirmed tonight. "And you are in fact a cop?"

I hold his gaze and nod once. My heart slams against my chest.

"She isn't. She's innocent." I'm quick to remind him that she has nothing to do with this.

"Of course she is. And I'll make sure we get her home since that's what you want."

A small bit of gratitude washes through me. My angel is safe. He leans forward and squares his shoulders and asks, "What else do you want, Kade?"

I shake my head and I take in a short breath. Once she's safe, I don't know what I can do. Gates told me to abort two days ago. But I couldn't leave yet, not if the report was false. I couldn't waste this chance..

Intel was collected between Ricky and Vic. They were planning my execution. Two days later and the only plan I have now is to get her home safe. Beyond that, I abort or I'm dead. I can't let that man live though. There has to be some justice, no matter how small. I can't leave and do nothing. "I like you, Kade. I've always had a weak spot for you. When I found out about your friend, I hurt for you. I still do." My blood chills at his confession. My brow furrows and then my grip tightens on the armrests. He lowers his eyes to something on his desk and fiddles with it, but I can't tell what it is.

"You knew?" I wasn't told anyone else knew. As far as the department knows, it was only a conversation between Ricky and Vic. And now Vic is dead.

"Of course," Gabriel answers easily. "It's my job to know who's walking through those doors." He clears his throat. "I almost killed you on day one." He holds up his hand and says, "No offense, Kade. I was just doing my job. But then I thought, maybe I could form a much-needed *partnership*. After all, you being a cop means that Ricky is your enemy, too."

"I'm listening." Although my heart hurts at the memory of James, hope fills my chest. We have a common enemy, and that can only work in my favor.

"Do you know who I don't like?" he asks me with a glint in his eyes. "I don't like Ricardo Stone. I don't like what he does, and I don't like how I'm inherently associated with him."

"I can understand how that would reflect poorly." I keep my voice even and wait for him to continue.

"I'd like him to die, Kade."

I nod my head once, relief flowing through me for the first time since I stepped into this office.

"His business is bad for my business. I want him dead, and I want all of his business gone. If that means I have to deal with you," he points his finger at me and then holds it in the air, "one last time before we part ways with no ill feelings, I think that can be arranged."

"What deal are you offering?" I ask him. I don't have anything to bargain with, but I need to know the terms if I'm going to make a deal with the devil.

He gives me an asymmetrical grin and says, "I have enough information on his contacts and operations that if they were to get into the wrong hands, *or the right hands*, well it would do me well to see that happen." Gabriel smiles at me and relaxes in his seat. "He dies, and everyone in this business knows that you did it and I had nothing to do with it." He holds my gaze. "And the information I give to you, you got from him."

"Is that all?" I ask. For the first time in years, I feel like I've made progress in this case. I'm focused on revenge and finally ending this.

"That, and the fact you've never met me or my Talia. You've never been here, and you don't know what they're talking about." He leans back in his seat. "I want this to be a win, win, win for me, Kade. If you make that happen, we'll part dear friends." He gives me a wide smile and says, "In fact, I'll owe you one."

"I'll make sure it happens," I say. I'm eager to accept his deal and finally see a way out of this. But first I need Olivia away from all this. I need her safe. For all I know, Stone will kill me before I can kill him.

Or Gabriel will, once I've done his dirty work for him.

Chapter 28

"I'M SORRY, ANGEL." I THINK I HEAR KADE'S VOICE, BUT MY eyelids are so heavy. I feel his small kiss on my forehead. I try to get up so I can kneel for him, but my body doesn't quite respond. I moan out for him, but they aren't the words I want. My head falls to the side.

"It'll wear off soon." I hear his voice, but I don't understand.

"I promise you, I'll keep you safe." I can feel his body carry me away, but I don't know where to. I can feel a cold breeze on my face, and the sounds of car doors opening.

Outside? Are we leaving? I try to ask, but I can't.

Kade sets me down against leather, and the sounds of a car starting make me realize we are leaving. I want to ask where, but I can't.

I try to roll my body and ask him, but I'm so heavy.

His hand cups my face and he kisses me. His comforting touch puts me at ease.

"Sleep, angel," I hear him say. I'd nod my head if I could. I want to sleep. My body's so tired.

As I drift off into a deep sleep, I swear I hear him say, "Forgive me, angel," and even softer, "I love you."

But I'm not certain of anything. It all feels like a dream.

My body stirs with the need to wake up. I've been asleep too long.

Beep. Beep. Beep.

Ugh. My head hurts so much.

I try to lift my body off this hard mattress, but my body is sore and the bright lights make me wince. *Beep. Beep. Beep.*

What is that noise? My head's killing me.

I slowly open my eyes and my body tenses. What the fuck? I'm in a hospital room.

"Kade!" I call out as I bolt upright in the seat.

My head's so dizzy I nearly fall back. I grip onto the cold steel bars on either side of the bed to steady myself. A nurse rushes in through the door, followed by another.

"Miss, please, lie back." She puts her hands on mine and I look around the room as she lays me back against the bed. I don't fight her, but I'm scared. What the fuck am I doing in a hospital?

"Where am I?" I ask her as easily as I can.

"You're at Union Hospital. You were admitted early this morning." My heart beats faster as I try to recall what happened. But I don't know. I don't understand.

"You had some drugs in your system, including rufilin. Can you tell me if you recall anything about last night?"

My body tenses as I shake my head. I don't understand what's going on.

"I don't," I say as I stare at the back wall.

Is this my freedom? He drugged me and left me at a hospital? Is he gone? Tears prick my eyes. He didn't even say goodbye.

I begged him to leave, but I didn't want this. This hurts. My heart literally hurts.

The nurse pulls up a stool next to the bed as the other gives me a small smile and closes the door behind her. She seems less anxious now that I'm not trying to escape.

"We were able to identify you from your license that was in your pocket, but could you tell me your name?"

"Olivia Bell." My voice is even and low. I feel distant. *He left me.* That's all I can think.

She nods her head and places her hand over mine. I can see sympathy in her eyes.

"You've been missing for quite a while."

Her hand pats mine.

"Can you tell me what happened?" she asks in a sweet voice.

I stare at her, not trusting myself to speak.

He left me. The last thing I remember is him pulling my back into his chest. He held my hand and kissed my neck. And then… he had to go? I don't remember. It's so fuzzy. I can't remember.

"I—" I swallow thickly, but I can't speak. I shake my head.

"It's okay," she says, and there's nothing but sympathy in her eyes.

"A missing person's report was filed. The police will be here soon."

I don't want to see them.

"I need a minute, please." I barely get the words out.

She taps my hand and gives me a sad smile. "We'll be right outside. Just press this button if you need anything."

I nod my head and wipe the tears from under my eyes I didn't even realize had escaped.

After a long time, reality slowly registers.

My throat closes and I cover my face as I lose all composure.

I don't stop crying until I hear a knock on the door and the police walk in.

Chapter 29

I'M WALKING INTO A SETUP, AND I KNOW IT. I HAVE NOTHING TO lose though.

I've got a vest on and three guns on me. I'm going with the one with the silencer first.

I shut the door to the car and take a look over my shoulder.

Gabriel and Andrew are parked across the lot at a café. They know it's going down. My heart beats chaotically in my chest, trying to escape. Andrew is Gabriel's right-hand man. He doesn't know everything, but he knows enough. I saw the surprise in his eyes though. I felt like a traitor.

It'll be worth it after today though.Gabriel may kill me the second I walk out of those doors. *If* I walk out. But if he gives me the paperwork and I can pull this off, everything will be worth it.

I could've called my handler, Gates. I could've been pulled. But I keep thinking about James and Olivia. If I leave now, it was all for nothing. His death and everything I put her through would be meaningless. Gabriel won't give me the papers until Stone is dead. This has to happen.

Gates wanted me out when he called. He said we had to abort. My boots crunch on the gravel as I walk up to the old packaging center. Ricky bought it for cheap, and his office is in the back.

No fucking way. Not after Gabriel offered me this deal. If he's telling me the truth.

She's safe. And that's what matters.

I push open the double doors and take a look around. A few men are playing cards on a cheap table to my right. One's smoking some skunked pot, and the scent fills my lungs.

I don't know who all knows I'm undercover. Intelligence says it's just Ricky. So I'm taking my chances. But it could be all of them. I nod at the men and they give me a nod back, and one even a quick wave.

I hope I'm right. I walk down the hall and all the way to the back. With each step my heart beats louder and louder knowing I'm walking to my death… unless I kill him first.

Being back here reminds me of what happened that night.

I thought about it the entire drive back up here. What would've happened if she'd never walked down that alley? I never would have met her. I never would have ruined something so beautiful. But I also wouldn't have gone to Gabriel. She's a bigger part of this than she'll ever know.

I stop in front of the closed door to his office and hesitate before knocking. I could still run. I could leave and never look back.

But I have to do this. I knock on the door twice with the back of my hand. *Knock. Knock.*

I can feel the sweat on my brow and I wipe it away as I hear him say, "Come in."

I take a deep breath and turn the knob. It opens slowly with a creak, and Ricky's right where he always is, smoking a cigarette behind the old desk. I take a quick glance around the room. No one else is here. I shut the door with a loud click and look at the man who thinks he's about to kill me.

"Have a seat, Maddox." The way he says my last name makes me want to cringe. It's like he's poking fun at it. He knows that's not my real name. Barrow's my real last name. How many times has he done that? How many times has it slipped by me?

I take a seat across from him and let the leather jacket I'm wearing slide up some as I sit back. My hands slip into my pockets, but the right one has a hole at the bottom. My hand slides through and I grip the butt of my gun.

My finger rests on the trigger.

"Kade, I have a few problems with the order coming up." Ricky leans back in his seat, his fingers in a steeple and taps his pointer fingers against his lips.

"We need virgins. They get the good money." I keep my eyes on his and nod.

"These used up cunts aren't bringing in what they used to." Every word that comes from his mouth disgusts me more and more.

"Did you see Vic yesterday?" he asks me. "He's supposed to be on the lookout for buyers, but he hasn't gotten back to me since he was on his way to you."

I play it off smoothly and say, "Didn't see him yesterday. Maybe I left a little too soon." He doesn't believe me. But it doesn't matter.

He leans forward and I follow suit, pulling the gun out slowly.

"Well, I'm gonna need two men to round up the product, now that that fucker, what was his name?" he asks me with his eyes narrowed.

"Who's that?" I ask him. My heart beats faster. *James.* I know that's who he's talking about.

He gives me a wicked smile as he nods his head and snaps his fingers. "That's right," he says as he pulls out a drawer to his desk.

My heartbeat slows and I pull the gun out. The metal slips against the leather, but I'm quick and efficient. Aim. Fire. Two shots. Both to the head.

The silencer is barely heard as his body jolts with each shot and he falls back in the chair, sagging with two neat bullet holes dripping blood down his face. And the gun he'd picked up from the drawer falls to the thin-carpeted floor with a low thud.

I push back in the chair and it topples over. Done. That fucker's dead. It's about time. If I die right now, at least I contributed some good to the world. I've sure as shit done my fair share of bad. But I'm done.

My heart beats rapidly and adrenaline surges in me as I leave the office, locking the door from the inside and closing it tight.

I walk out as casually as possible, waving goodbye to the fuckers playing cards and walk across the lot to my car.

Gabriel's standing outside the driver's door and as I unlock the car, he opens it for me.

"It's done?" he asks. I nod my.

"He's dead. Two bullets to the head."

Gabriel smiles and hands me a large manila envelope.

"I don't believe we'll ever see each other again."

"I don't think we will." I answer him with the same tone as I slide into the driver's seat and start the car. I make sure to do it while he's there, just in case. He closes the door and takes in a deep breath as I put the car into reverse.

I place the envelope on the passenger seat. I don't know what's in it, but I don't plan on looking until I get to the safe house.

"It's been fun, Kade. I'm sad to see you go, but I think it's for the best for both of us."

Again I nod. And I have to agree.

Our heads whip around to the packaging center as I hear a dim scream of anger and then another. They found him.

"Time to go," Gabriel says with a smile. "Best of luck to you, Kade."

"Same to you." We lock eyes before parting ways. As I drive out of the lot, I see Andrew give me a short wave from his truck across the road. I return the gesture and drive off. I'm still waiting for a bomb or a bullet.

I anticipate my death the entire three-hour drive to the safe house.

It doesn't hit me until I get there and park and look through all the documents that Gabriel handed to me, that it's finally over. It's really over.

Every contact, first and last name, alias and locations are all in neat, organized columns.

I lean back in my seat and rest my head against the cold window. It's over.

The hurt and hollowness in my chest doesn't move, and I stay in the car longer than I should before I gather the strength to go in and call Gates. I'll take pictures of the evidence and send them to him… just in case.

I get out of the car slowly and follow through with the orders Gates gave me days ago.

I sit at the desk in the back room and dial the number.

The phone rings and rings.

Finally, a man answers.

I give him the code words, and it's done.

My mission is done.

The only thing I want to do is to run to Olivia. I need to know if she's okay. I need to make sure she's alright. But I could never do that.

The world I've been living in vanishes before my eyes. The reality sets in.

Everything I did to her plays through my mind in slow motion.

I fell in love with her, but she should hate me for what I've done.

Chapter 30

Olivia

I LOOK OVER AT CHERYL HESITANTLY. I'VE BEEN HOME FOR A FEW days now. But I haven't left my room much. I haven't talked to my parents. They keep telling me they'll be there when I'm ready. But I don't see how I could ever be ready.

"Just talk to me," Cheryl says and reaches her hand out to me. I want to tell them all, but I know what they'll say. I confessed everything to the shrinks at the hospital and they gave me a pill and said I was sick. I'm not sick. I'm heartbroken; there's a difference.

I don't need anyone else talking to me about Stockholm syndrome. I'm thinking clearly, and functioning just fine. But I miss him. It hurts me so much to not know if he's okay.

It's almost like it never happened. Like I imagined it.

One day I was taken, and two months later I'm dropped off at a hospital. They filed a report even though I told them not to. Doctor-patient confidentiality apparently doesn't mean shit if my state of mind is unwell.

I didn't tell the police anything. I don't want to confide in anyone. I just want Kade back. I rub my chest where the pain is.

"I know they hurt you," Cheryl says and her voice cracks. She just wants me to talk, I know that. But I can't.

"Please don't." I shake my head and stop her right in her tracks. Tears prick my eyes. "Don't." I don't want to hear it. I don't want her pity. I don't want to know what they think happened to me. I know what they think, and I know what they'll say if they ever found out the truth.

"Tell me to do something then. Please." Cheryl's voice is full of desperation. "I feel so guilty." She takes in a ragged breath. "You have no idea. I love you so fucking much, and when you didn't come home I knew something was wrong."

Hot tears run down her cheeks. "I shouldn't have let you go there alone." She doesn't bother to wipe them away. It was just to an interview. I don't blame her in the least.

I hug her, making the bed bounce slightly. I tighten my arms around her to show her how much I love her. "It's not your fault. It's okay." She holds me back and doesn't let go as a violent sob is ripped from her throat.

"It's not okay." She pulls away from me and angrily wipes the tears. "You're not okay." I barely make out her words through the sobs.

She struggles to even her breathing. She's right; I'm not okay. I don't know if I'll ever be okay. I've never hurt this much before.

I feel abandoned and alone. Even though I'm surrounded by friends who are here for me. I don't want them though. I want Kade.

I take in a steadying breath and prepare to answer her, but a sturdy knock at my door stops me.

"Olivia?" My father's voice is uncertain.

"Yes?" I answer hesitantly.

"There are police officers here to see you." My blood turns to ice, and my body numbs.

I won't talk. I don't want to.

I look down at my body. I'm only in sweats and an old t-shirt. My pajamas basically. I've been wearing the same ones for two days now. They're clean at least. I don't have a bra on though.

"I'll be down in a minute," I answer loud enough for him to hear.

Cheryl's composing herself and wiping her nose with her sleeve as I open the dresser drawer and pull out a bra. Then I open the drawer below it looking for a nicer looking shirt. I turn my back to her to change clothes as quick as I can.

"Are you okay?" Cheryl asks.

I turn, slipping the shirt down and stare at my best friend.

"Are you going to be in trouble? Is that why…?" She doesn't finish, but she doesn't have to.

"No," I say and shake my head.

"What can I do to help?" Her wide eyes, glassy with tears, are pleading with me.

I hold my hand out to her. "I could use a friend." She's quick to take my hand and she doesn't let go as I walk through the hall and down the stairs.

My heartbeat seems to slow with each step and finally I'm in my dining room where an officer in uniform is sitting with my parents at the table and another officer is standing behind him.

"Olivia Bell?" the officer asks.

I clear my dry throat and try to answer, but it's so hard. It feels as though a lump is lodged in it, so I just nod instead.

"I'm Detective Dowers, and this is my partner, Detective Brown."

"Hi," I manage to squeak out.

"We have a few questions for you," the man standing asks. Detective Dowers' nearly bald head reflects the light hanging above the table. His eyes are a soft hazel, but they seem kind.

I nod my head again and pull out a seat, sitting across from the other officer. He's younger, but he looks tired with bags under his eyes.

His voice is deeper, too. "Do you know this man?" He sets a picture down on the table and everyone else in the room takes a look.

My heart stops beating. It's Kade. He's staring back at me. His power is reaching me through his picture.

Life seems to drain from me. I look into the officer's eyes, but I don't answer.

After a moment, he speaks. "We have reason to believe that he abducted you on September 16th."

"Is this the man?" my mother asks as she grips my shoulders and tries to look me in the eyes. But I don't move, I don't react. I feel trapped. I don't know how they found out, but I'm not saying a word. I refuse to say anything against him.

I won't do it.

"Miss?" Everyone's eyes are on me as I lick my dry lips and shake my head no.

"He admitted to kidnapping you."

My eyes flash to Detective Dowers. My heart races, and my blood heats.

"I need to ask you some questions. And you need to answer them truthfully." I slowly move my eyes to Detective Brown as he speaks.

"Olivia. Are you okay?" my mother asks.

"Olivia, you don't need to answer anything," Cheryl's quick to add. She looks up at the officers and says, "She has the right to a lawyer."

"We have no intention of pressing charges against Olivia. She's the victim here."

"What happened?" my father asks. And Detective Dowers looks more than ready to divulge information.

I don't speak as the two officers rattle off the last two months of my life as though it's a series of crimes. They have names and dates. They mention rape and sex slavery. All the while, my parents cry. Even my father.

I sit there numb, listening to it as everyone around me breaks down into hysterics. It's odd to hear what they think of it. Some facts I know could have only come from Kade.

He abandoned me, and then admitted to everything. I wish he'd told me. I would have never let him do it. I feel so betrayed by him. I'm sick to my stomach.

"We need you to answer these questions. And you're going to have to testify."

"What if she doesn't want to face him?!" Cheryl cries out with horror. She hasn't let go of my hand.

"I won't do it." I speak for the first time.

The officers stare at me for a long time.

"We're going to need you to speak to our psychologist." I shake my head. That's not happening either. No fucking way.

"If you refuse," Dowers looks at Brown and sighs as if he's burdened to tell me, "we will subpoena you. And if you fail to follow through with your obligations, charges will be pressed."

"How dare you!" my mother hisses across the table.

"Get out of my house." My father's voice booms through the room. My body shakes, and tears leak from the corner of my eyes.

"I'm very sorry for what's happened to you, but we won't allow you to compromise this case. We will prosecute you to the full extent of the law if you fail to cooperate."

That threat has echoed in my head every night for the past two weeks.

Each appointment, every interview.

And now as I get ready to testify against the man I love.

Chapter 31

Olivia

"MISS BELL, I ASKED YOU A QUESTION." THE OLD MAN distracts me from my thoughts. He stares at me through his glasses, waiting for an answer that I don't want to give him.

"I've told you everything." I feel sick to my stomach. I've answered every question they've thrown at me with complete honesty. Because Kade told me to.

The second I sat down, I'd planned to plead the fifth and not give them anything against him. But my eyes caught Kade's, and he mouthed to me to tell the truth. I've looked at him every time before answering. And every time he's given me an approving small smile and a nod.

"You've told us about many things, but you have not answered a simple question." The lawyer faces the jury and then looks back to me. "Did this man, Kade Barrow, or Kade Maddox as you knew him, did he or did he not take you against your will on the night of the 16th?" His voice is sharp. He takes his glasses off and purses his lips as he waits for me to answer.

"You don't understand—" I keep trying to explain it to them, but they aren't listening. Knowing now what he did… he saved me. I was in the wrong place at the wrong time. He did what he thought was best. And he kept me safe.

"I understand this man held you captive, and that you are suffering because of it. This man is withholding information on a Gabriel Durand. He's murdered his own partner in cold blood. He's committed crime after crime, and you've testified to those facts." His cold eyes bore into me as he asks, "Have you not?"

Tears prick my eyes and my heart squeezes with unbearable pain. I only did it because he told me to. Tears flow freely down my cheeks. I look back at Kade. He gives me a soft smile, and it breaks my heart. A sob is ripped from my throat.

"Yes," I answer barely above a murmur.

The man looks between me and Kade with disgust.

"No further questions, your Honor."

I grip onto the edge of my dress and hold my breath as I listen to the judge deliver his sentencing.

The hearing continues in a daze, as if it isn't real.

"How do you find the defendant?" the judge asks.

The clerk looks straight ahead as he answers, "The jury finds the defendant guilty."

My stomach sinks and churns with a sickness threatening to come up. The words sink in slowly, and my grip loosens. My lungs empty and refuse to fill.

The judge nods his head and addresses Kade. "Kade Barrow, although you engaged in activity you felt was required while you were acting on behalf of the police force, you've testified to several illegal activities that were in clear and direct violation of the law. You refused a direct order to abort, and therefore you will not be able to hide behind the guise of an officer of the law."

My ears fill with white noise and my vision goes black. My hands and body chill with a numbness as the judge sentences Kade to fifty years in prison.

Soft murmurs fill the courtroom, but I'm silent, refusing to believe what's happening.

"The jury is thanked and excused. Court is adjourned."

The gavel slams down hard with a loud bang and people stand around me. They're going to get up and do whatever it is that's waiting for them.

I stare at the back of Kade's head, waiting for him to look at me.

But he doesn't. He stands and walks behind the bailiff. He never turns.

My throat closes and my face heats.

A door opens to the left of the judge's bench for them to walk through.

I just need one look from him. Just one sign that I mean anything to him. I need to know it was real between us. That I'm not crazy.

But they walk through the door and it closes behind them without him ever looking back at me.

I collapse forward and cover my face with my hands. I don't care that they can see me. I don't care who hears me. I break down like I never have before. My heart is beyond broken, it's shattered.

Chapter 32

Kade

THIS ISN'T THE FIRST TIME I'VE BEEN GIVEN THIS OFFER.

I stare down at the sheet I'm about to sign. But I can't even wrap my head around it. I can only think about her. It's been ten days since the hearing, and every day I'm filled with regret.

I needed to do it for her though. I thought I was going away for fifty years. I couldn't let her even consider waiting for me. She would have, my sweet angel. I know she would have. And I don't want that life for her. She deserves a man who will be there for her, someone to give her children and a life worth living. With this deal, I can be that man for her. It'll be a few years. But I can give her that, if she'll wait for me. If she wants me.

"You aren't promising millions of dollars this time though, so maybe it's more believable," I say without any humor in my voice as I tap the pen against the table.

"You'll be heavily compensated for your enrollment in the program," the man in the suit, Mr. Smith, says. A Mr. Thomas was the one who offered me and James the deal that got me into this shit.

"It's three years overseas, or fifty years in jail." Mr. Smith stands up from the table, straightening out his tie. "Your choice."

I leave tomorrow. A plane's going to take me to Nepal and then god knows where else. For the next three years of my life, I'll be doing the government's bidding. Making up for my past crimes.

"We're here," the taxi driver says. I'm quick to get out and pull out my wallet.

I pay the tab, giving him an extra ten in cash and turn to look at the building.

It's her house.

I have one night of freedom. They gave me a single night, and I came straight here.

I never told her how I felt. I didn't get a chance to explain anything. I shove my hand in my pocket and feel the note I wrote her.

It's an apology for everything I've done.

A confession of how I feel about her.

And a promise to come back.

I walk slowly up the steps, my confidence slipping as I get closer. I don't know that she'll want me, but I have to tell her everything.

I hear her small voice as I come up to the front porch.

There's a porch swing and a huge window behind it. The window's open, and the thin curtains don't do anything to obstruct my view. I can see right inside. My eyes focus on her.

The beast that's been pacing inside of me since the hearing settles when I see her, my angel. She has a way about her that does that to me. She tames and calms me.

She looks beautiful in simple grey sweats and a pale pink tank top. Her ankles are crossed as she sits at a dining room table. Her hair's in a loose bun on top of her head.

She looks so relaxed and at home. She looks… normal. My heart speeds up as she turns to the window. I move out of sight as fast as I can, afraid she saw me. But she doesn't say anything.

"It's going to be alright, Olivia. We're here to help you," a woman's voice says. That must be her mother.

Olivia clears her throat as I peek back inside. I finally get a look at her face. She's so sad. She has bags under her eyes, and her lips are turned down. She's not okay.

"You don't understand," she says quietly.

"Well, tell me then. Please." Her mother's voice cracks and she sniffles, picking up a napkin to wipe under her eyes. My heart shatters in my chest. I'm feeling like a million splinters are stabbing me in every direction. This is my fault.

"You don't tell any of us anything." Her father's voice is hard.

"Harold, stop it," her mother snaps. "She'll tell us when she's ready."

Olivia's quiet. She doesn't respond. She sets her fork down and pushes the plate away.

"You need to eat, baby." Her father's voice is low and non-threatening.

They care about her. They're trying to help her. They're going to heal her when I can't.

Heal her pain that I caused.

I close my eyes and clench my fists.

What the fuck am I even doing here? I did this to her.

I crumple the note in my pocket and lower my head. I watch my feet move as I walk through the yard and down the empty street. There aren't any street lights. It's dark and lonely. It's what I deserve.

She deserves so much more than me. She deserves the life she would've had without me.

It's wrong of me to even ask for forgiveness.

I was in too deep. I refused to leave when I should have.

I'll do what I should have done from the beginning. I'll leave her alone. She's better off without me.

Chapter 33

Olivia

Three years later…

I CAN'T STOP SMILING. I ROCK BACK AND FORTH ON MY HEELS ON THE stage as the crowd claps and cheers. I hold my diploma tighter, feeling nearly unstoppable.

I have my degree in business and a dream job at a winery that I'll hopefully be able to take over soon. I can't believe how quickly life has changed for me.

I look out into the crowd, but no one's there for me right now. My parents' flight is delayed, and I haven't talked to Cheryl since I moved all the way out to California. Well, not like we used to. In all honesty, none of them ever understood why I felt that way about Kade. They never will, and that's okay.

"Are you ready?" Gwen squeals in my ear as we walk off the stage.

"Fuck yeah I am." I smile back at her and start to feel the excitement of being free from school. I've buried myself in work since I've started this journey of recovery. Inwardly I roll my eyes.

My heart was broken. It was shattered. But I'm okay now. I still miss him though. I can't help that. Some things stick with us forever, and Kade and our time together is something I'm choosing not to let go of. I know he's gone. He never loved me like I loved him. If he did, he never told me. I still dream that he did. Sometimes I remember his touch and I question whether or not I'm exaggerating it.

"Are you actually going to try to score tonight?" Gwen grips my hand

and pulls me through the crowd. As if by the time we get to the parking lot it's not going to be packed. There are hundreds of cars out there, I don't see the point in rushing just to sit in traffic, but whatever floats her boat I guess.

"One sec," I say and pull back on her hand so I can slip off my heels. She scrunches her nose and I respond by sticking my tongue out.

"At least you'll go faster," she says.

I smirk at her. "Precisely!"

I sway my hips to the beat of the music booming through the club. I slowly raise my arms with a drink in my right hand. It's dark, but the lights flash every few beats and the up lighting gives the club a hot vibe I've grown to love. This is our place to unwind. And I enjoy every minute of it. I like getting lost in the seductive beats.

Gwen bumps her ass into me and shakes it while sticking her tongue out, making me laugh. I look around, wondering who she's putting a show on for.

I don't see anyone staring back, so I smack her ass playfully and let out a laugh. I'm definitely buzzed and enjoying this night. I start work in one week, and I've gotta pack my shit up, move and get settled. I don't have much, but it's going to keep me busy. Tonight I can just enjoy myself though. I can have a little fun and take in the moment.

Gwen stands upright and turns to face me, mimicking my movements. She leans forward, unsteady on her heels. I quickly balance her, grabbing onto her arm and we both laugh. It's getting late and I think she's had more than enough to drink. I've had my fair share, and my feet are killing me. I'm more than happy to call it a night.

"Wanna go?" I ask her, practically screaming so she can hear me over the booming music.

"But Mr. McHotStuff saw!" she screams in my ear.

"Who?" I scrunch my forehead and look through the crowd as she points behind me. My heart stops in my chest, and my skin chills as I see him.

"He's all yours, baby! He hasn't taken his eyes off of you." I barely hear her voice.

Kade.

I stare back at him, not knowing what to do. I'm afraid to move, afraid to breathe even. I've thought I'd seen him a hundred times before, but it was never him.

I'm afraid if I blink, he'll vanish.

"Kade?" I whisper. And as though I've broken the spell, he turns and pushes through the crowd, leaving me.

Gwen grips onto my arm as I try to leave. "Where are you going?" she screams over the music with a worried look in her eyes.

I shake my head at her and point to the bar. "I'll meet you there in ten."

She points her finger at me. "Ten minutes."

I'd laugh at her trying to be the responsible one if I had any humor in me, but I don't. My blood pumps with adrenaline and anxiety as I push past the swaying hips on the dance floor and search for Kade.

I make it through the crowd and out to the other side in time to see Kade looking back over his shoulder and walking through the exit door.

I don't even hesitate. I'm not letting him get away from me.

I practically run in my heels to catch the door before it closes and yell out, "Kade!" as I see his back.

There are a few people out here smoking by the door. I barely notice them even though they stopped talking the moment I yelled. I'm sure they're staring, but I don't care.

Kade stops walking, but he doesn't turn around.

I take a few hesitant steps toward him but stay a few feet away. It's late and dark, but there are lights out here on the sides of the building. I can hear the low music get louder as the back door opens and then it dims as the door shuts with a loud click.

It's almost silent, save the sounds of the cars on the street at the end of the alley and the faint beat of the bass from inside the club.

"Kade?" I weakly call out to him. "Please," I start to beg him, but my throat closes and tears prick my eyes. I'd give anything to be with him. But he left as soon as he saw me. Nothing's changed. He doesn't want to be with me.

"You never loved me, did you?" I talk to his back, but that finally gets a reaction from him. He turns around, and my heart slows.

He still looks the same.

His sharp jaw has several days of stubble and his hair is grown out slightly, but the dominance and hard features are still present and they make me want to drop to my knees in this dirty alley. But I don't. I won't do that for a man who doesn't love me.

He opens his mouth, but doesn't say anything. He swallows thickly and watches the door as it opens, bringing the loud noises of the club along with it. He closes the space between us and puts his hand on my hip, although his eyes are on whoever left the building. I can hear their steps grow distant as they walk in the opposite direction and farther away from us.

Finally, he looks down into my eyes.

My heart clenches in my chest. I don't know why he's here; he's supposed to be in jail. I tried so hard to track him down that first year. But they wouldn't tell me anything. I felt pathetic for even trying to find him, but also like I'd failed him for never seeing him. But then again, I found solace knowing he'd never looked back.

In this moment, I know one of two things will happen. Either he tells me he loves me and we find a way to make this work between us, or he doesn't and I leave him behind forever.

"I just need to know if you ever loved me." I stare into his eyes and ignore the tears running down my face. It may kill a small part of me to hear he never did, but I'll survive. I just need to know.

He cups my jaw in his hand and runs his thumb along my bottom lip. My head falls back slightly and my lips part.

"I should tell you I never did. I should do that for you. I should lie." Hope blooms in my chest, and I take in a deep breath.

"But I'm a selfish man, and I love you so fucking much." My heart swells and hurts so much I can hardly stand it. This time it's a good pain.

"I don't deserve you, and I'll understand it if you send me away. I'll stay away; I promise I will. But if you have any feelings for me left at all, I want you, Olivia. I want to build a life with you. An honest life. I'm done with all that. I promise you."

I wipe the tears away from under my eyes, trying to calm myself, but it's so hard. I've dreamed of him coming back for me, but I never thought it was possible. I didn't think I'd ever see him again.

He loves me.

I want to beat my fists against his chest for leaving me. For throwing me away all those years ago. For not telling me the truth. For never looking back. Somewhere in me, there's anger.

But more than anything, I just want him to hold me. I miss him.

I lose all composure and wrap my arms around him, kissing him with everything I have.

And he holds me back just as tight, kissing me with passion and longing. He pulls my body against his hard, muscular chest. His tongue dives into my mouth and I lean into him. My body lights with a desire I haven't known for years.

He breaks the kiss and pulls away, both of us breathing heavily. "Not here, angel." He kisses my hair and looks back at the door.

After a long moment, I finally ask him, "You're really here?"

"I'm here, Olivia. If you want me, I'm here."

"I do want you."

"Somehow I knew you'd come back for me," I whisper into his chest. I don't know how, but I knew. Years later, I still feel like my heart belongs to him.

"I'm so sorry." He kisses my hair and holds me closer to him. "I wanted you to live your life. I wanted so much more for you than what I could give you. I'll make it up to you. Every day for the rest of my life."

"All I want is you, Kade. I love you." I need him. My heart and soul need him.

"I'm all yours, angel." He pulls away from me and kisses the tip of my nose. "I love you."

Epilogue

Olivia

"Y

OU TWO LOOK SO CUTE TOGETHER! HOW DID YOU MEET?" the waitress asks as we sit down to dinner. She looks sweet and innocent, but I hate it when people ask that question. I hate lying.

In the three years we've lived in the area, I've never been to this restaurant before. I love the seaside cabin feel of it. It's a good hour away from the winery, but I needed a vacation, and Kade said this is the first stop.

The renovations on the winery are seriously eating into its profits, but luckily Kade's investments are paying for this trip. He doesn't understand why I don't just quit since we don't need the money, but I like being challenged and learning the business. Maybe one day I'll sell it, and until then I have his complete support to pursue my dream.

I lay the white cloth napkin across my lap and smooth it out.

"At a club." I give the answer I always give. Kade reaches across the table and takes my hand. He knows I hate this.

"Oh, I love hearing these stories." She hugs the menus to her chest. If only I'd told her the truth.

"I'm starving," I not-so-subtly say to get this conversation moving. Kade chuckles at me and accepts the menu as the waitress hands one to him and then to me.

"You should try not to look so pissed when you answer that question," Kade says as the waitress leaves us.

"Well," I say as I open the menu and look down the list of fresh fish.

"Maybe we should come up with a different story." I wouldn't change anything between us. Not a damn thing. But I don't want to share it with anyone. They'll never understand.

Kade brings my hand to his lips and kisses my fingers.

"I don't want another story. I love *our* story." His confession makes my lips kick up into a small smile. "It's sad at times, and we went through hell. But I love you."

Tears prick my eyes. "I love you too, Master K." I blush as I say his name and he raises his brows.

"Don't start what you can't finish, angel." His voice is low and laced with a threat. A threat that makes my pussy clench. We'll be on vacation for days. I've been looking forward to this since I found out we were going.

"I would never." I look up at him through my thick lashes and see nothing but devotion in his eyes. Our story may not be the typical love story, but it's ours, and no one can take that away from us.

forsaken

They tempted me with her. And I couldn't resist.

I'm not a good man. I'm a hired killer, and damn good at what I do. Raised to be ruthless and forced into this life, I never had a choice.

Until she was thrown into my lap.

I didn't want to take the hit. It's too dangerous, and I can't afford these kinds of risks. I turned my employers down, but they sweetened the deal.

Gifting her to me.

She's scared, beautiful, and all mine.

She gazes at me with her gorgeous baby blues, and I can hardly resist taking her. She makes me want to break my rules… all because of the desire hidden in those stolen glances.

I'm addicted to her seductive curves and the soft moans that spill from her lips. She's tempting in ways she doesn't even realize. I'm practically obsessed.

They're going to want her back, but I'll kill them all to keep her.

Prologue

BEATEN. BROKEN. USED AS A BARGAINING CHIP. I'VE BEEN through hell. *He* can't do anything that hasn't already been done to me. Except show me tenderness, kindness… pleasure. And he has. In a way I didn't know I needed.

Goosebumps travel down my arms as I hear his heavy footsteps echoing in the hall. My steady heartbeat quickens.

He's come back for me. I'm almost surprised by the excitement I feel. The rush of adrenaline, and the anticipation of hearing the click of the lock on the door. *Almost.*

My fingers wrap around the thin bars as he enters. My captor. I could come out, I could let him have me. I know Gio wants me, and I'd be a liar if I said I didn't want him, too. His hard ripped body and the heat in his eyes tempt me to come out of my cage. The door's never locked, so I could easily leave. But I'm safe here.

He said he won't touch me, and he's held firm to his promise. So long as I stay inside of the cage, I'm protected. But I want to come out. I want his praise. *I've grown addicted to it.* His very presence is a drug.

I'm desperate for him, and he knows it. I want to resist. I want to hold out against whatever sickness is taking me over. But I can't. He's too much. *He's everything.*

There's a darkness inside of him, a dangerous beast. I know what he's capable of, but when he's with me, there's a sense of calm about him. Maybe

I'm naive to think I affect him as much as he does me, but the very thought that I do makes me feel powerful.

The sound of the door creaking open and his broad shoulders filling up the doorway make my lips part, and a moan of lust escapes my throat. My nipples harden, and my clit throbs with need. He's done this to me. He's trained me to react like this. I know it's the truth, but I can't deny I enjoy it.

"My princess," he says and his voice is rough and deep. It reminds me of how he groaned when he first took me. It's the sexiest fucking sound I've ever heard. He's just as obsessed with me as I am with him. It's only fair.

I lick my lips and shift on my knees, facing him and leaning forward. I don't leave the safety of the cage though. I want him to lure me out. Is that so wrong?

"I miss you," he whispers, crouching in front of the cage, his fingers curling above mine around the bars. My heart thumps hard in my chest, and my body begs me to just reach out. To climb into his lap and let him hold me. It's my choice. But the only choice I've been given.

I've never felt so loved before. Even if it's an illusion and nothing more. *But that doesn't stop me from craving it.*

"Tell me you missed me," e commands, and my mouth parts on its own. The words are there, right on the tip of my tongue. I flirt with the idea of saying them, but I close my lips shut tight

He tilts his head, narrowing his eyes and tsking me for disobeying him. Again I shift on my knees, questioning my decision to keep fighting him.

His expression softens as he sits in front of me, lowering himself as my eyes look down at him. I settle onto the floor of the cage across from him. Merely inches away, but so much farther than that all the same.

"I know you did." As he says the words, his dark eyes heat and a cocky grin plays at his lips.

I can't help my eyes widening and a smile slowly slipping across my lips. I wish I could hide it, but I can't hide anything from him. Not anymore.

I don't want to go back to the way things were. I know it's wrong, but I had nothing before him. I'm drunk on his touch, his words. He's everything I could possibly need. He's shown me that.

I may be broken. But I'm *his*.

Chapter 1

Gio

One month before

THE BRIGHT RED RUBBER BALL SQUEAKS AS I RELEASE IT, watching it sail far across my yard. Duke, my loyal black lab, turns and chases the ball as fast as he can, tearing up the grass in pursuit.

I smile to myself, looking out across the property. I like the seclusion and privacy of living outside of the city, and I was able to construct a home with everything I could need. I bought the place more for the land than for anything else. I'd be happy living in a fucking trailer if it meant I could do whatever I damn well please, but fortunately I get paid a lot of money to do what I do.

"You know we can't turn this down."

I glance at my father at the sound of his voice. He stands impatiently against a nearby tree, puffing one of the short, dark cigars he prefers. His receding white hair makes him look ten years older than he is. He's wearing his usual outfit, a blue dress shirt tucked into jeans with a brown work jacket over top and oversized brown boots that are nearly falling apart. He looks like a construction worker, or something blue collar like that.

He sure as hell works with his hands, but he's no fucking construction worker.

"You know that if we do it, the consequences could be extensive," I answer, feeling a chill run down my shoulders.

Duke grabs the ball and heads back, his tail held high in the air. My father huffs, shaking his head and then inhales deeply, looking past me.

His voice is low as he responds, "I understand your concerns, but this is beyond us."

"Exactly. It's too big to control," I answer, not bothering to look at him.

"Control?" He laughs. "There's no control in our line of work."

"Maybe the way you operate. But that's not how I do things."

He pushes off the tree and walks toward me just as Duke drops the ball at my feet. I pick it up and launch it again, sending the dog running. The smell of the cigar gets stronger as he walks closer.

"Listen, son. You know how much this means to me."

Guilt threatens to take over. The only man I owe shit to is my father. But he's falling for a trap. They'll never give him what he wants. "I know what it *could* mean, at least."

"We've been outsiders our whole fucking lives." His voice rises, letting his emotions come through.

"I know," I say, jaw tense.

"They think we're garbage and trash," he says, nearly spitting the words. "But this is our chance to show them that we're dependable. That we belong."

I grunt and watch the dog sprint off in the distance. My father's right, even though his motives are pretty fucking skewed. He's lived his entire life on the outskirts of the Romano *familia*, wishing he could be a part of them, but unable to join. He's only half Italian; his disgraced father ran off and fucked some Irish girl years and years ago. It doesn't matter to me, but my father never got over the fact that his full Italian Romano cousins were allowed into the *familia*, while he was kept at a distance.

That's probably why my father entered into this profession and trained me to work alongside him. Being hitmen means we're allowed to exist on the fringe of the *familia*. We've even earned some respect, though fear may be the better word for it. Over the years my father gathered a particular set of skills and passed them down to me, continuing the family tradition.

I don't give a shit about my inbred, shitheel cousins. I could kill them one by one if I wanted and never lose a wink of sleep. Blood means nothing to me.

I don't give a fuck about the *familia* like my father does. He has this chip on his shoulder and acts like all of our problems are due to the *familia* rejecting him. He can't see past his own petty need to be accepted by them.

Being an outsider suits me. I like my life outside of the city, and outside of the *familia*. I take their money and do their jobs because that's the life I know, but I don't want to be a part of their politics and their bullshit.

Taking this job offer though would destroy any semblance of outsider status and shove us right into the high-stakes world of mafia power plays. I don't fucking want that. I'm not interested.

"Think of the money," he tries to persuade me. "I know you don't care about the *familia* like I do." There's a hint of bitterness in his tone, and it makes my body tense. "But think of the money they're offering."

He has a good point. They're offering to pay us triple our normal rate, which is significant already. The target is difficult to get to and very important, but the money is absurdly good.

A man could possibly retire with that kind of cash.

"If we do this, our lives will change," I say, meeting his cold gaze.

"Exactly." My father smiles, his yellowed teeth showing for only a moment before he takes another puff of his cigar.

I shake my head. "You see it as a good thing, but to me this would destroy everything we've built."

His boots are heavy and his steps quick as he tosses the cigar aside. He walks up to me and suddenly grabs my jacket by the collar, bunching the fabric up in his fists. My hands clench into fists, but I wait. I'm used to this. I grew up with it.

I can see the anger in his eyes, the intense fury that dwells deep inside. It's a darkness that eats away at him, and I know that he drinks more than he should to try and keep it at bay.

I have the same darkness inside of me. It comes out in different ways, but it's there, slowly rotting me from the inside. I hate my father in this moment because I see myself in him, and it disgusts me. My knuckles go white and adrenaline pumps hard in my blood, but I keep it down, waiting for him to get out whatever's on his mind.

He better do it quick, 'cause I don't have time for this shit.

"You can't fuck this up for me," he growls. His face is close to mine, but I don't move. I don't give him the opportunity to see me weak. "The *familia*'s denied me for far too long. This is our chance to make things right for our family."

Duke returns without the ball and growls at my father. It's low and rough, from somewhere deep down in his throat.

"I'd let me go if I were you," I say softly, cocking a brow and looking my father in the eye. Duke doesn't have the type of control I do. But he'll always wait for my command.

"What, you gonna send that fucking dog after me?" He scoffs, but it's quick and panic is barely hidden beneath it.

"No," I say, staring him down. "You know I don't need his help."

There's a strained moment between us. I can see my father doing the math in his head, wondering if he could take me in a fair fight now that I'm older. We've come close to fighting in the past, though we've never actually traded blows. But we both know I have youth and experience on my side, and so he slowly releases me and takes a deep breath.

He picks up the cigar he dropped on the ground and takes a long puff, looking away as he walks back to the oak tree, ignoring everything that just happened. That's what he does. Thickheaded, thin-skinned and hot-tempered. That's the Romano in him.

I walk across the yard and bend down, picking up the ball Duke left, and throw it. Duke darts after it as if nothing happened.

"Just think about it," he finally says, forcing me to look over my shoulder and face him. "If we kill this fucker, we can be rolling in it for a long time."

"If we kill this fucker, we can start a war." I bite out my words. That's the real reason I don't want in on this.

He shrugs, rubbing out his cigar on the tree and letting out a deep exhalation of smoke. "Let's just wait and see what they have to say." He glances at me, a look of determination on his face, and then heads off back toward his truck.

I don't watch him go. I know he's pissed, and I understand that. Fuck, I can't even blame him, not really. Joining the *familia* is his lifelong dream, and if someone got in the way of what I wanted, well, I'd fucking kill them.

Too bad the old bastard needs me. The sound of his truck starting fills the chilly air as Duke comes back to me.

I'm his rightful successor. He's getting old, too old to go on hits, and for the last two years I've been taking on more and more of the load. In fact, he hasn't actually killed in nearly six months, which is strange for a man who makes his living in death.

He raised me to be a killer and to be the fucking best at what I do. From a young age I remember going to shooting ranges, and practicing knife skills.

My childhood was almost exclusively learning to fight, learning to stalk, and learning how to kill efficiently and quietly. My father trained me to be a hitman, and I quickly found out that I was damn good at it.

And I like it. I like tracking down my victims and taking their lives. They all deserve it. They have it coming to them. As far as I'm concerned, I'm doing the world a favor. I like the power and respect I get for being a skilled and in-demand assassin. Nobody fucks with me because they know who I am, and what I'm capable of. No one can push me around. They wouldn't fucking dare.

But I can't deny that it fucked me up. That it changed me. I can remember the way I was back when I was still a kid, back before killing became my life. The darkness wasn't there back then. I wasn't born with it. It was created.

As I pitch the ball across the yard again, I remember the day my father brought me completely into this life and forced me to kill a man for the first time.

My father stands over me in the cellar. My breath comes in ragged, short gasps.

"Don't be a pussy," he says to me, his voice barely above a whisper as he grips my shoulders. "You fucking afraid?"

"No," I say, but I'm lying. I'm terrified. I'm ten years old and I've never seen a man die before. Not in real life.

The old man's tied to a chair with a gag in his mouth, muffling his screams and pleas. I don't know him. His eyes are wide and brown. His hair is receding and he's probably fifty years old, but I didn't really know that back then. I was just a kid. I didn't know anything.

"What did he do?" I ask tentatively, and my voice cracks. My heart is beating so loudly I can hardly hear anything else.

My father whirls on me. "You fucking know not to ask questions." The anger in his voice makes me flinch. Ever since Mom died, it's been different between us. He takes his rage out on me. It's my fault.

"I know," I say, looking away from him. I expect him to hit me, and I wait for it… but he doesn't. My body is so hot. I feel like I can't even breathe.

"It doesn't matter what he did. All that matters is we get paid. These guys, they're all shit. You have to understand that." The man screams again behind his gag, but whatever he's saying is dampened. I wish I knew.

"I understand." I look at the man as my father walks over to him. He takes the man by what hair he has left and pulls his head back.

"Look at him, Gio," my father says. "Look at this man. Are you looking?"

"Yes, father," I say, staring at the man.

"This is our prey. He's our victim. He's nothing." My father releases him. "Are you a fucking pussy?"

"No," I say and step toward the man. My nerves are shaken, but I have to do this.

"Good. Very good, Gio."

The man struggles and tries to say something. He's panicking and trying to move again like he knows it's his last chance. My father backhands him across the face and his head droops. He's dazed, but not unconscious.

"What now?" I ask my father. I've been training for this since I was very young. I know how to shoot and how to fight and how to hunt, but this is the first time my father is making me watch.

Except watching isn't what he has planned. He holds his gun out to me, grip first. "Take it," he says.

I stare at him, shocked. "Why?" I ask.

"Do as I say."

Afraid, I take the gun. I expect him to hit me again for not following orders right away, but he doesn't. My hands shake.

I know something irreversible is happening. But I don't understand what, not yet.

"Press it against his head," my father orders.

I stand so close to the man I can feel the heat and desperation roiling off of him. His eyes are wide and pleading, staring at me, practically looking through me. He squirms against the restraints. I press the gun against his head. My throat is so tight, I can't swallow. I watch as the man begins to cry, deep heaving sobs. I hold the gun there, the cold steel feeling hotter as my hand starts to sweat, and I look at my father.

"Look back at him," my father commands. I try to swallow again, but I fail miserably. I stare at the man, but only at his temple where the gun is pointed. I can't look him in the eyes. "Are you ready, Gio?"

It comes to me in that moment, what my father wants. It's the reason he's not hitting me. Because he knows I'm about to do something important. I don't want to though. I don't want this. I hold the gun tightly, then grip it with two hands.

"I—I-" I stammer. I can't do this. I'm not like him.

"You will do it, or I'll untie him and let him beat you to death," my father sneers. My blood runs cold, and I finally swallow the spiked lump that has formed in my throat.

"I'm ready," I say in a voice I don't recognize.

Ten years old. My father puts a hand on my shoulder. His fingers dig in as he squeezes.

"Do it," he says.

I pull the trigger without thinking anything more. Bang! The man's skull explodes in a shower of blood. The sound, the feel, and the sight of the man, hung over and limp in the chair haunted me for years. But not the next man, or the next that my father had me kill. I don't even remember them.

I hate him for what he made me, but at the same time, I'm also glad for what he made me. I can take lives so easily now. They mean nothing to me. That first time was difficult, but it was also surprisingly easy.

One pull of the trigger, and it all ends. I'm safe, and the world is rid of a man who needed to die. The darkness inside of me needs this. It craves the rush and the thrill of a hunt and a kill, and if I go too long without a job I find that darkness coming up to the surface in the form of memories. Too much of my past still haunts me. I just need to focus on the present. *On the next kill.*

Duke returns with the ball. I crouch down and pat his shoulder, just now noticing how the sky has darkened and the air has turned bitter cold. "Good boy," I say softly. I relax as Duke nudges me, bringing me back to the present. "Next time, just rip off his nuts."

Duke licks my hand as I grin, pick up the ball, and throw it. He barks as he runs off, leaving me alone with the dilemma at hand.

My father wants me to at least hear what they have to say, and I can do that. I'll listen, because I owe him that much. But I can't imagine how they could change my mind on this one. Not when this hit could spark the largest mafia war in the history of the whole fucking city.

Chapter 2

Grace

Knock, knock. The hard pounding on my bedroom door forces my eyes open. I don't shake or shudder, and I don't flinch when the door opens without a response from me. I'm used to it now. My breathing comes in carefully, each movement calculated.

The door creaks and then shuts with a loud bang as I rise and blink the sleep from my eyes. I don't know how long I've been asleep, but it doesn't matter. It's not like I have anything else to do, or anywhere to go.

I restrain myself from stretching and sit up on the edge of my bed, my hands clasped in my lap as I watch my father walk toward me. I'm used to this, but my heart still races with fear. Everything else I can control, but not my heart. No matter how much I want it to remain calm, it always beats harder and tries to escape up my throat whenever he comes to get me. I never know what to expect, but I know how to behave. I've learned the hard way, but now I know how to survive. That's all I do… *survive.*

If I was a boy, it wouldn't be like this. But I'm a *disappointment.* A re-minder of my mother, and how she betrayed him. That's all I am. He never fails to make sure I know it.

"You need to do something for me," he says in a lowered voice. It holds the edge of a threat when he talks to me. It's always there, like he's waiting for me to give him a reason to strike me. Unless Uncle Toni's in the room. Just the thought of my godfather makes my heart calm slightly. He can't kill me with my uncle still around. My mother, yes, but not me. Uncle Toni would never allow it.

My father may be the Don of the Rossi *familia*, but everyone knows my uncle Toni calls the shots. They all look to him with respect, and they're loyal to him… not to my father. The very thought almost wills me to smile, but I'm not that foolish.

"The Romanos are up to something." I stare straight ahead, my neck stiff as he talks.

He crosses the room, moving to my window and then back toward me. "They've been circling our territory and looking for something." He continues talking without waiting for a response. He doesn't need one from me. We both know that.

I bow my head and keep my eyes down as he paces the floor in front of me. His suit pants swish as he walks and make up the only background noise. He usually doesn't talk *business* around me. He says it's not for women, and I honestly prefer to be left out of it. My fingers dig into the comforter as he speaks, knowing something terrible is going to happen. I don't want to know, but for him to be telling me these things… it's not good. "I don't like it, and you're going to fix this," he practically hisses, turning harshly in his spot and staring at me. I look up to meet his gaze, but only to keep him from touching me. My eyes meet his as I nod my head like I'm supposed to, but inside I'm screaming.

"The Romanos have been hanging around our restaurant; they're on our turf, looking for trouble." His pale blue eyes piercing into mine hold me hostage as my lungs pause their movements. "You're going out there as bait."

I don't react, but he still holds up his pointer and lowers his voice as if I've disobeyed him. Sometimes I can't prevent him from beating me, but it's best not to react, so I'm still as he says, "You don't have a choice. You're going to get us the information we need, and we'll get you out."

For a moment I question if he'll really come save me, or if the Romanos will get to keep me. I'm not sure it matters much. Although at least here I know what to expect. I rely on the comfort of familiarity. I search my father's face for answers, for reassurance. But there's nothing there. Only emptiness in his dark eyes.

"They're going to take you. You need to trust me and stay focused. Listen to what they say and when I come to get you, you'll tell me everything."

I'm numb to his words. It wouldn't be the first time he's used me for his own plans. I nod my head once, although I don't speak. He doesn't like it when I talk.

My heart leaps in my chest as he grips my chin in his hand and rips my head to the side.

"Answer me!" he screams at me. His stale breath fills my lungs as I heave in a frightened breath. After all these years I still cower. Maybe there's a part of me that isn't dead yet.

"Yes, father. I'll listen to everything." My throat feels so tight, but the words come out calmly. "I'll tell you everything." My blood runs cold. I ignore the voices arguing inside of me. One is telling me to run, and the other is telling me to fight back. Those voices are useless. *They both get me nothing but beatings.* I'm smarter than that now. It's not about fear, only survival.

"Good," he says as he releases me, and I fall back into place as he talks to me. "We'll drop you off at the restaurant, and you can walk back home. They've been scouting every day in the evening, so it shouldn't take more than a day or two before they get confident and take you."

I half expect him to tell me not to worry, but I don't hold my breath. I should be worried, and I am. More than that, he doesn't give a fuck if I live or die. Maybe he really needs the information, or maybe he's just looking to finally get rid of me.

I think about what he's asking, and hope rises in my chest.

I'll be alone. For the first time since I can remember, I'll be alone. I try to hide the excitement rising in me. *The hope.*

Maybe this will be my chance to run. I don't want to be the Rossi mafia princess anymore. I don't want to be a pawn in my father's games and get married off to whoever he wants to make alliances with. Although there's a faint hope that I can run and disappear, it's only barely there. It's faded to a mere whisper of what it used to be.

I've tried before to run, and failed. I have the scars to prove it's not possible to outrun the Rossis.

"Do you understand, Grace?" my father asks, practically spitting out my name like a curse.

"Yes, father." My eyes fall to the floor. It's better not to look him in the eyes, especially when I feel like this… when I feel hopeful. "Whatever you need me to do."

"Good." He turns and walks to the door with heavy steps, speaking without looking at me. "Get yourself dressed. We're leaving soon."

My hands ball into fists as the door closes, and my breathing comes in ragged pants. The facade leaves me quickly. I hate him. With everything in my being, I hate him. I rise from the bed and look out my window. It's nailed shut from the outside to keep me from jumping.

Outside, it's dark and grey with clouds covering nearly every inch of the visible sky. It reflects everything that I feel.

I walk to my dresser, my eyes darting to the door. Inside the top drawer, I dig under the pile of shirts and pick up a small bag of heroin. I wrap my fingers around it tightly. I've never done the drug, or any others for that matter. I stole it. I've collected a few baggies over time, and I know I have enough to easily overdose now.

I've been thinking about suicide for a while, but I haven't had the courage to end it. I don't want to die; I just don't want to live *this* life anymore. There's a difference. I stare at the heroin, feeling every emotion wash over me. I knew one day I'd need it.

I would be a fool not to take the heroin with me. I need a way out in case my father doesn't come for me and leaves me there. In case that fate is worse than this. I open the drawer containing my underwear and select my favorite push-up bra. Quickly, I slide the packet into one of the pockets containing the padded inserts. I just hope that whoever takes me won't search my clothing too closely, but in my experience the perverts I've been exposed to care more about seeing a woman naked than her lingerie.

But hopefully it won't even come close to that. He's giving me a chance to run. An opportunity I've prayed for.

Maybe God was listening. Maybe I'll be free soon.

If not, if I can't get away from my father, if I can't get away from the Romanos... at least I'll have a way out.

Chapter 3

THE HUSHED SOUNDS OF THE RESTAURANT AND MY OWN BLOOD pumping in my ears are the only things I can hear. My eyes flicker to the bay window at the front as the bells at the entrance jingle, and another member of the *familia* walks through the glass double doors.

The restaurant is so quaint and gives off a family-friendly feel. The dark green cloth table linens and plaid curtains on the windows make this place look like the quintessential Italian restaurant. Even the soft music playing over the speakers gives an air of comfort.

It's all bullshit. It's a front, and the entire city knows it. I glance up and across the room at my father, seated at the table farthest from me as he talks animatedly to someone I haven't met. He leans back as he laughs, the sound bellowing from his stomach. He looks jovial. That's fake, too. *Or is it?* Maybe he's happy that I'll be gone soon. I still don't know his intentions, but I don't care. I'm grateful. Scared shitless and trying to control my emotions, but grateful.

The bells chime again, and I whip my head up to see another man walk through the doors. The restaurant is closed tonight. But that doesn't mean anything.

I can feel their eyes on me. Everyone's looking at me as they talk in indistinct voices. I'm not supposed to be here. Some are confused by my presence. Others are visibly anxious. A man across from me doesn't bother to look away when I meet his eyes. His fingertips tap repeatedly on the wooden table. He clears his throat and breaks my gaze, running the back of his hand across his mouth and yelling out for someone named Joey to grab him a beer.

Maybe they all don't know what's going on, but some do.

I can't help but look over my shoulder one more time, searching for Uncle Toni. I don't know anyone in here other than my father. I think that may have been an intentional play by him. No one's talked to me, but I have no intention of talking to them either.

Two firm hands grip my shoulders as I turn in my seat. I nearly yell out from the sudden touch, but the sight of my father's cold eyes keeps me quiet. His fingers dig into my skin, and I wonder if the men can tell it hurts. If they do know, they don't show it. They don't try to stop him.

"Now." He nods his head, and I'm frozen in place from the intensity. "Start walking down Broom Street." He leans forward and plants a kiss on my forehead before releasing me.

His touch is gentle and unexpected. I have to blink several times before his expression changes back to the one I'm used to. The chair squeaks on the ground as I turn to do what I'm told. I'm still surviving. Just a little longer until I don't have to obey. *Until I can run.*

As I walk to the front, my legs shake and my nerves get the better of me. I turn to see the man from earlier looking at me again. As soon as my eyes meet his, he looks away from me. For some reason, my heart sinks. As if deep down I'd hoped someone would save me. How foolish.

No one in this building is coming to my rescue. I push against the heavy doors, knowing I'm the only one who can save myself.

The second the doors swing open, the cold air hits my face. They close behind me, leaving the sounds of the restaurant to fade to nothing as the noises of the night greet me. The wind lashes out at me, and I have to close my eyes and shield my cheek a moment with my arm. My thin jean jacket offers little protection against the brutal chill.

I heave in a deep breath and lower my arm. It's dark now, the sky nearly black with only a sliver of the moon shining above me. The street light closest to me flickers as I start to walk. It's only then that fear consumes me.

I'm alone. I've always felt alone, but protected in some sense. In an odd way, I've felt safe. Maybe not from my father, but safe in that I knew I'd live to see tomorrow.

The air hurts my lungs as I take in a breath, and I let out a rough cough.

It makes my eyes sting as I take another step and look over my shoulder at the restaurant. I could go back, but the very thought makes me start walking faster.

Never again. My legs move of their own accord, and I shove my hands into my pockets.

I know I'll never go back. Not willingly.

If only my conviction was enough to save me. I swallow the fear rising up my throat and turn the corner. I'm bait, but I can outrun them. I'll outrun all of them. I have to try, anyway.

I blink against the wind, hating how my eyes water. I haven't cried in so long. I sure as fuck won't do it now when my freedom is so close.

Of course I'm not dressed to run. I'm in heels and a dress, with a thin set of leggings. My father wanted me to play the part of an easy target, and he had to approve of my outfit. I'm tempted to kick off the heels so I can walk faster, but that's when I sense someone behind me.

As my pace picks up, so do the steps behind me.

Someone's clearly following me.

Tracking me.

There's nothing to listen to on this empty street other than our echoing steps and my anxious breath. The smacking of his shoes against the pavement resonates loud in my ears. The click of my heels is nothing compared to the thudding from whoever the fuck is back there. It has to be a man. The sound is too damn heavy to belong to anyone under 200 pounds.

Shit. Shit. Shit.

The Romanos. No. No, I refuse to believe they'd come this close to the restaurant. It's all in my head. I can't lose my chance at freedom so quickly. Maybe it's a Rossi. The thought should give me comfort, but it does the very opposite.

I'm too nervous to look back. In the movies, when people look behind themselves, that's when they have to start running. As soon as they glance back. They run, or they die. Even though in most cases running doesn't save them anyway.

I'm not fucking stupid; if I started running, I wouldn't make it one minute before he caught me. At least right now whoever it is back there is keeping some distance. For now…

I tell myself over and over, maybe he's not following me. I still have a possibility at freedom. He's just walking to his car. Or maybe he's just walking to his house or a bar at the other end of this street. But after a few blocks, the sound of him following me is unbearable. There's not much on this street. The lone gas station is closed down, and there isn't another building for a few blocks. Everything's run down and empty. My heart rate picks up as the reality sets in. *He's here to take the bait.*

A bad man is behind me, I know that much. Maybe it's the Romanos, like my father wanted. Like he planned.

Even if he's not from the Romanos, these streets are filled with bad men late at night.

If the stranger behind me had good intentions, he would've said something by now. There's no way in hell he's not following me. At some point he'll get closer. He'll gain more speed than what I have, and then I'll have to run. But I'm definitely going to make him work for it. If he wants to put his hands on me, then he's going to have to catch me first. And then fight me. I'm not going to be a good little victim. I'll do everything possible to scratch his eyes out before I give in.

I try to steady my breath, but it's so fucking cold out, just breathing hurts.

The man shadowing me is all I can think about. I didn't even pay attention when I turned the corner down the alley.

I was so consumed by what was behind me, I didn't see who was right in front of me until it was too late.

Chapter 4

Gio

Tʜᴇ Gʀᴇᴇɴ Pᴀʀʀᴏᴛ ɪs ᴄʀᴏᴡᴅᴇᴅ ᴀs ᴜsᴜᴀʟ. Iᴛ's ᴀ ᴘᴏᴘᴜʟᴀʀ place in a shit neighborhood on the South Side of Chicago. We come here all the time to meet with potential clients, but usually it's just to pick up payments.

Tonight, the stakes are higher. I sit at a table with my father, a glass of whisky in my hand while he puffs away on his cigar. I take a long sip and glance at him.

"Let me do the talking," I say.

"Why?" he grunts.

"Because I'll be the one doing the job." My voice is hard, but he doesn't seem to notice.

"Doesn't matter. I'm the elder here. They came to me."

"No," I say, trying to keep my annoyance under control. "If you want to do the talking, you can do the killing."

He looks at me, eyebrows raised. "That how it is now?"

I stare back at him, but we both know I'm bluffing. My father may be a piece of shit asshole, but I owe him everything. He's still family, even if sometimes I wish he wasn't. Without him, my darkness would have consumed me a long, long time ago. But at the same time, it's because of him that it's even there.

I don't have a chance to respond because up toward the front of the bar, the doors open and grab my attention. In walks Marco Romano, the second-in-command, and second most important man in the entire *familia*, followed by Alex and Angelo, two of my cousins. They're there for muscle and show, but they aren't necessary.

Nobody would dare touch Marco. He has the full weight of the Romano *familia* behind him, and any dumb fuck that came at him would invite the wrath of the whole fucking mob down on his head. They'd go for his family and torture them all in front of him and then kill him. The Romanos don't fuck around.

The tips of my fingers trail up and down the glass as they walk into the bar.

"They sent Marco," my father says to me underneath his breath, sounding surprised.

I have to admit that I'm surprised as well. Normally we don't deal with the top members of the Romano *familia*, at least not in person. Sending Marco here to talk with us is an honor. As much as I don't want to get too involved, I do feel a surge of pride that they're showing us this respect.

But it also means that this hit is very, very important to them. I knew that when we got the target, but now it's very clear how seriously they're taking it. My eyes dip to the floor and my body heats as I realize how pissed off they're going to be when I turn them down. I can already see that my father's excited and fucking delighted that they sent someone as powerful as Marco to this deal, and he stands up to show the proper respect.

I stand also as the men approach the table, but I'm prepared to disappoint them. I don't give a fuck who asks me to do it. I'm not going to be held responsible for this shit.

"Bruno," Marco says with a smirk, "you look good, you old bastard."

"Marco." My father and Marco shake hands. I'm pretty sure that they're very distant cousins, maybe related by a distant marriage. I'm not sure. It's all so fucking boring and complicated though. They're no family to me.

"Gio," Marco says, turning to me. We shake hands. "You look just like your mother."

"Thanks," I say. I suspect the reference to my mother was designed to throw me off balance, but I keep my face and tone neutral.

"Sit, sit," my father says quickly, gesturing to the empty seats. Marco takes a seat at the head of the table, the feet of the chair scratching along the floor as he pulls it out. Alex and Angelo sit at a nearby table without another word, looking serious and tough.

I give them a little grin, but they don't look at me, and don't make eye contact. I know they're afraid of me, and have been since we were all boys. I remember when I was ten and Angelo was thirteen. He tried to take my bike, and I beat the fucking piss out of him. He's been afraid of me ever since then.

And he should be fucking afraid.

"I'm honored that you came to this meeting," my father says, practically deep throating Marco's cock. I straighten my shoulders and turn my attention to Marco.

"It's an important meeting with our best men," Marco says in return.

We are his best hitmen, that's true, but he's buttering us up pretty fucking hard. I can smell the shit he's trying to shove down our throats from a mile away, and I know where this is going.

"Let's talk business," I say before my father can steal any more momentum.

"Okay Gio," Marco says, smiling at me. He's in his fifties, and only a few years younger than my father. His teeth are straight and white, and his hair is cropped close to his scalp. He wears a dark suit complete with a crisp, white pocket square, like always, and I can see the bulge of the weapon in the holster on his side. He looks like a used car salesman wearing an expensive suit, and that's more or less accurate.

Assuming used car salesmen extort, murder, deal in prostitution, and generally engage in all manner of illegal shit.

"You're offering us triple for this job," I say, leaning toward him. "That's more than fair, given the situation."

"I thought you'd think so." His eyes sparkle and his lips turn up, as if he thinks we're eager to accept.

"Except you neglected to talk about the politics involved." He holds my gaze, but that glint in his eyes fades.

"The politics?" he asks, feigning innocence. He waves his hand in the air as if dismissing it. As if taking out a major member of the Rossi *familia* means nothing.

"If we do this job, it'll spark a war. You know this, and yet you want us to do it anyway."

"I don't know anything about a war," he says, the smile still there.

"Okay, fine. It's none of our business, I know that. We're not in the *familia*."

"Yet," Marco says, cutting in with a glance to my father.

I can practically see my father salivating at the comment.

"But it will involve us," I say before my father can speak up, feeling my irritation rise. "Regardless of the outcome."

"Do you want more money?" he asks me straight.

"It's not the money." I shake my head slightly, keeping eye contact.

"You're hesitant. I can understand that. You're young, and don't know how the world works yet."

I clench my jaw and have to restrain myself from smashing his face into the hard maple table top. "This is a dangerous job regardless of my age."

"How about this," he says. "I'll throw in the niece of our, uh, target. You can take her and train her for us. Or at least break her down some. You know the drill. I hear she's quite a beauty."

I'm taken aback. A woman. They're giving us a woman. *What the fuck?* The *familia* has never made an offer like that before. That's not an aspect of this business I'm associated with. My father is though.

He quickly speaks up before I can even process the extent of what Marco offered.

To train? My body's stiff with the memories of my past flashing before my eyes as my father answers him. "We'd be honored, Marco," he says. "Gio will accept the woman and turn her into the perfect model of obedience for you." I've seen what they do. I know exactly what they want. I recall the sounds, the images. My father standing over a girl, a whip in his hands, a smile on his face. My heart races as I try to ignore my recollections. "You want a slave, he'll make her fucking perfect. Isn't that right, Gio?"

My father stares at me waiting for an answer, and I'm at a loss for words. I know what they mean by training, and I've seen it a million times, but I've never taken part. I've never done anything but witnessed it when I was a boy.

I'm barely able to nod my head.

"Very good," Marco says, and my father shakes his hand. "You two will do this contract, and you," Marco points at me, "will break the girl in. I'm sure your father has taught you a thing or two." Marco winks at my father, who grins proudly. "Then we'll discuss your full payment."

I blink, surprised. My father has a huge smile on his face. Before I can speak up and tell them that we won't be taking the contract, Marco stands. My father stands with him, and the two men glance at me. I stand as well, shaken and surprised at this turn of events.

"I trust that you two will come through," Marco says.

"Of course," my father responds.

"Good." Marco nods at me. "Gio, I'll send you the details so you can pick up the bonus."

Marco turns and leaves, followed by my cousins.

I grip onto the table as they leave us. "What the fuck just happened?" I hiss at my father.

"I accepted the job," he says, glaring at me. "What the fuck was that?"

"Nothing," I say, looking away. I can't admit to any weakness, especially not now. Not to anyone.

"We're doing this job," he says, his tone low and menacing. "You'll take the girl, and you'll do what you need to do. Understood?"

"We'll see," I push the words out through clenched teeth.

Chapter 5

IF I'M GOING TO DO THIS, I'M DOING IT THE RIGHT WAY.

That means planning. Preparation. Research. The days are long gone where a hitman could just run into a joint, shoot his gun, and run away. I need to be prepared for absolutely every and any possibility, because it's all happened to me in the past.

My father gives me shit over the planning, but he didn't have to deal with what I deal with back when he was still in his prime. Drones, DNA testing —hell, a single hair could give me away. I have to be aware of all of that, every little thing that could possibly give me away and ruin the hit.

This time it's different. This time I'm being given a new assignment, something I've never done before, but at the same time it's something I'm too familiar with.

I lean back in my chair and shake my head, trying not to let myself get lost in those memories again. I pull up my laptop and start researching the girl, Grace. It doesn't take me long before I find out most of her information.

She's beautiful, just like Marco said. She's a mob princess, so she's probably used to being treated like royalty. Except it's strange, there's not a lot of stuff about her on social media. I'd expect a mafia princess like her to have an active Instagram or something, but instead it's mostly a wasteland.

There are only a few pictures, and her Facebook profile is pretty dormant. It gives me enough to go on, and at least I know what she looks like, but it's very strange there isn't more.

I can't help but wonder about this Grace. Who is she? Who is this woman I'm going to have to break down?

I lean back and take a deep breath before standing and walking over to a window. Duke looks up at me as I walk past him. I don't pay him any attention, because he wasn't around back then. He doesn't know what it was like.

My father wasn't always in this business. Before he was a killer, he was a sex trafficker.

Maybe that's putting it too lightly. My father had a huge network of men in eastern Europe that would kidnap young attractive women and smuggle them over into the United States. From there, my father broke them utilizing a whole slew of methods, many of which he taught me over the years.

I'll never forget his favorite method, and the night he first showed me. It was late, probably after midnight, and I was already in bed. He came upstairs reeking of vodka and woke me up, then forced me to follow him. He took me out back into the old horse stable we had out there.

But of course, it wasn't a horse stable. The inside had been gutted and renovated, turning the old horse paddocks into cells with thick steel doors. Inside each cell was a woman.

I was ten years old.

He brought me into the first cell on the left where a girl maybe sixteen years old was huddled in the corner. My father told me to stay still and watch as he took his belt off and beat the girl until she obeyed him. By the time he was finished she was bleeding and crying, but at least she was down on her knees with her forehead on the ground, submitting to him.

"See, son?" he said to me. "That's how you break a girl for the first time. She needs to know that she's a rotten piece of shit, and without me, she's nothing." He spit on the ground before pulling me out of the cell, leaving the girl alone in her agony.

I hated him, but I didn't know why. His methods were cruel, brutish, and awful. But he had other methods, some clever. They played on the women's desires and fears, created a bond of friendship and trust. He only used those tactics on women that wouldn't obey him under threat of violence alone.

He gave up being a trafficker not too long after that night. His guys got pinched overseas, cutting off his supply of girls. Then a few women got away, forcing him to move away from the area, and he never got back into the business.

But everyone knows what he did back then. It's honestly a miracle that he never got caught, and probably entirely because he got out when he did.

That's why Marco is giving me this girl, though. Marco knows what my father used to be, and he knows that my father showed me some of his methods.

He's not wrong about that. I can break this girl and turn her into a sex slave if I want. I can do all the sick, disgusting things my father used to do. I can beat her and break her physically and emotionally without a second thought.

But I don't want to. I return to my laptop and look at her pictures again, frowning slightly to myself. I don't want to make this girl bleed and beg for her life. I have no interest in that. I'm a hitman and a killer, but I'm not a rapist and a woman beater. Maybe I have a darkness inside of me that needs to be fed, but I do still have some humanity left in me.

And she's so beautiful. There's an innocence to her pictures that surprises me.

The more I look at her pictures, the more I want her. It's completely unexpected, but I want to see her, touch her, and taste her so badly.

This deal is happening whether I want it to or not. I'm sure my father would be more than happy to take the girl and to break her, even though he's older now and not as strong as he once was. I'm sure he still gets off on that shit, no matter how gross and disgusting it may be. Which means I have to keep her away from him.

I have to take her. Maybe I'm doing it for the wrong reasons, but I need to make her mine. I'm in this already, and there's no turning back.

I reach down and absently stroke Duke when he comes over and curls up at my side. I know I'm trapped, and there's no turning back. I'm going to take Grace and make her mine, no matter what.

Maybe I'm doing it to protect her. Things would be so much worse if my father took her. Or maybe I'm doing it because I'm a selfish prick, and I'm drawn to her in a way that intrigues me.

Either way, I hate myself for it, but I'm going to follow orders. I'm going to take Grace, break her, and then I'll kill her uncle.

I turn back to my laptop and begin to make my plans.

Chapter 6

M Y EYES SLOWLY OPEN, AND I HAVE TO WORK HARD NOT TO groan at the pain pounding in the back of my head. The throbbing makes me wince. The floor I'm lying on is cold. *Where am I?* It's only a second before the memory comes back to me.

I didn't have a chance. My heart sinks as I realize how easy it was for them to take me, just as my father promised they would.

I was so full of hope when the guards stayed back and let me walk through the doors of the restaurant and out into the chill of the night.

I didn't have a chance to run away. I don't think I even made it ten minutes when three large shadows surrounded me and before I could even breathe, *whack!* The blow was delivered tight to the back of my head, and I collapsed into darkness.

My jaw clenches as anger rises in me. It was so fucking easy for them.

I deserve a goddamn chance! I wanted it. I want freedom so fucking badly, and I'd do anything to get it. But I'm too weak. Raised to be weak and helpless, that's all I fucking am. Hate consumes me, mostly for my father, but also for myself.

I finally open my eyes fully, and my heart starts to hammer. My body is like ice in that it's cold, numb, and still. I know better than to let my enemy know I'm awake and conscious.

There's a cloth hood over my head, and my hot breath goes stagnant in front of my face. As I swallow, I feel slightly dizzy. I close my eyes and focus on steadying my heart. It's only then that I take in my situation.

I can still run. If I got away from my father, I can get away from anyone. *But he let you get away,* a voice hisses in the back of my head. The pulsating pain comes back, but I ignore them both. He wants me to be a good little victim. To listen and do his bidding. Fuck him. Fuck all of them. I'll survive, and I'll escape. I won't stop until I'm free. Free or dead.

I just need to be smart and wait for the perfect opportunity. Quietly I swallow, filled with equal amounts of fear and conviction. My breathing is steady but hot, filling the bag.

My shoulder is sore, and the metal cuffs holding my wrists together behind my back are cutting into the skin. It hurts so fucking bad. I realize that I'm slumped against the wall, and I feel every muscle screaming in agony.

The pain dims as soon as I hear the door open to wherever I am. My body freezes, and nothing matters anymore. I'm alert, and all I care about is finding a way out. *My freedom.* I try to keep still and pretend I'm still knocked out, but it doesn't work.

They know.

A man's rough laugh cuts through the air as he says, "She's up."

My heart pounds, but I stay motionless. In this position, my options are limited, but I'm ready to fight. I'll do whatever it takes. It sounds like there are two men in the room judging by the two sets of steps that walk on the left side of me. I hear them sink into what sounds like a sofa, and I wait. I can hardly breathe, waiting for their next move.

This could be my chance. My father is who-knows-where, and maybe these men will underestimate me.

The fear of the unknown is what restrains my actions. I'm not going to be submissive for them. I'm not going to keep my head down and wait for them to tell me what they want from me, because I don't know if that will save me from whatever their intentions are.

In this moment I hate my father more than I ever have. I hate my life.

I hate myself for being so damn pathetic and not fighting hard enough. Death is a comforting thought, but I won't give in to that weakness. Not when there's still a chance.

Deep voices echoing Italian words that I vaguely recall from my childhood seep into my bitter thoughts. I never learned the language. My father didn't want me to. He enjoyed being able to speak without me understanding. He sends me in here to spy, and I can't even do that. *Pathetic.*

The Romanos are old school, but hopefully English will be spoken more than Italian.

I know some though. I know the words slave and princess. Both continually appear in the conversation, and I know they're talking about me. The Rossi princess. Slave. I guess that's what I am now, or at least what they want me to be. I swallow thickly, hating that my initial thought is to want to be back home. Back to that prison. No! I refuse. That's just the fear talking. I don't want to go back. Anything but that.

I turn sideways and scoot away from the sound of someone approaching. But it's useless. I fall to the hard concrete floor, my head and shoulder slamming onto the cement with nothing to break my fall. I wince from the pain and then scream from the violent hold on my arms, hauling me up and against a man's body.

I struggle against him and he shakes me violently, spitting Italian words that I assume are a threat, although I don't understand.

Stupid girl, be still. Save your strength for the right moment. The voice I hate calms me.

The thought makes my body still, and the other man laughs at my weakness.

If only they knew. With nothing to lose, I'm the strongest I've ever been.

Small shreds of light filter through the burlap bag over my head, and I realize I'm currently outside. I must be under a street lamp, because the light quickly fades and the sound of a van door sliding open fills my senses.

My heart speeds up, but I don't react yet. I listen and try to gauge what's going on. There's a third man. I can hear him now.

The one holding me tries to toss my body into the van, but I twist and kick out as hard as I can. However I've hit him, it's enough that he releases me and I fall back to the ground, nearly stumbling, but I right myself as best as I can, bound and blindfolded.

"Fuck!" he screams out as I weakly stand, balancing my body against the cold metal of the van door.

I try to run, but a fist slams into the side of my jaw. It forces me off balance, and I fall, my head slamming against the unforgiving ground. Fuck! The worst part is that I didn't see it coming. I couldn't even try to defend myself.

The pain is overwhelming. A foot swings into my ribs, and nausea threatens its way up my throat with stinging pulses of agony.

Stupid girl. You can never run from me. You can never hide from me.

My body freezes as the words of my father haunt me, momentarily crippling me.

Another kick to the gut forces a strangled cry from my throat.

A deep voice yells out, "Don't fucking touch her!" as I hear the loud crunch of a punch and the sound of someone keeling over. I'm worried about the implications of knowing they're fighting, but I don't waste a second. I can't. I need to run.

The fools didn't tie my ankles, and I take the one chance I'm given and bolt. The muscles in my legs scream with pain as I pump them, running aimlessly in front of me with my arms bound behind my back. Light and shapes whip past the bag over my head, but I have no idea where I'm going.

I don't care, I'm not wasting this moment. I can't. I can hear him chasing me, and he's right behind me, getting closer. The sounds of his ragged breathing, and his hard steps are getting louder. The world is nothing but flickering colors and madness all around me. I scream as his strong arms wrap around my waist, pulling me into his body and picking my feet off the ground.

I don't stop screaming for help and viciously kick out in every direction as I squirm in his grasp.

I gasp and instinctively try to reach up to my neck when I feel the sharp pinch of a needle.

"You're not going anywhere, princess," he says, and the voice is soothing, although the word princess ignites anger inside of me. I fall into darkness slowly, my hands tingling and body relaxing into a hard chest as I hear him whisper into my ear, "I've got you."

Chapter 7

WHAT A STUPID FUCKING MESS.

I toss an old box of ammunition aside and drag a bench piled with crap out into the hall. The gun room in the back of my house is surprisingly large and well built, but it's gathered a ton of shit over the years. Of course my father left me to clean the thing out alone while the girl lies there on the floor, drugged and unconscious. I have stacks of old weapons, ammo, and other nice surprises stashed away in there, and it took me forever to finally get the room more or less emptied out. It's perfect for this. Fitted with a biometric scanning lock for my fingerprint, a small full bath attached and no way of escape, it's fucking perfect.

When I come back into the room, I can't help but glance at the girl on the floor. She's still right where I left her, curled on her side in the corner of the room, and still just as fucking gorgeous as she was a few minutes ago. I can't keep my eyes off her, even though I know it's fucked up to have the sort of thoughts I'm having about a woman that's drugged and unconscious.

The entire situation is fucked up though. A few days ago I wanted to turn the contract down, but my father managed to swoop in and make the decision for me. Now I'm stuck with her, Grace Rossi, and I'm supposed to somehow turn her into a model sex slave.

I have some ideas about how to pull that off, but I've never done it before. Frankly, I don't feel like fucking doing it now. My father has a past in this shit. Not me. But I'm not letting him have her. No fucking way.

All of this is a pain in the ass, especially this goddamn mafia princess.

I don't need her or want her, but for better or worse I'm fucking stuck with her.

My heart hammers as I look over every curve of her body. *My princess.*

I sigh and drag a few more boxes out into the hall. Duke is snooping through them, and I push him to the side. He wags his tail and looks at me, panting and happy, completely oblivious. I ruffle his head and step back into the room, this time making an effort not to look at the girl.

Standing in the far left corner, uncovered from years of accumulated junk, is a large cage. I stare at it, smiling to myself. It was meant for bears, and I bought it years ago at a flea market. I figured I might have to lock up some asshole that I didn't want to kill immediately or some shit like that, but I ended up just storing it away and forgetting about it.

Now, though…

The girl stirs over in the corner.

She's beautiful. Fucking gorgeous. I keep thinking that every time I see her, my memory never doing her beauty justice. I kneel down next to her and gently lift her head up, making sure she's still unconscious.

I notice the wound on her head and grind my teeth, annoyed. That fucking asshole didn't need to hit her as hard as he did, but he got what he deserved in the end. I beat the shit out of him and his partner, the sick fuck that was kicking her on the ground. She's a tiny thing in my arms, light and easily carried. I lift her up suddenly, not really thinking about it, and bring her over to the bathroom.

I gently lower her into the tub before grabbing some rubbing alcohol and bandages from the medicine cabinet. I carefully clean and dress her wounds, then quickly check her for others. I need to make sure that the sick fuck didn't break a rib or cause some kind of internal bleeding.

There's nothing there, thankfully. Or at least nothing fresh.

Her body is covered in scars. Not every inch, but there are several in places that wouldn't normally show with clothing on, white welts in jagged shapes. I take a sharp breath as I look over them, marveling for a second at the amount of pain this girl must have been put through.

Who the fuck would do this to her?

I stand, shaking my head in anger. I adjust her so that she's in a more comfortable position in the tub, my mind straying to dark places, trying to imagine what happened to her.

My princess looks like she's been through something, though I can't be sure what. Maybe abuse, maybe some kind of accident. Either way, she knows pain, and that might be a bad thing. She might be stronger than she looks. I won't intentionally cause her that kind of pain, but things happen in my line of work that can't always be controlled, no matter how much I plan.

I get back to work, removing the mirror from the bathroom and any other hardware that she might be able to use against me or herself. When I finish, the room is just a showerhead, a tub, a toilet, and a sink. Everything else got stripped out.

Back in the main room, my mind drifts back to my childhood. My father taught me how to break down and reassemble every single one of the guns I owned while blindfolded. I carefully move the remainder out of the room and arrange them out in the hall, pausing only to pat Duke on the head. My father taught me how to torture a man, both physically and psychologically. I know every mental tactic there is. I know how to break a person and to make them completely mine if I really wanted to.

He taught me to ignore pain. He taught me to complete the mission no matter what. He taught me to be strong and capable above all things, and so far I've lived my life that way.

Even if I hate the orders, once I accept a contract I have to do what I'm told.

There's a part of me that hates how much I'm enjoying this. It's sick as fuck that I love the challenge of building her a prison in a short time-frame. I know the drugs will wear off in about another two hours, maybe even less, so I have to keep moving fast. I like keeping busy and building things, but I like staring at my princess. Her scarred body only makes me want to know her more.

Those are dangerous thoughts. She needs to remain just a subject to me, not a person. I can't risk getting close to her. That's the danger with this sort of thing: sometimes you see beyond the story you're telling yourself, and the thing in front of you can turn into a person.

Once the room is clear, I stand in the middle and look around. The cage is in the back left corner, the bathroom is on the right, and the rest of the room is empty. There are two small windows, but they aren't nearly large enough for her to get through. Plus, they're unbreakable and sound-proofed. She can scream, but there's nobody around for miles. I have video cameras set up in the ceiling, and I can see every inch of her enclosure, including the bathroom. The door is impervious to both blasts and tampering and will only open with my fingerprint. When I had this room built, I didn't spare any expenses. No one can get in or out without my help. It's the perfect prison for her.

I'm about to leave, when I suddenly have an idea. It comes to me like lightning. It's the perfect way to get to her, to peel back her layers and force her to show everything to me.

It's like a game, or maybe it's something like pity for what she's been through before. Either way, it's a tool.

The cage will be her safe space.

I stare at it and remember my childhood. I remember the girls and the men doing whatever they wanted to them. I remember how they cried at first, but quickly their faces became consumed with pleasure. They learned to enjoy it.

I remember how it excited me. I remember how ashamed of that I was, and still am.

I've decided. So long as she's in the cage, I won't touch her. That'll be the deal I make with her. If she stays in that bear cage, she'll be safe from me. It's a few feet wide and long, and large enough that she can stand.

But if she leaves it, then she's mine. She'll break and leave that cage with time, and I'll do whatever I want with her. *And I'll make sure she enjoys it.* If she retreats, I'll leave her alone. I'll give her food and water, and the comfort of a blanket.

My heart thuds in my chest. I glance into the bathroom and see her in the tub. She's fucking gorgeous, and I picture her crawling from the cage, begging me to come into the room and teach her a lesson.

I grin to myself. It's the perfect little game. I need to earn her trust if I'm going to make her mine, and the cage is going to be the key to that trust.

You can't just force a person to break. It doesn't really work that way. You can beat and starve them all you want, but if you never gain their trust, then it's all over. This cage will be her safety net, and I'll be the man who gives her that safety.

I can feel the darkness inside of me celebrating as excitement courses through my veins. I'm at war with myself, hating these sick little thoughts that I've been trained to embrace, and yet aroused at the prospect of play-ing with her.

It doesn't hurt that she's so fucking beautiful, and with a fight in her that I admire.

I walk into the bathroom and kneel down at her side. Her wounds are cleaned and bandaged, and soon the drugs will wear off. She'll wake up and she won't know where she is, but she'll be safe. I'll explain the rules of the game to her.

And then we'll play.

I reach into the tub and scoop her up, carrying her back into the main room and gently place her inside of the cage. I leave the door open, but I make sure she's completely in there. It isn't comfortable, but at least it's safe.

I give her one last look before I leave her room, shutting the door be-hind me.

Chapter 8

MY BODY'S SO SORE. IT HURTS FROM WHERE HE HIT ME. DADDY never hit me before. I don't understand…

I was so little, so scared. Right after my birthday party. Only six. Mommy said we should leave. She took me from bed late at night and carried me into the hallway. Mommy, no. "We can't leave Daddy!" She covered my mouth and stared at the door. It was their bedroom door. Mommy and Daddy's room. We can't leave Daddy!

I didn't understand. I was scared. My heart raced in my chest. The fear in my mother's eyes is something I'll never forget. We almost made it down the stairs. Her hand over my mouth as she carried me in her arms.

But he grabbed her hair. Daddy was so quiet until he yanked her backward, the pain on her face evident as I fell from her arms, crashing onto the stairs and tumbling down. She screamed as he hit her over and over.

It hurt so much. My hands covered the gash on my head.

No, Daddy! Why is he hitting her? No, stop! I yelled with tears streaming down my face. I ran up to help her.

Daddy's hurting her! Stop, daddy! Why is he hurting Mommy? Doesn't he know he's hurting her?

He kicked me. His hard foot landing in my gut, I fell harder. Smacking my head and shoulder on the wooden stairs as I fell down another step.

It hurt, but Mommy wasn't screaming anymore.

His hands were around her throat. I didn't know it then, but he was chok-ing her. Her fingers clawed at his hands. Her eyes turning red.

I screamed. I ignored the pain and ran faster up the stairs, hitting him as hard as I could.

Stop hurting Mommy! Daddy, stop! Please stop! My throat hurts from screaming. Someone help! Please help!

He let her go and she fell on the stairs. She wasn't moving and laid there. So still. Mommy? I just wanted to touch her. I wanted to make sure she was okay.

Her eyes were so red. "Mommy!" I cried.

His hand came down hard across my face. Mommy wasn't okay. Daddy wasn't either.

My hands covered my face where the sting from his hand pulsed. But my chest hurts too. Everything hurts. Nothing's okay.

My body's stiff as I groan, slowly opening my eyes. My head hurts. He hit me again. I feel so dizzy. The memories of my nightmare are slowly fad-ing. Fuck, how many times am I going to let them hit me? Over and over, that's all they ever do.

It takes a moment for my sight to come into focus. And when it does, I stay as still as possible, my limbs frozen with fear.

Where the fuck am I? My heart jolts in my chest as I realize the thin silver bars I'm seeing and the grated floor beneath me form a cage.

I'm in a cage. My skin pricks with fear.

Yesterday comes back to me in a flood. My hands instinctively fly to my stomach, remembering the kicks, and then my neck, the pinch. They drugged me and put me in a cage.

My initial shock and confusion quickly turn to fury. I moved from one fucking cage to another. Only this one is a literal goddamn cage! My heart speeds with anger, and my blood rushes in my ears.

I ball my fists and turn onto my knees slowly, barely making a sound and taking in my surroundings. I'm surprised by my rage; I'm not used to it. At least not used to it showing on the surface. It's a constant, but it's gen-erally buried under the fear and need to display obedience.

My eyes widen when I look forward and realize the door to the cage is open.

I blink several times and even creep out slightly, but not very far at all.

My hand reaches out, half expecting the door to slam shut, but it doesn't. How… odd.

As I move, a thin blanket that I was balled up in slips down my back and to my waist, exposing my chest to the cooler air. It's only then that I realize I'm naked, the breath stolen from my lungs. It looks like someone has neatly folded my clothes from earlier though, and they're sitting in a corner of the cage. I move to check my bra, and inwardly let out a sigh of relief when I see the baggie is still concealed in the padding.

I grip the blanket tighter around me, sitting on my knees. I take in a ragged breath and let a hand drift down to my sex. Did they hurt me? I don't feel any different. I don't think they touched me. Shame floods my cheeks.

I wish I'd run faster. If only I'd walked the other way. Maybe they wouldn't have been waiting. Maybe I could have gotten away. A lump grows in my throat, but I calm myself. *Ifs* are useless. They make me weak to dwell on them. I raise my head and focus on what's in front of me. I'm here now, and I need to figure out why and how to get the fuck out.

The grate on the floor makes my knees hurt, but I withstand the slight pain and look around the empty room. That's all it is. There isn't much I can see beyond this cage, which is large enough for me to stand, but only has a few square feet to move around in. There's a doorway, although it looks like the door has been removed, on the far side and then another door to my right.

Anxiety fills my blood.

Is this a game? Choose one door and what? I'm afraid to know.

It looks like the open doorway leads to a bathroom. It looks stripped and bare, but it's there. I imagine it's functional.

I don't dare leave the cage as I consider what the Romanos want from me. I slowly back deeper into the cage and nearly scream when my back hits a bucket. It's empty and it makes the only sound in the room other than my own voice. It scared the shit out of me. I'm quick to cover my mouth and silence the shrill scream that threatened to surface. It was only a squeak of what it would've been.

As my heart finally calms and the stupidity of my action weighs in my mind, I hear a faint beep from the door to my right and then a click.

Someone's here. Goosebumps prickle down my body as I clutch the thin blanket closer to me and back into the far corner of the cage, the farthest I can get away, kicking the empty bucket to the front. Right now my options are limited. There's not much I can do at all. But I'll bite, kick and scratch whoever's coming in here. I won't let them get away with this.

They took my chance at freedom. They better give it back.

The door slowly opens as I wait with bated breath.

I see a tray first. It's silver, and sitting on top is a small, dark blue plastic cup as well as something else. It's balanced in his massive hand as the man enters. My heartbeat slows as the door clicks shut and he turns, facing me with piercing blue eyes. They're almost like ice. His gaze freezes my heart and my rage, anger, and confusion all vanish. In their place is lust.

His corded muscles ripple as he walks toward me with confidence and an air of authority. His presence alone makes my heart stop. The way he carries himself makes it obvious that he's the epitome of power and control. It terrifies me while it also does something else. It ignites a fire in me that I didn't know existed. It's dangerous. *He's* dangerous.

His bright white shirt is pulled tight over his shoulders, and his faded jeans are hung low on his hips. So low that I catch a glimpse of the deep muscular "V" at his lower abdomen as he walks, and my lips part with a hunger to see more.

I swallow thickly as he closes the space between us. He's a Romano. Is he going to hurt me, kill me, or torture me? I'm not sure which. But whatever his plans are, maybe I can make a deal. I don't have anything he can truly want or need. I know nothing about my father's business, and I doubt they're looking to ransom me off. Taking me was a message. My father got that message, and now they can let me go.

I try to gather the courage to speak, to plead, or to fight. To do *something*. Instead my body remains paralyzed as he steps forward, setting the tray down on the floor in front of the cage.

He crouches on the floor and tilts his head, as if wondering what I'm thinking. Behind his eyes is a cold threat. His expression is completely devoid of emotion. Fear cripples me for a moment, but I gather my strength. I can't be weak. Not now.

"Wh—Who are you?" I'm ashamed of the stutter and the weak sound of my voice as it cracks. But at least I've managed to speak.

He clucks his tongue, contemplating his answer, and sits on the ground, looking into my eyes. "You can call me Gio. There's no harm in that."

My brows draw in at his comment. I don't understand. "You're a Romano?" I ask feebly. I don't think my father would lie about *who* took me, but I need to make sure.

He huffs a humorless laugh. "No, they gave you to me."

My lips part at his confession, the words slowly sinking in. *I'm a gift.* My body chills, and my throat closes and I feel as though I'm suffocating. The Rossis won't come for me. How would my father even know where I am, if the Romanos didn't take me? My breathing comes in frantic pants. No one's going to save me.

"Don't worry, Grace." My eyes dart to his. He knows my name. But I don't recognize his voice. "I won't come into your cage. You're safe there. From everything and everyone as long as you're in the cage."

He pushes the tray closer to me, and it scrapes gently across the concrete floor. It holds a cup of something, and a sandwich. The hunger in the pit of my stomach rumbles at the sight, and it makes the man smile. His teeth are a brilliant white, only adding more beauty to his gorgeous face.

It's not fair. Monsters should look like what they are.

"Eat, Grace," he gives me the command and sits at the entrance.

It pisses me off.

I'm not an object to be given away. Starting now, I don't take orders. All my life, that's all I've done. I've been told what to do, and been beaten for disobeying.

I refuse to let him do the same to me. I'm done with that. It's gotten me nowhere in this pathetic life.

"No," I barely breathe the word, knowing my defiance will earn me a beating. I don't care anymore.

He cocks a brow at me, and leaving the tray, he stands and leaves. The door closes and a moment later a beep sounds, followed by a loud click, indicating the door is locked. My heart beats faster, assuming he's coming back with something to hurt me with. I wait for a long time, staring at the door.

Time passes, and he doesn't return. I'm hesitant to think I've escaped punishment. Never has my father let a moment to beat me go wasted.

My stomach growls, and my eyes shift to the food on the tray. It's been awhile since I've eaten. I don't know what time it is, but judging from the dim light coming through the small windows, it's late. So maybe a day?

I won't eat it though. I won't give him that satisfaction.

I push more of the blanket under me and behind my back to stop the thin bars from digging into my skin and hurting.

I look straight ahead and into what's obviously a bathroom. I could leave the cage and try to find something in there to use as a weapon, but I'm terrified of leaving the safe place he gave me.

Shame consumes me. I don't even have the balls to look for a fucking weapon. My chest tightens, and I force my frozen limbs to move. I slowly crawl from the cage, my eyes on the heavy door he exited. My heart beats so hard in my chest it hurts. I don't want him to come back and beat me to the cage. *But I have to try.*

I take one step from the cage, but my fingers wrap around the bars, leashing me to it. I inhale a deep breath and let go of the bars, the thin metal slipping past my fingertips. My eyes tear away from the door and I move quickly to the tiny windows above my head.

I know it's impossible, but I have to try. I stretch on my tiptoes, trying desperately to even reach them. After a quick moment of failure, I take a step back and look at them. My body wouldn't even fit through those small rectangles. I could try dragging the cage over and climbing on top of it. I look at the rectangles again. They're so small. But I have to at least try. Even if it's just to open the window and flag someone down. Or scream for help.

I watch the door the entire time that I try my damnedest to move the heavy cage. My shoulders ache and the bars dig into my fingers, but it's useless.

I pull with all my weight, but it doesn't even budge.

Breathless and feeling pathetic, I give up the stupid thought and my eyes focus on the bathroom. I hesitate to walk the distance of the room, but maybe there's a way out. A larger window perhaps. The windows are close enough that if I heard the click or the beep, I could easily run back to the cage and make it safely inside before he could catch me.

The bathroom is too far. I'd never manage to outrun him.

But if there's an escape, or a weapon… I only glance at the door before my instincts take over.

As quickly as I can, I dart across the room, knowing I can't fail. If he comes in now, he'd beat me to the cage. And caught in the bathroom, I'd be cornered. My heart slams with fear as I take in the barren bathroom. My bare feet slap against the cold tile as my heart pounds in my chest. My eyes dart from the steel pipe under the sink to the showerhead. Those are the only two things I can think of to even consider as a weapon. Even the toilet tank lid has been removed, and the mirror is gone, too.

I crouch under the sink and pull with all my weight on the steel pipe, but my grip slips and I fall backward, my head slamming against the tile.

"Fuck!" I shout, grabbing onto the back of my head and wincing with pain.

Click. I swear I hear a click, and I move as fast as possible. My legs scream with pain as I sprint from the bathroom to the cage. My toenail scrapes against the concrete as I nearly trip, but I keep running. I don't stop. I ignore the pain and keep my eyes on the opening to the cage. To my safety.

I slam my body against the back of the cage and breathe heavily, staring at the closed door.

All I can hear is the blood rushing into my ears and my heart beating uncontrollably with fear.

But nothing happens.

My chest heaves, and I try to calm myself as I wait with panicked breath.

Did I imagine it? I pull my legs to my chest and stare at the door.

A long time passes, and I finally realize I let the fear get the best of me.

He's not coming in here. At least not in this moment. My eyes drift back to the bathroom and the tiny windows. They're both dead ends. No weapons, no escape.

I stare at the door and wonder when he'll be back, and what he's going to do when he does return.

He said he won't come into this cage, so that's fine.

I'll just stay here, but something has to happen eventually. Something has to change. I can't be stuck here forever. The reality hits me hard all of a sudden. I *can.* This could be my life now.

In the back of my mind, I remember the bag of heroin. Hidden inside my bra. Waiting for me.

I need to find a way out of here, or else I don't have many options. Tears threaten to show themselves, and the burning pain of unshed tears is all too familiar to me.

It's been too long since I've cried. I won't cry for this man. I won't cry for me when I failed at saving myself.

There's no one for me to blame but myself.

With the dark thoughts consuming me, I fall asleep against the cage, my eyes on the food that I refuse to eat.

∞

The days pass in a blur until I have no idea how long I've been here, and each day is the same. He comes in with a tray, taking the old one that sits at the front of my cage with untouched food. I don't even drink the water.

My mouth is dry, and my throat burns. A few times I went to the bathroom to drink from the tap, but the last few days have made me afraid to leave the cage.

During those first few days, I tested my confines. In the middle of the night, I would sneak out into the room and test everything. I went over every inch of the walls, every single corner, every single nook and freaking cranny. There was nothing.

I searched the bathroom. I ripped at the pipes, kicked at the toilet, did everything I could. My hands are bruised and my feet bloodied from the effort, but nothing helped.

Each day was the same. He came with food and that devilish, maddening smile. He speaks so softly, so intensely. His gaze makes me shiver. I have to look away, because I keep imagining things I never thought I would.

I have nothing left. I can't escape no matter how hard I try. Days slide by, and I sneak out and do what I can, but it never helps.

Finally, the only thing I can do to keep fighting is to refuse him.

I refuse his food. I refuse his questions. I refuse everything he tries to give me. Maybe I can't break out of my prison, but that doesn't mean I have to give in to everything he says and does. I listen and sometimes I talk back, but I won't ever give him what he wants.

I think the silence and lack of interaction have done more damage than good, but I don't care. I'm so pathetic. I moved from one cage to the next. But I won't give up.

Every day I watch Gio come in and I wonder if it will be the day I leave the cage and let him do whatever he wants to me. Sometimes I even want him to break his promise and come for me. It would be better that way.

I listen to his voice as he talks to me, but I don't really hear what he says. Only the commands to eat stand out. Which I won't do. I don't care if it kills me. At this point, I'd rather die than be a toy for him. I'll just stay here and try to sleep my way to death, ignoring the pain.

During the third night, I snuck out of the cage and tried to loosen the pipes in the bathroom. It was well into the night, and normally he didn't come when there was no light left filtering through the windows. It was pitch black, and he'd never come that late.

But this time he did. I nearly broke my neck diving back into the cage as he stood in the doorway, his arms crossed, his intense stare taking me in.

Shame and guilt, oddly enough, consumed me, but fear was the leading emotion.

I'm too afraid to leave the safety of the cage now, and my body aches when I move, so it's better that I just stay still. The first two days it felt nice to walk, but now it hurts. Maybe it's because I haven't eaten, or maybe it's because of dehydration, but I'm not sure.

All I think about is the one way out that I have left. Starvation is a slow death and painful, so I should use the bag of heroin and end it quickly. But I'm a coward. And I find myself looking forward to the small bits of conversation he gives me.

There's a bed and a chair in the room now. They look comfortable, but they're tools for him. I'm not a fool. He wants me to come out so he can play with me. And I won't do it.

I wish I had more options, but the door is locked. There's no way out.

Either I submit to him, or I live in this cage, or I die.

I've held on to hope for so long. For so many years, I thought once I escaped my father I'd be free.

I escaped him only to be put in a literal cage, gifted from my family's enemies to a man with bad intentions. My pussy heats as the only thoughts that have interested me flood into my mind. I don't know exactly what he wants from me, but I'm afraid to find out. I can't help but fantasize about him using me in a way that would give me pleasure, give me a reason to live. I've only been with one man. It was a mistake, one I paid dearly for, and when my father found out, Derek paid with his life. But I'm only human, and I have urges.

I drift slightly in and out of reality, not sure whether I'm daydreaming or actually dreaming. Sometimes I'm in the cage in the dreams. It's hard to know when I'm awake, but the pain is a good reminder of what's real.

Suddenly, I move my eyes from the back wall to the bathroom and I have to blink away the confusion. Did he move the cage? My mind is fuzzy, and I look behind me and then to the bathroom. He did.

I asked him… I think I asked him to move the cage closer. Maybe a day ago, maybe more. It's so hard to remember when time runs together. But he said I had to come out. He couldn't move it with me inside. And that's not happening. I'm not leaving. I won't give him my permission to touch me.

But now, I'm closer. The cage used to be on the far wall, and now it's right next to the bathroom. I question my sanity for a moment, but I know its position has changed. I know it has.

Did he move the cage while I was asleep? With me in it? Or did he come in here? I pull the blanket tighter around me.

He said he wouldn't come in though. He promised he wouldn't. And he hasn't.

With the size of his body and all that muscle, I imagine he could've moved it with me inside. I close my eyes and see him creeping into the cage and quietly lifting me. My heart hammers in my chest, but for a different reason than I'm used to. Not fear. Desire.

My eyes snap open and I quickly run from the cage, ignoring my thoughts and go to the bathroom now that it's close enough and alleviate my needs the fastest I ever have. My muscles ache with the quick movements; it's been so long since I've stretched. There's a pain in my stomach, too. It makes me hunch over and wince, but all the while I hold my breath with my eyes on the cage. I listen, waiting for the sound of his boots outside the door and the beep of the lock. But it doesn't come. I run back and climb into the cage, and I stare at the door with my fingers curled around the thin bars. I'm waiting for it to open. But it doesn't.

Maybe he wasn't watching. I look up at the camera to my right, and then to my left. Maybe he was, and he's happy I went to the bathroom.

He tells me he'd like me to leave the cage. Maybe I pleased him.

My head's dizzy with the thought, and my stomach hurts more than it did before, now that my bladder's empty.

Finally, my heart settles some and I move into a yoga pose, the rising sun, to stretch my aching back. The quick trip reminded me of how little I've moved; how little I've done anything.

The throbbing in my temples and the radiating pain in the pit of my stomach are constant symptoms that I'm unwell, but I can't give in. I can't live this way.

I stare at the food on the tray, but I refuse to eat it. I curl up on my side and fall into a light sleep. Only a few more days I think. A few more days until this is over.

The thought makes my heart clench, but I still ease into blackness just the same, ignoring the pain and welcoming what's to come.

It feels like only seconds have passed when the recognizable beep wakes me, and I turn slowly to face the door. Even the slow movement makes me dizzy, my mind fuzzy and weak.

Gio walks in, and his cold blue eyes are already on me.

I expect an object to be in his hand. He always brings something with him.

I'm right, there's a peach in his right hand. My mouth waters at the sight. *A peach.* The deep peach hue with a splash of gold on the side makes it look ripe. I'm sure it's sweet and juicy, and I can imagine the fuzz on my lips and tongue.

I swallow and rip my eyes away from it and stay stiff as he walks to me and crouches in front of the cage. His classically handsome face stares back at me. It's a face that both haunts my dreams and stirs fantasies in my mind. The rough stubble along his jaw tempts my fingers to touch him. I want to feel the texture. I want to spear my fingers through his thick hair and do so much more. I close my eyes as the thoughts overwhelm me.

What's wrong with me? This isn't okay. But I can't help it. I'm consumed with thoughts of him. The seeds of sin he planted have sprouted, and I can't escape the dark thoughts.

He did tell me he wanted me, didn't he? Or did I dream it? I can't remember.

"You need to eat," he says in a low, even voice. The smooth cadence and rough tone make my nipples harden and my pussy clench. I close my eyes, ignoring my treacherous body and hating him. But I hate myself even more.

"I don't want to," I lie. I do want to eat. I don't know why I'm doing this to myself anymore. I feel weak and sick, and I hate that I let myself be degraded to this. My eyes dart to the peach in his hand, and he holds it closer to me.

"It's for you, princess." His voice is mesmerizing. *It's for me.*

A sick part of me is thrilled for a moment.

He brought it just for me. My mouth salivates as I think of the taste, and the sweet smell fills my lungs. My head's dizzy with dehydration and I don't feel well, but the sight of the peach, the gift Gio's brought me, makes me want to take it in my hands.

"Come, princess. I want you to have this." He holds it out for me, and I fall victim to the trance in his voice. I slip forward and brush the fruit with the tip of my fingers. It's barely inside the cage.

My eyes find his, and my heart slams in my chest. I'm afraid to come out any farther.

"Go on, I won't reach for you. You're safe." His words comfort me, as though I believe they're true. It's not a trick.

As I reach for the peach, his fingers gently brush along mine, stilling my beating heart and causing an intense heat to flow through my veins. The spark ignited is so intense, I nearly drop the peach, but I catch it just in time with both hands. I barely come out of the cage and look up at him, his cold blue eyes are heated and piercing into me. I slowly back away as if moving too quickly will alert him to the fact that he could touch me if he wanted to. It would break his rule if he did, but he's staring at me with a hunger that I've never seen from him. An uncontrollable hunger that elicits both fear and desire.

I push my back up against the bars of the far end of the cage and wait with the peach, my prize and gift, held firmly in both hands. My body is tense as he finally stands and leaves me in silence.

I wait to hear the click of the door and beep of the lock before bringing the fruit to my lips, practically moaning from the sweetness and licking every drop of delicious juice, wasting nothing.

It seems as though I'd only just taken a bite when I look down and see it's gone, replaced with the pit.

It wasn't enough. I need more.

Chapter 9

SHE'S STILL IN THE CAGE. SHE'S ALWAYS IN THE CAGE.

It's impressive. Grace has gone so many days without eating, despite how weak she was when she first woke up. She was defiant, angry, and still refuses to leave the cage. She's finally accepting some food, but that defiance is still there, that beautiful fucking defiance.

In the early days, she would sneak from her cage when she thought I wasn't watching. I'm always watching her, though. I let her explore the room, test her boundaries.

I let her learn that there was no real escape.

I lean back in my chair, watching her. She barely moves, rocking side to side, humming something. I'm not sure what the music is, but she hums it sometimes when I'm not in the room. Maybe it's just nonsense and she's just passing time, or maybe it's a memory she can't help but vocalize.

I'm fascinated by her, far more interested than I thought I would be. I thought she was just another mafia princess, a spoiled little girl without a personality. I expected weakness.

Instead, I got the total opposite. According to the map of scars on her body, she's been through so much before she came to me. Because of that she has a strength inside of her that I'm not even sure she's aware of. She's resisting me far more than I ever imagined she could, and it excites me to no end.

I know that's fucked up, but I'm past worrying. The darkness is there, begging to be fed every single day. I honor my word and don't touch her when she's in the cage, which is all the time, but I ache for her to come out. I ache for the day when she finally crawls out and begs me to come into the room and touch her. I want her to beg for it so badly. I can give her a reason to continue breathing. I can make her body feel things she's probably never felt before and much, much more.

It will feel good to submit to me.

That's how I'll break her, I know. She'll finally trust me enough to call me into the room. I'll unwrap her from that blanket and bathe her, take care of her. And finally I'll slide my fingers gently along her skin and make her shiver until she pleads for more. I'll do it again and again, and soon I'll have her dripping wet on the floor, writhing with pleasure as my fingers do their work.

I'm hard as fuck just watching her on the cameras, imagining what I'd do to her. The whole thing is twisted and I feel broken inside, but I'll keep going forward. That's how I live my fucking life, just keep moving forward.

Suddenly, there's a knock at the front door. I stand up, pissed off at the interruption, and take one last glance at the monitors. She's not moving again. I leave the control room and shut the door behind me, locking it with a key. I quickly walk to the front door just as the knock comes again.

I pull it open and my father's standing there. "Son," he says.

"What are you doing here?" He never comes here. He only visits when there's a hit to be done. And that's only because he's reliant on me now.

"Come to check up on you. Gonna let me in or what?" he asks.

I nod and step aside. His heavy steps pause as he enters the hallway and looks at the mess of boxes and guns stacked in the living room.

"What's this shit?"

"It's from the gun room. I had to clean it out to make room for her."

"I know, but you didn't find a better place for it?"

"I've been busy," I say and clench my jaw and look away. "What do you need?"

"The Romanos have been asking about you." He walks into the kitchen as if it's his and grabs a beer from the fridge. He peeks his head over the open door and asks, "Want one?"

"I'm good."

He takes a seat at the table, making himself at home and takes a big swig.

"What do they want?" I ask. I lean against the wall with my arms crossed.

"They're wondering why that bastard Toni isn't dead yet."

"I've been busy," I say again.

"I get that. But he's just one asshole."

"He's a well-guarded asshole. I've been scouting him, searching for weaknesses." I set up surveillance to learn his routines, which are minimal. He has to know it's coming. He's not giving me an easy angle.

"What about the girl? She give you anything?"

"Not yet." My blood heats at his question. She's not a part of this. I haven't asked her a damn thing, and I don't plan on it. She's not a tool to use. She's mine.

"What's taking so long?" he asks.

"You know how long it takes. They always want to rush this shit, but it takes time to plan it out." I may be putting this off a bit longer than I should. But hits take time, and they know that.

"Yeah, I get it," he grunts, drinking the beer. "Still, they're getting on my ass about it. How much longer?"

I shake my head. "Hard to say. Weeks, maybe."

"Fuck, Gio." He finishes the beer and walks back to the fridge for another. I follow him, annoyed at this useless intrusion. I want to get back to my princess.

He knows better than this. Getting a little taste of the *familia* is fucking with his head. He knows how long it takes to research and plan a proper hit. He's complained many, many times over the years that they always want us to rush into it and get fucked, and here he is doing that same thing to me.

"Listen, I've overheard some shit," he says.

"What sort of shit?"

"There are some new meets going down. They're starting to let us in."

I raise an eyebrow. He seems excited, which is unlike him. The Bruno Luca I've known my whole life has been skeptical and quick to anger, but always patient when it comes to a kill.

I barely recognize this man. We've been growing apart for years, but now it feels like the break has finally come.

"I'm going to do it," he says, cracking another beer. I cock a brow at him and he repeats himself, "I'll do the hit."

"No," I say.

"I have a plan. You're taking too long. They want this shit done."

I ball my fists and have to take a deep breath before I clobber him to death. I almost want him to go forward with this hit and get himself killed. It would probably make my life easier if he just never fucking existed or suddenly disappeared.

Instantly I feel guilty about that thought. Although we're growing apart, he's still my father. I disagree with him over this situation, and there are a lot of things I hate about him, but he's still my family. My *only* family. I can't turn my back on him as much as I really want to. He's given me so much in my life already.

He fucked up as much as he gave, though. Maybe more.

"I can pull this off," he says confidently.

"I'm not having this discussion." I stare at him, and there must be something in the way I'm looking at him that makes him back off.

"Alright," he mutters and takes another swig. After a second of silence, he grins at me. "Hey, let me see the girl."

"What?"

"Yeah, let me see her."

"You know I can't do that." My back straightens, and I feel a prickle of unease down my spine.

"Come on, son," he says, leering at me. "I just wanna see the girl. I just want a little taste, you know what I mean?"

"*No!*" I say, more forceful than I expected. It surprises me and clearly surprises him, because his eyebrows instantly lift up in a questioning look.

I have to scramble to cover up my reaction. "You know how this goes," I say. "I can't have you going in there and fucking up my work. I need to build trust with her, make her want me above anything else."

"Yeah," he says slowly. "Right. I know how it is."

"You can't go in there. It's not a good time." It will *never* be a good time. My heart races with anxiety, but more so anger. *She's mine.*

"Fine, fine," he says, putting the empty beer can down on the counter. "Just take care of this shit fast, Gio. The Romanos want results."

"Fine," I say, and walk him to the door. "I'll do what I can, as fast as I can."

"Alright then, son." He gives me a look that I can't read, then leaves. I shut the door behind him, breathing fast as I lock it.

As I lean against the wall, taking deep breaths to calm myself, the memory of Grace's hand touching mine comes back to me completely out of nowhere. I feel that same electric spark and excitement course through me as in that moment, and I remember her surprised but angry stare.

I didn't stop my father because I want to break her, and the realization hits me with an undeniable force.

I stopped him because I want to protect her.

I don't want my father near her because I don't want him to hurt or touch her. It's completely fucked, but I'm protective of her. The princess is mine, all mine, and I won't have anyone else come near her.

Which makes things pretty fucking difficult for me.

I go into the kitchen and make her a meal, not thinking too much about it. I'm too busy going over every detail of my conversation with my father, wondering if he got an inkling of how I was really feeling. That last look he gave me was strange.

I'm going to have to be extra careful from now on.

I carry the food on a tray to her room. I touch the fingerprint scanner with my thumb, and the door opens with a click. I push my way inside and shut the door behind me, making sure that my face is blank. She can't sense my confusion.

She's lying in the cage like always, her eyes shut, breathing slowly and deeply. I walk over and put the tray down where I always do before taking a few steps away.

"Wake up, princess," I say softly.

She stirs a little bit.

"Princess," I say louder. "Get up."

Her eyes open. Her gorgeous eyes. She looks at me for a second, then looks at her food. She shifts her weight toward me, and for a second I think she's going to come out. I want it so badly, more than I could have imagined, but instead she stops moving, those eyes boring into mine.

"I'm here for you now, princess," I say softly. "So eat up. You're going to need your strength."

I smile at her, wicked and desiring, the darkness inside of me raging with delight.

Chapter 10

MY LUNGS FILL WITH THE SAVORY SMELL OF CHEESES AND meats, along with the sweet scent of fruits.

I lick my lips, sit on my knees, and then get up on all fours, my eyes steady on the tray. This is new. I've eaten everything he's brought me since the peach, but never has he made a tray like this.

"Come out, princess," Gio says from the entrance of the cage. My eyes dart to his, and my heart beats faster. Ever since our fingers touched, there's been a heat in his eyes that I thought I was imagining. But it's there, staring back at me. I know what it means, but I can't admit it to myself. Not yet.

"I want to feed you."

I look past him at the room that used to be barren. He's brought so many things into the room over the past few days. So many tempting items to touch. Textures I haven't felt in days… I think it's been days. No, it has to be longer. I try to remember how much time has passed, but I can't.

There's a pitcher of water on a small wooden table. I imagine it's plastic, but I'm not sure because I haven't moved. I wonder if there's anything I can break and use against him, but then I look back at his intense gaze and feel a shiver down my spine. I'm terrified that the second I creep out of here, he's going to come in and take me. Never letting me go. Never giving me a chance to run back here, into the cage. I can't live here forever though, and I want to come out and see everything he's brought for me.

"Gio?" I ask, my voice surprisingly level.

The corner of his lips pull up. "Yes?"

"If I come out and you feed me," my eyes rise to his, "will you let me come back in once I've finished eating?"

His eyes narrow at me and he tilts his head, considering my words.

"Do you think I'd take your cage from you?" His voice is low, as if daring me to tell him that.

"Yes," I say, trying to keep my voice calm and level. "I'm afraid if I come out, you'll never let me back in."

His chest rises as he sucks in a breath of air and slowly releases it, never breaking my gaze. "If you come out, I'll bring you to the table, feed you, and bring you back."

My body begs me to allow it. I need his touch. I haven't felt anything other than this scratchy blanket and the cold fucking bars against my skin.

And I've thought of what the rough pad of his thumb would feel like against my skin.

"Will you touch me?" I ask him.

"You mean, will I fuck you?" A small smile curls at the edges of his lips.

"Yes," I admit.

"No, princess. I won't fuck you until you beg me." My eyes widen at his confession.

I can't live in this fucking cage forever. I crawl out, my heart beating faster and faster as I get to the opening. It's been days since I've left the cage for anything other than rushed trips to the bathroom. My muscles ache from the movement. I stop at the very edge. He's so close to me. I can feel the heat of his body.

"Gio," I whisper so softly, I can't hear my own voice over the sound of the blood rushing in my ears.

"Yes, princess?"

"Please don't hurt me." I'm ashamed of how weak I sound. I want to be stronger, but it's been so long, and I can feel myself starting to break. But something in me is telling me that if I ask him not to, he won't.

He reaches his hand out to my face, but doesn't bring it beyond the invisible boundary. I move forward, letting him cup my cheek and pushing myself deeper into his touch. My heart swells with the gentle touch.

I need more, but I'm rooted in the cage and I don't trust him. At the realization of what I've done, I snap out of the haze that clouded my judgment. My lips part, almost as if to argue with myself, but somehow I find the strength to pull away.

I almost went to him. My heart thuds with disbelief.

I sit at the very edge of the cage, avoiding his stare. I can feel his eyes, but I don't look back at him.

My chest feels hollow and my stomach hurts. I can't live in this cage forever, but I don't want to cave to him. I feel like I've only just gotten my sanity back from the stupidity of starving myself. I have to resist him, even if I don't want to anymore. I won't let myself be weak like I was with my father.

"Sit with me, princess. I want to feed you."

I can't answer him. I can't talk to him. He confuses me and makes me question myself. I pick up the blanket and cover myself.

"Grace." His use of my name makes me look at him. There's admonishment in his tone. "You were doing so well."

The tenderness in his praise makes me question my resolve.

"I brought this in so I can feed it to you. That was the only reason."

My heart sinks. He's going to take it away.

I swallow the lump growing in my throat and shake my head.

He'll feed me something else. I know he will.

I ignore him and sit against the cage, used to the pain from the bars. He rises, leaving the tray at the entrance to the cage and stands there, staring at me, and I can't help but to look at it.

I expect him to take it, but he doesn't. Instead he says beneath his breath, "Just so you can see what you're missing, princess."

As he walks away, my fingers rise to my cheek. His warmth and touch felt… complete. I need it. I need more.

I don't want him to leave. I know this is a punishment of sorts. I refused him, so he's leaving me alone. And I hate that I want him. I want his companionship. I want him to talk to me, even though I refuse to talk back.

But I can't give in. I don't know what I'm doing; I need a plan. For now, my only defense is this cage. It's my safety but it's also a curse. I'm too scared to look beyond it. I need to though. I can't stay here forever.

I tried eating last night, and I couldn't even hold it down. I'd only taken a few bites before everything came up. I made it to the toilet, but just barely in time. I shouldn't have starved myself. I can feel my ribs, and every little movement hurts, even breathing. I need to get well. I look back at the plate of food Gio left. I need to eat.

I hear the door click open and peek up at Gio as he leaves me, the hard lines on my face softening as he turns to look at me. I watch him leave and say nothing.

Chapter 11

Several days pass, and I feel nothing but frustration. Grace barely ever leaves the safety of the cage. No matter what I do to try and tempt her, she stays hidden away from me, just out of reach. She only granted me that one touch. She tempted me, teased me with that touch. She stares at me defiantly when I enter the room and looks away when I speak to her, but I see something in her glances that always surprises me. I thought I was so close. She almost came out, but in the end it made her retreat further into herself.

Nothing works. I try comfortable things, attractive things, and delicious things. The hours tick past and she ignores it all, sticking to her horribly uncomfortable cage. I know she sneaks out in the middle of the night to use the bathroom, but she runs as fast as she can and doesn't linger for longer than she has to.

I let her. I don't tell her that I know. She probably assumes as much, anyway. There's a deep intelligence behind her uncooperative eyes that I haven't even begun to explore. I've thought about taking advantage of the situation and trying to catch her. Shutting the door to her cage and leaving her with no escape. But that's not what I want. I need her to want to come to me. But I'm getting impatient.

I can't help but question my tactics. I came into this assuming she was just another mafia princess, but my princess is clearly much more than that. She has this reserve of strength hidden deep inside of her that she's drawing from. I don't know where it comes from, not yet at least, but I want to know. I want to know everything about her.

The darkness inside of me rears its ugly head every time I go into her room, wanting to take her, use her, and destroy her. It wants to be fed, and its voice is getting louder and louder.

But there's another feeling inside of me keeping the darkness at bay.

I don't know how to explain it. It's something like a mix of curiosity and pity. I want to learn about the girl, to get inside of her head and pick its beauty clean. I also hate what the scars on her flesh mean, and I want her to give into me so that I can stop keeping her in a cage. I want her to break for her own sake as much as for mine.

But she's stubborn. Beautiful and stubborn.

I lean back in my chair, keeping one eye on the live feed of my princess in her cage while I go back through old tapes. I watch myself walk into the room with a comfortable chair and place it in the corner. I set up a table and cover it with a blanket and scarves and other warm, cozy things. She ignores it all, every single one of these items.

I stop when I get to the moment I'm waiting for. I watch as I walk into the room and get close to her cage. She moves away like she's afraid, but I pause and zoom in on her face.

It's grainy, but I can make out her expression clearly.

She's not afraid. She's *interested*. She's watching me with wide eyes, but her face doesn't betray an ounce of terror. Instead, it looks like she's watching someone she's curious about.

I skip ahead to the next day and find a similar moment. As I get close to her cage, I watch her face again in slow motion.

It's more pronounced this time. She's afraid, of course, but there's something else in her eyes.

She *wants* me.

The thought hits me like a train. My princess wants me. Her face quickly changes as I continue watching, but there's no mistaking it. I go back and watch again, smiling to myself, feeling something stir in my chest. It's a deep, deep desire for her body, a desire which I am beginning to realize she shares for mine.

I've seen that look on women's faces hundreds of times in my life. There's no mistaking it. I've had my fair share of women, and I know how they look when they see something they want. It's not always obvious, but if you know what you're looking for, it's always there.

Wide eyes. Lips parted ever so slightly. Tongue against the teeth.

My dirty little princess.

She wants to taste my cock sliding down her throat. She wants to feel my cock press between her legs as I whisper in her ear, telling her how slick her cunt is, how dirty she is for letting me have her body however I want.

I can already see it. She wants to be a filthy slut for me.

I look back at the live feed and frown again. Although she wants me, she's doing a damn good job of hiding it. She's resisting it with all of her willpower, and so far she's done an incredible job. It took me a while to even really notice it, but now I can exploit it. Use it. Break her.

Make her mine.

I feel newly energized, but my problems haven't changed. I need a new tactic, something to gain her trust.

She can't resist me forever. Hell, she doesn't want to.

I get up and walk into my main room, a plan already beginning to take shape in my mind.

I press my thumb against the scanner and the door opens. I step inside, my heart quickening the way it does every time I come near her. I slide sideways, carrying the chalkboard and the chalk in my hands.

She looks up at me, that gorgeous face almost openly curious. I walk toward her and she backs off, but I catch the look of desire. She can't hide it from me, not this time.

"Hello princess," I say, smiling. She watches me as I set up the chalkboard on top of the table facing her cage. I leave and grab a clock from outside before returning with it. I set up the clock next to the board and look back at her.

She's watching me closely. I want to walk into that cage and pull her out by her ankle and take her right here and now, but I won't. I can't do that to my princess, not until she's begging for it.

"Do you know what this is?" I ask her.

She watches me silently.

She looks thin and exhausted. I also know that she just needs to eat and sleep. The stress of the situation is making her feel ill.

"It's a chalkboard," I say. I write a time on the board: eight in the morning. I write another one down: six in the evening. I write two more times: nine in the evening, and one in the morning. She watches me the whole time, unmoving, quiet as a mouse.

"I'm changing the rules of the game, just a little bit," I say. "On this board are a list of times. Starting at each time, you have one hour to leave the cage. I will not enter this room, and I will not touch you."

She remains silent, but I can tell she's listening intently. She moves closer to me, closer to the entrance to the cage.

"You can do whatever you want during this hour," I say. "Sleep, shower, whatever you desire. If you're good, I'll give you more time. Maybe even a few hours at night so that you can sleep." I pause and smile at her. "But only if you're good."

"How do I know you're not lying?"

Her sudden speech surprises me. I stare at her for a second, feeling like I imagined it, but no, she definitely spoke.

"Have I lied to you yet?" I ask.

"No," she says.

"No, I haven't. And I'm not lying to you now." I crouch down in front of the cage and watch her, eyes hard. "I can come into that cage any time I want, but I don't, because I made you a promise. I will keep my promises to you, princess. I'll never break them."

She stares at me, but says nothing. At least she isn't recoiling away from me like she normally does.

Emboldened, I stand up and leave the room. Out in the kitchen, I get her meal together: a delicious soup, some freshly baked bread, and a tall glass of lemonade. I carry it on a tray back into the room and place it down on the table.

She watches the food, her eyes wide. I can tell that she wants it, and wants it badly. I've always given her food, but I'm a bastard. It's been mediocre and only there for nourishment. This is a treat. And she knows it.

"Come here, princess," I say softly. I crouch down near the cage's entrance again. "Let me hold you. Let me feed you."

"No," she says softly.

"Come," I say. "You'll be safe. I'll take care of you if you come out. I promise I'll only feed you this time." I'm hoping this time she'll give in. She'll crack, and whatever held her back before won't sneak up again this time.

She stares at me and moves closer to the entrance. Hope blooms in my chest. She's considering it. She looks me up and down with her brows drawn together. "Promise me?"

"I promise," I say. "I want to hold you and feed you. Come here." I hold out my hand.

She slides closer, close enough to touch. I reach in and gently take her hand.

My heart begins to pound in my chest. She's finally letting me touch her. I pull her toward me, being as careful as I can, but I see pain on her face. I frown, surprised.

I didn't think she was actually sick. But as I pull her out, I realize she's burning up.

She has a fever.

"How do you feel?" I ask her as I carry her in my arms to the table. I try to control my expression, but I'm worried. I didn't feel a fever two days ago. This is new.

"I'm fine," she says quietly.

I sit down with her in my lap. I can feel my cock stirring with excitement and the darkness begging to be fed, but I block it all out. I made a promise, and I'm going to keep my promises to her.

"You feel warm," I say softly. I take a spoonful of soup and bring it to her lips. She accepts it gratefully. I get another and another, and she eats every single one. *Good girl.*

"I'm fine," she says finally. I break off some bread and gently feed it to her. My fingers slip past her soft lips, and I feel the warmth of her mouth. Again my dick hardens, but I ignore it. I can feel my breathing coming in heavier, but I don't act on the thoughts screaming in my head.

I shift her weight in my lap. Her whole body rests against mine, almost like she can barely keep herself upright. She's so damn light, and I marvel all over again how easily I could break her if I wanted. She's not well, I remind myself. *I'm* not well.

It's so fucked that I keep having these thoughts. I keep thinking about taking her, breaking her, making her mine. I want to feed her and make her well again, but the darkness inside of me keeps warring against that, begging for me to go against my promises to her.

"What do you like?" I ask her, trying to distract myself.

"What do you mean?"

"For the room. What things do you like?" I need to know what the hell to get her. There's not much that I require. But nothing seems to tempt her.

She goes quiet for a second. "Music," she says.

"What kind of music?" It figures she'd ask for something that would fill the room so she can stay in that cage.

"Classical." Her voice is almost a whisper. "Piano. Quiet things."

"Okay," I say softly. "Music. What else?"

She bites her lip and looks away. "I don't know."

"That's okay," I say gently, tilting her head back to me, and feed her some more soup. Next, I hold the lemonade to her lips and she drinks it greedily. Her hands come up and hold the cup, but I control it.

"Books," she says after a few more minutes of silently eating soup.

"What kind of books?"

"I don't know. My father…" She trails off, and I can see the pain in her face.

"What about your father?"

"He didn't let me have many."

"I see." That little piece of information speaks louder than anything else has. "What else did he keep from you?"

"A lot of things…" She trails off again and I hold her close, my heart racing. I can't believe how vulnerable she is, and how much I love it. Normally I destroy vulnerable things, but right now the only thing I want to do is get her to open herself to me.

I want to drink her in.

"What did he do to you?" I ask.

"He's like you," she says suddenly. "Except also, he's the opposite." She shakes her head; confusion clear on her face.

"Did he give you these?" I ask, trailing my finger along the scars on her shoulder. She shivers under my touch and I feel my cock stir, the desire flowing through me.

She nods slowly, her lips parted, and shuts her eyes. "Yes," she says finally.

The desire leaves me in an instant. That fucking bastard. Anger boils through me, but I have to keep myself under control.

"What did he do to you?" I ask her again.

"Those were from a belt buckle I think," she says, her eyes still closed. She's practically trembling in my arms. "I was a disappointment. I'm still a disappointment. He wanted a son. But he got me instead."

"So he took that anger out on you?"

"Yes," she whispers. "For a long time. The scars are nothing. I can survive the scars."

Revulsion and hate flood through me. I realize with a jolt that I'm just like her father in a lot of ways. And I fucking hate it. I resist the urge to ball my hands into fists. He abused her for years. He controlled her, dominated her, and used her for whatever he wanted. I'm doing the same thing, although none of this was my choice.

She was forced on me. Now I'm just trying to do my job. *Lies*, a dark voice whispers. *You enjoy this. You're just as sick as he is.* I don't want this. I don't want to leave scars on her beautiful body. I want to leave pleasure with my touch. It's different. I don't want to hurt her. Not like that.

"Why did you stay?" I ask her, trying to stay calm although internally I'm at war.

"I couldn't leave," she says, shaking her head. "He locked me up. He bolted my windows shut. He kept me in a cage, a nice cage, but it was a cage."

"Like this cage," I say softly.

"No," she says, and for the first time I see her smile ever so slightly. "His cage was much, much worse." Her voice softens as she adds, "He could hurt me inside of that cage."

I finish feeding her the soup and place the spoon back in the bowl. She goes silent and doesn't say anything else as I feed her the last bits of bread. I can tell that talking about her father took a lot out of her, and I'm a mess of conflicting emotions on the inside.

When we finally finish, I look her in the eyes. "You need a bath," I say softly.

She shuts her eyes tightly. "You said you'd only feed me," she points out, and there's a sadness to her voice that shreds me.

"If that's what you want, I'll put you back. But you could use a bath."

"I'm afraid."

Her confession warms me. "Don't be afraid. Let me take care of you."

She lets out a noise that drives me fucking insane. It's a moan, or something like a moan. She doesn't open her eyes but she nods her head, giving me her permission.

I stand with her in my arms and walk to the bathroom, arousal surging through my body.

I want her. I want to take her. But I made her a promise, and I'll keep that promise.

Except her body is so soft and warm against mine, and my cock is so fucking hard. She's in desperate need for comfort, and I can give her that. I can show her what this is between us. I'm not sure I can keep myself under control. Not if she makes that sound again. I'll tear her to pieces and she'll love it, if only she'll let me.

I turn on the water, my whole body ringing with excitement.

Chapter 12

Grace

THE HOT WATER FILLS THE CERAMIC TUB SLOWLY. I WANT TO hold my knees to my chest, covering myself. I've never felt more naked in front of him. Which is absurd, because I've been naked this entire time. I hardly ever have my blanket around me now. But sitting in the white tub with his eyes blatantly on my body is different.

I can't hide myself. His large hand is firmly on my thigh, his fingers just on the inside of my leg.

My pussy is so hot for his touch. It's wrong. It's so fucking wrong, but I want him to slide his hand up higher. I want him to feel how much I want him. I lay my head back and close my eyes, but not all the way. Just enough to watch.

His piercing eyes roam over my body as he cups water over my chest. The warm water feels so nice, but it runs off my breasts, leaving the chill of the air behind. My nipples harden and I watch as his pupils dilate, and he licks his lips.

Yes.

Take me. I can picture him leaning down and taking a nipple between his lips, twirling his tongue around the sensitive nub. My legs slip open slightly as the water comes up past my hips. He finally releases me, but the look in his eyes holds a warning that I better hold still.

The threat does nothing other than prepare my body for more. Arousal pools between my legs. My fingers long to touch myself. To show him that I want it.

But I don't move.

It's one thing to fantasize, but it's another to invite the danger.

And he said he wouldn't. I trust that he won't. Even as my breath comes in short pants, and he runs the soapy washcloth over my body. The gentle touch is almost too much.

My heart rate increases as the minutes pass and when he turns the water off, it's all I can hear. The thudding of my heart, and the gentle swishing and splashing of the water.

"You're so beautiful, my princess." The words spill from Gio's lips, and the unexpected compliment takes me off guard.

"Thank you," I murmur.

He cups the back of my head and gently lowers me under. He massages me and rubs away every pain.

More. I want more.

I've never had this. In all my life, no one's ever cared for me this way.

He's gentle and takes his time with me. His touch is nothing but calming… well, maybe erotic. But that's my mind playing tricks on me. Wanting me to show him how he could touch me, if only he wanted.

A voice hisses inside of me to stop this. To remember who he is. To remember who I am.

But it feels so good. When he pulls the plug and I know it's going to end, a sadness settles against my chest. The cool air is harsh, but he wraps me in a blanket and lifts me into his chest.

I'm so tired. And he feels so right. I nestle my head into the crook of his neck and fall asleep in his arms. Before exhaustion takes me over, I swear I feel his lips gently touching my forehead and hear his sweet, soft words. "Sleep, princess."

My eyes drift shut, and I already know what I'm going to see. I think of his hands on my naked body. The water felt so good. The pressure of the stream, the warmth. But his hands were a million times better. My lips part and my fingers drift over my breasts, mimicking the way his felt, but it doesn't come close.

His tender touch was unexpected, and I loved it. I wanted more. I dreamed of him taking me.

I wanted him to lay me on the bed and not in the cage. I know he promised me, but I wish he'd broken it.

I'm snapped out of my memory by the sound of Gio approaching. Rather than shrinking back from the cage, I lean forward. I glance at the clock, and the hour is up. The hour he gave me to roam freely. He kept true to his word. I thought he would, but still, I haven't left the cage since he put me in here.

My heart races in my chest knowing what I have planned. After the moment in the tub, I've been warring with myself. I want him, but I hate him. I hate myself almost as much. I've been waiting for the right time.

I have the bag, and I'm ready to use it. But not on myself.

On him.

I can already see my sanity slipping. Loving his touch is a symptom that I'm not well. I'm falling into the depths of madness. I'll be shattered if I stay. I need to leave, and he has no intention of letting me go. So I have no choice. How badly I wanted him when he bathed me only proves that I'm so close to losing myself completely.

My heart lurches as the door beeps and clicks, slowly revealing Gio. I see the tray in his hand, and the cup sitting on top. And I know what I'm going to do. It makes me sick to think I can murder him.

But I need to get out. I don't know what lies beyond the door, but I know if he at least passes out, I can use his finger to get out and run for my life.

I can have freedom.

I stare into his gorgeous blue eyes and try not to show the sadness. I try to ignore the guilt weighing down on my chest. I don't know if this plan will work. But I think he'll drink from the cup if I asked him to. If I accuse him of poisoning it, and I wanted him to prove that he didn't.

I have to break eye contact as I think about how deceitful and manipulative I'm being. How wicked I am. This isn't the person I want to be, but this is what he made me.

"Will you come out for me, princess?" he asks. I nod my head, but wait at the entrance of the cage. The blanket is next to me and the bag is opened and waiting, hidden beneath it.

"Can I have a drink?" I ask him weakly. My voice cracks, and I hate that I'm showing weakness. A cold sweat breaks out along my skin. He's going to know I'm lying. My father always told me I was a shit liar. Anger courses through me at the thought of him. It's been a long time since he's been on my mind.

"Of course." Gio sets down the tray and I take the drink in my hand. It's tea. Hot tea. Perfect. I bring it to my lips and blow as Gio picks the tray back up. As soon as he rises and turns to place the tray on the table like he always does, I snatch the baggie and dump in the heroin.

I shove the empty baggie under the blanket quickly and spill a bit of the tea from the top. I gasp as the hot liquid splashes my skin and leaves a bit of a red mark.

"Careful," Gio says, quickly turning back to me. I can see the concern in his expression, and it nearly breaks me.

"You poisoned it," I say accusingly, but I can't look him in the eye. I watch him halt in his tracks at my words.

"I haven't poisoned anything, Grace." He walks over to me slowly as I raise the cup up to him. He doesn't come closer, and I stand. I step out of the cage and hold it out to him. I keep my expression level. I can't back down now. I can't let him see through me.

"Then drink it. Please. Drink it and prove it." I look him in the eyes this time, and pray he doesn't know what I'm up to.

If I'm honest, part of me hopes he'll refuse. But he takes it from my trembling grasp and lays a soothing hand on my shoulder. His thumb rubs soothing circles against my skin.

"I didn't poison anything, my princess." With those words, he brings the ceramic mug to his lips. I watch in horror as the truth of the situation hits me full in the chest. If he drinks that tea, he's going to die. I'll have killed the only person to ever show me an ounce of respect and tenderness.

He tips it back, and I can't help myself any longer.

I reach out and whip the mug from him, scalding hot water splashing against his skin. He yells with a mix of anger and pain as the mug shatters on the ground. I stare at it, chilled to the bone. My heart pounds in my chest and then when I look up at Gio, it stills with fear.

Anger stares back at me, attempting to pin me in place.

My heart thuds once, and I bolt. He takes a large step toward me as

I reach for the cage, and my fingers grip onto the bars as he latches onto my hip.

"No!" I scream out in horror. He's going to beat me. I rip my body from him, hurling myself into the cage. Scraping my knee against the metal and bashing my forearms against the grated floor. He reaches for my ankle, still outside the cage and I look back at him, whimpering.

His chest heaves as he releases me, and I crawl to the back of the cage. I pull the blanket to me by the hem and cover myself with it as though it'll keep me safe.

He was going to hurt me. He was going to beat me.

I know he was.

For the first time in a long time, tears spill from my eyes and I can't keep them back.

I hear him pacing in front of the cage, and then he kicks a piece of the broken mug. My body jolts at the sound of it smashing into the back wall. It's not close to me, but his fury is what's frightening.

I almost killed him. I was almost free. And now I have to suffer the wrath of my captor.

I sob into the blanket and try to ignore all the warring emotions within me. The guilt and sadness, the betrayal, the anger. I don't know what to feel.

The door clicks and beeps as Gio leaves.

I've spent so many days and nights in this cage.

But I've never felt this alone and broken.

Chapter 13

I CAN'T BELIEVE SHE DID THAT. ANGER EXPLODES THROUGH ME AS I pace the living room, slowly waiting for my mind to calm itself.

She never showed any aggression toward me before. Lashing out like that was strange, extremely unlike her. I quickly go into the control room and sit down at the monitor, watching her in the cage.

I can see her trembling, practically shaking. I can't hear any noise, but I know that she's crying. I watch her carefully, the anger slowly melting away, replaced by curiosity.

Then she moves. She rolls over and looks around the room, her eyes wide. She quickly crawls out of the cage, moving as fast as she can. She grabs a large shard of the broken ceramic cup and crawls back into her cage with it. The piece is large and jagged, and I watch as she finds a hiding spot.

She goes back to her old position, not moving at all this time. I lean back in my chair and sigh, shaking my head. I know she's scared because I got mad, but she knows better than that.

What the hell is going on with her? Maybe this is a part of her process. That must be what this is. I need to be firm, and her ass is definitely going to be punished for this.

I thought we had something. Feeding her, speaking to her, bathing her… it was something I'd never experienced before. Touching her skin that way and not taking her was more erotic than anything I'd ever experienced. My blood still rings for her, and my cock's still half hard. It took every ounce of my willpower not to slide my fingers along her skin toward her tight, soaking little pussy, and part of me wishes I had.

But then there's the anger and the teacup and now this. I can't allow her to have that shard. I don't want her to harm herself. I'm not worried about her hurting me with it, because I know I can easily disarm her and overpower her if it comes to that.

But I don't want her to turn it against her own skin. She might even be able to kill herself with it. Either way, I don't want another scar on her body, at least not because of me.

There's a small problem, though. I can't just kick in her cage and steal the shard back from her. I have to coax it out of her or at least convince her to leave the cage so that I can go retrieve it. I promised that she'd be safe while she's in there, and I'm dedicated to keeping that promise.

And I'm still puzzled by what happened with the tea. Curious, I rewind the video on the monitor to my right, keeping an eye on her on the other. I return back to the moment I gave her the tea and turned away.

I have to watch it twice before I notice what she did. My breath catches in my throat when I see: she slipped something into the tea.

Holy shit.

I watch the video over and over, slowing it down, frame by frame. Sure enough, she slipped something into the tea. Something I hadn't noticed. Something she smuggled in here.

How? Why? I can't be sure. Whatever it was, she must have had it on her before she was taken. I curse myself for being so fucking careless. She could easily have killed me. Whatever she put in that tea could have been a deadly poison or a strong sedative, and if I drank from that cup, I would be dead.

Careless, fucking careless. All because I let her have that fucking bathroom. If I forced her to use the bucket, this never would have happened. She wouldn't have been able to be so fucking sneaky.

Anger rises inside of me, clean and strong. I watch the video again and again, shocked and angered that she would try and pull something like that after what happened between us.

But slowly, I begin to calm myself. She didn't make me drink the tea. In fact, she stopped me. Whatever she had in there, she decided at the last second that she didn't want to hurt me.

I lean back and take a deep breath.

This is good. Her sneaking something into the tea wasn't, but her reaction was good. It means she's beginning to feel the bond between us, that it isn't just me. She's beginning to trust me. She could have let me drink the tea, but she didn't.

I smile to myself. The shock of catching her begins to wear off, and the implications of what actually happened settle in.

Grace didn't want to hurt me. She wanted to escape, but when it came down to actually doing it, she couldn't. She stopped herself. For whatever reason, she smacked that tea cup from my hand.

She's dangerous. But that excites me more than it should.

I stand up and groan, stretching. I walk slowly toward her door, not sure if she's going to listen, but I'm hopeful. I press my thumb against the pad, making the door click open.

Once inside, I stand near the door and watch her. She's breathing slowly, not moving, and she knows I'm there. She's trying to pretend like she doesn't notice me, but I know that she does. She's shrewd and smart, a cunning little minx. I can't help but smile.

She nearly killed me. But in the end, she couldn't do it.

Now it's just a matter of time before I take her.

"Princess," I say gently. "Is there something we have to talk about?"

She looks up at me. "No," she says and looks away.

"Princess," I say, coming closer to her cage. She doesn't move. "Are you sure about that?"

"Yes," she says softly.

I sigh and crouch down in front of her. I decide not to tell her that I know what she did, afraid that it might hurt more than help. I can revisit that later, when I've earned her trust. Instead, I decide to concentrate on the shard.

"You have something," I say.

Her eye twitches toward the remains of the cup and back to me. "No," she lies.

"Princess," I say, shaking my head, disappointed. "I know you're lying."

She looks away from me. "Just leave me alone."

"I can't do that. You know I'm always watching, but you tried to lie to me anyway. Why?"

"Please," she says weakly. "Just go."

"Princess. If there's going to be trust between us, you're going to have to tell me the truth. Do you have something you shouldn't?"

She looks at me, her face stricken. I want to reach out and touch her, feel her full lips under my thumb, hear her moan as I caress her body.

"Yes," she says.

"Good girl," I say, smiling. Pride and warmth fill me. "I need you to give it to me."

"Let me keep it." Her voice is practically a whisper.

"Why? What are you going to do with it?"

"I don't know," she says.

"You don't need it. I don't want to see another scar on that perfect body."

She stares at me. "It could be for you."

I smile at her brazen response. "We both know that won't happen," I say softly. I crouch down in front of the entrance to her cage and hold out my hand. "Give it to me, princess."

She chews her bottom lip, staring at me. "What will you give me in return?" she asks.

I can't help but smirk at her. "I'll give you whatever you want," I say. "All you need to do is come out of that cage and give in to what we both know you want."

She takes a sharp breath. I know she understands what I'm saying to her.

"I-I can't," she says.

"Yes, you can. Come out, princess. Give me the shard and then let me take what I want from you."

She hesitates, but she obeys; she reaches under the blanket and slowly draws the shard out. My heart starts to rush in my chest, beating like mad. I know she's inches away from doing what we both want. I can practically already taste her delicious pussy, her smooth skin against mine. I want to sink my thick cock deep inside of her and hear her finally moan the deep release she's been dreaming about for days now.

Her hand stretches toward me, but she's still resisting.

"Come on now-" I'm interrupted by a loud knock from the other room. I can hear it clearly through the still-open door. I resist the urge to look, but Grace's eyes are drawn to the noise, her body frozen.

I pause and cock my head, waiting. She pulls back into the cage, frightened.

I hear it again, and it's loud and insistent.

"Shit," I curse under my breath. I look back at her. "Don't do anything. I'll be back."

She nods. I turn and quickly leave the room, my jaw clenching and anger coursing through my blood.

Fucking shit. I nearly had her. I was inches away, and now some fucker is interrupting us. I can't be sure I'll be able to pick back up with her where we left off. The moment is destroyed now. And I'm fucking pissed.

I head to the front door and yank it open. My father's standing there, looking annoyed.

"What?" I ask him, angry. I almost forgot about him.

He pushes past me and walks into the kitchen. "Is that how you greet me now?" he says.

"I'm busy," I say, shutting the door and following him.

He leans against a counter and takes me in. "Doing what?"

"I'm making headway with the girl."

"You haven't broken her yet?" He laughs. "Pathetic."

"She's stronger than you know," I practically growl at him. "What are you doing here?"

"The Romanos want to know when the hit will be."

"I thought you were doing that yourself."

He grunts and looks away. "Things haven't panned out."

I sigh. That's fucking typical of him. He's gotten soft in his old age and he gets too excited about bad intelligence. He probably overheard some bullshit and took it as gospel like an idiot.

I won't fall for that, though. I take my time and work things out the right way, like he used to do. Like he taught me. He's a different person now, though, a weak person. He disgusts me, and I almost pity him.

"They have to be patient," I say. "This will happen when it needs to happen. And right now I'm busy. You got me at a bad time."

He huffs, but gets the message.

"I'm making headway," he says slowly, moving back toward the front door.

"What does that mean?" I'm frustrated, and he's being vague.

"I'll be back tomorrow," he says. "There's a meeting with the Romanos. I want to talk to you before I go."

"Wait," I say. "What are you talking about?"

He pauses at the door. "You'll find out soon." He grins and leaves, shutting the door behind him.

"Shit," I curse to myself. I stand there, wondering what the fuck that's all about. I can't tell if he's just trying to taunt me, or if that little meeting had an actual purpose.

Finally, I go back into the control room and sit at the monitors. Grace is fine. She's curled up in the corner of her cage like she normally is, not moving. I think she might be asleep.

The moment is gone. I'm not sure how to recreate it at this point. I'll just have to watch her very, very closely, and make sure to stop her if she decides to use the shard. At least until I can get it from her.

I lean back in my chair, thinking about her body, my father completely forgotten.

Chapter 14

I T'S ODD. AND HARD TO EXPLAIN. I FEEL LIKE I CAN'T COME OUT OF the cage. I don't think he's angry anymore, but I still stay in here. Even during the one-hour times that he gives me to roam. Even though I crave his touch, and I look forward to him coming in, I still stay within the safety of the cage.

He came in and cleaned up the mess I made. I laid the thick shard he knew I had at the entrance of the cage and refused to look him in the eyes when he picked it up and threw it away with the others. I gave him my weapon, my only hope of escape. I simply handed it over to him. What's worse is that as he swept up the shards, I felt guilty. It was my fault that the cup was broken. I was going to hurt him. He was angry after it happened, and I thought he was going to hurt me, but he didn't. He could have come into the cage. He could have broken his promise. But he didn't.

I can't explain why it causes me so much pain.

I must be broken, I must be sick, but I prefer to stay in here, only leaving the cage for short trips to look at something or to go to the bathroom.

Gio brought in a thick blanket, and I brought it to the cage. The grate on the floor just hurt too much. I couldn't take another day of the thin bars digging into my legs. I anticipated him telling me no, but it didn't happen.

The warmth and comfort of the blanket make me want more though. I keep looking at the bed, and I want to lie on it. I want to get in the bath again and feel the comfort of the steaming hot water. I want his soothing, gentle touch on my skin.

I look to the clock. It's the only thing that makes a sound in the room, and I know I have time. He won't be back for a little while. It's my hour of freedom.

My stomach rumbles with hunger. He left the tray for dinner. He wanted to feed me, but I wasn't hungry so he left it there.

I should eat. When I eat, the pain goes away. It lulls me into a deep sleep and for a moment, I'm better. Even when I wake up, I'm okay.

But the sickness always returns in the pit of my stomach. Gio left medicine on my tray, but I didn't take it.

I must have a death wish.

I don't even know how long I've been in here. I have no plan of escape, and I don't see a way out of here.

Maybe I should give in.

I close my eyes and remember his hands on me. The feel of his hard muscles against my body.

He's offered me safety, which is something I've never had in all of my life.

I know what he wants. And I want it, too.

I don't know how much longer I can fight it. This desire to let him have me and see where this takes us. Will he make me stay here forever? I don't think he will.

I should ask him. He hasn't lied to me, and I think he'd tell me the truth. He hasn't hidden anything from me. But I've hardly asked a thing.

A small huff of a dark laugh leaves my lips and sounds crazy to my ears, but I don't care.

My father wanted me to ask questions, to listen. What a fucking idiot. The Romanos don't even have me. If he knew where I was, he'd be furious. He wasted a pawn.

My shoulders shudder slightly with a laugh, and a smile plays at my lips. It shouldn't fill my chest with warmth, but it does.

He used me, and got nothing in return. And he has no idea where I am.

The realization lifts a weight from my shoulders, and I ease into the thick blanket. He's not coming for me. That's never been true in all my life.

My eyes open and I stare blankly at the wall, the smile slipping, but what life is this that I have?

I sit up and look at the clock and the chalkboard.

I asked him for music, but he hasn't brought me any. I have nothing. The reality is that I'm wasting my time, and my life.

I don't even know what I'd do if I were to ever get out of here. I'd run, of course. But when would I stop? And where would I go?

I remember a picture my mother had in her room. It was of her family. My nana and papa. I never met them, but it was taken back when my mother was a girl. The three of them were on the beaches of France. I'd love that.

I'd love to go there. If for nothing else than to listen to the waves, and pretend I lived in their time. That I could have shared that with them.

That's where I'd run, far away. I catch sight of the chalk next to the board, and my body stirs.

I need to write it down, so I don't forget. Happiness is something that's a rarity for me, but I have it now. I can't let it go.

I look at the time, and I know I'm still safe. I don't have to run, so I don't feel any anxiety. I even stretch, letting out a yawn that creeped up on me. It feels good to move. I almost walk directly to the board, but then I remember he put clothes in the closet. They were only meant to tempt me, and so I ignored them. But now… I want to see them. I want to feel them.

There are only three simple dresses draped on plastic hangers. There's a black one with a black lace overlay. Underneath is silk. The texture feels so soft and smooth. Has it always felt this way? It's so luxurious. I eye the other two garments, which are a short red spaghetti strap nightie, and an almost identical cream one. They look beautiful, but the black one calls to me. I feel like I need it. I don't put it on though, not yet, knowing that I'm going to be playing with the chalk. I don't want to dirty the beautiful fabric.

I lay it in the cage, wondering if I'll ever wear it and quickly grab the chalkboard. It's awkward to carry because of its size, but the cage is so large, it's easy to prop up the board and sit cross-legged in front of it. I'm careful to draw around the times that Gio wrote.

I lay the piece of chalk flat and make a wave, and then another. I layer them and use my fingernail to add details to the waves. I want them to look like the ocean is drifting away.

Like they've only just come up from the current, but they're already slipping back into the abyss to blend in with the others. But in this moment, they're different.

I stare at the sketch, which somehow has texture to it although I only have the one piece of chalk. One color to work with.

I want more. I need more. I'm not able to draw it like I can picture it in my head.

I could ask him for more, but I don't want to. I don't want to have to plead with him for anything. *Other than for him to take me.*

The dark thought makes me drop the piece of chalk. My heart hammers harder in my chest.

I only know two things in this moment. Two truths which are extremely clear to me.

I need to get out of here, and that starts with getting out of this cage.

Chapter 15

Gio

I SPEND MOST OF THE DAY WATCHING GRACE DRAW.

At first I didn't know what she was doing when she moved the chalkboard. I figured she might try to write some kind of message with it and hold it up to a window, or maybe she would break it into pieces and use them for something.

But when she began to draw, I was transfixed.

I watch every movement of her body. It's beautiful the way she draws in quick, short motions, shading and sketching. I'm not surprised that she can draw so beautifully. Everything she does is impressive, and this is just one more thing that makes me believe how special she is.

Initially, I have to wonder what she's sketching. It doesn't look like much, and I think maybe it's just doodles until she begins to sketch landscapes of the outside world. I catch her staring at the walls, probably imagining what the world is like outside of her prison.

I smile to myself. Duke curls up at my feet, and I reach down to rub his head. I hope I can let her outside one day, maybe even let her play fetch with Duke on my property. I bet she'd love it out there, and I have so much land. We could ride dirt bikes or horses, or go fishing if that was something she liked. Or maybe she'd be more into picnics and wine.

I laugh to myself. I realize I'm daydreaming about taking her on a date on my property.

What a fool I'm becoming. Maybe I'm going soft for her.

I watch her draw for another hour. I'm completely happy and content just marveling at her body and her beauty when there's a knock at my front door.

That jolts me back to reality. I remember my father saying that he'd be back today, and a nervous anger lodges itself in my gut.

"Stay," I murmur to Duke before leaving the control room. I shut the door, then let my father inside. He struts into the kitchen as always, not even bothering to say hello.

The arrogant bastard is getting on my nerves.

He needs to show some respect.

I follow him. He sits down at the table this time.

"You're back," I say.

"Like I told you I would be."

He seems angry and agitated, so I'll just get right to the point. "What's going on? You mentioned some fucking meeting."

"Yeah," he grunts. "We got to give the Romanos something."

"Well, give them what you have. Since you're taking care of it."

He glares at me. "I can't get an angle, and you know it."

"You can't?" I act surprised.

"Don't push me, boy," he warns.

I clench my jaw. "Fine. What are you going to tell them?"

"Like I said, I can't get to Toni. The fucking Rossis know there's a contract on him, I don't know how."

"Tell them that. We need more time."

"I have another way."

I cock my head at him, already not liking where this is going. "What is it?"

"Toni's mother."

I stare at him for a second. "The old woman? What about her?" I ask, but I already know the answer.

"If I kill her, that'll draw that Rossi fuck out. It'll set him off balance."

I have to ball my hands into fists to keep from jamming my foot down his throat. He knows that I hate fucking with women, and especially hate killing them. Grace is bad enough, and I wish I didn't have to put her through all of this. But I can't abide another woman.

"No," I say.

"No?" He laughs. "You act like there's a better way."

"Patience," I say. "That's the best way, and you know it. This mother bull-shit is just that, bullshit. You don't know what'll happen once she's dead, and that's bad. We can't plan for that."

"It's the best shot we have," he says, standing up. "Plus she's old as fuck. What's it matter?" He looks pissed, but I don't give a fuck. I want him to come at me. It'll give me an excuse to beat the piss out of him. It'll give me an excuse to hurt him for the way he fucked me up when I was a kid, leaving me with this deep darkness inside of me.

"There are lines that shouldn't be crossed," I say softly.

He grunts and finally looks down. "What about the girl?" he asks.

I shake my head. "I'm close. But not yet."

"Let me see her."

"No," I say.

"Gio." He steps closer to me, suddenly calm. "I need to give the Romanos something. Let me see the girl so that I can report back."

I stare at him for a second and finally nod sharply. "Just through the monitors, and only this once."

"Fine."

I lead him down the hallway and into the control room. Duke growls at my father, but I dismiss him with a wave of my hand. Duke slowly leaves the room, and my father glares at me.

"That dog is an asshole," he says.

"Duke just doesn't like dickheads." I nod at the monitors. "There she is."

He comes and stands next to me, and we both look in on Grace.

I can't help but smile proudly. She's in her cage, still drawing on the chalkboard, a beautiful and detailed realistic-looking shell. She looks to-tally absorbed and gorgeous, her face angelic and engaged in her task. I love the way she draws and how content she looks, wrapped in only her scratchy blanket.

Watching her like that, an idea strikes me. I need to get her some art supplies. Brushes, oils, canvas, all that shit. She'll love it. I smile huge. That'll bring her out of the cage. She just needs to express herself.

"What the fuck is this shit?"

I snap out of it, back to reality. My father is leaning over the monitor, squinting at Grace.

"She's in a cage," I say.

"I fucking see that. I mean the drawing."

"She's drawing," I say.

"How the fuck is that going to help break her?" he demands, standing and staring at me.

"Get out," I say softly.

He opens his mouth to argue, but he must see that I'm holding back my rage. He silently leaves the room and goes back to the kitchen.

I stand there and let the anger pass. If he had done anything but leave, I was going to beat him to death. I know it deep in my heart. I wouldn't have been able to stop. That stupid piece of shit probably thought I should be beating Grace to death, torturing my fucking princess until she did what I wanted her to do. That sick fucking freak.

Or maybe I'm the sick freak for doing what I'm doing. Maybe wanting to care for her while also making her mine is even worse.

I release a breath. No, I'm nothing like him and I never will be.

I follow him back out to the kitchen. He's leaning against the counter, his arms crossed.

"She's sick," I say.

"How?"

"I don't know."

"Don't let her die." He stares at me.

"No shit," I say. "I know that."

"We need her more than ever. We need her to be the perfect sex slave at the end of this."

The anger comes back full force, but I ignore it. "I understand."

"No, you don't." He steps toward me. "This is all falling apart. At the very least, we need to give the Romanos this mob slut as a gift if we can't get to Toni or if something goes wrong. If you can't get information from her, at least make her into a useful gift."

I grit my teeth. I don't fucking like the way he's talking. I don't like thinking about giving her back either. Now's not the time. I grunt at him, looking past him at the tray on the counter and nod. "I understand," I say, but the idea of Grace working as a sex slave for the Romanos makes my stomach turn.

There's a short silence between us. Finally, my father shakes his head and sighs. "Let's go," he says.

"What?"

"You're coming to this meeting with me."

"I thought you wanted to deal with them exclusively."

"I'm tired of being a fucking go-between, especially when you keep giving me bad news."

I watch him for a second. I don't want to go to this meeting and leave Grace alone. But I can't trust him to speak for me at this meeting. If there's something I can do to protect Grace, I need to go.

I have to trust her. I have no other choice.

"Fine," I say. "Let's go."

We follow my father to the front door. Grace is going to be okay. She doesn't want to disappoint me.

We drive in separate trucks to the meet. I don't feel like having him come back to my place after it's over, and he doesn't seem to care either way. The less I talk to him at this point, the better.

The meeting with the Romanos is at a diner at the edge of town. That doesn't surprise me, since I doubt they'd want to bring some outsiders like us into their central compound. I'm betting it annoys the fuck out of my father though. I want to sneer at him and tell him, *See? See? This is how they treat us, and you'll never be one of them.* That's useless and childish, and won't get me anywhere. He won't believe me. He'll always be looking for an in.

I need to outthink my father. I can't win this by sitting back and throwing insults at him. I know I've been too busy with Grace to concentrate fully on the hit, but I can't help myself. Now I need to figure out a way to buy myself some more time and to stop my father from going through with his awful fucking plan.

Marco rises from his seat at a corner booth and stands with his shoulders squared as we approach. The diner is full with locals and regulars, but it's really showing its age. The laminate table tops are beginning to peel, and the leather seats have holes and tears in them. The floors look like they're covered in a permanent layer of grime and grease. I suspect that this place isn't open because it does good business, but because it's just another front for the Romanos.

"Welcome," Marco says, shaking my father's hand first and then mine. "I'm glad you two are here." It's a firm handshake, but it's a mere formality.

"It's good to see you, Marco," my father says.

I nod at Marco, not wanting to debase myself by kissing his ass.

"Sit," he says. My father slides into the booth, and I sit next to him. Marco leans toward us, his hand folded in front of him, that sleazy smile on his face. "So, my favorite men. How are things?"

"Good, as always," my father replies.

Marco looks at me. "How's that little present I gave you?"

I hate that filthy smile. "She's fine," I say. My heart seems to beat slower, and my blood chills.

Marco laughs loudly. "Fine?" He shakes his head with disbelief. "That girl is more than fine, Gio. She's fucking gorgeous. You got lucky with this one."

"Yes," I grunt.

"Make any progress? I'd be interested in seeing."

I don't respond right away. I don't want him seeing. I know I have to, but I don't want to admit it.

"In fact, we were just talking about the Rossi slave. We're going to need to see how she's doing real soon." A sick smile snakes across his lips as he suggests, "Maybe a little video? Your father told us about the tapes." I turn to look at my father, that rat fuck. He should keep his goddamn mouth shut.

"We're very grateful for the opportunity," my father quickly says, that sniveling shit. "Gio here is working very hard on the girl. Right, Gio?"

"Of course," I say.

"Not too hard, I hope," Marco says. "You have a more important job to do."

This is the moment, then. I can practically feel my father ready to talk about his plan, ready to try and convince these impatient, stupid Romanos that killing some old lady would do any good for anyone.

I can't let him have this moment. "I have an idea about that," I say quickly.

My father looks at me, surprised. Marco smiles. "Go on," he says.

"Toni's well-guarded," I say slowly, the idea forming as I speak. "He's clearly the next in line for the Rossi throne, and his power is increasing every day. But what if we didn't kill him?"

Marco cocks his head at me, and my father scoffs. "Killing him is the job," my father points out.

I hold a hand up to him. "Wait. Hear me out."

"Okay," Marco says. "What are you thinking?"

"There's another man in the Rossi family that's just as important as Toni."

Recognition sparks in Marco's face. "The Don," he says.

"The Don," I agree. Visions of Grace's scarred skin flash before my eyes. *Yes, the Don.* I'm going to kill that piece of shit. I'll make it slow for her if I can.

"He's weak," my father says. "He's on the way out."

"Maybe," I say. "But he's still the Don. I think we can get to him more easily."

My father's clearly pissed. He's probably barely holding back his anger, but that's fine with me. He's the one that wanted to play these stupid fucking games.

There's no way we can really get to the Don right now though. It's possible of course, but not the way things currently stand. This is more about buying us some extra time from the Romanos to figure shit out and to plan a solid hit.

Besides, as far as I'm concerned, the Don is already dead. Maybe not today, maybe not tomorrow, but his death is coming. I'll be the one standing over him holding a smoking gun for what he did to my princess. If Marco decides to shift the target to the Don, then that'll be killing two birds with one stone, so to speak.

"Very interesting," Marco says.

"We can get to him," I say, half-lying. "He goes out with protection, but he still goes out. Toni never goes fucking anywhere. If the Don goes into the open, I can take him."

"He has guards," my father says. "That's a suicide mission."

"Not for a highly skilled sniper, it isn't," I say, staring back at him, daring him.

I can see the rage flash on his face, but he quickly gets it under control.

"Everything okay between you two?" Marco asks casually.

"Great," my father says, looking back to Marco. "Listen, I have a different plan."

"No," Marco says, interrupting him. "That's okay. I like this. I would love to see the Don dead. Toni will have to come out of hiding to take over the Rossi *familia* duties if the Don is killed, and then we can take him, too."

"That's right," I say, encouraging his line of thought.

"Good," Marco says, nodding. "Very good. I'll take this to my Don, but I know he'll be pleased." Marco stands and slides out of the booth. I get up next, followed by my father. "Bruno, I'll be in contact soon."

Marco shakes my father's hand. "Thank you, Marco," my father says.

Marco looks at me. "And you, good job today," he says. He shakes my hand and holds it tight. "Enjoy the girl while you can. And don't take too long."

I stare back and nod, but don't say a word. I don't trust myself to speak.

Marco releases my hand. I follow my father back through the diner and out into the parking lot. My mind is full of anger at that Marco prick, but my father suddenly whirls on me.

"What the fuck was that?" he asks.

I don't stop walking. "An alternative to your awful plan," I say.

"We didn't discuss that. You didn't want to kill any of them, and now you're trying to go after their Don?" I can hear the jealousy and anger in his voice.

"That's right," I say.

"You're going to get yourself killed," my father calls after me as I walk away from him.

"I doubt it," I say softly to myself. I climb into my truck, start the engine, and pull out of the parking lot.

I'm already thinking about my princess as I hurry back home to her. *Don't take too long.* Marco's words echo in my head. I need to speed this up with her. I bang my fist on the steering wheel and curse. I hate that they have anything to do with her. But if they want to see something, I can make it happen. I have to. I can't let them take her away from me.

Chapter 16

Grace

I'M DEBATING ON GETTING OUT OF THE CAGE. I'VE BEEN WONDERING about it. Wondering what he'd do if he walked in, and I was sitting on the bed. I don't know how he'd react.

Of course, he'd probably know I was there before he even walked in. I know he watches me. But what would he do?

He seems gentle and tender, although I know that he's keeping a part of himself hidden from me. I stare at the white sheets on the bed. They're perfect and crisp. Neither of us have sat on the bed since he moved it in and put the sheets on it.

I wonder what he'd think, if I was lying there, waiting for him.

My eyes snap to the door as I hear the beep, my heart thudding loudly. Usually I can hear him coming, but this time I didn't.

My brow furrows as he rolls in a TV cart. It's off for the moment, and encased in a large plastic box so none of the buttons can be touched.

I sit up and lean forward, my fingers wrapping around the bars.

He doesn't address me, which is odd. He always talks to me.

My heart hurts thinking I've done something wrong. I don't like that he's acting differently.

"Gio?" I call out to him without my own conscious consent.

He stops rolling the cart and angles it so it's facing the cage. Facing me. The black screen shows nothing.

"Yes?" he asks. His voice is a bit more hollow than usual. It lacks the side of him I've grown to expect. The hunger. Something's different. Something's changed, and I don't know what. But I don't like it. It makes fear rise within me.

I shake my head and shrink back into the cage. I reach for my blanket and cover myself.

Gio watches me closely, and his eyes reflect what I think is sadness.

I wanna know what's wrong. My mind is going crazy thinking of what's on that TV screen. Of what he's going to show me. It could be my father, or my uncle. Maybe it's footage of them being tortured. I have no idea, and the anxiety from not knowing fills my blood.

My instinct is to run to Gio. To ask him to hold me if it's going to hurt. It'll feel better that way. I know he can soothe the pain.

Before I can ask him anything or even move, he leaves me alone in the room. The TV is blank still and I don't understand, but he instantly comes back in with a large black plastic bag.

I sit up and wait for him to tell me what it is.

"I got you a gift, princess."

My eyes widen, darting to the bag and then back to his handsome face.

He smiles sweetly, and this is the man I'm used to. I slowly crawl to the entrance of the cage and almost slip out.

But before I can, I stop myself.

"Your drawing is beautiful." I look back to the chalkboard taking up so much room in here. I thought he might be mad. The idea that he might take it away from me also crossed my mind. So I kept it in here.

"You like it?" I ask him softly.

He walks to the cage and crouches in front of me, nodding his head. "I do," he says and his words warm my chest. "I got you more supplies. Whatever you need, princess."

My heart swells. I try to contain the emotion, knowing that something is wrong with me for even feeling remotely happy with Gio and his praise, but I ignore it and hold onto the sweet feelings.

He holds his hand out and waits. Knowing what he wants, I lean forward and let him cup my chin in his hand. He runs the rough pad of his thumb over my lips.

My heart beats faster. *Kiss me.*

I wait for his touch, but he doesn't move. I scoot closer to him, but still, he doesn't reward me.

"You'll have to beg me, princess, remember that."

My eyes widen and for a moment, I'm shocked. He's denying me? He has yet to do that, and for some reason it pisses me off.

I scoot back into the cage and resist the urge to pout like a petulant child. What the fuck is wrong with me?

Before I have time to think on it, he lets out a rough chuckle and clicks on the TV before leaving me alone again.

Sounds fill the room, and they're loud. So fucking loud. It's been a long time since I've heard music. I squint at the screen, not because the images are small, but because I just don't understand.

I don't recognize the people, and it's obviously a show.

It takes me a moment to understand what I'm seeing, but when I do, my hands ball into fists and anger consumes me. I stare at the door, willing him to come back.

It's fucking porn.

Chapter 17

Gio

I CAN'T HELP BUT SMILE TO MYSELF AS EXCITEMENT COURSES through my veins. I watch her staring at the television through my monitors, and her face is perfect. She's enraptured, angry, confused, and clearly aroused by what she's seeing.

The idea came to me as I was driving back from the meet with the Romanos. I needed something to speed the process along, but so far everything I've tried has either been interrupted and ruined, or failed entirely. I needed something to force her to confront her feelings for me.

I needed something to get her soaking fucking wet to the point where she simply couldn't resist any longer.

It came together pretty fast after that. I got an old TV, covered it in a plastic casing, soldered the power button down, wired a car battery to it, and streamed as much dirty fucking porn as I possibly could. I removed the volume buttons and the input buttons, so there was no way for her to turn it off or change it. She's stuck watching whatever I want her to watch.

Her eyes are wide as she watches the video. Playing on the screen, a half-naked slut in a schoolgirl outfit goes down on a thick cock. It's dirty, nasty, and the girl moans as she deep throats the guy's cock.

I'm half hard myself, imagining exactly how my princess would suck me off. Her lips are full and gorgeous, and I could see the horny slut deep inside of her begging to be let out. I know she'd take my thick cock down her throat, choke on it, gag and moan, but she'd keep working. I know my princess will work hard for me once she finally gives in.

She suddenly crawls toward the cage's entrance. She glances at the clock, and I can practically see her thought process. *You have an hour, princess,* I think to myself, smiling.

She quickly leaves the cage. I watch as she goes up to the television and begins to try and turn it off. She works the power button and tries the volume, the channels, the inputs, but nothing works. I grin, proud of myself for rigging this television. The porn continues to play.

She hits the TV out of frustration and then winces from the pain, shaking out her hand and looking at the television like it's her enemy. A rough laugh rises up my throat. She's pissed. I'm happy that she finally came out of her cage and is doing something other than sulking. Apparently, all she needed was a little hardcore porn to push her over the edge.

I lean back and watch her for a few minutes. She continues looking at the TV, trying to figure out a way to turn it off. I can tell she's considering just breaking it, but she hesitates. She's probably wondering what I would do if she broke it.

I'd just clean up the mess and bolt one to the wall. And up high enough so she couldn't reach it. I smile to myself. *Don't do it, princess. It'll only get harder for you.*

I can see the frustration on her face, but also something else. I glance at my own private feed of the porn she's watching. The girl in the uniform is getting her pussy reamed from behind. She shakes her ass, bucking her hips back against the guy, her face a mask of ecstasy. I look back at Grace and watch her reaction.

She's staring at the television. I can't really read her expression though. She's not upset or revolted by it, but she's clearly fascinated and can't look away. Slowly, she bites her bottom lip, and a smile comes to my face.

She's dripping wet right now. I can practically smell it from my room. She looks away, but I know she's thinking about how good it would feel if she let me give her the pleasure she truly craves. She's practically shaking, trembling for my touch. *Beg me, princess.* I know she will. She's going to be in need.

I stand, my cock hard, and quickly walk away from the monitors. I can't go in there yet and I know that if I keep watching, I won't be able to control myself. It's already taking everything I have to stay out of that room. I want to go in there, grab her hips, turn her, and press her against the wall.

She won't put up a fight as I pin her arms behind her back and fuck her tight, slick pussy from behind. Fuck, I can feel a bead of precum leaking from my slit. I've been dreaming of taking her. This better fucking work.

I walk into my kitchen and lean up against the counter, taking deep breaths. I clear my mind of any image of her. Duke comes into the room and I pet his head for a second, until finally the desire passes.

I open my eyes again and release a breath. That's better. I have to keep myself under control. She has a little time to herself.

I go to the table and check her medicine. She's been taking it, and I can tell that she's already feeling better. I can't be sure why she got sick in the first place, and I have to wonder if it was because of something I gave her. I hate the thought that I made her sick. I sure as fuck hope she doesn't think that.

I've tried to give her what she needs. She's a prisoner, but she's treated better than any prisoner could hope for. She has her own bathroom and tub, and can clean herself during her private hours. She has plenty of food, and sometimes she has delicious food. She has things to keep her mind occupied if she decides to leave her cage.

I shake my head, trying not to linger on this. I might have caused her illness, but I'm fixing it. I'm making it right.

I pat Duke again, then head down into my basement. The wooden boards creak under my feet, and I pull the light switch at the bottom of the stairs. The room is half finished, and there's another bank of video monitors against one wall, though smaller than the one upstairs in the control room. This is my secondary monitoring station, and it's dedicated solely to Grace's uncle.

I scroll through the feeds, skipping through the videos until I get to something interesting. Toni is surprisingly strict in his daily regimen and he never, ever gives me an opening. If he's ever out in the open, it happens late at night or at a random time during the day, and it never lasts for more than a few minutes. He's a very careful man, and I have to admit that I'm impressed.

But it makes it very, very difficult. Now that my princess is becoming mine, I need to move my plan forward. It's unlikely that I'll ever actually kill the Don, and so I need to find a weakness in Toni soon. I need to exploit that weakness and murder him.

Time passes as I watch the videos, one after the other. Nothing important appears as always. Duke curls up at my feet.

When I finally check the time, I'm startled. It's been at least two hours, which means that Grace has been alone in her room for much longer than I intended. I quickly finish up and leave the monitors to continue recording before heading upstairs, Duke at my heels.

"Stay out here," I mumble to him as I go in to check on Grace. I shut the door and pull up the video feeds.

She's lying down in her cage, staring out at the television. I glance at my feed of the porn, and it's a video of a woman riding a guy, working her hips over and over. I look back at Grace and zoom in on her.

I suck in a sharp breath when I get a closer look at her face. Her lips are parted with pleasure, her breaths coming in sharp and short. I pan down and realize that her hand is between her legs working in furious motions.

I zoom out and stare. My princess is touching herself while watching the porn. She finally couldn't take it anymore. Her legs are spread wide, and I stare at her pussy as her fingers slide in and out of herself, her head thrown back, loud moans escaping from between her lips. She's baring herself to me. She knows I'm watching.

My cock is hard as fuck, and I'm pissed. She isn't allowed to get herself off without me, no fucking way. I stand, shaking my head. There's absolutely no way I was going to let her touch herself, not without me at least. If she's going to get any pleasure, it's going to be because I say she can have it.

The dirty fucking girl. I bet she's thinking about me right now, her two fingers sliding in and out of her tight, slick cunt. I'm angry that she's daring to touch herself without me, but I'm also so fucking turned on. My cock is rock hard, straining against my jeans.

There's only one thing for me to do.

I head toward her door, intent on making her give me what I want.

Chapter 18

I'VE NEVER BEEN THIS HORNY IN MY ENTIRE LIFE. I'M NOT AN innocent. I've watched porn before. Videos just like the ones playing on the screen.

I felt perverted then. Ashamed, even. My fingers trail up and down my sides, hardening my nipples. I gently brush over them. The tingling sensation is directly attached to my throbbing clit. My head leans back against the cage.

I've been listening to moans for hours. To the slapping sounds of a man thrusting his hips against a woman's ass filling my ears. I can't tune it out. I can't unsee.

At this point, I can't even look away.

My pussy pulses with need.

I can't help myself. My head thrashes as my fingers circle my clit. I need it. I need the release. I whimper as my body heats. I need more.

I can't even breathe right. I move from my position, lying on my back and let my legs fall open, exposing myself. My inner thighs are wet from my own arousal. My breasts are perky, and I grip one with my left hand for the added sensation, squeezing roughly for a slight hint of pain. I need it.

I pinch my nipple as the woman on the screen reaches her climax. I need that, too. Please. I pull back and love the sharp sting from my own touch. My legs tremble, and I'm close. So close. My back arches, but before I can fall blissfully over the edge, I hear the faint beep and the door slams open.

My movements stop, and the heightened pleasure that overwhelms every inch of my skin dims. I almost want to cry at the loss.

The sight of Gio makes it worth it though.

He looks pissed, and I don't hold back the smile that shows on my lips. His chest rises and falls as his eyes move between my glistening pussy and my face.

I circle my clit once and moan from the sweet build of pleasure.

"Grace," he says in a low voice, making his way over to me in slow, deliberate steps. "You know better than to touch yourself."

I almost laugh at him. If he thought I'd beg him, he thought wrong. I'll stay in this fucking cage and get myself off until I'm limp and numb. Unable to move and soaked from my own cum.

I circle my clit again and the sharp sensation shoots through my legs, stiffening them and making my neck arch.

"Grace!" he yells, and the rough tone of his voice only makes me want to tease him more. To piss him off. To make him punish me.

A harsh moan is ripped from my throat at the very thought of him doing just that.

Pulling me out of the cage by my ankles and fucking me, filling me with his thick cock. *Yes!* Ruthlessly pounding into me without any mercy as I scream his name.

My legs try to close as the sensation becomes overwhelming and I whimper, shutting my eyes.

"Be a good girl for me, princess." Gio's voice is soft and full of lust.

"No," I say easily, staring into his piercing blue gaze. His eyes widen at my defiance, and I love it. I love that I can shock him and use this tactic against him.

I'll regret this later; I know I will. Faintly I'm aware of the edge of my sanity screaming at me. A part of me is furious, hating myself and him. *But it feels so good.* And I've wanted this for so long. No, I've wanted more. I've wanted him.

He crouches down low, and I meet his gaze as he stares at my body. "You're going to be in trouble if you don't stop."

His low threat brings me closer to my release, and I quicken my strokes against my clit. *Yes!* I stare at him, willing him to tell me how he'll punish me. I need him to send me over the edge. I'm so close.

I look him in the eyes and sink my fingers as deep as I can into my needy pussy. His eyes flash to my sex, and his breathing quickens. I slowly pump my fingers, curling them to stroke the bundle of nerves at my front wall and push my palm against my clit.

The sound of his belt buckle clinking as he struggles with his zipper makes me moan.

He's always shown so much control, but in this moment, he's undone. And I did this to him. My neck arches, and I have to tilt my head to keep my eyes on him as he unleashes his thick cock. My legs instinctively open wider and I rub my clit faster as he strokes his dick, his eyes darting from my pussy to my face.

"Come here, princess," he barely breathes, his chest heaving in air as his large hand moves up and down his massive length. I moan, thinking of how he'd feel inside me. How he'd stretch my walls. Would he even fit?

He'd force his way in.

The thought makes my back arch, and I strum my clit faster.

He leans forward, his free hand gripping the edge of the cage. The noise makes my body jolt, but I don't stop. He groans; anger and lust are clearly evident on his expression.

I love watching him. The sight is enough to push me close, but then he moans my name and it's my undoing.

My body writhes and my legs tremble and finally I explode, every nerve ending igniting at once. The sensation is almost too much for me to take, but now that I've fallen, I can't stop myself.

We cum together. Thick streams of his cum splash on my thigh, marking me, claiming me as his. The action only heightens the waves of pleasure rolling through my body. I try to keep my eyes on his, but my body tightens with a heated paralyzing pleasure that I can't control, and I throw my head back.

I try to breathe, but it gets caught in my lungs. Finally, I scream his name, loving the sweet tingling sensation ricocheting through my body.

My limbs sag against the blanket and he groans, forcing the last of his orgasm out. My eyes are heavy, but I look down and see the evidence.

My middle finger slides along my thigh and wipes up some of his cum.

I can't help the smile on my face as I slip my finger into my mouth and suck. My eyes are locked with his.

He tastes sweeter than I thought he would, with just a hint of saltiness. I fucking love it. So good. I wipe more of his cum off of my thigh and savor it. I feel smug that his plan backfired, and I'm still safe in my cage.

"When you finally come out of there," he says, and the anger comes back into his voice as he tucks his dick back into his jeans. It's still partially hard and I find my legs clenching with the sweet sensation of desire shooting through me as he continues, "You're getting punished for this, princess."

It takes a moment to register what he's saying. Instead of fearing the implications, I'm curious. I want to know. Is he going to spank me? Fuck me rough? My eyes roll back in my head and I relax on the blanket, wondering what he's going to do to me.

I hear the door close, and the soft beep… and then the moans of the television. I weakly turn my head and then let anger rise inside of me, groaning with frustration.

He left the fucking TV on.

Chapter 19

Gio

MY BLOOD RINGS WITH DESIRE FOR HER AS I COLLAPSE INTO one of my kitchen chairs. I can't think or concentrate on anything, and I'm not even sure how I ended up in the kitchen.

I can't get the image of her cumming out of my mind. Her perfect body, her full lips, her moans fill me with such intense desire. Though I didn't touch her, it was still the sexiest thing I'd ever been involved with.

The tension between us was incredible. As I stroked my cock and she watched, fucking her own pussy, I knew that she was mine. I can still feel the post-orgasm bliss as I sit here, slowly coming back to myself.

Grace is a dirty fucking girl, and now I'm sure of it. She's a fucking freak, and I'm going to bring the slut out of her. That was a good start, but there's so much more work to be done.

I'm going to make her my fuck slave. Once she gets a taste of my thick cock buried deep inside that greedy little pussy, she'll know she's mine. There won't be any other way. Once I make her back arch, her muscles clench, and her nipples hard, she'll be begging for more and more and more.

And I'll give it to her. I'll be good to her. *I'll give her everything.*

I finally get my shit together and stand. I glance at the clock and begin to prepare her dinner. I decide to make her something special, so I drink some whisky as I cook.

Duke comes into the room and watches me, head cocked, tail wagging.

"We're close, boy," I say to him, tossing him some scraps. He catches them, tail wagging. "She's driving me insane. That dirty fucking girl. She pretends to be all broken and innocent, but now I know better. Now I know what she's really like."

I go back to cooking, shaking my head. Listen to me, talking to my fucking dog. I must be really losing it over this girl. Duke eventually leaves the kitchen, heading back to lounge on his bed while I put the final touches on her meal.

A beautifully seared steak sits on top of buttery, garlicky mashed potatoes. French-style green beans sit to the side; French-style basically just means they were cooked in a shitload of butter. The delicious smell rises up to me, and I know she won't be able to resist this.

It's been two hours since I was last in there, and my cock is already stirring at the thought of going into her room. Watching her touch herself—that was just the start.

I'm going to get more, and soon.

The door clicks open, and I step into her room. I glance around at the space, smiling to myself at all of the luxuries I've provided her with. My gaze ends up on Grace hiding in her cage, the porn still playing in the background.

"Hello, princess," I say to her.

"Are you here to punish me?" she asks with a slight smile. She's breathing heavy and lying on her back in the cage. I can't tell if she's mocking me or not. It gets me hard either way.

"Not yet," I say, and place the tray down on the table. I know she can smell the delicious food.

I stand in front of the entrance to her cage. She stares back at me, not moving. The blanket covers most of her body, leaving her shoulders and her legs exposed. I stare at her skin and remember how she looks with her fingers pressed deep inside of her pussy. I know she's soaking wet and tight, and I know she's yearning for it as much as I am.

She's gorgeous, so fucking gorgeous, and she needs to be fucked. She needs my thick cock to teach her what she really wants.

"You look hungry," I say to her.

She glances at the empty table with her forehead pinched in confusion, then looks back to me. "No. I'm okay."

"I'm not talking about food." I kneel down in front of the entrance to her cage.

She watches me, curious. "What do you think I'm hungry for?" Her voice is breathless, and her eyes clouded in lust.

"I think your body is hungry for my touch," I say. "You sit inside that cage day in and day out imagining what I'd do to you if you finally came out, don't you?"

"No," she says, but she doesn't look away. Her blanket slides down ever so slightly, revealing the tops of her breasts.

"You're thinking about it right now. What would happen if you let me touch you?"

"Nothing good," she whispers.

"No," I say, smirking at her. "It won't be good at all. It will be very, very bad, princess. And right now, your body craves bad. Doesn't it?"

"I don't know," she admits in a small whimper, and that sends a thrill through me.

"I know," I say staring at her intensely. "You're aching for it. Right now you want to throw off that blanket and crawl over here. Go ahead, princess. Crawl over to me."

She watches me silently for a second, then obeys. She slowly gets on all fours. The blanket drapes loosely over her back, but I can see her perfect breasts, the incredible line of her flank down to her beautiful hips, and I'm hard as a fucking rock.

"What will you do if I come over there?" she asks.

"I'm going to give you what you want. We both know I can, princess. We both know I can make you feel things you've only dreamed about. You don't have to be in a prison with me. Submit, give in, and I'll make you feel free."

She stares at me, biting her bottom lip, and crawls toward me. I stay still, watching her. She stops near the entrance to the cage. I could easily reach out and touch her, but that would break my promise. She's still behind the entrance, and safe.

"What happens if I do that?" she asks.

"You know it won't hurt," I say in a low voice. "And if it does, you know you'll want that hurt. You want it because it'll make the pleasure that much sweeter. Let me make you feel it."

"How?" she asks.

My heart begins to hammer hard in my chest. This is the moment I've been waiting for.

"Turn around," I command.

She hesitates, and I wonder if she'll obey. I'm left dangling there for a moment, hanging on her every move, until she slowly turns around.

"Lift the blanket up," I order.

She does it. She lifts the blanket up over her hips, revealing her perfect ass and her slick, dripping pussy. Fuck, she's so gorgeous. I unbutton my jeans and slide my hard cock from my briefs, slowly stroking it.

"Come closer."

She takes a sharp breath. "I'm afraid," she admits.

"Don't be. You know you can trust me. Let me make you feel good, princess." My voice is husky and low with desire.

She slowly backs toward me. Slowly, agonizingly slowly, she lets her ass cross over the threshold, but then she stops.

I can barely hear over the pounding in my chest. I reach out and softly caress her round little ass. I want to slap it and make her moan, but not yet. I need to start with pleasure before I give her pain. I slide my fingers down her skin until I feel her tight, wet pussy.

Fucking hell, she's so turned on. I hold back a groan and the need to slam my dick deep into her cunt. She's absolutely soaked. "You dirty girl," I whisper as I slowly slide my thick fingers inside of her. She groans, looking over her shoulder and lowering her upper body to the floor of the cage. "You're dripping for me. You can't deny it anymore, princess. You want me."

"I don't know," she moans. "I don't know what I want."

"I do." I press my fingers deep inside of her tight little cunt, marveling at its slickness. She's so fucking pretty, pink and perfect.

"Fuck," she groans. "More."

"Don't tease me, princess. Come closer."

She inches closer. I grab her hip with my other hand as I tease her pussy with my fingers, sliding in and out, moving up to tease her clit before finger fucking her again.

Grace tips her head back, her moans getting deeper, more insistent.

I can read her body as her pussy gets wetter, and her moans get louder. I know what she wants. I know what she needs.

"Gio," she groans. "Oh God, Gio. That feels so good."

"You never really knew how good I can make you feel, did you? Now you know. Now you're going to beg me for more, aren't you?"

"Yes," she gasps as I press my fingers deep inside of her, curling them to find her G-spot, sliding in and out. The sounds fuel me to give her more. "Oh God, yes."

"What do you want, princess? Say it."

"I want more," she moans. "I want so much more."

"You greedy fucking girl." I grin, loving this. My cock is practically twitching, yearning to get inside of her. It's almost time. "Is that what I've made you? Just a greedy slut?"

"No," she moans. "I'm not greedy."

"But you are a slut for me. We both know that now."

"Yes, fuck," she moans. "I'm whatever you want, Gio."

"That's right. That's what I want to hear." I slide my fingers out of her, making her whine and glare at me. "Come closer," I say.

She slides a bit farther out of the cage. Half of her is outside. I spread her legs wide and gently caress her soaked pussy with the tip of my cock, teasing her, loving the way it makes her squirm.

"Gio, please," she says, and so I press myself deep inside of her.

"Oh shit," she gasps, tossing her head back. Her arms stretch out in front of her, and her fingers claw at the blanket.

"Fuck," I grunt. Her pussy grips me like a fucking vise as I press myself deep inside of her. I slide into her so easily. Her pussy is aching for me, so fucking wet for me.

"Gio," she moans as I slide back out and in, fucking her slowly at first.

"That's right," I say. "Take this fucking cock. This is what you're meant to do."

"Yes," she moans. I grab her hips and fuck her deeper, a little bit faster. I reach around her hip and find her clit, carefully teasing her sensitive spot.

"Oh God," she moans, her voice louder and lower, losing control. She tries to buck me off, trying to get away, but pushes herself back onto my cock not a second later, her legs trembling with need.

"That's right," I say, moving slightly back. She follows me, slowly moving out of the cage. "You're my dirty princess now. Ride back against this fucking cock, girl. Don't be a greedy slut."

She moans and starts to work her hips in time with mine. She bucks back, sliding back and back, riding hard against my cock. I grunt, pleasure threatening to overwhelm my mind.

I grab her hip with my left hand and spank her ass with my right. She groans, but it only makes her work harder and faster. I can tell she loves it. I know she's starting to realize that a little pain makes the pleasure sweeter. I slap her again and again, leaving light red handprints on her ass, but it only spurs her on. *Smack!* The sound fills the room, making my breathing come in short pants.

She rides back against me harder, her whole body shaking, her hair spilling down over her shoulders. We're moving backward as our pace increases, rutting and fucking there at the entrance to the cage.

Soon, only her head is still inside of the cage. I reach forward and tease her breasts, pinching her nipples as I rail into her. Pounding that sweet little pussy of hers and giving her every reason to love what I'm doing to her. We inch back, fucking deeper and harder, until finally, finally, she's completely out of the cage.

That sends me into a fucking frenzy.

"Fuck, Gio," she practically screams. "Yes, Gio, fuck me. Fuck me. Make me feel more." I give her what she wants, slamming into her, losing myself in the rough fucking.

I reach forward and grab her throat and pull her back against me. She gasps as she realizes where we are in the room.

"You're mine now, princess," I say into her ear, my cock buried inside of her.

She moans and writhes against me as I pick her up, one hand on her throat, my cock still buried deep inside of her, and carry her to the bed.

Chapter 20

MY PUSSY IS STILL SPASMING ON HIS THICK COCK AS MY HANDS dig at his fingers, trying to pry them away. Fear, bliss, and lust are all mixed within me and make my heart race.

He's not holding my throat too tight. It's just instinct making me try to push his hand away. He lifts me from the cage, and my heart beats faster as I weakly struggle against him.

I'm practically impaled on his dick with one of his arms braced against my front and between my breasts, his hand squeezing my throat, and his other hand gripping my hip.

I struggle to breathe as waves of a dim release threaten to consume me. *It's coming.* I try to writhe against him, both to get away but also to feel more. I need more.

He lays me on the bed and spreads my legs so he's straddling one thigh, his hand still firm on my throat and he squeezes tighter.

For a moment, only a fraction of a moment, my heart freezes with fear, a distant memory breaking through the pleasure. My mother. Her death. His fingers dig into my throat and I kick as hard as I can, uselessly. This is different. I try to separate the two, I try not to be afraid. But I am. I'm so fucking terrified.

Small white circles dance in my vision as he pounds into my pussy, thrusting deeper and harder, relentlessly taking from me. The moment of fear and conscious recollection passes, and waves of pleasure consume me.

My mouth opens with a silent scream as I cum violently. His grip on my throat loosens and he lets go as the ecstasy rocks through my body. He rides through my orgasm, viciously fucking me and making the intensity of my release that much higher. I feel lost in bliss, unable to do anything but claw at the sheets.

He thrusts into me without mercy as I scream with pleasure. Wanting more, but trying desperately to get away. My body is propped up, and I'm trying to just hold on. And then his fingers strum my throbbing clit, and I can't take any more. My lungs still, my body goes stiff and every nerve ending explodes with a fire I've never felt before.

He groans my name and his thick cock pulses inside of me, his hot cum filling me and leaking between us. It's only then that I can breathe, with his lips barely touching my neck as he pumps short shallow strokes, prolonging his release and sending shivers down my body.

He presses his lips to my neck and I breathe easy, a feeling of longing overwhelming me as I hold him closer. But as quickly as it came, it's gone. He pulls out and moves off the bed, leaving the chill of the room to creep closer to me. I watch his back as he walks to the bathroom, and the reality of what's happened slams against my chest.

My breathing comes in frantic pants, and my eyes go wide. I'm not safe. I don't waste a moment. I don't listen to what he's doing; I don't even try looking for him. I climb off the bed and run to the cage, not stopping until I'm in the very back corner and covered by my blanket. His cum leaks down my leg, and my heart squeezes in my chest.

What have I done? What's wrong with me?

I don't know what's worse, the fact that I enjoyed what happened or that I didn't even realize what I'd done until he left me.

He holds a spell over me, his very presence a trance. I can't escape it. He's like a drug, and I've grown addicted.

I watch as he walks back into the room, stopping only two steps from the bathroom. His brow furrows as he looks from the bed to the cage.

And then his eyes flash with something else. Something I've truly never seen from him.

Anger.

He looks fucking pissed. His hands ball into white-knuckled fists. His eyes narrow as he locks onto my gaze, forcing me to maintain eye contact and he stomps over to the cage.

I try to scoot back farther, away from him and his rage, but I can't. I'm cornered.

But I'm safe.

My heart beats faster.

He won't come in here. I'm safe here.

But I'm not.

He doesn't hesitate to bend down, walk straight into the cage and grab me by my ankle. He yanks me toward him, and I yell.

My fingers try to grip onto the bars, but they slip as he pulls me into his chest.

I scream and try to kick away.

No! He lied! He lied to me! My heart tries to climb out of my throat as fear consumes me.

"Stop fighting me, princess," he says quietly and his voice is gravelly low.

My blood runs cold, and I still in his arms from fear of what he's going to do. I knew it was too good to be true. I'm not safe. I never was.

He brings me to the bed, and I wait for his fury to be unleashed. My body sinks into the mattress, and I keep my eyes closed.

But nothing happens. I pull the blanket tighter around me, as if it can protect me. It never has before, but I have nothing else. There's nothing left.

After a moment passes with the only sound being his heavy breathing, I open my eyes.

The bed dips and groans as he sits on the bed, his back to me.

I don't understand.

"You won't ever do that again." Gio's voice is hard, unforgiving. And I cower behind him. "Do you understand? I'll take your cage away if you dare leave me like that." He finally turns to face me, and I can see the hurt in his eyes. "You will let me give you aftercare, do you understand that?"

My heart's racing, and I feel so confused. He leans down and kisses me. His tender touch is so unexpected. My heart swells, and tears leak down my cheek.

I don't understand it.

He pulls away with his eyes still closed and says, "You don't leave me after something like that. Not until I say you can." He opens his eyes. "You need to be comforted. Do you understand?"

"Yes," I answer weakly.

His eyes roam over my face, searching for something. "Are you okay?" His voice is so soft, so calm. It's a side of him I haven't seen.

I nod my head, but my fingers slowly rise to my throat.

An asymmetric grin pulls his lips up. "Did you like that?" he asks, his fingers touching mine and then sliding down my throat.

I can't lie. I didn't. I shake my head slightly, and concern is written all over his expression.

"Please don't," I shut my eyes and I can't continue.

"Shh," he leans forward and kisses my jaw and then down my neck and collarbone.

"I thought you enjoyed it… You didn't…" He clears his throat and looks away. "You didn't want any of it?" he asks.

"No!" I'm quick to correct him. "Just the choking."

He looks back to me and considers my words. I can tell he wants to ask.

"I watched my dad kill my mother," I say softly. I hold his gaze as it softens.

"My princess," he whispers, lying next to me and pulling me into his hard body. It's not until my cheek is against his bare chest that I realize I'm crying. I never cry. "Never again, I promise you."

"And I won't leave you." I say the words so quickly, and for a moment I misunderstand myself. Or maybe I meant it to be literal, I don't know.

He holds me until I've stopped crying and then kisses my hair, whispering, "I need to clean you up." He leaves my side and turns back to give me a look of warning. But I don't want to run. I want to stay. I don't want to hide from him.

I feel vulnerable and raw, and the way he holds me makes it seem as though that's just right. It's the way it's supposed to be.

When he walks back into the room, he seems different. I'm not sure why, but everything now is so different.

My thighs tremble slightly as he slides the warm cloth between my legs. I'm still on edge from hours of stimulation. He gentles his hand on my thigh and moves me to lay on the bed on my side. I curl up as he lays the blanket on top of me, tucking me in and moving behind me, his chest to my back.

He feels so warm, so strong. And his smell is so comforting. I fill my lungs with his masculine scent. It relaxes me. The tiredness of the day settles against me, lulling me to sleep in his strong embrace.

"I was supposed to punish you, princess," he murmurs and kisses my neck.

"Next time you touch yourself without my permission, you'll be punished. Is that understood?" His voice is hard, but he's holding me with such tenderness that the threat falls flat. Besides, I don't want to touch myself without him. I want him to take me like that again and again.

I want more.

"Yes." He holds me closer, and my heart beats frantically.

I'm vaguely aware that this is wrong and that I need to use this new development to my advantage, but the voice is so weak, drowned out by the steady beat of his heart, that it's easy to ignore. If only just for this moment.

Chapter 21

I POUR MYSELF A DOUBLE WHISKY ON THE ROCKS AND COLLAPSE INTO my couch in the living room. Duke comes over and curls up at my feet. I scratch his head as I sip the whisky, staring at the blank TV, my mind wandering over what just happened.

I've needed a strong drink since the second I first saw her. I needed to feel her tight pussy, to hear her scream my name, to know that I was making her feel intense and unbridled pleasure. Finally, I got what I needed, and my blood's practically ringing with incredible contentment. But I got more than I bargained for.

I regret going into her cage. I wish I hadn't done that. I promised her it would be her safe space, and I worked so hard to keep it that way. I just couldn't allow her to go back into her shell, not before I properly took care of her. She needed to be caressed, cleaned, worshipped. She needed to be shown how I feel about her.

Maybe I shouldn't have gone into the cage. I could see the fear in her eyes, and I hated that. But afterward, it was worth it. She let me take care of her, stroke her hair, whisper in her ear. Finally, when she was relaxed, I left her dozing on the bed.

She's dangerous; she makes me want to take her to my bed. To let her out. To share more with her. And that can't happen.

She's so fucking gorgeous. I can still feel her tight cunt wrapped around my cock. I can't get enough of her lips, her skin, her moans. It's all so fucking intoxicating. I know I have another job to do, but the idea of going out and killing again when I have my princess to train seems insane to me.

Now I'm faced with a new issue. I need to start that training, but I'm not exactly sure how to go about it. I've never actually turned someone into a sex slave before, and I still don't want to do that to Grace. She's my princess, not my slave, and I want to be the only one to have her.

I clutch my glass, the ice clinking against it as I feel my darkness rising up again. Lately it's been so quiet, probably because I was so content with Grace. But now that I'm faced with the prospect of killing her father and turning her into a slave, I can feel that darkness rising.

I want to make her mine. I want to dominate her. And I want to slit her father's throat for every bit of pain he's shown her. He fucking deserves it. The darkness wants all that, too, but for a different reason. The darkness in me wants it because it wants to destroy everything in its path. I want those things because I care deeply for Grace, much more deeply than I ever imagined.

My two halves are still warring, but I know which one is winning. I know my humanity is still there, and it feels stronger every day. There are moments, just like this one, where my darkness rears its revolting head, but I can get past it.

I will get past it. For Grace. *For my princess.*

I take a long sip and scratch behind Duke's ear. He looks up at me, head cocked, mouth slightly open.

"You want Grace to stay, don't you boy?" I ask him.

He pants a bit. I smile at him.

"Of course you do."

I stand up and knock back the rest of my whisky. As I head into the kitchen to get some more, I hear my phone buzzing back on the couch.

Annoyed, I head back and grab it. I don't recognize the number, but it's a local area code. I decide to answer it, though I don't usually take calls from strangers.

"Hello?" I say into the phone.

"Gio." I cock my head to one side. I vaguely recognize the voice.

"Who's this?" I ask.

"Where do you live?"

I narrow my eyes. "Who is this?" I ask again in a hardened voice.

"Where are you staying? Do you think it would be hard to cut off your fingers?"

My blood runs cold. The more he talks, the more I'm sure I know the voice.

"Listen, asshole," I say softly. "I wouldn't threaten me if I were you."

"We know all about it. What time's it going down, do you think? We're always watching you, Gio."

"Alessandro," I say. "That's you, isn't it?"

The voice pauses. "Soon, Gio. We're coming for you soon."

"Listen to me, you Rossi fuck—"

But he hangs up before I can finish.

I stare at my phone, not sure what the fuck to make of that conversation. My heart's pounding against my ribcage, and my anger starts taking over.

I can't be sure, but I thought the person was Alessandro, one of the Rossi cousins. I met him a couple times and he was just another one of their low-level scumbags, not someone I would ever worry about.

But that call is disconcerting. The mention of my fingerprints makes me think that he knows about my door, and my heart clenches at the thought. She's mine. No one else has a reason to go near her.

They didn't protect her from her father.

They can't have her back. I won't allow it.

I pace the living room, analyzing every second of the phone call. I need to be smart. I need to stay one step ahead.

I stop in my tracks, realizing they must know about the hit. Which means there's a rat. A rat with a big fucking mouth, ready to start a war. I have no clue how that's possible, since nobody that knows about it has any reason to tell the Rossis. The fact remains that the call happened, and it did not bode well.

I toss my phone aside and walk into the kitchen. I fill up my whisky again and as I head back into the living room, an uncomfortable thought strikes me.

Was my father so far gone that he would sell me out to the Rossis?

I stand completely still as my mind races through the possibilities. I know that the Rossis would love to have me, even before all this shit with Grace and killing Toni and their Don happened. I've killed Rossis before, and I'd probably do it again.

But no, no, that couldn't be it. My father wouldn't do that. He's an old man in a business that's not kind to old men and he's desperate to be relevant again, but he's not a fucking traitor. He's family. *We're* family. And that's an impossibility. Besides, he wants to be a part of the Romano *familia* so badly. Making a deal and selling me to the Rossis would destroy his chances at joining the Romanos. Even he would have to see that.

I'm just being paranoid. I walk over to the couch and sit back down again. This time, I flip on the TV and stare blankly at the football game, not really paying attention. Duke sits by my feet as I sip my drink, my mind roaming over the possibilities.

I can't shake my suspicion. I want to, but I can't help it. I keep imagining my father making a deal and selling me out, no matter how implausible.

"Fuck," I say and stand up. I finish my drink and feel the alcohol loosen my nerves. "I'm being stupid," I say to myself and walk into the kitchen. I put my glass in the sink then head into my control room to check on Grace.

I have to put the call out of my mind. It was meant to get to me. I need to be better than that. Better than this.

I can't worry about it just now. My father wouldn't betray me. I know he's close on a plan to finish the Don once and for all. He's come through countless times, and I know he'll come through now. I saw parts of the plan, and from what I can tell, it's solid. I wouldn't go with him on the hit if it didn't look like a serious plan.

The call was probably just some bullshit prank that the Rossis decided to test me with. I have to concentrate on Grace now that we're doing so well.

I sit at the monitors and watch her, slowly forgetting about everything else.

Chapter 22

I DON'T KNOW WHY I CAME TO THE CAGE. BUT NOW THAT I'M HERE, I can't leave. I slept so well on the bed. It was a deep sleep, full of comfort. But he was gone when I woke up. The sheets beside me were cold to the touch. And it left me feeling like I'd been cheated. I don't know what's wrong with me to think there's more to what this is.

Yesterday ruined me. It destroyed my armor. I don't recognize the woman I am.

I've sat here all day, feeling hurt and abandoned. As if I have a right to feel those things. What did I expect? I'm nothing to him. I'm no one. A piece of property that he was gifted.

My jaw clenches and I refuse to feel any more for him, but the second I hear the thudding of his boots in the hall, I take notice. My body turns to the door, and I wait for him. I'm eager for him. I hate it, but I won't lie to myself. As much I detest this side of me, I find comfort there. I even *enjoy* it.

At least I'm in the cage. My lips threaten to curl into a smirk, but I resist. If he wants to leave me, then I can leave him, too.

The door beeps, one of my favorite sounds now, and Gio takes two steps into the room. I watch his eyes as they move from the bed to the cage. Anger isn't present, not like it was last night, but there's something there. Or rather, something's missing. That spark and fire, the heat in his eyes. Something's different, and it throws me off balance.

"Grace," he greets me, walking to the large chair by the table. He sets the tray in his hands down and looks back at me, sagging into the seat. He leans back and waits.

I want to crawl to him. I want to put my head in his lap and comfort him.

I know something is wrong. I just don't know what.

My heart stills as I wait. Both of us are staring at each other, but neither of us are willing to act.

Finally, he moves forward, resting his elbows on his knees and resting his chin in his hand. "Come to me," he says softly. My body obeys before I give my conscious consent. I move forward on all fours.

I crawl to him, partly because I want to and partly because I know this is one step closer to my freedom.

Yes. I cling to that reason. I convince myself that if I'm a good girl, he'll let me go. I've gotten good at lying to myself over the years.

I'm not obeying because I want to submit to him, I want to please him. That's not why.

I'm not hurting for him because something's wrong. I don't feel for him. That's not what this pain in my chest is.

I can tell myself lies all day and night, but the moment I reach him, kneeling on the concrete before him, and he leans down, cupping my cheek in his hand and pressing his lips to mine, my heart swells.

I arch my back and moan into his mouth, my fingers spearing into his hair and pulling him closer to me.

Gio.

He breaks our kiss and sits back in his seat, his eyes never leaving mine. I stay kneeling on the floor, eyes wide and waiting for him. For whatever he wants from me.

"Do you think you can obey me?" he asks.

My eyes narrow, and for a moment I don't respond. But I swallow my hesitation and nod my consent. He won't hurt me. I trust him.

He rises and walks over to my cage. He looks back at me as he grabs the door that's been pressed against the side of the cage this entire time and swings it shut. Closing my cage, with me on the outside. The loud clicking sound ricochets in my head with disbelief.

My heart pounds with anxiety. I back away slowly on my ass until my back hits the wall.

Fear threatens to creep up on me, but Gio doesn't move.

He raises his hands in the air, and talks in low tones, as if he's approaching a wounded animal. And maybe that's just what I am.

"It's alright, princess. I just need you to know there will be consequences."

I feel like I can't breathe.

"You said you wouldn't take it away." I can barely get the words out. They're forced.

"I won't," he says softly, "it's just one hour." Instinctively, I turn toward the clock. One hour.

"Do you trust me, princess?" he asks.

My chest rises and falls with heavy breaths.

It takes a moment, but I can admit it. I do. I trust him.

"Yes," I whisper in a shaky voice.

"Come here." I start to stand, but he adds, "I want you to crawl."

I debate on whether or not I want to. Not because there are consequences, but because I don't want to obey. At least for that moment I don't, but I remember the look in his eyes when he came in here, and I move to him. I crawl, wondering if this will ease whatever troubles he has.

I want to ask him. But I don't know if he'll answer. As I sit on the floor next to him he reaches down and moves my legs so that I'm kneeling. He backs away, appraising me. It pisses me off.

"When you come to me, you'll sit like this." I look down at my body, and then back up to him. The cage is to my left, and it's closed. I bite my tongue. If it were open, it would be a different story. For a moment I consider how he'd punish me. What he'd do.

Would it be worth it to disobey?

"Now lie back and grab your knees so I can see you." He walks a few feet away and turns to face me, arms crossed, waiting for me to obey.

Yeah, it's fucking worth it.

"No." My voice is strong, and Gio immediately reaches for me. His hand is out like he's going to grab my throat and I shrink back, fear crippling the strength I have.

But he doesn't grab my throat at all. He picks me up by the waist and quickly walks to the bed, throwing me over his lap.

I don't even have time to react as he throws one of his legs over mine and immediately slaps a hand down on my ass. *Smack!*

My back arches as I scream out from the blistering pain, but he holds my shoulders down, forcing my upper body into the bed and continues the blows.

Again and again he spanks me. Each time in a slightly different spot, and they burn with pain. It radiates from my ass outward. Fuck, it hurts! My brows pinch, and I try to get away. But I can't.

Finally, it's over, but the cold air only makes it hurt worse. I try to move away, but he keeps me still.

Gio massages my sore ass and says in a low voice, "Stop running from it."

I wince from the pain and wriggle away, but he only holds me tighter.

"You want this," he says, moving his hand to my pussy. He shoves his thick fingers inside of me without hesitation and my body bucks in response, but he pumps them in and out, stroking my front wall and sending a heated bolt of desire through my body.

He pulls them away before I can climb toward my release, leaving me wanting. I'm surprised at how wet I am and how easily he pressed his fingers inside of me.

Bastard!

"Suck," he says, putting his fingers in front of my face. I could do it, and a part of me wants to. I want to get lost in this moment. My breathing comes in frantic. *I just need to obey.*

"Do it, princess. Don't overthink this." He leans down, whispering in my ear. "What we have is perfect. Enjoy this with me."

His words are my undoing. Just the acknowledgment that something is here between us makes me shed the last of my inhibitions. I take his fingers into my mouth and lick them clean, tasting my arousal. I moan while sucking on his fingers.

"Good girl," he says, kneading my ass. I wince from the sudden pain, and he chuckles.

"Now," he moves from the bed, leaving me alone on top of the sheets. "Get on your back and pull your knees up."

My heart slows, and I swallow my pride.

Is it wrong to give in when I want it? I shift on the bed, and a hint of pain from the spanking makes me suck in a sharp breath.

"On your back, princess." He waits while I make my decision and finally lie on my back for him.

I grab under my knees and lift them so he can see all of me. I watch his eyes heat, and it erases any trace of shame I have. He *wants* me.

I hide my smirk as he falls to his knees by the bed, so he's eye level with my pussy. He takes a languid lick and I moan, leaning slightly to the left.

His hand comes down hard on my inner thigh with a loud *smack!*

My body jolts and I quickly move away from him, but he drags me back to the same spot, holding me down.

"Don't move," he warns me. His eyes pierce into mine, daring me to talk back, daring me to move, but I obey.

Partly because of the shock.

He waits until I'm in the same position and then runs his finger down my pussy and up to my throbbing clit, circling it once. The pleasure makes me want to move, but I stay still.

"You're so perfect, princess," he says moving away from me and leaving me on edge. He takes a step back and looks me over appraisingly. My cheeks heat, and I feel a small sense of anxiety now that the heated look is gone from his eyes.

"Kneel," he says and I quickly move and sit in the position he wants. His large hand wraps around my thigh and moves my legs slightly apart.

"Like this." His hard voice forces my eyes to his. "Remember that." I hold his gaze and nod once.

"I want to train you," he says softly. "Would you like that?"

I speak before I can think, "Yes." My eyes widen at my confession.

"Good," he says with a small smile, and the look he had when he first came in shows itself again as he sits on the bed next to me.

I start to move, but then stop myself. I need to be still.

He chuckles and places his large hand on my thigh. "Training is over for today, princess." There's a sadness in his voice, and I don't like it. "Tomorrow we'll start again. Not today."

I slowly move, not understanding Gio's motivation. Something's changed between us, but more than that, something's wrong. I know it in the core of my very being.

"Are you alright?" I ask him. I can't help it. I don't like that something's bothering him.

He tilts his head and considers my words before nodding once. "Everything will be fine."

"What's wrong?" The only thing I gathered from that response is that something is not fine. And I want to know what.

He runs a hand down his face and then pulls me into his lap. I love the feel of being this close to him. I find myself melting into him. The comfort is something I've never had before, and I don't want to lose it.

"I'm supposed to do something that I don't want to do," he finally says.

"Don't do it then," I say simply.

He outright laughs at my response, leaning against the wall and pinching the bridge of his nose. "If only it was that easy, my princess."

I lean against him and listen to the steady sound of his heart.

The memory of everything that's happened flashes in front of me as I stare at the cage on the other side of the room. I look at the clock, and the hour is up.

I don't want to tell him though. I'm not ready to go back. *But I don't have to, do I?*

I frown, realizing my initial thought was that I should be in there. *In a cage.* I shouldn't be. I shouldn't even be in this fucking room.

I look up at Gio and wonder what he's thinking. I wonder what his plans are for me, but I can't ask. All the time I've been here, I've never asked. I know I'm a gift. I know he wants me.

Maybe this thing between us is real. Maybe he feels what I feel. I'll never know if I don't ask. But my blood runs cold. What if it's not the same for him? What if I'm mistaken?

"Gio," I gather the courage to ask, my breathing quickening with the fear of what his answer will be. "I don't want to stay in this room anymore." I can't look at him as I ask. But the lack of an immediate answer makes my eyes rise to his piercing blue gaze.

He watches me for a moment, and my heart clenches. Something's wrong with me to think that he'd care what I want. But I did. I thought… I don't know what I was thinking. Just before I move to pull away from him and search for the woman I used to be, he pulls me closer into his chest.

"This won't be forever, princess." He whispers his words. I don't resist, but there are so many unanswered questions, so much more that I need to know.

"If I'm good—" I start to ask, but he presses a finger to my lips, silencing me.

"You're perfect. And I promise," his eyes pierce so far into me, I'm mesmerized by his gaze. "Soon, everything will be different. I promise you."

His words are vague, but I trust him. I lean into his touch and press my lips against his. This is all I need right now.

Emotions overwhelm me, my body heating with a mix of anxiety and something more, something that's sinful and dangerous. Something vulnerable and raw.

Gio breaks our kiss, and I feel lightheaded and breathless.

"Come sit on your throne, princess," he groans, lifting me as though I weigh nothing and spreading my thighs apart as he lies on the bed and lowers my pussy onto his face.

His tongue laps at my sex as I grip onto his hair and nearly collapse forward from the sudden intense pleasure.

He doesn't let up. Licking and sucking and making my body shudder in utter pleasure, he's relentless.

I throw my head back and moan his name, "Gio."

He groans into my pussy and sucks at my clit, forcing a scream from my throat. *Yes!* I grind my cunt into his face, wanting more and being so close, so soon.

"Cum for me, princess," he whispers, lifting me off of him before spearing his tongue into my opening.

All form of common sense and survival leave me.

He's broken me down and made me something I never thought I'd be. I'm a slave to our desires.

I am only his.

Chapter 23

Gio

Thε night of the hit comes sooner than I thought it would.

Each day, I go to Grace and I train her. It goes slowly at first, but soon she warms up to the task. In fact, I can tell that she's enjoying it. She went from being afraid of leaving her cage to being out of it all the time. Sometimes she wears the clothes I give her, but more often than not she stays naked. I catch her drawing, reading, bathing, and she doesn't run like she used to.

She's finally submitted to me. My princess finally sees that it's better to give in than it is to fight.

Because I take care of her. I cater to her every need. It's true that she's still stuck in the room even though she doesn't want to be in there, but it's not much of a prison. She has everything she could possibly need.

And then some. At night when she's lonely, I can hear her softly begging my name. I love the sounds of her wanting me. I'll come to her then, in the middle of the dark long night, and I'll give her everything she needs. She arches her back under my touch as my lips graze her neck. I whisper in her ear, make her beg for my thick cock.

She wants her freedom. I understand that. She spent her whole life locked away and abused by her bastard father. My princess is tired of being locked away in a cage.

I told her it won't be forever, and I meant it. With each passing day, I try and figure out the best way to give her freedom. I need to find a way to keep her, to take her away from the Romano bastards. I need to convince my father to intercede on my behalf with the Romanos. I want her, and I'll have her. I don't want war over it. But if it comes to that… That's what it will have to be. A war. I'm not letting her go.

That's on my mind as I meet my father in a deserted parking lot on the edge of town. We're both wearing our usual hit clothing, black trousers with plenty of pockets filled with ammo and black turtlenecks. I have my rifle slung over my shoulder and he's strapped with two pistols and a shotgun. He grins at me as I climb out of my car.

"You ready for this, son?"

"Of course," I say. He laughs, clearly excited the way he always is on the eve of a hit.

I have to admit that I'm excited, too. I can feel my darkness roiling inside of my mind, begging to be released. It needs to be fed the blood and begging of my enemies. I know I'll be feeding it soon. The excitement I feel is almost too much. And it's her father. He's caused her so much pain. Of all the men to wind up on my hit list, this one is personal.

"Let's go over the plan one more time," my father says, leading me over to his truck. He spreads a map of the city out on the hood and I stand over his shoulder, watching.

"The Don has a poker game every Wednesday night," he says. "It's here, on the South Side in some shit rundown deli. He thinks nobody knows about it, but I've been staking him out." I follow my father's finger as he points to the various locations.

"Okay, so he plays poker. He's guarded though." I know he is. Every video feed shows at least three men with him. Men who could turn on me the second the first bullet flies out. I don't care for shootouts. I prefer a clean hit.

"Right," he confirms. "That's where I come in. I'm going to set their cars on fire, here," he says, pointing. "Once ablaze, they'll come out. That's when you shoot him from here." He points to another spot.

"What's that?"

"It's a building across the street. Abandoned, the perfect spot."

I nod, my face tight. It seems like a decent plan, though I don't like the uncertainty around the distraction. Still, this sort of thing has worked in the past, and I know I won't miss the shot.

"Before we do this, I want something," I say.

He leans back against his truck, raising an eyebrow. "What do you want?"

"The girl," I say.

He pauses, surprised. "You want that mafia bitch?"

"Yes." I don't like that he called her a bitch, but I let that slide. For now, at least. Until I have her, and she's safe.

"What the fuck for?"

"She's mine. I've grown… attached."

"Shit," he says, laughing. "You got pussy whipped."

I have to keep myself under control. I need his help in convincing the Romanos to let me keep her.

"She's not a good sex slave," I say. "The Romanos won't like her."

"You did it wrong, then."

"I didn't," I say fiercely. "She's just stronger than you realize."

He watches me for a moment, then sighs. "You really want her? You can have her."

I blink, surprised. I didn't think he'd give in so easily.

"Okay," I say. "You'll help me convince the Romanos?" It was his idea to begin with, and I have faith in my father. He can convince them. I know he can.

"They don't really give a fuck about her," he says. "If we pull this hit off, you can have as many Romano sluts as you want."

I clench my fist but instead of slamming it into his jaw, I just nod. "Good," I say. "Let's go then."

"Fuck yeah," he whoops. I can tell his blood is up and he's already forgotten about our conversation.

As we get into his truck and head over to our positions, that conversation is all I can think about. To my father, Grace is just some mob bitch to be used and abused until you're finished with her. She's just a wet hole to fuck and fill. But to me, she's become much, much more than that.

I'm protective of her. I'm possessive of her. I find myself wanting to be more tender, gentler, more loving than I've ever been in my entire life. When I'm in that room with Grace and she's giving herself to me, the darkness is completely silent.

Nothing silences the darkness. Or at least nothing had before, except maybe at the moment of the kill. When I'm with Grace, though, the darkness is totally quiet. There is only me and her and what we're doing, our bodies intertwined or just lying side by side afterward. She makes me feel something I'd never felt before.

She makes me feel at peace.

I glance at my father as we drive to the South Side of Chicago. He's probably never felt a moment of peace in his life. He has the darkness inside of him, too, just like I do. He probably thinks that the darkness will go away if the Romanos let him into the *familia*, but I know better.

Nothing so shallow could ever silence it. I don't know what could help him. I doubt anything at this point. He's a lost cause, but I'm not. Grace showed me that. *My princess.*

We finally reach the spot where the hit will go down. We park down the block, and my father points out the building.

"There, on the left, is the deli," he says, pointing. "And that on the right is your building." He points at a taller brownstone building that looks like it was once a shopfront with apartments on top.

"Roof access?" I ask him.

"There's a fire escape on the back. You can get up that way."

I nod. Fire escapes are convenient and cleaner. "Timing?" I ask.

"I'll give you," he checks his watch, "ten minutes to get into position. Then the fire starts." He grins at me.

"Fine. Plenty of time." My blood pumps with adrenaline. My body tenses, knowing the time has come.

"Remember, one shot. Then we're out of here. I'll be nearby waiting in case something goes wrong."

"I understand." I open the door and climb out.

"Son," he says. I look back at him. "Don't miss."

I grin. "You know I don't."

He nods as I turn and walk quickly down the street.

The block is quiet. It's a pretty normal-looking residential street on the South Side. The buildings are large brownstones some with flowerpots on the steps, but they're all in pretty bad condition. This is the neighborhood the city forgot about, and so crime is rampant.

It doesn't surprise me that the Don comes here to play poker. The Rossis have safe houses all over this neighborhood. It's their main turf. Besides that, he grew up in this place. He probably still has friends in the old neighborhood, and I'm betting he's playing with them right now.

I check my watch as I walk toward the building. Eight minutes to go. I find an alley between the buildings and head down toward the back.

I scout around the corner, and it's completely quiet. It takes me a second before I spot the fire escape. I walk over and climb up onto a dumpster before jumping up and grabbing the lowest rung. It slides down with a metallic grind. I dangle there for a second, watching, but nobody comes outside.

I pull myself up and climb. It takes me a few minutes, but finally I crest the roof and find myself standing above the block. I check my watch one more time. Three minutes to spare.

I get into position at the edge of the roof and crouch down to set up my rifle. I have a silencer at one end, a high powered scope, and a tripod on the front. I rest the tripod on the ledge and adjust the scope until it's perfect. The distraction should separate them enough. And with the fire escape, I'll be gone before they can get to me. Just one kill. The others can do whatever the fuck they want.

My heart is beating fast. I take a few deep breaths to calm myself, holding onto my rifle. I scope out the front of the deli and it's deserted, though that doesn't mean anything. There are clearly three mafia trucks parked outside. They're the only nice cars on the block.

I hold my rifle, waiting. I've done this hundreds of times before. I'm a damn good shot, and I never miss. I've never killed a Don before, but he's a man like any other. One bullet to his skull, and he'll go down.

Seconds tick past, and then minutes. I check my watch with a frown.

He's late. Eleven minutes pass, and then twelve. There's no fire down there, hell, there's no sign of my father.

When fifteen minutes come and go, I'm beginning to worry. My blood races with anxiety. Something happened down there. He's never late like this, not on an important hit. Maybe he's a piece of shit in our daily lives but when we're out on a mission together, he's as dependable as anything else in this world. He's a fucking rock.

Not tonight. He's late for the first time in our career together. I have no clue why, or what's wrong. We didn't set up walkies. I didn't even think about them because we never use them, but of course that was a stupid decision.

I turn and look back at the roof. I'm secluded, and I realize that my only way off is the fire escape. There's no entrance to the roof from the actual building itself.

A sound catches my ear. I look around, frowning. It's a low chop, a sputtering noise. It takes me a second to identify it.

It's a helicopter, flying low, directly toward me.

Suddenly, it clicks. The spot I'm in, the phone call, my father's lateness. It all makes sense.

I grab my rifle and whirl it toward the helicopter, taking aim. I fire off two shots, but it keeps coming faster than I expected. I have to reload as it screams toward me, descending onto the roof. I curse myself for not bringing something that holds more ammo.

My father. That fucking bastard. Panic and anger rise up in me as I prepare to fire off more shots, desperately trying to defend my impossible position.

Wind whips my body. It's going to fucking land a few feet away from me, and I'm suddenly cut off from the fire escape. I wasted my chance to try to escape by shooting at them like a fucking fool. There are some bullet holes in the front glass, but the pilot seems unharmed.

Four men with high powered rifles jump out of the helicopter. They're screaming at me, but I don't hear them. I fire off two more shots, clipping one guy in the shoulder before they're only feet away from me. I drop my rifle to the ground and throw a punch at the first man that comes at me. My fist cracks into his jaw with a meaty thud. I feel satisfied for half a second until someone hits me in the back of the head and I fall forward.

My fucking father. That bastard, that son of a bitch. He set me up. I don't know why he would do this to his own son. His own flesh and blood.

Feet smash into my body, and then I'm being dragged. Someone throws me into the helicopter and then the world is dropping away.

Blackness overwhelms me as I'm knocked unconscious from the butt of a gun slamming against my temple.

Chapter 24

GIO BETTER LET ME OUT OF THIS DAMN ROOM. I color in the sketch, shading it. I love this one. He's going to love it, too. I keep looking to the door. He's late tonight. He told me he would be, but I still don't like it.

I only get to see him. I miss… I miss variety, I think. I tried to explain it to him earlier. I need to get out of here. Soon. He always says soon. But I need a timeline. I love being his princess, his submissive, his… his everything. That's the way he makes me feel, and I love it. But I need to get out of this damn room.

I put the pencil down and hold the paper away from me. It's beautiful. In my periphery, I see the cage. It looks so small now. It's odd, how before it didn't seem to be. But I can't imagine going back in.

I turn to look toward the door as I hear Gio coming. My forehead pinches as I move to kneel for him. We always start the nights with training. It's basically foreplay for me now. I place my hands on my thighs, and my pussy clenches waiting for him. But there's something wrong. The footsteps sound… different. I jolt as something bangs on the door.

My heartbeat races with worry. *Gio?*

I hear a muffled voice, and then another. That's not Gio. My blood runs cold, and I scramble off the bed. Someone's here. The banging has stopped, but I hear them punching in a code. It won't work. Only Gio can open that door. I walk backward, my eyes on the door, wide with anxiety.

My throat closes, and I struggle to breathe. *Where's my Gio?*

I almost run to the cage, as if hiding would save me, but it won't. Nothing will save me. If these men are here, it means something bad happened to Gio. I know he wouldn't let them near me without a fight.

My chest tightens, and I look around the room for anything that can be used as a weapon. My easel. I run toward it, holding my breath. I nearly scream as a large thud on the door accompanied by shouting makes my body freeze with fear.

I crack the easel over my leg, and then split the large stick of wood into two. The edges are jagged. I hold both tightly in my hands, feeling the wood dig into my palms. I wait, moving back and forth on my heels, but I don't want to stand out here in the open. I have nowhere to hide though. I look under the bed, but it wouldn't give me much room to fight. Instead, I move to the bathroom and hide behind the tiny edge of the doorframe.

My heart races with anxiety. I close my eyes tightly, praying for Gio to come.

I cover my mouth with a sob and drop the one weapon as I realize he could be dead. My father. He's come for me! He better not have killed him. Not Gio. I can't bear the thought.

No!

No! Gio! I can't go back to my father and that wretched life. I won't. As the thought resonates through me, the door smashes open and the sound of several men coming into the room echoes off the walls. A large cloud of dust and smoke billows into the room, and I can barely make out the men. My heart sinks, and I slide down the wall, my fingers searching for the weapons I dropped in my panic.

I barely feel the tips of the wood with my fingers and I grab them with a force that nearly snaps them in two. I slide up the wall, waiting as deep voices speak in Italian. The smoke and dust is beginning to settle. Over the sound of the blood rushing in my ears, I can't make out a damn thing they're saying. Not that I'd understand, anyway.

As the footsteps come closer, I prepare to strike. At least one person is going to die. I'm not leaving. I don't want to leave.

The irony of the situation settles heavy on my shoulders. I couldn't wait to leave, but now all I want to do is stay. A shadow slowly creeps into the room.

I hold my breath, raising the stakes and as soon as the first boot lands on the tile, I turn and put all my weight into the blow.

I scream out and nearly collapse when I see who it is.

He grabs my wrist and my elbow, keeping the first stake from hitting him, but the second lands on his shoulder, slicing through the thin shirt and stabbing into his flesh.

Uncle Toni.

I scream, covering my mouth and hunching on the ground in shock and fear.

His face scrunches with agony as his piercing curse reverberates off the wall and the other men come in.

Uncle Toni rips the stake out as someone I vaguely recognize sees me and yells to someone else.

I huddle on the ground. "I'm so sorry." I heave in a breath.

The man throws me a blanket, and Uncle Toni kneels down. "Grace," he says and looks at me with such sadness in his eyes that I fall into his embrace, covered in the blanket.

I'm shocked and shaking with fear. The adrenaline and anxiety aren't even close to being gone. I start to say something. I want to rattle off questions and ask about Gio.

Does he know?

I need to know what's going on, but when I pull back to look my uncle in the eyes, the men have all gathered around me and there's only one I recognize well. Alec. He's always by my father's side.

I can hardly breathe, and the fear must be written on my face. I can't go back.

My body is cold and numb. I'm outnumbered.

"Shh, it's alright, Grace," my uncle says, pulling me in closer. My heart beats so hard, it hurts. I want to tell him everything. I need to know what's happened. But with the cold dead eyes of that man on me, I say nothing. I let my uncle appear to comfort me.

"We've got you now." He strokes my back. "That sick fuck is dead." My knees collapse inward and crash on the cold hard tile.

"Gio?" I whisper his name.

"It's okay, Grace. He's gone. He's never going to hurt you again."

No, I shake my head, violently. My lungs refuse to fill, and I struggle to move. I'm paralyzed. No, not Gio. He can't be gone.

I try to swallow and regain some sort of composure. I have to tell him.

"Move," Alec's cold voice says, and my uncle steps aside. "I've got her," he says, leaning down to pick me up. I start to push him away, but I see flashes of my father. I can't disobey.

I tremble in his arms and stare at my cage past him and in the other room.

He's dead. I blink away the tears. How could he leave me?

I grip onto Alec's shoulders as he carries me away, speaking to my uncle in Italian. The cage grows small, and eventually it's gone from my sight. I can hear barking outside, and part of me wonders what that is. A man walks by with scratches on his face, clutching his arm.

As I walk through his house, my heart splits in my chest, shattering into irreparable pieces. He can't be dead.

They can't take him from me.

I need him.

I won't live without him. I can't.

Chapter 25

Gio

THE WORLD IS JUST MOTION, LIGHT, AND SHADOW. I'M NOT SURE where I am, or when. I'm dizzy from the blow to my skull but I'm still alive, which is a relief.

Or maybe a curse. I try to move, but I can't. My chin is in my chest and my body aches; it's stiff and sore. It takes me a minute to figure out that I'm tied to a chair. My hands are bound behind my back, zip ties cutting into my skin.

I lean my head back and groan. My entire body hurts from the multiple kicks they gave me, and probably worse. Every tiny breath hurts. Fuck, I hope my ribs aren't broken. The room slowly begins to materialize around me as I get more and more of my faculties back.

Above me there's a bright spotlight shining directly down on me. It makes me squint as I open my eyes. I can hardly see out of my left. It must be swollen. I wipe my chin against my shoulder. It's dirtied with blood.

I groan and look straight ahead as the room comes into focus. I'm in a small room, maybe ten feet by ten feet. There's a drain beneath my feet, and the walls are bare white cinder blocks. The ground looks like it's unfinished concrete.

The unbelievable nature of my reality comes back to me slowly. My fucking father sold me out. It couldn't be anything else. They knew I would be on that roof with almost no way to escape. Trapping me like that was their only option. They had to set me up like that because if they came any other way, I would've killed them all. They sent a fucking helicopter because they were too afraid to face me, the cowards.

Why would he do that? What could the Rossis possibly offer him that would change his mind? We were so close to getting what we wanted. I would have gotten Grace, and he might have gotten a place in the Romano *familia*. Instead I'm fucking strapped to a chair, aching from a hundred bruises.

Oh fuck. Grace. My heart stills, and I struggle harder in my bonds. She's still locked in the gun room without any food. Fuck, fuck, fuck. I come fully awake at the thought of Grace stuck in there, slowly starving to death, begging me to come help her. I flex against my restraints and struggle, anger flooding me, desperate to escape.

I need to go to her. *My princess.*

I have to save her. I can't let her starve to death in that room. Fuck! My selfish need to keep her is going to cause her pain. I should have let her go. I know I should have. Things were going so fucking good. She loves it. And I fucking love her. I fucking know I do. I was too scared to risk her leaving me.

At least Duke is probably okay. He has his doggy door and an auto-feeding system. I know he'll be smart enough to run if they attack my place, and he can get food and water from the feeding system. At least I didn't get him fucked, too.

My darkness is there inside of me, raging in full force. It wants revenge against my father, while all I want is to run home and make sure Grace is safe.

"Hey!" I yell out. "Fuckers! Come in here, you fucking cunts!"

There's silence as I continue to struggle. Eventually, I tip over the chair and crash to the ground, smashing my face against the concrete floor. Fuck! I stretch my bruised jaw, moving away from the cold unforgiving ground. I grunt and nearly lose consciousness, but manage to stay awake.

A minute later, the door opens. Someone comes inside. I can only see his feet as he walks over to me. My breaths come in quickly as adrenaline fuels my blood.

The man grabs me and lifts me back upright. I stare into his face, defiant and angry. I hope he fucking drops me. I hope he kicks the fucking chair. He needs to. I need this chair to break so I have a chance. I need to get to her. As the plan formulates in my mind, I realize who it is I'm staring at.

It's him. The Don, Grace's father. The man I want to kill more than anything in this world for what he did to his daughter. To my princess.

"So," he says. "You're the one that was holding my daughter."

I stare at him, not saying a word.

"You're in a pretty bad spot now, Gio," he says. "We know all about you, you know. Have known for some time."

"Go fuck yourself," I practically spit at him.

I almost tell him where Grace is. I almost do, but I'm afraid of what he'll do to her. And as sad as it sounds, my father knows she's there. He knows what she means to me. If he ever loved me, he'd save her.

"Good. Defiant. Strong. I like that about you. I can see why my daughter is interested in you."

I stare at him, but say nothing, even as fear strikes through my veins. "We found her locked away." He tsks. He's just fucking with me. He doesn't know a fucking thing about me and Grace. I can't give in to his games. There's no way he has her.

"Tell me, Gio," he says as he walks behind me. I can hear him doing something back there that sounds like clattering metal. Finally, he comes back around. He's holding a wicked, large curved knife in his hand and he has a big smile on his face. "Tell me what you know about the Romanos."

I stare at him and say nothing. The smile never leaves his face as he carves a cut into the meat of my thigh.

I grunt, seething through clenched teeth as the pain floods me, but I don't cry out. I won't give him the satisfaction.

"Talk, Gio," he says. "I wanna know everything about the Romanos and their enemies. I want names. Your father already sold you out. Your very own flesh and blood sold you out for a position in our *familia*. Can you imagine that?" I hold back the pain, even though I already knew it. It fucking hurts. He clucks his tongue and shakes his head. "Well, he won't last long with us. We don't take kindly to rats, although I do appreciate him showing me where my Grace was locked away."

I grunt and flex against my bonds, trying to get free. Anger viciously tears through my body, and I know only violence will sate that anger. I can barely breathe at the thought of my father giving her back to him. Handing her over to a man who caused her so much pain. The betrayal of that is far greater than what he did to me.

My piece of shit father. This bastard, Grace's father. Both men are dead. I'm going to tear them limb from limb until they're screaming for my mercy. I won't stop. I won't ever stop.

"Go fuck yourself," I say to him just beneath my breath.

He laughs and carves into my other leg, the sharp knife slicing easily. I wince and grunt in pain, clenching my teeth and barely falling forward, but I still don't cry out. I've had worse. I can handle this.

I'd rather die than be a fucking rat. I'll let him destroy me if I have to, but I'll never talk.

It goes on like that for a while. I don't know how long. He asks me questions, I don't answer, and then he cuts into me.

He gets creative after a while, taking thin slices and pouring salt onto the open wounds. At least that makes it numb for a while. I'm in so much pain that my vision becomes blurred. They give me breaks, even feed me and give me water, but the pain comes back.

I sleep at least once. I don't know for how long. I'm in that room, strapped to that chair, and it's all I know.

I don't say a word. I'll never talk. I can feel my life hanging in the balance, and part of me wants it to finally end.

But the other part, the stronger part, wants to survive. I want to make it through this until I get the chance to have my revenge.

I'll kill them. I'll maim them. I'll tear them into pieces. For my princess. I have to live for her. I have to save her.

That's what sustains me. Rage and violence. Even through the torture, my silence never wavering, the only thing keeping me going is the rage. I worry about Grace every second, but my revenge will be for both of us.

Without her, my life is finished. I'm okay with that. I can handle that. When I'm through, I can join her, wherever she is.

For now, though, I survive. Cuts and kicks and bruises, I survive. A day, maybe two days, I can't be sure.

I don't know what time it is when Toni appears in the room. He stands near the door, his arms crossed, a smile on his face.

"The cameras were smart," he says, as if from a distance. "But you were never going to get to me. Maybe my brother, but never to me." He laughs.

"Fuck you," I mumble. It's all I say anymore.

"Right, of course. Fuck me." He grins, and I want to kill him slowly.

"I'm actually here to show you something, Gio. I think it might help you find your tongue."

I spit onto the floor and stare at him.

"Okay," he says. "I just want you to know that I hold no ill will toward you. I understand that you're just doing your job. Well, except with Grace. My lovely niece, Grace. She's wonderful, isn't she?"

I stare at him, my heart beating rapidly. I hate that he'd ever use her name. None of the Rossi family deserve her.

"You wanna see her, don't you?"

I won't give in to their tricks. It's just a stupid game they're playing.

"You're desperate to make sure she's okay. Well, I can do that for you. Would you like that?"

Yes, I want to see her. I want to make sure she's okay. But not like this. Not when I can't save her. I don't give him anything. Nothing. I'll give them all nothing. "Fuck you," I mumble.

"Grace," he says. "Come in here."

The door opens with a loud creak, and daylight filters into the room. The Don steps through, grinning wickedly.

Followed by Grace. Her head is held low.

I feel like I'm going to pass out. My heart is hammering in my chest.

It's her. She's safe. She's alive. She lifts her head to look at me, and horror passes through her expression.

They have her. But at least she's alive. At least she has a chance.

That gives me hope. I feel new strength surge through my body at the sight of her. She's so beautiful, so perfect. I know what I have to do.

I'm going to kill them. And then I'm going to take what's mine.

Chapter 26

I'M BARELY WALKING AS ALEC PUSHES ME TOWARD THE ROOM. I KNOW what door this is. The people who come in here never leave. Maybe my father's disappointment in me not knowing a damn thing has finally led him to kill me. I don't know, and I don't care.

My uncle's outside the door, and I can't even look him in the eyes. His arms are crossed and I can feel his eyes on me, but I don't return his gaze. I can't stand the sight of any of them. All those years I thought he protected me, I was a fool.

I thought he loved me, I thought he kept me safe. I was so wrong. He did nothing but keep me quiet. Maybe he prevented the beatings, but he never saved me. Not like Gio did.

The very thought makes my heart hurt.

They killed him.

I take in a sharp breath. At least Alec's shoving against my back eases slightly as we approach the door. My uncle may have some influence, but it's not enough. Not anymore. He let them hurt me. He was proud to tell me that Gio was dead.

I hate him. I hate all of them. I haven't said a word to any of them. The only thing on my mind is how to get out of here. But I have to kill my father first. That is the only thing I'm focused on. The only thing that's kept me alive since I've been back here, locked back in my room.

He hasn't even tried to talk to me. He doesn't give a fuck.

The only company I've had is my uncle. I couldn't talk to him though.

I didn't say a word as he told me they were waiting to kill him. It was all about him. Why he couldn't come to my rescue because it would have put him in danger.

I understand it. I do. But I don't care.

All the years I spent here made me weak. Gio gave me a reason for living. He gave me a strength I never knew I had.

And now he's dead.

My uncle's hand rests on my shoulder, halting me in front of the door. His hand is rough and cold. He leans forward and talks quietly, "It's going to be alright." His soft words sink in, resonating in my very being.

I look him in the eyes. "No it won't," I say, and he flinches from my simple response. "It's never been alright." Truer words have never been spoken.

My gaze is ripped away as the door flies open, revealing my father.

I don't drop my gaze. It takes everything in me not to glare at him. My hate has grown and consumed me. The wits I had before that kept me safe from his anger have all vanished. Beat me. Whip me. Humiliate me. I don't care. The last thing I do will be to put this man in his grave.

"Grace," he says, and his eyes are narrowed and his yellow teeth show through his sickening smile.

I don't respond. Instead I walk in, ignoring him and preparing for whatever it is he's going to do to me.

I only take two steps in and then I freeze. My legs go numb, and my knees threaten to buckle. I gasp, covering my mouth, my heart and body going cold. My eyes prick with tears. But I can't let them come. He's here. He's alive.

My uncle grabs my waist and keeps me upright. My body's trembling. He's alive.

"Gio!" I call out to him, and try to run to him. He's not okay. His face is bloodied, and he has bruises and cuts all over his body.

I can't stand the sight. Every inch of my body prickles with terror, and my blood runs cold. My uncle squeezes my forearms and pulls my back into his chest. I try to elbow him in his gut. I fight him, kicking and yelling for him to let me go. I can't take my eyes away from Gio though.

"Grace," he says and his voice is full of conviction as he struggles against the binds holding him to the chair. "Don't touch her!" he screams. Just hearing his voice mends a broken piece of my soul. My voice cracks, and the words refuse to leave my lips.

I finally tear my eyes away from him and fall to my knees, my hands gripping my father's shirt. "Please! Let him go!" My heart squeezes in my chest. If he ever loved me, he'd save him. A sob rips from my throat.

"He didn't do anything, please-" The back of my father's hand whips across my face. The force of the blow is so strong it makes my head spin as I land hard against the ground.

"You fucking cunt." I open my eyes, and through my blurred vision I see Alec's cruel smile and then my father's.

My heart collapses. They'll never save him.

I repress every emotion in me other than hate. A black void starts taking over.

I can hear the screaming. Gio and my father. The legs of the chair Gio's tied to are scraping against the floor. But it all turns to white noise. My body heats and an anger I've never felt grips hold of me, bolting me to the floor as it seeps into my blood.

"You're a fucking rat!" my father hisses as he crouches closer to me, close enough to hit me again. My head flings to the side, and my lips pulse from the impact. The stinging pain shoots from my heated cheek down my throat. I anticipated it though. I only use it to fuel me and my growing rage. My tongue darts out, and the metallic taste of blood fills my senses.

"She doesn't know anything!" Gio screams. I stare at the cinder blocks on the wall, focusing on my breathing, taking in the room. Looking for options.

It's quiet for a moment as my father paces. I know he's going to kill Gio. I can't let him. I won't be able to breathe if I watch him die at the hands of my father.

I look over my shoulder. My captor, my master, my everything is so badly wounded and scarred. But he's still fighting. I won't stop fighting either. Not till the very end.

Gio's eyes are darting from me to my father, the hardness in his features replaced by a vulnerability I've never seen as he says, "Just let her go." His breathing is coming in heavy pants as my father lets out a humorless laugh. "She didn't do anything. She didn't tell me anything."

I didn't. I have nothing to tell. But the truth isn't what my father wants.

This is just another reason for him to hurt me. Maybe enough to kill me this time.

"You're my daughter. A Rossi!" He screams so loud in my face it makes my chest hurt. I flinch out of instinct, and I hate it. I scoot back on my ass, the hard concrete under my palms and watch as my father moves to the edge of the steel table on the backside of the room. His rage is consuming him like the hothead he is.

Alec moves to the side as my father grips the table and flips it over, causing all of the knives and other weapons of torture to hurl into the air and crash onto the ground next to me. My arms cover my face as I turn my body.

Uncle Toni yells in Italian, grabbing my father by the arms and trying to keep him from beating me. Gio is screaming, his chair scooting closer and closer to me. But neither one of them can save me from the kick to my back. My father's hard boot slams into me.

"I have a rat for a daughter!" The spit from his sneer hits my face as he grips my arm and turns me toward him as he yells, "A fucking traitor!"

I see the knife. The sharp edge of it is shining in the dim light coming from the hallway. I don't hesitate to grab it, ignoring the kick to my stomach and quickly turn onto my back. It nearly slips from my sweaty palms as I grip it with both hands and reach up.

My father's eyes widen as he crouches closer, intent on beating me again.

Intent on hurting me like he's done for years. Expecting me to submit as I always have.

A violent scream rips through my throat as I plunge the blade into the side of his neck.

My heartbeat stills, and everything burns inside of me as I pull the knife out, blood gushing from his wounds and his body freezing in shock. And I stab him again, and again and again.

Chapter 27

Gio

THE DARKNESS IN ME SHATTERS AS GRACE PLUNGES THE KNIFE into her father. I'm helpless as I watch her struggle with the fear and anger and raw vulnerability shining in her eyes. Never has death seemed so real to me. And I can't do a damn thing but watch.

I struggle against the zip ties digging and cutting into the flesh of my wrists, the blood dripping down my hand from the wounds.

Fuck! I need to help her. I can't sit and watch. But I'm useless.

"You bastard!" she screams. She plunges it into his body again and again, the blade slicing through his skin.

"You bitch," he groans, finally falling against the wall as the blood spills from his neck. His hands try to stop the flow, but she's done enough damage. He's done for. He tries to fight, but he's losing so much blood too quickly.

I watch, totally helpless, unable to do a thing. I wish I could stand up and take the knife from her and finish the job myself. She doesn't need blood on her hands.

But part of me is grateful she's finally doing this. That she's the one to put an end to her pain. She's so fucking strong. I've seen this fight in her, and now she's using it. But it hurts me that she had to. I hate that it came to this. She's wanted freedom her whole life, and now she's getting it. Killing the man that locked her up and abused her for so long was one surefire way to exorcise him from her mind. He can never hurt her again, not after she stabbed him to death.

Toni stands by the door, arms outstretched. "Back off," he growls at the men that try to get past him and go to Martino's aid, even though the looks in their eyes reveal the shock, and in some of them the pride of seeing her take down her father.

Alec ignores Toni, grabbing a club that's stained with my blood from the ground. I push forward off the ground, desperate to save her from the blow, screaming and fighting again. My head smashes against the concrete, the chair landing hard in front of Grace. It's not enough, but it's all I can do. I prepare for the blow of the club to smash against my skull. Instead a loud bang ricochets off the wall. *Bang!* And then another *bang!*

My heart stills in my chest, fear crippling me. Not Grace. Please God, no.

I open my eyes and watch as Alec falls to the ground, knees first and then his upper body collapsing. His eyes are open and lifeless, a small hole in his neck bubbling blood. I watch as the blood seeps around his neck and soaks into his shirt.

"Let the girl finish this," Toni says from behind me, and I turn slightly to watch.

Grace breaks down into wordless sobs as she looks to her uncle, ignoring the cursing her father barely manages to mutter, and shoves the knife into her father's throat. With a final gurgle he's silenced forever, the blood seeping all over the concrete floor.

The blood runs down the concrete and slides into the drain underneath my chair. The Rossi Don is dead, and Grace is drenched in his blood.

Toni stares at Grace. He doesn't bother glancing at me, and I don't blame him. As far as he's concerned, I'm nothing. Toni probably never imagined Grace would have the balls to do this, but now it's done. It's something he should have done a long time ago.

And he's the leader of the Rossi family. By rights, he's the Don now.

Toni steps toward Grace. "Honey," he says softly, reaching his hand out to her. "Give me the knife." The men by the door stand and wait for their next command.

She stares up at him with tears in her eyes. "What?" she says after a long moment as if she didn't hear him.

"The knife, Grace. Give it to me."

"Give it to him," I say to her. She can't fight him, too. She can't fight the entire *familia*. He won't hurt her. None of them will. He better let her go.

She glances at me, taking in a ragged breath, then nods to herself. She hands the knife over to Toni. She needs to be held. I struggle once more, useless and feeling defeated. *She needs me.*

He takes it, then hands it off to one of his thugs. People gather at the entrance to the room, staring in at the dead body of the Don slowly bleeding on the ground. There's so much blood, and I'm betting that everyone is surprised at how much he's bleeding. I've seen it plenty of times before. The body holds a lot of blood, and it's always a shock to see it all spread out on the floor.

"That's a good girl," Toni says to her. He slowly helps her to her feet. I stare at them, not sure how I feel about this. He's being sweet to her, but I can see the shrewdness behind his eyes. He's already calculating what he can do with her and how he can use her for his own benefit. She needs to get away from all of them. They only see her as a pawn, and she's so much more than that. She deserves so much more.

"Let her go," I say to him.

His eyes flash to mine.

"I'll give you whatever you want."

He sneers at me. "What could you possibly have that I'd want?"

"I have names of contacts, the locations of warehouses." I know saying these things makes me a rat, but I'll give him anything and everything to let her go. "I know arrangements that are being made this very minute. But you know you're not upset Grace just killed your brother. You're the Don now. You got what you wanted."

He watches me for a second, his eyes narrowing, then looks at Grace. "What do you think, Gracie dear? Do you want to leave?"

"Yes," she says in a small voice. I can tell that she's still processing what just happened, and I can't blame her. This is the first time she's taken another person's life. She's in shock.

He pulls her toward him and rubs her back. It's comforting and without any eyes on his face but my own, I can see the hurt behind his. He may be a sick fuck, a killer and someone who's willing to sacrifice her if need be, but somewhere deep down he must care for her. "Okay then." Toni looks at me. "I have an offer for you. Are you ready?"

"I'm ready," I say.

"Why do the Romanos want war?" Grace turns in his embrace, her eyes on me.

I stare at him for a second, surprised at the question. I assumed that the answer was obvious, but the truth hits me in a sudden realization.

The Rossis have no clue why the Romanos are coming at them. Maybe they have guesses, but the Romanos haven't actually contacted them. As far as they can tell, it's just a random attack without any provocation.

"It's over territory," I answer him. "You made a deal with the Zhang Syndicate that the Romanos used to do business with. They cut the Romanos off, and they're pissed."

"How the fuck is their decision my problem?" He releases Grace and she backs away, but her eyes fall to her father and then to me.

"We could have negotiated," he says with a hard voice, his jaw tensing.

"It's easier to negotiate with a dead man," I point out.

He shakes his head, clearly considering what I've said.

"Let him go," Grace says, breaking the silence.

My princess. I look at her proudly.

Toni laughs. "He really fucked you up, didn't he?"

I glare at the asshole. Anger rolls through me, but I need to play my cards right. I keep myself under control. For now.

"Okay," he says finally. "I think I have a deal for you."

"What is it?" I ask, impatient.

"Take a message to the Romanos for me. If you do that, I'll let you live. If not, I'll have my whole *familia* hunt you down. Understand?"

"What message?"

He grins. "Just a little something. I'll tell you how to find it soon. Do we have a deal?"

I stare at him, and I know I should turn this down. I shouldn't accept without knowing exactly what this message is.

But then I look at Grace, and I have to accept. She can't be given back to these people, these fucking animals. She's mine and I'll do anything in my power to keep her and keep her safe.

"I accept," I say.

"Wonderful." Toni grins huge, then gestures at me. The thug with the knife walks in and cuts away my ropes and the zip ties from around my wrists.

Slowly, I stand. My muscles groan in pain, but I don't care how sore my body is. Grace pushes off the wall and runs to me. She throws her arms around my neck and I pull her close against me, holding her tight. My eyes never leave her uncle though, or any of the other men. I don't trust them. We need to leave while we can.

I can't deny the relief of holding her in my arms though. I hurt from a million bruises and I can barely stand, but I've never felt better in my entire fucking life.

She pulls back and stands at my side, facing her uncle. "I'm leaving with Gio," she announces with a firm voice.

He raises an eyebrow. "The fuck you are. You're a Rossi."

"I'm leaving," she says. "My father is dead, and I'm free now." The men shift uncomfortably, watching the two stare each other down. I move in front of her protectively. He has no reason to keep her, but he could if he wanted to.

Toni stares at her, then looks at me. "Is this what you want, too?" I can see the resolve in his expression. An immense pressure leaves my chest.

"She goes where I go," I say simply.

He shakes his head, his expression mystified. "What a fucked up pair."

I can't help but grin. *Maybe, but I wouldn't have it any other way.*

Toni sighs. "Fucking hell. Fine, girl, go with him. I don't give a fuck. But remember, if he doesn't live up to his promise, you're both dead." His expression turns to ice.

I take Grace's hand and we walk forward without another word. I'm limping more than I'd like, but that doesn't matter. I'm going to leave this place with Grace, and she's going to know that she's free.

We head past her uncle, past the thugs in the hall, and toward a door at the far end.

"This way," she says, tugging at my hand

We walk down the hall together and push open the door.

As soon as I we get outside, I hold Grace tightly against my body, taking a moment, just a small moment to really hold her. I'm so proud of her. "You did good, princess," I whisper into her ear.

"I killed him," she says softly. I can hear the pain in her voice, but what's more, I can hear the gratification.

"I'm proud of you."

She pulls back and looks at me, raw vulnerability in her eyes. "Really?"

"Really." I kiss her softly on the lips.

Chapter 28

I COULD FEEL THE KNIFE PLUNGING INTO HIS NECK. MY FATHER. THE Don.

I killed him.

I've wanted to kill him for so long. I fantasized about it. I wept for hours in my room after they told me Gio was dead, imagining all the ways I'd kill him. I didn't know how I'd do it, and now that it's done, I'm still in disbelief.

I didn't hesitate. I didn't think. I just saw the chance, and I acted. I grabbed the knife and I killed him as all of the fury and rage from my whole life spilled out of me in that moment.

I felt horrible. I felt broken. And I felt … liberated.

It felt *good.* Yet again, I feel as though I must be sick. I've killed, and I have no regrets. I've fallen in love with a man who took me prisoner. I must truly be sick.

"Princess?" Gio's rough cadence when he calls my name makes my body heat with need.

I look over, snapped out of my thoughts. Gio is looking at me, concern clear on his face. We're stopped at a red light. His truck is idling beneath us. We had to walk a few blocks, and all the while I gripped his hand with fear as though my father was coming for us. But he's dead. I have to keep reminding myself of that fact.

"I'm okay," I say softly. For some reason, I want to lie to him. I don't want him to be upset or to worry about me. I know that's crazy, but it's the truth.

"You're not okay," he says simply. "We'll be home soon." He reaches across the truck and takes my hand, a sudden and comforting gesture.

It's such a small thing, but I needed it.

Home. I've never had a home. Only a prison. I look at him from the corner of my eye and wonder if he's going to put me in that room. He can't. It will crush me if he tries. I'm finally free, and I know what I want. I want *him*. I want a life together. But I can't be caged anymore. *Never again.*

I lean back in the seat and nod my head. Gio is bruised and beaten, in horrible shape, but he's still going. He's the strongest man I've ever met. He was willing to do anything to save me, to keep me safe. Despite everything, I know the kind of man Gio is. He's the kind of man I want beside me for the rest of my life. I think he wants me too, but I need to hear him say it. I'm desperate for those words.

The image of my father's bleeding corpse keeps coming back to me.

I squeeze Gio's hand, and he squeezes back. I have to hold on tightly or else risk falling into my waking nightmare. Gio can help me. I know he can. He's been through this before. He's killed before.

We pull up to his house, the gravel driveway rumbling beneath the tires. I get a good look at it for the first time, the only time, without any fear. It's a beautiful house, built to look like a cabin, but I know it's much bigger than it seems.

It looks like a home. I can just picture the porch swing. I look to my left at Gio and I wonder if he'd build one for me. He's given me everything I've ever asked for. But things are different now.

They'll always be different.

"Come on, princess," he says as he climbs out of the truck. He walks around the front and takes my hand again. "Let's go inside."

"Okay," I say nodding my head and feeling so unsure, and let him lead me through the large front door.

I take a good look around as I enter. I vaguely remember the modern furniture and clean sleek lines as my uncle took me away a few days ago. Gio takes me into the kitchen and sits me down at the granite island on a bar stool. It feels strange to be in his house but not in my room. To be free for the first time. Even at my father's house, someone was always watching. I look up at Gio and wonder if that will be him from now on.

Something inside of me settles, knowing the answer already. Gio's different. I know he is.

It also feels normal to be sitting there with him. He goes into the refrigerator and offers me wine. He pulls a bottle out, dark purple, almost black. I can't read the label, but it doesn't matter.

"No thanks," I say in a soft voice, although I could use something for my nerves. I'm too shaken, and I feel on edge. But I need my wits. He nods and makes himself a drink. Whisky with ice. He sits down across from me, ice clinking in his glass.

We're quiet for a moment as I take in the place.

"Come here," he says, holding an arm out.

I stand quickly, needing his touch. I need his comfort; I need his reassurance. He reaches out and grabs my hips, pulling me toward him and into his lap. I bury my head into his chest, loving his warmth as he holds me there. I curl up against him and for the second time, I let myself go.

I sob into his chest. Everything seems to be too much for me to handle anymore.

He holds me, softly stroking my hair. "It's okay," he says softly.

But it's not okay. I killed my father. I murdered him with a knife in the most brutal way imaginable. There was so much blood, so much more than I could have imagined. I still can hardly believe that I did it.

I'm a sobbing, shaking mess, my body trembling and my breath coming in ragged, but Gio holds me tight and whispers gently into my ear. "It's okay, it's okay. I have you. I'll never let you go, princess."

That's what I need to hear. Never let me go. I can't live without him.

After a good hard sob, I'm an exhausted wreck. He releases me as I finally calm down. He wipes my tears and kisses my cheeks.

"You're safe now, princess," he says.

I shake my head, not feeling safe or secure at all. I wrap my arms around myself and take in a long inhale, just trying to calm down

"Trust me." He pauses and looks me in the eye. "You trust me, don't you?"

"Of course," I say softly.

I climb off his lap after a few minutes and pace across the kitchen. It's a large kitchen with a big island in the middle. The tile backsplash is a blue and green geometric pattern, and the cabinets are all dark wood. The appliances are stainless steel. It looks like a normal home. Like a real home.

"Can I have a tour?" I ask, trying to keep my mind off the images. The horrible images that keep flooding through my mind

"Of course. You can do whatever you want, princess."

I smile, then walk out of the kitchen. He follows me, drink in his hand, ice clinking against the glass.

His living room is sparse, but nicely furnished. There's a lot of light from multiple large windows and a sliding glass door in the back. I walk through the living room and he lingers behind me, not saying anything. He lets me wander around his home, looking at every little thing. I'm not taking it in though. I'm only distracting myself, and I'm sure Gio knows that. He's patient though.

I look into his bedroom, at his large bed. There are guns stacked in the corner.

The bed looks so inviting. I strip out of my clothes and crawl onto it, pulling the covers over my body. I look back at Gio, wanting to see his reaction.

I can't go back to the room. I just can't.

Gio gives me a small chuckle as he walks over to the bedside. "You can't sleep in the middle. I need room, too." He leans down and kisses my forehead, pushing the hair from my forehead.

A sense of relief washes over me, but it doesn't last long.

"We have to go, princess."

I look at him with a hint of worry, pulling the blanket closer to me. I don't want to leave. I just want to stay here and deal with everything threatening to consume me. I'm overwhelmed.

"I have to go see my father." It takes a moment for his words to sink in. I know his father's the one who sold him out. Tears prick at my eyes, but the anger keeps them away. "And you need to go to the safe house."

"And by 'see' you mean?" I ask with my eyes on the back wall, and a white-knuckled grip on the blanket.

"I'm going to kill him, princess. I'm going to kill him for what he did to you." Gio's voice is low and threatening.

"Don't leave me," I whisper. I feel weak, but I don't want to be left alone.

"I have to do this."

I look up at him, pleading, "Then take me with you." I don't know why I asked. It sounds ridiculous, but the thought of him leaving shreds me.

"I can't risk you. I can't."

"I don't want you to go." Tears stream down my face and I grip on to him.

He kneels on the bed and cups my chin in his hand. "My princess, I'll be back. I promise you. Let me take you to a safe place. I'll give you a phone, it's untraceable, but I'll know where you are and I'll call you as soon as it's done."

My chest pains, clenching in agony. "Please don't." The wretched words leave my lips even though I know he's going to go. There's no stopping him. This must be done.

He crawls closer to me, the bed groaning from his weight and he holds me close.

I can't resist the urge to take his lips with mine.

I pull him closer to me, gripping onto him, not wanting him to leave.

"Princess," he breathes the word, pressing his lips to mine, his tongue slipping along the seam of my lips until I part for him.

He groans into my mouth, pushing the covers away and letting his hands roam over my body.

We're both covered in blood and filth. But I don't care. I want him. I need him. I have to have him close to me, consuming every part of me.

"Don't leave me," I plead with him. Breaking the kiss only to help him strip his shirt off.

"Once more," he says, letting the shirt fall to the floor. His chest is bloodied and bruised, and it makes my heart clench with pain. I close my eyes and listen to his words as he adds, "And then never again."

He slowly lowers me to the bed, kicking his jeans off. When I open my eyes, I see his piercing gaze, full of devotion and so much more. Love. I know he does. But I need to hear him say it.

He pushes my legs wider, his hips butting against mine as he lines the head of his dick up at my entrance.

He eases himself slowly into me, moving back and forth, inching his way in. My neck arches, and my nails dig into his back.

I gasp, only then realizing that I'd been holding my breath as he slams deep inside of me, buried to the hilt.

Yes!

I need to feel all of him. Every inch of my skin comes to life as he moves in and out of me with a relentless pace. The headboard knocks against the wall as my head thrashes.

Gio grabs my chin and molds my lips to his, kissing me with the passion I have for him.

My heels dig into his ass, wanting more. I want the beast that's taken me, I need him now.

"No," Gio says, pulling away from me, but not stopping his merciless pace. "I need you like this. Raw and vulnerable and with me," he kisses me hard and with a desire that I can't deny. "Just like this." He pushes himself all the way in and pulls out slowly, taking his time and driving my release further and further up.

"Gio," I whisper as he kisses along my neck. My body heats and sweet desire stirs low in my belly, threatening to shove me over the cliff.

"I love you," I whisper the words as my back arches and my hardened nipples rub against his chest. The sensitive skin is directly connected to my throbbing clit and it brings me that much closer.

"I love you, Grace," Gio says, sucking in a breath and pounding harder and faster into me. His blue gaze pierces into me. "I love you so fucking much."

His blunt fingernails dig into my hips as he thrusts his thick cock into me over and over. A cry of pleasure tears through my throat as every nerve ending in my body blazes with a pleasure so intense I can barely stand it.

His eyes never leave mine as he rides through my orgasm, once, twice, a third time, before slamming into me and cumming with me.

We both lay in bed, panting and sated, clinging to each other. I hold onto him, every inch of my skin that I can manage touching his, not wanting to let go. I don't want him to leave me.

I'm afraid he'll never come back.

Chapter 29

Gio

I DRIVE SLOWLY UP MY FATHER'S WINDING DRIVEWAY, MY MIND completely focused on the task at hand. I know Grace is safe back at my safe house and nobody is going to come for her. Not a soul knows where it is. I don't know why I trust the Rossis to keep their end of the bargain, but Toni doesn't have any reason to go back on his word. And I know his niece has to mean something to him. She better. He'd be a fool not to want what's best for her.

He's the Don now, and as the Don he has to live up to some level of respect. If he goes back on the very first deal he made as Don, it would set a bad fucking precedent for the rest of his time in control.

I take a deep breath, getting my mind right. My father lives in a trailer at the end of a long dirt road. He bought several acres of land a few years ago and set up his trailer there, mirroring what I did on the opposite side of town. Except where I built a gorgeous house, he just kept his old shitty trailer and hoarded his cash.

Anger rules me, but I have to keep it at bay. My father betrayed me, went behind my back and nearly got me killed. Worse than that, he put Grace in danger. He gave her back to the man who made her life hell for all those years. Grace was forced to murder her own father and could have been put into an even worse position if she hadn't. All because my father was stupid enough to think the Rossis would have him. His greed. He's going to die because of it.

His time is over. He was strong for so long, and kept his shit together well. He built our business from the ground up all on his own. But now he's finished.

He went too far. He's my father and I'm supposed to love him, but I hate that piece of shit. I've always hated him, even as a little kid. We worked well together and he took care of me, taught me his trade, and made me the man I am today, but I despised him. Because of him, the darkness ruled my life, pushed me to do things I wouldn't normally do.

But it doesn't rule me anymore. That much has become clear to me. The darkness is silent as I put the car in park and stare at the trailer. Part of me is afraid that it's just biding its time, waiting for the perfect time to come back to the surface, but I can't live my life assuming that will happen.

I have Grace now. I have my princess. Watching her in danger, knowing I couldn't save her, it destroyed that part of me. It shattered its very existence. She's the cure I've needed all my life. And I'll never let her go. I know I need her, although I don't know why. It has something to do with my desire to take care of her, to bathe her, feed her, clothe her, and to give her pleasure. I finally have a reason to exist outside of my own desires. I have someone else to satisfy now.

I pull up outside of his trailer and park just across from his door. His truck is in its usual spot to the right, so I know he's home. I slowly climb out of the truck, a shotgun slung over my shoulder.

"Bruno," I call out. "Come outside."

There's silence from the trailer. I can imagine what he's thinking. He's probably watching me, shocked, not sure what to do. He knows why I'm here, but I don't know what he's going to choose.

"Bruno," I yell again. "Come face me. Come face the son you left for dead."

Slowly, the front door opens. My father steps out, his boot heavy on the ground, his eyes haunted as he stares at me.

He's visibly drunk. I bring the shotgun down into my hands and point it at his chest. He stumbles down off the bottom step wearing a beer-stained white wife beater and torn jeans. His eyes are red-rimmed and bleary as he steps toward me, his head cocked.

Fucking hell. He's been on a bender, that's for sure. Probably since the second I got taken. Maybe that should make me feel better, that my father does have some humanity left inside of him however buried, but it doesn't. I don't give a fuck about what's left of this husk of a man I once looked up to.

"How?" he croaks.

"You underestimated me," I say.

"No," he whispers. "I didn't."

"You did. You left me for dead. You sold me to the Rossis. But unfortunately for you, the Rossis made a different deal."

"Gio," he says, stepping toward me. "My son. I never sold you out. Never."

"Liar," I say in a strong, even voice that doesn't reflect what I'm feeling. Doubt is creeping in. I want to believe him, but I know he's lying

"How could I do that?" he asks. "You're my son, my flesh and blood. Please son, you have to believe me. I never would do that. Never."

"Liar," I say again, my finger steady on the trigger.

He comes closer and closer. I don't move the shotgun. Finally, the barrel is directly against his chest and he takes his hands, wrapping them around the barrel. He stares at me, his eyes wide, and I think I can see tears starting to form

He speaks with his forehead pinched. "I raised you. I taught you everything I know. I turned you into a man."

"You destroyed me," I say.

His eyes go wide as he understands what I'm about to do. I feel hollow, nothing but empty, and the darkness isn't there. I expected it to be, but it never appears. No anger, no emotion but an empty void. He's nothing to me. This is nothing to me.

"Goodbye, father," I say beneath my breath.

"Son—" The smile slips from his face.

I pull the trigger. The shotgun explodes into his chest, forcing him back. Blood splatters in all directions as his chest caves in. He slams to the ground with a single gasp, and then he lies still.

I walk over to his body, press the gun against his heart, and fire again. Just to make sure that bastard's dead.

I stand over my father's bleeding corpse and stare at his lifeless eyes. In all my years with him, I never once imagined it would end up like this. I always thought we'd die on a hit or rot away in prison. Never once did I think I would kill him. I never imagined I could betray him.

That changed when he betrayed me. He was dead as soon as he made that decision. Or maybe it happened sooner than that. Maybe Grace showed me what it means to be a real man, to stand up for what you believe in, to protect things you care about. Before I lived for cash and hits and that was it. But now I live for her.

My father would have gotten in the way of that. He never would have stopped trying to destroy me. And so he's dead now, the way he wanted it to happen.

I walk over to the truck and toss the shotgun in the back. I get out my large bowie knife and a roll of plastic sheeting. I walk over to my father's body and stand over him, taking a deep breath.

It's time to finish this.

I bend over him and do my work.

Several hours later, I find myself driving through the dusk hours as I head out to the Romanos main compound. I don't bother calling ahead because I know I won't be welcome either way. I'd rather this visit be a surprise than anything else. And to get it over with now, before I go back to my princess. I know she's worried, and I have the phone in my hand. But I can't call her yet. Not until this is done.

The Romanos often gather in a large Victorian house sitting on two acres to the north outside of the city. It's a beautiful little estate, probably owned by some fucking rich asshole back in the day, but now it's used as the center of one of the most powerful mafias on this side of the coast.

I pull up to the front gate and stop. A man holding a rifle stares at me as I lower my window.

"Gio, here to see Marco," I say.

"Who?" the man asks.

"Gio. Tell Marco that I have something for him from my father. It's important."

The man stares at me, then nods. He goes to his radio and calls up to the main house. After a short conversation, he heads back over to me.

"Marco says to come up."

I nod at the man as he opens up the gate. I drive up the path and park my truck out front. More men holding weapons hang around the front. They eye me suspiciously, but I don't care. I grab the plastic-wrapped bag next to me and hop out of the car.

"Hold on," a thug says. "Gotta check you for weapons."

"By all means." I grin at him as he pats me down. When he's finished, he gestures at the bag.

"That too," he says.

I open it for him. He recoils at what's inside.

"Anything else?" I ask.

"Uh, shit, no." He's clearly shaken, and has a look of disgust on his face.

"Thanks." I walk past him and into the front of the house.

Marco is waiting for me in the kitchen. Several of his men are scattered around the large room, and I can smell something cooking on the stove. It's probably some kind of tomato sauce and pasta, if I had to guess. It's a cliché, but pasta is easy as hell when it comes to feeding large numbers.

"Gio," Marco says, standing. "What a pleasure."

"Marco." We don't shake hands. He looks at me with a smile on his face, but I know there's menace behind everything he does.

"To what do I owe this pleasure?" he asks.

"I have a message for you from the Rossis."

His face darkens, and the smile disappears. "Since when do you work for them?"

"I don't," I say. "But he did."

I open the bag and dump my father's severed head out onto the table.

The men all take a step back except for Marco, who stands his ground without changing his expression in the least. Marco stares at the head with a shocked silence surrounding us, his men waiting for orders.

Fucking pussies. For a bunch of hardened criminals, they sure do act like a bunch of babies over one severed head.

"That's your father," Marco says at last.

"That's right. We were going to hit the Rossi Don, but my father sold me out instead." He clucks his tongue and takes a step back, narrowing his eyes and considering my words.

"How did… this happen?" he asks, gesturing at the head.

"The Rossis made a new deal with me. The old Don, Martino, is dead. His daughter killed him, and Toni is in charge now. Toni's offer for peace is that if I killed my father and brought you his head, we'd be square." I shrug and nod at the head. "That's what I've done."

"Why?" he asks, dumbfounded. "Why the fuck would he want that?"

"My father was a piece of shit. I think he's trying to tell you that the war is only going to get worse from here on out." I shrug. "I don't know, and I don't care."

"Why would you do this to your own father?" Marco stares at me, shaking his head and looking at me like I'm a rat, like I'm the piece of shit here. It pisses me off.

"You know him. He was a scumbag. You were never going to let him in." I begin to walk backward toward the door. "He betrayed me, and he paid for it. Now we're finished."

"Wait," he says.

"No. I'm finished with you, Marco. I'm finished with the Rossis, too. You're going to let me leave this place and never come back."

"Why would I let you leave?" he asks. "How do I know this isn't a trick?"

"You know me, Marco. If I wanted you dead, you'd be dead." I pause and smile at him. "Good luck with the war."

Without another word, I turn and leave the room. My back is to him to let him know he's no threat to me. My blood runs cold knowing they could kill me. But it would break code. There would be no honor in my murder.

My job is finished. Marco doesn't say anything as I leave and head back out front. Nobody comes after me, and nobody stops me as I get into my car and drive back toward the main road.

The gate shuts behind me, and I feel slight relief. But I won't be complete until I have my Grace in my arms.

I roll down my window and feel the cool breeze on my face. I feel free for the first time in my entire life. My father's dead, and my ties with the mafia are officially severed. The Romanos won't want me back, and the Rossis will probably kill me if they ever see me again. But as long as we stay away, they have no reason to come after us.

It's just me and Grace now. I'm nobody's fucking lapdog anymore. No more contracts from them, and no more killings. My life is in my own hands.

And the only thing I want is my princess. She's the only thing that matters anymore.

My heart hammers in my chest as I speed back toward her. I grab my phone on the passenger seat and dial up her number. The darkness is nowhere to be seen, and I feel optimistic for the first time in my life. I believe the darkness is gone, or at least it's buried down deep beneath this new feeling.

I can't wait to get back home. I can't wait to tell Grace everything. I want her to know how free I am. I want her to know how I feel about her. She's mine, she's completely mine, and she always will be.

I press down the accelerator and speed toward her, feeling light and ready.

She answers on the first ring. "Gio?" Her voice is low and full of worry.

"I'm coming, princess. I'll be there soon."

Epilogue

Gio

I STEP OUT ONTO THE BALCONY AND TAKE A DEEP BREATH OF THE fresh sea air. I raise the coffee cup to my lips and sip the fresh, strong French coffee as the city unfolds in front of me. Duke is curled up in the corner under the small table, dozing in the morning breeze. He's gotten lazier since we moved, just like a proper French dog.

It's a beautiful town, Saint-Tropez. Situated in the south of France between Cannes and Marseille, it's a small place that's not jam-packed with tourists. It's absolutely breathtaking, just like most of southern France, with gorgeous pastel-colored homes and a sprawling view of a deep blue ocean.

Grace picked it out. Out of everywhere in the world, she wanted to come here. It's our home now. And she loves it. That's all that matters to me. I don't remember how long it's been. Two months, maybe three. Time doesn't really matter anymore. Life is slow in Saint Tropez, which is exactly what I wanted.

I don't kill anymore. Ever since leaving Chicago, the cravings disappeared. The darkness never appears anymore, not even in my worst moments.

I take another deep breath, feeling calm and content for the first time ever.

I turn around and look into our bedroom. Grace props herself up on one elbow, smiling at me. The breeze from the open doors blows her hair out of her face. She's goddamn beautiful. I'm a lucky man.

"You're up early," she says with a yawn.

I walk in and kiss her gently on the lips. "I wanted to get your breakfast together."

"You're spoiling me." She laughs.

I shrug, smiling. "You're damn right I am. You're my princess."

"What's on the agenda for today then?" she asks, stretching her arms above her head.

"Whatever you want. I thought we might walk down to the market, get something for lunch and dinner, and then walk along the beach. Maybe stop for a drink somewhere."

"So, what we did yesterday?"

I grin. "Exactly. I also thought we could visit that little private outcropping of rocks…"

She laughs. "You dirty man. You're just trying to get into my panties again." She rests her head on the pillow and looks up at me as though she's innocent. She's just as dirty as I am. And she knows it.

"Damn right I am." I kiss her rough on the lips as the memory of fucking her on that public beach the day before comes back to me.

After everything went down, I picked up Grace and Duke from my house, packed some bags, and we left that night. We drove around the States for a while, living off my cash, until one day we met a guy that made fake passports in Philadelphia.

From there, we flew into London. We traveled around there for a while before heading into Germany. We hit up Italy, Spain, northern France, and finally settled in Saint-Tropez.

I ended up buying this apartment, and for the first time since we left my house, we settled into a normal daily life.

Well, normal enough. I still have a shitload of money saved up, which means neither of us are going to have to work for a very long time. If ever.

For her part, I can tell Grace is the happiest she's ever been. I made sure she got to visit everything she wanted and see and do everything possible. She had so many experiences to catch up on, and I loved watching her find herself in the world.

She's free. She's my princess, but she's free. She can leave at any time if she wants, but I know she never will.

Not when we're so stupid happy together. Not when it feels like we finally make each other complete, and the horrors of our past no longer matter.

I'm going to treat her like the princess she is for the rest of her life. She'll never work a day in her life if she doesn't want to. Or she can do any job she wants. It doesn't matter to me, so long as she spoiled, pampered, and happy.

That's my life now, and it's more fulfilling than anything else. We eat, sleep, fuck, and I take care of her. That's the way life should be.

"You shouldn't let me sleep in," she says finally, sitting up and taking a look around the room.

"You need rest now. You know that."

She sighs. "Just because I'm pregnant doesn't mean I'm incapacitated."

I laugh. "Sure it does. You have to let me take care of you."

"You already do." The soft smile that plays on her lips makes my heart clench.

I glance down at the ring on her finger. The wedding ceremony happened in Spain at an ancient church on the coast. We didn't speak a word of Spanish, but it was beautiful and perfect and most importantly, it made her happy. One look at the church, and she knew she wanted it to happen there. So I made it happen.

She sighs and stretches again. I walk over to the table and pour her some orange juice. She accepts the glass gratefully.

"You're still going to love me when I'm big and fat, right?"

I smirk at her. "You'll never be big and fat."

"Correct answer."

I crawl into bed next to her and kiss her neck. "You know, princess, we could always stay in."

"Oh, can we?" She smiles at me, a little mischievous. "And why would we do that?"

"You need your rest."

"You're not going to let me rest, and you know it."

"True. I'm a bad liar."

She laughs at my joke, and sets the orange juice down on the nightstand. I take my chance to crawl on top of her.

I kiss her full and deep, joy welling up inside of me. Soon, we'll be a proper family. I'll raise my son to love and respect people, and I won't let him have the life we had.

All that matters is that Grace can find herself and we can live together, peacefully, loving, a family in paradise. Her French is wonderful, and I'm getting better. Soon we'll be proper French citizens with little French babies.

I never imagined that in my whole life. But I couldn't be happier.

With Grace and our baby, I'm more content than I could possibly imagine. The ocean stretches out into the distance and I have her, my princess, my love, the only thing that keeps me going. I'll take care of her until my heart stops beating, and forever after that.

forget me not

I fell in love with a boy a long time ago. I was only a small girl. Scared and frightened, I was taken from my home and held against my will. His father hurt me, but *he* protected me and kept me safe as best he could.

Until I left him.

I ran the first chance I got and even though I knew he wasn't behind me, I didn't stop. The branches lashed out at me, punishing me for leaving him in the hands of a monster.

I've never felt such guilt in my life.

Although I survived, the boy was never found. I prayed for him to be safe. I dreamed he'd be alright and come back to me. Even as a young girl I knew I loved him, *but I betrayed him.*

Twenty years later, all my wishes came true.

But the boy came back a man. With a grip strong enough to keep me close and a look in his eyes that warned me to never dare leave him again. I was his to keep, after all.

Twenty years after leaving one hell, I entered another. Our tale was only just getting started.

It's dark and twisted.

But that doesn't make it any less of what it is.

A love story. *Our* love story.

Prologue

Robin

I CAN WAIT HERE LONGER THAN HE CAN STAND TO STAY AWAY. I KNOW that much.

A small grin pulls at my lips as I pick at the thread on the comforter. Always picking and waiting. There's nothing else to do in this room.

My head lifts at the thought, drawing my eyes to the blinking red light. And he's always watching. The sight of the camera makes my stomach churn, but only for a moment.

The sound of heavy boot steps walking down the stairs outside the closed door makes my heart race. I stare at the doorknob, willing it to turn and bring him to me.

I've waited too long for him.

The sound of the door opening is foreboding. If anyone other than me was waiting for him, I'd assume they'd have terror in their hearts. But I know him. I understand it all. The pain, the guilt. I know firsthand what it's like when the monster is gone and you only have your own thoughts to fight. Your memories and regrets. It's all-consuming.

And there's no one who can understand you. No one you trust, whose words you can believe are genuine and not just disguised pity.

But he knows me, and I know him. Far too well; our pain is shared.

His broad shoulders fill the doorway and his dark eyes meet mine instantly. He barely touches the door and it closes behind him with a loud click that's only a hair softer than my wildly beating heart.

It's hard to swallow, but I do. And I ignore the heat, the quickened breath. I push it all down as he walks toward me, closing the space with one heavy step at a time.

He stops in front of me, but doesn't hesitate to cup my chin in his large hand and I lean into his comforting touch. I know to keep my own hands down though and I grip the comforter instead of him.

It's a violent pain that rips through me, knowing how scarred he is. So much so, that I have to hold back everything. I'm afraid of my words, my touch. He's so close to being broken beyond repair and I only want to save him, but I don't know how.

We're both damaged, but the tortured soul in front of me makes me feel everything. He makes me want to live and heal his tormented soul. But how can I, when I'm the one who broke him by running away?

"My little bird," he whispers and it reminds me of when we were children. When we were trapped together.

He's not the boy who protected me.

He's not the boy whose eyes were filled with a darkness barely tempered with guilt.

He's not the boy I betrayed the moment I had a chance.

He's a man who's taking what he wants.

And that's me.

Chapter 1

Robin

One week before

"Doctor Everly?" a soft voice calls out, breaking me from my distant thoughts as another early spring chill whips through my thin jacket and sends goosebumps down my body. I slowly turn my head to Karen. Her cheeks are a little too pink from a combination of the harsh wind and a heavy-handed application of blush, and the tip of her nose is a bright red.

I grip my thin jacket closer, huddling in it as if it can protect me from the brutal weather. It's too damn cold for spring, but I suppose I'd rather be cold and uncomfortable out here. Today especially.

I give Karen a tight smile, although I don't know why. It's not polite to smile out here, or is it? "How are you doing?" I ask her as she walks closer to me.

She nods her head, taking in a breath and looking past me at the pile of freshly upturned dirt. "It hurts still. It's just so sad." Karen's only twenty-three, fresh out of college and new to this. I'm new to it too. Marie was the first patient I've had who killed herself.

Sad isn't the right word for it. Devastating doesn't even begin to describe what it feels like when a young girl in your care decides her life is no longer worth living.

I clear my throat and turn on the grass to face her. The thin heels of my shoes sink into the soft ground, and I have to balance myself carefully just to stand upright.

"It is," I tell Karen, not sure what else to say.

"How do you handle…" her voice drifts off.

I don't know how to answer her. My lips part and I shake my head, but no words come out.

"I'm so sorry, Robin," she says and Karen's voice is strong and genuine. She knows how much Marie meant to me. But it wasn't enough.

I try to give her an appreciative smile, but I can't. Instead, I clear my tight throat and nod once, looking back to where Marie's buried.

"Are you okay?" she asks me cautiously, resting a hand on my arm, trying to comfort me. And I do what I shouldn't. *I lie.*

"I'm okay," I tell her softly, reaching up to squeeze her hand.

As I tuck a loose strand of hair behind my ear, a gust of wind flies by us and a bolt of lightning splits the sky into pieces, followed a few seconds later with the hard crack of thunder.

Karen looks up, and in an instant the light gray clouds darken and cue the storm to set in. It's only the two of us left here and it looks like the weather won't have us here any longer, leaving Marie all alone. I think deep inside that's how she wanted it all along. She didn't want a shrink to give her advice.

Who was I to help her? The guilt washes through me and the back of my eyes prick with unshed tears as I take in a shuddering breath, shoving my hands in my pockets and turning back to her grave.

As much as I'd like to believe I'll let her rest now, I know I'll be back. It's selfish of me. She just wanted to be left alone. She needed that so her past could fade into the background. I know that now; I wish I knew it then.

"She's in a better place," Karen whispers and my gaze whips up to hers. She doesn't have the decency to look me in the eyes and I have to wonder if she just said the words because she thinks they're appropriate. Like it's something meant to be said when talking of the dead, or maybe she really believes it.

Karen turns to walk toward her car as the sprinkling of rain starts to fall onto us. She looks back over her shoulder, waiting for me and I relent, joining her.

I'm sorry, Marie.

As the cold drops of rain turn to sheets and my hair dampens, my pace picks up. It doesn't take long until we're both jogging through the grass and then onto the pavement of the parking lot, our heels clicking and clacking on the pavement with the sound of the rain.

I barely hear her say goodbye and manage a wave behind me as I open my car door and sink into the driver seat.

I just wanted to help Marie. I could see so much of myself in her. We were almost the same age. She had the same look in her eyes. The same helplessness and lack of self-worth. I wanted to save her like my psychiatrist saved me.

But how could I? I'm not over my past. I should have known better. I should have referred her to someone more capable. Someone who had less emotional investment. I pushed too hard. *It's my fault.*

The pattering of rain on the car roof is eerily rhythmic as I dig through my purse, shivering and shoving the wet hair out of my face. The keys jingle as I shove them into the ignition, turning on the car and filling the cabin with the sounds of the radio.

I'm not sure what song's on but I don't care because I'm quick to turn the radio off. To get back to the silence and the peace of the rainfall. I slump in my seat, staring at the temperature gauge. When I look up, I see Karen drive away in the rearview mirror. Watching her car drive out of sight, my eyes travel to my reflection.

I scoff at myself and wipe under my eyes. I look dreadful. My dirty blonde hair's damp and disheveled, my makeup's running. I lift the console and grab a few tissues to clean myself up before sluggishly removing my soaked jacket and tossing it in the backseat. The heater finally kicks on, and I still can't bring myself to leave.

I look back into the mirror and see that I'm somewhat pulled together, but I can't hide the bags under my eyes. I can't force a false sense of contentment onto my face.

I close my eyes and take in another deep breath, filling my lungs and letting it out slowly. I need sleep. I need to eat. It's been almost a week since I found out about Marie. A week of her no longer being here to call and check in on. Tears stream freely down my cheeks. I tried so hard not to cry; I learned a long time ago that crying doesn't help, but being forced to leave her is making me helpless to my emotions.

That first night I almost cried, but instead I resorted to sleeping pills. A wave of nausea churns in my stomach at the thought of what I did. It was so easy to just take one after the other. Each one telling me it'd be over soon. After downing half the bottle, I knew what I was doing. But the entire bottle was too much and it all came back up before I could finish it. Thank God for that. I'm not well, and I'm sure as hell not in a position to help others.

My hand rests against my forehead as I try to calm down, as I try to rid myself of the vision of Marie in my office, but other memories of my past persist there, waiting for this weakness.

I can't linger any longer. Putting the car into reverse, I back out of my spot, turning and seeing Marie's plot in the distance as I back up.

Grief is a process, but guilt is something entirely different. It's becoming harder and harder to separate the two, and I know why.

She reminds me of *him*.

Of a boy, I knew long ago. The turn signal seems louder than ever as I wait at the exit to turn onto the highway. *Click, click, click.*

Each is a second of time that I'm here and they're not. *Click, click, click.*

The cabin warms as I drive away, merging onto the highway.

Maybe all this has nothing to do with Marie.

Maybe it's just the guilt that summons the vision of his light gray eyes from the depths of my memory.

Maybe it's because I'm to blame for both of their deaths.

Chapter 2

John

THE FAINT SOUNDS OF THE RADIO DISAPPEAR WITH A LOUD click as I shut it off. It's an old ass black box, covered in oil and grime from the shop, but it still works. Without it, the garage is silent. I wipe my hands with the blue shop towel, picking under my short, thick nails and scrub against the rough callus on my left thumb.

I'm a blue-collar mechanic, and there's not much more to me. Day in and day out, I work at my shop on the outskirts of town. The old oak trees and converted barn on the far side of the property are everything I need. I like my peace and quiet out here. I'd be a liar if I said I didn't get a bit lonely at times, but I don't need companionship. I don't need anyone.

I turn to look over my shoulder at the banged-up cherry red Chevy truck. That's going to take a bit of work tomorrow when Steve gets in. Fixing that side door would be a pain in my ass to do alone. And now that Steve's gone home, it's just me.

That damn truck can wait till tomorrow.

All the tools are back where they belong except for a few wrenches on the bench. The shop itself is old, with a cracked concrete floor and chipped red paint on the far wall where the hangar's attached to the garage. When I bought this place, it was rundown and in desperate need of fixing up. I love the charm of it though, how it's beaten down but still standing strong. The history is what I look forward to when I come here every day. The property itself is large. An old pilot used to live here. He loved two things in his life, the ducks on the lake out back and his airplanes in the hangar.

Poor old man didn't live long after he sold the place to me. I've still got an old Ercoupe from the 1940s he left here. I meant to fix it up, but time's gotten away from me and work's been steady.

I toss the cloth onto the bench and stretch my back, reaching my arms over my head and letting out a deep sigh. My back cracks, and it feels damn good. It's been a long day of hard work. And I'll have another one tomorrow. That's what I live for.

The dim evening light streams through the open garage door, bringing a crisp breeze with it. It feels relaxing. I take in a deep breath and close my eyes, feeling the exhaustion flow through me. I don't know the last time I had a good night's sleep. Doesn't matter how many hours I seem to get, I'm never well rested.

I pull the thin, dirty white t-shirt over my head, feeling my sore muscles stretch even more. My denim jeans sit low on my hips. They're dirtied too, but I don't give a damn about them. I ball up the shirt and rag, tossing them into the bin and get ready for the short walk up the hill and to my house on the other side of the dirt road.

The familiar sound of the door to the shop creaking snaps my eyes open. My body tenses, and my muscles coil. The shop's closed, and there's no one else out here for miles. There isn't a single reason anyone should be walking through my shop right now. I can hear heavy boot steps walking back here to the garage.

I straighten my broad shoulders as I slowly and silently pick up the largest wrench on the bench, my eyes staring straight ahead at the open door to the garage. The cold metal easily slips into my palm, feeling just right as my heart thumps and my breathing steadies. I only make it a single step when Jay steps into the doorway.

He's just as tall as me, which would be intimidating to most. My arms are corded with muscle from years of hard work and manual labor. As are his, although I haven't got the faintest idea what he does. I've never asked.

We're both daunting men, the difference is that I try to hide it. I'm not looking for a fight or to scare anyone. I'm not sure Jay is either, but he can't hide the darkness inside him or the terror of his past that eats away at him.

There's a softness about my eyes and a gentleness in my rough voice. It's enough to make people comfortable enough with me to get along just fine. There's not a damn bit of that in Jay. There's a hard edge in his eyes that never leaves. His shoulders turn in just slightly like he's ready to fight at all times. He could maybe fool you with charm, since he's got some of that in him, but the way his eyes pierce through you is enough to send a chill down your spine.

I'm usually not intimidated or frightened by anyone. I can stand on my own and take care of myself when I have to. But Jay has a side of him I'm pissed to admit frightens me. Not because of what he'd do to me, since I know I can take him. And not because I think he'd come for me. I toss the wrench down on the old wooden bench and start walking toward him, wiping my palms down on my jeans.

Jay's not a threat to me; he's not my enemy.

The fear is because I never know what Jay's going to do. He's fucked up in the head from his old man. Anger management doesn't even begin to describe what he needs. He's got problems I don't know how to handle, and it doesn't matter how much I try to help him. Some things you just can't fix.

Nonetheless, Jay's been there for me when I had no one. And I know why he's the way he is. I don't see him much, especially not since I picked up and moved to this tiny ass town, but if he needs me, I won't turn my back on him.

Jay's eyes light up and a smirk plays at his lips as he saunters down the wooden steps to the garage and gestures at the wrench. "You think that'd stop me?" he asks with playfulness in his voice.

I grin back at him, stopping to lean against the Chevy's cargo bed in the middle of the large garage and shrugging my shoulders. A rough chuckle vibrates up my chest and I look back to my hands.

Jay's boots smack on the floor as he comes to my side, bracing a hand on the back end of the truck and looking over his shoulder at the door.

"You bring someone with you?" I ask him.

He frowns a bit, shaking his head and looking down at the ground. He never comes with anyone. I may be a loner to some extent, but Jay is something different. I'm not sure if he prefers it that way, or if it's because he just doesn't trust himself.

"I got a favor to ask." He stands beside me, shoving his hands into his jeans pockets and leaning back against the truck with me, mirroring my posture. He stares straight ahead and runs the back of his hand over his nose before saying, "You can't tell anyone." His voice is deadly low, and it makes my blood freeze in my veins.

I stare at him, waiting for more, but nothing comes. I clear my throat and try to relax against the hard metal.

I crack my neck to the side and nod my head. "You know I'm not going to say shit, Jay."

He nods his head slightly, his brow furrowing as he continues to avoid my gaze. He swallows thickly and says, "I'm gonna do something… and I need your help."

He finally looks at me, his eyes as cold as ice and narrowed. "There's a woman." My heart thuds once and my hands start to clench into fists, but I keep it from happening. Every bit of me is screaming to back out now, to tell him I don't want to hear it.

But I know what he's capable of, and I need to know who she is and what he's planning.

"A woman?" I ask. A chill flows in waves down my arms as if a cold draft has come through. I ignore the churning in the pit of my stomach. He'd never hurt a woman. Never. I know him. There's no fucking way he'd ever put his hand on a woman.

"She's broken, John." His voice is full of pain, and he breaks the gaze first. He talks to the ground as he adds, "She needs my help, but she's not going to want it."

"Then don't," I answer simply. If she doesn't want the help, there's no fucking reason he should approach her. He's got a warped sense of reality.

"She's hurting because of me," he admits quietly.

Tension grows in every inch of my body. I focus on my breathing, on staying cool and calm. Jay's violent and hot tempered. I stretch my jaw and look away, trying to convince myself it's going to be okay. That I can change his mind or stop him from whatever fucked up bullshit he thinks is going to happen.

"I have to," he says with conviction as if he read my mind.

It's only then that I see the dark circles under his eyes and how weary he looks. "Maybe you-" I speak without thinking, just trying to keep him appeased and take control of the situation.

"No," he interrupts, shaking his head before I can even finish. His body looks just as tense as mine as he pushes off the truck. I think he's going to leave, but instead, he starts pacing, running his hands through his thick short hair. "It's because of me," he confesses without stopping as his strangled voice repeats in nearly a whisper, "It's because of me."

My chest squeezes tight with pain watching him like this. It's been years. I haven't seen him break down since we were children. *Weak. Pathetic.*

The words whisper in the back of my head and he stops in his tracks, turning slowly, giving me a deadly look as if I said them out loud. For a moment, I think I may have. But he relaxes his stance and walks toward me slowly, stopping a few feet from me.

"She needs help."

"Then get her help from someone else." I answer him simply, licking my lower lip and hoping he'll reconsider whatever his plans are.

His eyes narrow slightly as he cocks his head, an asymmetric grin growing on his face. "She's going to help me, too." The way he says the words, so softly, with so much confidence and conviction, forces me to stare into his eyes, realizing there's no way to get him to stop.

"What are you going to do?" I ask, crossing my arms and trying my damnedest to just stay calm.

"I just want to get her alone and talk to her."

"Kidnapping-" The word is ripped from my throat before he cuts me off.

"It's not what you think," he says, his own hands balling into fists so tightly his knuckles turn white. The air is tense and thick between us. The sun setting makes the garage darker than it was only moments ago.

"You want me to help you kidnap her?" I ask him, not bothering to hide the disgust in my voice. The smile stays in place on his lips as he searches my eyes for something. He reaches into his pocket and pulls out a folded photograph. It's been creased twice, once down the middle and again at an angle off-center. He smooths it in his palm, finally looking away from me and answering, "I don't need help there, John." His voice is sad, as if he already regrets taking her.

He passes me the photo, flattening it against my chest with a hard thud and not letting go until I reach up to take the photo with my own hand.

"I just want you there to watch."

Adrenaline pumps through me at his request, anger rising in me. "And what am I going to be watching?"

"I just want to talk to her. I don't want to hurt her. I just want to fix her."

"Then get her help-"

"She's a shrink now," he says quickly. His eyes water slightly and he sniffs, looking away to take in a ragged breath. He licks his lower lip and looks back at me, willing me to understand. "She tried to kill herself," he says in an even voice I don't trust. "She grew up okay, you know?" He shakes his head once and pinches the bridge of his nose. "I didn't know she wasn't okay. I didn't know." I don't know if he's talking to me or to himself. His face is scrunched up with genuine pain.

"Who is she?"

"She's just a girl. I broke her, and I need to fix her." The strength in his tone solidifies his plan. He wraps his hand around the thin railing to the steps and mutters under his breath so low I almost don't hear him as he walks away, "And she's going to fix me."

"You won't do this without me?" I yell at his back, more a command than a question. I'll figure out something to keep him from doing this. I have to.

He turns to look over his shoulder, his face all raw pain and agony. He nods his head once. "I have to do this, but you need to be there. For me and her, John." His eyes dart to the floor, then back to me. "I'm going to-morrow night," he says and then turns back to leave, taking another step.

"I'll go with you," I tell him quickly. He only nods his head and keeps walking. I know he heard me, and I know where to find him when I finally get a grip on what the fuck is going on. I only have a few hours to figure something out. But I will.

It's only when I hear the faint click of the front door to the shop that I look down at the photo. I run my fingers down the creases to flatten it as best I can and take in the sight of a beautiful woman.

Her pale skin is complemented by the dark locks of her hair. I'm not sure where she is in the photo; it could be anywhere. The background is merely a brick wall as she looks off into the distance.

I don't know who she is, but she seems so familiar. The way she smiles, the look in her eyes, they strike something in me. A memory I don't have access to.

Jay's told me what happened when he was younger. The descriptions were so vivid I felt as if I was there. I run the tips of my fingers over her face, wondering if she's really the girl he talked about all those years ago.

I glance up at the empty doorway reluctant to believe Jay and to trust he's not going to hurt her. I can't help him do this, but I need to be there for her. I need to protect her. That one thought rings through my blood. I need to be there to help her. I need to get her away from Jay.

Chapter 3

Robin

Twenty years ago

M Y HEAD HURTS SO BAD. WHY DOES IT HURT SO MUCH? *I try to push myself upright, and the ground is so cold and hard. It's so uncomfortable, but my head is too heavy and I slump against the ground.*

Where am I?

I try to remember where I was. The sound of the carousel shrieking as it slowly turned from the blowing wind filters through my memory. The empty swings sway back and forth. The school playground is deserted. I thought everyone would be here today. But it's empty. The first day of summer and not a soul is here.

I remember how I looked up and the sun was far off in the distance, but still in the sky. Didn't they know we still had time to play? I'm younger than most of the kids, only twelve, but even the older ones usually play with me.

I sat on the swings for a while. I remember that. As the pounding in my head throbs harder I remember how the metal chains twisted and I let myself twirl on the swings over and over. I could wait for the other kids. I was sure they'd show up.

Did they?

I squint, trying to remember and I turn my head. My palms brush against the concrete floor, my cheek flat against the hard floor.

There was a man. He had a golf club and he needed my help. I remember how lost he looked. He said he hit his last ball into the trees and he couldn't reach into the bushes.

My heartbeat quickens as I remember, and my body goes still.

I knew to tell him a lie. I knew to turn around and run when he tried to take my hand in his. But he looked so hurt when I tried to pull away. He was genuinely upset, and all he did was ask me to help him.

The thin branches cracked under my sneakers as I went into the woods, following him to where he thought the ball had landed.

I open my eyes and I can't breathe.

He lied to me. My nails scratch on the ground as I clench them into fists and slowly look up.

No! Mommy, help me! Tears blur my vision of the cinder block walls.

No! This can't be happening. I pull my knees into my chest and try to stand.

Why does my head hurt so much?

"Are you okay?" a soft voice asks from behind me, encouraging me as I shuffle across the ground and push myself against the cold wall. It takes a moment for me to wipe my eyes and see him.

He's just a boy.

His knees are knobby and he's thin, but his shoulders are broad and he has a look about him that lets me know he's older than me. There's another look about him, too.

Sorrow and sadness cloud his eyes. Or maybe I just imagined it, because the moment my vision focuses, a hard expression stares back at me. He doesn't move from where he is, crouching only a few feet from me.

"Where am I?" I ask him quickly. I don't know where the words come from. I feel hot and cold, and I'm so confused. "I want to leave."

He huffs and shakes his head at me, pushing himself up from the ground where he was and takes a step toward me. He's taller than me. In that moment, he scares me.

"You can't leave," he says simply.

My face crumples, and I shake my head. "My mother will-"

"We're stuck here!" he yells at me, the anger in his voice making me flinch. He stares at the wall behind me, his eyes flickering to the floor then back to me. "We can't leave."

As I start to protest, I hear a loud rough bark outside. It's followed by a series of vicious barks that continue over and over. I whirl around and face the only window. It's small and rectangular, covered in filth and high up on the wall. There's barely any light coming through. Maybe there's a bush planted in front of it. I'm not sure, but at the very least I know there are dogs close.

"Don't try to run," the boy says behind me and again I turn to face him. Threats all around me, and it's my fault. It's all my fault. So stupid! I wrap my arms around my shoulders. "My mother-"

"Stop." The boy gives me the command, and I do. I stop because I'm a good girl. I've always been a good girl, but look at where it's gotten me.

It's quiet for a while, and the boy takes another step closer to me. I don't move. I don't know what to do or where I am, but deep down inside I know this boy isn't going to hurt me. There's something about him. Something broken and scared and angry even, but it's pure.

"What's going to happen to us?" I ask him weakly.

"He won't touch you. It's not about you."

"What?" I don't understand. I'm so confused.

"He's using you." He looks past me, anger evident as he clenches his jaw. "It's about making me do what he wants. He knows I won't..." his voice drifts off, and the anger changes into something else. Something I can't see because he turns his back to me.

I reach out to him, grabbing his arm to keep him from leaving me, moving purely out of instinct. The touch feels like a spark. As if I've put my hand to a flame, but before I can even process it, he whips back around to face me, a scowl of anger on his face as he stares at me. "I won't let him hurt you like he does me. All you are is a tool for him to use against me."

He takes another step closer to me, and for the first time I really get a good look in his eyes. The intensity almost makes me scoot back, but then I'd be against the wall. Trapped and cornered.

He parts his lips to answer me, but no words come out. Time passes, and the only thing I can hear is my heartbeat as he stares at me. His eyes don't break from mine, and I'm too scared to look away.

"I'm sorry," he says flatly, but then he turns away as if the sentiment were genuine.

For some reason, just hearing those words breaks me. The tears fall and as I wipe them away, he looks at me with distaste. I half expect him to tell me to stop, but he doesn't.

I struggle to calm myself and somehow I do. Maybe it's because I don't really believe him. I don't believe it's hopeless. My mother will find me, and she'll make that man pay for what he's done. Both to me and to this boy. I know she will.

"What's your name?" I ask to keep him from leaving me as he turns. I lick my lips, tasting the salty tears and wiping my cheeks. I don't want to cry. I want to get out of here.

"J-" he starts to answer me, but we both whip around and face the door as it opens, silencing us and making me instinctively back away from it.

I grab onto the boy's arm and try to hide behind him. I don't know a thing about him and the look he gives me nearly makes me run from both him and the man stalking into the room, but I don't get the chance. The boy grips my wrist with his other hand and pulls me closer to him, my front to his back and my back to the wall. He keeps himself deliberately positioned in between me and the man.

It's only when I grab onto the boy, my small fingers digging into the rough denim of his jeans at his hip and my cheek pressed against his back, that he lets go of me.

The boy may scare me some, but the man terrifies me.

Chapter 4

THIS SABBATICAL WAS A MISTAKE. I'M ONLY HOURS INTO IT, BUT I'm already feeling like I need to do something. Anything. I just can't sit here and not focus on work. It's what I've done since I was a child. It makes dealing with everything so much easier.

I pull the blanket tighter around me and toss the paperback novel onto my nightstand. I tried reading the first page at least four times. My eyes would travel along the lines, but not a word would register. I just can't focus. I can't relax.

I flick the switch to the lamp, turning it off and rub my tired eyes. I can't sleep either, but that's nothing new. My back cracks as I lie back down and try to stretch out my neck. It's sore and so are my shoulders, so I fluff the pillow and put my head back down only to be agitated by how hot the pillow is.

I'm just not comfortable. Not physically, not emotionally. And I don't think I should be. I deserve this.

I turn onto my side and then back onto my stomach, hugging the pillow close to me. I thought tonight I'd be haunted by the last session I had with Marie. I thought it would be her eyes I'd see that kept me from slipping into a much-needed sleep and letting the exhaustion take over. Instead, it's *his* eyes.

Red-rimmed and brimming with tears. They fall down his face and he doesn't acknowledge them, he just stares at me, whispering that he's sorry. He hadn't told me he was sorry other than the first day. But weeks later, my strong protector stared at me and it was all he could say. My chest tightens, and I remember how the fear weighed against me. "I'm sorry," he whispered.

I try not to cry. He already feels guilty, but he shouldn't. His father uses me to make the boy do things he doesn't want to. It's not fair to him. What's worse is that I want him to protect me. How selfish I am. I'm sickened by it, but the fear of his father keeps me quiet as the days pass.

As I swallow the spiked lump in my throat, twisting my fingers around each other and ignoring the emotions rushing through my blood, my eyes dart to the boy's arm. The bruises are already dark, and there's a large scratch on his forearm. The blood is so bright. Such a vivid color. I'll never forget.

"I'm sorry," he says and his voice cracks and this time he wipes the tears away with the back of his hand as he sniffles. I've never seen him like this. I shake my head with my eyes closed, ignoring how my heart squeezes and my body goes cold. His father is going to come for me. He's going to put me in the cage instead of the boy.

My mother isn't coming. No one is. It's been weeks. I knew the day would come when I would have to leave this room. I always thought it would happen after the boy was taken. Every time I'm alone in here, I'm scared his father will come back and he won't be able to protect me anymore.

But he let the boy come back to me with the threat that when he returns, he'll be taking me for his test.

I can't help but let the tears fall as I wrap my arms around my chest and try to keep the sobs from ripping from my throat. I can't blame the boy. He's kept me safe for so long. But he didn't listen. He wouldn't obey his father, and now the monster is going to come for me.

"It's okay," I say weakly, although the way my voice croaks, I don't even know if he can understand me.

He grips my shoulders with both of his hands. It's a bruising force that snaps me out of the fear of what's to come and captures my full attention. He's so close to me, so intense as he stares into my eyes. I don't think he's ever touched me before. Not like this, not since the first day when he shielded me. He doesn't like it when I touch him either. Especially when he has bruises.

He shakes his head, his eyes staying on mine. "React quickly," he tells me, and his face scrunches and he holds back his own emotions, breathing deeply before looking back at me with remorse. "He stops it if you show how scared you are."

His eyes pierce mine and I can't help but nod my head, although I'm not sure what he's talking about. He's never told me what happens when he leaves. He's not the same when he comes back and he likes to be alone, so I give him that space. "Don't try to be brave and hide it. He'll only make it worse."

I stare at him, but I don't answer. I can't do this. I need to be strong and not make this harder for him, but I'm terrified.

"Robin!" the boy screams my name, demanding an answer and my obedience, but before I can say anything, the heavy metal door swings open.

My eyes snap open and I struggle to take a breath, quickly sitting up and shoving the suffocating blanket off me. I take a ragged breath and reach up to my shoulders where he was touching me. I swear I can still feel his fingers digging into me.

He was just a boy, but he tried so hard to protect me. I pull my knees into my chest and rest my head on my knees, focusing on breathing. He didn't deserve the fate he was given.

I lick my dry lips, willing the memories to go away.

It's been so long since they've been this vivid. I know it's the guilt. I left him there. He took so much of the pain to try to save me. He's the only reason I could escape, and in return, I left him behind.

Small tears leak from the corners of my eyes, wetting my lashes and landing hard on my silk nightgown. I wipe them away and then reach for the bottle of pills on my nightstand.

I know I need to see someone for this. I can't keep taking pills just to sleep, just to keep the night terrors from surfacing, but I'm too ashamed to admit it all.

I'm too much of the coward that I was when I was a child.

I take two pills, hoping they'll help. Last night they didn't. Hours passed and sleep didn't come. It only makes the mornings worse, but maybe tonight, it'll come. I swallow the now room temperature water and set the glass down on the nightstand.

My back and shoulders hurt as I roll over again. I bunch the blanket between my knees and shift on the mattress. It's the best money can buy, but it can't soothe my sore body. It can't lull me into a deep sleep that keeps the nightmares from surfacing.

Nothing can save me.

It's a weird feeling when you know you're about to fall asleep. Your body seems to go weightless for just a moment. My limbs turn numb and everything feels heavy. So heavy but like I'm floating, a sweet contradiction that tells me sleep is coming.

I'm conscious of it, fully aware a deep sleep within reach. And that's when the floor creaks and my body wakes instantly, tense and stiff.

I keep my eyes closed, too afraid to open them. My heart races in my chest, and I'm too scared to move. *Maybe it's all in my head*, I tell myself, but the second I do, I hear the floorboards creak again with the heavy weight of someone walking into my bedroom.

My back is to my nightstand, but I know my car alarm is there. My keys are sitting somewhere on it in the dark. I need to move, if for no reason than to make a disturbance. I suck in a breath as I roll my body over, not looking at whoever is here.

I don't care who it is, I'll fight them. I won't go down easy and be a good little victim. I refuse to.

I knock the glass of water over, and it shatters on the floor. At the same time, the bed dips low with the weight of the intruder. I scream out as he grabs me, my fingers grasping at the ceramic cup that holds my keys, my earrings, my lip balm. The rim of the cup brushes along my fingertips as a rag covers my face.

I breathe in once, both of my hands reaching up toward my mouth. My fingers struggle to pry the large hand away, scratching as my muffled screams prove how useless my fight was.

His heavy leg lays over mine, pinning me down as I breathe in again. Chloroform.

I can smell it, and it's then that I know I'm fucked.

I struggle until I can't.

I scream until my throat's raw.

And when my body finally goes heavy and numb again, that weightless feeling taking over, my eyes roll back and I catch a glimpse of the man.

His eyes.

So gray. Even in the dark of night, I know it's *him*. The sharp lines of his handsome face are different from those I remember. My hand reaches up, my fingers brushing his rough stubble before falling without my consent.

He's alive. I will my eyes to stay open for just a bit longer. Just to be sure he's real.

The boy's alive. My heart squeezes, and the realization is too much to bear. It shatters my sanity, my composure.

And then the darkness takes over in one slow wave, and all at once, I surrender myself to him.

Chapter 5

Twenty years ago

I'M SO USED TO THIS ROOM. I DON'T KNOW HOW LONG IT'S BEEN, BUT *I don't bother to count the days anymore. I don't hope for Mama to come find me anymore. I know it's useless now, and it only makes me more upset.*

The only solace I have is lying beside me. I speak without thinking, just saying what's on my mind to break up the silence in the cold room.

"I wish I were a bird." I blink at the faint light shining through the small window so high up on the cinder block wall. "Then I could fly away." My voice lowers to nearly a whisper and I turn on the hard ground, facing the boy at my side. I tuck my arm under my head and swallow the lump in my throat as I avoid his gaze. It's such a serious look in his light gray eyes. I can hardly stand the chill that runs through me.

Some days I think he's angry with me. I can't shake the thought that he hates me; that he hates being stuck here with me, both of us helpless and at the hands of his heartless father.

"Both of us." I clear my throat and chance a look up at him as I add, "I mean I wish we were both birds." I turn to gesture toward the far wall as I explain, "So we could fly through that window."

The boy smiles at me, although I don't think it's genuine. "But it's closed," he says in a voice so rough and low it makes goosebumps spread across my skin. He clears his throat, propping up his head in his hand and leaning on his elbow to look down at me. My heart does a weird flip in my chest, fluttering when he leans closer to me. I can feel the heat of his body. He's older than me. He looks it, too. I feel my cheeks heat with a blush and I look away, turning back to the window and pulling at the thin gown I have on. It's not enough to keep me warm down here and I know if I were just a bit closer to the boy, I'd be more comfortable, but I keep my distance.

"Well, what animal then?" I ask the boy, curling on my side and tucking both arms beneath my head.

He's quiet for a moment, but then he answers, "A wolf could break it."

I resist the urge to turn to face him, closing my eyes as they roll and a small smile forms on my lips. A wolf could never fit through that window.

I decide to play along, feeling a warmth run through me as I hear him scoot closer to me. He never touches me, but he likes to be close to me. And I like it too although I don't tell him. "Well, you be a wolf and break the window, and I'll be a bird. Together we can run away."

"I saw a wolf kill a bird once on TV," he says, but the boy's voice is devoid of emotion and the shock of what he said makes me turn to face him, sitting up and pulling my knees into my chest.

"Why would a wolf do that?" I feel my brows pinch and my lips turn down; I know it's obvious I'm horrified from what he said, and it only makes him laugh.

He shrugs his shoulders and picks at a spot on the concrete floor, a satisfied smirk on his lips. Something about the look on his face makes my heart do that fluttering motion again and I find myself inching forward, my toes barely touching his thigh. But we both notice that they touch.

"A wolf doesn't have any reason to hurt a bird." I stare at him, but he still doesn't look up at me. "I don't understand."

The boy tilts his head to look at me and this time, the expression is something I've never seen before. There's a rawness in the light gray flecks, a heat on the outer edge where his eyes get darker. Almost like a flicker of a flame giving his gaze an intensity that makes my body freeze, but not with a coldness, with a burning heat.

"I think he did it," the boy starts to say, licking his lower lip and staring right through me, not caring that I can't even breathe when he looks at me like that, "I think he did it just because he wanted to."

Chapter 6

I PICK AT MY THUMBNAIL WITH MY TEETH AS I STAND IN THE CORNER of the dark room. I'm anxious, and adrenaline is pumping hard in my blood. Jay's a fucking bastard. He didn't tell me until it was already done.

I should go to the police and turn him in. I know that. Even as I pace in the small dark corner and stare at the woman on the bed, I know I should.

But I won't. Jay set me up. He said it was collateral, using my car and leaving evidence behind although he won't tell me what. I'm fucked. I grit my teeth remembering how he smiled at my anger.

I don't know what to do other than to keep her safe, but as the time ticks by I start to wonder if I'd do more harm than good. If being close and looking out for Jay would bite me in the ass. And in this case, the woman caught in Jay's gaze. I can't tell him no though. A low rumble in my throat pisses me off. I know Jay needs me and I'm fucked because I just can't walk away from him.

It reminds me of when we were kids. How I got along with everyone. A decent student and friendly by nature. Jay wouldn't come around to the playground often then. Very rarely. But some days I'd sit by the edge of the broken swing set, and he'd show up then. It scared me when he'd stay away for a long time. He wouldn't tell me where he went. All he'd say is that he wasn't wanted, but I shut that shit down. I wanted him around because I knew he needed someone. I could sense how desperate he was, but he was too afraid to open up. Too afraid to let anyone in. Except me, I guess.

The other kids didn't see him like I did. They mostly ignored him or, if they were honest with themselves, they were terrified to look him in the eye. That's the air around him that pushed everyone away. And the moment anyone would dare to approach us, Jay was gone. Uninterested in associating with anyone else. Despite all that, we got along just fine, better than fine most of the time. I knew how to be a good friend to him and he did the same for me when times got rough. We got close fast. Almost like brothers.

"Jay?" the woman calls out softly, and the sheets rustle as she turns onto her side, pulling her knees into her chest. Her voice is ragged, but not with fear, which is surprising. Just exhaustion. And it pulls me from my memories and back to the present.

She's even more gorgeous in person. I'm practically terrified to go any closer to her. She calls to me in a way I can't describe or justify. Her hair is a messy halo on the white pillow and her skin looks soft and smooth, so much of it exposed in the skimpy silk nightgown she's wearing. I only went to her to pull the thin sheet over her body, covering her curves although they're still prominent under the sheet.

"Robin?" I whisper her name and clear my throat when it comes out raspy. Jay's gone. He brought me here and left to get supplies. Things he said she'd need. I've never been to his home until now, but I couldn't have guessed for even a second it would be this nice.

He said it's for her. That it's always been for her, although he didn't know it until he was ready to take her. The way he talks about her has me on edge. He's obsessed, but only with healing her. Only in righting his sins.

All I know about her is her name, that she tried to kill herself, and that she has a past with Jay. He didn't give me anything else. He said she'd have to tell me.

"Jay?" the woman calls out again, her voice groggy as she rises on the mattress, bracing her arm behind her and slowly sitting up. She puts a hand on her forehead and lets out a small moan.

I hesitate only a moment more before taking three large strides closer before stopping at the foot of the bed. "You're safe," I tell her gently, raising my hands with my heart racing in my chest. "I promise I will keep you safe," I say and the words come out with strength. I will keep that promise if it's the last thing I do.

"Jay," she says softly, reverently almost and it shocks me. My brow pinches as I step closer to her, rounding the bed, but careful not to touch it. I don't even brush my knees against it. I don't want to give her any indication at all that I'll touch her.

"Jay went out," I tell her and try to breathe, I try to explain what's going on. "He wants to help you, and I'm here to make sure you're safe."

The small woman looks up and flinches. Her eyes go wide before she backs away slowly. So slowly it looks like the sheet barely moves as it falls down her body. She sucks in a breath and visibly swallows before I add, "I'm John."

"John?" she asks in a whisper before her eyes dart to the door and then back to me.

She's disoriented. The drugs are still coursing through her system, but the fear has finally set in.

"It's okay, I won't let Jay hurt you," I tell her, again raising my hands palms outward as though she's a wounded animal.

Her eyes fall to the sheet and then look back to me before she sits up to look at me, her gaze searching my face for something. She finally asks, "Does Jay want to hurt me?" Her eyes flicker to the door again and then back to my eyes.

The dim light in the room reflects in her eyes. Swirls of forest greens and flecks of gold. She has the most gorgeous eyes I've ever seen, but they're riddled with questions and fear.

"No," I answer her immediately. "He wants to help you."

She nods once and then the fear seems to dim although she unconsciously picks at the blanket on the bed.

"Are you alright?" I ask her, feeling deep down in the pit of my stomach that there's more between her and Jay than I realize. She's more afraid of me than him. I can feel it. "I promise, I have no intention of hurting you," I tell her and slow my movements to make it obvious I'm going to sit on the edge of the bed. I can't have her being afraid of me.

"I'm not well, no," she says softly, shaking her head just slightly but her eyes stay on mine, brimming with curiosity now. "Are you alright?" she asks me.

It throws me off. "No," I say after a moment. "This isn't alright with me," I add with my throat tight. "I didn't know," I explain, and I tell her more as a plea for forgiveness. I swallow hard and glance at the door. I should take her away. I can leave with her right now.

All the evidence will point to me though and if she presses charges, I'm fucked. But what other choice do I have?

"If you want to leave-" I start to say, but she cuts me off.

"What didn't you know?" she asks me, licking her lips and tilting her head to the right. Her eyes are wide with curiosity more than anything else.

"I didn't know he'd taken you," I admit to her in a low voice that's barely audible. She nods her head once.

"So you'd let me leave?" she asks in a small voice. Her eyes travel to the door as if watching herself simply walk away, but when her gaze stops, the lights turn on and Jay stands in the doorway. My eyes adjust to the light slowly, but they only focus on her and her reaction to seeing Jay. She hesitates a moment, her grip on the blanket tightening as she takes him in.

"Jay?" She whispers his name as if it's a question. As if it can't really be him.

My gaze turns to Jay, and I watch as his lips twitch up into a smile and his expression softens. He opens his mouth to say something, but instead he licks his lips and reaches behind him to close the door. A foreboding click echoes off the walls as he walks closer to her.

"How's your head?" he asks her.

"Jay, are you alright?" she asks and then crawls to the edge of the bed slowly, moving away from me and closer to him. Her eyes brim with tears, and she bites down on her bottom lip to keep them from spilling over.

He walks slowly toward her, and the sound of his boots smacking softly on the wooden floor is the only thing I can hear other than my racing heart.

He cups her chin in his hand and brushes his thumb along her lips, and she seems to lean into him. She reaches up and wraps her small hands around his wrist. "I know it's scary, but I thought you'd understand."

"You can't do this, Jay," she pleads with him as a tear slips down her cheek. The way she's talking to him, the way she pleads with him and ignores me completely shifts something deep inside of me. *She cares for him.* It's so fucking obvious.

"It's not just for me, little bird," Jay says in a pained voice. "I would have left you alone forever, I promise you I would have."

She shakes her head, rising on her knees to interrupt him. As the bed creaks with her shifting weight, he presses a finger to her lips, hushing her. "You wanted to hurt yourself," he tells her and her strength vanishes. She moves her cheek from his hand and seems to back away from him.

"Jay, you need help," she whimpers.

"Ah," Jay says. "And so do you, my little bird."

Chapter 7

Robin

I'M PRACTICALLY SHAKING. MY LEGS FEEL WOBBLY AND MY HEAD IS pounding, but I've never felt so aware.

It's him. It's really him. After all this time, he's finally come back to me. But this is a nightmare even I never dared to have. An outcome I couldn't have predicted.

"You're broken, Robin," Jay says and his voice breaks my thoughts. I stare at him, his eyes never looking so cold and his voice never feeling so devoid of emotion before. But he's right here in front of me. His jawline sharper, his shoulders broader and his body filled out.

He's no longer a scared little boy trying to protect me. He's become a man in every way.

"Why did you do it?" he asks me, and my blood turns to ice. I flinch as the memory comes back full force. The cold wind whipping across my face, the branches lashing out and striking me as I ran through the forest. I ran because I had no choice. *Liar!* a voice hisses in the back of my head. I didn't have to leave him behind. I'm a coward. I ran because I was scared.

"Why did you try to kill yourself?" Jay asks me and my eyes lift to his, my heart still hammering in my chest.

My throat feels dry and my voice comes out hoarse, but I'm grateful I misunderstood. I'm grateful he doesn't bring it up. I wish I could go back; I wish I could pretend I never left him. "I'm not well, but I'm-" I try to explain, but he cuts me off.

"Broken!" Jay yells at me, and for the first time real fear flows through me.

"I'm sorry I left you," I say. The words spill from me unbidden and I cover my mouth, hating that I've acknowledged it. I look up to him, watching for his reaction. But I get nothing, not a word or any recognition. "Please, don't hate me," I whimper. I feel so small beneath him.

Maybe this is what I've truly wanted. For him to punish me. For him to forgive me.

His large hand pats the back of my head, a comforting touch that brings me back to the first night I met him. When I lay on the ground crying until he finally reached out to comfort me.

"Don't be sorry," he says. "This isn't about that. It has nothing to do with how we left. It's only about who we've become since then."

"Why are you doing this?" I ask him. "You know it doesn't have to be like this," I say and my eyes search his, pleading and begging. "You didn't have to do this." My voice comes out as a hollow whisper.

"I did though," he tells me. "You have no idea what it's like. For me to know and be aware, and he… he doesn't. He doesn't see it."

I shake my head, grabbing onto the edge of the bed and the comforter as I insist, "That's not how this works, Jay!" I try desperately to get through to him. For him to understand. "I can't help you like this."

He breathes in heavy, and his eyes pierce into me for a long moment, like he's considering what I'm telling him. But eventually he nods his head. "Yes, you can. And I can help you," he says.

The hot tears flow freely now. "Jay, please," I beg him. My head starts to spin, and I feel faint. This can't be happening.

"You're going to stay here until we can help each other. Until you forgive me, and I forgive you."

It's like a spike to the heart to hear him talk of forgiveness. "I never blamed you," I say, telling him the truth. I never once blamed Jay for any of the fucked up shit that happened to us. "I hated myself for leaving you. And now-" my voice cracks realizing what he's become and how fucked up this all is. I should never have left him.

"You need help," I plead with him again, my voice wretched. I wipe the tears away with the back of my hand as I remember John. How he looked at me as if he'd never seen me before in his life.

"I know," he replies and his voice is raw and his eyes go glassy, but his expression is hard. "You can help me, and I can help you." He tilts his head, and it pains my heart.

My heart tries to leap up my throat. I feel sick as my stomach churns.

"This is your new home for a little while," he says. My heart squeezes in my chest, and I reach up to cling to Jay's shirt.

"Jay, no!" I cry out as he grips my hands in his and keeps me from holding onto him. I try to move toward him, to beg him to let me go. My nails scrape along his wrists. "Jay!" My pleas are useless.

"You don't have to do this," I urge as he backs away and I nearly fall off the bed. My eyes search frantically for the door and the moment they do; Jay squeezes my hands tighter. He squeezes hard enough so there's pain, but for only a moment and my eyes shoot to his.

My heart thuds in my chest, and the blood drains from my face. "Don't do this," I whisper, but my words fall on deaf ears. Jay turns his back on me and I scramble off the bed, but he's through the door and slamming it shut just a moment before I can reach him.

"No!" I scream at him, pounding my fists against the door. *Bang! Bang!* "Don't leave me in here!" I cry out for Jay as tears stream down my face and my voice goes raw. "Jay!"

Bang! Bang! I don't stop screaming; I don't stop pounding.

For so long I've dreamed of him coming back for me. I prayed he'd be safe.

If only I'd known.

I turn my back to the door, leaning against it as I slowly slide to the floor. My shoulders hunch and I feel useless, hopeless… worst of all, like a child again.

Yes, that's exactly how I feel. Like I'm back in the past all those years ago. But back then, Jay was my shoulder to cry on. My protector. *My savior.*

Now, I'm truly alone.

John. I hear him say his name in the depths of my memory, I see the look in his eyes and my own pop open.

He'll come back at some point. And hopefully sooner, rather than later.

John will come back, and I can use him. Tears prick my eyes, and my throat closes with emotion. I can't do that to him. I'm consumed by guilt. I can't stop having flashbacks of me running away.

But I have to try. Jay's not well, and I have to get him help. He's not okay, and I can't just stay here waiting around. Not for Jay, and not for John. I need to get the fuck out of here.

Chapter 8

I OPEN MY EYES SLOWLY; THE LIGHT IS STILL HARSH, AND MY HEAD'S groggy. The chill is starting to get to me, and I've only just now realized I'm still in my thin silk nightgown.

That fucking bastard. I clench my hands into fists and grind my teeth as I try to comprehend what's happened.

He's alive. Jay is alive.

That little bit of knowledge in and of itself is earth shattering to me. My head falls back against the door and my throat feels tight. My heart aches for him.

I struggle to breathe as I push up from the floor and lean against the door to stand. My eyes slowly focus on the room he's put me in, and it feels like a spike to my chest. A sob tries to escape, but I push it down, swallowing it and refusing to cry.

It looks the same as before… like a deliberate attempt to bring me back.

I shake my head. No, this isn't the same. "It can't be." The words creep through my lips as my shoulders quiver.

Cinder block walls yes, but the wall with the door is drywall. I blink the tears back, my eyes going glassy as I turn to face it and then the bed. It only has a simple frame with a mattress covered by a white fitted sheet and a thin white sheet on top. Only one pillow is on the bed, also white and still rumpled from where I was lying.

There was never a bed before. Was there? I don't remember one.

No, that's something I would remember. I'm sure of it. I lay on the ground next to him with a tattered blanket. Instinctively I look for the blanket, as if it'll be crumpled in a corner. The far right corner, the one farthest from the door. The one where we used to huddle together.

I swallow thickly, brushing my eyes with the back of my hand.

This room is made to look the same, but it's not.

That house was burnt down. I remember the smell. The ashes. I remember the fear that he was in there when it happened. That the boy had died, and was burned alive. I wanted to die myself. I screamed, and the officer held me close until my mother came to me.

She was crying, too. Even as she held me firmly against her chest, my tears soaked her shirt and hers fell into my hair.

The knowledge that there was no one inside didn't take the pain away. A pain that's never left me, a pain that's enough to render me useless in this moment.

My eyes feel heavy as I turn to the door again. It doesn't look like the old door. It was steel and gray. It was a door that couldn't be broken down. This one is painted white with a simple handle. No locks.

"No locks," I whisper and lick my dry lips.

I reach a hand out and then look up toward the ceiling. The far right is where the camera was all those years ago. I make a full circle, the sound of my feet shuffling across the floor accompanies me as I search for cameras in the room. But there are none.

Is he not watching? I find it hard to believe. I don't understand. A throbbing pulse makes me wince and I close my eyes until it goes away, holding both of my hands to the sides of my head.

What are you doing, Jay?

Why this? I open my eyes, remembering John. Maybe he convinced him? It hurts to think that way. It fucking shreds me, but it fuels me to move. I need to get out. I'm not safe here, and neither is he.

I grip the doorknob, expecting it to be locked, but it's not. My heart stutters and I test it again.

It's too easy. I jiggle the knob again, and it turns easily. The soft click fills the air as I turn it and pull the door open slowly.

I can't breathe. My heartbeat is too fucking loud.

I stand in the open doorway, too afraid to peek out, but somehow I force myself.

My brow knits as I rest my hand against the doorjamb and bite down on my lip, looking down a hall to what appears to be a basement. There's a door at the very end, faint morning light spilling in and a set of stairs leading up to the outdoors.

I cautiously take one step, my bare foot sliding across the cement.

Did he really just forget to lock the door? Or is this a test?

I don't take a moment to think. I don't try to understand.

He's not well, and he needs help, desperately. I can get him help. The thought pushes me to move faster, one step at a time as I look over my shoulder to a set of stairs that leads to the first floor of this house. I can't hear a damn thing other than the blood pounding in my ears and the slamming of my heart.

My palms turn sweaty as I keep walking.

I can leave and get help. I'll come back for him.

My body buckles at the thought, and I lean against the door to my potential freedom. The doorknob is cold in my hand.

I was going to come back, I almost whisper. I tried. I tried to go back, but the house was gone. I close my eyes, my body trembling and the memories flooding my mind.

His eyes are the same. God, his eyes are everything. The only thing I can see. The boy and the man looking at me are the same.

He needs help. I need to help him.

A low growl makes my body tense. It continues, long and low and threatening, and coming from my right.

I can't breathe remembering the dogs. No. No. I'm frantic as I rip the door open, pulling with everything I have and luckily, it too swings open and doesn't hold me back.

It bangs hard against the wall, the harsh noise joining with the loud bark of the dog. I can't help but look back, and staring straight at me are the dark eyes of a large black dog. His hackles are raised. He's snarling and his white teeth are exposed, drool dripping from his jowls as he snaps them shut and barks again repeating his vicious warning.

My legs seem frozen, yet they move me forward. Terrified and without any other option, I move so quickly my body slams into the concrete wall straight ahead.

I reach back to the door, my hand slipping on the metal doorknob as terror races through my blood.

I try to close the door, I try to lock him in the house and escape, but it's too late. The dog is too close. He charges for me. His large muscular body propels him at a speed I can't match. A scream is ripped from my throat as I take the stairs two at a time.

The dog's teeth clamp down on my legs near the top of the stairs and I fall hard, landing on my side with half my body still on the cement stairs and the upper half laying in a mixture of mud and grass. The dog releases me in an instant, but the moment I move my legs, a rough and vicious snarl rips through the air.

Jay.

My heart shatters in my chest.

His father had dogs too. How could he? How could he do this to me?

I try to get to my knees, to make a feeble attempt to run, but the black dog snarls and bites down on my arm the moment I lift it. He's so close, so massive. He must be ninety, or maybe a hundred pounds and built with speed and muscle.

I'm no match for him. My cheek rests on the grass as my body stills. I'm frozen with fear. The dog doesn't bite down, and he doesn't growl, he merely holds me in place.

Waiting for his owner.

The dog's teeth feel so sharp as I whimper. My body's shaking, freezing in the cold dirt and earth at the bottom of the cement stairs. The early morning sun rises, and it's enough light that I can see around me. Trees, open land… nothing else. Nowhere to go, no one to call for help.

Just like before. *He's dead.* I have to remind myself. The monster is dead. He didn't burn in the fire, but he was there, buried in the dirt.

It's just Jay. He's the one doing all this.

I pray that it's him. I pray for him to come to me and make this all go away. Make the memories go away.

The most fucked up part about it all, is that I don't hate him. I wish I could find it in me to focus on that strong emotion, but it's absent.

Even as fear cripples me and the sound of the dog's low growling vibrates up his chest and into my small body… I can't manage hate.

The sound of a man's strides makes me open my eyes. I force them to look back at the man walking toward me. His hands are fisted, his jaw clenched and a disapproving frown is on his face.

A low whistle pierces through the air, and the dog's jaws loosen before he backs away.

I still don't move. I lie there, my knees on the cement and the scratches from the dog bite burning and begging me to touch them. But I don't. I just stay there listening to the man approaching. I close my eyes as he nears, hating everything that's happening. Hating my failure, the circumstances. Hating everything but him.

He can drag me back inside; I won't fight him. I never could before anyway.

My eyes are too dry to cry, but that doesn't stop the guilt that smothers me when I peek up, his shadow blocking the light and I see the look of betrayal in his eyes.

Chapter 9

Jay

I KNEW SHE'D DO IT. I REMIND MYSELF OF THAT AS I CARRY HER BACK down the stairs.

She's so light in my arms. Her small body is hot and she clings to me as if she didn't just try to run from me. Her hot breath tickles my neck as she nestles her head there and stays still in my arms. She won't look at me though.

And for some reason that makes me feel justified.

It shouldn't though. I practically set her up for this, but it doesn't make it hurt any less.

I climb down the cement stairwell to the opened door and whistle for Toby to come in. He's a German shepherd I picked up after his partner, a police officer, died on the job. He was shot in the back and the fuckers got Toby, too.

He barrels in, taking glances at Robin, my little bird. He's curious but he'll stay away. I trained him well, and he knows how to behave and what to do.

"Good boy," I mutter under my breath as his paws patter in the basement and I kick the door shut. I think about locking it, but there's no point.

Robin sniffles and readjusts in my arms, but she's quiet. Her face is filthy, with a large smudge of dirt on her cheek, but she doesn't even try to wipe it away.

"I have a room for you upstairs, you know," I tell her as I walk her back to the room. It's just like where I first met her. Just like the room we spent months and months in.

She finally looks at me, those beautiful hazel eyes brimming with curiosity. With hope.

"It was your reward for being good for me. All you had to do was stay." Her eyes flick down and her body tenses as I push my back against the door to the room and walk her to the bed.

"I'm sorry, Jay," she whispers in a cracked voice. The light in here is bright. It's not like the one Father had. That one was dim and dirty, covered with filth that had gathered for years. This light is new. It's too glaring.

"You aren't though," I tell her as I set her down on the bed. I brush the sheets with my arm and look at her dirtied nightgown and the scratches on her leg from Toby. There's a trickle of blood on her calf and I'm almost proud that Robin stays still when I grab her just beneath her knee to look at it.

"He got you, didn't he?" The words slip out before I know it. I hate that he hurt her. Anger makes my body feel tight, my corded muscles ready to spring to life.

But it's not his fault. He was merely doing what he's been trained to do. As if hearing my thoughts, he whines from just beyond the closed door. My head turns to it, and I bite back the rage. It's not his fault she ran.

"I'm sorry, I really am." I look back at Robin, watching her pale lips part and then tremble as she waits for me to respond. Her eyes look everywhere but into mine.

"Scared little bird, aren't you?"

"Jay, you need help," she tells me again, her words a broken whisper. I nod my head in agreement though. My mind is fucked up, splintered and it hurts. It literally fucking hurts.

"I know," I whisper back.

"I can take you to the hospital…" my sweet little Robin says, as if that's the answer. As if there's a cure for this. There's not. I've already tried. I can't be like this anymore. The only cure for me is her.

I try to blink away the memories of the nurse holding me down to the bed. How they had to tie me down. I had to behave so they'd let me go. I had to hide who I was, and what I'd done. But with her, I won't have to hide.

"I won't go back there," I say and grit my teeth, my body tensing. "I'm not going anywhere, Robin."

"Let me go," she pleads with me, but that's quite the opposite of what I'll be doing.

I shake my head once and reach into my back pocket, my fingers slipping around cool metal. The handcuffs clink as I pull them out for her to see, and she dares to back away from me.

I snatch her ankle and yank her back toward me. Her fingernails scrape along the bed and she arches her back instinctively, but she lets me drag her close. It's so tempting, the desire to push her obedience. I hover over her, my dick hardening and my breathing coming in heavy.

"Jay, please," she whimpers with her eyes closed, her chest rising and falling.

"This wouldn't be necessary if you hadn't tried to leave me again," I tell her and my own heart squeezes with pain as her face crumples and she lets out a sob. "I'm sorry," she tries to say again, but it's a silent statement.

I feel bad for her, I really do, but it doesn't make the anger wane. Not in the least.

"I've waited so long," I confess to her. I lower my head to rest on her chest, feeling the dirty silk against my forehead and breathing in her sweet scent. It fills my lungs as my hands reach up and grip the bed on each side of her hips.

I've watched her almost every day. Well, night. The knowledge that I have to wait makes me even madder. I can only see her at night. But every chance I got to make sure she was okay, I took. I had to; there's a deep-seated need within me to ensure she's okay.

She's mine to protect. Mine to keep safe.

Yet she tried to hurt herself. "I knew you needed me," I whisper against her skin and lift my head to look at her. Her lips are parted as she breathes, her hair a tangled mess against the white sheets.

I catch a glimpse at a smudge of dirt on the white sheet and my blunt fingernails dig into the mattress.

"This needs to come off," I grunt through my clenched teeth, rising and gripping her nightgown in both hands. The handcuffs fall to the floor with a loud thud as she writhes under me.

"Jay!" she cries out my name, struggling to keep me from removing her filthy gown.

I let her arms flail, I let her nails scratch down my forearms, but I rip the thin silk fabric easily. It needs to come off of her. The memory of watching her lie on the dirty ground meshes with the sight of her running just now. I blink and there's a child in front of me; I blink again and it's her today.

My body sways as the memories taunt me. She left me. She didn't have to today. She didn't have to leave me again!

My body bristles with fury as I tear at the silk.

"Jay, please," she whimpers and backs away from me as I rip the muddy fabric from her and throw it onto the cement floor. She scuttles away from me until her back hits the wall. "Jay, no!" she screams.

The look in her eyes is what stops me. She's fucking terrified.

My body shakes as I calm my breathing. I blink again and again. My hands clench and unclench, and I stand there paralyzed.

A moment passes, and then another. I stare as Robin watches me cautiously and I wonder if John's here, but I know he's not. He'll come back in the morning. *It's just us.* I close my eyes and rest my knee on the bed, hanging my head low and hating that I've scared her.

"I-" I try to talk to her, to apologize and calm myself. "I need to clean you," I tell her although I speak with my head down and then raise my head to look her in the eyes. "You need your things," I say and try to sound sane. I know I'm crazy, I know I'm fucked in the head. But I'll never hurt her. I don't want to, anyway. "I'm sorry," I whisper and crawl onto the bed, slowly and making sure she knows I'm here for her. She tries to cover herself with her hands, and my blood heats with both shame and desire.

I grip the sheet, fisting it, I drag it up to her until she takes it.

I don't stop moving, and even as she tries to wrap the sheet tightly around her body, I lie close to her, like I used to.

"Jay," she says softly as I lie beside her and rest my head on the pillow. "I'm scared."

I nod my head, acknowledging her admission and knowing she has reason to be scared. It fucking hurts. I wish I wasn't like this. I wish I could have come to her and helped her without this fucked up head of mine. I close my eyes and wait for her to relax. She always did. Always. It didn't matter how bad the day was, or what had happened. Even the day he took her.

She let me hold her, and eventually she'd relax in my arms and fall asleep. *Always.*

I count the time, using her breaths as a measure. Slowly she molds her body to mine. Slowly her breathing steadies. It will come back to her. It never left me. Not a single day has passed where I don't imagine her in my arms. Some nights I swear I still felt her warmth, but feeling her now, I know I was a fool.

"Jay, talk to me," she says softly. She always wanted to talk. I run my nose along her hair and when I let out a heavy sigh, feeling the weight of so many sleepless nights come down on me, her hair brushes against my nose, lifting with my hot breath.

"I don't want to live like this, Robin," I tell her and each word scratches its way up my throat. I feel my walls break. She's powerful like that. Only her. *I'm so fucking weak for her.*

"Please help me," I beg her as my eyes sting. She was made for me. I knew it all those years ago; I knew she was sent to me for a purpose.

"I need you," I whisper against the pillow, my hot breath mingling with hers. I close my eyes as she reaches up and sets her hand down ever so slowly on the side of my face. Her soft skin moves along my rough stubble, and I open my eyes to find hers on me.

"For John?" Her eyes search mine as she asks, and it makes me feel weak. A pathetic huff leaves me as I swallow and stare at the ceiling. It's not like it was back at the old house. The home I grew up in. Or basement, rather.

"John has no idea." I turn to her and add, "He doesn't want to…" I can't finish. I can't talk about it. This is why I need her. I wrap my arms tighter around her and pull her in close. I shut my eyes, just for a moment.

She'll heal me, and I'll heal her. I swear I will.

I just have to be careful. My little bird is so easily broken.

My eyes snap open and I tell her, "You need to listen to me, Robin." My voice gets tight. "Even if you don't forgive me. Even if you want to leave me, you must listen."

Robin rises, propping herself up on her elbow and coming closer to me, holding me and lifting my chin so I'll look her in the eyes.

She shakes her head slightly, and I almost lose it. The anger is so close to the surface. It's always there, brimming just beneath my skin. "I forgive you," she whispers and keeps my gaze. "You never had to be sorry," she says but chokes on her words and with that I reach my arm up and pull her closer to me. She hangs her head low and I shush her again.

I rock her gently, thinking about how she looks at me like I can do no wrong. Like I'm broken and in need of fixing.

The thought used to make me hate her. I fucking hated being stuck with someone who gave me so much sympathy. I hated her for leaving. I hated how she had a normal life. How she wasn't fucked in the head like I was.

It wasn't until the sleeping pills that I realized. It wasn't until I heard her whispering my name in her sleep that I knew I had to take her back.

It was then that I saw things so clearly.

"Shh, Robin," I whisper as I rock her. "It's okay," I tell her even though I know it's not in the least.

Nothing is okay. Far from it.

Chapter 10

I'VE NEVER BEEN A GOOD SLEEPER. NOT THAT I CAN REMEMBER, anyway. My mother told me that I used to sleep like the dead. Once I fell from the sofa and my father grabbed me by the ankle and kept me from hitting my head. I just dangled there, fast asleep and completely unaware.

Of course that all changed when I was taken.

It's been years since I've fallen into a deep sleep and felt rested. Years since I've felt safe and able to sleep at ease.

Yet while I held Jay and let him hold me, it was so easy. So easy to drift into sleep. Maybe it's the drugs or the exhaustion… or maybe the weight of the guilt settling.

Only the guilty sleep in prison, and that's quite like what this is. I deserve to be here, because it's my job to heal him. I know it with everything in me.

He's broken because of me.

I roll slightly, feeling Jay's warmth cocoon me and slowly bring my hand to his chest. I never touched him back then, since he didn't like it. He'd always wake up, and I didn't want that. He needed rest more than I did. His gray Henley is unbuttoned at the top, and his broad muscular shoulders make the thin fabric pull tight.

I love his eyes; I always have even as they haunted me, but with them closed now I can focus on the small details of his face. How thick his lashes are, the rough stubble along his sharp jaw. The way his hair is short, but long enough to be messy.

A sad smile slips across my lips as I rest my fingers against his chest.

I wish I hadn't though, because he wakes instantly, gripping my wrist and making me gasp. His eyes pop open and the pale gray swirls in his eyes are full of emotion. He swallows visibly and with unease before letting go of my wrist.

He blinks the sleep from his eyes and turns to look over his shoulder, the bed creaking as he looks at the door and then back to me.

He wraps his heavy arm around me, pulling me closer to him so my body touches his and then shuts his eyes as if he's going back to sleep.

"Jay?" I whisper his name. I don't know what time it is, but it must be very early or very late.

"Robin," he says my name low, the deep rumble of his voice making the word linger between us.

"Let me touch you?" I try to be strong in my words, but they're weak. I've always been weak for him.

He stays still, but the moment I reach forward he grabs my wrist out of instinct. His blunt nails dig into my wrist. My breathing stalls and I stare at where he holds me, giving him a moment. "You want me here to help you," I finally say and look up into his eyes. He's staring at my wrist as well, at his fingers curled and gripping with a force that's unbreakable. I can feel the blood pulsing; his grip is so tight.

I swallow and add, "You need to let me do whatever I can to help you." My voice quivers, and I have to look away. It's selfish of me. So fucking selfish. I want to touch him, simply because I want to. So many nights he's held me. He's let me rest my cheek against his shoulder, and my lips have even rested against his chest. But never my hands. My hands need to be down.

"Tomorrow," Jay finally says and releases me, leaving my hand dangling awkwardly in the air until I submit and lower it to the bed.

Jay lies still, with no indication he's going to handcuff me to the bed. And I almost swallow my words, the plea for him not to. I don't want to remind him, but I need reassurance.

My lips part, but the words don't come out.

"What is it?" he asks me in a no no-nonsense voice.

"I don't want you to handcuff me," I tell him quickly. He lies still, with no reaction and my nerves get the better of me. I peek up at him through my lashes. His face is like stone, emotionless even. "Jay, please," I beg him.

My fingers itch to reach up and touch him, but I can't, so instead my fingernails dig into the comforter.

"You can't leave me," Jay says as if it's the only truth he knows.

This is wrong. He's not okay, and I'm not safe. But the two of us were never meant to be right.

I can't help what being with him does to me. I wish I could justify my feelings, but I know it's fucked up on too many levels.

All the feelings I have for him are hovering just below the fear.

The need to cling to him to stay safe is strong. It's hard to fight the urge to touch him. What's worse is that I don't want to keep myself from touching him.

"Go to sleep, Robin," Jay tells me, his large hand splaying along my hip as he adjusts me next to him like we used to lay, calming me and kissing the crook of my neck.

His rough stubble brushes along my sensitive skin, and my body bows to him. I can't deny the effect he has on my body. I can't help how I want him. I try to override my body's reaction to him.

"We need to talk," I try to tell him, but he shushes me. And I obey. Whatever fate Jay gives me, I'll take it. I know that with every piece of my being in this moment. I only exist because of him, and I'm guilty of a far worse crime than any he could commit against me. I'll bend to his will; I owe him that. *I owe him everything.*

"Go back to sleep," he tells me in an even voice. And for the first time in years, I do just that. I slip easily into the darkness and fall into the depths of a dream I once had long ago.

Chapter 11

John

THE CAMERA'S SET UP AND FOCUSED ON HER. SHE'S SITTING ON the bed with her knees pulled into her chest. There's a room upstairs full of clothes for her, yet she's wearing a white t-shirt that's far too large for her and a pair of men's blue flannel pajama pants. Something Jay must have left for her to wear. She's alone on a tiny ass mattress with nothing else in the room except a metal chair.

I let out a tortured breath and drag the chair across the room. The metal legs scrape on the cement floor, and the screeching only pisses me off. Rubbing the sleep from my eyes, I think about how I've canceled everything to be here. It's like an obsession, picking at the back of my brain, the anxiety making my body tremble. But more than that, I'm curious.

I don't know what exactly happened between them, but the way she looks at him and vice versa... I'm more than curious.

"How do you know Jay?" Robin asks me with her gaze still fixed on the sheet she's balling up in her hand. She dares to lift those hazel eyes to me, and I take a moment to consider what I want to tell her.

"We met when we were kids," I answer. I finally sit down a few feet away from the bed, but inside of the camera's field. I swallow thickly. "He helped me," I admit to her.

She picks at the sheet, but doesn't look down. Tilting her head, she asks me, "Helped you with what?"

"I was adopted and it was hard for me, but Jay was," I pause and clear my throat, remembering back to when we were kids. Both of us lost and feeling alone, feeling abandoned. "Jay was a good friend when I needed one." I nod my head once and then look back at her, but I have to rip my eyes away. It doesn't justify this.

"I see," Robin says softly and it reminds me that she's a shrink. A huff of a humorless laugh spills from my lips. "Are you analyzing me, Doctor Everly?" I ask her with humor in my voice, but she nods her head once.

"I hope you don't mind," she says in a soft voice, still picking at the sheet.

I try to swallow the spiked ball that's formed in my throat, but I can't. Instead I just talk. "I didn't want to do this," I tell her. "I'm afraid to not be here though." I look her in the eyes when I say, "When I came back here this morning, I was scared that I'd find-"

I shake my head, unable to continue. It makes me less of a man to leave. Less of a man to leave Jay with her. But there's something I don't know. It's like it's right in front of my face, something I know deep down inside that says it's all okay, that this is meant to happen like this.

"Jay doesn't want to hurt me," Robin says confidently, but then adds, "Maybe a small piece of him wants to. But I don't think he would."

I stare at her with wonder and ask, "Why would you give him the chance?" Her eyes narrow with pain and gloss over before she reaches farther onto the bed and pulls the sheets up to get comfortable.

"What do you know about me?" she asks me.

"You're a psychiatrist," I answer her. I almost add that I looked her up while she slept. That I know where she went to school and other details I was able to find online, but I shut my mouth. She's already frightened, and I'm holding on by a thread. "Did you want to become a shrink because of what… what you went through?" I ask her. My heart aches for her as I search her eyes for answers.

I've felt bad for Jay for so many years. It's why I could never leave his side. And I feel the same for her. Unabashedly so.

She shakes her head, her hair swishing over her shoulders as she looks past me and crosses her legs. She rocks slightly and says, "I wanted to go into law and make a difference, you know?" Her eyes find mine as her voice carries through the room.

"Law?" I nod my head and say, "I could understand that. I could see why you'd want to go that route."

I can see the red blinking light of the camera reflected in her eyes as she stares at it for a moment, and then she licks her lips and looks back at me.

"I used to think that the worst thing you could see before you die was the eyes of your killer," she tells me in a tone that's chilling. "And I wanted to stop that."

I take in an uneasy breath, rubbing the back of my neck and trying to ignore all the things Jay's told me of his past. They almost feel real as the images flash before my eyes.

"But it's not," she whispers.

I turn to look at her, my hand stilling on my neck and then slowly moving to my lap.

"Now I think the worst thing would be to see someone running away, someone ignoring your screams. Someone who could help you, but didn't." Her eyes tear up again, and she shudders.

"I don't think I could handle facing that," she says and waits for me to respond.

I fail to find the right words to tell her. I know it hurt Jay, because he's told me about the girl over and over.

"What else?"

"What else?" I ask her for clarification.

"What else do you know about me?" she asks.

"I know you were with him," I tell her, my blood chilling at the memories. "You were with him for a little while."

"For four months," she says and her voice cracks. She swallows and brushes a strand of hair from her face. "Two days over, actually," she says and smiles sadly. "I left him then," she says but chokes on her words.

"It's not your fault," I tell her honestly. I can feel the emotions from her. The disappointment and regret. "Anyone would have run," I add.

She nods, but her expression only turns more painful.

"So now you know why I'm doing this. But why are you?"

"I don't trust him," I tell her firmly. Surprisingly she simply nods, as if that's a given.

"So he's just a friend that you owe. Someone who's helped you, someone who's broken and fucked up and you feel like you need to help him to make sure he doesn't hurt me?"

I nod once at her analysis of the situation. My chest feels tight, and I hate how I feel restrained and like a damaged man for giving him this.

"Yes," I tell her and scratch the back of my neck as I consider how to word my next question right, but she cuts me off.

"What do you think of me?" she asks me, and it catches me off guard.

"What do you mean?"

She chews the inside of her cheek for a moment. "You know what happened." Her eyes dart to the door at the sound of Toby laying against it and making the door thud. "You know that I'm…" She doesn't finish, and instead she looks me right in the eyes and asks, "Do you think I'm crazy?"

My heart thuds in my chest, and I hesitate to answer. "I don't know everything-" I try to finish, but she cuts me off.

"Yes you do," she says quickly in a whisper. "I'll tell you a secret, John. No one left that house with a sound mind."

Chapter 12

Robin

I DON'T KNOW WHAT'S MORE DISTURBING, TALKING TO JOHN about what happened in the past, or staring back at the blinking red light. It's just like the cameras that were in the ceiling. The ones that watched us in our room.

"You gave it to him?" I ask Jay, and he peeks over his shoulder as he continues to lead me up the stairs from the basement to the main floor.

"Gave him what?" he asks me. I tighten my hand on his as the wooden stairs creak. "The camera," I reply, and the answer itself makes my heart hurt. My body tenses and I try not to close my eyes because I don't want to see it.

'I thought it would help," Jay says as if it's not fucked up.

He opens the door at the top of the stairs and warm light floods my vision for a moment.

"The room, the dog, the camera…," I say without thinking and pull my hand from Jay's to rub my eyes. When I pull my hand away, he's staring at me, a look of worry on his face. "It's not okay, Jay," I whisper.

"It's a second chance, little bird."

He shifts from side to side, but his body is tense. "You don't know what it's been like," he says in a tight voice, the anger coming through. "I'm trying, but some things need to be shown to him," Jay says, and my throat constricts at the thought of John.

"Jay," I speak softly, reaching my hand out to his, but he turns away and runs a hand through his hair. "Please listen."

"We do it my way first," he says, pushing the words through his teeth, his piercing eyes shining into mine and narrowed with authority.

"What if it makes it worse?" I ask him. He's playing with fire. I can already feel the creeping heat threatening to consume us both.

He licks his lips and takes my hand in his, looking past me as he says, "We're going to be alright, Robin." The way he says it reminds me of when we were children, only then it was the opposite.

He'd never admit back then that there was hope. Never.

"Let me show you your room," he says and then he blows out a low steady whistle. My muscles tighten as the large German shepherd trots into the room. With his tongue hanging out just slightly and his ears sticking straight up, he looks approachable, friendly even. But I can't breathe.

"Jay," I say his name like a warning.

Jay bends down, crouching on the floor and petting the dog's head with both of his hands. "We have to face our fears, don't we?" he says with a sad smile. I remember the scar on his leg from when he was a boy, and I take a hesitant step forward.

"Is that why you got him?" I ask him, but keep my eyes on the dog. My palms itch with a faint sweat, and my heart races. It took me years to overcome my fear of them. Even my family dog when I got home, a golden retriever named Chloe who was almost eight years old scared the shit out of me when she barked. I cried constantly, unable to stop the fear and the pounding of my heart, but knowing it wouldn't go away. It wasn't her fault. I loved her before, but the barking only reminded me of the terror I'd run away from.

Jay follows the dog, leaving me watching and forcing my legs to move forward.

The hall is small and short, and all of the doors are closed, but they have character. The house is old. Although the fixtures are new and the paint fresh, it's designed like an older home. The doors are carved and made of hard maple. My fingertips glide along the wall and then dip to a door and back up to the plaster wall.

"Whose house is this?" I ask Jay to change the subject.

"Mine," he answers without turning around and steps into a door at the very end. A door that's closest to the end of the hallway and the opening to the living room. I grip the inside of the doorway, partly to keep me from running, but also to make sure Jay knows I'm not leaving as I lean out and take a look.

The ceiling is tall, taller than I imagined for the hallway being so small. A large ceiling fan whirls and the small gust makes the floor to ceiling curtains sway. They're thin fabric with an organic quality to them.

Lots of browns. Dark brown floors, the tab top curtains and dark wood furniture are everywhere. The only hint of color is the dark blue sofa and matching love seat that sit in front of the large windows. With the curtains being so thin, I can see all the surroundings. Even through the gray of the sky and the slightly blurred view from the rain, it's picturesque, with the field of green and mountains way back in the distance.

But it sends a chill through me. I decided I'll stay, but I never really had a choice. The realization is sobering.

I focus on the furniture, on the living room itself. It's almost like a cabin, but modernized with a comfortable feel to it. It's homey, but barren in every other sense. There's no artwork. Nothing hanging on the walls. There are no candles or knickknacks. No books or magazines. No throw pillows or blankets. There isn't even a TV.

"Do you live here then?" I ask him, leaning back and looking over my shoulder to Jay. I still haven't stopped gripping the doorjamb.

He looks at me hard for a moment, as if debating on telling me and finally he nods once. "It's beautiful," I say just above a murmur.

I look down the hallway again and gesture with a nod. "Which is your room?" I ask him.

His voice is empty of every emotion when he answers, "The basement." My heart squeezes in my chest, and I have to tear my eyes away from him. All this time, I've been moving forward, trying to have a normal life. And Jay's merely been holding on to the past.

I have to close my eyes as the German shepherd rubs against my leg, the feel of his wiry fur sending chills through my stiffened body as he pants and leaves the room, laying with a loud thud in the hallway.

"He frightens you?" Jay asks me, and I whip my head to him.

"He bit me." I grit my teeth after saying the words because it's not quite true.

Jay takes three large strides toward me, closing the space between us and placing his hand over mine, still clinging to the doorway.

"Toby," Jay says with his eyes locked on mine although he's calling for the dog. He whistles low as the large dog rises and trots obediently to wait by his master.

I only resist slightly as Jay pulls my hand down, crouching and making me bend at the waist. I close my eyes, but continue to breathe evenly.

He won't hurt me. Not Toby or Jay. He won't hurt me. I repeat this over and over in my head, focusing on breathing.

The dog's tongue laps at my hand, feeling like rough sandpaper and I slowly open my eyes.

"He likes you," Jay says without looking at me, petting the dog and releasing my hand. "I knew he would," he says and pats the dog's head before standing up. The moment he does, Toby stops licking me and sits, waiting for another order.

"He won't let you leave," Jay says as he shoves both of his hands into his jeans pockets and stares down the hall at the door to the basement. He takes in a heavy breath and looks at me. "He's a good boy, but he won't let you leave."

I nod my head once, searching Jay's eyes for sympathy or guilt, but there's nothing there. The dog pants for a moment, and Jay waves him off with his hand.

"You didn't seem to mind the dogs before," Jay says as he turns his back, leaving me in the hall to watch as Toby stretches along the dark hardwood floor in the opening to the living room. The fan is on, and the faint breeze ruffles his fur.

It's only when I turn, pulling my eyes away from the dog that I register Jay's words. "What dogs?" I ask him as my heart beats harder.

I take a look at him as he walks into a nearby room. He picks up something small off the dresser, and I recognize it instantly. I'm stunned as I take a step into the room and realize it's not just any room.

This is *my* room.

"If you could be anywhere you'd like, where would it be?" he asks me.
I shift on the floor, my shoulder feeling numb. I pick at my broken nails

and look at the floor where I've been picking at the ground. There's never any-thing to do. Nothing but talk to Jay.

I can't stand it when he's gone. It's the fear of not knowing if he'll come back. The fear of not knowing what I'll become if his father takes him away from me forever.

"Hey," I hear Jay say softly, "just talk to me."

I stare at him, bewildered. He's different today. Softer in a lot of ways. "If you could go anywhere at all, where would it be?"

I pull my legs into my chest, feeling my back stretch as I close my eyes. "In a castle in Ireland," I say jokingly with a smile. Deep down my heart hurts be-cause I know what I really think. Back home with my family. But I'm not al-lowed to talk about that. Jay doesn't like it when I bring them up.

"Ireland?" he asks with curiosity. I shrug my shoulders and let out a small sigh.

"There's a picture from one of my books at home. It's a room in a castle." I feel my cheeks heat with embarrassment as I remember it's from a fairytale. I won't tell him that. I'm already younger than Jay. I don't want him to think of me like I'm a little kid although that's exactly how he sees me.

"I thought you'd say Disneyland," he says and laughs at me, rolling onto his back and passing the ball back and forth between his hands. It's odd to see anything at all in the room. The ball moves from palm to palm rhythmically and I see a smile grow on the boy's face. He looks so young, smiling as he lies on the ground, fiddling with a baseball.

It was a present, he told me, a present for being good.

I sit up on the floor, my palm brushing against the concrete that's all too familiar. "Do you think he'll let us go outside and play with it?" I ask him.

He stops his wrist in mid-motion, gripping the ball tightly in his right hand and almost dropping it.

"There is no outside, little bird," he says and then looks up at me, a small smile trying to curl his lips up, but it's so sad. I swallow the lump in my throat as he adds, "But we can pretend to be anywhere."

Although my heart breaks and tears fill my eyes, Jay sits up and hands me the ball, forcing it into my hand and sitting cross-legged across from me.

"Tell me about your room, Robin. I want to know all about it."

My eyes glide across the room, taking in every inch of it. Again, the ceilings are so high up. Higher than I realized at first, and the cream ceiling is fitted with dark wood beams that make my eyes travel up. A thin white chandelier with small crystals and lights that look like candles brightens the room. There are two smaller ones on either side of the bed which sits on the far end of the room along the wall. The headboard is the same dark wood as the beams, and it travels up the height of the wall.

It's hard edges and darkness are at complete odds with the bed itself, which is plush and littered with small cream pillows decorated with crystals and embroidery that my fingers long to touch.

"I made it for you," Jay says softly and I turn to him, not knowing what to say.

"Everything you need is here. I brought what you needed from your old place, too."

Your old place. The words make a chill travel down my spine, but I ignore it, letting my body move through the room, opening the drawers to the armoire and seeing my own things alongside others Jay's bought for me.

"I had to take your phone though and your computer, for obvious reasons."

"People will start to question-" I start to tell him, but he cuts me off.

"I've taken care of it." He sets down the object he's been playing with in his hands and its only then that I see what it is. It's a wooden owl, a trinket I got from my mom back in college. I watch him place it back on the dresser, exactly where it sat on my dresser at home. "If they text you, they'll get a message about you being on vacation and in an area with little reception. An email will get them the same thing."

"Take a look around, Robin. This is your new home, at least for a little while." My blood chills as he adds, "Your sabbatical is for eight weeks." I start to think about everyone who might call. My parents, maybe. My mom calls once a month. Other than her, possibly Karen. But this wouldn't be the first time I ghosted. They won't stop trying though. They'll come for me. The thought makes me tear my eyes away from Jay. I grip the bedpost as I try to calm myself.

I'm staying. I've already decided, and this changes nothing. I swallow the fears and take in the rest of the room, very aware of how Jay's eyes follow me.

My feet sink into the woven cream carpet as I walk toward the far wall.

There are curved shutters on the wall painted in a pale blue. Two sets of them that are shut and line up perfectly to form the shape of a leaf, the tips meeting in the very center.

They're exactly what I described to Jay so long ago. Like the shutters in the castle of my fairytale. My feet move of their own accord and I slide my fingers over the slats of painted wood and slowly open them. But behind them is nothing.

Not the mountains and green fields that I could see in the living room. Just the flat wall.

My fingers tremble as I close the shutters and slowly turn to Jay.

This is my room, and it's a prison of my own making.

Chapter 13

MY EYES FOLLOW HER AS SHE MOVES, ALMOST LIKE SHE DID the first night I saw her. She looked around the barren basement back then with different expectations.

My little bird likes her gilded cage, but she's not a fool. She knows that's exactly what it is. Seeing her here in my clothes, in the room I made just for her… it makes me want more.

I swallow as my blood heats and I watch her close the shutters.

"The bathroom is through here," I tell her, and she turns quickly to face me. I hate myself for bricking over the windows. She loved looking outside, but that was all she did, pined for freedom and somewhere else to go. I can't have that here. I can't give her any bit of it. I won't tempt her to leave me. She's already proven that I can't trust her. She ran the first chance she got. *I knew she would.*

She walks carefully toward me as I gesture to the door across the hallway. I let her pass me, following my instruction and getting a faint hint of her scent. That sweet floral is still there, but she needs to be bathed.

My dick hardens as I walk behind her, watching as she grips the oil rubbed bronze doorknob to the bathroom but then looks back at me for permission. My head nods on its own, somehow able to function even though internally I'm tortured by what I'm doing to her.

The light brightens the room and reflects off of the white marble tile. Everything is white and sterile in the bathroom, except for the black penny tile arranged in an ordered fashion on the floor. Even the curtain to the claw foot tub is a simple white.

She lets her fingers glide along the granite counter to the sink and I take a step through the door to get in with her. My blood heats as I close the space between us and she turns around to face me, surprised.

I'll give her what she needs, and she'll give me what I need.

"You need a bath," I tell her simply as I shut the door behind me. Her eyes flick to the doorknob and then back to me as she takes a step behind her.

"Jay?" she asks. She's always said my name like that. Like she's asking for permission, for comfort, for anything and everything when she breathes my name. Because what I say is true to her. There is only what my answer is and she will believe it with everything she has. There's so much power in how she expresses it. So much weakness in her voice.

"Yes?" I ask her, feigning nonchalance as I lean against the sink. I cross my arms and wait for her to say what's on her mind. I wait for her to address the fact that I desperately want to fuck her.

She can barely breathe as she stands in front of me.

"I've seen you plenty of times, Robin," I finally admit to her. I watch her eyes as I tell her, "I've come to your house a few times." I wait for her reaction. I expect fear or disgust, or maybe some mix of both. But she merely nods and slowly pushes the pants down her legs.

The bathroom is small and the sound of the pajama pants bunching and pooling around her legs and then at her feet fills the room. It's all I can hear along with the thumping of my heart. She's hesitant to take off the shirt though. Her fingers play along the hem and she looks back at me with nothing but insecurities.

"I'm not going to hurt you, Robin." I hate that she would ever think that. Her eyes remain skeptical, and she doesn't make a move to take it off. "There was only one time I ever wanted to hurt you."

That gets a reaction from her, but it's not one I want. It takes me a moment before I even realize how she's taken it.

I clear my throat and grit my teeth as my hand goes to the back of my head and I try to explain. "I was there that night when you took the bottle of pills and swallowed them."

"I've never been so angry, Robin." My breathing picks up as I remember.

By the time I ran around to the front of her house and broke in, she was already throwing up in the bathroom.

"You saw?" she asks softly. She covers her face and turns away from me. She shakes her head softly and the need to comfort and hold her takes over, but as soon as I approach, she turns around and takes a step backward.

I tell her as I take a step forward, "I'm not angry with you anymore." Her shoulders rise and fall as she waits for my next move.

She's my prey, small and scared. And trapped.

But I think she likes it this way. I think I'm her predator of choice.

"You were alone, and you carry so much guilt with you that isn't fair."

I wrap my hand around her waist as her legs hit the toilet and her hand brushes against the closed curtain to the tub. My blunt fingernails dig in as I pull her close to me. At first her hands come up, ready to brace her palms against my chest. But she knows better, and she quickly grabs on to the bit of her shirt on her upper thighs.

I let her chest hit me and hold her gaze as she stares into my eyes. "Robin," I lick my lips and then tell her, "I've wanted so much from you for so long."

I close my eyes as the years pass before me. My concern growing into an obsession. I open them to find her hazel eyes swirled with desire. Her breathing in short pants.

I lower my lips to her neck and whisper, "I don't want to wait any longer."

Robin reaches up just as the words slip past my lips. My initial instinct is to grab her, to force her back and pin her down. To protect myself. But her fingers spear through my hair and she crashes her lips against mine before I can admonish her. Her eyes are closed as she kisses me with long-ing, sweet and slow, but also a desperation that matches my own. I splay my hand along her back and trail my fingers up her thigh and over the dip of her waist. Her lips soften as I move my hand to her neck, my thumb brushing along her jaw.

I've dreamed of this moment for so long.

Her breath is hot and mingles with my own as I feel her soft skin, let-ting my hands roam freely and relaxing my grip on her. Her touch is soft, as I knew it would be. She's gentle but needy. Greedy, even. I pull back slightly and she lets me, but she's slow to open her eyes. She doesn't want it to stop. The thought makes my dick twitch and I grip her hips and move her ass to sit on the counter. Like the good girl she is, she parts her legs for me and I nestle my hips between her thighs.

"I want you, Jay," she whispers the words like a confession. Her eyes are still closed, and I can see how much it pains her to admit it. It's because I'm broken. She thinks this is wrong when it's the only thing that feels right.

I brush the tip of my nose along hers, waiting for her to look at me. She's out of breath and her eyes are a mix of emotions. She needs me as much as I need her.

I cup her chin in my hand and brush my thumb along her lower lip. "I would give anything to have all of you," I admit to her with absolute truth.

"Will you let me touch you?" she asks me, and my heart stops.

It's only my chest where I don't like being touched. I can still feel my father's hands slamming against me over and over. Pushing me backward. I don't fight it. I let him because if I don't, it's so much worse.

My blood rushes in my ears as I nod my head once. I should've guessed it was coming. I suppose in a lot of ways it was, because I'm ready for it. I want her to do what she wants to me. And I to her.

"I know I need this," I tell her. I'm so fucking aware of how damaged I am. "I don't want to be like this," I whisper and then pull the shirt over my head. The thin cotton slides up my back and over my shoulders until I'm facing her with nothing to hide me. Her eyes focus on my chest and dance along the faint scars.

They aren't horrible to look at, mostly faded from the two decades of time between now and then.

I can hear her breathe as she moves closer to me. She peeks up at me and I can almost hear my name on her lips. Asking me for permission, but I nod before she can do it. "Go ahead," I tell her with my shoulders squared. I may be broken, but I want to be fixed. I want her touch in every way.

Her hand shakes just over my chest. So close I can already feel the heat from her. I brace myself for it. For her touch. I want it more than anything. I want to feel her fingertips run along my scars and not cause me pain and shame.

If ever someone could do it, it would be her. I halt my breathing as she rests her middle finger along the dip in my throat and then slowly lowers it, trailing down the faint silver of a small scar. It's not the worst of them.

I wish I knew what they were from. I wish I still had the memories of what it was that left each of them. But there were so many, and time confuses things. The one on my leg was from the dog. The largest of the three. The one who almost killed me. That's the only scar I can place in my past. The rest are merely a summary of what my father gave me.

I grip her wrist out of instinct when she moves lower. She stays still, waiting for me. "I think that's enough for now, little bird," I say with my eyes closed and then look down at her.

"Jay, I promise I'll stay." Her voice is pleading but also sincere. I don't like her tone though. I gave her what she wanted, so she needs to give me what I want in return. "I promise I'll stay with you and beside you, and that I want what you want. I promise you," she pleads with me, and I already know what she's going to say.

"Just come with me to get help."

I stare into her hazel eyes as they gloss over with unshed tears.

Help. She is my help. She is the reason I'm like this. My breathing gets heavy as I resist the urge to snap.

Leave? No. We're only getting started.

She left me once, and she'll do it again. There's a sorcery about her, something that distracts me from the reality. Something that makes me feel as though just caring for her will be enough to heal all wounds. I bend down, picking up my shirt and put it on quickly, covering the scars from her view.

"Get a bath," I tell her and turn my back to her, opening the bathroom door and feeling the gush of cold air flood the room. "Don't make me regret leaving you alone."

Chapter 14

IT'S SO QUIET. EVERY SMALL MOVEMENT IS ACCOMPANIED BY THE sounds of the blanket shifting. There's not the faintest noise except the ones I create.

A little while ago the air conditioner kicked on, and it was heaven. A bit of white noise to drown out the silence. But the break was short-lived, so instead, I lie here in silence.

I turn over onto my side and pick at the threads on the comforter. They're small and so easily pulled.

I close my eyes and the vision of the basement flashes before my eyes. It was quiet then, too. But at least I had the steady sounds of Jay behind me. My throat feels tight as I swallow and try to calm myself down.

I think of the city noise and focus on it. So many nights it's kept me from this very nightmare. It's not so loud that it keeps me up or disturbs my sleep. But it's loud enough to keep me from going back *there* in my mind.

I grit my teeth and think of how he could hold me now. If he wanted to, he could be in here. I could sleep again.

The thought of falling into the depths of a dream with him makes my body move on its own. I throw back the heavy comforter and move from the bed with purposeful strides but hesitate at the door, my heart beating harder and my confidence waning by the second.

I swallow thickly, my heart beating slowly as fear creeps up and nearly stops me. But how many nights have I prayed to be close to him? How many nights have I wanted him to hold me? And he's so close. I only have to ask.

My heart aches in my chest as I remember how he'd whisper it. *If you need me, just ask.*

I need him. God, do I need him.

The lump seems to stop in my throat mid-swallow as I grip the doorknob and open it slowly. It doesn't escape me that there's no lock. Just like the bathroom. None to force me to stay in the room, and none to keep Jay out.

The door's silent, which is a blessing and a curse.

I don't want Jay to think I'm leaving.

Or worse, the dog.

I peek my head out of the doorway, opening it up slowly to reveal more of the hall. The moonlight spills into the front of the hall from the window in the living room and floods it with light. So much more than what I have in the room Jay gave to me.

I only take one step, my bare foot making the floor groan with my weight before I hear a low growl.

"Toby," I hear Jay's voice say the dog's name low and with an admonition in his voice just as the fear was about to take me. "Stay," Jay orders from the living room. I turn my head to look back down the hall to the closed door to the basement. That's where I was headed, but I follow the sound of Jay's voice and walk slowly to the living room, gripping the molding that cases the doorway and facing both Jay and Toby.

Jay's on his back in the middle of the floor. A thin blanket covers his lower body, and Toby lays close to Jay. He doesn't turn to look at me. He absentmindedly pets the dog once and then twice while staring at the ceiling. If not from his hand stroking the dog, I'd think he was asleep with his eyes open, his body is so still.

The dog merely lifts his head once, assessing me and then laying his head back down as if he's content with my presence.

"I wasn't sneaking out," I say quickly and the way I said it makes even me think that I was lying. My fingers twist around one another as I chance a step closer to Jay, just one, although my eyes stay on the dog.

"You should be sleeping, little bird," Jay finally says and then turns his head to look at me.

"I wanted," I start to say but get caught in his gaze. It's intense and the way his eyes look at night with him being so tired, takes me back to when we were trapped. Back to when he couldn't sleep at all.

"Will you lie down with me?" I manage to ask him, although I don't know how.

"No," he answers quickly and with finality. My heart feels splintered from his cold denial. I nod once, accepting it and trying not to think back to the bathroom. To the kiss. To the moment I thought we had. The moment I ruined.

It's my fault. It's all my fault.

"Leave the door open," Jay says softly, ignoring how I'm barely holding on.

I nod my head again and bite my lip as I turn my back to him, to go back alone to the room. It's only then that Jay says, "I can't, Robin. John will be here soon."

John. The way Jay talks about him makes my heart ache with a splintering pain that's nearly debilitating. I have to wait a moment, forcing all of the emotions away. Taking a look at this from my clinical background.

"What's the purpose of doing things this way?" I lick my lips after croaking out the words. I'm nervous to approach Jay; after all the years of training, I should be more confident. But it's Jay. I'm afraid to touch him, or to hurt him, to make him angry. Not because of what he'd do to me, but because of what my words could do to him.

Words are powerful, so much more than we realize.

"What do you mean?" he asks me, still staring at the ceiling, but his relaxed body is now stiff and his response makes me shift uneasily. I decide to sit on the ground, still in the entrance. The thin nightgown rides up but I pull it down as the cold wood floor presses against my thighs.

"Your way," I answer him and put my hands in my lap. It feels like a session in some ways, and the thought is comforting. "Why do you want to do it like this?" I ask him.

"John won't listen to me," Jay says. "He just shuts me down and he doesn't hear it."

"You talk to him often?" I ask him as I pick at the hem of my nightgown, each little bit of information helps me to understand.

Jay clears his throat roughly and looks away from me and toward the window. My throat closes, hating how much this wounds him.

"That's fine," I tell him to try to reassure him. "I understand, Jay." I keep my voice light and calm, feigning a casual air about such a serious conversation. "You know I'd never judge you." I try to speak the words calmly, but they're quiet at the end as the anguish rises and my throat seems to close. My shoulders rise slowly as I take in a deep steadying breath and close my eyes.

"He won't be able to deny you," Jay says and his words make my eyes open. He licks his lips as soon as my eyes reach his, and they draw my focus to his mouth.

My body heats, and I feel nothing but ashamed. The desire is there; I can't help it. But I'm ashamed that in this moment I want to comfort him in a primitive way. I have to tear my eyes away as I ask, "So you need me to tell him about our past? You can see why that scares me, can't you?"

He shakes his head and says, "You don't have to tell him anything you don't want to." My eyes flick back to his as he swallows and adds, "I just thought hearing it from you would help."

"Since he won't listen to you," I say as if it's a question, but it's only to clarify what I already know. I try my best to hide the genuine fear of revealing anything to John. But I fail at it, miserably.

A hesitant breath leaves me and I try to beg him one last time, "We should go-"

He cuts me off before I can finish and says, "I'll protect you. Always. I'll be there."

Always. The word is the final dagger. "You can't promise me that." I lower my head as the words slip out and I lose my sense of composure. I rest my head in my hands, my fingers spearing through my hair and I rock forward slightly. I'm not normally like this. The last time was my final session with Marie.

She reminded me so much of Jay. So much of me. So much of what we'd been through.

But this is nothing like what that poor girl went through. There's only so much a person can be pushed. Only so much pain they can handle before they break. She wouldn't take the medication I prescribed, and she couldn't turn off the nightmares.

I can't break down again. I can't let what happened to Marie happen to Jay. I have to be strong for those who can't. I failed her.

"I can, and I will. Please, little bird, my Robin." Jay rises and crawls to me. I peek up through my lashes, wet with the promise of tears that I hold back.

I don't resist him when he wraps his arms around me and pulls me into his lap. I stay still, not reaching up like I did when I was a child. He'd hold me if I promised not to hold him back.

But his grip on me is so different now. Everything is different.

The way the warmth of his strong body envelops me and heats my blood.

The way our breath mingles and begs me to arch my neck and press my lips against his.

The way I lean into his chest and breathe in his scent. He's slow to react when I place my hand on his thigh. He shushes me, cautiously, as if he's not sure that's what he wants to do. Slowly, he bends forward and kisses my neck.

This is so horribly wrong.

I need to be stronger than this. Stronger for Jay.

"How does this end?" I ask him.

He gives me a sad smile. "I don't know, little bird," he says looking down at me. "I don't know what will happen when he finds out."

I start to answer him, but the moment my lips open with a quick breath, he cuts me off.

"You need to go to bed."

"Can I sleep with you?" I ask him although I hate myself for it. I crave his comfort, and I know he craves mine. He gently pushes a strand of hair from my face and tucks it behind my ear, looking at me all the while with a tortured gaze.

"I want to touch you," Jay says and the sadness in his voice is outweighed by desire.

"Then touch me," I whisper, but it only cues him to stand, leaving me on the floor and staring up at him, the hope dimming with each passing second.

"I don't trust myself," he finally says and I shake my head, wiping the sleep and misery from my eyes.

The shame overwhelms me again. I'm so fucked up and broken for wanting him, but I do, so badly. Jay's hand grips my chin, forcing me to look up at him although the touch is comforting.

"It's not you, Robin," he tells me and before I can answer him with a sarcastic remark he says, "I want to make it hurt." His eyes are dark as he lets his hand fall. He turns his back to me as I let his words sink in. The muscles in his broad shoulders ripple in the dim light as he walks away from me, leaving me behind and he says with finality, "Now go to bed."

Chapter 15

Robin

I ROLL OVER WITH A GROAN. THE CLICK OF A DOOR OPENING AND closing wakes me from my sleep. My eyes hurt, and my head feels heavy. I didn't sleep enough, but the second I come to, I don't want to sleep.

Jay. I make a move to get off the bed, but my leg hits something hot and heavy.

I almost scream at the sight of Toby on the sheets, his jaws opening wide with a yawn. It's a lazy yawn, as if there's not a damn thing wrong in this dog's life. He stretches on the bed as I slowly creep away, my heart beating fast even though I repeat to myself over and over that it's okay. Not all dogs are the same. Just like people.

"He doesn't want to hurt me," I whisper with my eyes closed and when I open them, he's staring back at me.

I notice the flecks of yellow in his chocolate brown eyes. His tongue laps along his sharp teeth and it's all I can focus on for a moment, but only a moment before the big beast whines at me. The cry is strange as he whimpers and lowers his head, as if I've hurt him.

It takes me a moment, his big eyes on me before I climb off the bed, on the far side of the room. My toes hit the plush carpet and the absence of the warmth of the covers leaves goosebumps down my arms and legs. The silk nightgown is simply too thin for the early morning.

The dog's head raises and he springs from the bed, his large paws thudding on the floor as he rounds the bed. He watches me for a moment before pacing to the door. He's anxious as he looks back at me.

I worry that he won't let me shut the door, that he'll stay there in the doorway, both keeping me in here and also being too close for comfort. I've tried so long to rid myself of the fear of dogs and for a long time, it was bearable. But right now, it's just too much.

"I'm sorry," I tell Toby as he looks back at me with those eyes, like he doesn't know what to do with me or what to think of me.

"It's not you," I try to talk to the dog, feeling guilty because of the look in his eyes, but the sound of steady steps approaching stops me mid-thought. My heart sputters and turns in my chest as Toby moves out of the room and to the right toward the living room.

"Robin?" I hear his voice before I see him, and already I know it's John.

He stops in the doorway, his broad frame filling it, with nothing but denim jeans and a crisp white undershirt on although there's a black smear, obviously a stain on the lower left side. His boots are already on and I find myself staring at them, my heart aching and my throat going dry.

"Are you alright?" he asks me with a lowered voice, looking down the hallway before placing his hand on the middle of the door and pushing it open a bit more. He looks worried, concerned for me and like he's going to take me away. Like he thinks I want to sneak out.

There's more stubble lining his jaw today than there was yesterday, and his eyes are red. He didn't sleep.

"I didn't sleep well," I admit to him and avert my eyes as I pick at the hem of my thin nightgown. I wonder what John thinks of me. Of this. Of yesterday, or at least what he knows of it.

John runs his hand through his hair and looks back down the hall again. I can see the words on his lips, the promise to help. Asking me if I want to leave.

But I could never do that.

"When will you be back?" I ask him casually and tuck a strand of hair behind my ear. I take a step closer to him and cross my arms over my chest.

"I won't be long," he says with uncertainty.

"I'll be here when you get back," I tell him confidently and feign a smile. I'm sure it doesn't reach my eyes, but I don't care. It does what it's meant to. It gets him to leave without an attempt to take me away.

"I'm looking forward to our session," I say and keep my voice hopeful as I keep his gaze.

A confused look mars John's face as he leaves, Toby turning his massive head to follow him.

"I'll be back soon," he says looking over his shoulder and patting his hand on the doorway once, hesitating to take a step, but leaving me alone.

I nervously pick at my fingernails, remembering the camera, knowing that I have to go backward in time, back to what haunts me at night, back to what John doesn't know.

Chapter 16

John

I DON'T EVEN REMEMBER WORK TODAY. MY HANDS MOVED ON THEIR own, the task at hand blurring with what was consuming my mind.

The thought of her in the house. *Left with Jay.*

I finished one order. The only one I had that would bring anyone to my shop at all.

For now, and for the time being, the shop is closed. And every waking moment will be spent in that house with Robin.

I'm not leaving her again.

The doorknob clicks as I sneak into 401 Cadence Square, slipping the pin I used to unlock it into my back jeans pocket. My blood rushes through my veins. I know this is illegal, technically breaking and entering and I look over my shoulder before closing the door behind me. I swallow hard and let out an uneasy breath as I look around the living room.

Residence to Miss Robin Everly. Or former residence, unbeknownst to the rest of the world.

I walk easily into the cozy space. It's a small ranch house that's fairly dated, but her furniture and décor are modern and mostly simple. It's the pop of colors and textures that give it life. They seem odd knowing the bit of her she's shown me.

There's a professionalism about the room. Organization that seems more fit for a home design magazine, but the colors are cheery. Bright teal in the designs of the throw pillows and pale yellow stripes on the curtains and rugs. There are a scattering of teal flowers and motivational sayings like 'Live, Laugh, Love' on the pictures throughout the place.

As if she needs to be surrounded by something to keep out the stark and cold emptiness that would be left if those pieces were removed.

I ignore them for a moment, feeling my stomach churn at the thought of her being here instead of in the cabin. My phone is heavy in my hand as I watch the screen for a moment.

I have six cameras—not like the one Jay has set up in the basement. This way I can watch everything, at all times. He doesn't know a thing about them, and he doesn't need to. This is my insurance. I stare at the screen, watching how she sits across from the dog. She's cross-legged and the dog's laying down, but eyeing her curiously.

I wonder if Jay told her Toby is for emotional support. My fingers itched to touch her hand, to hold it while I let Toby approach her. Jay was right when he said she was damaged. He was right when he said she needed help.

I could help her. And I will. With or without Jay. If I'm going to do this, I'm going to do this right.

The only reason I'm not there now is that I need to know more about her. And see if I can find the evidence Jay left behind. The anger rises slowly. It's always like that when I think of Jay. A slow rise that turns to a simmer. Usually the thought that he can't help it is enough to calm me, but he fucking set me up. He forced my hand, and that's something that's unforgivable.

I slip the phone into my back pocket, turning my head to the window on the left side of the room as the gentle city traffic is disrupted with a honking horn.

I'm quiet as I walk through the house, greeted only by silence. My instinct is to go to her bedroom, but when the door creaks open and I peek in, I see her bed first. The sheets and comforter are in disarray and there's broken glass on the floor.

Fuck! Jay told me he left evidence, but I didn't expect it to be something so fucking obvious.

I grit my teeth and go back to the tiny galley kitchen, reaching into my other back pocket for the thin black leather gloves. I'm careful with every step.

The cabinets are old and worn. I have to go through three of them before

I find the dust pan. I take my time, cleaning up the room and wiping down every surface I can think of. All the while I take in every inch of her place.

What's most odd is that it feels like I've already been here. Especially the bedroom. It feels like I know her, like we aren't strangers in the least. I can't shake the feeling; I haven't been able to since I first laid eyes on that photograph.

I toss the rag I've been using to wipe down surfaces into the trash bag in her kitchen as the unsettling thought passes through me.

I make a mental note to take the trash with me on the way out. No piece of evidence left behind. I don't know when she'll be back…

I was going to let her go this morning. I was ready to take her with me. I'd do what I have to do with Jay and plead with her to stay with me until I figured a way out, but she was so willing to remain when I left. So unlike what I anticipated.

It feels like a trap.

I let the unfinished thought slip away as I think I hear someone in the living room.

My eyes whip up to the small doorway and I wait, listening to the blood rushing in my ears. *Thump, thump, thump, thump.* My heart races in my chest.

I'm quick to remove the gloves, shoving them in my back pocket and waiting for whoever it is to say or do something. I anticipate them calling out her name to see if she's home. But there's nothing but silence until Jay appears in the doorway.

A smirk slowly lifts his lips up with a knowing glint that sparkles in his eyes.

"Fucking bastard," I mutter under my breath. The smile widens and he walks closer to me.

"Cleaning up?" he asks me and then glances at the trash bag.

"Yeah," I answer him and bend down to tie it off. "Just on my way out," I tell him.

"You should go," Jay says, his voice full of something I've never heard from him before. Possessiveness, jealousy even. He leans his back against the doorway, blocking part of the exit and adds, "She's waiting for you."

There's an undertone to his voice that accompanies his narrowed eyes as he cracks his knuckles one by one. "You'll have to tell me what you think of your session."

I crack my own knuckles, mirroring him. "What I think about her, you mean?" I ask him, pushing him just slightly to see what his intentions are, to pick at the real meaning behind his question.

A rough laugh escapes his lips as he tilts his head and looks me in the eyes, crossing his arms as he shrugs. "I already know what you think of her," he says in a low voice, almost a murmur. Like it wasn't meant for me, which pisses me off.

"Is that right?" I ask him, feeling my blood heat and adrenaline coursing through me. It's been a long time since we've gotten into it. But I can feel it coming. Maybe not today while she's trapped at the cabin. But when she's safe, I know it's going to happen.

He relaxes his posture, as if coming to the same conclusion at the very same time. It does an odd thing to me and I want to bite the question back, but I can't anymore.

"Do you love her?" I ask him.

The smile stays on his face as he answers immediately, "Of course I do. If I didn't, I never would have let her go."

Jay admits to what I already knew. The love between them is obvious. The thing that shocks me is how hearing the words on his lips makes me feel. *Jealous.*

"Then let her go again. Let her make that choice," I tell him words I know are rational, even if what I'm feeling is anything but.

"We're only just getting started," Jay says as he turns to leave.

"You told me it was about her," I yell at him as he's leaving, letting my emotions get the best of me. My words halt his footsteps. He turns to look over his shoulders, his eyes smoldering with an intensity I've never seen.

"It's all about her. It's always been about her."

"I find that really fucking hard to believe right now," I spit as I take a step forward, meeting him halfway.

"Don't forget who will take the fall for this if something happens, John," Jay sneers my name, his eyes darkening with anger.

His threat means nothing to me; I don't care what the consequences are anymore. He smiles at me, a wicked grin at the thought. "She's just as much for you as she is me," he says and I flinch. "She has something she hasn't told you, John. Something you *need* to hear."

My body freezes as I watch him step back into the small kitchen. He carelessly touches every cabinet.

"What is it?" I ask him, not sure if I believe him or if this is a mind game to get me to do what he wants. But something feels off with her. A familiarity I can't grasp. A pull so strong that it makes me reckless.

He stops and looks back at me, a flash of fear in his expression, but only for a moment. "I want her to tell you," he says quietly.

I shake my head; there's nothing she could tell me that would change anything. But as I look up to tell Jay just that, he stares back at me with an expression I can't place. He drops his eyes and stares at the linoleum kitchen floor as a moment passes, letting the anger dim.

"I just need a little more time. Just a little longer before it all changes." He says the words so quietly, like they aren't for me. Only for himself.

"Before what changes?" I ask him as he turns to leave. He looks up at me like he forgot I was even here.

He stares at me for a moment, debating on answering me before saying, "Everything."

Chapter 17

Robin

THE RED LIGHT MAKES ME ANGRIER TODAY THAN IT DID THE first time.

A conditioned environment makes sense. If you want someone to remember something, you recreate it. You offer up any triggers, any objects or words that could have a mental association. Jay's plan has merit.

But it makes me angry because it takes me back there. Back to when I was helpless. Back to when I didn't fight. If I had known how it would end, I would have killed the bastard. I would have found a way. I would have killed him before he could hurt Jay anymore.

My shoulders are squared as I sit on the bed though. My back's against the hard cinder block wall. It doesn't slip by me that John's back is to the drywall, and he's the one who's forced to stare at the block wall. The same fucking stone that tortured my vision for four straight months.

"Do you feel comfortable?" John asks as he leans forward and puts his hands between his knees. I try to keep my eyes from moving to the blinking red light, but I fail.

I swallow the lump in my throat. "I could be more comfortable," I tell him and then look back to his steely gaze, "but I'll be fine."

"You seem…" his brow furrows and he leans back with an uncomfortable expression. "Better today," he concludes, finally settling on the words he wants.

"I'm more certain of what I need to do," I look into the swirls of gray clouds as I tell him and bring my knees up to my chest. It's an odd behavior

I've seen patients do, but I like it when they do it. It makes them vulnerable, which inherently means they're not defensive.

My eyes drift back to the red light, and I wonder who's really running this session. It needs to be me.

"Can I tell you something?" I ask John although it's a rhetorical question.

He nods his head once, not breaking my gaze and says, "Jay said you had something to tell me." My blood turns cold and I swallow the unforgiving lump in my throat, lowering my head to the comforter. I pull it up tighter around me, not wanting to address what John's said at all. So, I don't.

I pick at a loose thread. It's a habit because for so long, all I had was a blanket to pick at. This one is thicker, higher quality and clean, but it's a blanket nonetheless.

The thin thread slips between my fleshy fingertips before sliding past my nails as I start my story. "This story is about a girl named Marie." Just saying her name makes my heart squeeze in my chest.

Her face flashes before my eyes. Beautiful green eyes that were so clear and so pure, I felt she could see to the very depths of my soul. Her skin was pale and her hair was always combed just so. She kept it perfectly straight as though she were put together, but she wasn't in the least.

"Marie?" John asks me, and then crosses his ankle over his knee. The movement makes me look up as the memory of her voice echoes in my ears. *"Doctor Everly."*

I nod my head, hating how real her voice sounds.

It takes me a moment before I'm able to speak. "She had a very abusive father. Her mother fled in the middle of the night when she was only six and left her there."

The pain is nearly consuming as I talk about her in the past tense, but that's where Marie will always be. Never again to be here with me.

"He hurt her?" John asks, and it disrupts my thoughts. I part my lips to exhale and answer his question. "Badly."

"I'm sorry to hear that," John says with true sympathy. "You knew her well?"

My hair brushes my cheeks as I nod and say, "I was her shrink."

"For almost ten years he systematically abused her in every way possible."

"That's horrible," John says although his voice is absent. I feel the need to look up, to look into his eyes to see what he's thinking, but I can't. All I can picture is how Marie looked the last time I saw her. I knew she wasn't well, but they wouldn't let me go to her. They wouldn't let me keep her from leaving. She left me, and I knew it was the last time I'd see her.

"I couldn't save her," I whisper and let the warm tears slide down my cheeks. "I begged her, the last time I saw her, I begged her to take her medication but she didn't believe it would work."

Marie never had a chance. The moment she was saved from her father, the true beast destroyed her. Her memory.

The home she was in was temporary, and they didn't care for her. They just wanted a check. The city bus brought her there, and the program paid for it and her medication but she was always alone. The burden was left on her shoulders, except for the small moments I had with her.

"She'd gotten worse the last time I saw her. She started hurting herself." My breathing is ragged and I lean my head against the wall, closing my eyes and willing the images to go away.

"She needed more help than I could give her." There wasn't a phone call I didn't make. Marie became my priority, but I had no rights to her. I had no legal way to protect her or to take her like I so desperately wanted to.

"She's gone?" he asks me.

I wipe the tears away and take a steadying breath. When I lick my lips, the salt coats the tip of my tongue. It's only then that I come back to the moment, to what I can change. To what I can prevent.

"Her death affected me very deeply because it reminded me of-" I hesitate and swallow before I say, "Jay."

John shifts uncomfortably in the steel chair and the metal legs scratch the floor. "Because his father abused him?" he asks.

I'm careful about answering, but I decide to ask, "What do you know about what he did?"

John glances at the red light for a moment, as if distracted by it before looking back at me. "Jay has told me a lot," John answers with a tone that tells me he's uncomfortable.

"Did he tell you his father liked to see how much pain Jay could take before screaming for his dead mother?" The words slip out of me like a void. The brutality and tragedy seeming cold as ice on my lips. I look up into John's eyes as I explain, "It wasn't good enough unless his father believed it was genuine." He tortured him in so many ways. As if it were a game and he was simply trying to find the best tool that was most effective. But nothing ever would be. He would never win; he'd never be content.

"Is that what Marie's father did?" John asks, forcing my gaze back to him. To the present. To being in a basement twenty years later, brought back by the one boy I wish I could have saved.

If only I'd known.

"Yes, but that's not why she reminded me of Jay. When I left both of them, I knew they were going to their deaths." My composure crumbles as I state the words as a fact. Because it's so true.

I left Jay, and Marie left me. "Maybe I never deserved to help her," I croak out. Maybe if she'd been in someone else's care, she'd still be alive. That's the thought that keeps me up at night. The thought that made me down an entire bottle of pills in the hopes of ending my own life.

"I'm so sorry that you lost Marie, Robin," John says with such sympathy as he leans forward that it breaks me. "It's not your fault," he tells me as if it's a truth.

"I knew and I couldn't do anything. And when I left Jay-" My throat closes and refuses to let me take in a breath. My upper body collapses, and I hug my legs close.

Watching her walk away from me was every bit the same as when Jay turned his back on me in the field. He pushed me forward and said he'd stay behind for only a minute, but I knew it.

I knew it would be the last time.

And I still ran.

Marie never gave me the choice.

"Hush," I hear John say at the same time as I hear the bed creak with movement. I focus on calming myself as John rests a large hand on my back and slowly moves it up and down my back in soothing strokes.

His touch makes everything seem like it really will be okay. Like it's not my fault.

"It's alright," he whispers quietly into my ear. I creep closer to him, taking a chance to reach out and grab onto his other arm. And he lets me, he easily scoops me up and puts me in his lap. His arms wrap around me like they belong there, and it soothes something deep inside of me to be held by him.

"I've got you," he whispers and his hot breath sends a chill from my left shoulder all the way down my body. I let out a gentle moan and desire stirs between my legs. I just want to *feel* something other than this.

With him.

"Could you hold me close and stay with me?" I whisper my plea. Always afraid of being denied. "Please," I beg him when he doesn't answer immediately.

My heart stutters and flips as John slides me off his lap and leaves me. I nearly cling to him, I almost reach up to do just that, to grip onto his shirt and beg him to give me another chance, but I know better.

I watch as he walks to the door, leaving me breathing heavily and alone as the sound of it opening and then shutting again signals he's really gone.

My body trembles as I stare at the comforter, rocking on my own and focusing on the one loose thread. When a click fills the silent room and the door slowly opens, I chance a look up.

"Jay," I say and swallow thickly. I'm only slightly relieved when he nods at me. I close my eyes and let the wave of gratitude take over.

"Little bird," he says and his voice is so full of pain.

"Jay, please," I beg him, not caring how I look or how miserably I've failed him today. "I promise I'll do better, but please."

"This is for you too," he tells me softly as he walks to the bed and stops in front of me. I sit there on my knees, looking up at him as though he's my savior. "It's for all of us," he tells me, and it shatters my heart.

"Just hold me," I beg him although my voice comes out strong.

"It's too early to sleep." The memories of him denying me with that excuse rush back. It was always when he'd come back shaken. That's when he wouldn't hold me. It wasn't about me though; it was about him. His arms may have been the ones that wrapped around my body, but the comfort was meant for him. I can't accept that now. Not right now. I need him too much.

"I don't want to sleep; I just want you to hold me." I remember what he said last night, and it makes the pain that much deeper. "Please, Jay. You can hurt me if you want, I deserve it."

Instantly he pulls me into his chest, holding me closer and tighter than John did. Harder even. "Shh," he tries to calm me. "You aren't responsible."

"You needed me," I whisper against his chest. But I close my sore eyes and just allow him to calm me, rocking me side to side. Soothing me in a way no one else ever can.

"It was an impossible situation, Robin." He kisses my hair again like he did last night, and it makes a warmth spread through my chest. My fingers dig into my thighs, keeping me from reaching up to him.

"If you hadn't left, we wouldn't be here now, would we?" he tells me softly as he pets my hair with long strokes. It's relaxing, lulling me to sleep until he adds, "It's fate. Things are meant to happen a certain way."

I shake my head, hating his explanation and wanting to shove his hand away, but knowing not to reach up. *Fate.* Fate would mean Marie was meant to die.

"Please hold me," I beg him and it reminds me of the first time he ever held me. The first time we both knew we needed each other too desperately to ignore. Before I can add that I'll take the consequences, whatever they may be, he lies on the bed, making it dip and groan with his weight.

"For a minute," Jay says and my heart hurts all over again. But at least I have one minute. Just one to hold on to him.

Chapter 18

Twenty years ago

"**I**F I MADE A DEAL WITH HER, DO YOU THINK SHE'D HIT YOU?" my *father asks me as I sit in the steel chair across the room from him. My body shakes from the cold. My clothes are soaked, and the tips of my fingers are numb.*

A deal… is he finally going to let her go?

"I think she would. She wants to leave more than anything," he says more to himself than to me. I'm afraid to look at him. Afraid that if I do, he'll tell her to do it.

My little bird.

She's the only good thing in my world. The only purpose I have in life.

Do I think she'd strike me?

Yes.

She'd do anything to leave, and the thought shreds me. I could see him over her shoulder, whispering promises of freedom if only she'll listen to him. Just like he did to me for so long.

"Are you letting her go?" I ask him, and the words tremble from my lips.

A rough dry laugh fills the small chamber as he throws a towel at me. It's small and thin, but it's something. I keep my movements slow as he paces, still not looking him in the eyes. One day I'll be stronger than him. One day I'll kill him for what he's done.

But he likes to show me how weak I am, and he's right. I'm no one compared to him.

The rough towel drags over my skin, drying it as he says, "No, of course not."

He clears his throat, and I chance a look up at him as he stares at the back wall. He turns to look at me ever so slowly, and holds my gaze. My own eyes stare back at me. "She's too important, boy. And I have so many plans for her."

His words echo in my head, over and over. Through the screaming of the next session, through the sound of my feet pattering on the cold floor as he takes me back to her.

I only know two things to be true.

If she leaves, I'd rather kill myself than live another day.

And I need to get her out of here.

I promise I'll find a way out.

I wake up to my heart racing and my body feeling like ice. I stay still, perfectly motionless with my body tense. There's a thin layer of cold sweat covering me. The nightmares always feel so real. Like it just happened. Like I was back with him, helpless and stuck in that fucking chamber. It's only after a moment of calming my breathing that I feel her warmth as she stirs beside me.

My little bird. For a moment it makes me feel like I'm back there again, back in the room and I'm quick to look around. But we're on a bed, a comfortable one with sheets and a blanket. She's with me though; she came down here to sleep with me.

I open my eyes and peek at Toby, fast asleep by the open door. He's huddled in a ball and even he didn't wake this time. I turn over onto my side and pull her small body closer to me. I kiss the crook of her neck and look up, staring at the wall and the camera. It's off, but it's there, staring back at me.

Not only watching me, but it's watching her, too.

I don't want her here at night. It's too real with her in my arms. I whisper into the stale air, loving the feel of her soft body in my arms, "I'll always protect you, little bird."

The moment the words leave me, Robin stirs next to me, opening her weary eyes. They're still red-rimmed from earlier, and I know she's tired. No one is sleeping in this house. I give her a worn out smile and push the hair from her face.

"You left me," she whispers. I shake my head, denying it. Never. I'll never leave her. The accusation in her voice mixed with pain is a heavy cocktail, and I don't want to carry the burden.

"I'm right here," I tell her and when I do, a small smile tugs her lips up just slightly. It softens me and warms my chest. But then she reaches up. I'm quick to snatch her wrists. Quick to stop her. I can't help the reaction. I know it's part of my fucked up head. How once I didn't have my father to fight anymore, I found myself consumed with the past and tearing myself apart instead.

"I want to touch you," she tells me softly, and I stay perfectly still. She can help me. She wants to help me, and I desperately need it. I need her.

My fingers dig into the mattress, and I have to close my eyes as her hands slowly slide up my shirt.

"You're the only one I've let touch me," I tell her in a soft voice.

It was years ago, back when giving her everything was all I had left.

"It would have been different," I start to say, but my voice gets choked. The anger starts to rise, and my blood heats. I close my eyes, breathing out slowly.

It's not her fault, I tell myself. I knew what I was doing when I set her free. But knowing how it all played out… I can't help but feel animosity.

"Punish me, Jay," I hear her soft plea and it forces my eyes open. "Please," she begs me.

I hate how weak she sounds in this moment. I don't want that for her, and I quickly silence her before she can do it again. I crash my lips against hers, spearing my fingers through her hair and parting her lips to deepen the kiss. She obeys me instantly, arching her neck and digging her fingers into my thigh. Letting me know she's not going to move them.

I don't mind her being weak for me. But not when it's tinged with guilt.

She moans into my mouth, and my dick instantly hardens. I rock it into her, needing to feel something. A voice hisses in the back of my head, *mine*, as I break the heated kiss and catch my quickened breath.

"Punish me, Jay," Robin begs me in a whisper laced with desire. Her eyes are still closed as she waits for my answer.

"Would it make you feel better?" I ask her as I press my chest against hers and slowly let go of her wrists. "If I took it out on you?" I whisper the question, feeling the heat between our bodies mingle with our breath. I slide my fingers along her collarbone and then to the thin silk strap of her nightgown. I don't stop, my touch forcing the strap down her shoulder, letting it fall and exposing her left breast.

My cock is impossibly hard as I stare down at her gorgeous skin, trailing my finger over every inch and watching with bated breath as goosebumps follow my path.

Her pale rosy nipples are already hard as I reach down and pinch one with my forefinger and thumb, pulling back slightly and making her head fall back. A moan slips through her lips, and it forces precum to leak from my cock.

I've wanted her for so long, I know I have, but the anger has kept me from reaching out to her, from touching her. I harbor so much resentment for the day she left that I've feared this moment just as much as I've desired it.

"Jay," she whimpers my name as she shudders, and it's my breaking point. The last restraint I have snaps. I tear the nightgown off her body. The fabric comes apart with a loud rip, accompanied by her gasp.

She wants me to punish her. I will.

She wants me to have her. I'll take every piece of her and leave her with nothing. Nothing without me from this day forward.

I shove my hand between her thighs and her panties are already soaking wet. She writhes under me as I nip her neck and work my hand over her panty-covered cunt, pressing my palm to her swollen nub and ruthlessly forcing her first orgasm from her.

She doesn't expect the first release; it comes quickly and rocks through her body. As the ripples leave her lying limp, I tear through the thin lace and spread her legs for me. I kick off my jeans and boxers and stroke my thick cock just once.

I don't even hesitate. I'm not gentle; I don't give her a chance to acclimate. I thrust into her, slamming my hips to hers and taking her in one swift motion.

Her back bows and she screams out, but I'm quick to press my chest and lips to hers. It calms her as I pull nearly all the way out, feeling her opening at the tip of my cock and then shoving myself all the way back in. She's already wet and hot for me, making it that much easier for me to fuck her so ruthlessly.

I pound into her over and over again, feeling her tight walls spasm around my cock. Each hard thrust is met with a whimper escaping her lips. Her sharp nails digging into my back only spur me to fuck her harder, faster.

I take her with a punishing force, relentlessly pistoning my hips.

Even as she cums on my dick again, so hot and tight and sucking my dick in further, begging for my cum, I refuse. I groan into her neck, grinding my teeth and digging my blunt nails into the flesh at her hips to keep my release from surfacing.

She screams out my name over and over, but I stay still, holding my breath and ignoring the tingling at the base of my spine. My toes curl and my balls draw up, but I deny it. I stay as still as I can, buried deep in her tight cunt until her orgasm passes.

And then I do it again.

And again.

I spread her wider and fuck her deeper and harder each time. Letting the waves of her orgasms build and crash through her, leaving her limp and destroyed each and every time. Her breathing is ragged as she arches her neck and pleads with me.

"Please, Jay," she moans and her voice is a strangled cry. Her words barely audible. A cold sweat forms over every inch of my skin as I ride through her words, not letting up. Her body tries to roll away, in a desperate effort to leave me and I grip her throat tightly in my hand, squeezing as I piston my hips between her legs, forcing her small breasts to bounce. Forcing her hands up to clutch at my wrist. Forcing little cries of pained pleasure from her lips.

"Please what?" I ask her as her lips part with the need to breathe. Her fingernails just barely scratch at my hand, but she doesn't try to pull it away. It's only to make this last one the most intense. To shatter her completely and intensify it so that she'll be more than ruined.

"Please," she tries to speak, but the threat of another orgasm creeps up through her body, making her arch and writhe. As the silent scream is met with her body going stiff, her heels digging into the mattress, I pump my hips again and again, bottoming out against her cervix until my dick pulses and I relent.

I loosen my grip on her throat, listening to her gasp for air and scream my name with nothing but pleasure. My own orgasm finally tears through me, demanding its own relief and forcing her name from my lips. I whisper it in the crook of her neck, her hot breath on my face making my entire body chill.

Our mixed arousal and cum leaks between us as we both catch our breath. And I fall to the mattress next to her sated and mesmerized by the way she lies there panting for air. The way her eyes are dazed and her body trembles. Because of what I've done to her. Because of what I've given her.

She whimpers and tries to move when she realizes I've left her, but I merely splay a hand on her hip and she stills, waiting for me to tell her what to do next.

Her thighs scissor slightly, simply because I've put my hand on her but it's met with a small cry and her brow furrowing.

I lean over her, kissing her gently on the lips before pulling the covers up and around her.

"Don't leave me, please," my little bird begs me, and it destroys every bit of me.

"I won't," I lie to her just to ease her worry. "I'll be right here when you wake up."

Chapter 19

Robin

HE COULDN'T HELP BUT LEAVE ME.

It's all I could think while I stood in the hot stream of water. I run my fingers through my damp hair as I sit on the bed in the basement.

I'm not sure if John is coming or not. I haven't seen him since he left me yesterday, but it seems fitting to wait for him here. At least one of them will come.

I was foolish enough to think when the bathroom door creaked open and the hot steam drifted away from me that it was Jay, but it was only Toby. Hours later and still no sign of Jay.

My heart splinters as I cross my legs, and I have to close my eyes because of the aching reminder of last night. It was everything I thought it would be and more, but now I'm left alone, just like I was this morning.

I pull the lone pillow on the bed into my lap and lean against the wall, staring at the door. What a good little victim I'm being for him. My stomach sinks and my mouth dries up. I stay where I'm told to and spread my legs for him, begging him to ruin me.

I close my eyes and turn away from the closed door as Toby whines on the other side.

Jay's not the only one fucked up in the head.

I'm so busy wallowing that I don't hear John come in. It's not until he clears his throat and the door shuts with a thud that I realize he's here now. The air is tense and awkward between us, and I instantly wonder if he knows.

"There you are," he says and attempts a pleasant smile but he fails. "How are you feeling today?" he asks me cautiously, striding to the camera to turn it on and then fiddling with it as if there's anything new to focus on. I think it's just so he doesn't have to look at me.

"Used," I tell him flatly, watching for his reaction. He stills for a moment and my heart beats faster, but then he moves to the chair, the blinking red light greeting me as John takes a seat and the metal legs scrape and produce that irritating sound.

"Are you okay?" he asks me, leaning forward. It's feigned concern. He doesn't mean it. The realization makes tears prick the backs of my eyes, and I hold the pillow tighter.

"Why do you care?" I ask him out of anger. My words are shaky, and I use my middle finger to wipe under my eyes. I won't cry over this. I refuse to.

"Robin," John says my name with sympathy and compassion before rising from the chair and quickly coming to the bed. "Did he hurt you?" he asks me, and I simply shake my head. He rests a hand on my back, but he's holding back.

"You don't-" I try to speak, but my words are muted by the lump in my throat. "I'm hurt because I feel as though I don't matter to you." I tell him the truth, the raw honesty cutting me deeply. He doesn't even remember me. My eyes water at the thought, and I wish I were stronger. I take in a steadying breath and focus on him. How much he needs me.

"Do you like me, John?" I ask him. "Do you think if things were different, that you would like me?" The question carries a heavy weight to it. He has the ability to break me and crush me into a million pieces. I need him as much as I need Jay.

"Of course I do," John answers although he doesn't hold my gaze. I close my eyes, feeling my body turn cold and nausea stir in the pit of my stomach. The way his voice is tense, the 'it's-not-me-it's-you' tone is there. It feels like a breakup. I struggle to breathe for a moment while he speaks, but this is all my fault. I know better than this. It's Jay who makes me weak and stupid, who left me feeling like this. But I knew it would end like this. I'm the one who pushed.

"Yesterday, when I left-" he stops to rub the back of his neck and lets out an uneasy sigh. "I don't know how to handle this, Robin. You're fragile, and this situation-"

I cut him off and say, "It's intense, but I-" I ball up my hands in frustration and scoot away from his touch. "I need you to know that what you think of me is very important to me." I swallow thickly and gauge his reaction.

"What I think doesn't matter," John answers, shaking his head slightly.

"It does, John." I reach out slowly and risk placing my fingers in his hand, and that small touch is what breaks down his walls.

He wraps his strong hand around mine and sits closer to me on the bed, scooting back and licking his lips before looking up at me.

I can feel my eyes widen as I wait with bated breath for the truth. I can tell that's what he's going to say. "I feel for you," he says, and my heart thumps. "I feel a very strong urge to protect you, and to…" He trails off and waves a hand in the air as if he's looking for the right word.

"You don't have to sugarcoat it, John," I tell him as I keep my composure.

He looks back at me with an intensity that shocks me.

"This is fucked up," he tells me in a lowered voice, his eyes lightening as he says, "What I want to do to you is even worse."

I have to break his gaze and I stare at my fingers as I pull my hand away from his and grip the sheet on the mattress. I take a chance and peek at him. "What do you want to do to me?" I ask him.

"I want to take you away and keep you," he says, and a warmth flows through my body. He leans forward and I think he's going to kiss me, but he doesn't. Instead he puts his lips close to my ear and whispers, "I want to fuck you until you forget. Until you're only mine."

I close my eyes at his admission.

He backs away, and the chill from the basement air breaks the moment we had.

"But you're in love with Jay, and there's something between you two. I don't have a place interfering."

He's so wrong. So, fucking wrong. I part my lips to tell him just that, but as he sits back on the bed, straightening his shoulders, I see the blinking light.

Always watching.

I have to be careful. I have to tell John, but it would be so much easier if he could just remember.

Chapter 20

John

DAYS PASS EASILY, EACH ONE BLEEDING INTO THE NEXT. SHE'S addictive. The sound of her soft voice and the even cadence when she tells me stories charm me.

But they're about her and Jay. What her life was like before and after.

About missing him and how she could never forget what they went through.

What shreds me is her guilt, the way she describes moving on with her life as though it's a confession. It shouldn't be that way, but it doesn't matter how many times I tell her. That pained look in her eyes only gets worse.

The fluorescent light above my head flickers, and I look up to watch it. These sessions aren't moving things forward, and doing them in the basement is only aggravating me more and more.

"Is everything okay?" Robin's soft voice calls to me from across the room. She's on the bed as usual, her heels propped up as she hugs her legs, leaning back against a pillow with her head against the wall.

I clear my throat and glance at the camera, the red light blinking and wonder if Jay even watches. He doesn't ask about them in the least.

"What do you want to gain from this, Robin?" I ask her, my heart rate climbing. It's obvious she has no intention of leaving. What's happened between her and Jay has touched them both deeply, but I'm a conflicting factor. Every day it gets harder to leave. Every day I grow jealous. I get angrier.

This isn't the man I am. I need to get the fuck out of here.

"I want to know more about you, John," she answers me after taking a moment. She seems nervous as she watches for my reaction.

She wants me. I can fucking feel it, and I want her too. It only makes the situation that much more fucked up.

"What do you want to know?" I ask her, crossing my ankle over my knee and rubbing the rough stubble on my jaw with my thumb.

"Tell me about growing up?" she asks. It's an innocent question, but the look on her face is so serious. As if the answer will affect her deeply.

"There's not much to me," I tell her and sit back. "My story isn't like yours or Jay's." A sigh leaves me as I rub the back of my neck and look at the door.

"Tell me about your parents," Robin offers and my eyes flick to hers. I watch how she picks at the comforter as if her idle hands need to be taking notes. It makes me smile and reminds me there's so much more to her than the past she has with Jay. It also reminds me that she's probably used to this. Being the questioner and not the questionee.

"I was adopted when I was younger. And I was visiting the orphanage when I met Jay." The hint of a smile on my face vanishes at the memory. "My parents were young and they did what they thought was best when they gave me up, but Jay…" I can't finish the thought. He needed someone so badly. I saw how everyone looked at him. How they judged him.

I clear my throat and rub my palms on my jeans. "Anyway." I tell her the basic rundown. "I did alright in school, B student mostly. I wasn't really interested. I guess I was kind of quiet."

"And you're a mechanic?" Robin asks, and I nod my head.

"Yeah, I've always loved working on cars and bikes. It made sense." I nod my head and remember the shop just sitting there, but the bills aren't going away. "I enjoy working for myself but the downsides are the long hours and the lack of socializing."

"Are you a social butterfly?" Robin asks with a bit of humor. A rough laugh rumbles up my chest as I shake my head.

"Never really been into crowds," I answer her honestly.

"Not a lot of friends?" she asks.

"I'm not a loner like Jay," I answer her, feeling defensive. "A few guys work for me at the shop and we hang out occasionally. I can take them or leave them. I guess I'm a bit of a loner after all." I hadn't realized it until she questioned me. The bartender at the local pub and Steve a mechanic looking for part-time work are my two closest friends. And of course Jay.

"I'm a loner," Robin says, interrupting my thoughts. "I'm very much alone." She gives me this sad smile.

"Why's that?" I ask her. She shouldn't be alone ever. I could talk to her for hours and hours every day and be content with nothing else. She's the type of person you feel like you already know before she even lays eyes on you. She should definitely never be alone.

"I don't know why," she tells me and then looks down at the sheet. She stretches her back and then asks me, "Do you like to be alone at night?"

"Not in particular," I answer without thinking about anything other than her company in the evening. "I wouldn't mind company at night," I say and my blood heats as she holds my gaze and fire sparks between us.

"Why do you leave at night?" she asks me like it's a sin.

My brow furrows, and the pit of my stomach fills with guilt. "Do you want me to stay?" I ask her.

Her eyes search mine for a minute, as if she's not sure of the right answer. It fucking guts me.

"You love Jay?" I ask her, changing the subject and putting the attention back onto her. I know she does. It's why I can never have her. Why I feel compelled to carry on with this charade.

"I do," she says and my blood turns to ice. It's one more reason I need to leave. When I peek back up at her, she looks as though she's going to cry. It happens almost every day. When she breaks down and holds back from me.

I hate it. It keeps me coming back to her because I want to be the one to help her. The one she leans on. *The one she leaves with.*

I know I should tell her that it's okay. That it's natural to love him. That he loves her, too. But those aren't the words that come out of my mouth.

"I really hate that you get so upset. I just want to help you so you can move past this." *So she can get away from Jay.* I keep the thought to myself, but it's true. I want to keep her far away from him. But right now, she feels she needs him. She feels *for* him.

"Then help me, John," she says with a strained voice. Like she's so close, yet so far away.

"Tell me what you need," I tell her. And I mean it. I don't want her to be upset or hurt in any way. She's a strong, beautiful woman who should be happy. The past is where it's supposed to be, and she should know she deserves happiness.

"I need you to remember," she whispers and stares deep into my eyes.

"Remember what?" I ask her, my heart beating slow and my body heating. It's fear that keeps me still. Fear that I'm somehow involved in what happened all those years ago. I've tried so many times to think back to how I know this woman, but nothing comes to mind.

I must though, because she calls to me in a way I can't deny.

She gives me a small smile, but it's sad. Everything about her is a beautiful shade of sadness. "Can you tell me what you know of me again?" she asks me.

I sit back with slight relief, but the feeling that I'm failing her is so heavy on my chest I can't speak. "Can you tell me how we first met?" she asks me. Pushing me.

I try to answer her, I try to think but my memory is so hazy.

"Do you want to talk about something else?" she asks me, breaking up the throbbing headache and the overwhelming anxiety. Her hazel eyes shine with sincerity. "I just want to talk to you," she tells me and leans against the wall.

She's obviously lying, and it's then that it hits me.

This session isn't about her.

I'm not here to help her at all.

I'm not meant to interview her.

Jay set me up.

These sessions are all about me.

Chapter 21

Robin

I'M DONE SLEEPING ALONE. OR TRYING TO, RATHER. EVERY SECOND that passes is like a ticking bomb and I need to be close to him when it goes off. That, and I can't fucking sleep. Not without him.

It's been days.

Days of walking on eggshells and finding our footing. But we know who we are and what we want. And I'm tired of waiting.

The moment my heels hit the plush rug, Toby yawns at the door and stretches. He doesn't stand as I cautiously walk to the door, but his eyes are on me. He's slow to stand and make sure I don't go to the front door. That and the basement exit are the only two doors that set him off. Any other time, he simply follows me like a guardian rather than a warden. "It's funny that you used to scare me, you know?" I tell the dog as he looks up at me with the widest puppy eyes. I know there's a beast inside of him that could rip me limb from limb. I'm well aware of that fact. But the animal refusing to leave my side is just a big puppy dog.

I bend down and pat his head as he walks with me although my heart is racing.

I don't think Jay will deny me like he did the first night and if he does, I'm going to fight him on that. I don't think it will come to that though. He doesn't want to deny me, just as I don't want to refuse him of anything.

We need progress, not perfection, I think as I head to the bedroom across from the basement door. I don't try to be quiet at all. I want him to know I'm not sneaking around or trying anything.

The door's wide open and filled with so much more light than my own room. It's only moonlight, but the blinds are open and they send stripes of shadows across the bed. They lay on Jay's bare thighs and chest and all the way up to his chin.

I stop in the doorway, the floors creaking as I take in a steadying breath.

"You should be sleeping," Jay says without turning to look at me. Toby yawns again then arches his back before circling in the hallway behind me. The sound of his paws and the jingle of his tag are so loud. I swallow thickly, ripping my eyes away from him and taking a step into Jay's bedroom.

"I thought you slept downstairs," I tell him and he finally turns to look at me, although the rest of his body is still.

"It's different, knowing you're up here." His eyes travel down my body slowly, assessing me. The way his eyes heat creates an instant tension in the room that makes me shift slightly, ignoring the way my core heats. Jay has a power over me that's undeniable.

I walk toward the bed and sit down on the edge as I talk. "I think that's a good thing. It's change, and change is good."

My hands rest in my lap as I wait for him to respond. His eyes narrow, and he's quiet for a long time.

"Why aren't you sleeping?" he asks me, although he already knows the answer.

My throat gets tight as I scoot further into his bed and my knee brushes his. "I want to sleep with you," I push the words out and then look Jay in the eyes.

Slowly, ever so slowly, a smile tugs at his lips.

"Please?" I ask him and he hesitates but then shakes his head.

"You can't be here when John comes," he says although there's no conviction in his voice.

I ignore him and simply pull the sheet and comforter down and crawl into bed.

"You're getting bold, Robin," Jay says with a bit of an admonishment, but then he wraps his arm around me and pulls me closer to him. "I love it," he says with a soft smile.

I smile into his chest and then look up at him.

The faint light of the moon filtering in through the windows highlights the sharp lines of his jaw and his rough stubble. I nudge my nose against his chin and he lets out a huff of a laugh.

"You really should be sleeping," he tells me and I nuzzle next to him. I wish I felt warm fuzzy feelings, but I don't. I feel nothing but anxiety.

"I want to talk," I tell him and it makes him laugh. A genuine laugh that's rough and bubbles up from his chest. It's the sweetest sound to hear, and it reminds me of the first time I heard it. Pure joy from a man so devoid of any happiness.

"Of course you do." He runs a hand down his face and lets out an easy sigh before looking at me. "What do you want to talk about, little bird?"

"Anything," I answer him. "Just tell me something." I nestle closer to him, but keep my hands to myself. I love this. This easiness and openness. I want this forever.

"I feel better now with you," he tells me and it makes me smile, but the happiness quickly vanishes. "Before I thought it would be better if I just left." He looks into my eyes as he talks, absently trailing his fingers over the dip in my waist.

"I thought it would be easier if I was just gone."

"That's a horrible thought to have, Jay and you're so wrong-"

"Shh," Jay shushes me and calms me down by kissing my forehead. "I know that. I could never leave you anyway. Even if you had no idea I was there."

His admission only makes me feel that much worse. "I wish I'd been there for you," I whisper against his chest. I desperately want to rest my hand against his chest, but instead I move my fingers to the front of his pajama bottoms and slip them just over the edge so I'm comfortable.

"I can't tell you how many nights I wanted to get in bed with you," Jay says. "I know it's wrong. Stalking or whatever, but I wanted it. I wanted to go after you."

"I wish you had. I wish you hadn't waited."

"It's not like I could have shown up and asked you out for coffee." Jay huffs a chuckle, and it makes my body shake. His large arm wraps around me. "I wish things were different. I wish I wasn't broken for you." The smile vanishes as he rubs his eyes and lets out a heavy sigh.

"*We're* broken," I correct him. I chew on the inside of my lip, thinking about how to word the next question. The one thing that's really kept us apart.

"Have you tried to tell John at all?" I ask him and stay perfectly still, staring at the bedroom wall.

"He hates me," Jay says as if it's a fact.

"He doesn't."

"There's hate behind the pity. It's why he doesn't want to know," he says and it makes my heart clench.

"Can we talk about something else, little bird?" Jay asks and then kisses my forehead. "Or sleep?"

"He's the only thing holding us back," I tell him. I need more. I know I can't push, but I want Jay in my life fully and completely and I need more than this.

"Us?" he asks.

"Don't pretend, Jay. I won't let you do it, too," I say and there's a strength to my voice I don't recognize. I add, "I love you too much."

I want so desperately for him to say the words back to me. I want to hear it although I feel it deep in my soul already. I want him to acknowledge it more than anything.

It's quiet for a long moment. My breathing steadies and my eyes drift shut as I listen to the sound of his steady heartbeat and sink deeper into his comforting warmth.

"Do you love him too?" he asks me quietly a moment later.

I don't answer his question. I can't. Because right now, I know if I tell him the truth, it will break him. And I'll never hurt Jay. Never.

Chapter 22

I T'S NOT SNOOPING IF YOU'RE LOOKING FOR SOMETHING THAT WILL help a person you love.

I'm sure that's what parents say when they're searching their children's rooms and going through their text messages. I need to find something, anything that could show John the truth. Something that's irrefutable.

I'm sure all the evidence is burned and left in ashes, but that doesn't stop me from opening one drawer and then the next in Jay's bedroom.

If only I could find something. The thought makes my heart twist with pain. I don't want to be the one to show him. I don't want to be there when he's forced to face who he is. It's going to ruin him, but only then will all of us be able to heal.

The sound of the floor creaking makes my eyes whip up to the door, my heart racing. They travel down to Toby and I nearly smile looking at him stretch his back. An easy sigh leaves me, but then I jump at the sight of John.

I put a hand over my heart and try not to look guilty as I push the drawer back in. I didn't find a damn thing. Jay isn't one to keep things. Nothing worth any sentimental value. Nothing that reminds him of his past.

"Robin," John says my name low, as if he's afraid someone will hear him. Jay.

"What's wrong?" I ask him as my blood chills and my throat gets tight. "Is everything alright?"

"I think we need to leave, Robin." I nod my head once, thinking maybe

I could convince him to go to the hospital, but he's not in the right mind-set. He wouldn't believe a damn thing if I told him the truth.

I take a hesitant step toward John as he talks, "We can get out of here. I'll take you home or …to my place?" he asks as if it's a question. Like I'd need protection from Jay.

He has no idea it's him who I need to protect myself from. "John," I say and his name comes out like a plea.

"I know you feel guilty," John starts and I shake my head, turning away from him to look out of the window. I cross my arms, feeling trapped. Not by the solid walls, not by the men I love, but by my past. And hasn't it always been like that?

"It's not about that," I tell him honestly. "I can't go now. I see why Jay did this. Why he wants it this way."

I turn back to face John, and his expression has fallen. He's leaving. I've failed them both.

I reach out for his hand and he takes it before telling me, "I can't do this anymore, Robin; I need you to come with me."

His thumb rubs back and forth over my wrist with a soothing rhythm. I lick my lips and look deep into his eyes as I tell him, "I don't want you to go."

"You're not okay. I can see that you feel like you have an obligation to him. You love him, I get that, but this isn't right."

An uneasy breath leaves me as I watch every little move John makes. My lips part, but my voice is silent. I swallow thickly and refuse to let go of his hand when he starts to pull away.

"Can we go outside?" I ask him. I just need to feel like I can breathe.

He simply nods and walks beside me, not letting go of my hand, but not attempting to get closer either.

"I felt like we were making progress," I tell him and watch Toby as we get to the front door. It's a large heavy door made of solid wood and stained a dark brown. Toby doesn't have a problem in the least as John opens it. He almost closes the door right after him, but Toby slips out with us, staying close to my side and I've never wanted him more.

I reach down to pet him, feeling as though my breath is strangled. Sometimes progress isn't enough. It's not enough to keep John. It's not enough to ease the burden on Jay's conscience.

A chill sweeps across my skin and goosebumps spread along my arms as I shudder. The fresh air is what I needed though.

"There's a porch," I say with a bit of humor in my voice. I haven't stepped foot outside. It reminds me of the world outside of here. Of the life I used to have. The one we could share together.

John leans against the banister and looks out into the empty field, not looking at me as he tells me, "Jay will be back soon, and I'm going to tell him I'm not coming back here. I'm done with this."

The air gets colder and more tense as my eyes narrow and I watch him. "I thought we were doing better," I tell him although it comes out a question.

He turns to look at me, but quickly looks back out into the field of nothing.

I have to tell him. I have to push. Toby whines as the thought hits me, and I reach down to pet him again. I've never been more scared in my adult life.

I slowly sit, although my legs are shaky and this close to Toby's jaws reminds me of the vicious barking, the way he held me down that first night. I ignore it all. I have to give a piece to John. Something to keep him.

"John, I want to tell you a secret."

"What's that?" he asks and looks down at me, but I don't look back up at him as I pet Toby and try to think of what to tell him. It's been days and I don't know what I can say that he'd believe.

"I knew you when you were a child." My heart hurts as I confess. "This one time, you taught me how to whistle with a blade of grass." The memory is so fresh. I can still feel the bit of sunshine. A reward I was terrified would come with a punishment. "Do you remember?" I ask him.

I take a peek up to look at him, and his expression tells me everything I already knew. He doesn't remember a damn thing, and he won't believe me. All the time we spent together, none of it exists for him.

I hold the tears back as Toby rests his head in my lap. His warmth is so at odds with the bitter coldness that surrounds me.

"Are you alright?" he asks me, and my heart sinks even further.

"You don't remember me, but I'm not lying to you, John." I steady my breath. "I'm not crazy," I tell him and as the words slip out, I feel as though I am. I'm beyond sane at least.

"We never knew each other. The first time I saw you…" John starts, but doesn't finish his sentence. I wait, holding my breath and hoping for something, but also fearing it.

Please remember me. Please, John. I need you.

"You ripped it right out of the ground," I tell him, brushing beneath my nose with my forearm and not giving a damn about it. "And put it right to your lips." A smile forces its way to my lips and a laugh bubbles up. "I thought you were eating it," I tell him.

Silence greets me, and this time I don't look up to gauge his reaction. I let my body sway with Toby.

"I'm not the only one who's hurt, John. Neither is Jay." I whisper the words and half expect him to ask how it relates to Jay. Part of me hopes he will, but he doesn't.

Finally, he says, "I don't remember any of that."

"It's okay," I say and smile weakly. "I mean, I wish you did. I really wish you knew how much you meant to me."

"Then leave with me?" John asks.

"Will you listen if I…" I can't finish. He won't believe me, or worse, it'll push him farther away.

"Robin, whatever Jay told you-"

I shake my head and close my eyes. "This isn't something he told me, John." My voice is hard and unforgiving.

"I love you, John. You don't remember me, but I think you love me, too," I tell him, exposing everything I'm most afraid of. "Just don't leave me. Not yet. Not until I can tell you everything."

Chapter 23

Robin

I'M NOT USED TO WAITING THIS LONG. I PICK AT MY NAILS, wondering if I've ruined everything. Wondering if I should try to find him. I wish there were a clock in here. Something. Anything to fill up the silence.

My eyes drift back to the only constant in the room. The camera that's facing me.

The light isn't on, but it feels like it's taunting me that much more with it off. Like the cameras never mattered. Nothing did. It was going to happen regardless.

I slide off the bed, feeling restless and with an anxiety that won't go away. I hate that camera. I hate the blinking red light. I swallow thickly as I walk toward it. My throat is tight as I remember how the monster's breath felt against my neck like a sticky fog. How my body screamed in pain and the bed shook as he took something from me I could never have back. I stared at the red light through my tears. Watching it blinking and recording everything. Just watching it all happen to me.

And there wasn't a damn thing I could do to stop it.

I stopped screaming, I stopped crying. I had nothing left but the fucking light to take me away.

Pathetic. I'm fucking pathetic. The faint memory flashes before my eyes.

A cry rips through me as my fist swings in the air, slamming against the cold metal of the camera.

Fuck you! Then it crashes to the floor and I scream as I reach down and grab it before cracking it against the unforgiving floor again.

I was never pathetic. My teeth grind together as his face stares back at me. The face of a monster. Nothing but coldness in his eyes.

I hate him. I hate what he did to me and how I can never change it.

I scream out as I pick up the stand and slam it over and over against the broken camera. Small pieces of metal scatter as I recklessly destroy each and every piece I can. My muscles scream and the adrenaline pumps faster and faster, but I've never felt so alive. So liberated.

Jay's father did something to me; he changed me forever. But I won't let him define me. *That* will *never* define who I am.

My shoulders rise and fall with each heavy breath. No more fucking camera. No more of this. I won't do it anymore. I'm done with this shit.

I swallow my nervousness, my hands still trembling as I loosen my grip and let the leg fall to the ground. My body shakes as I look around, but instead of feeling crazed, instead of feeling scared by what I've done, I feel nothing but triumphant.

A creak to my right makes my body jolt.

I turn toward the door as it opens, breathing heavily, feeling invisible and empowered.

"Little bird," Jay tsks, his boots smacking on the cement floor as he makes his way to me. "That wasn't a very nice thing to do," he says with a hint of condescension in his voice. But the corner of his lips curls up into a half smile.

I break his gaze to look at the shattered camera laying in pieces on the ground.

"I fucking hate it," I mutter beneath my breath.

"So you broke it?" he asks me, his voice tinged with surprise. My palms turn sweaty as I look into his eyes, hoping to find approval. He stops in front of me, his broad shoulders and chest at my eye level and dominating me with his presence alone. There's a power about Jay that's undeniable, a confidence and demeanor that won't be denied.

"Yes," I answer him and wait for his reply. Clinging to the hope that he'll understand. It's not just a camera. It's something more. A pain I can't describe. He nods his head once and then looks past me at the pile of broken pieces on the floor.

"It's funny that you break what you hate… yet I seem to be the opposite?" Jay speaks in a riddle, not quite to me, maybe more to himself.

"I didn't mean to," I tell him quickly. "I'm just…,"

"Angry," Jay answers for me.

"Yes," I answer him in a whisper. He takes a step closer to me, filling in the space between us with heat. His large hands wrap around my hips and I slowly move my hands up to his lower back. Both of us are testing boundaries. My heart beats quickly as I tilt my head up. His hands move down and to my backside. He squeezes my ass and pulls me into him, hard and with a force that makes me gasp.

"It's easy to blame the anger," he says, staring into my eyes. His voice is like a hiss, like a spoken sin. He lowers his lips so they're close to mine, but he doesn't kiss me. "But you and I both know it's more than that. So much more."

I can't take the proximity, the intensity. I don't ask for his permission. I don't wait for him to make the move. I'm taking what I want.

I crash my lips against his and he's quick to react, to deepen it. To lift me up and force my legs to wrap around his hips as he lays me on the bed. His tongue parts the seam of my lips, and I open for him instantly.

Take me. Have me. Do whatever you want with me. I've always been yours.

My breath quickens and my chest rises chaotically as he peels my clothes from me. His fingers slip across my skin with a tenderness that's only thinly hiding the beast of a man Jay is.

His lips kiss and nip my skin, moving over every inch in a torturous fashion. My shoulders dig into the bed as my back arches and he swirls his tongue along my sensitive nipple. His hands, his lips, the roughness of his jeans brushing against my skin. It's all too much.

"Jay," I whimper his name. This is the only way I want his name to ever come from my lips again. My head is dizzy with desire and it takes a moment before the cool air makes me realize he's on his knees, upright and waiting for my attention. My eyes move slowly, trailing along every hard line of the muscles on his chest and shoulders. He waits to speak until I meet his hungry gaze.

"You want me?" he asks as his deft fingers unbutton his jeans. My eyes are drawn to the movement and I slowly crawl to him as if moving too quickly will make him change his mind.

I nod my head once and whisper in a sultry voice I don't recognize, "Yes, please."

"'Take it from me," he tells me as he shoves his pants down. He strokes his cock once and my eyes are drawn to it. I lick my lips and show him my intentions but his hand comes out, pushing my shoulders away.

I look up at him, a wave of denial threatening to steal my happiness, but his thumb brushes against my lips and he says, "If I wanted these fuckable lips I'd tell you. Give me your pussy," he commands.

I can barely breathe as I turn on the mattress, listening to it groan as I get on all fours and reach between my legs for his cock. As I do, he swipes his fingers through my slick folds and brushes my throbbing clit over and over. "You're so fucking wet," he groans and I half expect him to lose control, to take me like he did before. He says it like he's surprised, like I wasn't made for him.

"Please," I whimper and lower my head to the mattress. My fingernails scrape along the sheet. I'm close already. I want him that badly.

The only movement he makes is to gently stroke my ass. I peek back at him, willing him to take me as ruthlessly and savagely as he wants to.

"Show me how much you want me," he says under his breath as he towers over me, looking down at me with a heat in his eyes I'm sure is mirrored in my own.

In this moment, the only thing that matters is showing him just how much I desire his touch. How much I crave his affection and acceptance. His love.

I want him more than I ever have. More than I've wanted anything else.

I want him more than I want my own life.

Chapter 24

John

"WHAT HAPPENED TO THE CAMERA?" I ASK JAY AS I STAND in the opening of the bathroom door. There's still a bit of steam on the bathroom mirror and I watch as he wipes it off with his forearm. He looks over his shoulder at me, his hair still damp from the shower as he puts his t-shirt on over his head.

"The camera?" he asks, turning back to the mirror.

A tick in my jaw twitches as he ignores me. "The fucking camera is destroyed." My blood heats with anger. I'm tired of being a fucking pawn in this game he's playing. And how he likes to ignore me.

"She broke it," he says simply. The mention of *her*, of the sweet woman he's toying with does something to me.

"She did that?" I ask him with an air of disbelief, but also one of pride. She's stronger than she knows. She deserves better, so much better.

The past is the only thing that stands in her way. And that's just what Jay is.

"She fucking loved doing it," he says and there's a sense of pride in his voice and it echoes the jealousy in me. I clear my throat, wishing I could shake it off. Wishing I wasn't caught in between. *Wishing I could just walk away.*

"She's doing better," I say and watch the easiness about him slowly dim as I wait for him to respond.

"She wants you. You know that?" He cocks a brow at me meant to be friendly in nature, but it's not. I know he wants her. He fucking loves her, and she loves him. But I'd take her from him in a heartbeat. I want her just as much as he does. I can love her better. Treat her better. I can give her so much more.

"She should go now," I tell him, ignoring his accusation and the way my blood pumps harder and hotter. I can't look him in the eyes as the vision of having her again and again beneath me flashes before my eyes. *She'd love me more.*

"You want her too," he says, and my eyes flash up to his. "You want to fuck her. Marry her?" he asks me with that same wicked grin on his face. "You want to put a baby in her and ride off into the sunset?" he asks and tilts his head, egging me on.

"I'd give her a better life than you ever could." The words slip between my lips with a menacing growl.

He only laughs at me, then gives a sarcastic grunt and turns back to the mirror. Fucking prick. "You wish you could," he says beneath his breath, gripping the sides of the countertop as his expression hardens. The real him showing. The anger and the hate.

"You're using her," I tell him, feeling the swell of anger rise. I crack my knuckles on my right hand with my thumb, trying to keep from balling it into a fist.

He turns to look at me, waiting for more.

"All you are is using her."

"Maybe." A confident smile stretches across his face, and the danger in his darkened eyes is so apparent, so real. "I am using her. And she fucking loves it."

I can't fucking take it anymore. I love her. I fucking love this woman who's caught in a web of lies and hurt.

Adrenaline pumps through my body, burning up my skin. I hear the pulsing thud of my blood loud in my ears.

I won't let him get away with it. It ends now.

A snarl rips through me as I slam both of my fists into Jay's shoulders, landing hard and knocking into him with all my weight. I'm not used to this aggression. To this all-consuming rage, but when it comes to her, I can't hold it back. She makes me feel a side of me I've never known. She makes me want more. And I want her all to myself.

Jay's a fucking dead man.

He stumbles, smashing his shoulder and head against the bathroom wall. Before he gains his balance, I land a blow into his gut that nearly has him doubling over. But Jay's taken enough punches to know how to handle them. He mutters under his breath, "Motherfucker!" while ramming his shoulder into my gut. My eyes shut tight with the spike of pain that shoots up my body.

My legs lose their balance as my boot backs into the tub, tripping me. I grit my teeth and cling to the shower curtain as it rips the bar down, falling violently with a loud clank into the tub behind me.

I fall hard on my knees and elbows onto the tile with Jay's muscular frame crushing down on mine. I quickly wrap a leg around his calf and push my weight to the opposite shoulder, forcing him down on his back with me landing hard on his chest.

"She's mine," I tell him finally. "I won't let you hurt her," I say although I'm winded. He already has. He's destroyed her and ruined something so beautiful and pure. "I fucking hate you," I seethe at him.

My fist slams into the floor as I try to gain my balance and focus. It hurts like a bitch and splits my knuckles. My left hand grabs the collar of his shirt as I raise my bloodied right fist, eyes focusing on his pretty boy nose.

My breaths come in pants as he plants a punch on my left cheek before I'm able to gain my balance and take a swing at him. *Fuck!* I stagger back, both fists immediately going to my face to block any more punches. I land on my ass, but move to my feet the second I see Jay breathing heavy and struggling to get up.

"I hate you too," he says with a smile. There's blood coating his teeth as he sways in front of me. "I can't tell you enough how much I fucking hate you."

The venom in his voice is all too real, and I feel the same right back.

It's me or him when it comes to Robin. "Between the two of us, she'll choose me. Always," he says as if reading my mind. The smile stays in place as he wipes the blood from his mouth with the back of his hand.

He's right. My heart beats hard at the recognition. She'd choose him. And I can't fucking let it happen. She deserves so much more. Someone better than him.

My hands grip around his throat and at first, I feel flesh, real hot flesh that my fingers sink into, but the harder I push, the more I try to choke the life from this bastard, the less it feels real.

My vision shifts and he's no longer in front of me. My fingers are no longer around his throat, but instead on the edge of the mirror.

"Fuck you!" he sneers and he's back, his vicious eyes piercing into me with a threat of death and I smash my forehead against his.

Glass splinters against my forehead, it smashes around me. I hear the crack, I can fucking feel it, but when I open my eyes, he's there staring back at me. A smile on his face as he bashes his head into mine again and again and again.

A punishing abuse until I'm standing in front of a broken mirror, clinging to the edges of it and his image fades, leaving only my reflection.

My heart races, and my head's dizzy with pain throbbing and shooting through me.

Chapter 25

John

Twenty years ago

"**C**OME ON," I SAY AND MY VOICE IS LOW. SO LOW. I CAN'T SPEAK any louder, but she's moving so slow. I'm afraid he'll hear us. The keys jingle if I hold her hand. But I can't let go of her.

My heart races, beating uncontrollably at the thought of what will happen if he catches us. If he finds out that we're trying to escape.

He'll kill us. I know he will. He'll definitely kill my little bird. I can't let that happen. I turn back to look at her over my shoulder.

Her heels dig in and scrape against the cement as she resists me, and her fingernails scratch at my wrist to let her go.

"We need to go now," I tell her in a stern voice and her face crumples with fear. She shakes her head and her dirtied hair barely moves. Her eyes are wide with fear as she tells me, "We can't."

Her shoulders hunch when she hears the vicious barking of the dogs. "Close the door," she begs me, but I refuse.

I can hear him banging on the door. I can hear my father screaming. I'm surrounded by threats, threats that are promises for me, but empty for her.

"Right now, Robin," I say and grip her chin in my hand and look her in the eyes. "It's now or never," I tell her in a soft voice. My heart pains in my chest. Like nails scraping it slowly, shredding it piece by piece.

"I'm dead," I tell her. "If I stay, I'm dead." I only say those words for her. There's no other choice for me.

I've locked my father in the cellar. He's arrogant to think I could never slip by him. I only have one chance though. And as he rattles the door and screams at me, I nearly cower in front of her. I'm dead when he gets out, and I know he will.

The dogs I have a plan for, but she needs to go the opposite way. She needs to run without being followed.

"No, Jay," she cries.

"We need to go now," I tell her again and although the small girl's expression is only one of fear, she grips my hand tightly and finally moves. I don't give her a second chance, or myself one either. Every step is one more step away from losing her forever. One more step toward my death.

But it's for her. And it's worth it.

My life is so meaningless, but this gives me something.

I have to tug her wrist as we run up the cellar steps. The dogs are just outside the kitchen in the crate. The gate is closed, but they can get out. They have before. The lock on it isn't much at all. I'll have to hold it if I can't find anything to shove between the handles and strengthen the lock.

I stare out of the kitchen door only for a moment, knowing it's time to say goodbye.

"Jay, what do we do?" she asks me in a strangled voice.

"You need to run first, little bird." I stare at the dogs as they snarl and I tell her, "You have to go first. Straight through the field and into the woods. Keep going straight." I ignore her as she objects.

There's a road, it's a dirt road, but I've seen cars go by on it more than once. "Follow the road and I'll be right behind you," I lie to her.

I turn my back to the dogs and face her, managing a smile. How that's possible, I don't know. The tears in her eyes make me feel weak. Like I've failed her, but this is all I can offer.

I wish I had more.

"Promise me, you'll run no matter what you hear?" I ask her and it only makes her more scared. I hate myself for doing this to her, but it's the only way I know.

At the sound of the cellar doors smashing open in the basement beneath us, I quickly turn, gripping her wrist and pulling her with me as I rip the kitchen door open and yell at her to run.

∞

Clunk, the sound is so sharp. So crystal clear. The pain from the excruciating hit immediate, but also numbing.

I open my eyes and see my father. The memory flashes in my vision over and over. I'm on the ground, my hands in the mix of dirt and grass. It's so cold.

She's gone. She's safe. She left me.

My head falls back, and I cry. For the first time in so long, I cry without the tears being forced at the hands of my father.

"You fucking prick," my father sneers at me and I back away. Shuffling backward in the grass, the heels of my bare feet digging into the freezing cold mud.

It's not fast enough. No matter how much I'd like to pretend, I'm not bigger than him, not stronger than him.

I'm weak.

I'm only a child.

He raises the shovel up high in the air, and I don't try to block it this time, I don't do anything but sit there in a numb fear with the vision of her running away.

I only got a glimpse before Father came in. The dogs were furious, barking so loud and viciously. But I locked them in. I pushed a stick through the cages. I couldn't breathe until he ran from me to go to them.

In that moment, her foolish wish was also mine. I wanted her to be a bird and fly up so high. High enough that no one could touch her. Not the dogs, not my father.

I only wanted her to be safe.

But then my father came back. He dragged me out here and he's making me watch as he digs the hole.

The shovel raises up high again, and this time something's different. The sharp clunk as it smashes against my head, the hot blood that drips down my forehead.

I can't feel any of it.

It's not me.

My head hurts as I stare down at the boy. My hands can feel the metal in my hand, the wood of the handle as I watch the boy yank it away from the man.

It's not me though.

I stare in horror as he slams the shovel into the man's gut. He's a small boy, like me. He's skinny though, he's dirty. And he's a murderer.

His chest heaves as he beats the man several times with the shovel. Blood splatters on the ground. Over and over, even as the man lies dead and limp, the boy doesn't stop.

The boy is angry, and he's not well. I feel so sorry for him, but I'm too terrified to move.

I stay on the ground and watch as he slowly drags the man to the pit. It's not much, but he's tired and the boy can't do anything other than move the man to the shallow grave.

When he looks up at me, my heart stops. The boy's anger turns to something else, and his eyes narrow.

"Who are you?" he asks me. My heart beats fast and I don't know how to answer him. I don't remember who I am, I only remember my name.

"John," I tell him.

The boy sniffles and looks down at the dead man in the dirt and then back at me, nodding. "I'm not John," he says and it confuses me.

"My name's Jay."

Chapter 26

Robin

MY HEART IS RACING AND WON'T STOP; IT'S POUNDING SO hard it hurts. My fingers tremble as I push the bathroom door open slowly. It creaks noisily, and I can't even breathe.

I'm afraid of what I'll find on the other side.

I heard the screaming, the fighting. The shattering of glass.

There's no light on in the bathroom, but the stray light streaming in from the hallway reflects off the shards of mirror that litter the floor.

The door only stops when the knob hits the wall, and I stand there frozen in the doorway.

The cuts on his face and hands, the blood that drips down and covers his hand will forever be etched into my memory.

But the sight of him, the man I love so deeply and who I'm desperate to heal all the way down to his very soul, is wretched and it cracks my heart in two.

Sitting on the edge of the tub, his hands cover his face as he's hunched over. But he's alive. Wounded deeply, but still breathing.

"Jay," I whisper his name, terrified I've said the wrong one. I wait with bated breath, the pain in my chest only intensifying as he sits still, ignoring me and making me question what to do.

Call for an ambulance. It's obvious. He needs it. A psychotic break isn't something I can handle on my own.

I take a hesitant step forward, not daring to flick on the light switch. I'm only wearing a pair of socks, but I keep to the right, and gently push the sharp pieces of glass out of my way as I walk toward him. I just need to hold him. I need him to know that it's alright. It doesn't matter how bad it gets, it will always be alright.

The glass clinks as I kick a chunk to the left and take another cautious step toward him.

Finally, he peeks up at me. My body freezes, and I try to figure out if he's there. If Jay is present, or if John is the one sitting in front of me.

I can usually tell by the way he looks at me, but now they both know.

My heart sputters at the pain swirling in his light gray eyes. How his lip twitches with the need to frown and he shakes his head, looking away from me.

"It didn't go well," he speaks just above a murmur and looks away from me, staring at the wall as he lets out a heavy breath. I watch as he tries to relax in front of me, shaking his shoulders and brushing his fingers through his hair. Small pieces of glass tinkle as they drop into the porcelain tub.

Jay.

"You should give me a minute," Jay finally says as he stands tall and towers over me.

"I can help," I offer, but he steps around me, walking to the sink with the glass crunching beneath his boots.

"There's glass," Jay points out the obvious and then stares pointedly at my feet before turning on the faucet.

"I can get shoes," I say weakly. My thoughts are a blur, and his casual demeanor is not at all what I expected. "Can I just clean the glass from your hands so you don't make it worse?" I ask him. My fingers are itching to comfort him. To help him. I'm terrified he'll push me away.

"No," Jay says dismissively, running his hand under the water and looking up to a chunk of mirror still left on the wall. "What happened?" I ask him in a whisper. He looks at me over his shoulder and I think he's going to tell me to just leave, but thankfully he doesn't.

"John doesn't want to believe he did that to you."

I stand there numb, the tips of my fingers tingling. "Did what… did what to me?" I ask. Although I shake my head, there's nothing wrong. "You did nothing wrong."

Jay's lips part and a huff of a humorless laugh leaves him. He dries his hands on the towel, looking straight ahead.

"The day you left is what he's thinking about," he says and his voice is deathly low.

Tears sting at my eyes as I say, "Forgive me." I'll never forgive myself, but please, please I need him to know I regret it with everything in me.

"There's nothing for me to forgive, little bird. You did what I told you to do." He cups my jaw in his strong hand and I lean into his touch, desperate for it. For anything he can give me. "But John hasn't forgiven anything. He hasn't even begun to forgive himself."

I can't imagine the pain. I can't imagine what the man standing right in front of me is feeling in this moment. I just need to be here. And I am, but what good am I?

"I have to clean this up," he says as his hand falls to his side. "Just give me a moment, little bird," he tells me easily and with a small smile I so rarely see. There's a sadness in his eyes too though and I don't understand it. It makes me fear for him. I grab onto his hand, not wanting to leave and not willing to risk him.

"You're scaring me," I tell him honestly.

"I need to clean this."

"I can do it," I offer quickly. Anything I can do to help, but Jay snatches my wrists. The swift motion catches me by surprise. His fingers are forceful and his gaze down at me is intense.

"I need to be alone for a moment," he tells me, but it's the last thing I want for him. He's been alone for so long, and he just needs to let someone help him.

"I just want to help you, Jay." I'm terrified he's close to a break that's simply too much to handle. I can't let that happen. Not to him. Not to someone I love so deeply when I'm right here. "I can help you," I beg him and his expression softens slightly.

He turns my wrist and kisses it gently before letting me go. "Soon, little bird," he says and his voice is soft and drenched with hopelessness.

"It's going to be okay, Jay," I tell him, feeling the pain in my heart worsen each second that passes without him looking at me.

I follow his gaze to the broken glass and blood on the tiled bathroom floor. I can clean this up. I can fix this. *We* can fix this. "I can get you-"

"Go to your room, little bird," Jay says with authority, cutting me off.

My lips part with both disbelief and an objection but he adds, "I love you and I don't want you to see this right now."

I love you. I've known he loves me. How could we not share this to-gether? Two people so deeply intertwined and whose souls who cling to each other for comfort.

My lower lip wobbles and I reach out to him. I grip onto his shoulder without thinking until I'm clinging to his shirt and realize what I've done. But Jay doesn't react, he just lets me pull him and that hurts me deeper than anything. *His fight has waned.*

"I love you. All of you, and I'm right here," I tell him desperately, pray-ing he'll believe me. Every bit of what I've said.

A small trace of a smile forms on his lips and at first I feel like it really will be okay, as if he'll let me help him the way he needs.

"We should go," I offer although my words are shaky and my voice lack-ing confidence. I don't want him to withdraw.

"I'm not going back," Jay says with a hard voice. He looks me in the eyes as he tells me, "Go to your room, Robin."

My stomach sinks and churns. He needs help I can't give him. Jay kicks a large piece of glass and I look around. It can wait a moment. Just a mo-ment, but I have to force his hand. This can't happen again.

"I love you, Jay," I tell him with every bit of sincerity in me and reach up on my tiptoes to plant a chaste kiss on the line of his hard jaw before turning to leave.

"I was never Jay," I swear I hear him say as I step into the hallway, but when I turn around, he shuts the door faster than I can move, leaving me alone.

Chapter 27

John

Twenty years ago

THE GROUND FEELS COLDER TODAY; FALL OR WINTER MUST BE coming. It's hard to know without the bit of light from the windows anymore. He took it away.

"Please," she asks me again. She's afraid to ask me for things. At first I thought it was because she was afraid of me. But I think it's something else. A mix of sympathy and guilt. She shouldn't have either toward me. I hate it.

I lean my body so I'm closer to her, but still far enough away not to frighten her. She has a habit of inching closer to me; it's a habit I like. I love it even.

I love that she needs me.

"You don't have to ask, little bird," I say her nickname and she does this cute thing where she smiles and avoids my gaze. It almost makes me smile, but I can't. Not here. This house isn't a place for happiness. I'll smile when I get her out of here. Only then.

"Can you hold my hand, Jay?" she asks me softly, her eyes flickering to mine and then back down to the floor.

I pull the blanket up tighter around her and slip her small hand into mine, weaving our fingers together and letting her hold me like she wants to. She's been calling me Jay since the first day. I should have corrected her, but I don't want her to call me John. I don't want to be John. I don't want this life. I only want to be her Jay.

"I'll always hold your hand," I tell her.

"Always?" she asks, and I merely laugh it off in a huff and tighten my hand *around hers. Always is such a long way away. Too long to promise. I know it can't last forever and I won't make a promise I can't keep.*

I'll be Jay for her though.

I love her for calling me Jay.

For letting me exist again. Even if it's only for her.

The memory is so clear. My head pulses and I try to swallow as I lean against the bathroom counter.

What was I doing here?

Cleaning up the mess you made, a voice, Jay's voice, says so clearly in my head.

I look up to see who it is when the bathroom door opens, letting in the light from the hallway.

"Jay." Robin's voice is quiet, frightened. Jay. My body sways, and a shooting pain in my temple makes me wince. "You need help. I can help you. Please, Jay."

"That's not my name!" I scream at her, feeling lightheaded and my lungs refusing to fill. I'm not that sick fuck.

I refuse to believe it. I grip my hair in my hands and try to get the memory out. That never happened to me. I feel sorry for Jay. I can't separate the two.

I close my eyes, trying to figure out what's wrong with me. My head throbs and I can't get these visions to go away. It's because he's told me his past so many times. I close my eyes trying to remember when he told me, but in my memory, he's there, sitting on the chair, leaning against the wall, but then nothing. He's vanished.

"John," Robin says with her hands up. "You need help, John, and it's okay. You're okay, I promise you." She sounds scared and she takes in quick breaths as she speaks, walking toward me slowly.

Like I'm a wounded animal.

Calm for her. I hear Jay's voice and it only makes me angrier. She shouldn't fucking be here.

My vision blurs and for a moment it goes black, but I hold on to the counter. I'm lost right now. I can barely grasp what's real and what's not.

"It's fine," I tell her out of instinct. Because that's what you do when someone's worried for you. You lie to them.

"It's not, John," she says and shakes her head and her small hands wrap around my arm. "You suppressed memories for a reason." Her voice quavers and I wrap my arms around her instantly, hating that she's breaking down. She cries harder and tries to push me away, but I don't let her. I rock her back and forth.

She's so innocent in all of this.

"Just forgive me, please?" she asks me with tears in her eyes.

"For what?" I ask her, not understanding why she's so upset. She hasn't done anything wrong. I'm the one that's so fucked up. I'm the one who hurt her. The one who fucking kidnapped her.

My head spins at the thought. It's all me. Anger boils, but she speaks and I try to calm myself.

"For leaving you behind," she whispers her choked words.

My blood turns to ice as the memories come back again. They keep coming over and over. I try to shut them out but they make a pulsing pain shoot from the back of my head to the front where it stays and throbs, where it punishes me until I acknowledge the past. Until I face what I've done and what I've been through. "It had to happen," I tell her in an even voice, but the anger is there. I can feel it. I hated her for leaving me when I only existed for her. "I was selfish," I whisper as my hands start to shake with the mix of heated emotions.

A small sob leaves her as she shakes her head. "No, you were only a boy," she replies and tries to say something else but I can't hear her over the cries. She wipes her eyes and her shoulders shake.

"It's not your fault, little bird." The words slip out so easily. As if it's natural to call her that. I'm surprised by the presence I feel. As if I'm here holding her. For a moment, my vision splits. I can see me holding her, I can even feel my arm leaning against the wall. It's Jay who's holding her, Jay who recognizes her pain.

But I refuse to do it. I shut my eyes tight and hold her even tighter. I kiss her hair and a chill runs through my body, followed by a heat that boils my blood.

I may be aware that I am him and vice versa, but that doesn't mean that both sides of me are willing to merge.

"Go to sleep," I tell her in a deep voice. I look her in the eyes as I order her, "Go to your room, Robin."

"Now!" I yell and watch as she obeys me, looking at me with equal amounts of fear and defiance. I lick my lips, not knowing what to do. Everything's changed.

Chapter 28

John

"YOU'RE NOT TAKING THIS WELL, ARE YOU?" I look up at the sound of Jay's voice. He's standing against the doorframe to the kitchen, staring at me. A phone is in his hand. His phone. I look down at my own hand, and it's there. He tosses it back and forth in his hands, grinning at me and taunting me.

The decision is obvious. I need to call and turn myself in, but I can't fucking bring myself to do it.

I grip the phone tightly before shoving it away from me, but when I look up it's still there, still in *his* hands.

"You're not real," I tell him, refusing to rise and go touch him. Have I ever felt him? I can't remember a time I have. I'm crazy. Legitimately insane.

My mind plays tricks on me. Jay vanishes and my head throbs, memories changing in my head, turning fuzzy then sharp with the truth. The memories coming back.

He smiles, a thin, wicked smile and says, "Of course I am. I'm you."

"Make it stop," I grit from between my teeth, holding my head and rocking back and forth. I stand and scream, "You're not real!"

But who is it that wasn't real? *The life I lived was a lie.* I struggle to breathe as my stomach churns and I realize the very man I pitied, the life I saw as pathetic and disturbing… it was me. *It was mine all along.*

"All those nights I couldn't sleep," I hear Jay say and I look up to search for him, but he's nowhere to be found. I wince as I stumble and grip the wall, my head pounding harder and harder. "All the nights I had to go to her just to know it was real. That it really happened and it haunted her, too."

"Get out of my head!" I scream and seethe with anger. My eyes open slowly and I lift my head, seeing him watching from the corner of the living room.

"And what's worse? I knew I was fucked up in the head. So fucked up I couldn't go to her. I wanted to. So, fucking badly, but because of you, I couldn't!"

Toby barks and snarls, turning to face Jay, to face nothing. His hackles are raised as he exposes his teeth and a vicious growl echoes in the room.

"Jay?" I hear Robin call out from down the hallway, and closest to Jay. Closest to where Toby is facing. To what he sees as a threat.

Not my little bird. My body feels heavy and then light. He's gone and then I'm gone, a blackness taking over. But I fight it. The fur bunches in my hand.

I hear him whine, feel the dog's claws digging into the ground, and the sounds follow me, although I don't feel present. I'm here but not in control of my actions. Present but weak. Muted by the control Jay has, but conscious of it.

The basement door slams shut, and Toby claws and barks at the door. Over and over, the poor thing trapped but our Robin protected.

Our Robin.

"It's hell, isn't it?" I hear Jay's voice in my head as I come back to what's real. As I struggle to catch my breath and feel the blood from Toby's bite dripping down my arm.

When did he bite me?

"When you grabbed him from behind," I hear Jay say from the other end of the hallway.

"Jay!" Robin calls out from behind the closed door to her room.

"It's a bitch being there but not being present, isn't it?" Jay sneers. "It's fucking hell!" he screams and then stares at Robin's bedroom door.

"I'm coming out," Robin says from behind the door and both of us whip our heads to stare.

"Stay inside!" he screams before I can, but the words come from me, I can feel it. My body, but not my mind.

I don't want her out here, I think but don't say.

She's not a part of this, I hear in my own head. I look up and he's gone.

"You brought her here," I say out loud with spite.

"I can help, we need to talk," Robin says and her words are muted by the closed door.

"How could you bring her here?" I ask him as my body trembles. My poor Robin. She can't be here.

"You slept. Well you thought you slept, with not a fucking worry in the world. All the while, all I am is a fucking ghost of what happened to us! You kept me back to feel better," he spits the last two words.

"Selfish fuck!" I spit the words as the bedroom door opens. In two large strides I'm at the door and pulling the handle hard so it shuts.

"Stay inside!" I scream at her while Jay fights for control, or does he? I don't know anymore. My head pulses again with pain.

"I'm not going away, John."

I grab both sides of my head, falling against the hallway.

"Jay, please," I hear Robin call as the door creaks open again.

"Get out," I tell him as my hands ball into tight fists. They pound my head time and again.

"Please let me help you." She's cautious and doesn't move from her spot, but she opens the door slowly.

"You do this to me!" Jay's voice forces my eyes up to the corner of the hallway as Robin approaches me. He screams back at me, his eyes glossy and suddenly I see him for who he really is. "This is who you are!"

"Jay, please," Robin says and walks toward me with her hands up. She's walking into the fire.

She's not safe.

"Get out," I tell her as I press my hand to the wall and steady myself. "Get out of here," I bite out the words as she flinches and takes a half step back.

"I'm not leaving you," she says quietly beneath her breath, her eyes wide with both fear and disbelief. Jay's voice echoes in my head as he screams, but I don't listen.

"Get out," I say calmly, all the rage just beneath the surface. She tries to turn, to run back to her room, but I'm faster than her. I close the door and slam it shut before she can run. I cage her small body in, loving the heat and the feel.

I fucking love her, and that makes the pain in my chest only splinter deeper.

"Get out," I repeat again, feeling her hair in my face and resisting the urge to touch her, to comfort her as she trembles beneath me.

"I can help," she barely gets out as she turns in the small space between us.

"That's why I'm here," she pleads with me, chancing a moment to reach out to me. Her small hands reach up to my chest and I feel Jay inside of me. I feel him cower in pain and agony.

I'm a monster. "He never should have brought you here," I tell her and grab her wrists.

Her breath shudders as I tug her away.

"No!" she yells as she kicks me and runs to the living room.

I grind my teeth and follow her in, right on her heels. She grabs onto the first thing she sees, the sofa, and grips it as if it will protect her.

"John, no," she pleads with me, but she doesn't turn.

My breath stills and I feel Jay pace inside, hating me and wanting to kill me as I pry her fingers from the edge of the sofa.

She can't stay. I won't let her see this.

Jay's quiet as I fight her, holding her small body against mine and force her from the house. She kicks and begs me over and over, but I ignore her.

As I toss her outside, careful to keep her from falling too much, I know how this needs to end.

Chapter 29

Robin

FEAR LACES MY BLOOD AND THE NIGHT AIR IS BITTER COLD, making my hands shake as I reach into my pocket for his phone I took from him as he forced me out. I'm glad I had the presence of mind to put on my shoes when I went back to my room. I did it to avoid being cut by the broken glass in the bathroom but I should have realized this would be a possibility as well.

My shoes slam down on the porch steps, one after the other as I run forward. I look behind me, over my shoulder, breathing heavily from the terror screaming in my blood.

I knew there was a chance he'd break. Every moment with John I waited for him to remember. It fucking killed me for him to look at me with new eyes. No memory of everything we'd gone through. It was selfish of me, but I needed to know if he'd still love me even if I kept the truth at bay. That selfish desire stayed my hand. That, and the fear of how he'd handle it once he learned the truth.

Once he's learned who he truly is.

My Jay. The tortured boy and my savior in every way. But he doesn't see it as that. He never could.

My shoulder brushes against the bark of a tree as I try to catch my breath, breathing in the cold night air that makes my lungs feel like they've frozen. My muscles scream from running as fast as I did, but this is as far as I'll go.

I lean my body against the thick oak tree and look back at the house.

The sounds of him yell, pull more pain from my heart. The sob is suppressed as the light from the phone brightens the dark night and tears my eyes away from the lit windows in John's house.

There's no one for miles. No help can come soon enough.

There's no fucking way I'm leaving him. He's a danger to himself.

I stare at the screen, looking at the numbers to press to unlock it.

A password.

Fuck! I chew the inside of my cheek, looking back up at the house. I don't know his fucking number! In a moment of panic, I almost forget that there's an emergency call option at the bottom. I silence the sob that tears its way out from my lips and quickly call the police.

I clench my teeth. No rings. Pick up. Pick up!

A loud bang, like a crash from inside the house makes my heart leap in my chest and my body turns to ice as I look up. Nothing to see, nothing to hear but Toby's barking, over and over.

The click is loud as a calm female voice speaks clearly, "Emergency operator, what-"

"I need help!" I scream into the phone.

"What's your address, ma'am?" the woman asks me, and I freeze. Fuck! I look around, I look everywhere for a mailbox or a number. There's only a dirt road.

"I don't know! I don't know!" I scream into the phone, tears stinging my eyes. I look up at the house again, feeling like I'm failing him. "I don't know," I croak and cover my mouth, hating how weak I sound.

"Is the emergency at the location of your phone?" the woman asks me and I nod my head as I answer her, "Yes, please come fast."

"I've got your address. The police are on their way. I need to know what-"

As soon as she tells me they're coming, I drop the phone and bolt to the house. Finally help is coming for him. *Finally.*

"Jay!" I cry out as I grip the wooden railing and race up the stairs. The screen door slams open as I rush to get inside. As soon as I enter the house, I hear Toby barking again.

But it turns to white noise. Nothing matters as I sway on numb legs and stare at the ground.

The bookshelf is splintered on the ground, the books are strewn about. The lamp is shattered, and covering the floor with shards of thin glass are specks of blood that get larger and larger as I walk quietly to the other side of the room.

"Jay?" I call out, just as my eyes lock on his limp body in the middle of the room. The coffee table is overturned and he's lying next to it. Where he lay the first night I snuck from my room to see him.

"John?" I call out his name out of desperation. I walk faster when there's no response, falling to my knees next to him. His face is bloodied and bruised, as are his knuckles. A large mark on his face is bright red, covering nearly half of it and it's then that I realize he slammed his head repeatedly into the coffee table.

I put my hand on his chest, shaking him gently. "Talk to me, please," I whimper, but he's still. "Say something!"

I press my fingers to the side of his wrist, but fail to find a pulse. I press harder out of sheer panic. There's nothing. "Jay!" I scream a strangled cry and wrap my fingers around his wrist, holding his hand with mine.

"How could you?" I whisper. He can't leave me. "You can't leave me," I barely get out. "I love you. I love all of you and I can help you," I tell him in a ragged voice through the sobs.

Regret and fear are consuming me. *He can't die.*

It's only when I put my fingers beneath his nose and feel his breath that I'm somewhat calmed. But his pulse is so weak. "Help me!" I scream, knowing no one can hear. The tears fall down my cheeks freely, my eyes already are swollen and stinging from the pain.

I can't breathe as I hold his head in my lap, the warmth of the blood soaking through my clothes.

My body rocks back and forth. "Stay with me, Jay, please."

"John, come back to me."

"I love you both. I promise I'll make it better. I swear I'll never leave you again." As I whisper the promise I faintly hear sirens making their way toward the house. Help is coming. Finally, help is coming for him. I sniffle and hold him closer, lowering my head and whispering next to his ear, "I'm so sorry." I can't even voice everything I regret.

The sounds of the sirens coming can be heard in the distance, getting closer now.

"Just please come back to me."

Chapter 30

John

BEEP. BEEP. BEEP.

Each time the machine sounds, my head throbs with a pain that only brings back memories. I feel my forehead pinch and another shooting pulse, but I can't move my hand up to my head.

I groan, trying to move but I can't.

The images flash through my head.

My father holding me down. *Beep.*

His fist. *Beep.*

The dogs. *Beep.*

I go backward in time.

My mother dying. *Beep.*

I want to stay there. They're so happy. He holds her, and she holds me. *Beep.*

She's on the ground. *Beep.*

She won't wake up. *Beep.*

I scream out for her.

My head shakes and I try to move again, feeling closer to consciousness, becoming more aware of my body, but it's so heavy.

I shake her shoulders, trying to get her to wake up. Mom! I scream out. Mom!

The sound of my father's boots. The sound of the toolbox that crashes to the ground as he runs into the room.

My throat feels raw as I cry out again. *Beep.*

He pushes me out of the way.

No! Mom! *Beep.*

My shoulders shake as I watch him leaning over her.

Small hands shake me, but they aren't in the room with me.

Father! Help her! *Beep.*

His cold gaze finds me, his hands still holding Mom, but when he looks back at me, I can't cry out anymore. I can't speak.

His eyes are like ice as he sneers at me. What did I do? Why is he blaming me? I didn't do anything. I swear I didn't.

"Jay!" I hear a voice scream, and my eyes part slowly. My groggy head sways and I try to blink. The bright lights hurt though. My wrists sting as I pull upward, but they won't move. It takes a moment as my head lolls to the side to realize I'm in the hospital. Sedated and restrained.

"Jay," I hear her soft voice and vaguely feel her hands on mine. I turn my hand slightly and she laces her small fingers with mine. *My little bird.* I've held her hand so many times. Her hand belongs in mine. Everything's okay then. That's all I need to know that everything's okay.

Robin, my little bird.

She brought me here.

I expect anger, I expect to hate her. Instead I only feel weak and helpless. The pain in her voice is what does it. I've hurt her. I'll do anything, my little bird. Don't leave me. Not here, and not ever.

Slowly, the memories come back.

All twenty years and more.

My Robin. My sweet Robin.

I watch her run. I keep watching as the dogs bark behind me. They're so close, and I'm certain they're going to get out. It's only a large stick keeping the cage secured. It's going to break. I know it will. But when it does, they'll come for me.

I'll watch her though. I'll make sure up until the last moment my life slips from me that she's free, that she's running and the dogs stay here. My father will stay here. They can have me, so long as she's free.

When I turn behind me, finally ripping my eyes away from where she's gone, it's only because the sound of boots stomping against the cold hard ground is getting louder. It's only because I don't want him to touch me.

But the second I turn, the shovel slams against my skull and blackness consumes me. Only the briefest vision of my father follows me to the darkness.

"Jay, please. Stay with me," I hear her soft voice call out. It's like an echo in my head.

I'm here. I try to tell her, but my throat isn't working. My voice isn't here. I'm here, little bird. We made it. We both made it.

I remember standing outside her house. Across the street and shielded from the row of oak trees, I waited for her to be alone. She came to mine and I followed her home, too afraid of the police. I did that. I burned it down. It was all my fault.

But she has a family who holds her so closely.

And she never looked back.

My hand slips from the tree and the rough bark scrapes my arm. When she ran away… she never looked back. As the anger rises, I hear the footsteps behind me. I turn ready to fight, my movements sharp.

But there's no one there. Just a voice in my head. I shake my head again. The boy is there. He looks the way I want to look. Who am I?

"Jay!" Robin's voice is clear and strong.

"Robin," I finally answer her and I know she heard it.

Beep. "Turn off," I try to speak but my throat hurts too much.

"You were intubated, Jay. It's okay," I hear her tell me as I fight against the bindings holding me down.

I open my eyes as she yells at someone to turn off the machine.

They tied me up. I stare at the bindings, hating her. She of all people should know.

"Jay, it's okay," she tells me as she pats my hand over my clenched fist. "You had ICU psychosis and you tried to rip out your IVs, but you're okay." Her words barely register as I pull at the bindings, my muscles coiled, but I'm weak.

"Please, Jay. Please stop," Robin begs me, her voice strained. Her small hands grab my face, and they're so soft. Her tears hit my chest hard.

It's only then I see the wires, all the machines.

"Miss," a nurse calls out behind Robin as she comes forward to take my Robin away.

"Leave me alone!" Robin cries out and then looks back at me, her hazel eyes pleading with me. "Stay with me, Jay. Please. It's been days of this. Please, Jay. Stay with me."

Days?

I still my body, my heart beating rapidly and thumping so hard in my chest it hurts.

"He's fine!" I hear Robin snap at someone behind her and then sniffle. "Don't put him back under. He'll be okay. I know he will," she says and her voice is so strong.

"Robin, what-?" I can't finish my sentence as the last memory comes to the forefront of my mind. Over and over I smashed my head against the wall and coffee table, against anything. I wanted him out of my head. Jay... the memories of Jay.

I swallow thickly as Robin talks quietly and calmly, in an even cadence meant to avoid agitation.

"You hurt yourself," she tells me. "You're okay now, but I need to make sure you can swallow on your own and eat."

"Swallow?" I ask her.

"When you first came in, you woke up and... and they had to sedate you, Jay." Her small hand grips my arm tight. She's so sad as she tells me what's happened.

"Do they know?" I ask her and then swallow, my throat throbbing from the pain. I don't care if they hear. I need help. I can't hurt my Robin. I won't do it.

I see her nod in my periphery and it draws my attention to her. I try to pull my arm up so I can brush her tears away, but I can't and I've never felt a greater pain in my life.

"It's called Dissociative Identity Disorder... or split personality as it's more commonly called."

I nod once, I know already. I've known all along, but part of me has held it down. There is no cure. There are times when you may forget again and slip into psychosis, but constant therapy and a desire to be well are important. I used to think it was because my dad was crazy. It's not genetic. But it can arise from abuse and stress.

"Could you undo these please?" Robin's voice comes out strained as she angrily wipes under her eyes. "He's fine now," she says confidently. "He's back," she whispers.

I can't look as a nurse unties the bindings and tells me something. Not to hit, not to harm myself. It all turns to a blur as I think about her staying with me for days.

"How many days?" I ask her, although I stare straight ahead at the white wall.

"It's been six days," she says and I close my eyes tight. As the binding to my left wrist loosens, I quickly move it to my right, on top of Robin's.

"You stayed with me?" I ask her and she nods her head but says, "They couldn't let me stay with you at night at first. I had to get papers and orders."

It's quiet for a long time. And I whisper, "I'm sorry." I truly am. For everything I've put her through. She doesn't answer me, she only kisses my cheeks and then once chastely on my lips, but I can't open my eyes.

"Your name is John?" Robin asks me.

My voice is raspy as I answer her, "Yes."

I lay my head back, remembering how she ran again. How I gave her a choice and she left, but yet she's here.

I speak from the heart. Without thinking at all I say, "You don't owe me anything, Robin. I knew you'd run, and I knew I'd have to stay behind. You never owed me anything. You never had anything to be sorry for, Robin. This guilt isn't on you." I know she needs to hear it. It's plagued her for so long. My eyes stay closed, and I can't bear to look at her to see her reaction. I need to let her go for good.

"Stop it, John," I hear her say and turn my head to her.

"You aren't mine to keep," I tell her as my gaze finds hers. I want to keep her though. So badly.

"I was always yours, Jay." A warmth floods my chest, until I hear the name.

"Jay," I say the name with anger. I hid behind Jay. Or maybe I hid behind both. I don't even know which is more present in this moment.

"You've always been Jay to me. Always. And I've always loved you."

"I don't deserve you," I tell her simply.

"It's not about what we deserve, only about what's real."

"What's real?" I repeat her words with a sarcastic laugh. "My name's John." I talk out loud, but not really talking to Robin, my sweet little bird. Just at the mere thought of her nickname, the sight of her looking up from the floor of my father's cellar to the small dirty window flashes into my mind.

"You'll be alright, I promise you," she reassures me then cups my chin and kisses me on the lips. I grip her wrists, wanting to push her away. I don't deserve her love, and she shouldn't have to deal with this. With how fucked up I am.

"Hey," she whispers and tilts my chin slightly so I look her in her eyes. "Now that you know, now that you're aware, it will be much easier. I promise you." She licks her lips and stares deep into my eyes, willing me to believe her. "I know everything's going to be okay. It will take time, but just you knowing and accepting… you have no idea how difficult that is."

"It's because of you," I tell her. "He used you to make me-" I clear my throat and correct myself. "I used you," I confess and my heart splinters just admitting it. I can feel the urge to hold her tighter making my hands itch. The memories of my father coming on strong and making me want to cling to her. Everything was better when she was there.

"You did what you had to do," she tells me, but there's no way she can convince me that it's justified.

"I don't care what you think or where we came from," she says. "John, Jay, it's just a name. I love you. I've loved you for years. All I need to know is whether or not you love me."

Of course I do. She's the only one I've ever loved. I don't even know if it's possible to love someone else like I love her. She rests her hand against my cheek and my eyes drift to hers. "Do you love me?" she asks me in a whisper of a breath. The fear and insecurity apparent.

I tell her the truth. What I know to be more real than anything else. "I've always loved you, Robin. When I was jealous, when I hated what you represented, when I feared what you could do to me and what power you held over me." A sob rips from her throat and she covers her mouth with both of her hands as tears leak down her cheeks. I brush them away and put my hand on the nape of her neck, gently but firmly, just how she is with me. With a small push, she falls closer to me and I rest my forehead against hers and lower my hand to her back to rub soothing strokes up and down. "I've always loved you, Robin. And I always will."

Chapter 31

Robin

TWO WEEKS HAVE GONE BY, AND SOMETIMES JOHN FORGETS. It's remarkable that he was able to live a relatively normal life before. But I don't want him to have anything but a full life from this day onward.

I'll never leave him again. And he knows better than to pull that shit again.

The paper crinkles in my hand as I set it back down and then carefully fold it to put it back in the envelope. It's the report on John's mother's death. Margaret. He wanted to know, and I'm doing everything I can to find out every little piece of his history. An overdose.

The memories he has of his mother are pleasant, but the detailed history of her past isn't. I don't know how he'll take it, but it's one more piece of information he can digest.

I hear the tea kettle whistle in the kitchen and it rouses me from my seat at the dining room table. As I make my way in, I nearly stumble over the stack of empty cardboard boxes.

Thank fuck I still have a few more weeks left of sabbatical leave. Moving is a nightmare and a half. The kettle silences as I pull it off the stove and instantly hear the rumble of John's truck.

It's odd that the most unbelievable thing to me is that Jay's name was always and has always been John. I'm the only one to have ever called him Jay. A part of me loves it, and a part of me hates it.

The front door opens as I pour the water into the cup. I watch as the steam rises and the bit of calm normalcy is enough to make me smile as I hear his boots smacking on the hardwood floor.

I dunk the tea bag in and then again, watching as the light brown water turns darker and the color consumes the inside of the white ceramic tea cup.

My eyes lift at the sound of John picking up the boxes in the living room. The cardboard rustles as he lets out a heavy sigh.

"Why is there so much yellow?" he asks me. The question makes me smile into the cup and I nod my head once, recognizing the odd obsession.

"Yellow makes you happy," I say simply. "Just seeing the color makes you happier than you were before." I smile at him, but there's a sadness in his eyes from the admission.

He may think he's the fucked up one, but I needed him too. Desperately.

"Is this the last of it?" John asks and then leans against the doorway to the kitchen, ignoring my answer. His white shirt has a bit of dust swiped across the bottom which only makes him appear that much more masculine. His muscles flex under the thin fabric, pulled tightly across his broad shoulders and I absently blow across the top of the mug as I nod my head yes.

Slowly, we're making this place ours. A complete home. It's funny how even our décor seems to need each other for balance.

"Thank you for bringing it all," I tell him. I almost say Jay, but instead I say nothing.

It's odd calling him John, because he's always been Jay to me. He never told me, but I can understand why. In a lot of ways, we're learning more about each other, but in other ways, we're learning who we are ourselves.

Love isn't something we have to learn though. Love was a given from the moment we saw each other. Something in our very souls told us we were meant to be together. Without each other, we wouldn't have survived what life had planned for us. Not back then when we were only children, and not today or even tomorrow.

I need him as much as he needs me. It's the only thing I'm certain of.

"Thank you for staying with me," he says easily as he walks across the kitchen and wraps his arms around my waist. I set the cup down on the counter and the ceramic clinks before I look back up to him. I notice how his hands tighten on me as I lift my hands to his shoulders and rise up on my tiptoes to kiss him on the lips. It's short and chaste, but I want all the kisses from him. Every sort he has for me.

When I pull away and my heels hit the floor, his eyes are still closed. It's the raw emotion and truth that drew him to me. And maybe me to him.

"Tell me what you remember?" he asks me in a whisper and my gaze falls, but I rest my cheek to his chest and nod my head, listening to the steady sound of his heartbeat.

Together we'll get through it all. Together and always.

"I think you loved me when you saw me, didn't you?" I ask him.

"Which side of me are you asking?" he lets out an uneasy sigh, avoiding my gaze and the question.

"Both, neither, it doesn't matter really. I already know you did," I speak with feigned confidence. I want to hear him say it. I need to, really. I need to know that he's always felt this way. I know I have. I'll never stop loving him and I'm terrified that one day, he'll stop loving me.

"He showed me a picture," he starts to say and then covers his face with his hands. "I… I," John says. I bite my lip, hating how much pain it causes him when he tries to recall a memory and he reverts. But it's normal. He has to learn that. He has to accept it.

"When I saw you, all those years ago, I knew I was to protect you. When I looked at your picture. When I knew I was going to take you and face this… this hell in order to be with you. I looked at your picture and I knew I was going to love you." He nods his head, closing his eyes and I know it hurts, to merge the memories and meld the scene in his head. The medication helps the present, but the past is hard. Nothing's going to change that.

"I love every part of you, the man who wants to forget and the man who suffered for his father's sins." I cup his face in my hand and kiss him on his jaw and then softly on his lips.

He stares back at me with nothing but pain in his eyes.

"I don't know how you can love me," he says in a whisper.

"I don't know how you can think I ever didn't love you. Even when I ran. I've always loved you." A weak smile forces its way to my face as I struggle to use his name. He doesn't want me to call him Jay, but he's always been Jay to me. "My wolf."

John stares back at me, confused for a moment. Sometimes it's like this, when he doesn't quite remember, but then it clicks.

"Wolf," he huffs a sarcastic laugh and shakes his head. "You don't need a wolf, little bird. You needed another, someone just like you. You needed Jay."

I nod my head as my heart splinters. "I need *all* of you," I whisper against his lips. I can feel it, the moment Jay comes to the surface, the moment the possessive man inside of him moves his hands to the back of my head and deepens the kiss.

I pull back and look into his eyes whispering, "Jay?"

A small smile tugs his lips up, only just and he says quietly, "You can call me whichever name you'd like." He rests his forehead against mine and it's then that I realize our past needs to stay where it belongs. "You can call me Jay if you want. I'll be anyone for you. I'll do anything for you. I only exist for you."

I brush my nose against his, trying to lighten the mood. "Maybe when I'm mad at you I'll call you Jay," I tease and try to smile and when he does, my lips turn up easily.

"I love you, John," I tell him quietly, brushing my fingers against his lips. "And I love Jay, too. Both sides of you."

"I love you, little bird." He says the words just like he always has, with a hint of teasing and a touch of darkness.

I lean against him, and he holds me tightly. I wouldn't have it any other way. We're both broken from what happened to us. But the love that's come from it can't tear us apart. As long as we stay together.

"Always?" I ask him.

"Always."

John

I can hear the shower running as I stop in front of the shower door. The tips of my fingers tap against the wood. She's waiting for me, and so many times I think I should leave her. As if I'm undeserving of her and hurting her, keeping her back.

I close my eyes and let out a slow breath. When I inhale, the gentle smell of lavender fills my lungs. It's what my little bird smells like. And just that little bit makes the memories of holding her come back to me. They flood to me now. The bad ones I try to ignore, but the ones with her, *the ones with my little bird,* I hold on to them with everything I have.

It's why I want to let her go. And why I never will.

My eyes pop open wide, the selfishness and depravity making me hate the thought. She's a grown woman though, and she knows who I am in every sense of the word. As long as she wants me, I'm staying with her.

I push the door open slowly and the steam greets me with warmth and slowly passes behind me.

The anger surprises me sometimes, but more than that, the fear.

My father's dead and burned to ashes, but the fear is very much alive. I always knew the other side of me was filled with a darkness, but I wouldn't have thought it was fear.

But that's what creeps up more than anything. Especially at night.

Until my wife leans against me, giving me much-needed warmth. Until my hand splays across her belly and we both fall easily to sleep.

"I heard something about you always being right," I tease and then pull the shirt over my head. She peeks out from the shower curtain with a quip on her lips, something smart no doubt, but instead her eyes fall to my chest and the thought is long gone.

A deep groan of satisfaction rumbles up my chest and her eyes reach mine as a blush creeps up her chest and she pulls the curtain back into place to hide behind.

I fucking love it. I love her. And to think, I may have never had her.

The past can ruin a person forever. They may recover, but they're never the same. Never what they once were. The scar may be thicker than delicate skin. It may protect you from some things and give you a wall to hide behind.

But it's the gentle things that will cut it open and leave you raw and wounded once again.

Love is gentle and unassuming. It won't be denied.

My love saved me in so many ways, my little bird.

I could forget the pain and burdens.

I could forget the fear that the monster would return. Or worse, that I would be like him.

I could forget it all and leave it where it belongs, in the past.

But I can't forget Robin or the genuine love I felt for her. I can't deny that.

Not when I'm so desperate for her.

Not when she needs me in return.

And not when she's right here, loving me with everything she has and only wanting the same in return.

My memory destroyed me, but love is so much more.

You can't forget love, no matter how hard you try.

Epilogue

Robin

Two years later

"**T**OBY!" I CALL AS THE DOG RUNS FROM THE PORCH AND OUT into the field. He looks over his shoulder and halts in his path, but I wave him off. He can run if he wants to.

I sway easily on the porch swing, the chatter from inside muted by the screen door and the faint hum of the water flowing from the creek out back. I love it out here, on this property and in this house that John built.

Two years we've been here. Making steady progress. It may not always be perfect, but we're safe with each other. And John hasn't forgotten me and he believes what I tell him about our past. He remembers somethings too which makes days hard here and there, but together we'll pull through. That's the most important part. The trust and love between us are strong enough to keep us together.

Just as my eyes drift shut, the screen door opens with a long groan. I pop them open quickly, pretending like the exhaustion isn't getting to me.

"You coming back in?" John asks me. He's got a smile on his face and I know he loves this. "After all, the celebration is all for you," he says and his eyes drift to my swollen belly.

"It's not for me," I say with my eyes closed as the little one kicks my hip again. My feet slip across the porch floor as I shift on the swing and try to get more comfortable.

John lets the screen door shut and crosses the porch to sit with me. The swing dips when he sits and wraps his arm around me to pull me closer to him.

"They're here for you," John whispers into my ear and splays his hand over my belly. I love it when he does that. When his eyes light up with hope. We didn't plan this little one, but I'm so grateful and happy. And so is John.

I kiss him, feeling a rush of warmth flow through me. I would never have guessed our lives would turn out like this. It's nearly picture perfect.

At the sound of the door opening again, I pull away, feeling the heat of a blush on my cheeks. John just smiles as he stands and helps me to my feet. The wooden swing gently hits the back of my legs as I get my balance and say goodbye to a group of my coworkers.

"We're heading out," Karen says as she waves her hand, the other occupied by a paper plate covered with aluminum foil. A young woman who must be in her early forties, or maybe late thirties walks out with the group. She's in her gardening clothes and in an instant, I know she's one of our new neighbors. They live down the road and closer to John's shop. The closest neighbors we have.

"I really appreciate the invitation," she says as she stops in front of us. I've only had a few conversations with her, but she's a sweet woman, alone out here for the most part.

"Of course," I answer her. "I'm so happy you came." I can't help the smile on my face or the small yawn that comes after it as John makes small talk with her. I watch him as he talks. It's night and day from where he was just two short years ago. He's not perfect, but neither am I. Together though, we've gotten through everything. One thing that the memory can always hold on to, is love. There's never a doubt in either of us that the other person doesn't truly love them. That's rare and special and I can't get over how powerful it is.

"How did you two meet?" our new neighbor asks as she grips her drink in both of her hands. She looks between the two of us with a smile on her face. "You're such a good-looking couple," she says. I wish the smile that wants to come to the surface were genuine, but it's not.

She's not the first to ask.

And a part of me deep down is terrified that they'll all find out the truth. Another part wants to scream it out loud and tell everyone what we've gone through. Together.

I keep the smile on my face as my husband wraps his arm around my shoulder and pulls me closer to him. A lie slips so easily from his lips. It's a struggle every time, to listen to words that are false, meant to hide the truth.

No one wants to hear our story. The *real* story. When they ask how we met, no one would expect the harsh reality of our pasts. No one would be able to understand. They would judge us. And they'd never forget it.

I sure as fuck won't.

It's dark and twisted.

But that doesn't make it any less of what it is.

A love story. *Our* love story.

And I'm so grateful we got a happily ever after. Stories like ours aren't meant to end like this. It's only because we stayed together. Only because our love was stronger than our pain.

prequel to forget me not

something to remember

Chapter 1

I used to wonder what I'd done to deserve this. Why he hates me so much.

My stomach rumbles, and the aching pain that used to make me ball up because it was centered in my stomach now shoots through my body. I wince from the pain, but I don't scream. The stinging in my eyes isn't from tears. I refuse to shed them.

I've made my choice.

This room, in particular, is one I used to be terrified of. Cinder block walls that are damp and cold, and nothing but a blanket to cover me when I sleep on the hard cement floor. The fluorescent lights are horribly bright, and they remind me of the school's gym lights, but somehow the darkness, when he shuts them off makes the lights unbearable when they're on.

There's nowhere to hide when the lights are on.

I lick my dry lips as the pain settles and stare at the steel door until I feel like I can breathe easy again. I'm no longer afraid of the room. The punishment holding, as my father calls it. It will be my salvation. My escape from what fate has offered me.

Even at fourteen years old, I know what life and death are all too well.

I know my mother's dead. She never hears me when I scream for her. And I always do. I always cry out for her to save me when he makes me hurt and doesn't stop.

A chill runs through my body, but at the same time my forehead heats and a thin sweat covers my skin. I shudder and think about pulling the blanket up, but the blinking red light in the corner of the room reminds me that he's watching and I won't show him that I'm trying anymore.

I don't want comfort. I don't want to hope anymore. They're both useless and make trying and fighting seem reasonable when they aren't.

Maybe death is an exaggeration. After all I'm starving myself, and he's thrown me in here with the promise of food if I'll eat. I don't want to though. I can't keep living like this.

This isn't a life. When my mother died, it was my death sentence to be left in the hands of a monster.

Another spike of pain shoots through me at the same time as I hear the keys jingle on the other side of the steel door. I resist the urge to react to the pain although it's stronger and more intense than it's ever been.

I wish it weren't true, but even as I've accepted death as my fate, I'm terrified. I wish it wasn't fear that ran through me. I wish the adrenaline wouldn't spike in my blood and my natural instinct wasn't to cower, but I can't help it.

I've tried hard not to feel anymore, but the fear he's instilled in me is unbreakable.

Maybe that's why I hate myself so much. I'm weak and useless. Just like he tells me.

Some days I swear I don't feel anything anymore. Even the fear. It's as if it doesn't matter, like I don't matter anymore. How can I? How could I even be sane staring at the same walls each and every day? I barely move anymore. It must be days since I've decided not to eat. And since that day I've been in this room. Unmoving, unchanging other than the pain.

It's only a matter of time before he'll let me out of this room. It's just for punishments, or at least that's what it used to be. I don't know how many consecutive days I've been in here. Maybe it's my new home.

I scratch my fingernail against the cement, creating a mark. There are dozens of lines just like it. I think I started them to count the days, but it's turned into something else. Each one is the same as the last. Maybe I'm waiting for something to change them. Something inside of me or inside of this room to break up the monotony. Maybe I've just stopped caring.

I think Father's easier on me when I'm pathetic like this. It makes me feel even worse knowing he's the reason, he's the motivating factor behind it all.

I blink slowly and my thick lashes blur the faint light from the small window as the door opens with a protesting groan.

I expect the door to close just as fast as it opens, but when I chance a glance, he's left it open. His large body stands in the doorway, and his dingy off-white shirt and faded jeans are dirty from working outside on the farm and in the dirt.

His boots sound as if they're crunching against the ground as he walks. Each step getting louder and my heart racing faster. I stay perfectly still, resisting every instinct to run or to fight. Both are useless.

"Get up," he says and his voice is deep and rough. No room for negotiation.

My body flinches out of instinct, and I prepare for him to kick me when I don't react quickly enough. He always kicks me in the stomach and as I close my eyes tightly, disobeying him, I pray he does it hard enough to end this.

But nothing comes.

With the thin coat of sweat over every inch of my body, a chill goes through me, making my body stiffen. I nearly vomit from the intensity of the change, but I hold back.

"I've had enough of this, boy!" my father screams at me and I curl into myself. Embarrassment and shame flow through me from how weak I am, but I don't give it much thought. I already knew I was pitiful.

"I won't fucking tell you again!" he yells and leans down to haul me up by my shirt, but I scoot back and resist. If there's one thing I've learned never to do, it's to resist.

But I've wanted this. I have to remind myself of my death wish as the fear cripples me and the years of conditioning settle in and make my body tremble.

The back of his large, dirty hand whirls in front of my face, blurring from the speed as he snarls at me. The scowl on his face is only made more terrifying from his exposed yellowed teeth and the coldness in his dark gaze.

The last thing I see are his knuckles.

The last thing I hear is the crunch of my nose.

The last thing I taste is the metallic blood in my mouth.

The last thing I feel is nothing. So long I've waited for it. And it's finally here.

Chapter 2

UCK.

My neck is stiff, my jaw hurts and I know it's bruised. But what really fucking hurts is my throat. It's worse than a sore throat, raw and like it's on fire.

A groan slips out and I instantly regret it, my body squirming on a hard sheet of metal. I blink slowly, barely opening them and letting my eyes adjust to the dim light.

I know in an instant where I am. The kitchen.

The dusty plaid curtain on the window above the sink is the first thing I see, and that's all I need to know.

The kitchen, the table. Mother.

This is where she was a few times, I remember it well but I don't know what brought her here. Maybe it was him. I never thought about it back then, but as my eyes open wider, anger seeps in. *Did he hurt her like he hurt me?*

My muscles coil, and I try to sit up.

It only lasts a moment and then the pain in my throat makes me wince again.

Shit. It's only when I lift my hand to my throat that I realize the pain is only located there. It's no longer focused on my stomach in the least.

"I had to intubate you," my father says from the dark corner of the room. My heart thuds hard in my chest as he slowly stands and walks into the light of the room.

"Stupid fucking boy," he mutters and stands next to me. So close I can smell the dirt and whiskey that waft from him every day.

I try to swallow, but it only makes my dry throat hurt even worse. A sickness and hollowness threaten me. I can't even kill myself. I'm that pathetic.

I need to find another way then. Something fast.

"You need to knock this shit off," my father says as though he heard my thoughts. My heart stutters as I slowly raise my eyes to his. I don't dare speak though.

He looks tired up here with the morning light casting shadows down his face. He rubs his beard and clucks his tongue once before lowering his head to mine.

I instinctively back away as he says in a low voice, a roughness from his throat making his threat sound even more terrifying, "Don't make this harder on yourself than it has to be, you hear?"

Like the coward I am, I nod. My blood rushing and fueled by fear.

"I have something for you," he says as he backs away slowly. One step and then another, giving me space, but I don't trust it. "Sit up," he tells me. My body's stiff and my muscles sore. It hurts, it physically hurts to stay still, but I'm done with this.

Just let me die.

"Sit up!" my father screams, pounding his fists so close to my legs and rattling the table. My body jolts as I stare at his face, bright red as he spits, "Sit the fuck up!"

He grips my shoulders with a bruising force and rips me up so quickly my ass lifts off the table and for a moment I think he'll throw me off. Maybe into the old walnut cupboards. But he doesn't. *Thump, thump, thump,* my heart races, but I push down the fear.

There's nothing he can do to me anymore.

There's nothing left to take.

My shoulders shake uncontrollably, making me feel even weaker as he looks me in the eyes and reaches into his back pocket. It's a wrinkled polaroid picture, and I can't help how my eyes dart to it and then to his face. I wait, still as stone and cold as one too as he flicks it with his fingers, not showing me fully and teasing me with it.

I don't know what it could be. Really anything, I suppose. Whatever it is, it's a threat and it won't work. There's nothing more threatening than simply living at this point.

He flicks it again and the thwack of the paper just annoys me. My teeth grind together as I slowly turn away from him. It doesn't matter. Whatever he has to threaten me with, I don't care. It'll all be over soon.

My throat seems to clench, painfully scraping as I take in a sharp breath. The sight of my father's hand so close to my face prepares me for the inevitable blow. But it doesn't come. It's only when he takes a step away that I finally look down at my lap. The photo is face down against my worn dirtied jeans and I almost don't pick it up.

Almost. But the curiosity is too strong.

I flip it over, prepared for the worst, but my forehead scrunches when I realize what it is.

It's just a girl. Huddled into a small ball, her t-shirt and jeans are dirty like she's been dragged through the mud. Her sneakers are still on her as well. It takes a moment for me to understand what I'm seeing, but when I do, my heart stops beating right. She's in my room. That cement floor is the same floor I was just sleeping on.

She's in the punishment room.

"Get her out," I say and the words are pushed through my lips the second they reach me as a thought. I will my tired body to move, but my father's quicker than I am. So fast that the back-hand smacks against my cheek and mouth, splitting my lip open and flinging my head backward. My body flails as I attempt to stay on the raised metal table, but my fingers slip along the smooth metal and I fall. I stumble down on the ground, my side hitting the knob of a cupboard on the way down and my elbow landing hard on the linoleum floor.

I suck in a breath between clenched teeth, but remain still on the floor. Not daring to move from my awkward position. Another lesson my father has taught me well.

My heart races in my chest, feeling as though it's trying to get away. Trying to go to her. But I stay still.

I need to listen. "Don't hurt her," I say the words in a hoarse voice but it's nothing but a plea. A pathetic plea that will fall on deaf ears. "Please," I add weakly and hang my head.

I don't want her hurt. No one should ever go into that room. It's a place for nightmares and monsters. Maybe my father should be locked away in that cell. But not her.

I chance a peek up at my father, watching as he nods slightly and then runs his fingers over his jawline. His knuckles are split from striking me and the knowledge makes me smile slightly. But I hide it. The tip of my tongue runs along the cut on my lip as I look down and away, trying to remember every detail of the girl on the floor.

"Is she okay?" I dare to ask him.

"Fine," he says gruffly, stopping in his tracks and walking toward me. He has to shove the table to the side in the narrow kitchen to bend down close to me. Again his scent drifts toward me, and this time it's stronger. So strong I nearly vomit, but I hold it back.

"She's going to be good. I already know that," he says and I can feel his eyes on me. Waiting for a reaction and my response.

Whatever I do, I need to save her from this fate. I take a steadying breath, making sure I don't react in the least. I just need to get to her.

"Do you want to see her?" my father asks. "I got her for you."

Finally, my eyes reach his and my chest rises with a disbelieving breath.

"All you have to do is listen. And she's yours." I watch as the smile slowly stretches across his face as he adds, "Listen to me and she stays safe."

Chapter 3

I want to get closer to her, but I stay right where I am.

I can see she's breathing, and that's what matters right now.

Listen to me and she stays safe. My father's words echo in my head repeatedly as I wait for her to awaken. I was desperate to get in here. I needed to see her to protect her, but with every second that passes… I start to hate her.

I was so ready to give in. So ready to end all this shit. And now, because of her, my fate is worse than it's ever been.

Yet, so much better.

My fingers itch to push her hair away from her face. She's young; younger than me, I'm sure. She's pretty in a traditional sense. Her hair is ruffled though, and she needs to be taken care of.

There's a scratch on her cheek, like a scrape more than a scratch I guess.

My back leans against the cinder block wall, and it's cold and hard, but it's giving me stability. The thing I hate most about this situation, is that I'm still helpless.

There used to be ointment in the medicine cabinet. The mirror has a patina from where you have to grip the edge to open it. But in the old mirror cabinet, there was an ointment for scratches. I don't know if there is now.

A weak humorless smile makes the corner of my lip twitch as I pick at the frayed end of my jeans. I can't even get her something for the scrape.

Pathetic.

That hasn't changed in the least.

She doesn't know though. She doesn't know anything beyond these walls. I lean my head back, tearing my eyes away from her for the first time since I've been let back in.

She doesn't know. And she needs someone to protect her, even if it is only just enough to prevent a worse fate. Surely, it'll be enough?

For her. My teeth grind together and my knuckles turn white as I ball them into fists.

It better be enough. It has to be. It's all I have to offer, and now she's changed everything.

Chapter 4

My head hurts so badly. Why does it hurt so much? I try to push myself upright, and the ground is so cold and hard. It's so uncomfortable, but my head is too heavy and I slump against the ground.

Where am I?

I try to remember where I was. The sound of the carousel shrieking as it slowly turned from the wind blowing filters through my memory. The empty swings sway back and forth. The school playground is deserted. I thought everyone would be here today. But it's empty. The first day of summer and not a soul is here.

I remember how I looked up and the sun was far off in the distance, but still in the sky. Didn't they know we still had time to play? I'm younger than most of the kids, only twelve, but even the older ones usually play with me.

I sat on the swings for a while, I remember that. As the pounding in my head throbs harder I remember how the metal chains twisted and I let myself twirl on the swings over and over. I could wait for the other kids. I was sure they'd show up.

Did they?

I squint, trying to remember and I turn my head. My palms brush against the concrete floor, my cheek flat against the hard floor.

There was a man. He had a golf club and he needed my help. I remember how lost he looked. He said he hit his last ball into the trees and he couldn't reach into the bushes.

My heartbeat quickens as I remember, and my body goes still.

I knew to tell him a lie. I knew to turn around and run when he tried to take my hand in his. But he looked so hurt when I tried to pull away. He was genuinely upset, and all he did was ask me to help him.

The thin branches cracked under my sneakers as I went into the woods, following him to where he thought the ball had landed.

I open my eyes and I can't breathe.

He lied to me. My nails scratch on the ground as I clench them into fists and slowly look up.

No! Mommy, help me! Tears blur my vision of the cinder block walls.

No! This can't be happening. I pull my knees into my chest and try to stand.

Why does my head hurt so much?

"Are you okay?" a soft voice asks from behind me, making me shuffle across the ground and push myself against the cold wall. It takes a moment for me to wipe my eyes and see him.

He's just a boy.

His knees are knobby and he's thin, but his shoulders are broad and he has a look about him that lets me know he's older than me. There's another look about him, too.

Sorrow and sadness cloud his eyes. Or maybe I just imagined it, because the moment my vision focuses, a hard expression stares back at me. He doesn't move from where he is, crouching only a few feet from me.

"Where am I?" I ask him quickly. I don't know where the words come from. I feel hot and cold, and I'm so confused. "I want to leave."

He huffs and shakes his head at me, pushing himself up from the ground where he was and takes a step toward me. He's taller than me. In that moment, he scares me.

"You can't leave," he says simply.

My face crumples, and I shake my head. "My mother will-"

"We're stuck here!" he yells at me, the anger in his voice making me flinch. He stares at the wall behind me, his eyes flickering to the floor then back to me. "We can't leave."

As I start to protest, I hear a loud rough bark outside. It's followed by a series of vicious barks that continue unceasingly. It makes me whirl around and face the only window. It's small and rectangular, covered in filth and high up on the wall. There's barely any light coming through. Maybe there's a bush planted in front of it. I'm not sure, but at the very least I know there are dogs close.

"Don't try to run," the boy says behind me and again I turn to face him. Threats all around me, and it's my fault. It's all my fault. So stupid! I wrap my arms around my shoulders. "My mother-"

"Stop." The boy gives me the command, and I do. I stop because I'm a good girl. I've always been a good girl, but look at where it's gotten me.

It's quiet for a while, and the boy takes another step closer to me. I don't move. I don't know what to do or where I am, but deep down inside of me I know this boy isn't going to hurt me. There's something about him. Something broken and scared and angry even, but it's pure.

"What's going to happen to us?" I ask him weakly.

"He won't touch you. It's not about you."

"What?" I don't understand. I'm so confused.

"He's using you." He looks past me, anger evident as he clenches his jaw. "It's about him making me do what he wants. He knows I won't...," his voice drifts off, and the anger changes to something else. Something I can't see because he turns away from me.

I reach out to him, grabbing his arm to keep him from leaving me, moving purely out of instinct. The touch feels like a spark. As if I've put my hand to a flame, but before I can even process it, he whips back to me, a scowl of anger on his face as he stares at me. "I won't let him hurt you like he does me. All you are is a tool for him to use against me."

He takes another step closer to me, and it's the first time I really get a good look in his eyes. The intensity almost makes me scoot back, but then I'd be against the wall. Trapped and cornered.

He parts his lips to tell me something, but no words come out. Time passes, and the only thing I can hear is my heartbeat as he stares at me. His eyes won't break from mine, and I'm too scared to look away.

"I'm sorry," he says flatly, but then he turns away as if the sentiment were genuine.

For some reason, just hearing those words is what breaks me. The tears fall and as I wipe them away, he looks at me with distaste. I half expect him to tell me to stop, but he doesn't.

I struggle to calm myself and somehow I do. Maybe it's because I don't really believe him. I don't believe it's hopeless. My mother will find me, and she'll make that man pay for what he's done. Both to me and to this boy. I know she will.

"What's your name?" I ask to keep him from leaving me as he turns. I lick my lips, tasting the salty tears and wiping my cheeks. I don't want to cry. I want to get out of here.

"J-" he starts to answer me, but we both whip around and face the door as it opens, silencing us and making me instinctively back away.

I grab onto the boy's arm and force myself behind him. I don't know a thing about him and the look he gives me nearly makes me run from both him and the man stalking into the room, but I don't get the chance. The boy grips my wrist with his other hand and pulls me closer to him, my front to his back and my back to the wall. He keeps himself deliberately positioned in between me and the man.

It's only when I grab onto the boy, my small fingers digging into the rough denim of his jeans at his hip and my cheek pressed against his back, that he lets go of me.

The boy may scare me some, but the man terrifies me.

Chapter 5

"**I** WANT TO GO HOME," THE GIRL WHIMPERS. HER WIDE DOE EYES dart from mine every time I look at her. We're on opposite sides of the room, and that's how it's been since I came back. That's all she keeps saying as she's bundled up in the corner and crying.

She's terrified, and has every right to be. But after what my father's done to me, I don't want to look at her. Partly out of shame. Partly out of hate. I was only gone for an hour, but an hour is enough.

He did it on purpose. Taking me the moment she woke up, and showing her how easily he can break me. He knew what he was doing, and it worked. And I did nothing to stop him. No fight in me… for her. And now, I can't even look at her.

I can feel the bags under my eyes, the desperate need for sleep. But I can't. Not with her here and not knowing what my father will do next. I force my dry throat to swallow, the pain still present and lean my head against the cold wall as I stare at the door. Sleep's come easily to me this past week when I had nothing left to give, but I won't let it take me now.

"Please, can you just tell him to let me go?" she asks weakly. I can see her lean forward slightly, hesitant and praying for mercy from me. But I can't do anything for her. I'm so fucking helpless, and it only makes me angrier. Doesn't she know I'm pathetic? My father made sure to show her as much.

"I just want to-"

"Stop it," I tell her harshly and hate myself even more. I glare at her, ready to tell her how she needs to be quiet. How there's no way out and that her crying is only going to piss me off, but then I see how glossy her eyes are, how her lips are turned down in a way that makes her seem even more vulnerable.

My heart beats in a weird way, like it's skipping instead of beating. It hurts and my stomach churns with a sickness at who I am. Who I've become. I don't want to be like this. I don't want to be this person.

"Jay," she says and I look up at her. Her voice is soft. It doesn't matter how angry she is with me or I with her, we're all each other has.

I stare at her, waiting for her to say something, but the tears fall down her cheeks. They don't even require her to blink.

"I'm scared," she whispers. Her voice is hoarse and her shoulders crumple inward. My blood rings with adrenaline to move, to go to her and cradle her in her arms. But I don't want her to touch me back.

"I said I'd look out for you, right?" I ask her. Offering her a small smile. It's not genuine in the least, but I try. I mean it. I will look out for her. I don't know what I've done, but I know she didn't do a damn thing wrong. "I won't let him hurt you," I tell her.

"How could he not?" she asks in a murmur and her voice cracks at the end. "He's a bad man," she says and then licks the tears from her lips. "Bad men do bad things." She wraps her arms around herself and then looks back at me with an expression I can't place.

My skin heats, every inch of it feeling like it's on fire. "I'm here," I tell her simply.

"Hold me please," she pleads with me, wiping the tears from her eyes and looking away. "I'm just scared and I need…" she shakes her head, not finishing her thought.

"You need to sleep," I say, finishing it for her and she whips her eyes to mine. There's nothing but fear in hers. Her body is stiff and she slowly looks at the door.

"I'm here," I tell her softly and offer a hand out to her. I don't know why I do, I shouldn't. But she's quick to crawl across the cement floor to me. She drags the blanket with her and glances at the door as she comes over to sit next to me. I keep my distance when her knee bumps into mine. I scoot away, keeping a gap between the two of us.

The look on her face is like I smacked her, and she immediately withdraws. "I don't like to be touched," I tell her with a tense jaw.

Her head lowers and she slowly pulls and tucks the blanket around her. She hesitantly offers a bit of it to me, which makes my lips tug up into a smirk and I shake my head.

I don't want to be anything close to warm. The chill keeps me up at night. I nestle my back against the wall and stare straight ahead. She's close, and hopefully feeling better, but there's not much else I can do for now. I've already started calculating a way to sneak her out. If we both run, he can't get us both. *I just need a chance.* How many times have I prayed for just that, only to go unheard?

But Robin isn't tainted like me. Maybe fate will have mercy on her.

"Sorry," she barely whispers the word and my eyes are drawn to her as she huddles under the blanket. She doesn't look at me as I ask, "For what?"

"I didn't mean to touch you, it's just so cold," she answers weakly.

I stare at her a moment, only because it doesn't feel cold to me really. A little chilly, but then again, maybe she's not used to this. I snort a humorless laugh, a huff really at the thought and that gets her attention.

When she looks up, her eyes dart to the rip in my shirt.

My father did that on purpose, too. She slowly reaches her hand up and I grab her wrist, my fingers wrapping easily around her as a small gasp comes from her lips. "Don't," I warn her, my heart beating wildly.

Her eyes look back down, past the tattered cotton and at the smattering of scars.

"What happened?" she asks me with sadness so evident in her voice.

I want to shove her off my lap, to leave her in this filthy cell. But I don't. Instead I stay perfectly still until I can lower her arm back down. If I leave her, I have nothing.

She'll judge me. Pity me. And use me.

But I need her. Without her, I have nothing.

My eyes drift to the cement floor. I should tell her that I don't know how to really help her. But I can't.

"I want to leave, Jay," she says and her eyes beg me as well and I want to tell her I'll find a way. But I'll never lie to her.

"I do too," I tell her the truth. I can give her a small bit of it.

If I can find a way, I'll make sure she gets out of here.

I swear to it. I'll do whatever it takes.

It's the only thing I have to live for anymore.

sexy as sin

From *USA Today* and the *Wall Street Journal* best-selling author Willow Winters, comes a sexy second-chance MC romance.

I took the fall for a crime I didn't commit, and it cost me everything. Including the only woman I ever loved.

I'm not the man she fell in love with. Four years behind bars made me harder, colder … with a temper I can't control.

But then I look at her and nothing else matters. I'm broken without her and a shell of the person I used to be.

She is my one and only. My addiction and my sanity. I could never imagine how time would change everything and how far we'd drift apart … but she can't deny this tension and she can't hide the way her body reacts to mine.

She was mine once and nothing can ever change that.

I only hope the secrets of the past four years don't tear us apart the moment I make her mine again.

Prologue

Kat

I F I HAD KNOWN WHAT WAS GOING TO HAPPEN ... I WOULD HAVE begged him not to go. I would have even fought him to keep us from walking through those doors. That's the thing about fate, though—you're never given a heads-up. But I should have known because everything was just right. When everything is perfect, it's eventually all going to crumble and there's not a damn thing you can do to stop it.

Four years ago

As my heels click against the cement stairs and I walk into the garage, I note that it feels like home. I know every square inch of this place. I've practically grown up inside of these four walls. With an arm wrapped around my waist and the bite of the night chill outside waning, all I can do is let a smile slip into place.

Everything is familiar, from the smell of the oil that's ever present to all the mechanic tools hung neatly on the walls. Any item you could ever need to repair or build a motorcycle is here. Hell, I don't care in the least about the work that's done here, yet I bet I could name most of the tools, just from Cill asking me to hand them to him over the years. At a glance I could tell if any of them were out of order—that's how much time I've spent here. Hours and days and years. Basically my whole life. It may seem strange to other people, but the rumble of bikes paired with the loud laughter and hollering that come with the men who are always here is my kind of heaven. I bet ordinary people feel like this when they walk into a cozy living room.

My leather jacket presses against Cillian's leathers with a faint squeak as we squeeze by the narrow opening to the rest of the three-story building.

The best part by far is holding Cillian's hand, just like I've done for years. His fingers loop easily through mine like we're meant to be together. We *are* meant to be together.

I can't remember a time when I didn't have a crush on him. In high school we started dating with approval from both of our fathers. My heart warms to think about him as my high school sweetheart. My father said it would make sense; his father said it was a business decision done right. Mob connections from my father, MC from his.

I'm head over heels for the boy I've always been told I'm meant to be with. Now that we're older, it's only gotten more intense.

An hour ago, we were in his bed. With his hard body pressed against mine and a cold sweat slipping across my sensitized skin, I cried out his name and he murmured his love for me in the crook of my neck.

Cillian's tall, with hard but lean muscles that work against me. I just barely come up to his shoulders. I don't think anyone could imagine a man like him saying the sweet things he does to me when he comes, whispering his adoration and promises for our future. It's like he's showing me some secret part of him that no one else will ever get to see. I hold that secret close while we walk into the garage together. He pulls me tighter as we move through the door to the staircase at the side of the building.

One thing everyone does know: he's my ride or die and I'm his, and we're both protected in every way imaginable.

With the rec room on the second floor only a threshold away, he bends down and kisses me. "I wish I could take you back to bed," he murmurs, his voice throaty and laced with sin and sex appeal.

A shiver runs through my body and travels lower, bringing a blush to my cheeks.

"You should," I tease him, nipping his bottom lip. I'd fuck him all night, every night. On more than one occasion we've fooled around till dawn. Nothing is better. He knows my body, every inch of it and every secret. Cillian's my first, and I don't want any other men.

"You want to turn back then and not go to Sunday dinner?"

"Yeah," I say and capture my bottom lip between my teeth before adding playfully, "Let's go before anyone sees us." Tugging on his hand is useless and I already know it's not going to happen.

Every Sunday, we have to be here for dinner. No exceptions. After all, it's both a family and MC occasion.

He laughs and with his gaze lifting past me to the threshold, he seems to consider it. The rough pad of his thumb glides along the stubble on his chin before he looks back down at me, a wanting look I know well in his light blue gaze. "They'd wonder where we went. They'd talk about us."

"Who cares?" I slip my arms under his leathers and tug at the fabric, making my desire known as I slide my fingers up his back. "They already talk about us."

If our fathers weren't in charge, the whispers would be heard far more often. I don't care what people say. I only want Cillian. Everything I dreamed of in high school is right there in his eyes. Our whole future.

"After dinner. I promise," he tells me with a handsome but cocky grin. "I'll take you back to bed after dinner."

The tip of my nose nudges against his as I let out a small moan of protest; it's nearly a mewl of want. Cill's deep groan as he backs me up to the wall and lowers his lips to mine forces a simper to my lips that grows into a full-blown smile as he kisses down my neck. His rough stubble and roaming hands are everything I want and need.

Just as my head falls back and my breathing turns heavy, Cill backs away and then cracks a smirk at my mouth opening in protest and disbelief.

He chuckles at me and I smack his chest. "After dinner, Hellcat."

Swatting my ass, he keeps me moving and I don't miss a beat, getting on my tiptoes to nip his lower lip.

The guys are already gathering in the rec room and someone must catch a glimpse of us because they call out for Cill. A low groan of annoyance leaves me and Cillian gives me a rough chuckle in response. It's like one big family, and I love that too. One big happy family with Cillian's dad in charge after mine handed him a business deal he couldn't refuse. I don't know exactly what they do, and if I'm honest, I don't want to. Cill says not to worry; my father tells me to do as I'm told and not ask questions. All in all, I'm aware they go out on runs for weeks at a time. When they leave,

Cill is anxious and calls me every night. When they come home, he can't keep his hands off me.

He's loyal to me and all Cill's ever asked is for me to stay loyal to him, to trust him and not to worry. I'll take that response over my father's any day.

There's already a crowd in the rec room, the chatter intensifying as we walk in and Reed, his best friend, greets us with a tip of his chin, a smile on his face. He looks like the cat that ate the canary and I wonder what he knows.

My mind slips back to what I thought Cill said last night. I could have sworn he mentioned marriage. It seems silly to be nervous like I am for him to ask, since we both know we're meant to be married. But he hasn't yet and every day that passes by, I know he's going to ask soon. I feel it in the pit of my stomach.

"You want a beer from the back?" Reed questions, gesturing to the other side of the floor.

"Hell yeah," Cill answers and I nod too. I'm only eighteen and Cill's nineteen, but liquor has always flowed easily for us here. Maybe that's another reason I prefer this place to home.

Part of this open space is an expansive kitchen, separated from the rest by a countertop, and there are leather couches, an old coffee table and a professional pool table on the other end. The rack is on the table next to some chalk, but the cues are hung up because no one's playing right now.

A couple of women, two friends I've met a handful of times but I forget their names, sit on the side of the coffee table, leaning forward and talking to Finn and Cill's uncle, Eamon. It didn't take me long to learn everyone's roles. Finn is the treasurer, which seems at odds with his large stature and weight. He's first generation and formed the club with Eamon and Cill's father decades ago. His accent is thick, as is his Irish temper.

Eamon is the road captain … but also the enforcer. He's much leaner and again it seems to go against natural thought until you see the man in a ring. Cill's uncle loves to tell stories of "back in the day, when I was a fighter …"

If another person walked in right now, they might be intimidated. The room is riddled with leather and tattooed skin. Not everyone gets it, but I do. I'm not afraid.

Unlike one of those women, who has a nervous laugh that still hasn't left her. I watch as Finn's brow raises and he leans back. Both he and Eamon are older than the two blondes, one platinum, one dirty blonde, both of them gorgeous. The two men have always had hangers-on and it's never sat right with me. I get that they don't want commitment like the others; they don't want "old ladies." The term makes me roll my eyes. But seeing women come and go is uncomfortable. It's family dinner and if they don't intend on them being family, they shouldn't be here. It's not like it's an intimate gathering. There are over a dozen people here already and another two dozen or so to come. But still ...

I've always found his uncle Eamon a bit disrespectful when it comes to things like that, but as Cill says, they're old school. Which again, makes my eyes roll.

I start to take off my jacket, but a chill blows in and I think better of it, opting to leave it on even though Cill takes his off.

All the windows in the rec room are open. Fresh fall air comes in through the screens. It's early autumn, but already chilly at night. The sun is just starting to set and through the blinds it's easy to see it sinking into the woods behind us.

Nerves settle through me as Cill's hand parts from mine and he has a hushed conversation with Reed. Tonight's the night we're going to tell our fathers our plans for next year. Any other daughter would probably be excited to tell her parents she got a college acceptance letter. My father, though, doesn't like the idea of me leaving and lately he's been kind of off. My mother passed two years ago and he's been downhill ever since, falling into the bottle every night. Part of me feels guilty for leaving, but like Cill said, I have to live my life and I'll show my father it's for the better.

I start college in town next fall, and Cill's happy for me. He's proud, even if he'll be staying with the club. After all, it bears his family name: Cavanaugh Crest. He has to because he's vice president of the Cavanaugh East and this is our home. But we're going to get our own place together halfway from here to State College.

The crack of a beer snaps me out of it and Reed smiles as I look up at him, tipping my head in gratitude.

"Thanks," I say, accepting the drink with a mock cheers and he and Cill don't miss a beat to continue their conversation. My gaze filters through the room, but I don't see Missy anywhere, Cill's aunt. She's practically his mother since Cill's mom passed when he was just a baby. She's probably out grabbing a few more things for tonight. I'm restless without her here, telling me what I can do to help.

Someone comes down the stairs from the third level, footsteps loud and unselfconscious. It's mostly offices up there on the top floor of the three-story construction and a few bedrooms for people to crash if they need them.

"Kat's going to college," Cillian blurts out to Reed. "She got into the pre-med program, isn't that fucking amazing?" His fingers slip through mine again and he brings my knuckles to his lips, then kisses them.

My cheeks flush at the compliment, but I don't have much time to react other than to hug Reed back because my phone is ringing.

I hear Reed ask about my father's reaction as I dig out my phone from my pocket. Reed knows how it is, and speak of the devil, my dad's name is on the screen.

He's probably on his way and forgot something or he's running late. He's been late to everything recently.

"Hey, Dad."

"Are you already at the garage?" His voice sounds different than expected, anxious maybe.

"Yes." I huff a laugh at him a little. "Can't you hear it?" It's far too loud in here and it just got louder with Missy yelling out *coming through*, a pan of something in one hand and a bag in the other.

It's too loud to hear what my dad is saying.

I have to drop Cill's hand. I hate letting go of him, but I'll only be gone for a few minutes. He looks down at me and I tilt my head toward the stairwell. He bends to kiss my cheek, his rough stubble grazing against my skin and I catch a hint of his masculine scent that I love. It's woodsy, but fresh like the ocean. Plugging one ear, I make my way through the crowd to the little empty space at the foot of the stairs. Cill watches me go as I try to hear what my father's saying.

Something about going somewhere quiet. No shit, I can hardly hear him.

"Kat." My name is nearly a curse hissed through the phone with impatience.

"Sorry, Dad. I couldn't hear you. Say that again?"

"Did you find your mother's mug?"

My whole body goes cold with a numbing chill. *My mother's mug.* I cross my arms over my chest instinctually, hoping I didn't hear those words. The party is still pretty loud, even in here. Maybe I got it wrong. "What did you say?"

"Did you find your mother's mug?"

The blood drains from my face and it's hard to keep my expression neutral. It's our code phrase. It means I'm in danger.

We made the phrase before my mom died, and just the mention of her makes my stomach sour. My dad has only used it once before while I was at school. I walked out the front doors without telling anyone and came to the club. Everything was fine and it was only a test. Which I'm hoping he's doing again. Just testing me, even though it would be fucking cruel to do it today.

"I'm already here, Dad." My voice tightens when I realize that it could be he's the one in trouble. Something might have happened to him.

"Is there anyone around you who can hear me?" My gaze lifts and locks with Cill, only a few strides away through the threshold. He mouths to me, "Everything all right?" and I can't answer.

"Kat, answer me," my father demands at the same time that Cill motions for me to come back to him. I slip closer to the chaos that is the rec room but stay just on the other side of the threshold where most of the noise is blocked.

Cill looks down into my eyes, keeping me there as he asks in a hushed tone, "Are you okay?"

All I can do is answer, "No."

My father hears me say it too. "Good," he states over the phone.

I almost correct him to tell him I'm not alone and that Cill may be able to hear, probably everyone else around us too, but Cill takes my phone out of my hand.

His expression turns from concerned to serious in an instant. He's silent as he raises his hand.

Fear slips down my spine and then over my shoulders, burrowing deeper inside as Cill's expression hardens. Frozen to the core, all I can do is watch. With Cill's hand raised, one by one the room is silenced. One by one their eyes move to the VP and then to me when they realize it's my phone in his hand. The laughter stops. We're surrounded by his uncle and his dad. Their friends. Members of the club. They're all friends with my father too.

They were friends growing up and now I grew up here. Cill grew up here. That's how we're part of the MC. We belong here. I tell that to myself over and over again. I belong here. I'm safe here. I am.

I've always been a part of this club, but as the room goes silent and Cill puts the phone on speaker, careful to mute himself first, I feel the walls caving in.

This must be some kind of nightmare.

"The cops are coming," my father says into the dead silence of the room. If I wasn't paralyzed with fear, I'd fall over or run. I can barely swallow, let alone move a limb.

"He says the cops are coming," Cill says, loud enough for everyone to hear.

"Kat. You're going to be safe when the cops come," my dad continues and I wish I could tell my father he's on speaker, but he would want everyone to know too, wouldn't he? If the cops are coming, everyone here should know about it. "Just let them arrest you." My eyes widen in shock and then my mouth drops open. "They're going to let you go, but you're going to be arrested for your protection. You understand me?"

Cill's dad, the head of the MC, the president, the man in charge, reaches in for the phone. As I peek up at him, his gaze is filled with a hate I've never seen from him. My hands tremble and I instinctively take a step back, my shoulders hitting the wall behind me.

It takes Cill wiping my cheek to realize there are tears streaming down my face.

"I don't understand. I don't understand any of this," I barely get out as Cill's father turns his back on us and everyone in the rec room moves at the president's command.

Cill stays in the hall with me, comforting me of all things and as if on cue, the sound of sirens can faintly be heard sneaking in through the open windows.

My heart hammers and I still can't wrap myself around what's just happened.

I know, without my father telling me, there won't be enough time to run. He's giving me this information with only minutes to spare. My dad isn't at the party because he knew this would happen and he didn't want to risk getting arrested.

"He's a rat," I whisper as reality grips me and Cill pulls me in close to his chest. "It's going to be okay," he says. "I've got you."

Oh, God, how could my father do this?

Cill rocks me and kisses my hair, whispering something but I don't hear it over the pounding of my heart.

It's surreal. This is the moment I know everything has changed and there's no going back.

For four years, I live with this memory. The memory of everything crumbling before my eyes. Even with Cill's arms around me, I knew nothing would ever be the same. I couldn't have imagined what I'd have to live through next. What we'd both have to live through.

Cillian said it would be okay, and I wanted to believe him so badly. He promised he'd help me. He'd make it all right. I stood there trembling as he disappeared into the back of a squad car with his hands cuffed behind his back, the red, white, and blue lights scattered across the pavement.

They thought since he was only nineteen, he'd get a lighter sentence. And he might have, if he'd named names.

But he didn't give up a single person. He took the fall for the club with a sentence of ten years, with the chance of getting out early for good behavior.

My father ran, but I stayed.

And my world changed forever.

Chapter 1

Kat

Present time

THE GIRL I WAS AT EIGHTEEN IS LONG GONE. AFTER EVERYTHING that went down, she's a forgotten memory and the woman I face in the mirror is guarded and reserved … for good reason.

In the last four years, nearly everyone I've ever known has avoided me at all costs. I suppose I'm lucky to simply be ignored and left on my own. Worse things have happened when crime families excommunicate members. It's partly because I was only eighteen, Lydia told me.

From both of my past families, only one person remained my friend on each side. Lydia, thankfully, told her family to fuck off when they warned her to stay away. No one wants to be associated with a rat. Even if I didn't do it, and it was all my father, I'm guilty by blood.

On the other side, the MC, it was Reed who made sure I was all right … that changed, though, so really I only have Lydia.

Just that thought makes my blood run cold.

"You feeling all right to go in?" Lydia, my best friend since we were itty bitty, pauses outside my house. She dyed her brunette hair a shade darker recently and the moonlight hits it just right, highlighting a bit of red as her fingers toy with the ends. Her gray sweatshirt is a size too big, making her look even smaller than she already does in those worn black skinny jeans.

"Feeling all right to go in?" I echo and her deep brown eyes widen as she looks back at me like I'm crazy.

With my free hand I dig the keys out of my purse, ignoring the uneasy feeling. They're always falling down to the very bottom corner. Almost like they're trying to get out.

"Seriously," Lydia presses, a hand landing on my shoulder as she glances from me to my front door. "Are you sure you're okay to go in?"

"Yeah, it's fine," I say and shrug, fiddling with the keys and then dropping every ounce of fear to move forward regardless.

"I mean, someone broke in, so it's not fine," she says, emphasizing the words *broke in* and waits for me to meet her eyes.

I shrug again. "I try not to let it get to me."

That's the best attitude for moving through life, I've learned. Don't let things get to you or you could worry yourself sick and find yourself crying every hour of every day. Give yourself a few minutes to feel your emotions and get on with it. Keep your chin up.

That's all I could do after everything with the MC fell apart, and it's all I can do now. It's made me a stronger person. Some people might have collapsed under the weight of that life change, and God knows I wanted to, but I didn't. I carried on. Even when my dad vanished into witness protection and left me with nothing, I kept going.

I shift the bouquet of flowers in my left hand to the other one as we go up the steps, keys jingling as we go.

The benefit of working for the florist just outside town is that I get to take leftovers home on Friday. We're closed on Saturdays and Sundays, and my boss lets me have some of the blooms that look like they might not make it through the weekend. Only the freshest flowers for our customers. This bouquet of white peonies will have a happy home in the mason jar that's centered on the hand-me-down table in the small kitchen-dining room combo.

"Well, I'm coming in with you," Lydia says and crosses her arms over her chest as if I'd object.

"Good," I tell her and point the flowers at her, pausing with the keys slipped into the lock of the door, "'cause I have two bottles of red that aren't going to drink themselves."

Lydia cracks a hint of a smile, but she doesn't let up that the break-in isn't something I should make light of.

Swallowing down that thought, I push open the front door and I'm met with the *beep beep beep* of the new alarm system that requires a code I quickly punch in.

The moment I hit the little green button, it's silent save for Lydia pushing the front door shut and letting out a sigh of relief.

"See, safe and sound. The alarm system was a good idea," I tell her as she looks around like she hasn't been here nearly every weekend since I rented out the place.

It's a small house, a little rough around the edges but with good bones. The inheritance my mom left me was supposed to go toward my college tuition, but that fell through. Just like most everything in my life.

"What did the police say?" Lydia asks as we go in and I toss my keys on the kitchen table, then hang my purse over the back of one of the wooden chairs. Setting the flowers down, I follow Lydia's gaze. She scopes out the house like she doesn't trust it, her eyes wandering from room to room.

"You know I didn't call the cops." Lydia stares at me, eyes wide with exasperation. She's silent, though, 'cause she knows that's not something I'd ever do.

Her mouth opens and closes with a silent protest, but then they form a thin line.

"You ready for a glass?" I ask her and she reluctantly nods, slipping her bag off her shoulder and draping it over her chair. "Let me just have a look around," she says without actually asking permission. With my head in the cabinet, snagging two glasses, I listen to the old wooden floors creak as Lydia goes about her way.

I have everything I need here. A little kitchen, a little living room. A bathroom. Two bedrooms. It's plenty of room for me, but barren for the most part.

I can't imagine what anyone would want to steal. Nothing was taken but when I came home, the front door was wide open with the small glass panel busted out, answering the question of how the intruder got in. I'm not going to lie, I was terrified at first.

That's the only reason I called Reed. I had to.

I didn't see anything out of place and he didn't see anything that made me worry. The alarm was his idea, though, and he had it done in a day. Emotions toss and turn as I remember the way he looked at me and how I couldn't even look back at him.

With a long exhale I snatch up my glass of wine in one hand, grab scissors for trimming the flowers in the other, and take both to the table.

I've spent some time putting the place together. I found the dish towel that hangs on the oven at a thrift store last winter. I liked the look of the owl embroidered on the front, with teal streaks running through it and a floral pattern in the background. I hung new curtains just before the break-in happened. They have a bit of blue in the pattern that goes with the dish towel. I have a teal teapot I'm in love with and a thick floor mat by the sink that cushions my feet when I'm washing dishes.

It's cozy and cute and I'm sure whoever broke in was sorely disappointed. If only they'd known I was broke and barely making it by.

"I still wish you'd called the cops," Lydia murmurs as she makes her way back into the kitchen, striding right for her glass of wine.

"I called Reed," I tell her as if it's no big deal, but my attempt at a casual tone is anything but.

"Did they help you at all?"

They. Lydia doesn't say MC, and a chill creeps down my spine. I can't ever think about the club anymore without feeling an empty pit in my stomach. Loss and sadness. They were my family, and I lost almost all of them that night.

"Reed said he'd look into it for me."

"And?"

I shake my head, focusing on tossing the stems of the flowers and not looking her in her eyes. I know there will be questions there and I'm not ready to answer them. "Haven't heard anything."

One of the things I love most about Lydia is that she knows when to push and pry versus when to drink wine with me talking about nothing, pretending like it's all okay.

"You okay otherwise?"

"Yeah." And I really am okay. It took a long time to feel normal after what happened that night four years ago and seeing Reed brought it all back and then some. "Yeah, I'm fine," I tell her and myself both.

It took a long time to stop waking up with tears in the corners of my eyes. I still miss the MC and I never drive down Cedar Lane just to avoid any thoughts of the garage and the club. I think anyone would miss a group of people who were like a family to them. But I don't cry about it anymore. At least not much.

Lydia sighs a little. "You want a snack?"

"You know I do."

"Chips?" She's already digging through my pantry like it's hers too. That's how it's been for most of our lives. She's as comfortable in my kitchen as I am in hers. I could sleep in her bed as easily as I could sleep in mine.

"You know I'm going to miss this," I comment and wish I hadn't. I know she already feels guilty about leaving me here while she takes off, living out her dreams.

"It's not like I'll be gone forever," she chides, the bag of sour cream and onion chips crinkling in her hands.

With an audible inhale, I tell her she better not be.

I center the flowers on my countertop and riffle through the pile of mail, grimacing at the bill I've been avoiding, the one stamped red. "Ah, fuck it, I'll deal with it on Monday." I toss the mail back onto the counter, feeling free of it. Bills can wait for one more day. I want to savor this time with Lydia. It's going to go so fast. "Why do you have to leave me again?"

"College."

"Right, right, right." I grin at her to cover up the ache in my heart. "The whole doing better for yourself and all that," I joke.

I laugh at her and she fake laughs back at me until we're both actually laughing. I'm going to miss her so much. She's been the only constant in my life for so long. But it's what's best for her. She's going to be a doctor one day.

"So …" The tone of the conversation shifts with that one word and I'm on alert again. I stare her down, but she stares into the red of her glass, her fingers fiddling with the skinny and tall stem. "You feeling okay with Cillian getting out soon?"

My stomach drops at the casual question. I'm frozen with my glass at my lips, ready to take another sip. Finally I do it just so I can complete the movement, then put it back down on the countertop. I don't taste a thing. "I didn't know Cill was getting out. No one told me."

Lydia's dark eyes go wide and then narrow. "But he's staying with you?" She makes the statement almost like it's a question.

"What?"

"That's what Reed said. He couldn't convince him otherwise." My head falls back with disbelief. He was just here. Standing right where she is.

"What?" Pure nerves crush into my stomach. "When did he tell you that?"

"Last week," she answers nervously. "How didn't he tell you?"

"How didn't anyone tell me?" I respond, pushing my wine away.

"Cillian is coming here?" Emotions swarm through me, making every thought harder to focus on.

"I swear to God that's what he said. He came in and—"

"Reed came in?" I interrupt her to clarify and while she's rushing out an explanation of what happened, panic takes over.

All I can see is Cillian, standing in this small rental, taking up every inch of the place and staring back at me with his sharp blue eyes, asking why I stopped coming, why I stopped calling. My body goes cold and I can barely hear a word Lydia says.

You stopped calling too, I can already hear myself answering.

And his imagined answer makes my fingers go numb: *'Cause you stopped loving me, Hellcat.*

"Are you okay?"

"What?" I snap out of it and have to wipe under my eyes.

"I'm so sorry, Kat," Lydia says and rushes over to me but I put a hand up, stopping her.

"I'm fine."

"I should have told you the second Reed said something but I just assumed you didn't bring it up 'cause—"

"I'm fine," I repeat, hardening my voice and she's silenced by it.

"I should have told you."

"Do you know when?" I ask her, not bothering with should haves and could haves.

Staying with me. That means staying here, in this tiny house. The one that's meant to be a bridge away from the past. No one said a word to me. Not Reed. Not Lydia. I had no idea.

"I'm not sure … soon, though. In order to be released, he needs a place to stay. Reed didn't tell you anything?"

"No." No one told me anything. "Don't I—don't I need to sign something for that?"

"Well, Reed helped you get this place, right?" The chair protests against the floor as she takes her seat again, holding the glass with both hands.

"Yeah." I needed someone to cosign with me. *Fucking Reed.* If he were here, I'd lay into him. How could he do that, knowing what happened?

A voice answers all on its own. If Cill told him to make it happen, he'd do it.

I nearly voice the thought; instead I swallow it down with another large gulp.

I don't know what to think. I don't know what to say. I feel numb and light-headed, like I might pass out any second. "He's coming home and he didn't tell me. He's coming here and Reed didn't tell me."

"Everyone's been keeping secrets," Lydia murmurs, and she gives me a look full of sorrow before taking a swig. "You want me to stay with you?"

I whisper, "Yeah. Can you just stay 'til I fall asleep?"

"Of course," she answers, reaching out for my hand and I let her take it. A million thoughts overwhelm me. Every single one about Cillian. Every single one, a regret.

Chapter 2

THE RUMBLE OF THE BIKE BENEATH ME ALMOST BROKE ME earlier today, when the sun was setting across the horizon and the pale hues brushed against the barbed wire of the fence I left behind me.

The grip of the handle, the rev of the engine only inches below me and the wind against my face. Four years went by in a blur, yet the life I left behind feels as if I barely know it anymore.

"You sure?" Reed questions as he parks his truck, and the alcohol swirling in my blood makes my head sway.

The idea of being released early on probation was one thing, and the expectations I had for this night were low, but tonight is anything but the celebration the men claimed it to be as beer bottles clinked and they cheered.

Longing for what used to be sunk its claws into me. As I stare at Kat, the light from her kitchen against the dark night giving me every detail, I sink deeper into the worn leather seat of Reed's truck; regret and something else I can't articulate weigh me down.

Who is she now? This woman I used to love and now a woman I don't recognize. Four years and her absence changed what was once between us. I barely remember what we talked about the last time we spoke, but I know she didn't tell me she loved me. Her calls had stopped months before, but I kept calling her.

Until she didn't say those words back. That was over a year ago and yet somehow I thought this would be the right thing to fucking do the night I get out of prison.

"Fuck," I say and my hand runs down my face as I lean my head back, letting the reality sink in.

"You can stay with me," Reed states as if it's decided, turning the key over and the ignition protests just as much as I do. He keeps telling me that. He's been saying it for weeks trying to get me to change my mind.

"I'm going in there," I say and my voice bellows with more anger than I realized I had.

What's between Kat and I may be different. I'm sure as hell different; colder, meaner even. Hell, I don't know how anyone could love me after what I've done behind bars. A tremor runs through my hand and I form a fist to stop it.

"I dreaded a number of things," I confess to my best friend, clearing my throat as I do and making sure to keep my voice even. "I dreaded seeing my father's grave, I dreaded seeing my uncle Eamon, now the pres, who barely spoke to me while I was away. I dreaded seeing the fucking club—"

"Don't say that—" He tries to interrupt me, his voice thick with sympathy I never fucking asked for.

The leather groans as I turn to look him in the eye. "It's the truth. Some nights I blamed the fucking club. But I never dreaded seeing you or her." *Until now.*

Gripping the handle in my right, and the strap to a duffle bag with essentials in my left, I swing open the old truck door and listen to it creak as I step out. Spending the night with Reed made me certain of one thing: we're still the same.

"Now I need my hellcat back." A nervousness prickles across my skin as the wind creeps up my leather jacket. "Even if she doesn't want me," I murmur beneath my breath as I hear the slam of Reed's door and then his heavy footsteps quickening to catch up to me. "She fucking owes me."

All I could think about every night was walking up these concrete porch steps. As Reed races to beat me to the door, using the iron knocker, I'm all too aware of how I pictured walking right in. Not stopping or hesitating in the least. She'd stand there, her eyes wide first with shock, then relief and adoration.

Sometimes that's what I pictured as I fell asleep on that hard bed with images of her writhing under me in my head.

Other times, my eyes stayed open as I stared at the cracked ceiling of the cell, imagining how she'd back away, how she'd tell me she couldn't be with a man like me. That she knew what I'd done and that I was all wrong for her. That everything we ever were was a mistake.

She told me then, in these fucking terrors that kept me wide awake just like it did last night, that she regretted ever being with me and it was over.

I prepare myself for whatever it is she has to say as a voice I know all too well calls out, "Coming!"

If she's going to leave me, she's going to have to do it to my face.

"I think this is a mistake." Reed's murmur is spoken just beneath his breath, as is my response.

"I'll add it to my fucking résumé."

The crickets are the only sounds I can hear over my racing heart until the door opens.

Thump, thump. The light of the foyer creates a golden halo around her. Standing all of five feet two, Kat stares up at me, her gorgeous eyes working their way up from my chest until she meets my gaze. Her expression isn't at all how I pictured.

Time pauses for a moment. It's gone too fast, but it stills long enough for me to take in her cherry lips, her hazel eyes and the shock that disappears far too quickly, replaced with a shadow that hides a woman I used to know.

Thump, thump. The door opens with a groan and she stands to the side, her gaze moving easily from me to Reed as she tells us to come in. Her cadence is soft but confident, and I nearly second-guess everything until she peeks up at me and her grip on the door tightens.

There's the look I've been dreaming up, staring back at me through a glossy gaze. It's nearly gone as quickly as I see it, but I know damn well it's there as she glances to the floor and licks her lips. I don't take my eyes from her and she's quick to bring hers back up but it stops at my mouth.

Heat spikes through my blood. *That's my needy girl.*

Even if she doesn't openly admit it, even if she's wary, she wants me still. The tension crackles between us, although it's quickly extinguished.

"I could smell the beer and whiskey from all the way in the kitchen,"

Lydia states evenly with a touch of humor as she leans against the open doorway through Kat's home.

I've seen pictures of this place, Reed showed me. He kept tabs on her for me. And although the compliment is there—*I like your place*—there's not a word that could leave my dried throat right now even if I tried.

It's silent and awkward between Kat and me as Reed makes small talk with Lydia and I share stolen glances with the woman I never stopped loving.

Her thin cotton nightgown barely hides her curves although it's baggy on her small frame. I know I've aged while I've been gone, with dark circles under my eyes that never used to be there and lines from constant stress and worry, but Kat's changed too. Without an ounce of makeup on her, there are bags under her eyes and I wonder if it's because she couldn't sleep knowing I'd be knocking on her door tonight. Her hair is shorter, cut just above her shoulders and dyed a pretty blond that complements her olive skin tone.

Kat walks past me, careful not to brush against me, to stand beside Lydia and motions to the stairs at my right. The instinct to slip my arm around her waist and pin her against the wall is only stopped by her statement when she says, "The guest room is ready for you."

Thump, thump. I want nothing more than to hold her but instead I'm paralyzed where I am. A fucking guest room?

A chill flows through me, keeping me where I am and threatening to take her away again if I say or do anything at this moment.

Reed clears his throat and Kat crosses her arms, refusing to look at him. A beat passes and I finally speak.

"You two not friends anymore?" I motion between the two of them, although my gaze traps Kat's and my pulse rages against my veins. She swallows thickly before answering me with a gentleness that tells me she's feeling the same thing I am. That all of this is balanced on a cord wound so tight it may break.

"He didn't tell me you were coming," she says and licks her lower lip before adding with a sigh, "I had to find out from Lydia."

It's only now that I realize I'm far too drunk for this. *Fuck.*

I stand there, time ticking away, just taking her in. My eyes roam down her body and back up and although I want her more than anything,

I can't help but to notice how her bottom lip wobbles and she catches it between her teeth. It's telling me the same thing that her glossy eyes and her defensive posture are.

Two strong hands press against my back. "We had a lot to drink, so," Reed states, pushing me forward but I'm far from ready. Even if the alcohol is wearing on me, making my head spin and throwing off my balance.

The question comes out without my conscious consent. "You don't want me here?"

"I didn't say that—" She raises her voice for the first time, her gaze piercing through mine with thinly veiled desperation.

Reed shoves at my back. "You're drunk, man, come on."

My grip loosens and the duffle bag drops to my feet. "I need to hear you say it," I blurt out and then catch myself. Fuck, she makes me weak. She has me under her thumb and doesn't even know it.

"Say what?" she's quick to ask and that eagerness promises she'll say what I want to hear, but I'm too much of a bitch to risk it.

"Tell me you want me to stay here," I say instead and then I'm quick to amend it. "That it's all right that I stay with you."

Reed bends at my side, picking up the duffle bag and not looking at either of us.

Lydia looks anywhere but at us too and all the while, I wait.

"Of course you can … I'm just," she says and glances down, then back up at me, "… I'm just surprised you want to." Her voice nearly breaks and the corners of her lips turn down.

Fuck. I hate this. I hate every moment of it as a cold sweat breaks out on the back of my neck.

It kills me how she looks as if she's on the verge of breaking down. Lydia must see it too because she's quick to tell me to get my drunk ass upstairs. "Welcome home," she adds before stepping between Kat and me.

I can't help myself, though. I ask her, "Did you think I forgot about you? I know you haven't forgotten about me."

"Let's go," Reed says and grabs my arm, pulling me to the stairs as Lydia takes Kat's hand, taking her away from me.

In all the ways I imagined coming back to her, this sure as hell wasn't the reality I expected. That's all I can think as I climb up the stairs, wishing I'd had enough beer to pass out at the fucking bar so I could have avoided all of this.

At one point I was strong for her, but after four years, all I feel is broken or pissed off and there's no in between until I look at her …

I barely know who I am anymore, but all I want to know is whether or not she could love me again.

Chapter 3

Kat

SEEING THE TWO OF THEM TOGETHER IS SURREAL. REED … AND most notably Cillian. My heart is all sorts of crushed yet still able to beat. Furiously and nervously at the same time. With my fingers numb and barely able to breathe, I watch, unable to say a word.

Although I grimace as Cill stumbles and my chest flips with an ache. My Cillian. My rock and my ride or die … he's a shell of the man he used to be.

He's still handsome and every bit of how I remember him … but four years in prison aged him, obviously so. He doesn't seem to have slept a bit, given that darkness under his eyes. He's more than toned now. The muscles that ripple in his shoulders and down his arms pull at the cotton of his shirt as his leather jacket falls to the floor.

Sexy and sinful … but there's a brokenness that's undeniable. Even as he attempted to hide it when I opened the door, I felt it. In the very marrow of my bones, my body ached in mourning of what's become of him.

I always knew him to be deadly and brooding even, but this is a different brokenness.

It takes everything in me not to gather him up myself and let out these sobs.

It's been a year since I've seen him and that year must have been hell.

Regret pulls my gaze away as Reed mutters, "Come on. You're drunk," yet again.

Judging by Reed's scowl, he's on the verge of pulling Cill out of my house by the arm and back to his truck. I should let him do it. This whole thing—Cill staying with me after his release, no warning—it shouldn't be happening. No one has the right to show up at my house and demand to stay with me. But I know I'll never forgive myself if I let this happen.

Cill is in no state to go anywhere else. He's drunk, and there's a darkness in his eyes that scares me because I don't think he's able to hold back a single thing. It also begs me to comfort him.

My fingers itch at my side and as they do, Lydia tugs at my arm and silently mouths the word *no* as if she could read my mind.

I hate everything about this moment.

The tension between the four of us is so thick it makes my heart pound. Reed's about to get physical with him. Drag him out of here, back to his truck.

"You shouldn't even be driving," I tell Reed without looking at him, my arms crossed as I sink back into the chair, Lydia standing as if she's my warden by my side.

Reed mutters, "I'm not driving."

"You drove here," I bite back and peek up at him, but he's still focused on Cill.

"I'll walk home. I needed to drop him off. But we'll both leave now." Both leave. My heart stalls in protest and everything goes cold.

"No," Cill states with finality.

Cill's hardly spoken to me but I could easily hear the slight slur in his voice, and I can barely look him in the eye. I have no idea what Reed told him about me. I don't know what Cill knows. Which only intensifies the betrayal that overwhelms me.

Two drunk men, four years of hell for all of us, and a stubborn man who doesn't know what's good for him anymore … shit.

This is going to turn into a fight. It's an invitation for the cops to get nosy. Cill doesn't need that. I don't need that.

"Let him go and head home," I tell Reed. "You can come back for your truck in the morning."

"You sure about this, because—" He doesn't get a chance to finish as Cill interrupts. "I'll go upstairs," he says, then clears his throat and the cords in his neck tighten as he swallows, "and you walk home. She's right."

Cill shakes off Reed's arm and balances himself on the banister. My God, the pull I feel to him as he closes his eyes and steadies his breath.

Reed tosses Cill's duffle bag toward the foot of the stairs, nodding. Lydia offers him a ride, which he rejects and then he and I share a look. One that brings that ache back tenfold.

"Come on," I say and open the door for Reed. I shoo him away, but I stand on the porch and make sure he doesn't drive. I don't think Reed is as drunk as Cill, but he definitely shouldn't be behind the wheel.

When he's gone, I shut the door and lock it, then push the deadbolt shut and set the code too. I can feel Cill standing behind me. His very presence is throwing heat into the room.

So for a long moment, I keep my back to him, doing everything I can to not tremble and keep my composure.

Lydia shuffling around in the kitchen is the only thing I can hear. I wish the creak of the stairs would tell me Cillian's doing what he said he would, but he's not. When I turn, he's right where he was before but fully turned around, his light blue gaze focused right on me. Those big, wounded puppy dog eyes don't match the brutality of this man in the least.

A cabinet opens and then closes to the left of us.

Lydia's lingering in the kitchen to give us space, I bet, and I'm glad she did. I can't have this moment with Cill in front of anyone else. Not her. Not Reed.

"I think I might be drunk, Hellcat," he rumbles and his lips kick up into an asymmetrical smile I've missed. All of that apprehension vanishes and it's something else that forces me forward, one step at a time.

Hearing that nickname in his voice, drunk and scratchy and tired, makes me go weak in the knees.

My response is gentle and somehow comes out even. "You should probably go to bed, then." Standing a safe three feet away from him, I cross my arms over my chest to keep my hands where they are. His gaze drops, making note of it. A sad smile on his face is all I'm given.

I swallow thickly and head up the stairs to the second floor, past him, my arm brushing against his. And when we touch, my God, that small touch. My eyes close and I breathe in deep, quickening my pace when I hear the stairs creaking behind me with his weight.

A narrow hall leads to a bedroom in the back. Cill appears beside me with his duffle bag slung over one shoulder. He looks at the room. The bed. The window. It's not much, but enough for a guest to be comfortable.

"You want me to go somewhere else?" he asks again.

"No," I say and my answer is firm even if it is just a whisper between us. I don't need any time to think about it. It surprises me how much I mean it. I don't want him to go anywhere else.

"Stay here," I tell him and back up when he takes a half step forward. "You're drunk tonight," I explain as his arm drops to his side. "Tomorrow." I say the word like it's a promise.

With a nod and a hint of that asymmetric smile, he repeats, "Tomorrow."

"Good night, Cill."

"Good night, Hellcat."

I almost give in. I almost recklessly go to him. Even with every logical thought that's guarding my heart, part of me wants to feel his lips on mine again more than the rest of me wants to confess my sins and tell him what happened.

But in the end, I pull the door closed.

The act pulls on strings I'd rather stay still. I only hold it together then and there to tell Lydia she can go home if she wants. She only hesitates a moment.

My hands tingle with anticipation as I climb the stairs, my heart thumping with every step.

Before going to my room, I check on Cill's but the door is closed and I don't have it in me to open it.

My own bed feels empty in a way it never has before.

My body craves to be wrapped around Cill, but my fingers tangle in my hair instead. There's so much to tell him and each line runs wild in my mind. There's so much I already should have told him.

Sleep evades me. The thought of him down the hall, alone under the covers, is too much. It keeps me awake.

I toss and turn, the sheets uncomfortably tight and all wrong. Every time I glance at the clock, it's only been ten minutes and yet hours tick by. And then another. All the while I stare at my bedroom door.

Should I go to him? I don't even know if Cill would want that. Even if he did right now, he may not after we talk.

Time changes everything.

Tears form at the corners of my eyes and I brush them away, struggling to hold on to my sanity. It's difficult not to dwell on the negatives, the thoughts that keep me wide awake. Instead, I think about what used to be. How at one point, I thought all we had left was our happily ever after.

With the memories playing back like a movie, sleep comes and goes in short spurts.

Dreams tempt me and they show me how it once was when we first got together.

Morning comes all too soon with a stubborn alarm and tired, reddened eyes.

"Fuck," I mutter as I smack the clock, hating that I didn't turn it off last night. Six a.m. is far too early and puts me at only three hours of restless sleep at most.

Still, I don't bother to stay under the sheets.

As soon as I remember—Cill's here—I'm out of the bed, my bare feet on the cold wooden floor. It's not far to his room, but when I get there the door is wide open. I know what that means before I step through the threshold.

My palms are clammy as I steady my breathing.

He's not there.

With a quick check in the bathroom only to find nothing, I head downstairs. I rush down, taking the stairs two at a time. The house is quiet around me. When I don't see him, I call out his name and it echoes in the empty house.

He's not here either. I circle the living room to look for signs of him. There are none. He didn't sit on the couch, or pull the throw blanket over his legs.

Swallowing thickly, I do everything I can to shake off the uncertainty.

I don't know why I care so much. He spent one night in my house, and it's not like there would be plenty of evidence that he was here. As the heat of panic creeps up my arms, I just need some proof. Some little thing to say Cill's really back home and last night wasn't a dream. He was here with me.

As I head to the living room to grab my phone that's charging, ready to text Lydia, I see the note.

A slim piece of paper from the notepad I use to make grocery lists. He didn't leave me with nothing after all.

It's from Cill.

I have to take care of a few things.
Like getting a phone …
I'll call you and I'll see you tonight.
If you need anything, or you need me, call Reed.

Six years ago

A younger version of Cill, only seventeen years old, leaned over the pool table. Shot after shot, he cleared the table with ease. He was a shark even then. I remember thinking he probably learned how to play from his dad, but I didn't care about that. All I cared about was how hot he looked in the dim lights of the rec room. He wore a tight black T-shirt that showed off his muscular arms. Sinking a ball into one of the pockets, easy as can be, he looked up at me. A smirk immediately met his lips. He didn't disguise how much he wanted me and I didn't attempt to hide anything either. He let his eyes linger on my face for a long time, until I blushed.

Our fathers were doing business upstairs. They did that a lot and left the two of us alone. I met Cill's father before I met Cill. He told me more than once he thought Cill and I would get along well. Which is probably why my father never brought me to the MC club … until that night.

"You want to play?" Cill asked.

"I don't know how."

"Bullshit." He grinned at me and every inch of me went hot. "You're Angelo's daughter. You trying to hustle me?" My teeth caught my lower lip, although it didn't help hide my smile. "Little con artist, aren't you?"

"Maybe." I picked at the torn jeans I wore.

"What were you going to bet me, then?" I blushed deeper, imagining all the things I could say if I had the courage. "'Cause I was going to bet you a kiss."

"If you won, you wanted a kiss from me?" I questioned him. The idea of Cill wanting a kiss from me was like winning the lottery. Even if it never happened, that didn't matter. He wanted a kiss from me, and I could barely breathe with how excited that made me.

I knew he could tell. I wasn't very good at hiding anything. His growing smile forced away any insecurity I had.

Unfortunately, it didn't last for long.

Both our fathers clattered down the stairs at that moment, their voices coming into the rec room ahead of them. I didn't get to hear Cill's answer, if he gave me one. I fell in love with him in that moment. I never stood a chance. He was sexy and sinful ... but charming and easy in a way I'd never felt before. There was an attraction I couldn't deny on my side and he wanted me back. Nothing was ever going to top that.

Nothing.

Chapter 4

Cillian

FOUR YEARS MIGHT AS WELL HAVE BEEN A FUCKING LIFETIME. Slipping the new phone into my back pocket, I attempt to take in everything that's changed and what has stayed the same.

Life used to be routine and easy. I loved every fucking day.

Monday through Saturday I worked my shift in the garage, fixing up whatever came in. Unless we had a run, in which case it was days on end with the growl of the bike under me. Either way, work came and went easy enough and with good company.

Church, a.k.a. the club meetings, on Sunday and then family dinner after.

My father told me when I got out, he'd make sure everything was like it was before.

Now he's six feet under and I would give anything to hear him offering me any advice at all to get through this.

The slow rumble of the truck keeps us company as I keep my ass in the seat, not knowing what to expect next.

"You look like today kicked your ass," Reed comments half-heartedly as I turn off the engine and close the door to his truck.

"Thanks." I huff a laugh and think back on Kat's house. It's small and in need of a powerwash and weeding. The whole house could use fixing up here and there.

I could do that. I could so easily take care of it for her.

"Rough night?"

I shrug before dragging my focus back to him. His hands are already covered in oil, just as mine will be in a few hours. My uncle didn't waste any time putting me back to work. One other thing has stayed the same as well. Church is on Sunday and I'm damn well looking forward to that. Until then, he told me to stick with Reed in the garage.

"It was all right. Slept off the beer and snuck out before she got up," I tell him.

"Snuck out?" He lets out a chuckle, a smile growing on his face. "I know I keep saying it," he starts, "but I missed you, man. We all missed you."

At that remark, my thoughts run back to Kat. Reed must know it because he tells me, "She missed you. Trust me, man, she missed you."

I stopped by her bedroom door at the crack of fucking dawn this morning and thought about pushing it open, but I didn't.

Reed left his keys to the truck on the kitchen table. I drove it to get a few things I needed, texted Reed I'd meet him here at the garage and waited and waited. He only lives a few houses down and I thought about heading to his place instead; I couldn't fucking stand to stay inside the garage. Being there when it's empty and ghosts linger in every room, was more than I could take. So I stayed in the truck, waiting for his ass to get here.

I've never felt so fucking out of place in my life.

As our boots crunch on the gravel, he passes me one of the two cups of coffee from the corner shop. It's cheap, like it's always been, but hot. "You and Kat talk last night?"

"No."

"You sleep all right?"

Nodding, I comment, "Pretty good," which doesn't do it justice.

For the first time in years, there were no lights shining in my eyes in the middle of the night. No fights. No screaming. Nobody losing his shit from being behind bars. It was the best sleep I've had since I went away. Only way it could have been better is if Kat was in the bed with me.

We go up to the third floor, past the garage on the first, then the rec room on the second where my life ended four years ago.

The office is different. It's still shabby in the same way, with second-hand office furniture and filing cabinets, but it's not quite like I recall. Reed takes a seat in an old office chair behind one of the desks and I take the leather sofa across from him that I don't remember from before. At least one thing has been updated.

The garage doesn't open for another thirty minutes, so we've got time to kill.

"What's it like with my uncle being in charge now?" I remember back in the day when he and my dad would go at it.

Reed's thumb taps on the armrest, a telltale sign that's always given away when he's anxious.

"If I'm honest, I miss your pops."

He died while I was in prison. I didn't get to attend his funeral, and it's one of my bigger regrets. I should have been there for that. Instead, I was in a cramped cell reading a warden-approved paperback book about metalworking.

"And things are still unsettled?"

"It's more about the leadership now." Reed rubs a hand over his face. "Duncan Tray, that prick from up north, tried to step in and negotiate with our contracts … so when your uncle insisted on voting for change, we went with it at first."

"At first?" I hate that fucker Duncan with everything in me. When I was locked away, I know he paid people on the inside to fuck with me. He's lucky he's still breathing.

"Some of the members want to move into a bigger space and expand the operation. And others want to stay where we are, with what we have."

"What do you think?"

Reed searches my eyes for a moment before telling me he's one of the few who doesn't feel comfortable expanding. "Your uncle wants to, though, and he hasn't dropped it. It's just … we're heading past the territories we have agreements with."

He's tense, barely moving other than the nervous tap of his thumb. "The pres won't let it go."

I can only nod, taking it in and unsure of what this Sunday will be like.

Church was never contentious that I remember. I was young, practically a kid, and I figured things would stay the same forever. Church was for brainstorming ideas for the garage, for fucking around and giving each other a hard time. For splitting cash after handing off deals for the organizations that relied on us. The Cross brothers up north, and the Valettis down south with their connections to the docks. We acted as a go-between and took a hefty chunk of change to make it worthwhile.

"I don't see why we need to expand unless things have changed? Have we lost deals or taken smaller cuts or what?"

"No," he says and his voice raises slightly as he shakes his head, "money is good. There's no reason, that's what I'm saying." He hesitates and pauses his tapping before saying, "It should have been you who took over."

All I can do is swallow down his statement with both bitterness and loss. I always knew eventually I'd take over my dad's place in the MC. Years and years and years from now when my pops was gray haired and didn't want to do it anymore.

Life's a bitch.

For the second time today, I miss my father. If I closed my eyes right now, I could see him sitting there in place of my best friend. He sat in that seat nearly all my life.

My throat is so tight, I can't even offer an opinion. I haven't been back long enough to know which path is the right way forward. I haven't been out long enough to know what I want to do with myself, let alone make a decision that would affect the club.

"You'll vote with me on Sunday?" Reed questions nervously and I don't hesitate to nod in agreement.

"Yeah," I answer, my tone reflecting my apprehension given everything that's changed.

"Sorry, man … it's mostly good." Reed shakes off the tension and relaxes his shoulders as he changes the subject. "You looking forward to seeing everyone?"

The coffee hasn't cured my hangover yet and I don't want to answer questions about prison. Many of the guys in the MC have been in jail for one thing or another, but I'm the most recent, the youngest … and I took the fall when any of them could have done it instead.

The more I think about it, the angrier I get.

"Yeah." I clear my throat and tell him, "It's good to be home, I just … need a moment to get reacquainted I guess."

I took the fall for the raid, and they've been careful since then. It makes me bitter to think about it. If Kat's dad hadn't fucked around the way he did four years ago, I wouldn't have lost her, I wouldn't have gone away and I would have been here when my pops's health started going south.

Leaning back, I settle on something that brings a smile to both of us. "I'm looking forward to working on my bike," I say.

"Working on her?" He grins and tells me, "I fixed her up so she's practically brand new."

I chuckle, nodding my gratitude.

My mind wanders to Kat. Thinking she's all sorts of new to me too.

New and apparently off-limits. Or so she thinks.

Even if I can't touch her, I want to be in that house. Wanting that soft bed with her scent on it. In prison I had to sit with all these feelings. There was literally nothing else to do. I could try to jog them out in the exercise yard, but I was in my cell most of the day. You learn to deal with the waves of rage. Some guys do, anyway. Other guys go crazy in there. Who knows? Maybe I was one of them.

Reed eventually does some work on the computer. He makes a few calls. My uncle comes in and the three of us have a conversation that feels like it goes on forever, but only lasts about fifteen minutes. I'm getting back to life in the club. This is life in the club.

The garage is where I lose most of my time, remembering what could have been.

Working with metal and surrounded by the nostalgic smell of oil, the feel of labor bringing a burn to my muscles forces the time to tick by. For the first time since I've been out, there's a moment of peace and ease. And naturally … my mind wanders back to her.

It always comes back to her.

It's not until I climb into Reed's truck, and he gets in behind the wheel that he brings her up. "You two …? What's going on there?"

"I haven't spoken to her in a year," I tell him. He's busy nodding his head while I admit, "But I want her back. I want us back."

I keep my last thought unspoken as he turns over the engine: *I need her back.* If I have her, everything else will be right again. I fucking know it will.

I'll make it right. I'll make her love me again.

Chapter 5

Kat

LYDIA LEANS AGAINST MY KITCHEN COUNTER AND LOOKS OUT the window into the yard. Her takeout container is open on the countertop next to her and she pokes her fork into it, then scoops out another minuscule bite. "I'm going to miss this."

"This restaurant is only good about half the time," I joke, downplaying her somber mood.

"I'm going to miss you, Kat."

She rolls her eyes at me and laughs, but I know the emotion behind her words is real. Realer than most things in my life, anyway. Some things turned out to be cruel jokes and I didn't know until after the fact. C'est la vie, I suppose.

"I'm happy for you. I truly am." I snag a wonton and add, "But I'm going to miss you like crazy." I can't even look her in the eye as I say it. Just in case some part of me decides to get weepy.

I know how much she's wanted to go to college and how excited she is to start her new life. Part of me actually considered leaving to stay with her, at her suggestion a few months back when she got her acceptance letter in the spring. But … I don't think my life is anything to dismiss, either. My job at the flower shop is a good one, I love it even. I have a kind boss and reasonable hours and I enjoy putting the orders together. It's meaningful, what I do, even if it is small. It's just not college. Lydia going off to college feels like another world away.

In reality, it's only a two-hour ride on the train. I know which ticket to buy to visit her and how long it'll take to get there. I even know some of the places we can check out when I visit. We mapped it all out over a bottle of wine when we checked out the campus together. In all honesty, I've never been so thrilled for her. Lydia's eyes were so bright when she took in the buildings.

With my fork halfway in the air, I cock a brow and ask with a smirk, "You sure you have to leave me all alone down here?"

She's drinking wine with her takeout—we both are. I'm not drunk, but I feel the effects of the alcohol. Maybe that's why I'm only thinking of Cill every five minutes. I'm aware it's every five minutes because I can't stop checking the clock. He texted me when he'd be home.

He said *your place,* rather than home.

I'll be at your place around seven.

It's six forty-five now.

With the cabernet sinking in sip by sip, I'm less nervous and more excited than I've been all day. Warm. A little bit calmer. Lydia takes another swallow of hers.

"I'm not leaving you alone." She glances toward the stairs. "Am I?"

I can't think of what to say to Lydia, so I grab the wine instead. I'm anxious with the thought of him in the house. Anxious, and attracted. Another sip down and I shrug, licking the sweet liquid from my lower lip.

All my feelings for him came back in a rush with that simple text message. Thinking of him in that guest bedroom made it damn hard to settle down at night. I'm not the kind of girl who tosses and turns over things she can't control, but Cill? He's like a thunderstorm. I never know when he might break apart.

My gaze flicks to the clock again as I lean forward in anticipation. Shoving the food away, I can't eat anymore with these butterflies.

He wants me. I don't know everything and I have to tell him what happened. But the man I've always loved wants me and there's still something there.

My only worry is that once I tell him what happened, or once he finds out, he'll never look at me the same. But last night, that look he gave me ...

"How did it go last night?" Lydia asks, bringing my attention back to her although she's focused elsewhere. She's watching out the window again.

"Not a peep from him after I showed him the room, and when I got up

… he was gone." I rub under my still sore eyes. I'm exhausted, but there's not a chance in hell I'm going to bed until I see him.

"You sleep at all?"

"Not at all." I can barely manage a fake smile. I don't count those hours when I was half dreaming close to the morning. That wasn't restful sleep.

"Kat," she says, her tone scolding. "You have to rest. You can't start losing sleep over—"

"I'll be all right. Just getting used to things. It was the first night." And I didn't know it was coming. All things considered, things could have gone a lot worse. Cill's back home and he's safe. I was safe in my house. No one tried to break in. If losing a night of sleep is the worst that happens, I'll be counting my blessings.

"You know," Lydia says, "you are the one in control here. If you don't want him here, you tell him that. He can find somewhere else to go."

"I know."

I understand the worry that lingers in her eyes. I do. I get it. But it's Cill. And if there's something there still, how could I possibly let that go?

I took it upon myself to be independent so that I'd never be caught off guard the way I was that night at the clubhouse. No one would ever throw my life into disarray again. But I know, right away, that I won't kick Cill out of my house and I won't say no if he wants me. I don't think I have that in me. Even if he is turning my emotions a bit upside down.

A bit—okay. Totally upside down.

"And …" She takes another small bite of her food. "If you don't want to be with him, you don't have to be."

"I know."

"Then why do you look like that?"

"Like what?"

"Like you're stuck and hopeless. And maybe like you're a lovesick lost puppy." Lydia softens her statement with a smile.

She's right. I couldn't even nap today. I spent an hour on the couch trying, but all I could think about was whether Cill would come back or whether he'd disappear out of my life again. I thought about his note. I thought about him … and then he texted me.

"It's kind of insulting to my ego that a single text from a man can make me feel this way," I admit out loud and, without my conscious consent, sneak a peek at the clock again.

Lydia snorts a laugh and pushes her hair out of her face, elbows on the table while dragging out the words, "Oh my God. You still love him!"

There's that twist in my chest and the knowledge I have to tell him everything, but still I nod.

"So you're a mess over him, even after four years?"

"Because I want him with me more than anything," I admit. "But when he finds out what happened …" Emotion makes my throat close.

"So you haven't told him?" Lydia questions.

"I betrayed him, Lydia." The clock reads six fifty-five. "I honestly thought about texting him … and then hiding at your place." A heavy exhale leaves me.

"He wasn't here," she tells me and I'm shocked by the hard tone she uses. With my gaze trapped in hers mostly from shock, she repeats, "He wasn't here and a lot happened. He changed and so did you, and if he can't understand that, it's on him." Her swallow is audible when she finishes and she gives me a curt nod as if to ask, isn't that right?

There's a flop in my chest, one that's dull and thuds on its own for a moment.

"How do I look him in the eye after he's gone through hell and tell him what happened?" I've thought of it a million times, but even in my imagination, I open my mouth and no words come out.

"Kat." Her voice goes soft and serious. Lydia puts down her fork and my stomach twists at the conversation I know is coming. "You aren't the only one, and he needs to know—"

The front door rattles, then opens with a familiar creak. I jump, feeling guilty and caught, and barely manage to catch my wine before it sloshes all over my kitchen floor.

"We're back," Reed says. "You here?"

"In the kitchen," Lydia calls out. With only a few steps Reed appears in the threshold, wearing his leathers, complete with a Celtic cross, and an easy smile. Until he sees me, and it slips for a moment.

Then there's Cill … appearing right behind him and all that nervousness and fluttering and every emotion that I can't control, it all comes up full force with no way to stop it.

Chapter 6

Cillian

WITH A SOFT CLICK, THE FRONT DOOR SHUTS BEHIND ME and my gaze roams down Kat's backside as she enters a code into the security system.

My body's hot and my blood pounds as I slip off my leather jacket and wait for her to turn around.

To face me and face this situation we're in.

It's so quiet in her place that I can easily hear her swallow as my jacket is placed over the back of the simple wooden chair.

"Well, now they're gone …" she says and trails off as she ambles her way into the kitchen, her bare feet padding on the floor. With her arms crossed over her chest, she hides the fact that she's not wearing a bra under her dark navy sleep shirt.

"Do you need anything before I go to bed?" she asks, brushing her hair off her shoulder, her wide hazel eyes peering up at me.

"Why does what you say to me, not match what I think … you're thinking. What is it you really want to say?" I take a hesitant step toward her and the floor creaks beneath me.

My little hellcat stays where she is, her breath hitching as I reach out and let my thumb slip down her arm. The small touch is like a spark, cracking and igniting the faint tinder into a blazing fire.

She swallows again, her chest heaving with a desperate inhale before brushing my touch away and ripping her gaze from me as well.

I haven't felt so nervous, so close to the edge of something that could break me since I sat in that small barren room of the courthouse, signing confession papers and knowing it meant I wouldn't see freedom again for years.

That's what her simple act of rejection does to me … it's worse than that even. Fuck.

"I um …" She clears her throat, her back to me as she gathers the wine and glasses, cleaning up the small space and avoiding me entirely.

With both hands gripping the back of the chair, I'm careful as I ask her, "Do you want to talk? Do you want me to help?" It takes everything in me to keep my voice steady as I confess to her, "I'll even take small talk, Hellcat."

I'm only given her profile as she rinses out the glasses, the sound of the water rushing from the faucet taking up space, but her laugh, feminine and warm, drowns it out. She still loves to be called Hellcat. Hope lingers and the heat rises.

I may be nervous, but I'm not letting her push me away.

"Small talk, like what?" She peeks up at me, turning off the faucet.

"Thought you preferred beer."

She huffs a short laugh, wine staining her bottom lip. "Things changed …" In an instant, that warmth vanishes. She's hot and cold. "I have to tell you—"

"No you don't." My response is harder than I thought it would be.

"I don't want to talk about … whatever the hell it is that keeps stealing you from me."

"I can't—" Her head shakes and her reluctance shows as she grips the counter, no longer facing me in the least when she adds, "I can't stand seeing you without telling you—"

Reed did this same shit on and off before I got out. Everyone wants to fill me in on the bad shit.

"Stop," I say, cutting her off. Everyone I love is holding back and, for the love of God, I just need them there. "I just got out," I tell her. Emotions riddle the words and because of that, and maybe because I take a step toward her, she faces me again. Vulnerable but wanting. I soften my tone, offering her the parts of me she loves. "Can't I just have a moment where I see you smile again?"

I used to tell her that her smile made it all okay. No matter what shit we were in, no matter how fucked anything got, if she was smiling it would all be all right and just like back then, she offers me one. Her gaze falls to the floor as the shy smile I've held on to for years to carry me through this hell settles on her lips.

With one more step, I close the gap between us to tell her, "That's my girl." This time I cup her cheek, my thumb falling on those lips I used to devour.

Both of her hands wrap around my wrist and I think she's going to pull my hand away, but she doesn't.

Longing is etched into the shards of green and gold in her gaze. Then in a blink, it's over. "I'm really tired," she tells me and it's my cue to drop my hand.

"Didn't sleep last night?"

"Yeah ..." she answers and peeks up at me again, the tension still there but held back so carefully. "... just wanted to stay up in case you needed something."

"I'm good," I tell her softly and add, "You should go to bed."

There's a moment I think she'll kiss me. That she'll pop up on her tiptoes like she used to and give me even the smallest of pecks. My chest thumps and my blood rushes, knowing if she does, I'll fucking devour her.

I'll take her right here and now.

Instead, the moment passes and I watch her go. I wait for her to look back, and she does, at the very top of the stairs. She grips the banister and her lips part like she'll say something, but then she stops herself and all I'm given is another *sleep well*.

I could. Ten seconds before she's gone and that's when I can breathe. With both hands on the table, I lean over forcing myself to stay right the fuck where I am.

I'll give her a moment. I'll let her climb into bed and then I'm going up there.

Rounding the table, I tour her place, picking up odds and ends here and there. Getting a good look at who she is now. Little bits of her show in accent pillows with deep jewel tones and soft blankets laid out on the back of the sofa.

It's not until I open the drawer in the coffee table that my composure crumbles. There's not only a framed photo of the two of us tucked away, but also my leather patch I gave her. The one my mother used to wear that I gave Kat the day after I told her I loved her for the first time.

It's right there, in the heart of her home, but hidden away so no one can see.

Slamming the drawer shut, I run my hand through my hair and second-guess my plan, but only for a moment. Taking the stairs two at a time, I head upstairs and any hesitation I had vanishes when I see her bedroom door open.

It wasn't this morning. It was firmly shut.

It's pitch black inside and as I push the door open, it creaks. It takes a moment for my eyes to adjust.

And a moment for her to see I'm there.

"Cillian?" she asks in a hushed voice, breathless even.

"Is your bed big enough for the both of us?" I question, my hand already on the door to close it.

With the light filtering in from the stairwell and the lights left on downstairs, they offer a halo around Kat and I'm able to see her nod a yes.

Thank fuck, I nearly groan in satisfaction as I close the door.

My boots come off first, followed by my jeans and then my shirt. My back was to her for the first part, but as I tug off my shirt, I catch sight of her watching.

If we were as we used to be, I'd tease her. I'd ask her if she liked what she saw.

In my mind I see her, I see us: a different version that was never broken and she'd bite her lower lip, sitting up and teasing me back to come see for myself.

A pang in my chest of regret and guilt stays with me as the comforter rustles and the bed groans as I climb in.

She's silent and perfectly still on her side of the bed. Waiting, and more than likely overthinking things.

As casually as I can, I roll onto my side and tell her, "I want to hold you."

It's dark and the shadows play on her gorgeous face but I can perfectly see her defenseless gaze. Carefully, I lay my arm on hers and my brow cocks as I add, "Please?"

A moment passes and then another before she rolls over to the other side, scooting closer to me so I can wrap an arm around her.

There's space between us but as the minutes pass, both of us lying there, our warm bodies slowly shift closer together until she settles her ass against my crotch.

I take my time as I slip my thumb down the crook of her neck. Every action is measured. Even when I nuzzle right there and kiss below the shell of her ear.

Her hushed gasp is fucking everything I need to continue. My thumb finds the swell of her breast and she presses her chest into my touch.

It may have been years but I remember that soft gasp where a touch of surprise lingers. The way her eyes nearly close, heavy with lust, is a detail that hardens me even more, although I didn't think it was possible.

As I press my splayed hand against her lower belly and then lower, her back arches, bringing her ass to press against me. Only the thin fabric we both wear under the covers separates us now.

A deep groan leaves me, one of primal need that I can't control.

Kat peeks over her shoulder, looking up at me with a concoction of emotion swirling in her gorgeous hazel eyes. She swallows audibly, not breaking the gaze to tell me, "I used to dream of that sound." The moment she's spoken, it's almost like she wishes she hadn't. As if she'd reach up and grab the words, hide them and never admit that again if she could.

There's a wretched pain that burrows into my chest as she attempts to look away, but I crash my lips against hers, taking the kiss I snuck in here to claim.

Maybe I shouldn't be here. Maybe we shouldn't be doing this. But as she turns in my arms, her hands gripping my shoulders, her legs wrapping around my hips as she clings to me, greedy for more, I don't give a fuck.

She has always been mine. Even though she broke my heart. Even after years of being apart.

She's mine. She'll always be mine.

With my lips at the shell of her ear, I whisper, "Get undressed for me." I'm already aching hard for her, but her eagerness is everything I need.

I swear if she gripped me, if she wrapped her fingers around me in this moment, I'd come undone in an instant.

It's been so damn long and I need her. Fuck, how I need her.

When she's fully undressed, but still hiding from me under the covers, I pull them down and turn her over how I want her.

"I'm going to move the pillow here," I tell her before settling it under her hips so her ass is higher, so her pussy is right there for the taking.

I groan in approval as my hand cups her ass and then finds that sweet entrance between her legs.

"Already wet for me," I murmur and then lean forward, grabbing the back of her neck. "If I didn't come in here to take care of you, were you going to do it yourself?"

As her lips part to answer, I rub circles around her clit and my little hellcat jumps beneath me, writhing from the touch.

Giving her ass a quick smack that makes her jump again, I scold her. "Answer me like the good girl I know you are for me."

"No, I wouldn't have," she groans and when my hand returns to her swollen nub, she moans the sweetest sounds into the pillow.

I only pull away to remove my boxers, taking my time so I'm sure she's aware.

As I get into position, I place my hand on her shoulder, keeping her where I want her.

I whisper, just to be certain, "You want me?"

Her whispered answer is immediate. "Yes."

With my head at her slit, I command her, "Tell me how much."

Turning her upper body as much as she can, her eyes find mine and pierce through me as she whispers, "Please. I need you."

Her chin tilts for a kiss, longing evident in her eyes and the moment my lips meet hers in a gentle kiss, it turns bruising and I thrust into her all the way to the hilt with a single stroke.

Her cries of strangled pleasure fuel me to fuck her faster and harder. To take her and ruin her. I wanted to take it slow and love her for our first time together since all this shit happened.

But the moment I'm inside of her, I can't stop mercilessly taking her with every thrust, each one nearly violent. It's been too fucking long without her. I need to feel her come on my dick more than I need to breathe.

Chapter 7

"**I** DON'T WANT YOU TO THINK ABOUT ANY OF THIS SHIT OR WORRY. I just want you to love me," he whispered as I lay limp in bed. "Do you understand?"

As he asked the question, he cleaned between my legs with a wet towel and the sudden touch made me jump, but I was sure to tell him yes. The word spilled from my lips as easily as my pleasure came, one orgasm after the other after the other, bringing me closer and closer to sleep.

It was his kiss, though, soft and gentle on my shoulder and my cheek, then on my lips after he whispered, "Good girl," that lured me into the depths of my dreams.

If he hadn't kissed my shoulder so sweetly as he tucked me in, I'd have thought he secretly hated me. For a moment I truly thought that he hated me. That he knew and he hated me. He fucked me so roughly, so ruthlessly … leaving me so deliciously used. But the way he held me, melted every insecurity away.

If it weren't for the ache between my thighs, I would keep questioning, *Did last night really happen?*

That's all I can think when I wake up.

Slowly, because of the wine I had last night with Lydia.

Memories filter into the last moments of sleep. Cill next to me in the bed. His mouth on mine. His hands on my body like he had never missed a day of touching me in his life.

Did we really?

I turn over on my back and stretch, feeling the soreness in all my muscles … and elsewhere. His muscles were hard next to the soft touch of the blankets. It was like waking up after a long, deep sleep, so deep you hardly know you're dreaming until it's over. Everything about it felt right. And … dangerous.

Dangerous in a way I didn't expect. I don't think Cill would hurt me. Not physically. Never that. Even in his anger, he'd never lay a hand on me. Emotionally, though … My heart races, thinking back to last night. I'm still in disbelief that he wanted this from me. That he still wants me at all, after four years and the very last year.

Footsteps from the kitchen catch my attention, breaking up my wandering thoughts. I climb out of the bed faster than I ever have. It doesn't take me long to fetch a clean pair of pajamas and I'm still pulling the shirt down as I head downstairs. My heart never stops this weird racing in my chest. Like if I'm not fast enough, it never happened. If I don't see him now, before he leaves, it all goes away.

I find him in the kitchen, standing at the counter staring out of the window by the sink. In worn jeans and a black cotton T-shirt, with bare feet and stubble lining his jaw he appears laid back, yet still has this intensity and pull about him. It's overwhelming and keeps me from going to him. Instead I stand in the threshold of the kitchen.

Cill turns his head at the sound of my feet padding on the floor. "Morning," he says, letting his eyes drift down my body.

"Hi," I offer shyly and then blush as he gives me a charming, yet cocky smirk. "You look far more rested," he comments and then he turns back to the coffee machine. It drips slowly into the pot.

"I had a little help." I clear my throat and add, "A sleep aid I highly recommend." I can't help my smile as I go to the fridge.

I can feel his eyes on me as I get out a pan and the eggs and start the process of cooking them on the stove. A new pack of English muffins waits by the toaster. Scrambled eggs today. My hands aren't steady enough to get the yolks right any other way. Especially with him watching my every move.

Nervousness and insecurity worm their way into my mind again.

I steal a peek at him over my shoulder and find Cill watching me. He's not smiling and my own vanishes.

"You okay?" I ask him.

He blinks. I wonder if anyone else is asking him whether he's okay. Checking in with him, the way people should after an experience like he's had.

"Yeah," he answers, seeming to shake off the seriousness that overcame him. "I'm good." It doesn't leave me, though. Last night was a moment for us.

Was it only a moment? My pulse seems to skip and a numbness creeps up the back of my neck as I put English muffins in the toaster. I take another covert glance at Cill and watch him run his hand over the back of his neck, like he feels the same. A pricking knowing that even if last night was heaven, we're still living in a hell we didn't choose and can't control.

"Do you want to talk about it?"

Another glance at him. The coffee is almost done brewing. "Do I want to talk about what?"

"What happened in there … and while you were away." It's better to ask him the question even if he refuses to answer me. I want him to know I can handle the topic.

His sharp blue eyes don't leave mine when he says, "I want to talk about why you stopped coming."

It's so blunt that it feels like a punch. A chill sweeps down my body as the events tip over like dominoes in my mind. Once the first one fell, they couldn't be stopped. I swallow thickly and try to focus on the pan in front of me. My motions mechanical, I pull the plate closer and tip the eggs onto it. Then the other for Cill.

I don't want to tell him. I don't want him to know anything about what happened.

"So we both have some things we want to keep to ourselves?" he questions.

"You scare me, Cillian."

I look back at him and find him staring, his eyes wide. "Why's that?"

The English muffins pop up and I toss them onto the plates, burning the tips of my fingers in the process. Hissing *fuck* under my breath, I'm quick to stick the tips of my fingers into my mouth.

"You all right?" he asks, the concern real in his voice.

"Yeah," I answer him and gather the courage to answer his question.

All the while, I butter the bread automatically so it melts into the little crevices. As if this isn't a conversation I've been dreading. "You're—you're intense. On edge. Your shoulders are rounded in like you think someone's about to hit you. You look like you might get into a fight."

I part my lips to tell him I saw it happen. I watched him change into this man every time I visited him. Then his father … then everything that happened after.

He's the one who changed first, though. "I just … I'm not used to it being like this." I answer him honestly and my voice cracks at the end. I hate it.

I'm reckless as I toss the butter knife into the sink, and I immediately wish I hadn't. I'm calmer as I put the butter back into the fridge.

His gaze burns into the back of me and I pretend the tension isn't heightened.

"You know I'll never—"

"You'd never put a hand on me," I say, cutting him off, turning to gaze at him so he knows I mean it. "But that doesn't mean … it doesn't mean things aren't different and that we aren't different people now."

"And that we both have secrets," he notes as I reach for the plates.

Swallowing thickly, I answer him, "Yeah, we both have secrets," and place both plates on the table, taking my seat. He stands for a moment, watching and with a fork in hand I look up at him, then motion to the plate.

"I'll tell you something if you tell me something," Cill says, taking the seat across from me and picking up the fork but not eating just yet.

Cill clears his throat and he doesn't look at me while he speaks. Instead he stares at his plate. "The first time they tried to kill me was in the cafeteria."

"What?" The stunned word leaves me as my fork falls and my body goes numb.

"Competitors … That fuck Tray, I'm pretty sure." He swallows thickly, then finally looks back at me and says, "Reed made a few calls and found some people, so it didn't happen a lot, but in the beginning … I thought they were going to kill me, Kat." His voice is hoarse with raw emotion although his eyes don't reflect it. His body is tight until he turns his attention back to the plate.

Tears prick the back of my eyes. There's something about how he sits there, so matter of fact that they tried to kill him and that's why he changed. He had to fight for his life. The boy I loved had a tenderness about him that's all but hardened into unforgivable stone. I watched it happen and I couldn't stop it. I couldn't help him … I didn't even know what he was dealing with. Before I have a chance to calm down and blink the tears back, they leak from the corner of my eyes.

Fuck. It comes out of nowhere.

It's all the pent-up feelings of the last four years coming out of me in a rush. I'm out of my seat, hiding my face from Cill before he can see. I reach for a mug and pretend like I'm not losing it from his confession, but a sob is torn from me. He thought he was going to die. That they were going to kill him and he never told me or anyone. He lived with that fear.

I could never imagine—

Strong arms wrap around me and Cill turns me in his arms, holding me tighter as I try to bury my face in his shirt. It only makes me cry harder. It's been so long since anyone held me like this. He rocks me as he holds me, kissing my hair. "Don't worry, Hellcat. Don't worry. Everything's all right now."

"I'm so sorry." Embarrassment heats my cheeks. "I can't control it … I just." My throat is tight and the right words won't come. "Neither of you told me." I barely get out the words as Cill loosens his grip slightly to look down at me.

"Why would I, Kat? You couldn't do anything to help me. No one could."

My hands tremble as I furiously wipe away the tears and try to stop. "I'm sorry."

"You didn't do this." He kisses my cheek. "And I don't want to hear you say that to me ever fucking again."

I nod. His grip on me is strong. Stronger than it ever was when we were younger. His years in prison hardened him, aged him. They made his body different than I remember, yet it still feels familiar enough that I crave it.

His hand stays on my back, rubbing soothing circles as I sniffle and make a cup of coffee like I didn't just have a fucking breakdown at the very beginning of our conversation.

Even as I scoop sugar out for the cup, my hand trembles. I just can't imagine, day in and day out, trying not to die.

"Now you tell me something," he murmurs into my ear. Cill doesn't release me as easily as I thought he would. He squeezes me tighter for a second before he lets me go. It hurts to push away from him. I steady myself with a hand on his shoulder and he lets me.

"I—" It's so difficult to speak, even more difficult to focus on one thing. But through my racing thoughts, one truth begs to be spoken. Something that might make him happy. "I stopped coming … but I wrote to you."

His hand stops and falls, leaving a chill where his warm touch had soothed me. "I didn't get any letters."

I have to brace myself and gather my composure in order to show him. I don't like that it requires putting any distance between us, but he needs to see this. Shaking off the sadness and putting an end to it, I head to the other end of the kitchen. If I'm ever going to tell him the truth, he has to know that I didn't give up on him. As if I ever could. I never stopped needing him. I just didn't have it in me to face him after what happened.

I didn't deserve him anymore. I still don't.

"I kept the notebooks in a drawer next to the sink." I speak out loud, to drown out my thoughts, and I doubt he can hear me. Sniffling, I reach in and pull out two worn and used-up notebooks. They're nothing special and a number of pages are smudged and crinkled from tears that fell on them during the harder nights.

I present both of them as Cillian stands behind me. Turning to him, I put them in his hands. "I wrote something to you every night." My words are barely a murmur, my tone somber.

He opens the first and closes it quickly. "Why'd you stop coming? Is that in here?"

I shake my head. It's not. I can't even look him in the eye.

He opens it back up.

I don't know what he'll find. I can't remember what I said when I wrote to him, but I remember how I felt. I confided in those pages because it was the only way to keep surviving without him. The notebooks would hold my emotions and I'd be able to go about my life.

Every night, I wrote something down about Cill that I missed, or something I wanted him to know.

It was the only way to keep him from haunting my dreams. I had sound nights and even dreams sometimes when I wrote to him. If I forgot, I'd wake up in a cold sweat from a nightmare. I know that sounds crazy. It's true. I bite the inside of my cheek to keep from telling him that, because I know it sounds ridiculous.

I can't help reading them upside down as Cill skims the entries. I never truly thought I'd get to experience this moment. There was always a chance I wouldn't see his eyes moving over the page and his hands holding the edges of the notebook so carefully.

Sept 5

We went to get our palms read today and I remember the groove on your palm that's split. You remember how I showed you that one time? When Missy showed me how to do palm readings? I think you might have believed her, even if you pretended to be skeptical. I miss her. I miss the club. I miss you the most and I was thinking about that groove. She said that when the lifeline groove is split it means there's going to be an uncertain time. Do you remember that? Do you think that's what this is? It's only a moment that's uncertain? 'Cause if it is, I'm ready for it to end, Cill. I miss you. I miss you so fucking much. I don't know how to make it right, though. I wish I could hold your hand right now. I hope you feel it. Even if I'm too fucking chickenshit to call you or go to you … I hope you can feel me holding your hand. I love you.

Sept 6

Today was really hard. I think it's my karma. I deserve it. If I'm honest with you, I'm really struggling and I'm lonely and I don't really know what to do, Cill. I didn't get the job at Mac's Hardware. I don't know where else to apply. I don't know what to do, and I want to call you so damn bad, because I know you'd know. You always know, Cill. But if I hear your voice … I just can't. I can't do this anymore. I'm too damn sad all the time. Can't we just go back? I wish we could just go back and we'd never gone to the club that night. I wish the car had broken down. I wish a storm had flooded the street.

I hate the club. I hate what they did to you. I hate my father. I hate them all. All but you and Reed.

My eyes are ripped from the page as Cill speaks and closes the note-book. It's only then that I realize the emotion in his gaze.

"They should have taken care of you." His voice is deathly low.

Before I can even speak, the breath stolen from my lungs, he continues, "I went away, taking the fall for them and they knew who you were to me."

"Cill—" I start to argue that they did in a way. For a moment they pretended at least, but he cuts me off.

"No, you weren't okay and where the fuck were they?"

"Reed was—" I swallow the words and instead place both palms on Cill's chest as he drops the notebooks to the counter. It takes everything I have to steady my breathing.

"We'll go," Cill states. "The two of us."

"What?" I whisper.

"The clubhouse. It's time for you to go back."

"Things changed when you went away." My voice shakes a little. Lots of things have changed. One that's irrefutable is that I left that world. I don't belong there anymore.

"I said we're going."

"Cill—" Anxiousness overwhelms me. "I don't—"

"Do you work today?" he questions.

"No." I shake my head with the whispered word.

"Good," he says with finality, tapping the notebooks on the counter once before turning his back to me and heading toward the stairs, both books still firmly in his grip. "Get dressed. We're going."

Chapter 8

Cillian

WHICH HAPPENED FIRST, SHE LEFT ME OR THE CLUB LEFT *her to fend for herself?*

My text goes unanswered. Reed saw it, though; it's marked as seen. He's my best friend. Betrayal ran deep during the drive over as I constantly checked to be sure he hadn't responded. I grew up in the life of loyalty and family.

Where the fuck was that for me? Where was it for Kat? She's not the one who betrayed the club. We were kids at best. My father's words scream at me as I recall that night.

He begged me to run, to be anywhere but on the scene when the cops arrived. I should have listened to my old man. Regret is a bitch but betrayal … it's unforgivable in this world.

The entire way to the club, Kat was silent and if I pressed a subject, she'd only give me one-word answers. She was too busy picking at the sleeves of her burgundy sweater and a hole in her torn skinny jeans. She was too busy avoiding me and the conversation.

My leather jacket was laid in the back seat of her car and I left it there.

Being home is nothing like I thought it would be. There's a constant anxiousness that has me on edge. Even as I drove Kat's car, taking her back here to the club, I struggled with reaching out to hold her hand.

There's a part of me that's dead and gone. And a part that's mourning what used to be. More than anything I want it back, but as her pace slows with us nearing the club, I question what it used to be. What loyalty meant and whether or not it ever existed.

It hit hard when Kat asked if we were taking my bike.

The dreams of her on the back of my bike carried me through hell and yet, I couldn't bring myself to do it. Not for this.

None of this feels right. It's not what I was told it was. It's as if I've been living a lie. It's eerie as I slip my fingers through her hand and walk through the same door that led to our end four years ago.

"Cillian?" My name on Kat's lips holds fear, insecurity and the threat of her turning around and leaving me as I push open the door.

She pulls back, her boots stumbling in the gravel and her hand leaving mine.

"Don't you dare leave me," I say and the words leave me before I'm able to stop them. With my pulse pounding in my ears, I tell her with a gravelly tone, "You are mine."

Her hazel eyes peer back with more concern than I anticipated, more fear, like it'll kill her to go back to what used to be our home, our haven, the place of nearly all our firsts. "Cill, please," she begs me in a whisper, and it's my undoing.

With one hand wrapping under her thigh and the other on her waist, I lift her up in a swift movement and brace her back against the wall, capturing her lips and reminding her who she belongs to. Even if neither of us will say it out loud. I love her. I need her.

And this hell the club put her through? Seeing her write that she hated the club and feeling deep down that I do too? I can't fucking stand it.

It only takes my lips on hers for my little hellcat to mold her lips to mine. To part the seam of them and grant me entry. Although I'm hard with my kiss at first, my touch softens, her body heats and soft moans pour from her like they used to.

It's only once I'm satisfied she won't run that I pull back and stare into the haze of emotions in her gorgeous eyes.

"The club had no right to leave you." All I keep thinking today, the one thought that won't stop demanding to be heard, is that she would have stayed with me if only they did what the club stands for. If only they'd protected her. She was more mine than she was her father's daughter. She was supposed to be my wife, my everything. "They should have stayed by you until I was out."

A concoction of emotion swirls in her green and gold eyes that I can't place. "I don't know that that's true."

"I do." There's not a second of hesitation. "They knew what you meant to me. Every single one of them." They knew I was going to propose. They all fucking knew. "And that's enough. Do you hear me?"

She nods, swallowing thickly as I slowly lower her to stand on her own, her back still against the old brick wall of the club.

"They need to accept you because you're mine," I tell her firmly and the lack of her denying that is what fuels me to say and do whatever the fuck I have to in order to make this right.

"I am," she murmurs, her gaze still captured in mine.

This time when I gather her hand, she holds it back, walking beside me as I push open the door and lead the way past the garage and upstairs to the rec room.

"Cillian?" my uncle calls out when he first sees me. Standing by the pool table, a whiskey glass in hand, there's not a billiard ball in sight because some kind of plans are laid out on the table. He's quick to gather them, as if they're not for me to see. "You're early," he adds, his voice dropping and his gaze lowering to land on Kat. His nondescript tee and worn jeans are at odds with how I remember this place. It feels empty and cold.

"And you brought company," he states and his voice drops even lower.

Heat blazes across my skin. "Yeah, church isn't for another hour," Finn calls out from the other side of the room. Unlike my uncle, Finn's got his leathers on as well as a pair of reading glasses and a yellow legal pad.

"We're just going over the numbers, something's off," Finn adds, his Irish accent thick, and then sets the pad down on the kitchen counter. It's all the same in this place. The same but older; less thrilling, less wanting.

Is that what they're doing? The fucking accounting?

"Where is everyone?" I call out. It's Sunday so the garage is closed, but this place … it was never empty. There was always someone here. Footsteps echo down from the stairwell to my right in the narrow hall, the one that leads to the third floor. They're fast paced and light, and it doesn't take long for Reed to come into view.

His expression not at all surprised, and very much carrying the guilt of what my last message said to him.

"You should probably wait for church to start …" My uncle's voice gathers my attention, "… so you can find your place."

My teeth grind as I take a step forward, Kat protesting slightly as I pull her in behind me.

"You get my message?" I question Reed, who stalks in after us, carefully following.

"Yeah, I got it," he answers, his glance moving between myself and Kat. They share a look and it's one I don't fucking like.

"Maybe we should go?" Kat asks as I walk to the right of the hall. To the left is the pool table, the television and a sofa which is new and takes up the depth of the room. To the right is the kitchen and before that, the dinner table.

Ignoring Kat, I count the seats and then glance up at my uncle to say, "How many are coming to dinner?"

"Cill—" Kat starts, raising a hand but Reed stops her, murmuring softly, "It's okay." I don't have time to react to them as my uncle answers, "The same as always. Ten."

"We'll need to make that eleven," I state and then stalk to the back where two armchairs with old rubbed leather are seated under the windows.

Snatching one of them, I drag it across the room to make eleven chairs around the table. "I hadn't realized Kat stopped coming, but that mistake has been rectified," I call out across the empty room. It's maybe fifty feet from my uncle to me, but there's not a damn thing that separates the tension.

In only hours all the patched men will be upstairs in the office for church and after that, it's Sunday dinner with all our families. Or that's how it used to be.

Ten.

The number is so damn low.

When did the club dwindle to that? It's not until the legs of the chair are under the table that it hits me. There used to be nine in church alone.

What the fuck happened?

"I can go," Kat speaks and Reed silently watches her.

"You're not going."

As she stares back at me wide eyed and Reed glances between the two of us, the only thing that races through my mind is that I should be the one leading church. I was lined up to be president.

"We need to talk," I announce to my uncle and he's silent, his deep brown eyes boring into mine. I add, "When are we talking?"

"With her here?" the prick dares to question.

Agitation wars with my common sense and anger bristles within me.

"Cillian, calm down." Kat's voice is meek, so unlike her.

"Calm down, man. Let's talk," Reed adds. All the while, my uncle only watches. Finn does the same although it's different. Finn has the decency to look confused and lost. His hands raise and he asks what's going on. He doesn't know what's wrong and that's obvious.

My uncle does, though.

"I left and you turned your back on her," I say, then look my best friend in the eye and he stares back at me like I've sucker punched him.

"It's not like that, and you know it."

Just as I make my move toward Reed there's a crash downstairs from the door being thrown wide open and a deep voice I don't recognize bellows, "We have a warrant to search the premises!" The stairwell of this old place is narrow and the four cops who climb the stairs show one by one, guns pulled and at the ready. Three men, one woman, and none of them look friendly to me.

My heart pounds as I take them in, knowing full damn well I'm on probation and that there's a gun in the waistline of my pants.

Fuck, fuck, fuck.

"What the fuck?" Finn roars from behind me, and Reed takes Kat by the shoulders, pulling her back as the cops enter. Two continue up the stairs and two stand in the doorway as we each raise our hands in the air.

"We're unarmed," Finn tells the two male officers at the same time the pres questions, "Warrant for what, exactly?"

I can't stop staring at Kat. I'm about to lose her again. In the same goddamn place I did years ago, and she didn't want to come in here. She didn't want to do it.

Fuck, I fucking hate myself. Heat flows over my skin. Reed's look of shock must match my own.

Poor Kat stares up at me as I walk quietly to her with eyes full of terror that dart to my waistline. She knows all too well I never leave unarmed.

You never know, in this life, when you might need it. Especially when you're fresh out of prison with blood on your hands.

After a round of clears the officers lower their weapons. The two upstairs slowly make their way down.

Uncle Eamon holds an expression of near annoyance. "The fuck is this?" he asks and snatches the warrant from the tallest of officers who holds it out. They're all dressed in their blues and make their way in just as Kat backs up and presses her back into my chest, like she can hide me from them.

My poor hellcat. Regret won't let go of me as it continues to bury itself deep down.

With both of my hands steadying her shoulders, I'm prepared to tell her I love her and I'm sorry. To whisper it into her ear as the officers ask for identification for each of us and Finn argues that we don't have to give them that.

Instead I'm met with her hand, reaching up my back and then into my waistband. I struggle to keep a straight face as she takes the gun.

"Unless the warrant—"

"It's a search and seizure and includes the persons of any Cavanaugh East club members who are on the premises," the cop who seems to be leading the pack announces clear enough for all of us to hear. Kat quietly slips the gun into her purse and stills, with the top flap of it open as the officers approach us.

"I assume that includes everyone here?" he questions, taking a moment to look each one of us in the eye.

"You're his son, aren't you?" the officer asks me, the skin between his eyebrows wrinkling as he narrows his eyes at me.

"Who do you mean?" *His son.* Anger boils inside of me, this prick bringing up my father when he's long gone.

"The founder of the club, Ronan Cavanaugh."

"Yeah, I'm his son."

"I figured, you look just like him." His gaze moves to Kat and every muscle in my body tightens. "And you?"

"She's my girlfriend. I don't imagine the warrant includes who we're fucking, does it?" I ask as I lay a hand on her shoulders, moving closer, and closing the flap at the same time as I step forward to muffle the noise.

"I'll start with you then?" the officer says. He's got a hard jaw and a clean shave, unlike his partner, whose beard is neatly trimmed and who calls over Reed. Reed stands with his arms out and we both allow the officers to do their job. All the while I watch Reed, who keeps looking at my uncle, who's waiting his turn for the pat down as the other officers search this floor of the club.

With my own hands held out, the officer frisks me, then grabs my wallet and calls in my ID. I know he can't arrest me; I don't have shit on me, but I don't know what the hell is in the club. There shouldn't be a damn thing here.

As if reading my mind, Reed glances up at me and shakes his head, letting me know we're safe as the officer calls in our names, asking if there are any warrants for arrest. Fucking prick.

"There's nothing here," Finn states as he takes the paper from the pres and then flicks it. "Fucking harassment from the DA. Search whatever the fuck you'd like, then get the hell out."

Although the three of us are silent, Finn doesn't let it go. "The hell is this about, anyway?"

"We received an anonymous tip," the lone woman officer answers, standing in the doorway. Her makeup is minimal, her hair pulled back into a tight bun at the base of her neck.

I don't recognize any of these faces. Not from growing up, when I had plenty of run-ins with the law. And not from that fucking night four years ago.

It doesn't take long for the officer to hand back my wallet and ID.

"You okay?" Kat whispers, breaking up my thoughts. Her arm wraps around my waist as she presses herself into me, her grip tight like she refuses to let me go.

"There's nothing here, Daniels," an officer speaks across the room to the head officer in charge. His voice is low and I can't help but note that it was damn fast that they searched. It's almost like they were told where to look. And whatever it was, wasn't there.

"Keep looking." The officer lets out a long exhale, giving out more commands. It's quiet as we stand in silence, watching the men of the law make chaos of the rec room, searching through every cabinet, ripping up every cushion. They don't leave any inch unturned.

"Church is canceled until further notice," the pres, my uncle, says beneath his breath, his eyes focused on the officer leading the charge, Daniels.

"Yeah," Finn confirms as the rev of motorcycle engines can be heard pulling up to the garage.

Reed's busy texting away, most likely warning whoever it is who showed up at the same time an officer takes the stairs down two by two.

Chapter 9

THE KETTLE WHISTLES ANGRILY AND EVEN AS I HEAR IT, I DON'T. The heavy feel of that gun in my hand consumes my thoughts until I snap out of it. It's been hours, but the tension lingers.

It always seems like a good idea to go back to the kitchen. You can count on things there. Even when life seems unstable, most kitchens have the basics. A sink, a countertop, and a humming fridge. That's where I go when we get back to the house. It helps that there's usually alcohol in the kitchen too.

It's been silent between us since we left. Apart from him kissing my hair and the occasional touches, he hasn't done anything but think. I can practically see the thoughts that wind in his head.

There's a rat. Someone tipped them off and I don't know what exactly the tip was, but I know I could have lost Cill again. All over a fucking gun. All over the fucking club.

Biting down on my lip, I check my phone again.

He didn't say a word to Reed and neither did I when the cops said we were free to leave, much to their chagrin after hours of searching. The expression on Reed's face haunts me and the fact that he didn't respond to my text only makes me worry more.

All I asked him was if he was okay. I know he saw the text, but he hasn't answered.

As I pour the boiling water into the mug, eager for a cup of mint tea to calm my nerves, Cill gets up abruptly, leaving the wooden legs of the kitchen chair to scratch against the floor as he does. He goes upstairs, his footsteps heavy.

"You all right?" I call after him.

"Fine, I'll be back," he answers.

His footsteps keep going. I listen to every one of them. My chest is tight with emotion. He's anything but fine. All of this is fucked. Hating all of it, every last bit of today, I lean against the counter next to the stove and pull out my phone to text Lydia.

> **Kat: We went to the club. There was a raid.**

She texts back right away. Thank God.

> **Lydia: Oh my god. The cops came?**

> **Kat: Yeah.**

> **Lydia: Are you guys okay? What the hell happened.**

> **Kat: Yeah. As good as we can be. I almost tell her wrong place, wrong time jokingly, but I can't do it. I can't make light of what happened.**

The cops came, and this time, they didn't take Cill.

> **Kat: It all feels like a lie.**

> **Lydia: What lie?**

> **Kat: That it was ever safe. That I ever belonged. That I was ever a part of it, a real part. I thought Cill was part of it too. I never thought they'd let him take the fall like that.**

With a shaky hand, I put down my phone and breathe deep. The tea is next. I focus on it even as the phone beeps with another text. I harbor so much anger toward all of them. Even to his father who's long gone. Cill never should have taken the fall.

Inhaling the calming tea, I pray for all of them to get what they deserve. After a moment, I'm able to check my phone again.

> **Lydia: I never thought it was right.**

I'm too wrapped up in my thoughts to hear Cill come back down, so he's able to catch me off guard as his arms fold around me the next second.

"Hey, Hellcat." His tone is calmer than it's been all day, which instantly soothes me. It doesn't go unnoticed that we were tense around each other earlier, but after what happened at Cavanaugh Crest, he hasn't stopped touching me.

I couldn't be more grateful. I need him to be steady for me.

"You okay?"

"No," I admit. The back of my throat is tight. I'm not on the verge of breaking down, but I'm angry. "There's so much that's just fucking wrong." The bitterness lingers after the words are spoken. A part of me expects him to deny the reality, like my father used to do, but he doesn't and that's all the more shocking.

"I know," he answers in a whisper. He adds, "I'm going to make it all right. I promise," and I wish he wouldn't.

How could he promise such a thing? It's all fucked. I catch my bottom lip between my teeth before it trembles and Cill looks me in the eye, the comfort changing to something else. Something darker and something more sinful.

"You're going to need a safe word, Kat."

My head tilts immediately to the floor, thinking of the phrase my father gave me and hating it, hating him. The rage is instantly subdued as Cill grabs my chin between his thumb and forefinger, bringing my attention back to him as he tells me, "So when I whip your ass for taking my gun, I'll know if I'm going too hard on you."

"Cillian," I murmur, my eyes widening with shock but my body heating with anticipation.

"Word, my little hellcat," he commands, his voice still soothing even as the threat of punishment looms.

"Mulberry," I speak without thinking. Mulberry is the street where an old pizzeria used to sit on the corner. Cillian first "punished" me behind that pizzeria.

It wasn't much of a punishment if you ask me, getting fucked raw while he played with my ass. A tingle heats my skin at the memory.

He smirks at the word, maybe knowing exactly why I picked it, but it falls as quickly as it came to grace his lips. "You aren't going to do that again, do you understand?"

"Yes." Although the answer is instant, my internal agreement is not. For him, I'd do it all again. If I can protect him in any way, I will.

There's no way I could stand by and watch like I did before. I couldn't live with myself if I did.

"I mean it, Kat," he murmurs and I wonder if he knows what I'm thinking. "If they took you away, I … I don't know what I would do." His voice is tight with emotion.

Cill holds me tighter and kisses my cheek, then my lips. It's far softer than he's been with me since he's come home.

As he pulls me in closer, my front to his, I can feel how hard he is. It ignites every nerve ending instantly.

"Being apart from you has been hell," he murmurs against my lips before kissing me again. My hands slip up his shirt to his bare shoulders, eager to touch him.

He lets his hands roam over my body, and when I don't pull away, he starts pulling at my clothes. One by one he strips them off until I'm naked. The chill of the air dancing along my skin as if it's part of the foreplay.

"Stay facing the counter," he says, his hands reaching down to unbuckle his belt.

I obey, the warmth between my thighs clenching with a new heat and desire.

In the reflection of the kitchen window, which thankfully faces an empty field that leads to woods so it's all shades of dark moss and sage, I watch as he pulls his shirt over his head, his muscles rippling. Then he steps closer to me again and arranges my hands on the sides of the counter.

The leather of his belt sings as it's pulled through the loops of his jeans. A shiver rolls down my shoulders and it's immediately halted by Cill's strong grip. His thumb travels in a soothing stroke up to the base of my neck and back down with each word.

"If I ever scare you, I want you to tell me."

His somber tone is unexpected, given the predicament.

"I'm not scared of you, I'm scared of …" I start to say as his expression reaches mine in the reflection, "… losing you, but also everything that comes with being with you again."

"But you are with me."

"Yes," I answer eagerly. It's only then that I realize how deeply I mean it. Even if he doesn't know what happened. Maybe I'll never have to tell him. It doesn't matter, does it? If I love him like this. If I'm willing to do whatever he wants?

"Good because I can't lose you again," he says and then his head falls to the crook of my neck. His grip on my shoulder loosens as he plants a kiss on the tender spot below my ear. My eyes close and my nipples pebble as he drags the edge of the leather down the curve of my side.

"Then don't leave me," I beg him.

"I won't leave you, so long as you don't leave me."

"I won't. I promise," I tell him in a desperate rush.

Brushing my hair to the side, he kisses my neck and whispers, "That's my good girl" before pulling back, leaving only his left hand gripping my shoulder.

"You need to obey, though, my little hellcat," he says as his tone darkens and I nod, knowing what's coming.

"Count to three for me," he says and before I can agree, the first lash lands across my ass.

I hiss in a breath, seething as he massages the mark with the palm of his hand, kneading my heated flesh.

"Count," he reminds me, his lips at my ear and then he kisses my cheek as I breathe out the word, "One."

"Good girl."

Two and three come back-to-back, leaving my lips parted as the stinging pain makes my toes curl. Before I can even exhale, his fingers find my clit and he rubs ruthless circles.

"Two and three," I murmur as I bend over the sink, holding on to it to keep me upright.

"Good girl," he says, complimenting me again in that deep, soothing tone of his.

I love it. I love this.

Cill eases my feet apart with one of his and strokes between my legs. Ruthlessly and demanding my desire. As I moan, his left hand grips the globe of my ass, bringing a heated sensation of pain that heightens the pleasure.

With my teeth sinking into my bottom lip, I give in to the need to mewl as the waves threaten to crash around me, drowning me in the sinful need.

The sensation pulls tight in the pit of my stomach and then rages outward, paralyzing me and all the while, Cill plays with my body, kissing along my exposed neck and plucking my nipples at a whim.

Once my orgasm has peaked, he pulls my hips toward him so that he can angle himself to my opening and push inside. I let out another soft moan, reaching for something to grip as he fucks me deeply and without mercy.

"Damn, you feel like fucking heaven," he says low into my ear. "You feel just like I remember. My first and only."

His words force me to tense. I'm not how I always was. And he's no longer my only. Cill's not the only one I've been with. I wish we'd had the kind of life where we could have stayed together. I wish I wasn't carrying around this guilt. He fucks me with even strokes while that horrible guilt fills up my lungs.

"It's all right, Hellcat," he says like he already knows.

My voice is thick with unspoken secrets. "I don't know if it is, Cill." Does he know? Please, let him know. Let him know and still love me regardless. *Please still love me.*

He doesn't stop. Instead he reaches around in front of me and circles my clit with a fingertip.

"You can tell me whatever you want," he says gruffly.

Pleasure builds between my legs. My head thrashes with the undeniable heat.

"How am I supposed to tell you things if—if they'll ruin this moment?"

He takes a deep breath and lets it out, pulling nearly all the way out and then slamming back into me, my hips butting against the edge of the counter, nearly bruising.

"I'm inside you," he says finally. "It's where I wanted to be every goddamn day for the last four years. You can tell me whatever the fuck you want, and it won't ruin a damn thing." He doesn't stop and the pleasure doesn't let up. Neither does the burning secret begging to spill from me.

He thrusts into me slowly as he tells me, "I want you and I'll never stop wanting you."

Kisses greet my side, his hands roaming along my sensitized skin. It's all too much. His touch is gentle and it strips down the boundaries I've been holding around myself. I can't tell him the whole story. I'm not ready, and neither is he.

"I'll ask you questions," he says, stroking in and out of me steadily. "How about that?"

I'm barely able to utter a word, but I agree, nodding my head as the pleasure rises. He grips my ass as he thrusts in deeper and harder.

"How many men were you with while I was away?" he questions and my eyes open wide, my heart thumping in fear of being torn to shreds. "Don't lie to me, Hellcat."

Only a moment passes. All the while, he keeps up his pace. With my breath unsteady I answer him. "One," I say.

He swallows hard, so hard I can hear it, and I think he might drop it until he asks, "Did he treat you right?"

Every thrust forces my hips to hit the counter and heat engulfs me as I nod.

"I'm sorry," I say, the tears falling, the pleasure and the pain intertwined. "I'm sorry, Cill."

He pulls out of me and I almost crumple across the countertop. *No. No, please. Don't leave me.* The words are trapped at the back of my throat, and they're kept there by Cill's bruising kiss. He turns me to face him and lifts me up to perch on the edge of the counter. Then he thrusts himself inside of me and braces my back with his forearms as he fucks me like he always has. Possessively and with a passion that's undeniable.

I bury my head in the crook of his neck, my warm breath suffocating me as I realize what I've just told him.

"Look at me, Hellcat."

Sharp blue eyes pierce through me and hold me in place as he takes from me. It's a punishing fuck, hard and deep.

All the while, I struggle between the push and pull of pleasure and pain, praying he doesn't ask me who.

Chapter Ten

Cillian

S HE HAS A WAY OF CALMING ME. I SWEAR TO GOD THE LAST year in that hell was unbearable because she left me. Every time I think back on it all I know is that my father passed, we had an argument and then things changed.

Staring down at the texts from Reed, that began last night until this morning, I know I should be focused on the club, but I want answers from my hellcat.

Why is she so fucking scared now, walking into the club like she doesn't belong?

What happened—what really fucking happened that drove her away? Was it me? Or was it something else … was it someone else?

Reed (7:14 pm): You two all right?

Reed (8:09 pm): The police just came knocking now.

Reed (8:10 pm): They haven't stopped since you left. Every couple of months there's something.

Reed (10:26 pm): Can we talk?

Reed (10:47 pm): Can you at least let me know that you're still fucking alive and they didn't arrest you again?

Reed (11:14 pm): I just drove by her place and talked to Lydia. Look, I'm sorry. When your pops left, and Eamon took over, things changed. In a lot of ways and I wish they didn't but we have to talk.

Reed (9:15 am): I think there's a rat. I think whoever it is either wants you back in jail or they were after me this time. I was moving supplies when you came in. I only put it back and stopped because I heard your voice downstairs. If you hadn't come just then, I would've been holding it. I wouldn't have had a chance to hide the shit.

Cillian (9:15 am): Delete that shit right now.

Reed (9:16 am): Then let me come over. Fucking talk to me.

Cillian (9:18 am): Come over

The rustling by the sink brings my attention up to Kat. The morning light kisses her face through the kitchen window as she rinses off the pan. Her hips sway as she dries it. I must be addicted to her, because even with the world crashing down around us, all I want to do is lay her on the table and fuck her until she comes undone with my name on her lips.

"Reed's coming over," I speak out loud, if for no other reason than one of us will know we have company soon and I can't strip her down unless we want to get caught.

Her hair falls down her shoulder, exposing the thin strap to her satin nightie. "Right now?" she questions in a breathy voice and it's only then I realize she may want to change. The fabric is thin and as my gaze drops to her chest, I note her nipples are pebbled.

"Yeah, you may want to change," I comment as I lift the cup of coffee to my lips. I'm not given a chance to take a sip, though.

The knock at the front door is followed immediately with him opening it. "It's me," he calls out before shutting it. We can only hear him as I answer that we're in the kitchen.

When he comes into view, it's obvious he didn't sleep for shit. His clothes are rumpled and the bags under his eyes add to the pathetic demeanor. The sight of him is exactly what women must see when they say he looks like a lost puppy.

"Hey." Reed's greeting is complete with a nervous swallow. My entire body tenses but I tell him hey in return. I don't know if the man standing in front of me is my best friend or a fucking traitor.

He glances at Kat and respectfully averts his gaze to me, leaving her standing in the corner of the kitchen as he takes the closest seat which puts him straight across from me at the table and her at his left.

"You want coffee?" Kat asks and Reed nods, his gaze focused on the wilting flowers in the center of the table. With a deep breath in he gets right to the point. "It had to be a setup."

"Who? Who would have even known I was heading in?"

"It could have been me they were setting up," Reed offers but then hesitantly looks over his shoulder at Kat, still standing in the corner of the kitchen by the sink. Watching silently.

"Back when Missy—"

"Don't bring up her name," I say, cutting him off as my voice drops deathly low. Just the mention of Missy, a woman who was like a second mother to me, the woman who kept the club together and then ratted, makes my blood boil.

Reed is silent, staring back at me like he has something to say. He doesn't say a word, though. "Who could be the leak? Who's the rat now?"

"They're saying it's Kat, but I don't think it is."

"Who the fuck is saying it's her?"

"Me?" Kat's tone echoes both disbelief and fear. "I wouldn't dare," she says, barely getting out the choked words.

"Who the fuck said it's Kat?" I say harsher, slamming my fist down to get their attention.

Reed looks me dead in the eye when he tells me, "Your uncle."

"Fucking hell," I say, gritting the words between clenched teeth. Everything runs cold and I look up at Kat to find her expression fallen and true fear in her gorgeous eyes.

"I'll kill them before they think to say that shit again ... let alone touch you."

"It's not her," Reed says and then glances up at Kat to add, "I know it's not you. We all know you wouldn't."

"Then why the fuck was her name even mentioned?" The cords in Reed's throat tighten as he swallows. "Is it because of her father?" I ask, my anger barely contained. Before I can help myself, before Reed can even answer, my decision to go back there is final. Leaning over the table, I stare down Reed and ask, "How did you let this happen?"

"I think maybe you should calm—"

As my fist slams down on the table, I can feel the rage boiling. I've always had anger issues, my pops used to say I was temperamental. Prison only made that worse.

"They turned their backs on her the moment I left." I still have the ring I was going to give her. The memory of it only makes the pain worse. "It's a betrayal and it needs to be dealt with."

"Cill, it's—"

"We're going back," I say and my tone holds no room for negotiation as I meet each of their gazes. It doesn't escape me that there's worry buried inside each of them. When did conversations about the club get met with fear? "We're going back." It takes everything in me to keep my voice calm and lower it to add, "We're going to do another vote and I'm going to put it all back to the way it was."

Even as the words leave me, I know it'll never be what it once was. If that's what I want, the family the club used to be, I might as well start over.

That very thought echoes in Reed's eyes.

"They don't want me in there and that's fine. But I would never—" Seeing my hellcat give in, seeing her cower under the idea of going back … I fucking lose it.

"It's not fine! Who the fuck said they don't want you there? My uncle?"

"Calm down, Cillian."

"It's my fucking club," I scream, my muscles coiling.

"My father's," I add and my voice splits with emotion I have no fucking intention of dealing with. "I should have been there," I shout, each word emphasized with the slamming of my fist.

"How could they make you feel like you weren't welcome?" I say and stare down Kat, my everything. Her eyes are glossy and I can't fucking take it.

"Reed, how could you let this happen!" I'm met with nothing but silence, both of them staring at me like they would a wild, uncaged animal. "I should fucking kill him …"

"No one's killing anyone right now, Cill. Man, you just got out," Reed points out, attempting to temper my anger.

"I need you to calm down so I can tell you—" Kat does the same, although she doesn't finish.

"Tell me what?"

"When I … when we stopped …" My hellcat grips the counter as if she needs it to hold her up. "I was with someone and your uncle found out, and that's why."

"So fucking what? So what if you slept with someone. That's between us. It's none of his fucking business." I don't care that she fucked someone. I care that he wasn't good enough to keep her and that she's mine now. That's all that matters. My uncle can go to hell if he doesn't like it.

"Cill … it's who."

"Who? Who was it?"

"I think you should calm down," Reed offers, no longer sitting as he steps away from the table.

"I have to tell him. I have to, Reed," she says and Kat's shoulders crumple on his name. What the fuck is going on.

Who could make her break down? My hellcat. I only survived that first year because of her. What the hell is going on?

"Cillian, just sit down, man." Reed glances to Kat, his agony in her pain … I finally put two and two together.

It's a bullet to the chest. Shocking and paralyzing as I realize it was Reed.

"Was it you?" I manage, the words sounding heavy and deep as the room blurs and all I can see is my best friend's face.

"You fucked her and dropped her," I speak the reality out loud. It was him … and he let the club drop her? He let her turn into this weak version who's more afraid than I've ever seen her.

"You did this to her?" My body's heavy as I stand, the legs of the chair scraping against the floor as I straighten my back.

"No, it wasn't like that," Reed insists, taking a hesitant step away from both Kat and myself.

Kat's apologies are drowned out by him telling me to calm down.

"You fucked her?" I ask although they've already admitted it. Denial and betrayal bring my hand to form a fist, the skin across my knuckles stretched so tight they turn white.

With a single glance down, Reed's hands fall to his side, resigned to the fact he's about to get the karma he's had coming.

I get one in, one solid punch before he yells out something incoher-ent and as I go in for another, purely fueled by rage, he slams his fist into my jaw, the crack and blister of pain barely registers.

Just like I can hardly hear Kat's scream.

Kat

"You don't understand. It wasn't like that," Reed tries to explain as if Cill's in any state to listen.

"She was mine! Mine and you were supposed to protect her."

I beg him, "You're scaring me Cillian, please! Please! Stop!" I can't get out the words: they have to stop yelling.

The cops can't come.

"Stop," I cry out, watching the two of them barreling their fists at each other's faces. Reed throws his weight into Cillian and the two of them slam into the kitchen table. It gives instantly, splintering between the two of them as they crash onto the floor.

Make it stop.

"Please! Cillian, let go!" Reed's attempt to back away is denied. Cillian's hell-bent on getting his anger out and as much as I can't blame him, I can't let it happen.

He can't go to jail.

"Please, Cillian," I cry out again and as they scream at each other, their voices getting louder and louder, I act without thinking. My body wraps around Cillian's back, my arms over his shoulders and my legs around his waist, my face buried in his neck.

Everything is hot and turmoil rages inside of me as I beg him to stop, knowing it's all my fault. I did this.

"Off me, Kat! Get off before you get hurt!"

"Run, Reed!"

Cillian's hands wrap around my arms as he grits between his teeth, "Off, Kat. Get off before you get hurt."

It's enough time to give Reed the chance to get out of the rubble and the moment I see his feet steady on the ground I yell out for him to leave. "Get out! Go!"

Cill attempts to stand but my weight throws him off and he staggers back, falling and my shoulder bashes against the cabinet.

"You're protecting Reed!" Incredulity is clear in his voice and for the first time in my life, I'm afraid of him.

"Please! Please! Mulberry." My world spins and my body trembles pressed tightly against Cillian's hard body. "Mulberry," I whisper again and hate myself. "Please, Cillian. Please."

"Let go of me, Kat." His voice is lowered as the front door shuts. But I can't let go yet. I have to give Reed time. Unable to speak, I shake my head.

"I need you to let me go." Betrayal sinks into his words.

"I can't, Cillian. Please. Please just … I can't."

Chapter 11

Kat

MY HANDS WON'T STOP SHAKING, NOT EVEN AS I CLEAN UP the chunks of glass and the shards of ceramic from the debris left behind from Reed and Cill's fight.

The table's broken and Cill's face is already bruised on the right side across his sharp jawline. Tears spill silently as I clean up the mess, attempting any semblance of sanity.

"I'm sorry," I repeat in a whisper as I pull my legs into my chest, leaning against the counter and feeling the cold against my heated cheek.

Everything happened too quickly, far too quickly and it's at odds with how slow and long the last four years have been.

More importantly, everything is broken. It was always the three of us and when Cill went away, time shredded any chance of us staying the same.

Cill's hands run through his hair as he paces in the threshold.

I'm grateful Reed's gone and they've stopped. I'm grateful Cill knows because he needed to. And that's all I'm grateful for.

I wish I would fucking die right now. Truly, watching the pain Cill's in, I pray for death as I choke on my sobs and apologies.

"I need to ride," he says and I can only nod.

I swallow thickly and agree with him. "Okay," I manage and then the selfish part of me spills out when I say, "Promise me you'll come home."

"You still love me?" he questions as he stands by the broken table, towering over me as I'm on my knees and it's torture that he has to ask.

I did this. I deserve to feel this hell that rages inside of me. The turmoil causes my cheeks to burn.

"Come with me now."

"Cill?"

"I can't stay here. You fucked him here, didn't you?" His words slap across my face and all I can do is nod.

"I don't want my bike right now," he decides, his tone holding no negotiation. "Put on your clothes and get in the car."

I can barely look him in the eye as I push up off the ground and brush past him to get clothes, but he grips me first. His hand lands on my arm and pushes me against the wall.

My back hits the threshold and before I can object, before I can do anything but gasp, his lips are on mine.

My body's reaction is instant, holding him back for dear life. My pulse races and my blood heats.

His kiss is possessive, harsh and brutal. But it's him. He kisses me and I savor it, in case it's the last.

When he stops, he doesn't move anything but his lips away from mine and I stand there breathless and waiting for judgment.

His gaze moves to my shoulder, where there's a small scrape when he asks, "Are you all right?"

Nodding gently, ever so gently so he doesn't move, so he doesn't let me go, I tell him, "I'm fine."

With his forehead pressed against mine he whispers, "Get dressed. Now."

I do as I'm told, quickly dressing to make myself presentable. All the while my thoughts race, the regrets and the raging emotion.

My heart pounds as I make my way downstairs to a waiting Cillian. He gets in my way when I try to take the keys. He doesn't say anything, just pushes past me and gets into the driver's seat.

A minute later we're speeding down the street away from the city and thankfully the opposite direction of the club and Reed's place.

All the while, I glance at a brokenhearted Cillian, hating that I put that scowl on his face. Hating the bruise that's already marred his stubbled jaw. He barely looks at me and I struggle to speak. To tell him how much pain I was in. How it was a mistake … but how I fell in love with Reed and needed him.

How I ended it because it was wrong. I ended it with Reed. I ended it with Cillian too.

Cill makes a right, then a left. My heart pumps adrenaline throughout my body. I want to believe it'll turn out okay, but I haven't felt this scared since Cill was arrested.

A gas station comes up on our right. The lights above the pumps are blinding against the night sky.

The corner of the street is nearly dead this time of night. A tire store on one end is closed although the parking lot is packed with the cars of men who are a block down at the strip joint. On the other side is a gas station and the corner store. It's a bit run down but that's the way it is in this city. The lower down the hill, the worse the condition. As you drive up the hill and the blocks go from Twentieth Street up to First Street, the houses are nicer, the parks cleaner.

I think it's the way all old cities are.

"No fucking way," says Cill under his breath. His tone alerts me that something's wrong.

I turn my head and see the parked car. *Fuck. No.*

Before I can stop him Cill pulls over, the brakes screeching. We're facing the wrong direction on the road.

"Please," I cry out, "Cillian, don't!" It's like fate set him up. "He's not worth it," I say as Cill finally stops nose to nose with the parked car. My heart races.

No, no. Please, Cillian. Tears prick at the corners of my eyes.

He's angry and right in front of us is an object of his hatred. Duncan Tray. The fucker who tried to take advantage the moment Cill was locked away and then again when his father passed.

I know the cherry red muscle car is his and as I glance from it to Cill's expression, my chest tightens with a knowing dread.

He's always been a problem for the MC. My father used to tell me to keep a lookout for him. There was a rumor in the club that he gave the police some of the information they used to arrest Cill. I'm certain Cill heard it too.

If nothing else, the guy's a creep and belongs behind bars for that in and of itself.

"Wait. Cill, stop."

He shoulders open the driver's door, leaving the keys in the ignition which sound off in a *beep, beep, beep* as Cill steps out into the street.

I take in the gas station but I don't see Duncan Tray anywhere.

"Cill, please stop," I beg him, managing to get out even though my body's numb.

He doesn't even hesitate as he opens the trunk and I beg him not to.

"I know you're upset. But please, Cill, don't do this."

His shoulders radiate angered power as he palms the tire iron.

"Cill, please …" I trail off as he closes the trunk with a thud. My vision spins and blurs with the fear of cops being called.

On the first swing, he shatters the driver's side window of the other car.

It shatters and the glass sprays.

"Get in the car, Kat," is all Cillian says before he swings for the back window. His rage has taken over his body.

Cill smashes one of the side mirrors, then the other. He's raining dents down on the body of the car. One foot stomps down on the front bumper and it collapses into the street. The windshield is next. It takes the most effort.

Holy fucking shit.

My pulse is out of control and I can't breathe.

The cops are going to come. They're going to arrest Cill, and he won't get another chance. He's on probation.

"Cill, you have to stop." I raise my voice to be heard over the sound of metal on metal. "Cill. Cillian. The cops are going to come."

He breaks through the rest of the windshield, sending shattered glass flying onto the front seat. I run to his side before he can take another swing. He puts his fist through the broken glass instead. It cuts him. "Stop," I beg him, screaming so loud the words feel as if they're ripped up my throat. "You have to stop."

Cill blinks down at me, his eyes flashing. "No."

"Yes. They're going to arrest you."

I take a big step back, then another. I can't breathe.

"I can't lose you!" I tell him and my body trembles. Glancing across the street, eyes watch us. Fuck. I force my body to move. I can't let them call the cops.

"Where the hell are you going?" He narrows his eyes. I turn around and check the street for traffic, then run across.

Cill follows me across, dropping the lug wrench with a loud clang. His face is red with anger but he's not destroying the car anymore. Not that it matters. The damage is already done.

Just as I get to the glass door, Cill puts his hand on the door and tries to keep it shut. "You're not going in there, Hellcat." Rage still has its grip on him, making him a fucking lunatic.

"Yes I am," I shoot back. I push his hand away.

He's fucking crazy if he thinks we can just drive away and no one will tell. They know who he is and who I am. I have to fix this. I push all my weight against Cillian, screaming *look what you did*, and he seems to snap out of it, only slightly. Enough that I can rip the door open, a bell chiming far too sweetly for the moment.

I have to do something. I can't let him go to jail again. I can't.

The cashier's eyes are wide as I rush up to the checkout. Cill's presence isn't helping anything. He stalks behind me, his hand bleeding. I put both hands on the countertop and swallow thickly.

"Listen to me. Please." My voice is shaken. "I need you to do something for me. I know you have security cameras. I need you to delete the last few minutes of footage. The last ten minutes. That's all I need."

"I can't do that." Her head shakes as she looks from me to Cill with genuine fear.

"It's right behind you," I say as I point and then tell her, "The guy who owns that car hurt a woman in our club years ago. Please." Hearing Cillian move behind me, I turn to see his hand run down the back of his head as he looks out of the doors.

When I look back at the cashier, a young woman, younger than me even with a high ponytail and wide eyes, I beg her, "Please."

"I don't want to get in trouble," she whispers and Cillian's tone of regret can be heard behind me, reality setting in.

"Please," I repeat.

"He went to jail for me, and he can't go back." I suck in a breath, panic setting in. We need to get out of here before Duncan Tray gets here. It's already been too long. Minutes have passed. Cops will be here soon. Fuck. Fuck.

She opens her mouth, and I just know she's not going to do it.

"Please," I beg again. "Look at me and try to understand. I just need this one thing from you, and I promise you, it'll mean the world to me. It would be everything to me if you deleted this footage."

She swallows thickly. "There are two other stores," she says hesitantly. "I'd have to call around and ask them to do the same thing."

"Do they like you?"

"What?"

"The other people at the stores. Do they like you enough to do it?"

She nods.

"Cill, give me your wallet." My hand shakes as I hold it out to him. I'm praying that nobody else walks in right now. I just need to get us both the hell out of here. Quickly.

Cill digs in his pocket and hands me his wallet. I open it and take out all the cash, sliding it across the countertop to the girl. It's a decent wad. There's got to be a few hundred there.

"Please call them," I say urgently, shoving it across the counter and glancing back at the two cars, one fucked up and then mine which still has the driver's door open. My chest heaves with my chaotic breathing.

She bites her lip and glances out at the pumps. All the while, madness bristles through me.

She disappears into the back room.

"I'm sorry, Hellcat," Cill manages the moment she's gone. My broken man stands by the doors like he knows this is the end.

"I'll fix this. I promise," I tell him with desperation although I can already feel him slipping away. His temper has always gotten the better of him.

Always.

"The last ten minutes didn't happen." I hear her before I hear the door swing open.

Relief floods through me at the same time that I hear sirens wail in the distance.

"I'll call them," she tells me as she reaches for the phone and her face pales. "The cops are going to come here. What do I tell them? The other stores are one thing, but I don't know about the cops."

I look her straight in the eye. "Tell them it was four guys in a Chevy. You got it? Four guys in a Chevy got out, wrecked the car, and drove off."

"I don't know ..."

"The club will have your back." I'm gambling huge by saying this. I'm not part of that group anymore, but I'll go back to them if I have to. "You know who I'm talking about?"

"You sure about that?" she questions, her eyes darting outside.

"I'm sure."

"Okay." She gives me a fast nod. "I got it. Go before they get here."

"Thank you," I barely get out before taking Cill's hand and tugging him toward the door.

"Fuck, Hellcat," he says, realization of what he risked in his voice. "Fuck, fuck, fuck."

"Come on." We break into a jog outside the gas station. I run around and get into the car on the driver's side. My fingernail catches on the mechanism to adjust the seat and breaks. Cill slides in next to me and I put my foot on the gas. Blue and red lights are just barely seen in the rearview mirror.

"I've got this," I say under my breath. I pull out into the street like we never parked on the wrong side of the road and gently accelerate over the next block. I stop at an intersection, then keep going. As soon as I think it's safe, I make a left turn and keep driving.

If they start looking for us, I don't want to go back to my house. My heart pounds and protests. Everything is at war inside of me. As if today could get any worse.

Headlights in the rearview mirror scare the shit out of me.

"Someone's behind us."

Cill twists around in his seat, the leather groaning as he does. "It's Reed." His voice is thick with emotion.

I'm hanging on by a thread and although I know there's tension, I need Reed. Cillian needs Reed. My words are caught in the back of my throat as I gauge Cill's expression. With an open cut on his hand, blood on his shirt and the bruise on his face, I'm torn to shreds over how broken my first love is.

For years, all I've known is that I couldn't fix anything. That life was shitty and I didn't trust myself let alone anyone else. It has to change. I have to fix this.

As I take in a steadying breath, I pull off into a public parking area that almost no one uses behind the old strip mall and park.

Cill's swallow is audible as he turns in his seat, staring ahead with a deadly glare.

Reed pulls up next to me. The seat belt clicks as I unlatch it and I take one glance at Cillian before getting out.

Reed follows my lead, and it's the first chance I have to take a good look at him. The cut on his brow is swollen and red and his left cheek sports a bruise that matches Cillian's.

Emotions storm through me. Regret and anguish most of all.

As I heave in a breath, barely standing straight, I feel ragged and shaken. I can barely believe any of the events of today have happened.

Before I can speak a word, Reed states, "You've gotta leave the car, Kat. Don't drive it anymore tonight."

"How do you—Were you following us?"

"No. I got a call from my buddy … the bodyguard at the strip joint. He saw everything but it's taken care of."

He doesn't look me in the eye and he doesn't look to Cill either. The man in front of me is a man who came out of a debt he owes.

"Are you okay?" I question, feeling the weight of it all.

He offers me a sad smile with the shake of his head, his deep brown eyes echoing a sorrow I know all too well. One of loss and regret. One that's given up but still has to move on.

"Reed—"

He cuts me off. "I'll take you wherever you need to go. Neither of you should be driving right now."

With my eyes locked on his, I wish he could feel everything I feel. I wish he knew everything I'm thinking. For a moment, it feels as if he might.

"I just want to fix this," I whisper but I doubt my words are heard over the sirens that steal our attention.

I turn around and poke my head into the car. "We're going with Reed."

"No we're fucking not," says Cill.

"We need to go to Nello's … by The Ruin," Reed speaks over me, easily heard by Cillian.

It's a restaurant that has a private back room. It's hours away, in Desolation, New York. Club members go there when they want a private conversation, or to wait out a complicated situation. It's a nice restaurant, fancy even. I certainly can't afford it on my own. That's maybe the best cover of all. People don't think members of the MC would eat at a place with white tablecloths.

"Come on, Cill," I say softly.

"We'll walk," Cill shouts out the window at Reed. "That'll be enough time to get them off our backs. We'll fucking walk there."

"You're not going to walk there like that. I saw you come out of the gas station. I know you're bleeding," Reed answers.

Cill is silent for another long moment, then he curses under his breath and gets out.

I climb into Reed's car first. Cill's still pissed, and I don't blame him. I would be furious and heartbroken. I would be a fucking wreck.

"We just need a place to calm down," Reed says. "We can talk while we're there, man."

"There's nothing you can say."

"I think there is," Reed replies. "I think there are things you need to know. Fuck, Cill. This isn't how I wanted this to play out. I sure as hell know you wanted it different. We all did. Get in the car."

Chapter 12

Reed

One year ago

WHEN I OPEN THE DOOR TO KAT'S PLACE, THE FIRST THING I notice is the broken frame in the foyer. My blood spikes with adrenaline as I search for any evidence of a break-in.

"Kat?" I call out her name, attempting to close the door quietly behind me although it creaks.

"In here," her somber voice calls out and I'm given a fraction of a second to feel relief until I hear her crying.

Kicking the door closed, I bypass the broken glass from the destroyed frame and head to the kitchen to find Kat covering her face at the sink. The water's running and when she peeks up at me, her eyes are swollen from crying and her reddened cheeks are tearstained.

"You okay?" Every step I take is careful as I approach her. In satin pink pajamas and without an ounce of makeup on, she's both gorgeous and utterly raw. A primitive side of me wants to console her; another side craves to comfort her in the way I know she needs.

She sniffles and turns off the water, giving me her back as she reaches for the kitchen towel to pat her face dry.

Tossing the towel down she gives me a careless shrug as if she hasn't lost all composure.

"What happened to the picture?"

"I threw it," she admits with feigned strength and then her composure seems to diminish, leading her to confide in me.

"He yelled at me. Like I'm the reason his father died? He just … he's losing it and I can't help him."

As tears well in her eyes, she grips the counter to hold her balance. "I loved his dad too. What can I do? I don't know what to do."

She loses it, and as she covers her face, turning away from me, I casually approach her. She's wounded and I know the feeling. Cill's father was a second father to me.

His death was sudden and I know Cill's not taking it well.

None of us are.

But he shouldn't yell at her. "He's just angry right now, but he loves you."

"I'm angry too," she sobs. She's anything but angry. She's broken. Both of them, my two best friends, are nothing like what they used to be.

"It's going to be okay," I whisper, and when I reach out to her, she leans into my touch. At first it's only slightly, but as the grief takes over, she falls into me.

I'm grateful to hold her, to give her this. Because I'm struggling too.

I feel us all falling apart and I don't know how to make it right.

When I kiss the top of her head and whisper into her hair it's going to be all right and that he loves her, I mean it, and I have to stop myself from telling her I love her too … because at this moment, I know I mean it just the same.

Present time

"I'm not here to fight you." That's the first thing I have to say to Cill, even if it's not quite true. Hell, maybe we are here, in the back room of Nello's, next to The Ruin, to fight. Maybe we're here to have it out. I'd rather have him punch me than some asshole across from the gas station. I won't send him to jail.

My body's still ringing from earlier today in Kat's kitchen, even after the nearly two hours of silent driving to get here. I think we all needed a moment of quiet and time to think. But two hours wasn't enough. I don't know that any amount of time will prepare me for this.

The dim lights in the back room only make Cill's bruised cheek look worse. He'll get over it, just like I will.

My shoulders straighten with barely contained anger as I take in a heavy breath. Although I know the anger isn't justified, it's still there.

I never should have touched Kat, but inside all I can think is that he never should have left us. All of it was fucked.

"I don't want to fight you," I tell him again. "What happened between Kat and me is long over." As I say the words, my heart is in agony. It feels like this is it for all three of us.

I fell in love with Kat, I fell hard for her and I only wanted to love her, because I knew CIll couldn't. It wasn't supposed to happen like it did. I never stopped loving her, though. Just like I never stopped wanting to be the friend Cill needed either.

We were both missing him. Both broken … hell, all three of us were.

Glancing over at Kat, sitting beside Cill in the circular booth and across from me, I know she'd choose him ten out of ten times. I'm the piece that has to go for them to be together now and it's my fault. I know that, but I can't stand that it has to happen.

Clearing my throat, I face Cill head-on, doing what needs to be done. "You need to know what happened with the club, even if you hate me right now. I want to tell you everything I know."

The stark white tablecloth is gently lit by the candle in the middle of the table, and a basket of bread wrapped in a white cloth napkin to keep it warm separates us.

It's quiet back here and the waiter is more than aware that we need time to discuss business so I doubt we'll see him again until Cill calls for him. With the location so close to The Ruin, Nello's is used to this. They're paid well, even if we don't order a damn thing to eat.

I could confess everything to Cill in this room. Spill every detail and I don't know what will happen after. I dread what will come. But it has to be done.

"What the hell happened to the club?"

"Things changed when your uncle took over."

"You keep saying that." Cill looks me dead in the eye. He's wary of me now and I don't blame him. I would be too if he fucked the love of my life without me knowing. "Tell me the truth, Reed. You owe me that."

It's not always best to tell the truth. Anyone who grew up at the Cavanaugh Crest knew that. Sometimes it's best to keep your damn mouth shut. Everybody loves to talk about how honesty is the best policy, but it's bullshit. Not saying anything is the best policy. Keeping your head down and doing what you're told is what we're expected to do. I wish I hadn't, though. I wish I knew what was really going on so I could have stopped it all.

"I think your uncle …" I say and swallow thickly, knowing how this is going to sound and praying he'll believe me, "set it up. All of it."

"What do you mean 'all of it?'" His eyes narrow and Kat's gaze moves to her clasped hands on the table.

"Can we eat?" Kat pipes up between us, her nervousness not at all disguised by her sweet, feminine tone. I've always thought she was beautiful, but more than that, careful and intelligent. She has intention behind every move.

Cill peers down at her. "I'm not hungry." The way his eyes search hers is telling. He still loves her deeply, even if there's pain there.

I'm thankful for that. I would never forgive myself if he stopped loving her. How could he, though? The two of them need each other.

My throat is tight as I swallow and watch her tell him, "I think we should get some food first." Kat puts her hand over his. "I think we would all feel better if we had a bite to eat. A lot happened tonight."

While they share a hushed discussion and then call the waiter who silently brings silverware and menus, I think about how it got this bad. I remember every day that led to this hell.

The only thing worse than losing Cill and watching everything turn to shit, was figuring out that his uncle had been behind it all. For a while, I couldn't even admit it to myself. If I thought it was true, I'd have no choice but to tell Cill.

That would tear him up. When I finally decided it was real, a few months after his father passed, though I didn't have any proof, I found reasons not to tell him. If I told him while he was locked up, he'd go crazy. Cill could never sit around and let shit happen to him. He had to take action. At least he had to find out why something had happened, and maybe solve the problem. Going to him with vague rumors while he was in jail would cause havoc and put him in jeopardy.

I couldn't tell anyone. I did what we were told to do all our lives, keep our heads down and do what we were told.

All the while, I watched and caught on to the shit Eamon was doing and now I know too much.

When the waiter finally comes around, with a paper pad in his hand, I can barely find my words. It's like I've been slowly unraveling the last year, when all of this started after Cill's father died, and now there's nothing left of me.

As another waitress quietly comes into the room to refill Kat's goblet of ice water with the silver decanter—neither Cill or I have touched ours—our waiter asks what I'd like to order.

I peer across the table to ask what Kat and Cill ordered, a glass of red and two fingers of whiskey. Yeah, I'm probably going to need alcohol too.

Clearing my throat, I ask for the same as Cill. When the waiter's gone Kat speaks up again, her fingers slipping down the stem of her goblet.

"I think we each have one drink to calm our nerves, we eat to settle our stomachs and then we can talk," she states softly but in a matter-of-fact way, only lifting her gaze to reach each of ours once she's finished.

"We've spent hours in the car in silence, what's another hour here?" she points out as if it's an innocent question.

The tension still bristles from Cill's shoulders but he peers at me, waiting for my answer.

"Yeah," I reply, "I think that's best."

Turmoil stirs in the pit of my stomach as Kat orders us appetizers of bruschetta and burrata that sound far too eloquent for men like us, but the way she reads it and admits she loves the glaze has me nodding my head in agreement.

We all order meals. I go with the same meal I get every time we're here simply out of habit. Capellini with crabmeat. Cill and Kat do the same; filet and shrimp for Cill, and lasagna for Kat.

It's quiet while we wait, each of us thinking maybe. Taking small sips of my drink, I watch the two of them touch. Occasionally she holds his hand and he squeezes hers. It feels like an ending, like I'm forced to watch it, to sit in it so it's burned into my memory what real love is and how I almost destroyed it.

The whiskey is gone sooner than I'd like. I pick at the bread, not tasting it until the meals are served.

Kat was right. It's helping Cill, at least. He's not as tense. Kat watches him even more than I do.

I didn't know how things would go when we showed up on her front porch this past weekend. I was scared to death. If she kicked him out, I didn't think Cill was going to recover. She barely speaks to me anymore. She stopped talking to him too.

Now, staring across the table, I know everything happens for a reason.

It was one thing for him to lose his freedom for four years. It would have been another thing to have the one girl he loved most shut the door in his face.

Cill's plate is gone in minutes. I've barely touched mine and Kat's made a small dent in hers. But he inhales his dinner.

A faint smile tugs at my face when I remember the time we were here last and Cill was going off about something. She said he needed to eat and then he wouldn't care about whatever it was he was complaining about. I remember laughing but not paying attention to whether or not it was true back then. It's only a joke but I wish it were true. I wish a good meal and a conversation were all it would take to fix this.

Kat pushes the basket of bread in front of him. It's the best bread in the city. The inside is soft and the outside is crusty. It tastes like home. This restaurant is almost as familiar as the rec room at the garage. I know this bread like I know the recliners in that room. We must've spent hours there watching football and poker games.

Cill's eaten enough food for the three of us but it's done him some good. He might be different than he was before, but he's still my best friend. The hurt look in his eyes has faded a bit. Enough that we can talk.

The waitress brings dainty mugs of coffee once the waiter has cleared our plates. It's all done silently. Kat has tea instead. She stirs in sugar, the spoon clinking against the ceramic. I can feel her discomfort as well, though she's trying to hide it. For Cill's sake, I think. She glances over at me.

I take that as a signal to start talking.

"I think …" I start, then trail off and lick my lower lip, knowing what I'm about to say is a bombshell that could destroy Cill. But he has to know. "It wasn't just Kat's father who ratted four years ago."

Cill narrows his eyes, his brow pinching. His tone is level and low when he says, "The hell do you mean? Everybody knows it was him. He's the one who called Kat to warn her what was happening."

"And that didn't seem off to you?"

"No," answers Cill.

"It seemed off to me. The more I think about it, the more it doesn't make any sense." I look at Kat. "If your dad knew ahead of time, he wouldn't have let you go to Cavanaugh Crest that night. He didn't want you mixed up in all of that. He has his sins to pay for, but he loved you. It just doesn't fit."

Kat looks down at her empty plate. Cill's still looking at me, his eyes questioning.

"I don't think your dad died of a heart attack either," I tell him. I've held this knowledge for so damn long, and it's a relief to get it out into the open. "I think your uncle wants it all and he's working for both sides. The Ruin and the feds."

My mind races with a million things.

The fact that Missy went missing and his uncle claimed she was a rat and that she took off. Yet her house was cleaned out months later and she hadn't taken anything.

"I think he set her father up. I think Missy caught on and your uncle killed her. I think we have the cops come every other fucking month because he's slowly taking out anyone who stands in his way. I think it was supposed to be me that left when the cops came last."

"Slow the fuck down," Cill demands, his eyes locked on mine, his voice so low it's barely heard. Barely moving at all, he commands, "Start from the beginning."

With a racing heart, I swallow and tell him everything.

"When you left and her father disappeared, the charges they brought against you … her father didn't know it all, you know? He didn't know about the frequency of drops … it had to be someone else and Missy brought that up." I can barely breathe remembering how it all went down, but how Eamon played it like it happened differently.

"When she disappeared, he said it made sense because she was asking questions and poking around. He said she had to be a rat.

"But the questions she was asking weren't something a rat would want to know. She was trying to figure out who else was in on it—"

"Missy was like a second mom to me," Cill says, his hand firmly wrapped around Kat's.

"I know. So did your father." His eyes whip back up to mine at the mention of his dad.

"He wasn't with it like he was before you went away. But he never believed Missy could do that to him. I think he caught on. I think he figured it out. 'Cause they said he died of a heart attack, but I heard them fighting before that, Cill. He and your uncle were going at it. Everyone who's questioned your uncle Eamon left shortly after. Either they died or they were a supposed rat who disappeared."

"Why didn't you tell me?"

"I didn't have proof until Kat's place got broken into." A heat breaks out across every inch of my skin as I look at Kat. "I didn't tell you, but I found two bricks of coke in your guest room. The same stock he had me moving during the bust. He knew Cill was getting out and he planted it and was going to wait for the perfect time." I look back to Cill.

"It had to be Eamon. He was the only one with a key to the stock. He planted it at Kat's place and I bet his plan was to take me down as I was moving it, and then to get you for possession, blaming it on me. Then we're both out of his way."

I don't even know if what I said makes sense to them. If they'll connect the dots like I did. "It sounds fucking crazy, but it's the only explanation."

My pulse races, praying they believe me. I almost add that he's why I let Kat go. Eamon is why when she broke down and told me she couldn't ever see me again, that's why I let her back away. If she stayed close, he could see her as a threat too.

I was still there for her. Still someone she trusted and I would be there any time she was in need, but at a distance.

I can't bring myself to speak about her, though. There's too much that's already been said.

"Say something, man," I plead after a long moment of silence. "I've felt like I'm going fucking crazy and paranoid for a year now. Ever since your pops died."

"You think my uncle sold out my father, his brother?" Cill's voice breaks when he adds, "You think my uncle killed him?"

There's a long moment of staring into my best friend's eyes, telling him something there's no way in hell he'd want to believe and having no evidence at all, only a gut feeling. "Yeah."

"No." He's quick to deny it, shaking his head. Kat, though, she stares back at me, realization clear in her gaze. "No, you're wrong." I hear the betrayal in his voice. I felt the same thing when I figured it out. The Cavanaugh MC wasn't about backstabbing bullshit and stealing power. It was about the bikes, and goddammit, the family. Founded by two first-generation brothers and their buddy Finn, something like this … it's soul shattering.

"I know it's hard to believe, but—"

"They were supposed to have each other's backs." He stabs his finger on the table, emphasizing his point. Readjusting in his chair, he starts to say something and then stops.

And then he does it again, choosing his words carefully. "My uncle was supposed to be the example. He's supposed to take care of all of us. And now you're telling me he's turned? You're telling me he killed my father?"

"I think he—"

"That's one fucked-up thing to say if you don't know—"

"Yes. They fought and then your father died suddenly of what they said was a heart attack, but the autopsy didn't confirm that. Then Missy started poking around and she died. He lied, said she left but I know she's fucking dead. Everyone who goes against him disappears and I know it was him who broke into Kat's house. I know for a fact it was him.

"I don't have evidence of everything, but I know he planted evidence in her home."

"What did you do with it?"

"The coke? I dumped it."

"When did you start thinking he killed my father?"

"It was only a thought a year ago when he died, but then it made sense when Missy disappeared. I just … I didn't want to believe it."

Chapter 13

Cillian

EVERY MEMORY I HAVE OF MY UNCLE FLASHES BEFORE MY EYES as I watch Kat and Reed share a glance. The fear that lingered in his gaze turned to comfort the moment he saw she was worried.

I don't miss the way she speaks to him, with a tone and submissiveness I once thought she held only for me. And with the expectation that he'll make it all okay. That he'll fix it. That he'll keep her safe.

"My uncle ..." When I clear my throat the two of them stare back at me, and Kat's quick to place her hand in mine. I pull it under the table, squeezing it tight.

With a heavy breath, Reed looks between the two of us. I've never seen him look the way he does. I know four years changed us both, and neither of us for the better.

"It was just too much, too heavy ... for it to be true."

"What you're saying ..." I can't even finish a fucking sentence. Something deep inside of me is screaming that it makes sense. That ever since my father died and my uncle didn't even come in and see me, ever since then I knew.

Swallowing thickly I tell him, "Even if he's not a rat, even if he's not working both sides, if he killed my father, his only brother ..." I leave the last part unsaid. I'll fucking kill him.

Reed's statement is spoken lowly, his eyes peering back with mourning. "I know."

It's silent for a long moment.

"Back in a minute," Reed says, getting up from his seat. He heads down the hall into the main restaurant and when he opens the door, the din of the other patrons slips into our private room for a small moment until it's quiet again.

Kat flips our hands so she's holding mine. "You okay, Cill?" Her soft voice is the only sound I've wanted to hear all this time.

"Lots of memories here," I say gruffly. It's true. I used to come here with my dad. We would sit in this same room and talk about whatever came to our minds. Usually it was something to do with Cavanaugh or school. I thought we'd be doing this until he was an old man, but he never got the chance.

Now Reed's saying it's our own family who killed him. Anger scorches inside of me, rising up like a slow tide and exhaustion is the only thing keeping it down. If my uncle is behind all this, then I took the fall for nothing.

"I'm starting to doubt everything," I admit to her. The statement comes with a wave of sadness and regret.

Her gentle murmur makes me take it back though, "Everything?" she asks. Her wide hazel eyes beg me not to regret her and damn, if she ever thought I'd give her up or that I would take back anything between us, she's gravely mistaken.

With my fingers slipping under her chin, I whisper against her lips, "Not you, my little hellcat." With a soft kiss against her lips, I add, "Not us."

"What Reed just said is heavy and this place has to be difficult to be in," she tells me once I drop my hand from her chin. Nestling in next to me, she molds her side to mine, but stares at the door.

"Yeah, it's getting to me." I bite my tongue before saying the second half: *and I believe Reed.*

"You want to go home?" Kat murmurs.

"Not yet."

I want to sit here until I figure something out. I don't know what, exactly. Just something. I don't want to take this unsettled feeling back to her place with us.

The owner pokes his head in the door before coming out to see us. The sight of Nello makes my lips pull up in an asymmetric smirk. He's older than I remember him, with gray hair around his temples that was never there before and wrinkles around his eyes when he grins and says, "Cillian, how are you doing, young man? Is there anything I can get you?"

"No, thank you, Mr. Russo. I appreciate you letting us have this table last minute."

His hands clasp in front of him as he fiddles with his red tie. With black suit pants and a crisp white dress shirt, it's obvious he's the one in charge of this place. "Of course. It's the least I could do. I'm so sorry about your father," he adds, his tone somber.

Immediately, that bit of warmth I held vanishes. "Thank you."

He seems to regret his condolences, quickly turning his attention to Kat. "Is there anything I can get you, dear?"

Dear. He's forgotten her name. I know she hasn't been here as much as me, but she came with me a handful of times.

"No, thank you," answers Kat. She tries to put a smile on her face, but it's not real. Kat gives up halfway through. That scares the hell out of me. She always could do that. Smile when everything was going to shit.

With a nod, I think he'll leave us to it, but before he turns, he asks me, "You doing okay?"

"I'm glad to be out."

"You have everything you need?"

I've known this man for almost as long as I can remember. What Reed said has me questioning everything.

"Can I get you dessert?"

I didn't think I could eat another bite, but Kat perks up when she hears about dessert.

"Chocolate cake sound okay?" he asks her.

"Sure does. Maybe to go?" she adds and he says, *of course.* That's what he always says. He's amenable to men like me.

He glances down at our hands on the table as Reed comes back into the room. "What happened to your hand? You need anything for that?"

It's kind of him to ignore the matching bruises Reed and I are sporting. I flex it, stretching out my fingers and shaking my head as Reed takes his seat. "I tried to become a handyman and did something dumb with a hammer. Won't make that mistake again."

"Be more careful," he scolds, smiling with his eyes.

"Hey, Nello," I say before he can exit the room completely.

"What's that, Cill?"

"If anybody asks, we were here a little earlier. In fact, we've been back here all day."

He nods shortly, his gaze staying on mine. "You got it."

The moment the door closes, giving us privacy once again, Reed speaks, "Well, you didn't kill me. So I take it, what I said about what happened and about your uncle—"

Readjusting in my seat, I cut him off. "We'll talk about it later," I tell him and then glance between the two of them. "I want to," I start but shut my mouth as the waiter enters the room.

He brings chocolate cake packaged in a little black box tied with a red ribbon, halting the conversation.

I'm short with him, but my voice is as even as it can be. "Just the bill and a few more minutes, please."

"I want to talk about you two," I tell them both the moment the stiff silence greets us once again. "What the hell happened to you?" My gaze is solely on Kat.

She swallows thickly and pulls her hands into her lap. "What do you mean?"

"You're not yourself." I know it's hypocritical coming from me, but it's true. "You're scared and unsure and you," I say and bring my attention to Reed, motioning toward him, "you fucked Reed ... was that before or after you ended it with me?" I didn't mean to say that last part. Fuck, I don't want to know. "I never thought you'd do that. What happened to my hellcat?"

"I—" Kat looks down at her chocolate cake, then back up at me. "I lost everything. I lost you ... and then ... I felt like I didn't deserve you."

Tears shine in her eyes and her face flushes. It kills me to see her this way. She isn't like she used to be. This strong woman who could handle anything. Hell, maybe it's me who remembers her differently ... or maybe it's just because we were kids who didn't know shit.

I grab her hand again. "I love you, Kat."

Her eyes meet mine, disbelieving and filled with tears. "Cill ..."

"I love the woman you were," I tell her and make sure she's staring back at me when I continue, "and the woman you are now. Let me see you smile again. I want to make you smile again."

"I don't know if I can do that right now," she murmurs.

I let my mind unravel, every thought slipping out, "You weren't scared of anybody. You didn't cry yourself to sleep at night. You didn't refuse to smile. And you didn't fucking cheat on me."

Her eyes come to mine, glossy with tears. She doesn't deny it. That it happened before she ended it with me. *Fuck.* Dread pricks across my skin.

"Why?" I'm barely paying attention to Reed anymore. He hasn't said a word and I can't look away from Kat. "Why did you do it?" My throat's tight and dry.

She glances at the door. "We shouldn't have this conversation here. If you want to talk, we should go home."

"I'm not going home until you tell me why you thought it was better to cheat on me than wait just one more year." My pulse races. "You stayed through the hardest shit. Even when my father died …" I'm losing my shit, and I know it. Emotions surge through me and make me want to punch something, or fuck something. It blew a hole through my chest to hear about her and Reed. I'm not going to spend another second sitting nicely at the dinner table while she keeps this secret from me. Hiding it does even more damage.

"I just don't think—"

"Why, Kat? Why did you do it? I was in prison, I lost my father." I can't help that my voice raises as I pound a fist to my chest. "I deserve an explanation."

Kat snaps, the fire coming back into her eyes. She digs her fingernails into the tablecloth. "You were angry," she says, her voice shaking with emotion. "Everyone hated me, and I lost them. I lost everyone."

"There's no way they hated you," I tell her, but I'm not sure. I don't know. I wasn't there, because I was in prison. I should have been by her side.

"Your father was the only one that still accepted me at Cavanaugh. He was there when my father left." Her voice tightens and she takes in a heavy breath before continuing. "And you were so angry and hateful and turning into someone I didn't recognize." Her voice drops. My hellcat is beautiful when she's pissed like this and all her angry energy is focused on me. Tears glisten on her cheeks but they're not a sign of weakness. It's like she's crying broken glass and doesn't care. "And I just wanted to be held for a moment. I wanted someone to say I wasn't crazy and that it was going to be okay, and you—you—"

She shakes her head, pulling back. The blaze in her eyes becomes less heated.

"You had too much, it was too heavy and I couldn't hold any more, Cill. We got into that fight—"

"It was one fight—" I argue back. I remember it well. I raised my voice at her. I vented. I took my anger out on her. I know I did. I apologized a hundred times, but I know I lost her that day. How could I have possibly kept her? I was fucking locked in a cage. I couldn't make it right.

"It wasn't just a fight. It was me realizing I couldn't help you anymore."

"So we got in one fight and you—"

"You're not listening," she says, cutting me off, her anger blistering between us. This … this is what I know. The woman here I know how to handle.

"I needed you. I couldn't have you."

"So you went to Reed?"

"He came to me … and I couldn't say no, because I needed someone to love me. I'm sorry"

"I never stopped loving you."

"It wasn't your fault. I'm not saying that." She's on edge, barely containing herself. "I'm sorry." She's at war with her anger and I've been here before with this woman. Only then she didn't hold back, she let me have it. Which is exactly what I deserved.

"Kat, I never stopped loving you."

"I love you, Cill. I've always loved you. I was just so lost and upset. And so damn alone."

"Come here."

I pull her into my lap and kiss her. I can taste her tears on her lips, but as soon as her mouth is on mine she's fully my hellcat again. I taste her like I haven't had the chance for four years. I kiss her like we might not have another chance when we walk out of here. Kat pulls back and I let out a sigh. It feels like I've been holding it in for my entire life.

"What was that?" she questions.

"My hellcat just came back to me." I put my hands on the small of her back and hold her closer. "Hit me."

"What?"

"Hit me, Kat." She puts her hands on my shoulders instead. "Curse me out. Do whatever you need to, but don't you dare leave me."

She laughs and wipes away her tears. "Where would I go, Cill?"

"Anywhere you wanted."

"It wouldn't matter," she tells me. "You're in my head, and in my heart. You'd still be with me. Except I wouldn't have you to talk to, and that would be hell. I know it would be, because it was hell when you went away."

"It was hell for both of us."

"You were fucking stupid to take the fall and say it was yours." There she is. That's my hellcat. I'm so damn relieved she's back. She would call me out back then, and I want her to do it now. "Possession and distribution. You should have kept your mouth shut and not said it was yours."

"I know. I was stupid. I thought I was doing a good thing. It didn't take long to realize I had fucked up."

"I hated you for it, Cill," Kat admits. She knows I can take it. That's what I wanted from her all along. I don't want her to treat me like I'm made of glass. "I hated that you did it and I watched you wither away." Her eyes shine with tears again. "I still loved you, even when I hated you."

"Well, I'm back, and I'm not going anywhere. I love you, Hellcat."

"I love you too."

She leans in and gives me a sweet, soft kiss. It reminds me of the way we used to kiss when we were teenagers and still figuring out how to do it right. Kat's always done it right. She can be a hellion, but she always kissed like we were in love.

I guess we were.

I know we still are.

Kat looks into my eyes, and I get lost in the moment. It's too damn much for the dinner table but I don't care. The only way I was going to walk out of here is if I solved something. Now we've solved it. And if there's still bullshit with Cavanaugh to be dealt with, at least we have an understanding of one another.

Her eyes go wide. "Oh no. Reed—"

We both turn to where Reed was sitting and find the chair empty.

Chapter 14

I'M EXHAUSTED WHEN WE GET BACK TO MY HOUSE AND THE heartache is too much to deal with. The night has been far too long. "I just want to lie down," I tell Cill as I lock up behind us.

The keys hit the table and then I check my phone again. No reply from Reed. He left without a word, but Cill's car and keys were waiting for us in his place.

"On the couch, or in bed?"

"In bed." I need to be completely horizontal or I won't make it. Everything we talked about at the restaurant feels unfinished and painful. It's like a chilled dread that simply won't go away. Being on my feet one more second can't happen, though.

We both take quick turns in the bathroom and when I come out Cill is standing at my bedroom door. "I'm not sleeping anywhere else tonight."

That scares me, because it means he wants to keep talking too. And if we keep talking, I'm going to have to tell him all of the truth. There's a part I left out. A part that still hurts to talk about.

Yeah, he yelled at me because I was the only person there.

Yeah, he was stupid and then angry and there was nothing we could do about it.

Yeah, we were all dealing with the loss of his dad.

Yeah, without his dad there, I wasn't welcome at the club.

But there's a piece he's missing.

The bed welcomes me with its soft sheets and blankets I picked out with Lydia when I first moved in here. I burrow against the pillow while Cill climbs in next to me. He takes out his phone, and I see Reed's name on the screen. Text messages. Cill glances over them and puts the phone facedown on the table.

I move in closer to his side and let him put his arm around me. He reaches over and turns off the light.

With the room dark and quiet, I thought I'd be able to give in to the weight of the day and pass out. Instead my thoughts race and apparently so do Cillian's.

"Was it something specific I said that drove you away?"

Thump. My heart is heavy with every beat. "No … I just missed you and what we had before," I begin, and I know it sounds awful as soon as the words are out of my mouth. "I didn't mean that I was trying to replace you, or … or that you could be replaced. But I missed you. I was a wreck without you. I felt like there wasn't a reason to keep going. I'd wake up in the morning and think about going back to sleep for the entire day."

Cill rubs my back. "I thought about that too."

I roll over under the sheets and scoot closer to him, resting my cheek against his chest. He's quick to wrap an arm around me, holding me there. "There wasn't really anyone else who understood. Reed was the only other person who missed you like I did. Well, almost as much. I couldn't talk about it with anyone from Cavanaugh. I didn't even want to be back there. I would have been totally alone without Lydia and Reed, and Lydia didn't understand the way I was feeling."

He doesn't say anything. I know how this must sound. Me, complaining about how difficult things were for me when he was the one who truly suffered.

"I'm not comparing it," I murmur. "I know it was hell for you. You never should have gone away."

"It was worse than hell." Cill must have so many things bottled up inside, but he doesn't add anything else. I wait for a while to make sure.

"It was about missing you," I explain, hating how stupid it sounds. "It was about trying to live with that emptiness. That's all it was."

His hand moves again on my back. "When did it happen?"

I wish I could just fall into the darkness with him and forget all of this ever happened. The sheets rustle as I maneuver under them, playing he won't push me away. Denying the past won't get rid of it. It won't change what I did with Reed. All it will do is force me to spend more energy pretending that my life played out differently. I don't want to do that.

"The first time was after your dad died." Reed and I had both gone to the funeral. I felt like my dress was choking me. The service was filled with people from Cavanaugh Crest and all I wanted to do was escape. I didn't want to keep the life I had. "The funeral was hard. Reed was devastated that you couldn't be with us. He said it was fucked up that you couldn't be there. He wouldn't drop it."

"How long after?"

"A few weeks." I steel myself to continue. "Then you stopped answering my calls and when I went in, we had that fight."

Anger spills out of him. "So you thought it would be better to fuck my best friend?" I begin to pull away, but Cill holds me tight. "Kat—I'm sorry. Fuck."

"I know. I know. I'm sorry."

"It already happened," Cill says. I get the impression he's repeated this to himself many times over the past four years. "It's done. It hurts like hell, but it's done."

The words are right there, wanting to be heard, but he continues instead, "Not being able to see you was the lowest moment in my life. And then you stopped coming altogether."

I can feel him hesitating over a question.

"Just ask," I plead. This is so damn painful. It's the hardest conversation I've ever had because I need us to come out better after this. I can't lose him again. Cill's the only reason I'm not crying already. I sure as hell want to. The tears are nearly ready to flow. The guilt churns in my stomach.

Far off in the distance, almost so far we can't hear it, a police siren disturbs the city.

"And you still have feelings for him?" Cill asks although it's not so much a question, just a known truth.

I don't lie to him. "Yeah ... I still have feelings."

"Did he wear a condom?" Cill asks.

I knew he would say that, but my stomach drops. "No."

"You could have gotten pregnant."

My teeth lock together like they don't want to let out the words. I don't want to give voice to the words. Every day I've tried to come to terms with this. To accept it as something I did that's not any better or any worse than anyone else's actions. But it is worse, because it was Reed. Because Cill had lost his freedom. I still had mine, and I used it to royally fuck up.

I can't speak. The longer my hesitation lasts, the surer he's going to be.

"You told me not to hold back," Cill says gruffly. "Now you don't hold back."

"I did." There. He knows now. I said it, and he knows. "I did get pregnant."

As he props himself up to stare down at me, I fall to the sheets, the tears flowing, but nothing else does. "Hellcat …"

I've made it this far without breaking down. That won't last forever.

"I found out two months in when I miscarried."

Cill sucks in a breath. The shadows that line his face highlight the pain in his expression. I swear I see him wipe under his eyes just as I look at him, but I can't be entirely sure because he leans down to kiss the crook of my neck the moment I think he's crying.

I made a mistake and I suffered it alone.

Besides watching Cill get arrested, the miscarriage was the worst experience of my life. At first I didn't know what was happening. I hadn't been paying much attention to my cycle because I couldn't bring myself to care about anything. Everyone knows that stress can cause you to be late. That's what I thought, if I thought about it at all.

Then the bleeding started. The pain was what made me realize it wasn't normal. I was only eight weeks along but it hurt so badly I couldn't stand up. Every time I tried, I'd get dizzy. I thought I might die in my own bathroom.

Nobody else was there.

I wasn't talking to Reed after what happened. It was awful what we'd done.

Cill wasn't talking to me either. We had the fight and then I went silent and he gave me the silent treatment back.

So when I realized … all I thought was that I deserved to go through that pain alone.

Lydia was at work with her phone off.

I caved and called the only person who could take me to the hospital, but Reed wasn't answering. And the person who I wanted to hold me and promise me it would be okay was locked in a prison cell.

That pain hits me all over again and I push Cill's arm off me and try to stand up. Cill won't let me leave. He pulls me back into the bed with him.

"I have to go," I say, my voice thick with tears and shove my hand against him. "I don't want to do this in front of you."

His strong arms wrap around me and pull me close to him, bringing me into a comforting warmth.

With his lips brushing a kiss in the crook of my neck, he whispers, "That's not true and you know it." Without an ounce of fight in me, I give in, letting him pull my body as close to his as possible as he runs his hand over my hair. "You missed me like I missed you, Hellcat. Don't try to lie to me about it."

"Why should you watch me cry over this? It was my mistake. I deserve to work through the consequences on my own. You shouldn't feel sympathy for me, Cill. I knew it was wrong and I did it anyway."

"Yeah. You were hurting and you tried to seek out comfort. You think I can blame you for that? I did the same damn thing, only there was nowhere to go but inside my head. I'm partly to blame for all this shit happening anyway."

"No you're not."

"I could have seen you sooner," he admits. "After the fight. I thought if I put you out of my mind, the time would pass quicker. It was bullshit. And by the time I got over it, you had stopped coming."

"I felt too guilty to come. I couldn't look you in the eye knowing what I'd done."

"I'll look you in the eye any time," he says, and I finally let myself melt into his arms.

"Will you be able to do it in the morning?" I question. I don't know if I'd be able to, if I were him. I might get up and walk out like he did that first night he stayed.

"I'd look at you any damn morning, Hellcat. I don't care what happened."

"Yes you do, Cill."

"I care. But I only care because it's you. I want you to be okay."

Deep, even breaths are all I'm able to focus on and the warmth of his chest against my back. I listen to his heartbeat for a while. A long while maybe, his arm a comforting weight around me, holding me close and re-fusing to let go. His breathing steadies long before mine does.

"That's it," I tell him. "I didn't do anything else while you were gone. I hope you can believe me when I say that."

"Hmm?" Cill asks sleepily. I blink up at his face. It's mostly hidden in the dark, but I'm pretty sure his eyes are closed.

"I'm glad you came back," I whisper, and then I curl up against him and fall asleep too. "I love you, Cillian."

Chapter 15

CILLIAN AND REED SIT CLOSE TOGETHER AT A NEW KITCHEN table Reed brought over this morning and the two of them put together in silence while I slept. Cill's still in his gray sweatpants and a white tee. Reed's at least dressed in jeans and a dark navy Henley.

With sleep still in my eyes, I came down to see the two of them putting the last screws in. Reed can barely look me in the eye and the only thing he's said to me is that he's sorry he didn't answer last night. He had a lot to think about.

There's a sadness between us that doesn't fit right but I've tried to swallow it down all morning.

I made them coffee an hour ago and I know for a fact it's cold by now. Neither one of them seems to have noticed. They just keep talking in low voices that make it impossible to hear a damn thing.

I should be grateful that they're both there, sitting side by side, not murdering each other.

"More coffee?" I ask, holding up the pot. I've had two cups and it's still not enough to make me feel awake enough for whatever's going on.

They don't answer. I pick up the two mugs. They don't notice. I dump them out in the sink. Still nothing.

"Are you going to let me in on what you're planning? I know it has to do with Cavanaugh." I fill up the mugs with fresh coffee and take them back to the table.

"I don't think this is something you need to be a part of, Kat," Reed says, accepting his coffee and still not looking me in the eye. I fucking hate it.

Blowing out my frustration, I close the cabinet door carelessly after putting the sugar back and say, "Cillian, if you're going back to the Crest to deal with your uncle, I deserve to know about it."

"When it's all said and done, Hellcat," Cill answers, blowing across the top of his coffee. He doesn't look me in the eye either.

I bang my fist on the table between them. It finally makes Reed shut up. "Tell me," I demand. "I don't know what the hell you two think you're doing. You didn't tell me shit back then, but you're going to tell me everything right now or I'll fucking lose it, Cill. You too, Reed. What the hell is going on?"

Cill's lips pick up in a smirk. "Well good morning, Hellcat," he murmurs, his pale blue eyes piercing right through me in a way that's sinful.

I'm caught for a moment as he sips his coffee.

"I thought you could hear us, Hellcat."

"How could I possibly hear you when you're whispering?" I bend down and kiss his cheek, leaving both palms on the table and leaning down low enough that I'm more than sure he can see right down my baggy sleep shirt. "Tell me. Now."

Reed and Cill share a glance that would piss me off if I wasn't sure I had their attention. "We're figuring out what to do with him," Reed says.

"Who?"

"My uncle," Cill says. Pain flashes in his eyes as fear engulfs me. "We're comparing notes. Figuring out what really happened."

Reed stands up from his seat before Cill is finished speaking. "I've got to go call someone. I'll be back in a minute."

"Where are you going?" I ask.

"Just to the porch," he answers and knowing he's not going far settles the unease inside of me.

"Don't do anything stupid," I tell him although I'm not sure he hears as the front door shuts, my throat thick with frustration. This was how they were before Cill went away. Planning things together. Getting in trouble together. I could talk them out of things, but honestly, I didn't most of the time. I was always riding in the passenger seat and chiming in to tell the stories later at Cavanaugh. Nothing major. We never got arrested. But I was Cill's hellcat, for better or for worse.

I'm older now, though, and someone has to think about these things.

"What exactly are you two going to do?" I say and glare at Cill. An amused smile curves his lips and he stands up from his seat at the table. My heart pounds like they're taking action right this minute instead of just making plans.

"Don't be scared, Hellcat."

"I'm not scared." The words stumble off my lips as I make my way back to the corner of the cabinets, leaning against the counter. "I'm pissed. I'm fucking pissed, Cillian." I take refuge in my mug of coffee.

He crosses the kitchen, the legs of the chair scraping across the linoleum floor as he gets up.

"You don't look pissed," he counters, his steps steadily bringing him closer to me. The mug clinks on the counter as I set it down, my attention never leaving Cill. "Fine ... maybe I'm scared."

He closes the distance between us and rests his forehead against mine before kissing the tip of my nose and whispering, "Yeah. Me too."

As much as I love his comforting touch, I pull away, making sure he understands how serious I am.

"I'm scared to lose you—I can't go through that again." His lips brush against mine in an attempt to silence me, calm me, or just love on me, I'm not sure. But I can't shake this uncertainty so I gently push him back. "If your uncle planted shit here when he broke in—if he's already trying to fuck you over—I'll fucking kill him." The words leave me without a second thought. Peering up at Cillian, I watch his brow raise and then the grin grow on his handsome face, his cheek still bruised.

"My little hellcat," Cillian says, and he kisses me. Not just a light peck. It's not a move to soothe me. It's a kiss I know he needs just as much as I do.

And just like then, his mouth on mine makes me forget to fight everyone.

It makes me forget we're up against his uncle, and seemingly the rest of the world. He flicks his tongue against mine and I forget it all. I forget to be heartbroken that Cavanaugh let me down after Cill's arrest. I forget everything but how good it feels to be with him.

The hum of the refrigerator kicks on and I fall deeper into the kiss.

Cill pushes me up against the counter, the space between us lighting on fire. As he presses up against me, I'm made aware that Cill's hard and I tease myself by rubbing against him until he groans. "If you're going to do that, Hellcat, we should find a bedroom."

Just then Reed comes back in, the front door slamming shut behind him. "Damn it," Cill says. He kisses me one more time and pulls away.

Reed's footsteps are heavy and I'm still catching my breath as Cill turns to face him. It doesn't make sense that I should feel as guilty as I do when Reed catches my eye.

"What did he say?"

"Yeah. He meets every other week." He paces through the kitchen, his hand running through his hair. Cill glances back at me as I ask, "What's going on?"

"My uncle was seen with a man a few times. Reed hired someone to follow him after he found the coke upstairs. He's an agent."

"An agent? Like—"

"Like, an agent of the Federal Bureau of Investigation ... my uncle's the rat."

Reed chimes in. "If he's working for the feds, what the fuck are we going to do?"

"I'm not leaving," Cill says.

Reed stares at him. "Why the fuck would you stay? I've wanted out since you left. It's been fucking hell."

"You think there's nothing worth fighting for? What about Finn?"

"He thinks the same," Reed counters. "He's counting the fucking days. He told me when you got out—someone was going to die. I can feel it, Cillian."

Cillian's silence speaks to his disagreement.

"You don't know how far it's gone." Reed is quiet and serious.

"Nobody else is going to jail because of him. If someone's going down, it's going to be my uncle."

"Then I hope it's only him that's a rat. 'Cause if it's anyone else, we're fucked."

My stomach knots as my mind speeds ahead through what that would mean.

If Cill's uncle has gotten his claws into Cavanaugh, they're already against us. If more of them are working with the feds, then it means there's no safe place for Cill to be anymore. Just avoiding the club won't be enough. They'll be looking for ways to put him back in jail.

But more than that, it'll mean that the family we once had is as good as dead.

"It's worth it," Cill says. "If there's a chance to put it back together again, we have to take it."

"It's not fucking worth it," Reed argues. "Do you hear what you're saying? It's not worth it for you to be in jail!" Reed's voice breaks on the last word. Everything he feels echoes in myself.

"Cillian, please—" I start to say, trying to reason with him.

"If my uncle comes after us, that's just as bad as being locked up. Fuck it, Reed. I'm not going to spend the rest of my life looking over my shoulder. If you really think he's all there is to Cavanaugh, then by all means, don't try to take him down. But I think you know better."

"Damn it, Cill." Reed shakes his head.

Cill looks at me. "What do you think, Hellcat? You think it's over at Cavanaugh?"

All of my earliest memories of the club flick through my mind. I was at home in the rec room, and the garage. I never felt out of place there. Even as a little girl, if I wanted to know something about one of the bikes, some tall man wearing black leather and a grin would explain it to me.

Cavanaugh's the reason we're all standing in this kitchen together. If we hadn't had that, we wouldn't be here.

And Cavanaugh's been dead to me since Cill's father was buried six feet under.

"If your uncle's working with the feds, I think you tell the Cross brothers, you tell the Valettis. You let it leak to the men who can take care of it and we get the hell out. Ask someone at The Ruin where we can go."

"Where's my hellcat?" Cill murmurs, disappointment evident.

"Protecting you, Cillian. Keeping you from getting in deeper when you never should have been involved."

"Listen to her, please, man," Reed pleads with Cillian who looks between the two of us with disbelief.

"It's the Crest … what are you two fucking saying—"

"The Crest is dead!" Reed screams, desperate to get through to Cill. He closes the space between them with heavy steps and the air suffocates me.

"The club is down to ten people including the two of us. Six men I hardly know anymore, a traitor and an old man who's waiting to die." I reach out to steady Reed, slipping between the two of them as the tension rises. He's losing it.

"Hey, hey, let's just have a seat," I offer, gentling my touch. I've only seen Reed like this once before. The day Cillian's dad was found dead. My hands rest against his shoulders and Reed's arm wraps around my waist, pulling me in as he buries his head in the crook of my neck.

I'm surprised but only because Cill's behind us.

"I can't do it," Reed murmurs before coming to grips and slowly releasing me. He lifts his head, his eyes red and drops his trembling hand. "I can't watch you kill yourself for a family that doesn't exist anymore."

Everything in me wants to hold on to him as he takes a step backward.

He stares at Cillian and I'm hesitant to look back and see his expression. I expect anger from Reed holding onto me like that. Maybe even toward myself for getting between them. I expect a lot of things, but when I turn around, Cill is right there, reaching around to pull Reed in. I'm caught there, between them both, as Cill pats Reed's back with firm slaps.

"I'm right here, brother."

"Don't fucking go back, man. Don't fucking leave us again."

As I slip away from their embrace, the two men hug it out, neither willing to let go. "We have each other," Reed says and emphasizes, "that's enough."

Cillian's silent and I'm not certain he's convinced.

"Can we just wait to do anything?" I offer again. "We have time, don't we?"

The two men look over at me before they each take a step back, emotion riddled in their lost expressions. My two broken and lost men. "We have each other, that's what matters," I tell them.

Cillian looks between the two of us, swallowing thickly. "How exactly is that?" he questions and a chill sweeps down my back.

"What do you mean?" Reed questions in a single breath even though both of us know what he means. There's love between us all, and I can't deny that I feel more love for Reed than I should.

"I mean … the two of you … If I wasn't here, you'd be with her, wouldn't you?"

"No, the club isn't safe—"

"If it was safe," Cill says and inside I'm screaming for Reed to let it go. I love him, but he knows I'll always be Cill's. I can't lose him as a friend, though. Neither can Cill. We need each other. It's as simple as that.

Instead, he says the worst thing he could.

"Yeah." He swallows, his hands slipping into his pockets, as if signaling he doesn't want to fight, or maybe that he's willing to take the punch without punching back. "If you weren't here and it was safe, I'd be with her. Of course I would."

Thump, my heart races and a heat engulfs me.

"And you would too," Cill states softly, without judgment as he glances at me.

"But you are here," I say and the words are pleading as they pour out. I can't lose him. Please, no.

"I know I am, Hellcat. I'm not going anywhere," he tells me as I rush into him, my hands fisting his tee. He chuckles. The bastard chuckles a genuine laugh as he looks down at me, smoothing over my hair before kissing my temple.

I've never felt such confusion.

"The thing is," he whispers at my temple, his warm breath slipping down my shoulder, "Reed still wants to fuck you and you want him too." He keeps me close to him and before I can object, Reed agrees.

As I turn to face him, breathless, Reed is standing closer than before, only inches behind me now. "I never stopped wanting you and I never will, Kat."

Cill kisses the side of my neck, stealing my attention back. "What do you say, Hellcat? You want to be shared?"

Cillian

Kat keeps looking back at me like this can't be real. Every time her wide hazel eyes search mine, I kiss her harder, wanting that look of uncertainty to vanish.

The moment the three of us are inside her bedroom, I kick the door shut and tell her to strip. I'm the first to make a move, pulling my shirt over my shoulders and letting it fall to the floor.

Kat stares back but I don't have to ask her twice.

Her sleep shirt falls to the floor easily enough and she shimmies her thin lace panties down to the floor. Leaving her completely bared to us, her rosebud nipples peaked and her hair cascading around her shoulders.

Her wide eyes dart between the two of us, her shoulders rising and falling with each heavy breath. The flush in her cheeks and her hardened nipples prove she's turned on, even if nervousness clings to her.

"How do you want me?"

"On your knees, Hellcat."

I help her get into position exactly how I want her. On the edge of the bed, her mouth facing Reed who's still standing there, his shirt removed but his pants still on. I'm the first to drop my pants, palming my cock and stroking it once.

The bed groans as I climb up behind her. I'm vaguely aware that Reed has hardly moved. If he wants her, if wants to keep loving her like I know he does, this is the only way he's going to get her.

"You taking her pussy?" he finally asks lowly, just above a breath.

I only nod, knowing damn well I want her coming on my cock and I'll be coming inside of her. I get her first. She's mine, after all. I'm only sharing.

He crouches down and runs the pad of his thumb across her bottom lip as he asks, "You want me in your ass then, my little sex kitten?"

Her body tenses slightly and I run a soothing hand down her curves. "You did that?" I ask them both, purely out of curiosity.

Kat's head shakes and Reed says, *not yet.*

My cock hardens even more at his statement: not yet. There's so much pleasure we could show her together. So many things we've never done.

Excitement runs through me, but I focus on playing with her, on readying her.

"How about your mouth then?" Reed murmurs, leaning down to kiss her and she moans into the kiss. My heart races watching them.

It's not what I expected. There's no jealousy, only a need for more.

I press the head of my cock between her folds and then lower, spreading my precum around her clit.

She gives me a sweet little mewl and I focus on her rather than Reed, who's only watching so far.

Leaning down so my chest is closer to her and I can nip the lobe of her ear, I push my fingers inside of her, stroking and then pulling out to rub ruthless circles against her clit.

"You're so fucking wet, Kat." I nip her shoulder as I pull back and add, "Are you wet for him too?"

She doesn't answer at first, although I know she heard and I spank her ass, once. The slap reverberates in the room.

At first she cries out, but she's quick to answer, "Yes."

"That's my good girl." Reed says the words that were just about to come from me.

I settle on the next step as he gets into the position he wants, finally playing along.

"Arch your back how I like," I say and I watch as her ass raises and her shoulders drop.

"Keep that mouth of yours available for Reed while I fuck you," I tell her and just as she's answering, I slam deep inside of her in a single thrust.

Her gasp is fucking everything. I fuck her ruthlessly, thrusting into her at a deep and steady pace. Her nails dig into the comforter and she struggles to keep her head up as the pleasure tenses her body.

A part of me wants him to see what I do to her, how she's perfect for me. How easily I get her off and how gorgeous it is when she comes for me. The other part of me, a very curious part of me, wants to know if Reed can satisfy her too. I want to know if she makes those same sounds for him.

Licking his lower lip, Reed unzips his pants and lets them fall to the floor. Palming his dick, he watches me as I grip her shoulder, pounding into her mercilessly as she moans and struggles not to writhe under me.

Watching him hold her like that, her gaze pinned on his with his hand wrapped around her throat, is addictive in a way I've never felt. "You want me to throat fuck you while Cillian comes inside your tight little pussy?"

Wrapping her hair around my wrist, I fist the hair at the base of her neck and hold her steady for him.

"Open up that sweet mouth of yours," I command her and she obeys.

Her pussy tightens around my cock as I thrust myself as deep as I can inside of her.

She moans around the head of Reed's cock, her cheeks hollowing as he pushes himself in her.

His left hand stays around her throat as his right moves lower, so he can cup her breast in his hand. He plays with her, teasing her and I crave more of it.

His hips thrust and I watch as she tries to take him. My little hellcat takes what she can, her eyes watering and when she swallows around him, I nearly lose it.

Reed's head falls back and at the same time, she tightens around me. She loves it. The desire and the primal need that tenses every muscle in me are unimaginably sinful.

I fuck her harder as he pulls out and she heaves in a breath.

Her lips are swollen as he palms his cock, strokes it and then lifts her head back up. "You can take more of me," he tells her and she obeys, opening her mouth into that perfect O even as she moans from the hard thrusts I give her.

Fuck. I find my release, pulling out as quickly as I can and only exhaling as I come on her back.

"Take her pussy," I tell him, barely getting out the words as I heave myself up. With a hand on Kat's hip, I turn her over. It's careless, and we'll need to change the sheets once he's done, but I want to see him fucking her.

Selfishly, I want to be the first to throat fuck her.

"Spread your legs for Reed," I tell her and my little hellcat obeys, her pink pussy already swollen. Reed doesn't hesitate to climb on the bed as I get off. Breathing heavily and trying to wrap my head around how fucking hot this is.

If a man laid a hand on Kat or looked at her twice, I'd kill him. But Reed giving her pleasure like this? It's something I didn't know I'd enjoy like this.

Bringing her knees up, he pushes himself inside of her, and her head falls back, her eyes close and he thrusts as if he's meant to be fucking her. As if this is how he did it before. There's comfort in the position, his groin pressed against her clit, like he's all too aware that's how she likes it.

I wait for the jealousy, I wait for the anger, but all I can do is watch as he rocks inside of her and Kat opens her eyes to stare at me. Her eyes are wide until they close again, the pleasure taking over.

Reed chuckles a deep rough sound before kissing her neck, and it snaps me out of it. "Look at Cillian," he commands Kat, who's barely with it. "He's giving me a smug look, like your pussy only feels this good because he warmed you up for me."

Kat's bottom lip drops as she peers back at me, lust covering her gaze. With every thrust, she lets out a moan.

I wish I was hard again. I wish I hadn't come at all. I'm already planning on how I want to fuck her with Reed again. Next time I'll take her mouth first. And that sweet ass of hers is going to need to be prepped.

A low groan of approval leaves me and I crouch down to be closer to Kat.

"Be a good girl and please us both," I whisper as I kiss her. Her hazel eyes are half lidded as she moans my name. Mine, not his.

"I'm not the one fucking you right now, Kat." Reed lifts her knee up, slamming into her deeper and harder. "Come on his dick like you did for me."

It doesn't take long for them to each find their release and all the while I wait for the anger, for anything other than a deeply satisfied content.

Even when he comes in her, I fucking love it.

Even as her hand slips between her legs to keep from making even more of a mess, all I want is to replay what just happened over again.

It's quiet as he leaves her, gathering a hand towel from the bathroom and bringing it back to her.

She doesn't look at me and he doesn't either, not for a long time. Not until I help Kat up and the vulnerability stares back at me.

I kiss her. At first it's quick and then she reaches up for more and I mold my lips to hers.

"You able to stand, Hellcat?" I nip her lower lip as she straightens herself. "Barely," she manages and then blushes as she peeks up at me.

She's utterly gorgeous, with her hair a messy halo and her cheeks flushed. "I just need the bathroom." With a smirk on my lips, I help her get to the door. All the while Reed's in the background, taking off the sheets and laying down the comforter so we can sleep on that tonight.

Leaving her in the bathroom, I make my way back.

The moment we're alone, Reed questions, "So, you're not going to kill me then?"

"Is that what you thought?"

"For a moment … I questioned it."

"Figured you'd try to get laid one more time before I ended you then?" I joke but he doesn't laugh.

"I mean it. I love her but I love you too. I just … I don't want to lose either of you. I barely made it this last year."

It takes every bit of the man I am to admit to him the truth I had to accept last night, "I don't think I can keep her on my own. Not when I know she loves you like you love her."

"You could. She loves you more."

"Who would I be without you, though? I need you and if you're going to be here, you're going to be around her." I lick my lower lip, cutting him off when he takes pity on me, rather than simply accepting it.

"It's always been the three of us. I want to keep it that way and if it means, I share her … then that's what it means."

I'd rather share her than lose her. Right now she might choose me, but when I fuck up again, and I know I will, I don't want her to question it. I want her to have my best friend right there, so she can confide in him and love on him until she's not angry at me anymore.

"I might lose her if it's only me, but together we can have her forever."

"You're talking like this is more than just a one-time thing," he states although it's more a question.

"It's whatever we want it to be. I want to take care of my uncle and get the hell out of here, maybe disappear to the West Coast?" Ever since Kat said the club was dead, it's slowly sunk in. Maybe I just needed to hear her say it, or maybe I needed the fear of losing her to settle deep into my bones. "All I know is that I lost you and her once, I'll do whatever we need to do, but I want to deal with my uncle before we head out."

Reed only stares back at me, nodding before telling me, "I'll see what I can find out."

Chapter 16

I T'S LATE AT NIGHT WHEN I GET THE MESSAGE FROM MY GUY AT THE Ruin. He knows somebody on the West Coast—a guy named Derrick who used to be tight with someone named Seth, the right-hand man of one of the Cross brothers. We were given the blessing to leave, to take refuge there with new IDs, new passports, a new life.

It's a gift in exchange for the information about Cillian's uncle Eamon. The Ruin verified it and said they'd take care of him, and it would be the end of the Cavanaugh Crest.

They didn't say we couldn't kill him first, though.

"Promise me you two won't do anything stupid." Kat's words ricochet in my head as the engine revs beneath me. She's made me make that promise a thousand times. I ride behind Cillian in the dark of the night on the way to the Cavanaugh Crest, gripping the handlebar as the vibrations travel up, warning me that keeping that promise is going to take a fucking miracle.

We don't find Cill's uncle at the club. That would be an amateur move. I used my contact at The Ruin to set up a meeting at a place outside the city limits. There's a large reservoir there, and once something comes in, it doesn't come back out.

Still risky as hell to do this. We have no guarantees that someone else won't show up.

Hell, I'm relying on my contact from The Ruin to get Eamon here. I half expect Finn to be with him or serving as his lookout, although I was assured he'd come alone.

We park down the hill from the reservoir, side by side on our bikes and kill the lights. Fear and doubt creep in as we wait. "We could keep riding," I suggest to Cill. "We could pick up Kat and get the hell out of town."

I don't want her mixed up in this. It broke her heart when Cill went to prison. It doesn't need to happen twice. We can figure things out on the road.

Just us, getting the hell away. Ever since he suggested it, I can't stop thinking about it. It's the only thing that feels right anymore.

"If he killed my father … you know he did. I know he did. I'm not leaving here till he admits it." With a nod, I follow him down to the meet. It's a hill between two old warehouses, the moonlight and security lights are all that help us see.

There's a good chance Cill's uncle doesn't show, either. There's a chance all of this is another setup.

We wait about five minutes and a light appears at the bottom of the hill. An old man, a touch overweight in dark jeans and a black hoodie, checking a cell phone. It's Cill's uncle.

"Holy shit," Cill says under his breath. "There he fucking is." My pulse spikes.

Although we see him, it takes him about halfway to realize it's us. He stops in his tracks as it registers. I wonder if he knows then. All I can think is he has to realize at some point tonight that we know. "Hey, Eamon," I call out, keeping my voice even and trying not to raise suspicion as his hand falls to his waistband. I can't come back alone. The thought is buried deep in the back of my mind.

The crickets and the night sounds surround us until all I can hear is my blood rushing in my ears. Eamon's eyes narrow. "You're not who I'm supposed to be meeting with."

"We got a message too." I keep my tone even. I don't want to scare him off. "It said to meet here and ask about Missy … is that what you're doing here? Something about a rat?"

He laughs, nervousness filtering into it and I know he hears it just like the two of us do. Clearing his throat he adds, "Now they didn't tell me that. That's," he shakes his head, one hand running down his jaw, the other lingering over the gun tucked in his jeans.

"That's what?" Cill questions. "You sure she was a rat? We heard it might be someone else. We heard it might be you."

A moment of silence hangs over the hill.

"It's a shame," Cill's uncle says.

"What's a shame?" Cill asks.

"That it has to end this way," his uncle replies.

He pulls out the gun, recklessly in an attempt to be fast. I'm faster, though, prepared and aiming it at his skull without stumbling. His is still aimed at the ground, his hoodie having slowed him down.

"Lift it and I pull the trigger, Eamon," I tell him, my tone deadly.

"How about you drop it?" Cill says, the heavy gun in his hand slowly rising to aim at his uncle. "Tell us what happened. Did you kill my father?" A faint click tells me Cill's a hairline pull of a trigger from ending it all. A cold sweat breaks out across my skin.

Eamon's gaze goes from me to Cill. Gun or not, he's still outnumbered. He's going to have to hit us both if he wants to walk away from this place. There's no way that's happening. He swallows loudly and then gives a half-hearted smirk.

"Don't you boys think this is all a bit overblown?" he says, the breeze in the chill of the night carrying his voice to us. "This is a misunderstanding. Put down the fucking gun, Reed."

"A misunderstanding?" Cill says it slowly, like he can't believe his uncle just said this to him. "Did you call my dad's death a misunderstanding?"

"That was a heart attack," his uncle snaps.

"That's not what I've heard," Cill says. "I heard different. I heard it was you." Emotion carries into his words. The mourning, the betrayal. "Are you gonna deny it?"

He waits and the silence stretches.

"You'd have done the same thing," spits his uncle. "Your father ran the club into the ground when you left. He refused to take the opportunities we were given … so I took one instead."

Cill takes an uneasy step forward, a step too close for my liking. "You decided to get in bed with the feds and pick people off."

"At least I didn't get in bed with your old lady, like Reed did," Eamon shoots back. Cill's jaw clenches and for a second I'm worried he'll lose his temper, but he ignores the taunt.

"You set me up … set Reed up?" He motions toward me with the gun and glances at me. His uncle doesn't, though, and I keep my focus on Eamon.

Bitterness seeps into Eamon's tone. "I did what I had to do."

"What the fuck?" Cill almost laughs. "Admit it. Admit you killed him."

Two things happen at once: Eamon lifts his gun and fires at the same time I pull the trigger. Cill's too lost in his emotions to act quickly enough, but I saw it. I saw Eamon's thumb move back. I pulled it as quickly as I could, but still, his uncle got off a shot.

Bang. Bang.

Heat overwhelms me and I'm paralyzed as I watch both of them drop. Eamon falls backward, a bullet ripping through his throat. Blood sprays and I take two steps forward, watching his hands attempt to keep the blood from gushing out of his neck, even as he chokes on it.

Training keeps me focused on him, even though fear cripples me. "Cill." I call out his name as the life drains from Eamon's body.

"Cill!" I call out louder as Eamon's eyes fall back and his body stills, his hand drops to the ground. His chest is still. I don't trust it. I move forward once more, aim the gun and shoot two more bullets into his chest. They thud one after the other, jostling his body from the force. There's no sound, no expression.

He's dead.

It's only then that I can move, turning to find Cill propped up on his knee. Thank fuck. Relief floods through me but I can't stop my hands from trembling.

"I thought you were dead." Adrenaline rushes through my veins. "I thought he got you."

"I'm all right," he tells me, although he stays focused on Eamon. "He didn't say it."

"I'm sorry, Cill." I know he wanted to hear it, he needed to. Fuck, I did too. I settle on a single truth. "He's a coward."

It takes two of us two drag him to the edge of the reservoir. We weigh down his pockets with rocks and throw him in. Doesn't take long for him to disappear under the water. Even after it's done, it doesn't feel real. None of it does. Not until Cill tells me, "Let's get home to Kat."

I only nod, keeping my answer to myself, but he says it. He says the exact words I was thinking, "I need her."

Kat

Cill and Reed thought they could tiptoe out of my house without me knowing, but they were wrong. I heard them leave.

I swear there's some part of me that just knows when they're in trouble. Like my soul is attached to theirs. And right now, it's worried.

I tried to fall back to sleep, it's what Cill would want. Instead I either stared at the spinning fan, thinking the worst, or tossed and turned … also thinking the worst.

They're gone long enough that after an hour of uselessness, I get out of bed and make a hot cup of tea.

It feels better to wait in the kitchen. Lying under the covers and hiding has never been my thing. Maybe for a couple of days after Cill got arrested, but you can't hide under the damn blankets forever. Eventually, the world finds you anyway.

Time slips by and I text Lydia. Her response is to call and the moment I answer she asks, "Want me to come over?"

"No, that's okay. I'm just—"

"Waiting for two men who are nothing but trouble," she half jokes, sleep evident in her voice.

"I didn't mean to wake you."

"I wasn't dreaming of anything special so I don't mind," she tells me. A sad smile graces my lips as I sit down at the table.

"How are you two?"

I chew my bottom lip at the word *two*. "We're … kind of like old times, kind of like new," I admit to her and pull out the chair at the table, debating on what I should tell her. I want to spill everything, every last detail.

"Does he make you happy?" she asks.

"Yeah, happy but worried."

"But happy?" she asks again and I let out a short laugh, pulling one knee into my chest balancing my foot on the edge of the chair.

"Yeah, he really does make me happy. He makes me feel like me."

"It might take some time not to worry, you know?"

Swaying in my chair, I know she's right. I hate time, though, it hasn't been good to me.

"Yeah," I agree with her and then ask, "Want to take my mind off of it? Or is one a.m. a little too late and you'd rather sleep."

The sound of her rolling over in bed filters through the phone before she lets out an easy sigh. "I may have met a man," she says and then hums. I'm grateful for her, for friendship, for her stories. I try not to think about the fact that I probably won't see her very much once this is all said and done.

Instead I laugh along with her and decide I'm grateful phone calls exist.

It's not long after that I hang up, thanking her and telling her to have sweet dreams of her dark-haired mystery man that I hear their bikes.

Breathing in deep, I down the last of the decaf tea and head to the sink to wash out the cup. I grew up to that sound, the rev of the engines. I know it so well, I can clearly hear two of them.

I don't know what exactly is going on with the three of us, but I'm grateful both of them are coming home to me. Whatever it is we're doing, I want it. I want both of them however I can have them.

Reed comes in first, holding the door open for Cill. Adrenaline pushes me to move to the threshold and fuck I wish I hadn't. I'm paralyzed by the sight of Cillian. Tremors run up my spine.

He's covered in blood. His shirt is stained.

"Oh my God," I nearly fall to the floor, my trembling hands covering my mouth. "Hey, Hellcat," he says. "It's not mine," he clarifies and although that's fucking horrible in and of itself, the relief is immediate.

"Are you all right?" I ask and look over both of them, still standing in the threshold and too scared to move. Reed closes the door and I note there's a bit of blood on him too that's smeared across his shirt.

"We're both fine." Reed adds, "Promise."

"What did you do?"

"We ended things here."

Things. I know exactly what that means. It's his uncle's blood.

"Do we need to leave?"

Cill nods, catching my eyes as he pulls the shirt over his head. "We'll pack up and move tonight.

"Tonight?" Surprise is evident in my rushed-out word.

Cill nods as if it's not a big deal to pick up and move in the middle of the night. "We're starting over. Just us, and Reed."

It takes me a minute to process what he's said, my head spins with all of this happening at once. "Reed too?"

"I think the three of us should keep doing what we are ..." Cill says and lets his gaze drift down my body. "What do you think, Reed?" He looks over his shoulder at Reed, who's stripping down to take off the bloodied clothes.

His muscles ripple as he does the same, looking me up and down like I'm some kind of meal for the two of them to enjoy together. He even licks his lower lip before nodding and saying, "I think that's exactly what I want."

My body flushes from head to toe. I can't believe he just said that. I can't believe that Cillian is standing in the middle of my kitchen with someone else's blood on him, and talking about sharing me with his best friend.

Something in my heart clicks into place. I meet Reed's deep brown eyes, feeling shy. I can't speak. I never dreamed that Cill would suggest something like this. I didn't think I'd want him to, but now that he has, I can't imagine it being any other way.

"You like that, don't you?" Cill questions.

I'm hesitant to nod, but I do it. "I just want to love you two." I swallow down every apprehension.

"Good," he says with finality. "'Cause that's all I want too."

"Same," Reed adds. "We love you, Kat."

I stare between the two of them, not believing while also eager for this to be true. "I love you both too."

Epilogue

One week later

REED DRIVES WITH THE WINDOWS DOWN AND ONE ARM OUT in the California breeze. It's taken us over a week to get here. We could have made the trip faster, but none of us wanted to. Their bikes are in the back and we got a notice that everything we packed up and shipped arrived at the new place.

We're almost there. I have no idea what it'll be like. But I know I'll have both Reed and Cillian, so I'll make it home.

I was content enough at the flower shop, but nothing compares to being on the open road with Reed and Cill. We find out-of-the-way motels that have been lovingly cared for by the owners and stay up all night in bed together. We stop at half of the roadside attractions on the way out west. We drive in the desert under the stars. We eat at diners that have menus the size of a phone book. Every single thing we ever talked about doing when we were young and dumb and thought life ahead of us was going to be an easy road, we do.

Our motto now is to live with no regrets and every day we accomplish that, I believe it more and more.

I have my feet sprawled across the back seat. Cill rides in the passenger seat. He's looking out the window at the scenery, his face relaxed.

Kat: We finally got to the coast!

Lydia: Took you long enough :D

Kat: There were lots of sights to see ;)

Kat: You should come out here with us. Everywhere we've been is absolutely gorgeous

Lydia: You trying to set me up with Reed?

I smile at the phone. I know she's joking, but I'm going to answer her honestly. It feels good to say it out loud. Or type it, I suppose.

Kat: No. I meant it when I told you I'm claiming both of them.

Kat: But I mean it. You should come out here

There's a silence, and I wonder if she's thinking of what to say. I told her we're a throuple the other day and she thought I was joking at first. I know it's not normal, but when the hell have our lives ever been normal? At this point, I'll settle with safe and content. I just want to be safe, and I am when I'm between them both.

Lydia: You gonna run forever?

Kat: We're not running. We're just … making a new start.

It's easy to hope with these two men.

A sign passes by on the side of the road.

"Reed," I call up. "Take the next exit."

"How come? We're not quite there yet."

"I want to see the ocean."

Cill turns around and smiles at me. "You want to look at something big and all-consuming, Hellcat? If you do, I have another idea."

"Take me to the ocean," I tell him, teasing. "And then you can show me how all-consuming you are."

He doesn't have to show me.

I already know.

Cill

I didn't just tell Finn that I sent the info to The Ruin, I didn't tell him shit and as far as I'm concerned, I don't owe it to him. I don't owe anything more to Cavanaugh Crest than I already gave. He'll make assumptions maybe, ask questions and possibly put the pieces together. But the old man will be fine without me. Just like he was for the four years I was away. The thing about prison is that you learn to keep your mouth shut, and I did. I spent four fucking years locked away. My best friend and the love of my life lived in hell, and my father was murdered.

But that's all over now. We're on the other side of the country, with sunny skies and an open road. Nobody out here knows what I did. Nobody's ever going to know, except the two people in the car with me. They're the only ones that matter.

A club can be a family, if you let it. But when push comes to shove, you learn who your real family is. My hellcat's mine. I'll spend the rest of my life giving her what she needs, which is both of us.

The ocean comes into view as we pull off the freeway. "There it is, Hellcat. The Pacific Ocean."

She leans up between the front seats to look. It's a sight to see. Something about all those waves in the sun. This is why I'll never tell her no.

"Is it everything you ever dreamed of?" I say, joking.

Kat turns her head and kisses my cheek. "I never dream of the ocean," she says. "All I ever dream about is you." She settles down, biting her bottom lip as she peeks at Reed, a blush creeping up her cheeks, "And you."

This "the end"
comes with a *very sinful*
happily ever after

For a sexy—and explicit—extended epilogue of the three of them together in their blissful happily ever after, subscribe to my Patreon:
www.patreon.com/WillowWintersAuthor
I had a lot of fun with these three and I hope you enjoyed their story!

Don't stop reading!
Dive into *All He'll Ever Be* today and fall in love with
the Cross brothers.

about w winters

Thank you so much for reading my romances. I'm just a stay at home mom and avid reader turned author and I couldn't be happier.

I hope you love my books as much as I do!

More by Willow Winters
www.WillowWintersWrites.com/collections